THE
SALAMANDRA
GLASS

Also by A. W. MYKEL
The Windchime Legacy

THE SALAMANDRA GLASS

A. W. Mykel

ST. MARTIN'S PRESS
NEW YORK

Note: This is a work of fiction. Though some of the characters and events in this work were modeled after real people and actual events, it *is* a work of fiction and a product of the author's imagination. To the best of the author's knowledge, the events as portrayed in the work have never occurred.

Library of Congress Cataloging in Publication Data

Mykel. A. W.
  The salamandra glass.
  I. Title.
PS3563.Y49S2   1983   813'.54   83-8618
ISBN 0-312-69738-4

First Edition

10 9 8 7 6 5 4 3 2 1

For my Dad. He was my best friend, and I loved him.

THE
SALAMANDRA
GLASS

Prologue

DRESDEN, GERMANY, 1936: What had begun as a light steady snowfall at the start of the journey was now a raging blizzard. It was definitely not a night that the young officer would have chosen to course the 110 miles south from Berlin to the city nestled astride the Elbe River. Nor was it the night he would have chosen to listen to a lecture on the history of Dresden and its renowned culture. But when a general talks, a newly commissioned lieutenant listens, despite the long and close association that existed between them. Rank still had its privileges.

It was not, however, for the lessons in history that these two men had come to Dresden. They had come to see a man of remarkable skill—a glassmaker—and the finished product of a commission issued many months earlier. It had been an expensive undertaking. The glass-maker's time was valuable, and his thriving business had suffered from the many hundreds of hours this commission had demanded. He had told them that what they wanted *was* possible, but only for an artisan with his skill and understanding of the unique chemistry involved. They had known what they wanted, and the glassmaker had known what they would pay to get it. They had accepted his price without question.

The car was parked several blocks from the glassmaker's studio. The men walked a careful route to be sure that they were not being followed. The lateness of the hour should have precluded that possibility, but with the state of affairs inside Germany, nothing was assumed.

The two men entered the studio. The intense heat of the work area was a sudden contrast to the cold outside. For just the shortest of moments, activity in the studio stopped as all eyes looked to the two men who had come at such a late hour. Then just as suddenly the work resumed, all bodies going about well-practiced routines.

The two officers cautiously regarded the four men working with immunity to the heat. These men composed the master's "chair." Each worked with clearly defined duties, the signatures of their stations and learning. One of these men caught the particular notice of the young officer. He was a boy, actually, but tall for his age. His face said that he was perhaps thirteen or fourteen, but it was more than his youth that held the lieutenant's attention. The boy was a Jew. That was unmistakable. And his eyes were the only eyes to return to the two men coming in from the cold. There was an uneasy, assessing quality to his quick glances, which became an intense glare when the young officer's interest was noticed. They were defiant eyes, cold and hard—the eyes of a clever mind.

The sound of a door being opened caught the young officer's attention, and his eyes swung immediately to the small smiling face of the glassmaker.

A warm greeting was extended to the two men. After a brief exchange of pleasantries, the glassmaker invited them to accompany him into the gallery, affording them escape from the oppressive heat of the furnaces.

The young officer didn't have to see the eyes of the apprentice to know that they followed him to the gallery; he could feel them. And it amused him a little to think that one so young as the apprentice possessed an ability to intimidate with just his eyes. Too bad he was Jew; he would have had promise.

The young officer took a position at the side of his superior, who spoke quietly to the glassmaker. The general had a precise, authoritative manner of speech. In contrast, the glassmaker spoke with a soft high voice, sounding on the verge of laryngitis. The voice did little, however, to belie the self-assuredness and pride of the man behind the bespectacled, weak-looking face and thinning hair. After several moments of conversation, the glassmaker moved from the gallery to an adjoining room, leaving the two officers to themselves.

The young lieutenant looked slowly around the room, examining with interest the works on display. He could not help feeling admiration for the formidable talent that went into the creation of such works. The crystal was breathtaking. So fine was the stemware that he was sure that too hard a glance would shatter it. There were magnificent Persian pitchers and vases with delicate millefiori composition, plates, bowls, and vessels with intricate latticinio patterns and spirals with

2

coloring seemingly possible only with an artist's brush, but entrapped within the glass itself.

He turned and continued the inspection. His eyes stopped on the shelves of intricate lampwork miniatures. There were ships, delicate glass nests, and animals of all descriptions with awesome complexity and accuracy of detail. He saw two pieces in particular that absolutely astounded him. The first was a convoluted glass tree of impossible detail. The second was a stunning glass bird of prey poised in the attack position. Every piece was a revelation of beauty and skill. It was only the sound of the glassmaker's return that broke the spell of fascination.

The glassmaker carried two flat cases. The first was small, about three inches square and an inch thick. The second was thin like the first, but longer. He held out the small case. "I think you'll find it to be quite satisfactory," he said, the pride in the yet unseen work evident in his small eyes.

The general accepted the box and opened it slowly, revealing a pendant one and one-half inches in diameter, mounted on a silver backplate. It depicted a three-headed salamander of remarkable detail. The main body was black, with flecks of gold and rainbow colors looking like tiny glistening scales. The center head was positioned straight out at the viewer, the other two heads turned slightly to either side, but with all eyes visible. The body of the salamander curled to the left, with the tail swirling back to the right, across the bottom of the pendant. The finite detail was incredible, right down to the exactness of eye structure.

The glassmaker held out a magnifying glass for closer inspection. It was quite a bit more than they had thought and hoped possible.

If the lampwork had left the young officer impressed, what he now looked at left him speechless. How could it be possible? he thought.

"And the others?" asked the general.

The glassmaker held out the second case, opening it for inspection. "They are exact," he replied, the slightest trace of a smile breaking across his thin lips.

Both men examined the pieces closely.

"And the possibility of duplication?" asked the general.

"Impossible," the glassmaker responded.

"That is part of the beauty and genius in using glass. All of the pendants are made from a single composite glass cane. To make that one master, over eight hundred separate glass canes were required. Each of those was crafted individually, so that when pulled to the required thinness each would bear its own distinct quality, like a finger-

3

print. Microscopic examination of the pendants will reveal that each corresponding glass cane composing the pendant set is identical. There are over eight hundred identical and irreproducible sets of canes in each. Also, the unique coloring accomplished with the various metal oxides could never be executed to exactness again. It is, therefore, doubly impossible. The pendants are truly one-of-a-kind duplicates, and a hundred master craftsmen could not reproduce a single one to exactness again."

The two men were satisfied beyond all expectations.

"You have met all of our requirements, Herr Haupte," the general said, handing over the balance of payment for the commission. "I trust that no record of this transaction will exist?" he added.

"We have never met," the glassmaker said, smiling pleasantly.

"And the others out there?" the young officer asked.

"I needed the assistance of only one of them. The rest know nothing," the glassmaker responded.

"Which one?" the lieutenant asked.

"The apprentice," answered the glassmaker.

"The Jew," the young officer said.

The smile fell from the glassmaker's face. "The . . . boy . . . has very promising talent, and I trust him completely," he said flatly.

"He is a Jew," the lieutenant repeated coldly.

"He will be the finest glassmaker in Germany one day," the man responded. "You took great pains to admire his work earlier," he said, pointing to the glass tree and the attacking falcon that the young officer had been so taken by. "He is already possessed of more talent than most of the glassmakers in Germany. He can be trusted completely, I will guarantee that."

The young officer looked at the lampwork display, then back to the glassmaker, and nodded.

The passage through the infernolike studio was a swift one. Once again the lieutenant felt the penetrating stare of the apprentice, and he made eye contact for only a brief moment. He felt very little consolation in the glassmaker's assurances as they left.

Outside, the two men walked away in their cadenced step without conversation.

"The security aspects—I don't like them," the young officer said, breaking the silence.

The general walked on awhile before speaking. "Are you familiar with the painter Hans Grundig?" he asked.

"No," the lieutenant responded, puzzled.

"He has just completed a painting that I was privileged to see. He

4

calls it *Vision*. It shows Dresden, and a sky filled with planes. It was a night sky, ugly with the orange glow of fire. The flames were from Dresden, being destroyed by that fire, its beautiful buildings charred to rubble and waste, its people dead and dying in a firestorm from hell. That hell was war. Do you believe in people having 'visions' of the future?" he asked his young subordinate.

The lieutenant thought for a short moment. "No, I don't. The future is what we will make it," he replied.

"Yes, what *we* will make it," the general repeated in a tired voice. There was so much for his young protégé to learn.

The lieutenant was a bit perplexed. The general's words had nothing to do with his comment regarding the security aspects of the pendants. They walked on, the lieutenant electing not to push the subject for the moment.

"The security aspects will be taken care of when it becomes necessary," the general said at last. But the importance of security was not what was on his mind. He held only one thought, one image. He saw Dresden—beautiful Dresden with all its culture and charm—in a storm of flames with enemy planes overhead.

Chapter 1

SPRING LAKE, NEW JERSEY, MAY 1982: The highly polished Mercedes of Christian Gladieux paused momentarily beneath the flagpole before completing the left turn onto Third Avenue, which served as the business district for the small, charming oceanside community. It was a warm spring day and through the open window Gladieux could hear the huge American flag ripping and cracking in the brisk wind coming in off the ocean.

He drove slowly down the main drag, throwing a few friendly waves to those who had spotted the car of Spring Lake's resident bestselling novelist. Christian Gladieux was a point of town pride.

He had already been a well-established author when he came into the community in 1960, taking a large, stately home just one block from the ocean.

The two children of Christian Gladieux had assimilated easily within the community. Michael had been a scrapping fourteen-year-old about to enter high school. He had already been tall and strong, taking after his father, and proved to be an immediate boon to the athletic program of the regional high school in Manasquan. Gabrielle had just turned ten, and before the first summer was over had won the hearts of half the boys her age. Her young beauty was as disarming as Michael's athletic abilities were imposing.

The early years in Spring Lake had been exceptional to Christian Gladieux. He could be seen on countless days by the beach with notebook in hand, drinking in the inspiration offered by the rhythmic, almost hypnotic beauty of the ocean.

But things had begun to change in the mid 1960s. It wasn't evident at first to the people who knew him. Things deep within the man that had been so well held back for so long had begun to gnaw into his consciousness. His wife had sensed the subtle changes in him long before they became more profound and began to affect the relationship between them. It had come like a slow cancer, spreading, choking off vital parts until the inevitable direction had become clear. A shocked but respectfully silent circle of friends had watched the sad course evolve. In 1968, the marriage ended.

Michael had already dropped out of his premed studies at Ohio State University to "find himself." He wound up in Vietnam, a cruel theater for a young man searching for vital answers about himself. Gabrielle had been graduated from high school just prior to her parents' separating. She went to the west coast to attend the University of Southern California, undertaking studies in journalism.

Denise had chosen not to remain in Spring Lake following the divorce and had also moved to California, where she eventually remarried.

Despite the things that had forced them apart, and the unpleasant episodes prior to the divorce action, Christian still loved Denise. It hurt him deeply when she remarried, though it never showed on the outside. The high quality of his work continued as though not even the slightest disruption had entered his life.

Michael had ended up serving three tours of duty in Vietnam, and later completed his studies for a degree. He had spent a lot of time traveling after Vietnam, both on his own and in various forms of employment. He seemed never to have found all the answers for which he searched. He was remarkably independent and curious, and adventured often into new experiences of the wildest nature.

Christian admired the independence of his son, and knew that he would someday find all of those answers. He would be a remarkable young man, rich with the education of his experiences and inner knowledge of himself. Perhaps his son was closer to that day than even Michael realized himself. He was currently in Central America conducting research for a book on the rain forests of Costa Rica. It was the first major commitment he had made since leaving the highlands and rice paddies of Nam.

Gabrielle had turned into a beauty, very much like her mother. After completing her studies, she returned east to pursue a career in journalism. It was the unending joy of Christian that both his children had found their own paths to writing. He had never pushed them toward it, always maintaining that they must choose their own way, following their hearts to do the things they wanted to do. He had seldom questioned them or found disappointment in their choices.

One near disappointment came when Gabrielle decided to get married. It wasn't that he had objected to his daughter's marriage, or that he thought she might stop pursuing the career she wanted so much. Inside, he had questioned her choice of a husband. His name was Daniel Preston, and he was a member of the New Jersey State Police. Christian had always hoped, and expected, that she would do better in the "hunting" department. She had grown up with the benefit of wealth and all its advantages. A policeman . . . Well, how much could he offer her? It had pleased her father somewhat that she kept some sign of her independence in the name she chose, Gabrielle Glady-Preston, but in his heart he had feared that the marriage would not last beyond the physical aspects of the relationship. Unhappy marriages were a common plague to the profession of law enforcement.

His fears had changed in time as he grew to know his son-in-law. He found an intelligent, hardworking young man who truly loved Gabrielle and who was tremendously supportive of her career goals. His own career with the State Police advanced rapidly, and he was already a very highly regarded sergeant of detectives.

Gabrielle's career had blossomed nicely, too, without the influence of her father. A young family also began to grow with the coming of two beautiful daughters, Alexis and Sandra. All things considered, Christian Gladieux was proud of the way his children were turning out.

The Mercedes pulled into the driveway of the Gladieux residence. It was a spacious, rambling house, made larger to Christian by its emptiness. But it held many warm memories, and he truly enjoyed living in Spring Lake. He had no intention of ever leaving it.

It was only four months ago that Christian Gladieux's writing had started again after more than a year of sudden inactivity. It had been a very troubled, dark time that had tested the extreme limits of the man, his conscience and his beliefs. His editor and publisher were not aware of the reasons behind his silence, but were understanding; there was nothing wrong with taking a well-deserved rest. He was far from being in financial need, and an invigorated, well-rested Christian Gladieux would return with a blockbusting theme, they were sure. But it was not the sudden birth of a brainchild theme that sent him to the desk for pencils and paper. It was, instead, the decision to disregard the great personal risk he would face to tell a story he knew must be told.

To his readers it would be another riveting story in the tradition of Christian Gladieux. But to others, who would most surely recognize it,

9

it would be a threat to their existence. And to those who would threaten that existence, it would be the means to end it.

Christian Gladieux pushed the button activating the automatic door closer as he left the garage. He walked the distance from the separated garage to the house in the late rays of the bright sun.

He could smell the ocean and the life so recently returned to the professionally manicured grounds. The combination of scents and the clear beauty of a brilliant blue sky would have inspired him at any other time. He hardly noticed them now as he entered the house through the side door. There were few things these days that elicited happy response from him.

His entry brought him into the kitchen. Before proceeding further into the house, he put a pot of water on the range and readied a cup with instant coffee and artificial sweetener. It would be a while before the water reached boiling, and he decided to check the mailbox on the front porch. He passed through the large formal dining room and through the open sliding doors into the center hall. Within a few moments he was thumbing through the envelopes as he stepped back into the house. He began walking back through the center hall, reading the return addresses on the envelopes, when he looked up, his eye catching a glimpse of something on the stairway leading to the second floor. He changed direction and headed for it.

His first thought was that Sophie, his housekeeper, had come by earlier than expected and left him a note telling him so, or perhaps a note containing phone messages she had taken. As he neared the stairs, he saw that he had been wrong. There was no mistaking the slanted block letters hastily scribbled across the face of the envelope. Letters in the same hand had been arriving for eight weeks now.

Gladieux was filled with rage as he reached for it, for this one bore a new significance. It had not been sent in the mail like the others—it had been *placed.*

They had dared to violate the privacy of his home. He tore the envelope open and removed the single sheet, unfolded it, and began reading. It was in his native French:

> Collaborator,
> It is the considered verdict of the Court of Justice of the Firewatch Brigade that you are *guilty* of the charge of collaboration with the enemies of France during the occupation years of 1940–44.
> Your actions of treachery and betrayal were directly responsible for the arrests, torture, and deaths

of hundreds of your fellow freedom-loving Resistance fighters of the group known as "Defiance."

Proof beyond all doubt is in our possession that you conspired with the filthy occupiers of our beloved France, revealing to them the identities of your fellow countrymen and the details of their efforts against the enemy.

It has been decided that the sentence of this court for your past crimes shall be *death*.

May you forever rot in hell, and your memory bear the mark of your treachery.

Firewatch

"Proof beyond all doubt," he murmured. The fools! When would they ever stop their witch hunts? Their justice dated from a time when a pointed finger or an unsigned denunciation was "proof beyond doubt."

Christian Gladieux had been a hero of France. Few men would have or could have done the things he had done during that dark period of France's history. And they dared to call him a traitor, declare him guilty and sentence him to death by that same justice—with "proof beyond doubt"!

"Well, let them come," Gladieux growled, crumpling the letter. He would be ready for them.

He turned and headed for his library. There was a gun in his desk, and he intended to carry it and to use it if necessary.

The room was dimly illuminated by the traces of sunlight managing to sneak by the drawn drapes. The light allowed ample visibility to sight the desk clearly. He did not turn on the overhead light as he entered.

He had taken no more than two steps into the room when a sharp punchlike blow landed in the lower right side of his back. Before he could turn, a second more savage blow was delivered to the same spot. With a sudden and complete loss of breath, he fell to his knees, struggled to turn and face his attacker, and never saw the baseball bat that slammed into his face.

He was aware of himself lying on his back, unable to draw breath. The sudden swiftness of the attack had left him stunned and almost without pain. He was aware of the blood covering his face and filling his mouth, and of the smashed upper teeth and nose. He rolled slowly from his back to his side and attempted to rise to his hands and knees, when he felt his upper body being jerked upright by the arms from behind into a kneeling position. Then Christian Gladieux became aware of a man holding him tightly while a second man slipped a wire loop over his head. He became aware of the deliberately slow tightening of the garrote and the sound of profanities being directed against him. He was made aware of how slowly and without grace death could be made to come.

Justice, as rightly or wrongly as it may have been placed, had been served.

Chapter 2

PRINCETON, NEW JERSEY: Gabrielle Glady-Preston looked up from the bathtub as the phone rang. She ran the back of a wet hand across her forehead to push away several strands of loose hair.

"Danny, could you get that, please?" she asked her husband. "That should be my father. He said he might stop over tonight. He' probably calling to confirm his plans."

Danny smiled and nodded, then dropped the towels for the two youngsters being bathed to the floor beside Gabrielle. He hurried out of the bathroom to the master bedroom and snapped up the phone. "Hello?" he said.

"Danny?" the voice inquired. It was a familiar voice. He couldn't place it immediately.

"Yeah, speaking."

"This is Tom Waller, Danny," the voice announced, then hesitated.

Danny knew Tom Waller. He was on the Spring Lake police force. There was no reason for Tom be calling him at home. The uneasy feeling set in quickly.

"Yes, Tom. What can I do for you?" Danny asked cautiously.

"You'd better get over here, Danny. Your . . . uh . . . father-in-law's housekeeper called in here a few minutes ago in a terrible panic. A body has been found in the house."

"Jesus!" Danny exhaled in shock. "Is it him?"

"We're not sure," Waller replied. "The responding officer doesn'

12

really know your father-in-law. And ... well ... there's been ... uh ... there's been some disfigurement. Some mutilation of the body. It was a homicide."

Danny was rocked by Waller's words. He suddenly felt the need to sit down, but remained standing. "Who's coming in on it?" he asked quickly.

"Monmouth County Prosecutor's detective staff has been notified."

"I'm on my way, Tom. And thanks for getting to me so quickly. I appreciate it."

"I'm sorry, Danny. I'm heading over now and will meet you there. I sincerely hope it's not him."

"Right. I'm on my way," Danny said and hung up the phone. He clipped his Detective Special to the back of his belt and pulled on a light jacket to cover it. He moved out of the bedroom and quickly down the hall.

"Was it him?" Gabrielle called from the bathroom above the playful squeals of the children.

Gabrielle! What could he tell her? He quickly decided to get all of the facts before saying anything. There was still the possibility that the body in the house wasn't Christian's.

"No, it wasn't him," he said from outside in the hallway. He thought fast. "It was Hoag from down at the station. He can't find the file on a case we wrapped up last month. He's got to have it. Something about the colonel wanting it fast. I'll be back in a little while."

"Can't it wait until Monday?"

He stuck his head into the bathroom, trying desperately to look as nonchalant as possible. "No, it can't wait, and I'm in a hurry. Be back in a bit."

She rose from the tub, her arms dripping wet, and walked over to the doorway. "You sure that a certain new 'lady bear' with big knockers hasn't got you sneaking off to the station for a little overtime?" she asked in a low playful voice so that the kids wouldn't hear.

He tried to smile, but the attempt was a weak one. The usual snappy rejoinder was absent. "I'll see you in a little while," he said, then turned and headed for the stairway.

Gabrielle watched as he moved down the stairs. There was a strange look in his eyes that she had never seen before. She had the very clear feeling that something was wrong.

"Mommy! Sandra won't stop splashing me," Alexis complained with a loud urgent whine.

Gabrielle returned to the bathtub to restore order. But the strange feeling stayed with her, despite her attempts to dispel it.

The frenzied drive to Spring Lake was a record breaker, though it seemed like an eternity to Danny. All he could think about was how to break the news to his wife if the body did turn out to be Christian's. No cop likes making notifications of death. As a young trooper he had learned many ways to make the duty easier when it couldn't be avoided. Usually a close relative or a priest or a physician who was well received was greatly instrumental in the notification. If all else failed, he knew that he could just walk away from it when the job was over. But this was one that he couldn't walk away from.

He decided to call the parish priest from Spring Lake, who had been a longtime friend of the family. He knew that a doctor would be needed, too. Gabrielle would undoubtedly need his services, if for no other reason than to relax her to enable her to sleep. One of their friends could watch the children until the initial reaction was past.

"God," he prayed, "let it be some other poor son of a bitch."

He saw the police cars as soon as he turned onto the block of his father-in-law's house. It evoked an eerie sensation. He had seen the setting countless times, but it had never touched him personally before.

He stopped the car at the house and spotted Tom Waller immediately. Tom faced him squarely as he approached, reading the question in Danny's eyes. A moment's eye contact preceded Tom's words, and it was enough to tell Danny that his prayer hadn't been answered.

"I'm sorry, Danny," Tom began. "It's Christian."

The sinking feeling began.

"We'll still need a positive I.D. from a family member. It's better that Gabrielle not see him this way," Tom advised.

Danny was past him almost before the sentence was finished. He bounded up the front steps with Waller in close pursuit.

The photographer had just finished the last of the mandatory shots from assorted angles. He shook his head at no one in particular as he passed through the library doorway. Danny walked past him and went right to the body.

Seeing a dead body wasn't new to Danny. He had lived these scenes more times than he cared to remember. So many, in fact, that viewing "dead meat" was not disturbing to him, unless it was a child. But seeing Christian Gladieux on the floor was not like viewing dead meat. He had known this man, had come to like and respect him a great deal. He was filled with silent anger as he viewed the desecration inflicted upon the corpse, taking personal offense at the deed.

The eyelids had been pinned closed with ball-headed map pins through the pupils of the eyes. The left ear had been severed and was not in evidence in the room. Christian Gladieux's tongue had been cut out and in its place had been stuffed his penis and testicles. The tongue had been left in the cavity where his testicles had been. There was also general disfigurement from the blow to the face.

Danny had seen such mutilations before, in gangland-style killings, where specific offending parts of the victim's body were targets. The violated sexual organs and mouth were the insult to the victim and his family. For the executioners, they were signs for the reason of the justifiable killing.

There was one additional aspect of the mutilation that stood out, and obviously bore the most significance. A steel spike had been driven into the chest in the ultimate act of desecration, violating that part of the body that is the center of life and soul of mortal man. The spike had also passed through a wrinkled letter.

Tied to the spike was one more element that would add to the mystery of what had happened. This was a pendant. A pendant of intricate design, bearing the image of a three-headed salamander.

Chapter 3

CORVOCADO NATIONAL PARK, COSTA RICA: The loud reportlike crack of tearing wood and the violent shudder of the platform jarred Michael Gladieux out of the suffocating nightmare. His sweating chest heaved spasmodically as he gulped in huge breaths of air like a near drowning man just reaching surface after a desperate struggle for life. Perspiration rolled down his face and he imagined himself back in Vietnam for that brief startled moment between sleep and consciousness. Then the sounds of the wind and crashing plant life began to filter through the confusion and started to register in the brain, gauging the strength of the approaching storm. The ugly tangled knot of memories faded quickly and the hands reached, as if by reflex, to check the buckle of the safety belt securing him to the platform ninety feet above the rain forest floor.

To his discomforting surprise, the belt was not secured. It was a small mistake, but three tours of duty in Vietnam had taught him not to make small mistakes. They killed you. A flak jacket left open, an unguarded light, the sound of a half-empty canteen, or some other small detail ignored because you were too tired to care bought you the long rest and a trip to Dover in a steel coffin: Welcome to the halls of glory—*contents not for viewing.*

He secured the safety belt as the full force of the tropical deluge hit. He admonished himself for the carelessness that was not typical of him. The sudden onset of such storms was common in a tropical rain forest and made the safety of a tiny four-by-eight platform ninety feet above the ground of doubtful relevance.

Another loud cracking noise followed by the crashing sounds of lower vegetation told him that a second large branch of his tree had been lost to the storm's high-force winds. The sounds of similar casualties could be heard at varying distances throughout the rain forest. It caused wonder as to the strength of the shallow-rooted sanctuary guarding his well-being. Nobler giants fell with alarming regularity during such storms, and Michael Gladieux felt the same helplessness that he had experienced in Vietnam in the helicopters when they came under heavy ground fire. You could hear it, see it coming up at you, feel it, and all you could do was hug metal, stay low and pray, "Not me, God, not today . . . please!" The first form of answered prayer came when the "flexies" opened up, pissing back down their own dose of death and fear.

The storm raged with accustomed violence, leaving little doubt as to the power of nature, and with it the unmistakable awareness that you were sharing both its beauty and its danger. Then, almost as quickly as it had begun, the wind stopped, leaving only the sound of the forceful rain on the plastic roof of the platform. The fine wetting spray being blown through the insect netting also stopped, and the rain began to slacken until it became an unrhythmic tattoo. Within a few minutes, only the intermittent patter of drops from higher vegetation sounded, and the feeling of relief set in, like in the helicopters when the ground fire grew distant and out of range. Another prayer answered. You tried to remember it exactly as you had screamed it in your brain. Every word, every inflection, exactly. You said that prayer over and over because you knew it worked. "Just one more time, God," you always added. "Just one more time."

Michael checked the luminous dial of his watch. It would be at least another two hours before sunlight would begin to filter down through the higher emergent layer of the forest to the canopy. He tried to sleep again, but couldn't. He felt the exhilaration beginning to fill his veins as it had always done back in Nam after the moments of extreme fear had passed. It was like speed, bringing a rainbow all its own—the promise of deliverance—"one more time, God."

The power of nature had always awed Michael. The tremendous forces of creation and destruction were so out of man's control. It was nature's right to destroy what it had created, but it always renewed after the destruction. Michael had seen man's power demonstrated, too, though it was all destruction. With a simple ease, he had seen entire expanses of beautiful highland forest totally reduced by chemicals and giant Rome plows and long slow fire. He could still almost smell the white smoke from the phosphorus and the deep black smoke from the napalm that could suck the air out of your lungs. *Deny the enemy valuable resources and cover.* Killing the enemy was man's right, and if killing a forest was necessary to exercise that right, then it was justified. They killed such beauty to reach such ugliness.

The highlands of the Annamese cordillera were not unlike other rain forests of the world. There was a hidden, haunting beauty to them that had infected Michael. War had exposed him to them, both from the air and on the ground, where fear and death lurked in the dark rotting tangle in the form of an enemy you could seldom find, much less beat.

More than eight years had elapsed between the time Michael left Vietnam in early 1970 and the time his scientific interest in the rain forests peaked. He completed a rather long and well accepted thesis on the environmental interrelationships of a single acre of tropical rain forest at Finca La Selva, Costa Rica. He established himself in the scientific community as a sound observer with a refreshingly aggressive approach to rain forest research. His articles were widely published and considered authoritative.

Scientists the world over knew that only by rapidly understanding these incredibly rich, diverse pockets of evolution could their importance to the very survival of the earth be emphasized and brought into proper focus. Armed with enough facts, they could possibly wage a successful war to stave off the shortsighted, greed-prompted rush to irreversible ecological ruin. They applauded the efforts of men like Michael Gladieux and others who strove toward attainment of that knowledge.

Michael Gladieux had never been busier or happier in his life. He had found the direction that he had been searching for since he was twenty, when he had left college to find answers about himself. Vietnam had taught him much of that, and it was there that the seed of curiosity and understanding of the rain forests had been planted. The return of the nightmares he had thought long dead was a recent development, and he considered it a modest price to pay for happiness.

Daylight broke gently and seeped into the upper canopy below the woven crowns of the tallest trees. Michael ate a fast breakfast of bananas, dried fruits, and condensed milk, then readied himself to inspect the complicated web system from which he worked for possible damage from the storm.

Working in a rain forest was no simple matter. A rain forest is a complex multilayered environment, and research went on at all levels within the system. Michael's current work was limited to the upper canopy.

To work effectively within this environment, he had to learn highly developed rope-climbing techniques, knowing that to study the system properly he must be able to exist and move freely within it. Borrowing from techniques devleoped by other rain forest biologists, Michael constructed an intricate web system of supporting ropes across great expanses of canopy. Using a harness and stirrups, he moved by means of pulleys, while suspended, with relative ease and silence to get quite close to fields of observation. As a base of operations he constructed a four-by-eight platform, complete with plastic roof and roll down insect panels. It was his home within the environment.

Each new storm necessitated careful inspection of the rope network for signs of damage. His life depended on the integrity of the network. It was all that kept him from plummeting ninety feet to his death. It was a duty he never shirked or shortcutted. Absolute certainty was the only acceptable standard.

The morning was a long and tiring one. Two of the ropes had sustained damage, one being completely torn away. Repair necessitated restringing with a crossbow and monofilament line, then taking a cumbersome roundabout route to the target tree, followed by the drawing in of the monofilament with the new rope attached to its end.

When the web system was completely repaired and up to standard, he returned to the platform for lunch and a brief rest before resuming his observations. Throughout his lunch of freeze-dried spaghetti and meatballs his jungle-trained ears traced a distant movement through the lower tangle at ground level. The years in Vietnam had taught him the differences between animal and man-made sounds, and the sudden silence of his immediate region told him that the man was near.

Few men traveled alone in the rain forest, unless they were very familiar with it. Either another scientist, a park ranger, or a poacher

Michael thought. A sudden crash and the instant eruption of curses in the familiar voice told Michael who his visitor was.

Carlos Caesar raised himself from the tangle of tough vines that had snared and felled him. The first loud curses had not been directed at the forest, but at his own clumsiness. Caesar was a deputy administrator in the National Parks Department in the Ministry of Agriculture under the Forest Service. He spent little time behind the desk of his pleasant little office in San José, the capital city. He preferred spending his time in the many beautiful national parks he helped manage.

Corvocado, which borders the Pacific Ocean in southwest Costa Rica, was one of his favorites, and he spent nearly one-third of his time here. Michael often let Caesar use his platforms and had taught him how to negotiate the observation webs he had painstakingly assembled. In fact Caesar had helped him construct the last two, including this one. Caesar, although not a trained scientist, was a superb amateur ornithologist. He had spent many days with Michael, observing the incredibly rich bird population of the canopy and emergent layers.

But he came to the forest today carrying no observation equipment, no cameras or climbing gear. He came with news for his American friend. News he did not know how to tell him.

"Carlos," Michael called out. "Do you come up, or do I come down?"

"Down," Carlos's voice said, too weakly to be heard. He cleared his throat and tried again. "Michael, I do not have my climbing gear with me," he said in excellent though accented English.

No climbing gear? Michael thought. He had not expected Carlos to come today, though his friend was always welcome. It was not like him to come so deep into the forest for just a social call. Michael readied the seatlike harness and foot stirrups along with the necesary ascenders to the access rope for his climb back up.

Carlos watched as Michael rappelled through the middle-layer roof with the swift agility of a monkey, wondering how he could tell him the unpleasant news. Too soon, Michael was on the ground, his tall strong body approaching, the bearded face smiling with joy at the sight of his good friend.

"No gear? I can't carry you up to the platform, my friend," Michael said in fluent Spanish. Like his father, Michael had a talent for languages, speaking those that he had mastered almost without trace of accent. French had been natural to him, being spoken in his home equally with English. German and Spanish had been learned quickly, as had the various dialects of Vietnamese, Montagnard, and Cambo-

19

dian he had needed in his thirty-nine months of duty in Southeast Asia

He shook hands with his friend, and immediately read the uneasiness in the large dark eyes.

"What is it?" he asked, not attempting to guess.

"Michael, my friend, I don't know how to tell you," Caesar began A long uncomfortable moment of silence followed. He held out a folded telegram, a genuine sadness in his eyes. "This came for you today. I'm sorry. Very, very sorry."

Michael took the telegram with that sinking feeling inside. He knew from Carlos's face that the news was of crushing significance. He unfolded it and read:

MICHAEL
URGENT YOU RETURN HOME STOP FATHER
DEAD STOP SEND AHEAD FLIGHT INFO
STOP MEET YOU EWR OR LGA ADVISE END
DAN

Michael nearly collapsed from the sudden shock of the news.

Carlos grabbed his American friend by the elbow and put a hand to his shoulder. "Are you okay?" he asked, looking into the eyes for the real answer.

Michael looked at him as though puzzled, or dazed, like a fighter who had just gotten up from the canvas not knowing what day it was He nodded slowly and turned back toward the tree.

"My notes. I . . . I can't leave them up there. I'll climb up and get them. Wait for me here," he said in a low, weak voice.

"I will get them for you," Carlos said quickly. "Give me the harness and stirrups."

"No . . . no, I . . . can get them. I'm all right," Michael returned.

"It will be no trouble," Carlos said. "Perhaps you shouldn't climb—"

"I'll do it," Michael interrupted softly but with finality.

He stepped toward the ascent rope and turned back to his friend "I'll need to make arrangements. Can I use the park radio?"

"They are already being made for you," Carlos said. "I will take you back to San José in the Forest Service plane. You will be on the first available flight. You can call home with the flight information after we have confirmed it. If we leave here soon, we can be in San José in about three hours."

"Thank you, Carlos. You're a good friend," Michael said.

Carlos returned a slow nod.

Michael started up the rope, raising the seat harness extended along the rope while pushing himself up on the locked stirrups with his legs. The upper ascender automatically locked and he raised the stirrups and second ascender while sitting in the harness. The process repeated itself with more rapid and powerful movements until it looked like a smooth caterpillarlike motion.

The expenditure of energy was necessary for Michael. He used as much strength and speed as he could to help release the explosive feelings building up inside. Heavy perspiration started, and the strong, well-conditioned muscles were pushed to make them tire and hurt. If there had been records for such ascents, he would have just broken them.

He reached the platform, now out of Caesar's field of vision, and breathed deeply. The perspiration burned his eyes and rolled down his face and through his beard. His face, chest, and back began to cool from the breeze at the high level of the forest. He grabbed the notebooks in which he recorded his data and drawings, and snatched up his camera and equipment bag with the film he had shot. He quickly secured anything that could be blown off the platform and rolled down the heavy transparent plastic panels over the insect screening to help reduce the effects of the wind on the platform while he'd be gone. Then he sat on the edge of the cot and buried his face in his hands.

Michael's last image of immortality had just vanished. Certainly, any of the self-immortality of youth had been left in the jungles and rice paddies of Vietnam. That was one of the cruelest lessons of that time in his life. He had forfeited his youth as so many other young men had. But somehow, that everlasting image of his father, tall and vital and brilliant, had never been affected.

He thought of the last time he had seen his father over a year ago. He remembered the goodbye as clearly as if it had happened yesterday. How could he have known that he would never see him or talk to him again? A handshake had been the last goodbye. He wished now that he had hugged him and kissed him and told him the words he could never tell him again and had never told him enough—"Dad, I love you."

Carlos Caesar could hear the crying that Michael tried to muffle, and he knew he would say nothing about it when his friend's strained, reddened eyes looked at him next. Indeed, the rain forest that both men loved so much hung in reverent silence. All of God's creatures, great and small, that we often regard so lightly, knew the sounds of sorrow and hurting grief, and offered their quiet respect.

Chapter 4

TIME and exhaustion had no relevance in the mind of Michael
Gladieux. He hadn't slept since the morning of the storm at Cor
vocado. The long hike out of the rain forest and the one-hour flight to
San José in the battered, sputtering single-engine plane of the Forest
Service seemed like a fog-covered dream. His body had moved me
chanically, the eyes and muscles taking care of business while his brain
numbly tried to accept the news of his father's death and prepared to
confront the reality of the fact. It was while calling Princeton with his
flight information that his brain received its cruelest shock. The detail
of his conversation with Danny replayed wickedly in his mind as the
United wide-bodied jet streaked its way at cruising altitude from
Miami to Newark.

"How did it happen?" he had asked.

"It was a homicide," Danny had said after a moment of hesitation
When he said it, it was with the detached objectiveness of the cor
speaking for the man, but for Michael, the word "homicide" had
landed like a well-aimed blow to the solar plexus. It was paralyzing
The silence seemed endless before Michael began asking questions that
Danny knew better than to answer at long distance.

"How?" came the first one, strained, almost choked.

"We don't know yet," Danny lied. "He was found Saturday night
by Sophie. The postmortem is scheduled for Monday morning. I'll
have answers when you arrive."

"Who did it?" The second question was immediate.

"We don't know that, either. All the available evidence has been
collected. The State Police have officially entered the case, and the

22

crime lab will get started Monday on what was taken," Danny replied.

"Has a motive been established?" Michael asked.

"We just don't have answers, Mike," Danny lied again.

"God damn it, you have to know something," Michael shouted into the phone.

"Mike . . . listen—"

"Tell me!" Michael demanded.

"Mike . . ." Danny stopped and gave a sigh of exasperation into the phone.

"Tell me!" Michael repeated.

"We just don't know yet," Danny said.

Michael squeezed the phone with all his strength and anger. "You're a cop, god damn it. Your people are conducting the investigation. You have to know something," Michael insisted.

"Mike, I'm a part of the family. That leaves me outside the circle of investigation. They won't tell me anything until they're ready for an official release of information. Nothing will be disclosed until after the autopsy Monday morning. I'll know more by the time you get in Monday afternoon," Danny told him. "We'll have time to talk then."

Michael knew that he wasn't thinking objectively. His emotion was getting the better of his judgment. He should have realized that Danny wouldn't be privy to the early information and that it was the policy of police agencies worldwide to keep personally involved individuals out of investigations to protect the evidence qualitatively. It was one less nightmare for the prosecutor's office to contend with, and prevented self-styled justice from precluding due process. Simpler complications had blown otherwise airtight cases right out of the courts, to the benefit of the guilty and further tragedy of the innocent victim or his survivors.

"I'm . . . sorry," Michael said in a calmer tone. "How's Gabby holding up?" he asked.

"Not well, Mike," Danny answered. "The doctor has given her something to calm her and to help her rest. She's sleeping now. Father Piela is here now, too, and your mom and Ray are on their way in. They should be here in about two hours."

"How's Mom taking it?" Michael asked.

"Better than Gabrielle, though still not well. I talked to Ray, mostly. Your being here will help a lot."

Michael reviewed the arrival information and apologized to his brother-in-law again for his outburst. Danny understood and told him that he'd be there to meet him in Newark.

Newark was now just a few hours away for Michael. He didn't like

23

the thoughts going through his brain, but he couldn't stop them as he put his head against the seat back and closed his eyes.

He had seen the visions of death in all their ugly forms in Nam. The naked bodies of an ambushed patrol, stripped clean by the enemy, with the cruel effects of the VC knives in making sure of their kills. Ghastly poses of death frozen in response to impact, and the peaceful poses of bodies in long rest; bodies with pieces missing, faces blown away, chests or backs gaping open or gone completely. He had seen death in living faces, too, just before being thrown from helicopters or shot in the head by grinning South Vietnamese interrogation specialists. He saw death in such mass that at times the ground couldn't absorb it and you walked in it, were covered with it, and smelled of it. The impersonality of group death became such that seeing masses of bodies was no more traumatizing than seeing a dead cat by the side of the road.

There were scary deaths, too. Like the "charmed" grunt who had survived everything that the war could throw at him. Everyone used to flock around him because nothing could happen to him. Every outfit had one. Michael had seen him on the latrine pot covered with his own blood after having just cut his own throat—dead with a fucking smile on his face. Some men died from wounds so small that they couldn't be found without exhaustive search. Others gave their belongings away because they knew it was their "day." They had seen it, and they died as they knew they would.

He had seen men scream from such pain that they prayed for death, and men suddenly die who hadn't even realized they'd been hit. He saw poor bastards live who should have died, and wounded men die who shouldn't have, from shock, or fear, or just the belief that they would. Everybody thought about his own death and how it would come, whether easy or hard. And Michael wondered about his father, and how death had come to him.

He hadn't even considered the possibility of murder when the news first reached him. He thought the cause to be something like a sudden heart attack or a car accident or maybe a plane crash.

Michael's thoughts went to the memories he held of the man he loved. He had always enjoyed a good relationship with him, especially from the time he went away to school, and a special closeness had developed between them. It was no longer a relationship of authority and subordination like that between a father and his child. It was love and respect and friendship between men.

He remembered with some guilt the time he told his father about the deep confusion within his mind, and explained his reasons for wanting to leave school for a while to discover himself before committing to a life in medicine. Although Christian did not agree, he acceded to letting Michael follow his own mind. Neither of them could have known that a Marine Corps enlistment and Vietnam would follow.

He remembered, too, the extended leave after his first tour of duty in Nam had ended. Like everyone there, he thought of home to the point where in his mind it was better than it had ever really been. Not finding what he expected was very disappointing. There was little comfort in being home and with his friends again. Nothing was the same; he was not the same, and it was obvious. He could see it in the eyes of people. Eyes that stared suspiciously or with pity or with disdain, as though he was some kind of stupid dope-shooting donkey not smart enough to have kept himself out of it. Some eyes had an almost fearful quality in them as though they were looking at some kind of animal expected to become suddenly wild and dangerous. Nowhere did he see respect in the eyes, except in the eyes of his father. His father knew the changes that war made in a man and although respect was evident, so was sorrow. And in the eyes of Michael Gladieux, Christian had seen the absence of youth, the innocence stolen from them by the horrors they had seen. The gentle, intelligent eyes were no longer there. They had been replaced by the eyes of a hunting jungle cat wary of everything that moved and that didn't move, growing increasingly restless from confinement and hungry for the life it remembered.

Christian had assessed his son well, for his mind was filled with thoughts of the highland forest and the rice paddies, and concentrated on remembering the feelings that had been so dreaded when he was there, but were suddenly, desperately needed. The exhilaration of danger and survival was gone, the ultimate test of one's self no more. After the experiences of Vietnam, how could anything make one feel high on life?

Michael remembered the early-morning walk he and his father had taken on the beach. They walked for almost an hour before Michael's words described what was in his mind. It was a long talk, and the understanding displayed by his father was what Michael needed more than anything to help let the feelings out.

They returned from their walk to a magnificent breakfast. Michael ate with the appetite of a wolf, and for the first time seemed happy. Christian excused himself from the table in the middle of the meal and climbed the stairs to his son's room and sat on the edge of the bed looking at the banners and mementos of his son's happy youth, and he wept silently for the son he knew would be leaving the next day before completion of his leave to request a second tour of duty in Southeast Asia. There were still answers back there that had to be found.

The announcement to fasten seat belts for the final approach into Newark International Airport snapped Michael back into the present. A fresh realization of why he had come home hit him. He stirred uncomfortably in his seat with the wave of sudden emotion. He concentrated on the ground and the landing to distract himself.

Danny watched through the broad windows of the United gate pod as the large wide-bodied craft taxied through its last turn before making its way to the waiting ground crew at the gate area. He didn't feel nervous exactly, though there was some apprehension about facing Michael with the facts that he could no longer avoid telling him. Michael would be greatly disturbed by them, and he knew his brother-in-law's feelings for the system, especially in regard to justice. He would be hard to control, hard to hold back from attempting revenge before the authorities could act. Danny was a part of that system and knew the inequities and faults inherent to it. But he was a part of it and stayed within the established bounds.

The plane docked at the gate, and people waiting for friends and relatives began to crowd around the gate exit. Danny stood well back from the others, but in a direct line with the rampway so that Michael could spot him easily. He was the sixth passenger into the terminal and spotted Danny immediately.

As Danny watched Michael approach, he could see the image of Christian Gladieux as he had doubtless been in his youth. There was much about Michael that was like his father.

The two men greeted each other with a warm handshake and half-embrace. Michael backed away to arm's length and looked at the light chiseled features of his brother-in-law. He looked like a cop, Michael thought.

"I wish I could say it's good to be home," Michael said.

Danny nodded. "Yeah, I know. It's good to see you, anyway, Mike. Let's walk," he said. "Do you have luggage?"

"I'm wearing it," Michael said. "I don't need much in the rain forest. I left all my gear at the Forest Service office in Corvocado. All my real clothes are at the house in Spring Lake. Can we get into it?" he asked as they walked up the enclosed rampway to the terminal.

"Yeah, that's no problem. It's not cordoned or anything. They've gotten everything that they need out of it. I've already picked up one of your suits from the house for tonight. We'll be staying at Christian's house starting tonight until the services are completed tomorrow. We'll need maybe another day or two to go through his effects, if everyone is up to it. I'm sure he had insurance policies and financial matters that will need taking care of."

"The insurance information will be in his safe-deposit box, I'm sure. So will the rest of it probably. My father is . . . was a very organized guy," Michael said, the last words choking off weakly.

Danny could hear Michael's struggle to retain composure in the quiet throat-clearing coughs and the occasional quick sniff of his nose. His silence was a part of it, too, and that was okay with Danny. He wasn't looking forward to the conversation that would be starting soon.

The two men maintained silence through the terminal and to the parking area situated below it. Within a few minutes they were clear of the airport complex and headed for the New Jersey Turnpike for the trip to Princeton. The conversation began again as Danny reached cruising speed on the turnpike.

"I want to know how he died," Michael began suddenly.

Danny had rehearsed the answer to that question a dozen times while waiting for Michael's plane. Now the accepted words didn't offer themselves as he had wanted them.

"The autopsy determined the cause of death to be strangulation," Danny began almost clinically. "Two knife wounds to the lower back of the rib cage were inflicted prior to strangulation, as well as a rather severe blow to the face with a large blunt instrument. Whoever killed him expected a struggle and inflicted disabling injuries to reduce his defensive capabilities.

"It's my bet that the knife wounds came first by surprise as he entered the library, to restrict his breathing capacity. The face blow followed to stun and further disable him. The strangulation followed. Death wasn't meant to come quickly, or the knife would have gone to the throat, or a handgun would have been used. I'd also bet on two killers, not one."

Michael ached with such pain inside at the thought of the slow death his father had suffered that he felt as though the knife were in him, twisting and tearing violently at life-sustaining organs.

"Who did it and why?" Michael asked.

"It seems that a group called the Firewatch Brigade in France believed that your father was a collaborator during the war. The Firewatch Brigade is a communist organization made up of a relatively small number of fanatics, much like the communist Red Brigades. They're at the extreme radical end of the spectrum and, like the Red Brigades, resort to violence and acts of terrorism, often to achieve rather doubtful goals. A note was found indicating that he had been tried in absentia and found guilty. The killing was an execution in accordance with the Firewatch verdict. That makes it entirely possible that our killers are not from this country and may already be out of it."

"Are you telling me that there's nothing we can do about it?" Michael asked.

"I didn't say that," Danny replied. "But it'll make things a great deal more difficult. It's not just the killers to go after here, they were only the instruments of death like the weapons they used. The people responsible are the decision-making members of this Firewatch Brigade. Even if we caught the actual killers and brought them to justice, the real culprits would remain untouched."

"Brought to justice? Whose justice?" Michael asked cynically. "Do you really think that you can bring any of those people to justice in this country? I don't."

"It can be done, Mike. It takes time—"

"Bullshit!"

". . . time and a lot of cooperation from French authorities," Danny continued. "It may turn out in the end that we don't get them for this crime, but I'm sure we can get them for something if enough heat is applied."

"And just who is going to apply this heat?" Michael asked. "Dad wasn't the ambassador to France, you know, or a general attached to NATO command. Outside of us, who's going to care enough to apply heat? Nothing will be done about it beyond the local level. It will end up being just another unsolved case for the New Jersey State Police files. It'll collect enough dust, then be forgotten."

Danny drove without comment. He couldn't respond to those words.

"You said something about proof before," Michael began again. "What was this proof?"

"It wasn't specifically mentioned what this proof consisted of. But another aspect of the crime makes me believe that it's in our possession now. There was some . . . mutilation to the body," Danny said, wincing inside at the expected reaction.

Michael leaned forward in his seat and turned toward Danny, squinting hard at him and clenching his teeth. "What kind of mutilation?" he asked with smoldering rage.

"The type we commonly observe in mob killings where the offenses are symbolic of the justification," Danny answered.

"Don't use the word 'justification,'" Michael said loudly. "It was *not* justified. I don't care what somebody else may have believed, he was *not* a collaborator, and I won't hear that word imply that he was, intended or not."

"Mike, I'm not saying—"

"I know what you're not saying, what you don't mean. Just don't use that word. Go back to the mutilations. Describe them to me."

Danny described the mutilations in vague detail to try to lessen the pain he knew it would bring. He ended by telling of the spike that had been driven into the chest with the note and pendant attached. "I suspect that the pendant is the proof in question," he said.

Michael's brain had stopped recording beyond the description of the mutilation. He had seen every type of imaginable mutilation to corpses in Vietnam. Ears were commonly taken to verify a kill or to help establish a body count. He had taken them himself, but not out of some morbid satisfaction. Other mutilations to the eyes, mouths, genitals, and other body parts were done either out of benign savagery or as ultimate insult. There were all kinds of redundant mutilators—eye shooters, part collectors, and crazies who got their jollies desecrating a fallen enemy.

Slowly the words "proof" and "pendant" filtered through to his brain. "What did you say about a pendant?" he asked.

"The pendant attached to the spike is probably the proof referred to in the letter," Danny repeated. "It had the image of a three-headed salamander on it. It must have some kind of significance."

"Does Gabby know about the mutilation?" Michael asked.

"No. No one does right now except for the authorities, you, me, and Sophie. Those details have been blocked out to the media. I told Ray because I felt I had to, but he hasn't said anything to your mom."

"That'll mean a closed casket," Michael said.

"Not necessarily. We'll make that decision before things get started tonight. If there's any doubt, we'll close it."

"What kind of arrangements have to be made yet?" Michael asked.

"Everything has been taken care of. The wake will start at seven this evening and will last until nine. Then again tomorrow morning from nine to eleven. The funeral will take place at two in the afternoon, and there will be some kind of short reception at your dad's house afterwards."

Michael fell back into silence for the remainder of the trip, his mind filling with hatred for blank faces that he vowed to find.

Danny turned off the turnpike at Exit 8 and took route 33 west, then 571 into Princeton. The ride had taken about an hour. He pulled into the long driveway and parked near the side entrance to the house.

"The kids are with a neighbor," Danny said. "Gabby may be sleeping. Your mom and Ray are here now."

Michael got out of the car in silence and followed Danny into the house. Ray Barry, his mother's husband, was the first to greet him.

"Mike," Ray began, looking into his stepson's eyes. "What can I say?" he offered, shaking his head in disbelief.

Michael nodded, the pain fresh again. "Thanks for coming, Ray. How's Mom holding up?" he asked.

"Not bad right now, but it'll get a lot worse tonight. I think she'll need you here. She's with your sister—" He cut off the sentence at the sounds on the stairs behind them, and turned.

Michael looked past him to see a grief-shattered Gabrielle being helped down the stairs by Father Vincent Piela, the priest from Spring Lake, and his mother, who looked only slightly better than her daughter.

The sight of Michael standing there gave Gabrielle a sudden rush of strength. She negotiated the last stairs and ran across the room to him.

There was a long moment of silence, interrupted only by the soft sounds of Gabrielle's sobbing, her head buried against Michael's chest. She looked up into his strong features, her eyes bloodshot and swollen, tears streaming down the cheeks of her tired face.

"Daddy's dead," she said weakly. "What are we going to do?" she asked, her voice trailing off into pathetic sorrow.

"Don't worry, Gabby," he said, pulling her head gently to his chest again. "Don't worry, Sis. I'll take care of it. It's not going to end like this. I won't let it. I promise," he said softly.

Denise Gladieux Barry watched her children tearfully. Michael looked into the sad eyes of his mother. Her pain was evident, but so was her strength. Michael extended an arm, and she too came into it, kissing her son and stroking his hair and bearded face with her hands, studying the striking resemblance between her son and his dead father. Tears filled her eyes, and she kissed him again, then embraced both her children, turning her kisses and comfort to her daughter, who needed them so much.

Michael fought back the sounds of his grief, but could not hold back the tears that welled up in his eyes, blurring them before rolling down his cheeks. He saw the priest approach through his tears, the unclear figure of him growing more familiar as he drew near. He extended a hand to the priest.

The priest took it, giving a nod that acknowledged Michael's unspoken thanks and offered his own thank-you for the strength Michael's presence gave. Then Father Piela stroked Gabrielle's soft brown hair, and in silence blessed the children he had watched grow, and asked that their sorrow be eased and turned to strength for the days ahead.

Indeed, the need for strength would be real.

Chapter 5

SMOKE curled from the lips of Detective Sergeant Robert Caldwell as he sat in his parked car concealed across the street from the Holiday Inn in Bordentown, New Jersey. Ten minutes had passed since he had watched Colonel Alan Kendrick enter the motel through a side entrance and his driver leave the area in the sparkling state-owned vehicle. It wasn't standard procedure for the Superintendent of the New Jersey State Police to be left without the presence of at least his bodyguard-driver in close proximity. Caldwell hadn't expected Kendrick to show up for the intriguing command performance, even though he was sure the order for the meeting had originated from his office.

He crushed out the short stub of the Camel and tried to ignore the hunger pangs from the missed lunch. There had been time to eat, but eating lunches on hot days made him slow in the afternoon, and he wanted to be fully alert. The surveillance of the motel was his own idea, to try to determine the reason for the unusual request. It wasn't that secret meetings were unusual. Indeed, his life seemed to be filled with them. Meetings with informers and contacts were always closely guarded to protect them. But this was not a meeting of that nature. It had been called for selected department members. There was no reason to hold departmental meetings in secrecy, unless someone who did not want his attendance on record was going to be there. Kendrick had already verified that fact about himself, which was curious enough in its own right.

Caldwell lit up another unfiltered Camel as a second car he recognized pulled into the side lot and parked. His immediate superior, Captain Stephen Bach, got out of the car and hurried in through the same side entrance. He hadn't been expected either, since he was off on vacation. This was getting better all the time, he thought as he pulled hard on the cigarette, inhaling its smoke deeply.

Another ten minutes went by before he started his car to meet his appointed arrival time. No sooner had he driven into the lot and parked his car than his new partner, Anthony LoIaccano, arrived.

Both men got out of their cars carrying small attaché cases containing the meager facts they had gathered on the case they had just been given.

The two men exchanged greetings and headed for the same side entrance the others had used. Caldwell saw another car pull in and its occupant get out and stretch stiff muscles before gathering two boxes into his arms. This man was William Henry, one of the top evidence specialists of the New Jersey State Police crime lab.

Caldwell and LoIaccano entered the side door as Henry began to cross the parking lot. They slowed their pace until Henry caught up to them. Caldwell introduced LoIaccano and Henry, who had never met

"I don't understand why we're here," said Henry after the introduction, addressing the statement to Caldwell. "Who else are we supposed to be meeting?" he asked.

"Got me," Caldwell replied. "What have you got in the boxes?"

"Homicide evidence taken from Spring Lake by the Monmouth County detective staff," Henry answered. "Got everything here but tissues and fluids taken from the corpse. We haven't even finished going over all of it yet. This isn't sound procedure to be moving material around like this before we've finished with it."

"Well, someone's got something important on their mind. We'll find out in about two minutes what's going on," Caldwell said as the three men reached the door.

Caldwell knocked and waited. About fifteen seconds later came the sound of the chain lock being removed and the door was swung open. Captain Stephen Bach stood at the open door.

"Good, you're right on time. Come on in," he said.

The three men entered, Bach locking the door behind them again

Caldwell looked around the room. Kendrick and Bach he had seen enter. But there were three other men that he didn't know and hadn't seen arrive during his stakeout. There was a brief moment of awkward staring before Colonel Kendrick began his introductions Caldwell carefully noted the faces and the names of the three strangers.

The first two were with the Federal Bureau of Investigation and the third with the Central Intelligence Agency.

It was a strange combination, Caldwell thought. The Bureau and the CIA; it was like having two female cats in heat in the same garage. He couldn't wait to see what had brought this act together.

Kendrick finished the introductions and motioned for the men to take chairs before going further.

"You've been asked here today to discuss a case of homicide that has just become the responsibility of the Division," Kendrick began. "That is the murder of Christian Gladieux. Some of us knew him personally, and those who did not, knew of him either through his son-in-law, Dan Preston, whom you troopers know, or through Gladieux's success and renown as a novelist.

"The death of any celebrity is a news event that brings a lot of public interest, especially under circumstances like these. People expect fast answers and good competent police work in bringing about a swift solution to the crime. That was one of my reasons for sending in the major crimes unit so early. I do not mean to imply that the Monmouth County detective staff is not capable of bringing the case to a swift conclusion—they have a fine department. Let's just say that I felt we have more ships in the water and that our ships have bigger guns. You understand what I mean," he said with smile.

"The other reasons are, of course, more personal in nature. It touches us all when one of our own, or a member of his family, becomes the victim of violent crime. And it would be an obvious lie for me to say that my feelings in this case remain disconnected from it and that only cool, objective reasoning prompted my reaching for it. I knew Christian Gladieux and considered him a friend. Dan Preston is also a friend of mine, and an outstanding member of the Division. And that, too, is a part of it.

"But I didn't have you come here to justify my reasons for taking the Gladieux case. Before I go on, however, I must point out to you that the very fact of this meeting, as well as its purpose, must remain confidential. Is that clear to you all?" Kendrick asked, waiting for affirmative responses from his men.

"Good. I feel it important to tell you that you were carefully selected, and that I trust you all completely, or you wouldn't be here."

He paused a moment as though to organize the facts in his head before starting again.

"News of the Gladieux murder was spread quickly by the media, along with some of the mysterious details of the case involving the motive for the murder. Our friends here from Washington became interested in the puzzling aspects of the crime and some of the evidence known to have been collected, and they contacted me directly. This meeting was requested to review all the known facts and to make available to them any information that we have developed. We will also be keeping them informed as we progress on the case," Kendrick explained.

Caldwell felt for the pack of Camels in his pocket, hoping to find it relatively full. He sensed that a long night lay ahead. In a way, it didn't puzzle him that these men would show an interest in the case. The involvement of an extremist group known to have ties to terrorist activities and associations with other groups of even more notoriety was cause enough to generate interest in a lot of places. Whatever their reasons for being here, he was certain he would learn a great deal more about them from the questions they asked.

Kendrick's final words were somewhat lost on Caldwell as he was sizing up the three government men. Something inside told him to remember everything they said, especially regarding pieces of evidence that held their special interest. If his intuition was right, as it usually was in these matters, he'd be making a phone call at the first opportunity after the conclusion of this meeting.

It wasn't long before the focal point of their interest became plain to Caldwell. They reviewed all the facts carefully, but a single item, which had been the first inquired about, was the unmistakable apple they had come for. Their line of questioning seemed always to lead back to it.

It was enough for Caldwell to know that his call would have to be made. An important aspect of this case would also be of interest to other people as well, although he couldn't sense the significance of it yet. Whatever it was, a pendant bearing the image of a three-headed salamander had excited someone in Washington enough to send three people asking questions.

A dull nervous feeling began to enter Michael's gut as they neared the funeral parlor. The director of the funeral parlor had told Danny that he was certain they could conceal any traces of the disfigurement. But he had said that before seeing the body, and Michael wondered if they really could. He would find out shortly, he knew, as the car pulled into the empty parking lot thirty minutes before the start of the seven-to-nine viewing.

The sun was still shining brightly on the warm spring day as the three men exited the car. Danny turned to Ray. "Would you stay with the women while Mike and I preview the situation inside?"

"Sure, I'd be glad to," Ray replied.

"Would you rather that I do this alone?" Danny asked Michael.

Michael's eyes had been fixed on the building that held the remains of his father. He looked back to Danny and shook his head.

A young man in a black suit greeted them politely as they reached the entrance. Standing a few feet inside the open doorway was the director of the funeral parlor. He was also dressed in a black three-piece suit with a dark striped tie.

"Hello, Dan," he said softly, extending his hand. His eyes moved to Michael. "You're the son," he said. The resemblance left no doubt.

Michael nodded, taking the offered hand.

The director nodded. "Accept our condolences, Mike."

"Thank you."

The director looked back to Danny and motioned toward the viewing room in which Christian was laid out. The three men started walking toward it.

Michael's eyes immediately saw the placard on the wall bearing the name of his father. He was filled with a sudden apprehension and nearly stopped. The sensation had actually begun before seeing the name, as the sickly sweet fragrance of the commingled scents of flowers hit him upon entering. It was the smell of death. Not only of funeral parlors, but of actual death. It was the same sweet odor that Michael had observed at scenes of fresh, violent death in which a large spillage of blood and body fluids had occurred. For reasons that he could not explain, the scents of sudden and violent death were often quite similar to some of the milder fragrances emitted by flowers.

"Were you able to fix him up?" Danny asked.

"Yes. I think you'll be pleased," the director said as they neared the room.

"What about the postmortem?" Danny inquired. He knew the effects that an autopsy could have on a body, even one not previously marked.

"Clean job," the director said. "Nice and neat, easy to work with."

Michael saw the foot of the casket as he neared the door, and again his apprehension nearly stopped him from entering. But he continued into the doorway behind Danny and the director, who still shielded the body of his father from his vision. When they neared the front of the room, they began to move to the right, and his eyes caught the first sight of his dead father. A hammer would have had less effect.

The initial reaction passed quickly, and his concern switched to the appearance of his father. As he approached more closely, his eyes began searching frantically for any telltale signs on the sleeplike face, but there were none.

35

Danny stood close and looked down at the face of his father-in-law. It was remarkable. The face looked normal and proportioned, with no residual evidence of the blow to the face. Danny leaned forward over the body and looked to the left ear. The longish-styled hair was neatly placed, and the pillow nestled just a little higher than usual. Only very close observation indicated that no ear lobe was visible below the hair as on the right side. One would have to look for it specifically to tell.

Danny backed away. "You did a great job. He looks good," he said.

"He looks dead," Michael shot back, his voice laced with bitterness.

The director looked at him, puzzled, almost fearful of the tone.

Michael continued looking at the face of his father, then looked at Danny and the director. "I'm . . . sorry," he said.

"We do try our best to give a natural sleeping appearance," the director said nervously.

"Well, you did just fine," Michael remarked as he looked at the pink-hued lights which cast a soft lifelike quality on the face. He looked around the room at the crush of flower arrangements offering tribute to the man who was so well liked and admired.

The director looked back to Danny, who gave a rapid nod to indicate that everything was all right.

Michael placed his hand on the crossed hands of his father and uttered a silent pledge to make things right. It could not, and would not, end so simply.

The two hours that followed were a dull blur to Michael. The stream of people was endless. The offered condolences went unheard by ears that seemed to listen but were deafened by a brain crying out for retribution. It was only the enormous, pathetic grief of his sister that moved him periodically to unrestrainable rises of emotion. Her pain was his pain, and he could do nothing to protect her from it. His mother had Ray, and her sorrow was a hurting one, but not hysterical. She was a wonderfully strong woman.

It was ten minutes to nine when Father Vincent Piela entered the room. The remaining people hushed as he approached the casket. He knelt and looked into the face with sincere sorrow and prayed. Then he rose, touched the hands of Christian Gladieux, and turned to the silent waiting faces. He spoke with heartwarming eloquence as his words touched everybody, then led them in prayer.

The priest concluded his brief service and spent a few moments talking to Gabrielle and then to Denise. He walked to the back of the room and took Michael's hand, extending his condolences. Michael took the opportunity to thank him for all that he had done.

"You know, Michael, your father and I had become quite close over the past year or so," the priest began in a low voice. "He was a very troubled man."

Michael's eyes registered some surprise. "Did he ever confide in you as to the reason for it?" he asked.

"No, but I always had the feeling that it was over a matter of belief."

"Belief in God?" Michael questioned.

"No, your father had a very healthy philosophy about God and faith. He believed in God, but not in the ritual surrounding religion. He felt that religion was a personal thing between a man and God. It didn't matter if they reached their understanding in a church pew or on the beach or on a golf course. I couldn't argue with that.

"But your father also talked about self-belief. He would say that real faith started here and here," the priest said, touching his chest and head. "And that before a man can really believe in anything, he must believe in himself. He said that the struggle to believe in one's self was the most difficult of all, because in ourselves we find all things good and all things evil, and we must choose those things upon which we will build our faith.

"I felt that this was where his trouble lay, as though he were facing some challenge to those beliefs. Somehow, the peace within him had been upset by that challenge and caused a great conflict within his mind."

Michael's first thought was of the charge of collaboration, and the proof beyond doubt that had been referred to. He would not believe that his father was a collaborator.

"And he never gave you a hint as to what it might have been?" Michael asked.

"No, not really. Though once he did mumble something about how a man's ideals can change and words which I could not distinguish about loyalty. He wouldn't repeat it, dismissing it as a passing notion of some kind. He became very pensive for a while after that though."

"Did he seem to be troubled up to the time of his death?"

"No. Strangely enough, he seemed to have been relieved of some great burden for the past several months," the priest replied.

"Can you be more specific as to how long?"

The priest thought for a moment. "I would say for three or four months. I could tell, because our conversations became much lighter and covered many more topics. He seemed to have worked his way through some of his problem," the priest said. "I only wish now that he would have confided in me. Perhaps I could have helped him. I don't know if it would have avoided any of this . . ." He trailed off, shaking his head.

"It wasn't the state of *his* mind that made this happen," Michael said.

"I know, I know. Such a terrible thing. I pray that it will be resolved."

"It will be, Father. You can bet the deed to the church on that," Michael guaranteed.

The tone of his meaning was not wasted on the priest. "Revenge isn't God's way, Michael," he said.

"The Bible mentions justice, and the right to expect it," Michael countered.

"There are laws and people to execute those laws, my son. We cannot take it upon ourselves."

Michael held the priest's stare for a few moments. "Thank you, Father, for all that you've done for my mother and sister, and for the friendship that you gave to my father. I'm truly grateful to you."

The priest nodded. "It was the least that I could do. Michael . . . I wish that you would come and talk to me after the funeral," he said, troubled by the seeming state of Michael's mind.

"It won't change anything, Father," Michael said.

"Perhaps not. But we could talk."

"I won't promise," Michael returned.

"You didn't say no. I'll accept that much for now. I'll see you tomorrow," the priest said, shaking Michael's hand.

Father Piela walked away, had a few words with Danny, then left.

The evening ended at about half past nine for the family. The emotions rose again on leaving, but the levels of grief were much more controlled. Acceptance had begun to settle in.

They would now be heading back to the house in Spring Lake, and Michael wanted that very much. He didn't know what, if anything, would reveal itself, but he was going to begin the search.

He already knew something that the police didn't. Something had disturbed his father very much and for a long time. He didn't know what it was yet, or if it even fit into the picture. At least it was a beginning. And it was all that he needed right now—a place to start, to take that first step. It would be a long road, to be sure, and he was ready to travel it—every step of the way.

Chapter 6

SERGEANT Robert Caldwell stepped into the phone booth outside the closed service station and tapped out a zero, followed by the 212 area code and the seven digits of his desired number on the dial-first phone.

"Operator four three three. May I help you?" a pleasant voice asked.

"Yes. I'd like to make a collect person-to-person call to a Mr. Clayton Cargill."

"Your name please?" the operator asked.

"Winston Bass," he said.

"Thank you."

He listened to the clicks and whirrs and the split second of silence before the ring on the other end began.

"Unitrol. May I help you?" a male voice said.

"Yes, I have a person-to-person-collect call for a Mr. Clayton Cargill from a Mr. Winston Bass. Will you accept charges?"

"Yes, operator, we will accept charges," the voice said.

"Go ahead, sir," the operator said to Caldwell.

"Thank you," Caldwell returned as the operator clicked off.

"Is your location sterile?" the voice asked, inquiring as to the absence of possible wiretap.

"It's public. I've used it before," he replied.

"Hold for verification," the voice instructed.

Caldwell held his ear to the silence. About fifteen seconds passed before the voice returned. "You're clear. State your identification code and clearance."

"Bass, eleven-oh-one-seven-seven. Piper Delta Zebra," he complied. He could hear more clicks and whirrs. A computer was working.

"Clearance accepted," the voice announced. "Please hold."

After nearly a minute of waiting the familiar voice of his contact came on. "Yes, Bass, what do you have?"

"The homicide of one Christian Gladieux. Last name spelled George—Lincoln—Adam—David—Ida—Edward—Union—X-ray."

"Got it. Go ahead."

"There has been interest from Washington. FBI and CIA. They were not specific as to their reasons, but I suspect that they have a file on this man," Caldwell told his contact.

"If they do, we'll know about it. Go on."

"Apparent interest seemed to be in possible connections with the Firewatch Brigade or other subversive elements, possibly neo-Nazi in opposition to Firewatch. A strong interest was expressed in one particular piece of evidence. This was a pendant, made of glass, about the size of a half-dollar, slightly larger, bearing the image of a three-headed salamander. It is multicolored, primarily black, affixed to a silver backplate. This was left on the body by the killer, or killers, with mutilation to the corpse. A letter was left stating that the reason for the 'execution' was collaboration with the Germans during World War Two. Firewatch tried the decedent in absentia, finding him guilty. The killing was the carrying out of the sentence."

"Firewatch," the voice said. "Small but nasty. We'll go to work on it. Can you obtain the pendant?" the voice asked.

Caldwell thought for a moment. "I can get photographs," he said. "This material is tagged evidence. I don't think I can get it."

"Evidence is only important if it gets to court," the voice said. "If this was Firewatch vengeance, it will never get there. The evidence will be meaningless to your organization. I would also suspect that pressure from Washington will result in its removal from your custody, anyway. And probably very soon. Especially if that is what they were interested in, as you suspect.

"We could always obtain it once Washington has it, but that would be extremely difficult compared to getting it now. I suggest you endeavor to obtain it in the best way you can," the voice said.

Jesus Christ, thought Caldwell. He remained silent for a moment. "All right. I'll think of something. But remember me when I'm out of a job," he said.

"At your earliest convenience. We'll arrange the drop upon your notification," the voice said.

"Yeah, swell," Caldwell said with mild sarcasm. "I'll call you."

"We'll be waiting," the voice said, then the phone went dead.

Caldwell hung up the phone and ran his hand through his hair. Fucking great, he thought to himself. Now all I have to do is steal evidence. It wasn't that hard to do, actually, when the evidence was old and not of immediate interest. That wasn't the case with the pendant. At least he knew exactly where it was and had access to it. The longer he let himself think about it, the harder it would become. He decided to take it tonight, before his own brain began to work against him. With luck, he'd have it within the hour.

He went back to his car, lit up a Camel, and drove off into the night.

Michael stood in the library of his father's house, staring at the spot where the body had been found. Dried blood still soiled the Oriental rug covering the center of the floor. Aside from that trace of violence, the room and the rest of the house seemed quite in order.

Danny entered the room quietly, and watched Michael as he walked slowly around it. Michael went to the file cabinet beside the desk and opened the top drawer. After a moment he closed it, then walked to a table beside the recliner chair that his father worked in, opened the fold-down door, and bent to look inside. Then he straightened up and turned to Danny. "Were these dusted for prints?" he asked.

"Everything in the room was," Danny replied. "Why do you ask?"

"Was my father working on a book?"

"Yes, he was," Danny answered.

"How far along was he?"

"I don't have the slightest idea. Why?"

"Because whoever killed him took all his material, that's why. I've watched him work enough to know how he did things. He always put his research files, character notes, outline workups, and rough drafts of his chapters in those two places. They're empty now. Someone has taken everything."

"Are you sure?" Danny asked.

"Positive. I suggest we contact his publisher in the morning. If he was beyond the outline stage, they'd at least have a copy of that. If he wasn't, they may know what he was working on."

"Why would they want his material?" Danny asked.

"I don't know. But I don't buy the collaboration theory for one minute. If that had been the sole reason for his being killed, they wouldn't have given a damn about his work."

"Maybe he just put it somewhere else," Danny suggested.

Michael looked at him, shaking his head. "That table and that file cabinet were the only places he kept his unfinished work. I know what I'm saying. Come on, I think it's time we talked to my mother," Michael said.

The two men left the library and went to the kitchen, where the rest of the family was making a weak attempt to eat the food prepared and left by thoughtful neighbors.

"Would you like some coffee?" Denise asked in her slight French accent as they walked in. Michael nodded. So did Danny.

A moment later she was pouring two cups of her excellent coffee, then joined them at the table.

Michael wasn't quite sure how to begin without starting the flow of pain again. There was no way but a direct approach, so he took it. "Mom, you're aware of the note that was found beside Dad, aren't you?" he asked.

She looked at him for a brief instant before answering "Yes. I know what it said."

"They called Dad a collaborator. Why would they do that?"

She waited a long time before answering. Then she looked down and away before slowly raising her eyes to her daughter and then back to Michael. "I think it's time to tell you both something," she said.

For an instant Michael felt his stomach sink, fearing that he was about to hear words he had not thought possible.

"Your father," she said, "was *not* a collaborator. He was a very brave man and a hero, recognized by De Gaulle, the Free French forces, and the British for his courageous, unselfish efforts for his country during the war. It was a terrible time in our history, and a great many people suffered and did unthinkable things for the best and worst of motives. Your father never talked about those times, for many reasons. And I understood them, even more than he realized.

"You see the war was very hard for him. It was hard for everybody, but your father had more than his share of suffering from it. I'm sure that you don't know what I'm going to tell you, and I hope that you will understand.

"I did not see your father often after the war started. At first he was fighting with the army. He was wounded and discharged at about the time France surrendered. He made his way to me at my father's house, but stayed only a short time before leaving to join the Resistance. I saw him only three times after that until the war ended. And he never confided in me as to the horrible things that happened during those years, although I learned something about them afterwards from his friends, and . . . I sensed others.

"Your father belonged to a Resistance group called Le Groupe

42

Défi—Group Defiance. He became the second in command behind a courageous young woman named Edna-Marie DeBussey. She was a remarkable woman.

"Both she and your father carried a heavy responsibility. They commanded many people, and watched so many of them die and go through such horrors. Group Defiance had one of the highest casualty totals of any Resistance group in the war. Each one weighed heavily on your father, especially one—a woman. I found out about her after the war. But inside I had known. A woman does," she said with tears beginning to fill her eyes.

"Christian loved her very much. And he felt her death to be his fault, because he could not save her in time. You see, she died after the liberation of Paris, killed by French patriots who took her for a collaborator. She used . . . herself to gain information from Germans in high places. Her role was known only to your father, Edna-Marie, and a few others. The Frenchmen who killed her had no idea of the part that she played for France.

"I saw a picture of her once, standing with your father. She was very beautiful."

Denise looked at her daughter and smiled. "Her name was Gabrielle. Gabrielle Dupuy.

"When the war finally ended, your father returned home, a weak, shattered image of a man. He was numb and listless from grief. So many had died, brutally murdered by the Germans. Gabrielle had died, and it seemed as though your father had, as well, inside.

"Then one day that I shall never forget, men came to our home. They informed your father that he was under arrest as a covert collaborator, responsible for many of the deaths he mourned. It was not true, but charges had been made by another Resistance group which claimed to have proof. An unknown collaborator *had* existed within Group Defiance. There had been many informers. But this one had been especially helpful to the Germans and had betrayed hundreds of his own people. His identity was never learned.

"Your father was put on trial, and his friends from Group Defiance flocked to his aid. The proof turned out to be weak circumstantial evidence based upon mere supposition and hearsay. He was declared innocent by a vote of four to one and released. The one guilty vote came from a communist judge. The charges had been brought against your father by a powerful communist Resistance group led by a man named Pierre Falloux.

"Your father was released and cleared of all charges, but he knew that a specter of doubt would always hang over him. He was outraged that the country for which he had suffered so much would do such a thing to him. The very men who had sat in judgment of him had been guilty, themselves, of collaboration in one form or another before opportunely realigning their positions when the outcome of the war became clear. A great many 'heroes' suddenly appeared out of thin air near the end.

"Your father was hurt and angered beyond redress, and he left France to come to the United States. He never set foot in France again, and never spoke of the past."

The phone rang, breaking the spell of the listeners. The hour was late for a phone call, and Michael's eyes expressed as much to Danny Michael went to the phone and answered it.

"Who is this?" a nervous voice at the other end asked.

"This is Michael Gladieux. Who are *you?*"

"This is Paul Terrence, Mike. I'm . . . I was your father's editor," the voice said. The tone was frightened.

Michael flashed a quick glance at Danny and pointed a finger toward the other extension in the living room. Danny was off like a shot.

"Just a second, Paul," Michael said, to give Danny time to get there. The faint click a moment later told him that Danny was on the line. "Okay, Paul. What can I do for you?" he asked.

"I'm . . . I'm sorry about what happened to your father," the strained voice said.

"Thank you, Paul," Michael returned evenly.

"I have to talk to you. It's important that I talk to you soon."

"All right. When would you—"

"I . . . I have his outline," Terrence interrupted. "I think it has something to do with his death."

"Go on," Michael urged.

"I can't. Not on the phone. There's just too much. I have to talk to you in person. I'm sure that your father knew—"

"Knew what?" Michael asked.

"He knew. He knew it could mean trouble for him. He told me as much in strict confidence, but I didn't . . . believe him," the voice said, starting to cry. "Now nothing is left."

"Paul, you have to tell me more," Michael urged.

"I think that I'm in danger, too," Terrence said. "I *must* meet with you. Someplace safe."

"How about here at my father's house?" Michael suggested.

Terrence didn't answer.

"It's safe here, Paul. There are a lot of people here. My brother-in-law and I can protect you."

44

"That's not enough," Terrence said nervously.

"I can get half the god damn New Jersey State Police here, if you insist. We can control this house. We might not be able to control an area that we're not familiar with," Michael said.

Terrence was quiet again. Michael could almost hear him thinking.

"Okay, your father's house, then," Terence said at last. "But early. Five o'clock in the morning," he said.

"Why not right now?" Michael asked.

"No. When the roads are empty and I can see that I'm not being followed. Five o'clock. No, four. Four o'clock. Is that okay?" Terrence said, sounding terribly confused and frightened.

"That's fine, Paul. Do you know how to get here?"

"Yes . . . yes, I've been there before. I'll see you . . . at four."

"All right, Paul. We'll be waiting for you," Michael promised.

The phone went dead.

Michael hurried out of the kitchen and met Danny, who had already started back in.

"It sounds like you could be exactly right about your father's work being important to someone else," said Danny. "Whatever it is, it has this guy Terrence scared out of his senses. He didn't sound too good to me. He's confused and not far from panic. It might have been best if we went to him."

"I think you're right. But it's too late for that now. Let's hope he's not too scared to show up. If we can get our hands on that outline, then maybe we'll know what's going on around here."

Chapter 7

THERE were still too many cars on the road at 2:00 A.M. to suit Paul Terrence as he approached the Tappan Zee Bridge from the Tarrytown side. He now wished he had chosen a later hour to arrive at Spring Lake, allowing him clearer highways. Enough cars were moving in his direction to make it impossible to tell if he was being followed. The only vehicle he was certain of was a pickup truck with a loose headlight that bounced as it was jarred by the bumps in the road. But that truck had passed him long ago and certainly hadn't been following him.

His Volkswagen Rabbit sped smoothly toward the long sweep of the bridge. He nervously checked the rearview mirror. At first he didn't know what to make of the headlights not far behind him, except that he noticed one of them bouncing rapidly from the road vibration. It was the pickup truck again. He couldn't remember passing it, but then he had driven with such intensity of thought that he didn't even recollect passing familiar points that he knew well. He gave it no further thought as the fuel-injected import hummed onto the bridge. He estimated an hour and a half yet to Spring Lake. Every minute into the early morning hours would mean less traffic to worry about.

It wasn't until he had left the superstructure and passed the halfway point on the bridge as it dropped nearer the water that he noticed the pickup truck in the lane beside him.

It was a four-wheel-drive vehicle, and the cab sat considerably higher than his own position. He tried looking up with some difficulty, only to see a face staring back at him through an open window. Then, very quickly, an arm shot out holding what looked like a flare gun.

Terrence had only begun to feel fear when the window of the back door shattered. There was a muffled pop and a sudden bright burst of flame on the back seat. A roaring rocketlike sound followed and the car filled with a choking black smoke.

The car began to weave from the combined effects of the smoke on Terrence and his struggle to reach the copy of the manuscript outline on the back seat, which was already in a mass of flames.

He screamed as he pulled his burning arm back. He shook the arm frantically as the fire covered it in an oozing, spreading fashion.

He coughed, and choked, and screamed from the pain as the glass of his door window shattered in on him. The second thermite device landed squarely in his lap after deflecting off the dashboard and steering column. It, too, erupted into incendiary fury, quickly engulfing the screaming editor. He clawed wildly at his burning clothing and flesh chunks of his skin coming off in his hands.

The Rabbit began to swerve uncontrollably. The pickup truck kissed the front fender hard, driving it toward the rail. The import climbed the low wheel barrier and struck the rail heavily, spinning and taking out a large section of the safety retainer.

By this time, the interior of the car glowed white from the intense reaction of aluminum powder and iron oxide. The car crashed through four more sections of rail before tipping over the side. But it did no fall. It hung suspended, spewing smoke and flames.

Cars that had been on the bridge stopped, their occupants watching helplessly as the truck stopped just ahead of the suspended car, shifted into reverse and rammed over the low wheel barrier into the Rabbit and the portion of rail holding it to the bridge.

The car plummeted from the bridge. Tremendous columns of steam and smoke billowed upward as the car sank quickly, the thermite reaction continuing below the surface of the water with an unstoppable fury.

All four wheels of the pickup truck belched smoke and rubber as it strained to free itself from the tangled rail. It broke free as helpless bystanders watched, and sped off. Some of the witnesses rushed to the torn edge of the bridge and stared in horror into the murky water at the eerie sight of fire burning below its surface, in what looked like a vision of hell itself.

Paul Terrence had been right about the outline's importance to people unknown. And whatever its contents, he had taken its secret with him.

The sounds of the surf and the wind and the wet slaps of his feet renewed Michael as he ran on the beach. He had done this same thing countless times in his younger days, but usually in the waking hours of dawn. Those runs had always been enjoyable. But running at three in the morning under a clear, star-packed sky with the cold pinch of a spring night was even better. He was the only living thing in sight and he felt incredibly free.

He had tried sleeping, but was unable to. Despite the many hours without rest, his mind and body were too keyed up to sleep. The prospect of getting his hands on his father's outline and possibly learning the real reason for his murder was acting like a hit of speed.

He had kept a hard pace, breaking a good sweat. The cold May ocean stung his feet as the surf's roll carried up through his line of running. He made no effort to avoid the water.

His mind drifted as he ran, summoning repressed memories from long ago. Memories of a place a half a world away—the highland rain forests of Nam. So much of that time had come back to him during the past months with the return of the nightmares and sudden flash memories. The death of his father had brought back the worst recollections.

He had spent thirty-nine months in Vietnam, living most of that time by his instincts like an animal. He had received a quick baptism by fire, surviving an ambush on his first patrol, in which 80 percent casualties were taken. A week later, he survived a direct hit on a bunker, and was the only man to walk away. He quickly became the "charmed grunt" of the outfit. He got into a lot of heavy shit pretty early, and guys all around him kept getting the grease, while he'd never be touched. Everybody wanted to be near him because he was safe. The trouble was that they never got saved, just him.

Then he saw the charmed grunt who had cut his own throat in the latrine. He wanted no more to do with that handle after that.

He volunteered for long-range recon patrol (lurps) and got the duty. Michael Gladieux proved to be more than just charmed, he was downright spooky in the way he learned to understand the highland forests. The jungle became his friend, and he felt comfortable in it. He moved through it as silently as a gentle breath of air, without stopping its sounds.

As a lurp, he spent days and weeks at a time in the heavy bush. Even most other lurps, who were all generally thought of as animals, came to regard him strangely. He began spending more time out than in, and that scared shit out of people. But he wasn't chasing some kind of death wish like many thought, it was just that he felt safer out there where he could control events. Being a part of a fearful huddling group in an underground bunker and "waiting" wasn't his way of staying alive. Making it happen and controlling the event was. He went home while a lot of "play it safers" didn't.

He spent a lot of his solo "walk" time working with the mysteriously primitive people of the highlands, the Montagnards, who often hired out to American Special Forces as mercenaries. They respected "Glad-jo" because he scared the living hell out of them. Many thought that he was a ghost who couldn't be killed, and who could appear or disappear when he wanted to. He'd be there one second and gone the next. Even they didn't know when he moved by their encampments.

But it wasn't only the ways of the forests that Michael had to learn in order to guarantee cooperation from the "gnards." The VC used the basest form of violence and terror to get it. Glad-jo learned those ways and never hesitated in using them when he knew they were needed to break the VC spell. Just the sight of him or the knowledge that he was near was enough to guarantee their cooperation. They did what Glad-jo told them to do, whatever it was, without hesitation.

His reputation became well known to certain members of Command staff as well. One particular event had more than caught their attention. It was during the siege of Khe Sanh, and involved the Special Forces A Camp at Langvei, five kilometers southwest of the Khe Sanh combat base. The camp was garrisoned by twenty-four Americans and over four hundred South Vietnamese special troops. Com-

48

nand called it impregnable. It was heavily fortified, well bunkered, and perimetered with triple rows of barbed wire and German razor wire, dense patterns of claymore mines, and had enough firepower to stop a division of crack NVA regulars with death enough left over to spare. It was no wonder that they dismissed Glad-jo's report saying that it could be and would be taken.

"It isn't possible," they had said.

But it was, and he told them how. His report never got beyond the major and his roomful of "experts."

Just past midnight on February 7, 1968, Langvei fell in a single swift surprise attack. The North Vietnamese brought in nine light Russian tanks, Soviet T-34s and 76s. They penetrated the perimeter and used satchel charges, bangalore torpedoes, tear gas, and napalm on the bunkers through the air vents and machine gun slits. It was a rout, in which fifteen of twenty-four Americans and three hundred of four hundred South Vietnamese specialists died, the rest escaping into the jungles. Half-crazed from the utter terror and style of the defeat, these survivors related the grim details. Tanks had come from the jungle to crush them. Tanks!

"Tanks? Impossible," they had said just days before.

Glad-jo had told them that they would use tanks. He had also penetrated the perimeter of the camp by himself, undetected, and diagramed the entire complex set on twin hills above the border with Laos. That wasn't supposed to be possible, either, they had said. But he had done it. Why wouldn't they believe it?

"Begging your pardon, Major," Michael had said at the conclusion of the meeting, "but you're all full of shit. Langvei is going to be taken—with tanks," he had told them, then left.

Mention the word Langvei to a member of the Command even today, and you'll see skin crawl. They just didn't listen.

Glad-jo's intel reports were never distrusted after that. His first tour ended shortly after the relief of Khe Sanh in April of 1968. But not before he impressed certain figures in Command even more with his actions, when twice he called in heavy artillery fire on his own position, directing hits against enemy encampments. He had crept close enough to hear and understand their conversations.

When he returned for his second tour of duty, Glad-jo was a legend in I Corps. People didn't know what to think about the 4th Division lurp who operated alone and who couldn't die. People around him died, too regularly, but he didn't. That was scary, and had the opposite effect of his earlier charmed status. People stayed away from him, and he liked that just fine. It made people happy to see Glad-jo paint up for night walking. It improved their odds of staying alive another day, or week, or however long he was going to be out.

It was at the beginning of the second tour that he was called into Danang to meet with some men who had taken a special interest in his record.

It was refreshing for Michael to talk to people who really knew what was going on, and who didn't hide behind the media props that Command carefully built to paint an illusion of victory. Men who didn't make decisions based on maps and graphs with colors and lines that they made up, which often had no bearing on the real situation. Men who didn't call Langvei a clever trap that the enemy had fallen into, or Khe Sanh the cleverest ploy of the war. Men who knew that they had been lucky that the NVA didn't attack with the five full regiments that had been hidden in the forests around Khe Sanh. Men who knew that the enemy could have taken Khe Sanh at any time if they had wanted to. Victory wasn't coming, and it never would. Michael knew it. These men knew it.

These men approached Michael with an interesting proposition. They were looking to assemble a very small and select group of men who were capable of highly efficient work of independent nature. A number of unique problems had begun to present themselves, and many more were foreseen in the future. These men were to help eliminate those problems, operating independently of Command responsibility, reporting only to the small group responsible for this program. Special training would be required, and would be given on an individual basis.

The offer intrigued him, and after carefully thinking about it for almost a week while on R and R at China Beach, he accepted. His training program commenced immediately, with his transfer out of the 4th Division lurps. The new team, which was composed entirely of reconnaissance-type personnel, was given the name "Dawgs." It consisted of five men. They had said small and select, and they meant it.

These five men met seldom during their training, but did come to know one another by reputation. They were all men of the same mold, representing an awesome, deadly potential.

They learned things about their bodies and minds that they never imagined, and developed both to withstand tremendous hardship. They were taught exercise patterns which toughened sensitive and vulnerable parts of their bodies. They were conditioned and taught to absorb and deliver maximum force in hand-to-hand struggle. Death pots and pressure points were taught beyond those introduced during basic and recondo training. Their minds and discipline were toughened by extensive sensory deprivation techniques designed to maximize their performance capabilities over extended periods of solo operation, and to strengthen the inner processes of the mind. Mental discipline was vital to the nature of the work they would be asked to perform.

They had all learned the ways of the heavy jungle before selection to the group, and were taught things that increased those capabilities till further. They learned how to survive without carrying any food or water, and to conduct warfare almost invisibly, silently, like ghosts. Their aims were no longer directed against divisions, battalions, or patrols of the enemy, but against individuals. Individuals considered dangerous—regardless of the side they were on.

Michael's first assignment concerned itself with rumors of Caucasians fighting on the side of the enemy. They were believed to be converted POW's or ideological turncoats, possibly even Soviet specialists or mercenaries.

After forty-three days on the assignment, Glad-jo returned with seven left ears. He dropped them on the table in front of his "coordinator" along with five sets of American dog tags. The other two had been mercenary types—one German, the other Belgian.

His coordinator, known to him only as "Tripper," the name over the right breast pocket, smiled and gave him his next assignment. Two names, both generals, one South Vietnamese, the other American. Their involvement in black market activities and drugs had gone far beyond allowable limits. Their activities were to be terminated, by whatever means convenient. And so began the last twenty months of Michael Gladieux's service to his country in Vietnam.

Michael sprinted the last two hundred yards to the pool pavilion with all the kick he could summon after his three miles on the beach. His chest heaved, the cold air biting in his lungs. The sweat rolled down his face, chest, and back, and his heart pounded like a rapidly firing cannon. The pain felt good.

He continued to walk, shaking out his arms and legs so that they wouldn't tighten, then he picked up a gentle pace again around to the street side of the pavilion and toward his father's house.

Paul Terrence would be arriving within the next forty-five minutes. That would leave plenty of time for a good hot shower and a few minutes of relaxation. Michael couldn't wait to get his hands on the outline that the frightened editor was bringing them. Terrence had felt

certain it was connected to his father's death, and Michael was begin
ning to believe the same, even without the knowledge of what it con
tained. It was already clear to him that some deep mystery existed and
that his father had been murdered because of it. Someone else had had
a stake in what his father had known, and now Michael stood on th
brink of learning it as well.

Michael had no way of knowing that that "someone else" had
already taken steps to remove the threat posed to him by Paul Ter
rence. And that the stake held was an enormous one . . . to be protected
at all costs.

Chapter 8

ANTICIPATION yielded gradually to impatience, then to irritatio
as the hours slipped past the agreed meeting time. By 7:00 A.M., bot
Michael and Danny were resigned to the fact that Terrence was no
coming. Danny had almost expected it, from the level of fear that th
editor had conveyed. Michael, however, was mad as hell at the los
prospect of getting the information he wanted so badly.

He thumbed through his father's address book until he came t
Terrence's name. He went to the phone and tapped out the New Yor
number. The phone rang and rang and rang. He slammed it down in it
cradle.

"God damn it!" Michael said, walking to the large living roor
windows, looking out to the street for the hundredth time. "Where th
hell is he?"

"He could be on his way," Danny said. "He might have gotten
late start for any number of reasons."

"Bullshit! He's not coming," Michael insisted. "We should hav
gone to him. It was a mistake on my part."

"No, I don't think so," Danny said. "He's just scared. He'll call u
again when he's feeling a little braver."

"I can't wait that long," Michael said, letting the curtain fall bac
into place.

"It looks like you don't have a choice. Is he married?"

"I don't know. If he is, his wife's not home, either," Michael opened the address book again and stared at the entry under Paul Terrence's name. He had called the right number.

Scribbled in the space below Terrence's was another number. It said simply: "Rye—(914) 471-9203." He showed it to Danny.

"Do you suppose this guy may have another place?" Michael asked.

"Could be. It looks like the entry was made for Terrence. Call it."

Michael went to the phone and tapped out the number. It rang fifteen times before he hung up. "Nothing," he said flatly.

Ray came quietly down the stairs. He entered the living room and looked around. "He didn't show, huh?"

Both men shook their heads.

"How did Mom sleep?" Michael asked.

"It took a while for her to fall off, but she slept well. She's still asleep. What about Gabrielle?" he asked Danny.

"The pills did the trick. She needed it," he replied.

"How about you guys?" Ray asked.

"I got about two hours," Danny answered. "Mr. America here ran his fool head off on the beach this morning at three A.M. I'm surprised he's still standing."

"So am I," Ray said. "You're going to cave in if you don't get some rest soon," he commented to Michael.

"I will, once this day is behind us," Michael said.

"Come on. I'll fix you guys breakfast, California style," Ray said.

The three of them filed into the kitchen.

About thirty minutes later Denise and Gabrielle came down. Ray put mugs of coffee in front of them and broke eggs for the omelets. They both looked well rested.

"I take it from the looks on your faces that Paul didn't show up," Denise said to her husband and Michael.

"No, and he's not at any of his numbers," Danny said.

"Maybe he called in to his office," Gabrielle suggested. "Someone there may know where he is. Ted Featherston would probably know, if anyone does," she said, referring to the president of Bonaventure Press, her father's publisher. "He'll be at the funeral today. We can talk to him afterwards."

"What if Terrence shows up while we're gone?" Ray asked. "He may not stick around."

"I've thought of that. I don't really think he'll show, but we have

to expect it. Someone's going to have to stay behind through the morn
ing viewing," Michael said.

Ray looked at Denise. She nodded, as though to tell him that she'd
be all right without him.

"I can stay," Ray volunteered.

Denise repeated the nod to Michael and it was settled. They fin
ished eating and prepared to leave for the nine-to-eleven viewing.

Like the previous night, the number of people attending was im
pressive. A large number of Danny's colleagues came to pay their sin
cere respects. Among them were Colonel Alan Kendrick, his wife, an
son, who was a first-year attorney with the State Attorney General'
office. There was enough capable force in that room to fight a smal
war, Michael thought. If Terrence showed up, he'd feel safe for sure.

Michael paced anxiously, taking trips forward to his sister an
mother, and to the entrance of the funeral parlor.

It was after ten when Ted Featherstone arrived. Michael had me
him a few times as a young boy, and recognized him immediately.

He waited until the publisher had paid his respects at the caske
and to the women before approaching him.

"Mr. Featherston, my name is Michael Gladieux," he said extend
ing his hand.

"I'd know it in a minute," the publisher said. "Please, please, ac
cept my deepest regrets. It was a terrible shock. I just can't properl
express it."

"Thank you, Mr. Featherston."

"Please, call me Ted," the publisher returned.

Ted Featherston was a smallish man, neat and aristocratic in hi
appearance. He had small, handsome features with thin, distinct lip
that moved exaggeratedly with his precise speech.

"I had hoped that perhaps Paul Terrence would be coming wit
you," Michael began. "You wouldn't happen to have heard from hir
today, would you?"

"No, I haven't. And frankly it has me a little worried. It's ver
unusual for Paul to just not show up at the office without explanatior
He had no outside appointments, according to his secretary, and
couldn't track him down anywhere. And I'm sure he wouldn't mis
attending this."

"Did you talk to his wife or family?" Michael asked as Dann
approached. The two men had already met when Featherston arrivec
and there was no need for further introduction.

54

"Yes, and his wife said that she hadn't seen him since yesterday and was nearly hysterical with worry."

"You talked to his wife?" Danny asked.

"Yes," the publisher replied. "I called quite early, hoping to catch Paul before he left for the office. I was going to have him ride down with me to attend the funeral."

"Does she work?" Danny asked.

"I think so. Why?"

"It may be nothing," Danny answered quickly. "Do you know what kind of work she does and what time she might leave in the morning?"

"What's going on?" Featherston asked, perplexed.

"Paul called us last night, Ted," Michael said. "He was frightened and seemed to think that his life was in danger. It had something to do with the reason my father was killed."

"My God!" the publisher exclaimed, truly shocked.

"Will you be coming back to the house with us?" Danny asked.

"Yes, I had planned to."

"Good. I think we should postpone the rest of this conversation until we can talk in privacy. In the meantime, I'll get a few wheels rolling on checking into the whereabouts of Paul Terrence," Danny said.

He walked over to Colonel Kendrick and a few of his colleagues and spoke quietly to them. When he finished, Kendrick spoke to his men and made some notes on a pad. Two of the men left immediately. Danny then returned to Michael and the publisher.

"We'll have fast action on it. NYPD will be asked to check out the Manhattan address, and the New York State Police will check Rye," Danny told them.

Paul Terrence had still supplied them with something by not showing up. It was stronger than a hunch in Danny's mind now, and Colonel Kendrick had agreed. There was more behind the murder of Christian Gladieux than a crumpled letter had indicated.

Ted Featherston lit up his two-dollar cigar a little uneasily in the library of Christian Gladieux's home. His eyes returned nervously to the bloodstains on the Oriental rug.

"Just what is it that makes you think Paul Terrence is involved in this?" Featherston questioned.

"Don't misunderstand," Danny began. "We're not saying that he's involved in the murder in any way. But whoever killed Christian may have an interest in Paul Terrence as well. Paul believed himself to be in danger; he made that very clear."

"Why would Paul be in danger? As I understood it, the reason for Christian's death had something to do with his past in the Resistance," the publisher stated.

"Yes, that's what the evidence said," Danny began. "But Paul felt that the book my father-in-law was working on was a part of the reason, or possibly the whole reason for his murder. Paul had the outline in his possession and said that Christian confided that it could mean trouble. Paul was supposed to meet us this morning with the outline."

"You must have more copies of that outline at your office," Michael said. "Could you get one for us?"

"Certainly. If I remember correctly, there should be two more copies. I can get you one. But why should you need copies at all? Surely, your father had a copy and the original."

"It's gone. Everything is gone," Michael said. "I discovered that much before Paul's call. He just confirmed my early suspicions."

"Everything? All of it, gone?" Featherston asked in disbelief.

"Every scrap. And I don't even know what it was about or how far along on it he was," Michael said.

"I can help you with some of that," Featherston said under an eruption of aromatic smoke. "As I recall, your father submitted the outline to us last January. It came out of the blue. We weren't even aware that he was working on anything. He came into the office one day carrying it with him. He met with Paul and they had lunch together. It was a long lunch. I remember that clearly because Paul missed an afternoon meeting with our graphics people about the jacket design of a hot spring release. We were already behind with it, and the meeting was important.

"I ceased being put out over it when I learned that he had obtained an outline from Christian. Your father hadn't submitted a thing in over a year. That made up for it nicely. Having your father ready to go again was big news."

"Four months," Michael mused aloud. "If it was to be done at his usual pace, he would have been almost halfway into the first draft. That means a lot of material is missing. Did he ever submit completed chapters?"

"No. Just the outline. It was his habit to submit the entire, completed work."

"But you did read the outline, didn't you?" Michael asked.

Featherston frowned. "No, I'm afraid I didn't. I enjoyed your father's work so much that I usually waited to treat myself to a finished manuscript. I was never worried about his choice of story line. I left that to Paul and your father."

"Then you don't know what it was about?" Michael asked.

"No. I'm embarrassed to say that I don't," the publisher said a little sheepishly. "And I might add that Paul never mentioned your father's concern over the subject matter, either, or I'd have read it."

There was obvious disappointment in Michael's face.

"But don't let that bother you," Featherston said. "Paul is completely familiar with it, and I'm sure others have read it. I have a personal copy of the outline in your father's file. I can have that for you tomorrow."

"Do you remember the title?" Danny asked, hoping that some light might be shed about its content.

"Yes, as a matter of fact, I do. It was entitled, tentatively, *The Salamandra Glass.*"

Michael and Danny looked quickly at one another, but said nothing. The phone rang and was answered in another room. A moment later there was a tap on the library door and it opened.

Ray leaned in. "Danny, it's for you. A Sergeant Caldwell," he announced.

"Right," Danny said, leaving to take the call.

There were a few moments of silence before Michael spoke. "Did Paul ever say anything about the story line?"

Featherston shook his head. "Only that it was very strong and one of your father's best. I'm sorry, I just don't know any of the details."

Michael nodded at the publisher's response.

Danny returned to the library. The unmistakable expression on his face told them that he had just heard from Colonel Kendrick.

He looked first to Michael, then to Featherston. "Paul Terrence is dead," he announced. "And so is his wife."

Featherston's face went ashen. He moved slowly in a hunched walk to a chair and sat down, unable to comprehend what he had just been told.

"How?" Michael asked.

"Incendiary devices. Apparently while he was on his way here. An attack was made against him from another vehicle. His car was then forced from the Tappan Zee Bridge into the Hudson. There was very little left of the interior. Nothing that could help us," Danny said.

"And his wife?"

"Beaten and strangled in Manhattan. The apartment is in absolute shambles, and is cordoned for evidence. Robbery could be a motive, but with what we already know, I'd say it was a search."

Then four words which Terrence had muttered through his crying the night before came back into Michael's mind. "Now nothing is left," he had said.

Michael began to charge from the room.

"Where are you going?" Danny asked, catching his arm.

"I'm going to start tearing this house apart," he said.

"What?" Danny asked, not understanding.

"Terrence said, 'Now nothing is left.' I think we're going to find that there are no copies of the outline at Bonaventure. And he knew that. There has to be something in this house that will tell us what that manuscript was going to be about, and I intend to find it."

Danny thought for a second, then nodded. "All right, we'll search this place from top to bottom. But not now. It's almost one o'clock, and the services will be starting soon. I'll get somebody here to watch the house while we're gone. Then we'll start tonight, as soon as we can get everybody out."

"If you get somebody in here, then anything we find will be taken as evidence. I'm not going to let that happen," Michael said with finality.

"Don't worry, that's not going to happen," Danny returned. "I'll call someone I can trust to keep quiet."

Danny went back into the living room and picked up the phone. The name that had popped into his head was that of a man who had helped him the day that Christian Gladieux had been found murdered. Tom Waller had breached protocol once for him already by notifying him quickly, enabling him to get early bits of firsthand information that might otherwise have been withheld from him because of his familial connection to the victim. He was sure Tom Waller would help him one more time.

A second thought also occurred to him as he made the call. Another person had gone beyond protocol to give him information. And he hadn't even been at the funeral parlor when the request was made. Danny had no way of knowing just how much help Robert Caldwell would offer before this day was past. Indeed, there was a great deal of help awaiting them.

Chapter 9

THE weather was dramatically appropriate for a funeral. A somber gray drizzle filled the cold air as the final services were conducted for Christian Gladieux.

Michael held an arm tightly around his sister, whose tired, drawn face was highlighted by eyes reddened and spent with grief. The most difficult moments were past them now with the touching last farewells before the closing of the casket.

Michael looked like he was about three days into a heavy drunk from the effects of no sleep. He felt the crush of exhaustion hit him as soon as he returned home from the funeral. The activities of the reception registered vaguely in his tired, aching head. He managed a moment of alertness when Gabrielle brought him a cup of coffee and sat on the arm of the chair beside him.

"You really do have to sleep," she said softly, running her fingers through his hair.

"Keep that up and I don't think I'll last another minute," he replied.

"You deserve a long rest. You've held us up for days," she told him.

He drank some of the coffee and closed his eyes for a moment. They felt lead-heavy, and he could feel the cells in his brain start to shut down. But he fought back and pulled all systems to alert status. There was a lot to be done yet. He knew that he couldn't rest.

"You're fighting it," Gabrielle said. "Why don't you go upstairs and get some sleep," she urged.

"I can't. Not yet. But I will tonight, I promise."

"How about a little walk then? We could just talk."

"Sure. They won't need us around here for a while."

"How about the boardwalk?" she asked. "The air will do you good."

"Sounds nice. Let's go."

The air was chilly as they walked through a wetting mist. Arm-in arm, they looked more like lovers than brother and sister.

"What's happening to us, Mike?" she asked. "It seems like the whole world is collapsing in on us. First Daddy was killed, then his notes and papers were taken, and now Paul Terrence is dead too."

"And we've lost any opportunity to learn what Paul knew. It seems that Dad confided the matter only to him. Damn! We'll never know," Michael said.

"Can Ted give us any answers?" Gabrielle asked.

"I sure hope so, but I'm not holding my breath expecting it. I don't think he's going to find anything back at Bonaventure. I think that's what tipped Paul off and made him run."

"Someone at Bonaventure must have read the outline. Didn't Ted?"

"No, he didn't. Apparently, he never read any of Dad's outlines. He preferred to wait for the finished manuscripts."

"But there must be other people who have read it."

"Ted felt sure there were. If only we had Dad's notes and work sheets. I can't help feeling there's something in that house that can give us answers."

"If anything is there we'll find it. With five of us looking, we're bound to find something," Gabrielle said.

The heavy cloud cover brought the darkness early. Michael checked his watch.

"I think we should get back to the house. Ted could be trying to call us right now. If he went straight back to Bonaventure from the funeral, he may have had time to find something," Michael said.

"Then let's go. The sooner we get everyone out of the house, the sooner we can get started on going through it."

Michael put his arm around her shoulder and gave her a squeeze. Then they headed back to the house.

The fire crackled loudly in the big stone fireplace of the living room, throwing welcome comfort into the room. The cold dampness outside had begun to penetrate the old house. Danny started up the furnace and lit the fire in the living room to provide some immediate warmth until the heating system in the large house could catch up.

The family sat in the pleasant warmth, grateful that the last guests had left, and looking forward to the rest they all needed so badly. They had discussed the necessity of a search, and had even put forth a plan of attack on the old house. They agreed that one room at a time should be searched thoroughly. Anything that bore even remote significance would be discussed by the entire group.

Danny recommended starting the search the following day, after they had all slept. One night wouldn't make a difference. In the state they were in, it would be easy to miss a small, important detail. It was agreed unanimously.

Sleep had come quickly to everyone except Danny, who lay awake in the bed beside Gabrielle listening to her soft, regular breathing. He had a decision to make that troubled him. He knew that involvement in any form of investigation into the death of his father-in-law, official or private, would be expressly forbidden to him. He knew that he should not even be considering it. But this was a family matter. His family. He had admired his father-in-law greatly, and held Michael in equally high regard. And Gabrielle—he couldn't have been luckier in his life than to have her. The thrill of loving her had never left him. Holding her and kissing her and making love to her were still as exciting to him as they had been when they first gave themselves to one another.

He wanted the same answers that Michael did, and he knew that Michael would pursue them with or without his help. Michael would go after his vengeance and risk death himself to get it. Danny knew the real decision he faced was to either abide by the law he upheld and believed in, or to violate it in search of the vengeance that Michael would have—to help him break that law as safely as possible, and to see to it that he came out of it alive. Law or justice. He had to choose.

The knock on the door downstairs brought Danny out of his dilemma. He pulled on his pants and made his way quietly downstairs. No one else in the house had heard the knocking. He opened the door and was both surprised, and not surprised, to see Bob Caldwell standing there.

"Bob, come in," he said quietly. A quick check of his watch told him that it was about eleven o'clock.

Caldwell could see that he had gotten his friend out of bed. "I'm sorry to get you up like this, Dan. I saw that all the lights were out, but decided to try anyway. I have some information I think you should know about."

"I wasn't asleep. Come on in."

Caldwell stepped into the house and followed Danny into the kitchen, where their conversation would be less likely to disturb the others.

"How about a beer?" Danny offered.

"That sounds real good."

Danny took out two Löwenbräus, opened them, and handed one to his friend.

"Thanks," Caldwell said and took a long swallow. "That hits the spot." He reached for his Camels and lighted one. "Please accept my condolences, Dan. And my apologies for not attending personally before now."

"Apologies aren't necessary. And I'd like to thank you for your call earlier regarding Terrence. I appreciate you sharing that information with me."

Caldwell shrugged it off. "How's it going here?" he asked. "Is Gabrielle bearing up okay?"

"It started off pretty rough, but she's holding up real well now. As far as what we've got here, it's a real mess. Something is going on that we can't figure out yet. Terrence's death confirmed that. We're aware of the collected evidence, but have come across some less obvious facts that point to a lot more than a charge of collaboration. It has to do with a book my father-in-law was working on. His outline and partially completed manuscript are missing, along with all of his notes and files pertaining to it. Terrence was his editor, and called here stating that he felt the book was the cause of Christian's death, and that he was in danger himself. There's little doubt to the truth of his fears now. And we don't have the slightest notion of what was in that outline or manuscript, except for a title. And that ties in with a part of the evidence found with the body. It was tentatively entitled *The Salamandra Glass.*"

Caldwell nodded. "What else have you got?"

"Nothing. We plan to search through the house, starting tomorrow, in the hope of finding something that will offer a start."

"Kendrick intends to remain firm on your noninvolvement in the investigation. I don't have to tell you that," Caldwell said.

"I know," Danny said, nodding.

"In fact, it came down today that he's about to have you reassigned to the Academy to instruct in criminal investigation to keep you out of the field for a while."

"That I didn't know." Danny frowned.

"Hey, it's a good job. Nine to five. Take it. I know some guys who'd give their left nut to land that Academy job."

"Well, I'm not one of them," Danny said.

Caldwell smiled. "Neither am I."

"You said you had something for me. What is it?" Danny asked.

Caldwell pulled hard on the Camel. "Washington has come in on t," he said through a cloud of smoke.

Danny narrowed his eyes. "Who is it that's interested?"

"The Bureau and the Company. High-level interest. They came in esterday, real quiet like. Kendrick pulled a few of us into the Holiday nn in Bordentown. Hush-hush, nothing-leaves-the-room deal. Their easons were predictable: Firewatch, possible connections to other sub-versives, ranging from transnationals to neo-Nazi. They're gonna dig ard, trying for anything. Sounded like they had transnational escala-ion in the U.S. on their minds. But most of it was cover bullshit. What hey really want is the pendant that was found on the body. They tried ot to be too obvious, but I read them right from the start. Based on vhat you've told me about the title of your father-in-law's book, you night be right on track with what interests them, too."

"They gave no indication why they wanted the pendant?" Danny isked.

"No. They were real coy. But I can tell you this much, they want it ɔad. This case is going to go beyond our jurisdiction. We won't stand a ɔhance in hell of solving it. Washington stands a better chance, but I lon't think it will go beyond knowing what happened and why. The ʒuys who did it will never be brought to proper justice here, if at all."

"It smells like they already know something," Danny said.

"I'm sure they do, and I don't think we'll ever learn what that is hrough our investigations, unless we get very, very lucky. And I don't hink we will."

"That's great! I can just hear myself now, telling Mike we can't do anything but let the guys who did this get away with it. He's ready for ɔlood. He ain't gonna swallow that pill.

"Christian knew something that got him killed. It also got Paul Terrence and his wife killed. I'm not going to be able to stop Mike rom going after the people who killed his father. You don't know him. He's smart, and capable. Very capable," Danny said.

"I'm not saying you should stop him," Caldwell said, crushing out he stub of his Camel.

"As I see it, I've got two choices," Danny said. "I could let him try t alone, in which case he'd try to kill half the people in Firewatch, ʒetting himself killed in the process, or I can do my best to help him. At east I can try to keep him alive."

63

"You know what you're up against," Caldwell said. "No govern mental law enforcement agency, local, state, or federal, would ac knowledge, support, or acquiesce to an investigation of a homicide by civilians or sworn law-enforcement personnel who have a familial con nection to the victim. You might be treated with some deference by ou department, but you'd be kept out of it. Anything you might turn up or your own would have to be handed over to the agency of jurisdiction and you stand the very real possibility of compromising any evidence you get near, and could face disciplinary action from the Division.

"But you do have one recourse. You could hire a licensed private investigator to work on your behalf even though his work runs paralle to and concurrent with the official investigation. That is within you rights and the law.

"Furthermore, there's every reason to suspect that aspects of thi case will lead outside the legal borders of this country. You're on you own there. You have vacation time and compensatory time built up Maybe you have to help Gabrielle clear up matters of Christian's estat in France," Caldwell said with a wink.

"From the perspective of the Division, you'd be out of our hair. I would assure that you wouldn't interfere in any investigations or com promise available evidence. You'd keep your job and meet the mor important obligation to your wife and Mike."

Caldwell paused to light up another Camel and finish his beer. H was giving Danny time to think. The true purpose of his visit was abou to emerge.

Danny sat in silence. He slid his untouched Löwenbräu across th table to his friend, who had just presented him with the solution to hi problem. His commitment to his wife and Michael was easily the mor important to him. He could meet that while staying within the techni cal bounds of his commitment to his profession. The only gray area stil remaining, and the part that troubled him the most, would be trying t control Michael if, and when, they learned the facts. But he could dea with that when the time came.

Caldwell lowered the half-emptied Löwenbräu. "Well, what d you think?" he asked.

"I think it can be done," Danny answered, nodding slowly.

"I know someone who can help you," Caldwell began with an other eruption of smoke. "His name is Bill Pheagan. He runs a bi operation out of New York called Omega Enterprises, and he's got lot of strong international contacts. It's a very effective low-profile out fit. His people are real pros. They're good, Dan. Real good."

64

Caldwell scribbled Pheagan's name and number on a piece of paper and slid it across the table to Danny. "You think about it. If you and Mike decide that you want to use his services, call that number. I think you'll find him very interested."

Danny took the paper as Caldwell finished his beer.

"I've got to run," Caldwell said, rising from his chair.

Danny accompanied his friend to the front door.

"Thanks, Bob. You've been a big help. I really appreciate it."

"That's what friends are for, pal. I know you'd do the same for me if the tables were reversed."

The two men shook hands and Caldwell left.

Danny went back into the kitchen and turned out the light, then climbed the stairs to the bedroom. He put the paper with Bill Pheagan's name on it into his wallet and crawled into the bed. He felt as though a burden had been lifted from his shoulders. He lay back and closed his eyes. Within minutes he was asleep.

Chapter 10

It was nearly noon when Michael awoke. He descended the stairs to find the others in various stages of late breakfasts, again prepared by Ray. They had not been up much longer than he. Everyone looked well rested and ready for the long day ahead.

Danny had prepared a list of the items that could be the most likely to tell them something of significance. Expense records, travel receipts, passport, pocket calendars and notebooks, letters, recording tapes, phone bill receipts, anything that might trace Christian's movements and suggest names of people he might have talked to over the past eighteen months. Anything having the appearance of outline material or notes would be thoroughly scrutinized.

Michael and Danny discussed the possibility that Christian could have hidden valuable information in his safe-deposit boxes at the bank. They decided to check them first, while the rest of the family began the search in the kitchen.

"Does Dad's attorney have to be there in order for us to get into the boxes?" Michael asked.

"No. Only the presence of a bank official is required to guarantee that we don't take anything of value belonging to the estate until an audit of the boxes can be made," Danny replied.

"When are we supposed to meet with the attorney for the reading of the will?" Michael asked.

"Next Monday. We were originally set for tomorrow, but he had to leave town and won't be back until sometime this weekend."

Within thirty minutes they had found the keys to the safe-deposit boxes and had left for the bank.

"I'm glad that we got this chance to be alone," Danny said as he drove.

"What's on your mind?" Michael asked.

"Bob Caldwell came by last night. He gave me some interesting information," Danny said.

He told Michael about Washington's interest in the case and the pendant, and related the entire conversation in full detail.

"Do you know this guy Pheagan?" Michael asked.

"No, I don't. And I've never heard of Omega Enterprises, either," Danny answered.

"It's not that I don't trust your friend. I realize he went out on a limb to tell you things he shouldn't have. We both appreciate that. And I agree with his opinion that we'd be smart to use a private investigator to help us. I understand the position you're in, too. I think his recommendation is the only way around it for your sake. But if we're going to use someone like this Pheagan, I'd like to know a little bit about him and his agency," Michael said.

"I'm sure I can learn something before we meet with him, and I think we should do that soon, tomorrow, if it can be arranged," Danny suggested. "I can make a call today to set it up. I'll contact Featherston, too. We may as well stop in at Bonaventure as long as we're going to be in the city. Perhaps Terrence wasn't the only one to read the outline. We could learn something."

"That sounds fine with me," Michael said. "I'm for anything that will get us fast answers."

"Let's hope they're all right in there," Danny said, gesturing to the bank as he pulled into the parking lot.

Christian Gladieux had maintained two large safe-deposit boxes. In terms of their search, Michael and Danny found little of significance. Just a current passport, which told them that Christian had not gone abroad in the two years since it was renewed. They were both disappointed that the passport hadn't yielded important information.

But disappointment was replaced by amazement at the other things they found.

Michael knew that his father's estate was considerable, and Danny had known that as well. What was presented, however, was many times greater than either had imagined.

They found the usual documents of title and insurance for the house and car. They also found documents for other valuable properties they didn't even know he had owned, and stock certificates for thousands of shares in various corporations. Christian had been a large investor in a small company called Haloid in the mid to late 1950s. That company later became the veritable giant known as Xerox. Those stocks alone were worth millions. He had invested in numerous companies and new ventures which had become pure gold, and in mining and drilling operations, and in fledgling companies involved in aerospace and semiconductors. They found certificates of deposit and money market notes, precious metal futures and records of past investments that aggressively built a gigantic portfolio. He had kept meticulous records of these transactions. They found descriptions of all his current financial affairs and a projection of potential moves in investments as far as one year ahead.

Every important document that was a part of his life was in those boxes, from his contracts with Bonaventure, to his divorce settlement. Certificates of assessment for all of his personal belongings with accompanying photographs were found as well as an estate valuation showing a net worth in excess of thirty million dollars.

Two metal tags were also found, bearing impressed eight-digit numbers. They had no idea what these were. The bank official present recommended that they contact Christian's attorney regarding them. He would, no doubt, be aware of their relevance, if any, to the estate.

Their search through the safe-deposit boxes had taken nearly two hours and had left them weak from astonishment. They were permitted to remove all insurance policy information, and a copy of the estate valuation was made for them. They made a record of the numbers on the metal tags and took the passport to include with the other materials they expected to find back at the house.

When they returned to the house, they shared the information regarding the estate with the others, who had finished their search of the kitchen. All that had been found were two unidentified keys to Yale locks, some gasoline receipts, a receipt for office materials he had recently purchased, and a repair voucher for an IBM typewriter that had been left at a local shop for routine maintenance. They broke for a late lunch before continuing the search of the house.

As their lunch neared its conclusion, Danny excused himself and went into the living room to make his phone calls. The first number he called was the one Bob Caldwell had given him.

A pleasant female voice answered the phone and Danny asked to speak to Pheagan. He waited approximately thirty seconds before Pheagan came on the line.

"Bill Pheagan," the crisp voice said.

"How do you do, Mr. Pheagan?" Danny began. "My name is Daniel Preston. I was given your name by a friend of mine. He recommended you very highly and said that you might be able to help my family with a rather delicate problem."

"Preston. Yes, I was told that you might call."

"Then you've spoken with Bob Caldwell?"

"Yes, briefly this morning. He gave me a quick rundown on your situation. I saw the incident on the news and read about it in the paper. Please accept my condolences. Your father-in-law was a fine writer. I was a fan of his," Pheagan said.

"Thank you, Mr. Pheagan. Since you have a brief background from Bob, you know what we're up against. My brother-in-law and I would like to discuss the aspects of the case with you. It's rather involved, and I'd prefer not going into any of the details over the phone. You understand."

"Yes, certainly. When would you like to meet?"

"At your earliest convenience. Your office will be fine."

"All right. How about tomorrow morning at ten?" he asked.

"Ten is fine. We'll be there. I'll need an address," Danny said.

"Are you familiar with New York City?" Pheagan asked.

"Yes."

"It's six six six Park Avenue. Tenth floor. Look for Omega Enterprises. It's a large suite, you can't miss it."

"I've got it. Is there anything special that you'll need from us?"

"Anything pertaining to recent travel, phone records, expense records, recent financial transactions, and the like usually provide us with a good place to start."

"We're already on it. I guess I ought to ask what your customary fee is in such matters."

"Based on the background from Bob Caldwell, and the resources that I would expect will be required, I'd say that one thousand dollars per day, plus unusual expenses, should cover it."

"You're in a good business, Mr. Pheagan. I hope you're worth it."

Pheagan let go a small laugh into the phone. "See you at ten, Mr. Preston."

"We'll be there," Danny said, then put the phone down in its cradle. Jesus, he thought. A thousand bucks a day. I'm in the wrong fucking business.

He picked up the phone again and touched out the Bonaventure Press number from Christian's address book. He asked for Ted Featherston, giving his name to the phone receptionist. The wait was a short one.

"Hello, Dan," Featherston's voice greeted.

"Hello, Ted. Have you come up with anything?"

"Some good, most bad," the publisher replied. "Mike was right about the outline, there isn't a trace of it anywhere. I brought it up at our marketing meeting this morning, and have two editors who had scanned it when it first came in. Paul's assistant had also read it, and so has one of our subsidiary rights people. It won't be as good as having the outline, but it will give you a good idea of what it was about."

"That's really good news," Danny said. "Listen, Mike and I will be in the city tomorrow. Could you arrange a meeting for us with these people? Say at about twelve-thirty?"

"Surely. I'll have them all here waiting. I'll have lunch brought into the office to save us time. I've asked them to try to remember as much about the outline as they can. I'm sure that between the four of them you'll get a pretty good picture."

"That's super. We'll see you tomorrow, Ted. We appreciate it."

"You're very welcome. I hope we can help. See you tomorrow."

Danny hung up the phone and held back the urge to race back into the kitchen to tell the others about Featherston's news. He had one more call to make first.

He tapped out the 212 area code and his next number.

"Thirteenth Precinct. Sergeant Thomas speaking," a voice answered.

"Can I talk to Detective Sergeant Peskrow, please?" Danny said.

He waited for over a minute before the line came to life.

"Peskrow," the graveled voice said.

"Hey, Peter. Dan Preston here."

"Danny Boy, long time no hear. What's new in the boonies?" Peskrow asked in a heavy New York accent.

"A lot. Most of it bad."

"Yeah. Yeah, I heard. I'm sorry, Dan. Tell the wife for me that I feel bad, huh? It was a lousy thing to happen. Is there somethin' I can do?"

"As a matter of fact, there is, Pete. That's why I called. I need a rundown on a P.I. by the name of William Pheagan. He runs an outfit caled Omega Enterprises, located at six six six Park."

"What do ya wanna know?" Peskrow asked.

"Whatever you can get for me. I need it fast, by tomorrow morning."

"That's fast all right. I don't know the guy or his outfit offhand, but I'll get somethin' for ya. Where can I reach ya?"

"I'll call you, Pete. Nine-thirty tomorrow morning."

"Okay. Just spell the name for me. That's F—"

"No, it's P-Paul, H-Henry, Edward, Adam, George—"

"Wait a minute, I broke my fuckin' pencil. Hold it a second." There was a short delay. "Okay. I got P-H-E-A-G. Go ahead."

"Adam, Nora. Got it?"

"Got it. I'll have somethin' for ya in the morning."

"Thanks, Peter," Danny said.

"Any time, pal. Hey, if there's anything else I can do, just let me know, huh?"

"I will, Pete. This is plenty, thanks."

Danny hung up the phone and went back into the kitchen, where everyone had finished eating.

"I've got some good news and some bad news," he said to attentive listeners. "The bad news is that none of the outline copies can be found at Bonaventure, just as you suspected, Mike. The good news is that Featherston has found four people who have read the outline. He'll have them waiting for us at twelve-thirty tomorrow in his office."

There was no hiding Michael's elation at the news.

"We'll be able to get some kind of picture from them. At least we didn't draw a blank," Danny said.

"That's outstanding," Michael exclaimed.

"We're set up for tomorrow morning with Pheagan, too," Danny said.

Gabrielle's face grew puzzled. "Who is Pheagan?" she asked.

"A private investigator. We're going to get some outside help to enable us to conduct our own investigation," Danny told her.

"And when was all of this decided?" she asked, a little hurt at not being included in the decision-making process.

"This morning," Michael answered. "It's the only way we can do something ourselves without jeopardizing any kind of case that can be built."

70

"I didn't say anything this morning, because I wanted to be sure he'd be willing to help us," Danny said.

"I take it, then, that he's willing?" Gabrielle asked.

"Yes, he is. And he wants us to bring everything we find. That means we have a lot of work to do between now and tomorrow morning," Danny replied.

"We'll never be finished by morning," Denise commented.

"But we might find enough to help him get started. Mike and I will take it in to him, and then stop over at Bonaventure to see Featherston. In the meantime, you guys can continue the search. If anything turns up, we can bring it in to Pheagan when we've finished the rest of the house."

"I suggest we start in the library, where Daddy kept his records," Gabrielle said.

"Okay, then let's get started," Michael said, the first to get up.

Together they left the kitchen and headed for the library, determined to find the threads that would unravel the mystery of Christian Gladieux's death.

Chapter 11

THE first complete day of searching yielded little. They worked well into the night, finishing the first floor. Christian's records revealed only that he had been virtually inactive for almost two years, which was not like him. The phone records for that time yielded nothing of immediate value, either. But everything would be turned over to Pheagan for closer examination. Perhaps his trained eye, guided by detached objectivity, could identify bits of evidence that they just couldn't recognize.

One of the Yale locks belonging to the keys they had found earlier was uncovered and a number of blank cassette tapes were also found. The tapes were patiently run through end to end as they searched, to be sure they were completely blank throughout.

One finding had offered them a tiny glimmer of hope. That was the discovery of the monthly Daytimer calendars that Christian had habitually used. They found them neatly in order for a five-year period. All but two for the months of July and November of 1981 were accounted for and examined carefully. Knowing her father's work habits well, Gabrielle said that the November Daytimer should hold some promise if they could find it. November would have been the month he started his outline for the January submission. There could be notes pertaining to it in that calendar.

They discussed their poor findings over breakfast the following morning, before Michael and Danny left for their meetings in New York. Michael expressed strong feelings that the expense records had been made deliberately sterile by his father to cover his movements. He felt certain that valuable information still lay hidden in the house, and that they would find it all in one place when they did hit upon it. The others agreed to start the day's search while Michael and Danny were in New York. They left immediately after breakfast.

About ten minutes from the Holland Tunnel, Danny pulled the car over to a row of pay phones near Exit 14 of the New Jersey Turnpike.

He dialed Peskrow's number at the nine-thirty time agreed upon.

"Peskrow speaking," came the familiar voice.

"Peter, this is Dan Preston. How'd you make out?"

"Pretty good, Danny Boy. I think I got what ya need."

"That's great. Let her rip."

"Your guy, Pheagan, has had his P.I.'s license for eight years. He must have big bucks backing him, 'cause he's got a big operation. It was big right from the start. Omega Enterprises has three offices, in New York, L.A., and Chicago. New York is the headquarters. He's got a staff of fifteen at the Park Avenue location, including a full-time attorney. Chicago's got a staff of ten, and L.A.'s got an even dozen, including another attorney. They hook up by computers, which they own outright. That gives you an idea of the bucks involved. They specialize in private sector interests, and do some work for some of the big insurance companies. That means the guy's gotta be good, real good. Them insurance companies have their own top-notch outfits, and if they go outside for help, it's to the best. It also tells ya that the guy is well connected internationally. Omega is privately owned by three people. Pheagan is one of them. A guy by the name of Thomas Lazzarus is another, and runs the L.A. branch. The third owner is a retired Naval Intelligence officer named Richard Wentworth. He comes from money and is about seventy years old now. He's probably the big money man in the deal.

"We got no complaints outstanding against the guy or any of his

72

staff here in New York. I'd say what you're looking at is a top-notch outfit in the big-bucks league. That's all I got. I hope it's what ya needed," Peskrow concluded.

"That's exactly what I needed, and wanted to hear. Peter, I can't thank you enough. If there's ever anything that I can do for you, just give me a shout," Danny said.

"You bet, Danny Boy. I was glad to help. Don't be a stranger, huh?"

"I won't. Thanks, Pete."

Danny hurried back to the car and filled Michael in on Peskrow's report as they battled the tail end of the morning rush-hour traffic through the Holland Tunnel. It was just a few minutes past ten when they stepped out of the elevator at Pheagan's Park Avenue address. The doors to Omega Enterprises were clearly marked.

They stepped into a tastefully decorated reception area, and approached an attractive middle-aged woman at the reception desk. She took their names and announced them to Pheagan's secretary over the interoffice phone. About a minute later an extremely good-looking brunette entered the reception area. The receptionist pointed to the two men, and she approached them.

"Hello, my name is Marcie," she said in smiling self-introduction. "Mr. Pheagan is expecting you. Please come with me." The look on her face plainly indicated that she liked what she saw when she looked at Michael.

They followed her through a door into a large open suite divided into roomy cubicles by colorful five-foot-high partitions. Everything seemed to be hustle and bustle, the air filled with the sounds of a busy office. They crossed the large suite, weaving through the mazelike layout toward a closed door with William Pheagan's name on it.

The girl knocked lightly on the door and opened it inward, motioning to the two men to step inside. A man stood silhouetted against the large windows, his back to them as they entered.

"Shall I bring in coffee?" the girl asked.

"Yes, please, Marcie," the man said, turning toward them. "Just bring in a pot, we'll be a while."

As Pheagan faced the two men, he looked directly into Michael's eyes.

The shock struck like a bolt of lightning when Michael recognized the face of the man they had come to see. It was closely followed by the realization that they had, indeed, become involved in something of greater significance than met the eye. He stared back into the sharp, dark features and ice-blue eyes of a face he would never forget, a face he saw often in the dreams that filled tormented nights. The name he put on it, however, was not Pheagan, but Tripper, his Dawgs coordinator in Vietnam.

"Mr. Preston?" Pheagan said, extending his hand toward Michael as he approached them. The obvious intent of Pheagan was to keep their past association unknown to Danny.

"No, I'm Michael Gladieux," he said flatly, an intensity emitting from his eyes that could crack stone.

"My apologies. I'm very glad to meet you, Mr. Gladieux," Pheagan said, taking the steellike grip of the hand that drifted up to meet his own.

"Then you must be Mr. Preston," he said to Danny, extending his hand. "Please, sit down," he said with a gesture to the two well-cushioned chairs in front of his elaborate cherry desk.

Michael didn't move at first, as Danny stepped forward to one of the chairs. He fought every instinct inside him that shouted to turn and leave the office.

"Please, sit down," Pheagan repeated.

Michael moved forward slowly and lowered himself into one of the soft chairs as Pheagan rounded his desk and sat himself behind it.

"I guess a first-name basis would be a lot more comfortable," Pheagan said. "Please, call me Bill."

"That's fine," Danny said.

The door to the office opened, letting in the sounds of the busy atmosphere just beyond them. Marcie carried in a tray with a pot of piping hot coffee and two cups for the visitors. She poured coffee all around, then left the office.

"I've already spoken with Bob Caldwell, as you know, and am familiar with the general aspects of the case. But why don't you start from the beginning with what you know, then we'll get into anything that you might have brought with you," Pheagan recommended.

A brief moment of awkward silence followed. Danny looked to Michael, expecting him to start. When he didn't, Danny began, recounting every possible detail—from the discovery of Christian's mutilated body to the ongoing search of the house.

Pheagan listened patiently through Danny's monologue, jotting a few notes on the legal pad in front of him as the story progressed.

Danny finished by telling him of the phone conversation he had with Featherston and about the meeting that was scheduled later that same day with the people who had read the outline. He added that he intended to tape the entire meeting for later review.

"And you brought what little you were able to find in your search of the house?" Pheagan asked, looking at the two bags on Michael's lap.

"Yes," Danny replied.

"Let me see it," Pheagan said.

It took Michael a second to realize that both men were staring at him, waiting for him to hand the two bags over to Pheagan. He snapped out of his pensive mood, realizing that for the appearance of normalcy, he must be a part of the meeting. Michael had no idea why the people Pheagan represented would be interested in the death of his father, or whether Pheagan still, in fact, even worked for them. He knew that Pheagan had been involved six years ago, when he had last seen him. He was still called Tripper back then. He decided to go along with Pheagan's charade until the first opportunity permitted him to pose direct questions.

Michael's mind jumped to Bob Caldwell as he handed the bags across the desk to Pheagan. He wondered how much his actions had been truly inspired by friendship. Caldwell had been the conduit to Pheagan. It had been smooth. That was typical of them. There was no doubt in his mind that these people were aware of his attitude toward them, and that a direct approach would have met with immediate rejection on his part. So they had sucked him in sufficiently to where he now wanted to know the reasons for their interest. That meant he would listen, which is more than he would have done with a direct approach.

Pheagan dumped the contents of the two bags into separate piles on his desk and began going through them in an almost cursory manner as he spoke.

"I think that your conclusions are all sound, based on what is known. But I also think you've overlooked the very important and obvious element of collaboration," he began, starting several piles of papers on his desk according to his own assigned significance. "True, the outline of Christian's book bears obvious relevance to the pendant by its title, but we don't know what that outline contained. We do know that a charge of collaboration had been leveled at him as the reason for his execution. We also know from the story related by your mother that Christian was tried for the same charge in 1945, and that a major collaborator did exist who was never identified. The one aspect of Christian's outline that you have not considered, and most definitely should, is that he may have learned the identity of the collaborator and threatened to expose him. There's no telling what station in life this man now holds, but he would very definitely not want that discovery to be made known to others, to avoid a similar fate to that which befell Christian. This collaborator could have engineered the entire accusation, trial, and execution to protect himself. He may even be a part of Firewatch and have used the association to his advantage to remove the threat to himself," Pheagan surmised.

"But wouldn't the recovery of the outline and partially completed manuscript only help point out his guilt to Firewatch?" Michael asked.

"Not if it didn't reach their attention," Pheagan responded. "He may be in the upper ranks of their organization, or have had a say in the choice of assassin, or assassins, in which case he could have selected people who held a particular loyalty to him. There's no guarantee that Firewatch is even involved. The killers could have been hired professionals who simply followed the instructions for which they were paid, without the slightest regard for what was in the manuscript. I may be able to find out whether Firewatch will hold to the claim of responsibility for the act. That will tell us a lot if I'm right.

"The next piece of evidence that we need to focus on is the pendant and its relation to the missing outline. What is it? What part did it play in his past? Was it the 'proof beyond doubt' mentioned in the letter, or was it a form of signature by the responsible party?

"Whatever Christian Gladieux knew, it threatened someone so acutely that murder was the only way out. Taking his information was easy, but removing all traces of it was not, and the attempt was not successful enough to prevent the connection from being made. The real person behind the killing may feel secure—even though he knows we will make certain connections—because he knows that his trail is well buried in a forty-year-old mystery. What he doesn't know is the level of your determination to start from the beginning to unravel that mystery. Something sparked Christian's curiosity and enabled him to learn enough to be dangerous to this person. We have to find that same thing to give us our starting point.

"We, therefore, have three objectives. We must hope to learn the content of the missing outline, as it should contain many of the answers we need. We must determine the significance of the pendant. And we must pursue the obvious theme of collaboration. Somehow, they're all connected to the person who was so threatened that the order to kill was given. You have a great deal more to start with than you think, especially with the resources of Omega Enterprises working for you. The one fact which must be kept in mind, however, is that this person has already given an order to kill to protect himself. He'll do it again without hesitation if he feels threatened. Be prepared for it—and prepared to counter it. Make no mistake, if you embark on this, as you

seem determined to do, you will encounter increasing danger to yourselves as you progress toward the solution."

In his reaction to the initial discovery of the missing outline,
Michael had failed to connect it to the obvious collaboration charge.
He had simply rejected collaboration as it pertained to his father, and
did not consider it further, precluding the theory of the real collaborator's identity being threatened, as put forth by Pheagan. It had been a
product of Michael's emotional response, of which Danny was also
guilty in part. Pheagan's objective approach was not clouded by emotion, and his points were all well taken.

"And what do you make of Washington's interest?" Danny asked.

"Their interest is in the pendant. Caldwell seemed certain of that.
So is ours. I have close contacts there that can shed some light on their
reasons. That will give us valuable information.

"I think that you two had also better make plans to go to France
somewhere along the way. That's where the most important answers
will lie regarding this collaborator," Pheagan said.

Pheagan took a short break to pour more coffee into the empty
cups, then reached for two of the smaller slips of paper in front of him.

"According to this receipt, your father owned an IBM Selectric
typewriter which he brought in for servicing four days before his death.
In your search of the house, did you find any of the carbon film cartridges he might have used?" he asked.

Michael thought for a second. "They would have been in the library where he did his typing," he reflected out loud. "No, I'm sure we
didn't find any."

"According to this second receipt, he bought six cartridges last
November. Did he do his writing at the typewriter?" Pheagan asked.

"No," Michael answered immediately. "He worked his drafts
longhand, in pencil. Then he typed out the finished work after all
rewriting was completed."

"Then whoever killed him also took the cartridges. They were very
thorough," Pheagan told them. "Since he typed only finished material,
the last thing of significant length that he would have typed may very
well have been his outline. The typewriter was not in the house when
he was killed, and the cartridge in that machine could not have been
taken. If your father brought it in for servicing with that cartridge still
in it, we may have the outline yet. I'll check on that today."

He picked up another piece of paper, bearing the two eight-digit
numbers found on the tags. "What are these?" he asked, showing them
to the two men across the desk.

"We don't know," Danny answered. "We found two oval metal

tags with those numbers impressed on them in his safe-deposit box. The bank official recommended that we contact Christian's attorney regarding them. I tried calling, but he was out of town. We have a meeting scheduled with him next Monday for the reading of the will and to attend to matters of the estate."

"What is the attorney's name?" Pheagan asked.

"His name is Paul Axel," Danny replied. "His office is in Wall Township."

Pheagan jotted down the information.

"I see that the estate is quite substantial," Pheagan said. "Do you know how many different publishers Christian may have contracted with in the past?" He asked.

"As far as I know, he's always been with Bonaventure," Michael replied.

Pheagan sat back in his chair and looked at his watch. "When is your meeting scheduled at Bonaventure?"

"Twelve-thirty," Danny answered.

"It's twelve now," Pheagan said. "I still need a lot of background information on Christian. Since you're going to tape the meeting anyway, why don't you go downtown to keep your appointment," he said to Danny. "Mike can supply me with the information I need and fill out the necessary forms for our records. He can meet you there in less than an hour. Then I suggest that you both return here after your meeting at Bonaventure to review the tape with me. It may provide important information."

"Mike?" Danny said, looking to him for his opinion.

"That'll be fine," Michael said. There were some matters of background that he wanted to get straight, himself. This provided him with an opportunity to be alone with Pheagan.

"Okay then," Danny said, rising from his chair and extending a hand across the desk to Pheagan, who had risen with him. "Bill, it was a real pleasure meeting you. I feel like we've accomplished something today. I hope when we talk later that we'll have a lot more to put into our efforts."

Danny looked back to Michael. "See you in a little bit," he said.

A second later Michael and Pheagan were alone in the office. Pheagan had reseated himself and stared into the eyes that had narrowed and grown diamond-hard.

"You're looking good, Mike. It's been a long time."

"Which is it, Pheagan or Tripper?" Michael asked.

"Pheagan—for now," came the reply with a wry smile.

"You're beginning to develop the annoying habit of turning up in my life when you're the last person I want to see," Michael said. "But I have to admit that you're getting slicker as time goes by. I had no idea what I was walking into this time. Your boy Caldwell handled that nicely."

Pheagan made no response to the mention of Caldwell's name.

"Now suppose you give me the *real* reason why the *group* is interested," Michael demanded.

"We're interested because Washington is interested," Pheagan said. "And I didn't come looking for you on this one, Mike. It was just the luck of the draw that made it your father who was killed, and my name to pull the assignment. We'll both just have to live with that fact, and each other, for as long as this thing takes."

"Let's get one thing straight between us right up front," Michael said slowly, deliberately. "I have no desire to act on the group's behalf now or ever again. You said that it was the luck of the draw that brought us together. Okay, I'll buy that—and live with it because I have to. My only interest lies in finding out the real reason why my father was murdered, in clearing his name of a collaboration charge, and in finding the people responsible. I don't care whether or not you ever get what you want out of this, whatever that is. I need help, and recognize that maybe I can't do this thing alone. I'd take help from anyone who was in a position to give it. It happens to be you—and I know you're good at what you do. That's my bonus. But make no mistake, I'm *paying* for that help. A thousand bucks a day, plus expenses. So, *you're* working for *me,* and that's *my* choice. Don't start rapping on me about that patriotism bullshit and love for my country like you did fourteen years ago in Nam. I'm not a kid anymore who can fall for that shit. This is a straight business deal. I ask for information and you get it. I pay for that with U.S. dollars, not my soul. And don't ask me to help you unless it helps me learn what I have to learn, because I don't care about your causes. Do I make myself clear?"

"Perfectly," Pheagan answered, knowing it would do no good to counter with argument now. When he knew better, himself, exactly what it was that Sub Rosa felt it needed to learn, he could begin to work his magic on Michael. Right now they both needed answers and were in a position to help one another. He, too, would leave it at that.

"I won't give you an argument, Mike," Pheagan said. "I guess I don't fully understand your reasons for feeling the way you do about the group. You obviously feel that way, so I guess that's all there is to it.

"You spent two years with us in Nam. That wasn't an easy time for anyone. We weren't responsible for that war and the things that went on. You knew we weren't a part of the government and that we exercised our own policy there, thanks to connections in the Pentagon. For all intents and purposes, you were a civilian during those last twenty-four months in Nam, although your record shows otherwise. We knew what was wrong there, and that we couldn't win. We knew the position the government had taken in its stand on the war, and we knew what it would do to this country. It tore the heart and innocence out of this nation. Two world wars couldn't do that. Korea couldn't. But Vietnam did. It affected this country like nothing else in this entire century. It was not one of our prouder moments. That's precisely why *we* did the things that we did. Because our concern was for this country and its survival of that unpleasant episode in our history.

"You don't know a whole lot about the people you worked for back then, and now isn't the time to tell you. But I will someday, when the time is right. We appreciate what you did for us in the past, and we want you to know that.

"In seventy-six, when we sought you out, we did so again out of concern for this country over an issue which threatened to tear deeply into old wounds. You were the only man who could have gotten us the kind of information we needed. We would have gone elsewhere if we could have. But you knew the forests of Nam and Laos better than anyone. If American POW's were still being held and could be located, you could do it better than a small army. One man, working alone, who knew the land and could move through it like a ghost was what we needed. We came to you because we knew you were the best we had."

"And it was a mistake on my part to accept your request," Michael shot back. "Your mistake was in thinking that I was still a part of the group. I left it, and you, behind when I left Nam."

"But you did go back there for us," Pheagan said.

"I told you, that was my mistake."

"It was no mistake. You knew as well as we did that American POW's were still being held. You cared, pal, whether you want to admit it or not."

"Yes, I cared," Michael said angrily. "And I also know that you did *nothing* with the proof I brought back." Michael's anger had taken him to his feet. He leaned across the desk, glaring at Pheagan.

"Those poor bastards are still there," he hissed. "They're not even men anymore. They've been treated like animals for so long they can never come back. Their only hope for freedom is death. If you weren't going to take them out, then you should have at least given them that."

"Bringing them out was not our decision to make," Pheagan offered in defense. "We gave our information to our highest contacts in the Pentagon. It wasn't believed."

"*Wasn't believed?* They knew! That proof was irrefutable. You couldn't have given them better evidence," Michael fumed.

"The decision was not ours to make," Pheagan repeated.

Michael looked at Pheagan without speaking, his rage smoldering inside.

"We believe in this country," Pheagan said. "In all the things that are right *and* wrong with it, because it's all that we have. We try to make it better, Mike. We really do try."

"I don't want to talk about this anymore," Michael said. "Other things are more important to me. My priorities are different now. All of that is behind me, and I won't go back to it. I can't believe in it."

"I'm not asking you to," Pheagan said calmly.

"Oh, but you are. Not in your words now, but they'll come. I know they will. Don't waste your breath on me, Pheagan. I'm here only for *my* reasons now, and I'll help you only so long as doing so helps me."

"You've already made that plain," Pheagan said.

"And let's keep it that way for the record, shall we?" Michael said. "You've made your point."

"Now, if you need information about my father, I'll give it to you. And if I have to sign forms of agreement, or anything else, get them so I can get it done. I don't like being here. That meeting at Bonaventure is far more important to me right now than trading ideologies with you," Michael said, returning to his seat.

Both men felt the discomfort of their strained alliance. But it was an alliance that would become vitally important to both of them as they began a journey through mysteries that neither man could solve alone.

Chapter 12

SINCE the plan called for a later meeting with Pheagan to review the tapes to be made at Bonaventure, Danny decided to leave the car parked where it was. He caught a cab, which proved to be a lesson in frustration.

The ride should have taken no more than twenty minutes with the expected traffic. But, as often happens in New York City, the traffic flow took on a sudden resemblance to quick-setting cement. At one point, the traffic stopped so completely that it looked like an I.Q. exercise, which no one in attendance had the wit—or the willingness—to solve. It was only the artful persuasion of one truck driver that finally put people's attitudes in a more cooperative vein. He simply rearranged the fender of the car sitting across his path to get the point across that he didn't like the fellow blocking his way. It worked magic.

Danny's next bout with frustration awaited him just inside the doors of the triangular Flatiron building on Fifth Avenue, which housed Bonaventure Press on the top three floors. Two of the six ancient elevators were out of service, and when, after ten long minutes one of the tiny slow-moving cubicles arrived, it stopped at every floor and seemed constantly to be packed. This was not turning out to be one of his better days, he thought as he looked at his watch. He was an hour late when the doors opened for the nineteenth floor.

Danny entered the small reception area and gave his name, explaining that he had an appointment to meet with Featherston, but was an hour late. The receptionist buzzed Featherston's office and told Danny that someone would be right with him. He spent the time looking at the books lining the wall shelves displaying the spring season's

ottest releases, as well as some past big sellers, including Christian's
ast book. It had dominated the best-seller lists for months.

A tall, plainly attractive woman slipped around the corner and
pproached him.

"Mr. Preston?"

"Yes."

"My name is Julie Taylor. I'm Mr. Featherston's secretary," she
aid. Her searching eyes told him that she was also looking for Michael.

"Mike should be here any minute," Danny said. If Pheagan was
ight about how long Michael would be delayed and if he had fared
etter with the traffic, the statement would be accurate.

"I have to apologize for being so late," he said to her. "I don't
now what to blame more, the traffic or the elevator."

"I know what you mean," she said, laughing. "Mr. Featherston
as everyone waiting for you."

"Fine. I suggest that we not wait for Mike. We can start the meet-
g and brief him when he arrives."

"Come with me," she said.

They walked down the narrow corridor leading to Featherston's
ffice, which occupied the odd triangular point of the floor. The closed
oor to his office was just ahead of them, his name prominently let-
red on the clouded glass of the upper half. Julie walked directly in
ront of him, and he was taking full appreciation of her rather hand-
ome figure when the bomb went off. The blast was enormous. Like a
ow-motion nightmare, the door exploded out at them, along with
ieces of the wall around it. The last thing Danny saw was Julie's body
eing blown back into him, amidst a ferocious spray of shrapnellike
ebris. Then there was nothing but darkness and pain, until uncon-
iousness swept away all sensation.

The dark eyes squinted through the window of the Chinese restau-
int at the mad scene across the street. The force of the blast had been
great that it literally shook the restaurant and surrounding buildings.
atrons of the restaurant began rushing to the window and out into the
reet to get a closer look at what had happened.

The sidewalks around the Flatiron building were covered with
ass from the shattered windows. Dozens of people injured by the
lling glass were sprawled on both sides of the street. At the pointlike
p of the building there were chunks of heavy debris which had fallen
om the blast site. All that remained of Ted Featherston's office was an
gly blackened hole in the building.

A slight smile broke the plane of the man's lips, and his hand went

unconsciously to his mouth, the thumb and forefinger raking gentl
through the thick mustache, barely touching the scar of the faintl
noticeable harelip.

He looked at his watch. It had been right on time. But then h
knew it would be. His associate, Scalco, was a pro at such things. That
why he had chosen him.

He turned his six-foot-three-inch frame from the window an
shouldered through the crush of curious patrons to the phone at th
back of the restaurant near the restrooms. He deposited a dime an
dialed a number.

"Yes," said the answering voice with some apprehension.

"It's over," he began in his native French. "It went like a charn
They'll need a spoon to carry out what's left."

"And a mop, I guarantee," Scalco returned. "What's left to do?"
he asked.

"Not a thing but to get home. Our work is done here. I'll conta
you in the usual way within seven days."

"Very good. As always, it has been a pleasure," Scalco said.

A smile broke across Renaud Demy's face. It had, indeed, been
pleasure, he thought. "In seven days then. Go safely."

The phone clicked dead.

Demy returned to his table and dropped a ten and three singles t
cover his bill and the tip, then slipped his trench coat over his har
angular body.

He made his way to the door and stepped out onto the street int
what had quickly become a mob scene of curious onlookers. The a
was filled with the sounds of sirens and voices screaming in pain an
confusion. It was all music to his ears.

He pulled his trench coat closed, turned, and walked down Fift
Avenue away from the blast site. He went through a mental checklist
be sure that no loose ends had been left dangling. Christian Gladieu
was dead. All traces of his work had now been erased, and anyone wh
mattered had been eliminated. Certainly their efforts should have bee
sufficient to kill off any threat ignited by Gladieux. All in all, it ha
been a good week's work. Somewhat easier than he had expected it
be, actually. He had hoped there would be more challenge.

What a marvelous city New York was, he thought as he walke
So large, so vital—so *vulnerable*. It was a pity they had so little time t
play in it. It would have been such fun.

It was four-twenty when the rest of the family arrived at St. Vi
cent's Hospital to meet Michael. He intercepted them quickly to r

84

nove their fears. With the tremendous emotional shock and suffering hat Gabrielle and Denise had gone through during the past six days, nstant relief was a must.

"He's okay," Michael said, taking a trembling Gabrielle in his rms. "He was knocked unconscious, has a few cuts and bruises, and is till a little confused. But nothing is broken and there's no permanent lamage."

Gabrielle held tightly to her brother. He was the only strength she ad left in this nightmare that surrounded them. "I want to see him," he said, wiping her tears away.

"Come on. He's awake."

The family passed through the reception area and to the elevator. A few minutes later they were entering the private room Michael had rranged for Danny.

"Danny . . . Honey," Gabrielle said, rushing to his side.

The bandages covering his cuts and swollen cheekbone below the eft eye gave a worse impression of his condition than was actually true.

"Are you all right?" she asked, smothering him with gentle kisses.

"I'm fine, hon. I'm fine," he said with a weak smile. But his eyes were telling Michael just how close they had both come to dying. Had ney made that meeting on time, they would both be dead. Danny adn't been told that the others had died, but the force of the blast left o doubt in his mind that they had.

The phone on the table beside the bed rang. Michael answered it. "Yes."

"Mike, this is Bill Pheagan. I'm downstairs. How is he?"

"I'll be right down," Michael said. "Meet me by the elevators."

He hung up the phone. "Pheagan is downstairs. I'm going down to ee him. Would you like anything?" he asked Danny.

"Yeah, to get the hell out of here."

"Tomorrow maybe, if you're a good little boy." Michael smiled.

"Mike, I'd like to come downstairs with you to meet Pheagan," ay said. "We found some things that you and he should see."

Michael nodded, and the two men left the room and headed for ne elevator. When they stepped out, Pheagan was waiting for them. Michael made a quick introduction.

"How is he?" Pheagan asked.

"He'll be okay. A few cuts, mild concussion. He was lucky on two ounts. One that a good deal of the force of the blast was directed utward, due to the odd configuration of the room and the presence of) many windows; and two that someone was directly in front of him) take the force of the explosion. That saved his life," Michael said.

85

"Right now the figures stand at seven dead and twenty-six in jured," Pheagan told them. "All five people in Featherston's office were killed, and one woman on the street below was killed by falling debris. Featherston's secretary died about thirty minutes ago.

"I'm arranging for some of my people to set up protective surveil lance on your brother-in-law's room, just in case someone decides to make another try. I suggest that we find someplace private for the rest of this conversation," Pheagan said.

The three men went into the hospital coffee shop and found a corner table that offered them ample privacy.

"You're to carry this," Pheagan said, sliding a small-frame Llama automatic across the table to Michael, concealing it as much as possible with his hand. "And carry these," he continued, handing Michael per mits covering New York and New Jersey. "They'll hold up. By the time they can be checked out, they'll be on file."

Michael lowered the gun into his lap, checked it carefully, and stuck it into his belt beneath his light jacket. He put the permits in his wallet.

"You stay close to the rest of your family, especially your sister. Whoever tried for you two today may consider her equally threatening. You're to take no chances. If you doubt, shoot. I'll take care of any mistakes you may make."

That was the group speaking, Michael knew. The ability to ar range such details was clearly within their power.

"I've already checked on the typewriter repair shop. The cartridge was not in the machine. That means that we'll have to go on without the prospect of learning what the outline could have told us," Pheagan said.

"I have some things that should be interesting," Ray said, raising bag he had brought to the table. "We found these in a footlocker in the attic. It was the second Yale lock," he said to Michael.

Michael dumped the contents onto the table. The first thing to catch his attention was a passport folder. He reached for it and opened it. It showed a clear picture of his father, but the name to which it was issued was Claude Tremblay. Place of residence was listed as Montreal, Canada. It showed that Christian had made two trips to France, one in July and the other in November, both in 1981. Also on the table were the missing Daytimer pocket calendars for those same two months that had not been found with the others in the earlier search.

Michael handed the passport to Pheagan and then opened the July calendar to the dates corresponding to the trip to France. Christian had

86

been in France for six days. There were tiny notations in the Daytimer which were not clear to Michael. They were obviously in some kind of code his father had devised. What seemed clear, however, was that Christian had met someone referred to as Leopard on the third, fourth, and fifth days of his stay there. The word "Circus" appeared prominently on the last meeting day. There were abbreviations and sparse cryptic notations which had been of obvious importance to Christian, but suggested nothing to Michael. He handed the July Daytimer to Pheagan and opened the November calendar to the corresponding dates of Christian's second trip to France. There were more notations which looked like code names; "Fox, Albatross, Ferret," and again the name "Leopard."

Michael handed the November calendar to Pheagan and picked up several envelopes addressed to his father in hastily scribbled block letters. He opened one of the envelopes and read the single sheet it contained, then checked the postmark. He arranged the other envelopes according to date and began reading them in order of receipt. There were four in all. When he finished them, he handed them to Pheagan, who also read them.

"He started getting the threat letters in March," Ray said. "They're all signed, 'Firewatch,' and all refer to the charges of collaboration. He never told anyone that he had been getting them."

"Well, I think this confirms an important supposition," Pheagan said, waving the Daytimers. "Your father had a contact in France and met with him in July, and probably again in November. The name 'Leopard' is repeated in both Daytimers. That's probably the code name he used to identify him. I don't know what to make of these other notations yet, but the word 'Circus' is prominent enough to indicate that it had added significance. I think there's no question that your father learned whatever it was that got him killed *in* France, and that you're going to have to concentrate your search for answers there. We've got to find this Leopard. He ties this whole thing together, I'm sure."

"Where do we start?" Michael asked.

"I would imagine the best place would be with the people who were most closely associated with Christian during the war, his fellow Resistance fighters.

"Have you finished searching the house?" Pheagan asked Ray.

"No, we still have to go through the second floor bedrooms," Ray answered.

"I think you ought to consider spending the night in the city,"

Pheagan said, tossing a key onto the table. "We maintain a VIP suite at the Plaza that you're welcome to use. It's big enough for all of you."

Michael handed the key to Ray. "You and the girls use it. I'm staying at the hospital tonight to keep an eye on Danny."

"I can arrange the protection for Danny," Pheagan said.

"Then you arrange it for Ray and the women. I'm staying with Danny. If they try for him, I want to be here," Michael insisted.

"Have it your way," Pheagan said. "Call me tomorrow before you leave the city." He looked down at Michael as he got up to leave. "And remember what I told you," he said, tapping his side, belt high, to indicate the handgun. "If they show, it's for one reason only. Don't hesitate to act, because they won't. They're outwardly prepared to use violence, but may not be expecting you to be. Use it and worry about mistakes later, because one is all you'll get. Don't make it."

It was six-thirty when Pheagan returned to his empty office. He unlocked the right-side security drawer of his desk and pulled out a phone. He lifted it from the cradle and tapped out a seven-digit number.

"Unitrol," a man's voice answered.

"This is Phoenix, seven-seven-zero-four-zero. Clearance, triple-Delta-Queen. I need a contact with Horatio. I'm on the sterile Omega-David line."

There was a moment's delay while the computer ran its lightning-speed verifications.

"Accepted," the voice said. "You will receive a ring back on the Omega-David line within the half-hour."

"Clear," Pheagan said, hanging up the phone. He reached farther into the drawer and pulled out four folders. They were labeled with the names of Christian Gladieux, Michael Gladieux, Gabrielle Glady Preston (née Gladieux), and Daniel Preston. They were complete dossier files that he had read through at least three times already. One of those files, Michael's, he had helped accumulate prior to and following their association in 1968, when the small but elite Dawgs unit was assembled. Pheagan knew that file by heart. He had become quite familiar with the others by this time, as well. One folder, however, would be read and reread dozens of times until the nature and character of the man became rote to him. He opened Christian Gladieux's folder and began reading it once again from the beginning, wondering how much of a man's complexities could ever really be understood from words on paper. If only they knew what Christian Gladieux had discovered.

He read for nearly twenty minutes before closing the file. He again reached into the drawer, extracted a jeweler's box, opened it, and stared down at the pendant that Bob Caldwell had successfully obtained upon instructions from Sub Rosa. Why was Washington so interested in it, he wondered. . . .

B-r-r-i-i-n-g!

Pheagan snapped up the phone. "Phoenix," he said into it.

"Horatio here," the mellow voice of his superior said. "What have you been able to learn?"

"We're out of opportunities on the outline, unless something very unexpected turns up," Pheagan said. "The family has found something of importance, however. A false passport, under the name of Claude Tremblay, issued to a residence in Montreal, Canada. It was used by Gladieux to travel to France twice in the last year. Once in July, and then again in November. He developed some kind of a contact, who may have furnished him with what he knew. I believe it's imperative for the family to concentrate their efforts in France, trying to run down the collaboration aspect, and the identity of the contact we think to be referred to as Leopard by the father. In the meantime, we should attempt to develop the background on the pendant."

"We have already begun on the pendant," the voice said. "Based on Washington's information, it goes back to World War II, and the later discovery of three identical pendants, whose existence was made known during the war trials at Nuremberg. One of Britain's most sucessful moles worked right inside the German High Command throughout the entire war. It was a brilliant plant. He worked diligently for the German war effort, the value of his information far outweighing his efforts for the enemy. He was never suspected, and rocked members of the High Command at the trials when his true identity and role were exposed. During the final hectic weeks of the war when their efforts were concentrated on destroying files and documents, this agent came across information in a personal file of a Wehrmacht general that told of a secret organization believed to have been formed to continue efforts after the war. The organization was called the 'Salamandra.'

"Shortly after his testimony a second witness appeared in secret session, attempting to bargain for his life, offering information regarding the Salamandra in exchange for immunity to all charges against him. This testimony is *not* a part of official record.

"He gave the names of three individuals who were the governing committee of Salamandra. The revelation was shocking. He had named three men living in three different countries—the United States, Great Britain, and France—who were heirs to some of the largest private fortunes in those countries, and were destined for political positions of highest influence. Each was said to be identified by a pendant fitting the exact description of the one in our possession.

"The witness said that the Salamandra was still young and poorly structured. though large in scope. Within a week of his testimony, all three individuals named were dead by suicide, and their pendants discovered. It was never known how they had become aware that their identities had been revealed. because the information was held under the strictest security.

"A death oath had been sworn by the Salamandra pendant holders to protect the security of the organization should their identities ever be learned. They kept their pacts. The witness was found dead the day after his testimony had revealed the information regarding the oaths. His death was from cyanide poisoning.

"His last testimony included the belief that the deaths of its governing committee would certainly destroy the Salamandra organization. as it had not been sufficiently organized at levels below its leadership. and the basic plan had been known only to the committee.

"The governments of the three countries agreed to a pact of secrecy over the Salamandra issue. and a further understanding was reached to maintain a close watch for signs of resurgence of the organization. The presence of a new pendant. therefore. quite understandably caused great concern in Washington. especially when it was later determined that all three pendants were still in place in the respective countries of their discovery. What we have is. in fact. a *fourth* pendant." the voice concluded.

Pheagan thought for a second. "Then the theory that Gladieux had knowledge of an identity is sound." he said.

"Yes. it would seem so." the voice agreed.

"But why. then. would the pendant surface? The removal of Gladieux and all traces of his outline. as well as those exposed to it. should have removed the threat. To show the pendant is a dangerous. illogical step." Pheagan submitted.

"Or one of desperation." the voice offered.

"Desperation? Explain."

"Let's suppose that the Salamandra had not died with its leaders in 1945. and that a succeeding committee had. in fact. been appointed before the deaths of its three exposed leaders."

"But what about the testimony of the witness?" Pheagan asked.

"I haven't finished my supposition." Horatio said. "The testimony of the witness could have been *arranged,* to add substance to the theory

90

of the death of the Salamandra. Say that there were, in fact, three more pendant holders. That would present a new situation altogether, would it not?"

"Yes, it would. But that still doesn't explain your theory of desperation," Pheagan countered.

"Let's suppose further that a triumvirate still exists, and that the identity of one of these men is in serious jeopardy of exposure, and that he does not want to take his own life without first being certain that his identity has, indeed, been compromised. His fellow committee members would, for their own safety, just as soon see him dead. But he has convinced them that he can cover all traces sufficiently to keep the committee out of danger. Say they agreed to give him a chance to prove it to their complete satisfaction by offering the severest test of all," the voice said.

"Yes, I see. If he survives this, then he lives. But why would the Salamandra risk exposing themselves when they've managed to stay so well hidden for so long? I think the credibility of your theory is strained," Pheagan reasoned.

"No, it's more than theory. You see, the existence of the Salamandra has never been a secret to Sub Rosa. The Salamandra was formed *before* the war, when the clouds of that conflict were only faintly gray. The revelations at Nuremberg offered the perfect opportunity for the Salamandra to *disappear* from existence. But in reality, only the name died, along with those parts they chose to make visible. The names revealed at Nuremberg were not the leadership of the Salamandra, but merely the heirs to that leadership. They were expendable—and replaceable. The Salamandra still exists, though we know it differently, and engage in a constant war against it. It's a war which you help wage daily. I think you know what I mean."

"Trinity?" Pheagan asked almost hesitantly.

"Trinity," Horatio repeated. "Trinity and the Salamandra are one."

Pheagan knew with crystal clarity the meaning of Horatio's words, and the extent to which that war was being waged to protect the private sector of this country and to preserve world order. The fight was endless. He knew well the success that Sub Rosa had attained through difficult, thankless effort in fighting those battles against transnational terrorism, which was shaking the rest of the world. There were still plenty of terrorist activities, and hundreds of organizations within the United States whose bombs could kill and maim as readily as those planted by the transnational groups. And these numerous small groups, no doubt, received assistance and guidance from Trinity. But the "main event" terrorist episodes had been successfully prevented in the United States, while they were frequent news in other parts of the world.

Pheagan knew, too, that the absence of main event activities was not due to the lack of trying, for quite the contrary was true. Sub Rosa's tremendous success in stopping the main event lay in their worldwide intelligence-gathering capabilities, and in their ability to intercept terrorists of the transnational league before they could act They had secretly killed and maimed hundreds of them over the years and the battle was growing more intense, made exceedingly more difficult by the increased potential offered by sophisticated weaponry, and the stepped-up efforts of domestic terrorist organizations here in the U.S.

The battle was escalating too rapidly, growing more difficult for Sub Rosa to control. This, they knew, was due to the planning and efforts of the centralized core that controlled those terrorist activities and remained invisible to the world. This core of evil was known to those who fought it as "Trinity."

Trinity was the force of destruction and chaos that threatened every form of government and private sector interest in the world They choreographed and directed ruthless applications of massive terror and disruption against a system of world order they opposed, without ever offering a better plan beyond social control through fear Disapproval of the system was all the moral justification they needed.

The leadership of Trinity was like the wind, exerting its force without ever being seen. The organization was tremendous in size and so well insulated that it was impossible to penetrate more deeply than a few layers. There were too many individual groups each chasing a cause of its own, too many levels of command to find a death spot at which to take aim. Only taking the head could kill this animal—if the head could be found.

"*Before* the war," Pheagan mused. "It had nothing to do with a Nazi comeback then, did it?"

"Not even remotely, though they were apparently ready to carry on business regardless of which side won," Horatio replied. "You see the Salamandra that started in the thirties was very much like Sub Rosa, which started twenty years before it. Sub Rosa was committed to preserving the strength of the United States; to protecting its interests abroad; to ensuring world order; to cultivating economic growth and development; and to helping strong, stable governments dedicated

92

o democracy and free enterprise. It was no accident that America emerged as a world power. And it was no miracle that we remained one. Sub Rosa helped to ensure that.

"The Salamandra began very much along those same lines; its interests, however, were for a strong, unified Europe. The people who started the Salamandra controlled a good deal of Europe's wealth, and for awhile got off to a good start. But the real dream of unity ended as the inevitability of war approached. We can only guess at what went wrong after that, though there were obvious differences among the Salamandra's leadership over the opportunities that a world at war would present and a course of action to adopt.

"The war brought enough problems of our own to solve, and when it ended, the Salamandra, as we knew it, no longer existed. Its evolution into Trinity had begun, and though it wasn't a rapid one, it soon became clear to us that an enemy, and not a friend, would be the end result.

"Trinity has become bigger and stronger than Sub Rosa today. We can't withstand their forces forever," Horatio continued. "And when our efforts cease, so will those of the less capable who are dependent upon us. And then the world will lose its war of survival."

"This identity is the one chance we have, then, of ever striking deeply at the core of Trinity, isn't it?" Pheagan asked.

"Perhaps the best and only chance we'll ever have," Horatio clarified. "Kill enough of the brain, and the body will die," he said.

"One man's identity won't be enough," Pheagan returned.

"Perhaps not, but it's an opportunity that we must seize. We don't know what Christian Gladieux knew, except that he had tapped more deeply into the core of that evil force than we had ever been able to do ourselves. One of three identities is dangerously threatened. The Salamandra pendant bears three heads. We can remove one of them. If that is the limit of our ability, then we must achieve it, if for no other reason than to demonstrate that we *can* do it. If we get lucky, and use that identity properly, it may yield more than we dare to hope possible," Horatio concluded.

Find one man, and hope that he will lead them to the others, Pheagan thought. Perhaps, with luck, it could be done.

"I'll need some things from Intelligence Central," Pheagan said.

"You'll have whatever you need. All our resources will be at your disposal," Horatio told him.

"Good. Then here's what I'd like them to get started on."

The war of survival had begun.

Chapter 13

Danny slept soundly through the entire evening after the activity surrounding him had died down. Being the closest person to the blast to survive, Danny had become the prime subject of interview by the police. He could tell them nothing except that the door blew out at him and Featherston's secretary as they approached it. The police inquired into the reason for his visit to Bonaventure, which he covered by telling them that he had gone to obtain an up-to-date statement of Christian's royalty account for purposes of the estate valuation.

No, he hadn't known any of the people in the room, except Featherston, with whom his meeting had been scheduled. He apologized for not being able to help them, but there was just nothing more he could tell them.

Red tape delayed Danny and Mike from leaving the hospital early the next day as they had planned. A final examination by the doctor cleared a part of the formalities, but obtaining the necessary paperwork was a joke that both men took poorly. Matters were finally cleared up and Danny was released.

Less than thirty minutes later they were on their way back to Spring Lake to join the rest of the family, who had headed back earlier in the day to resume the search.

It was nearly dusk when Danny awoke. He stood in front of the bathroom mirror staring at his face and upper body. The left cheekbone was swollen and discolored. Small bandages covered three of the worst cuts on his face, which had required stitches. He peeled off he bandages to assess the damage. There would be small scars over the left eye, left upper lip, and the right cheek just above the lower jaw line. The rest of the cuts were superficial. His left upper chest and shoulder were also discolored and bruised from flying debris. The left thigh also had a few nasty gashes but had not required stitches.

Julie Taylor hadn't been so lucky, although after what the glass and debris had done to her, death might not have been the worst thing that could have happened. At least it had been fast, and although she lived for three hours after the blast, she was unconscious and seemingly without pain. Danny had heard later from a few of the detectives he talked to that those in the room had been brought out in pieces. So a few aches and pains, and even a few scars, did little to detract from the realization of how lucky he had been.

He thought about Gabrielle and the fear he had seen in her eyes when she first came into the room at the hospital. Jesus, she had been through enough, he thought. He wondered about the possible danger ahead. If only he could persuade her to stay in the U.S. while he and Michael went to France to pursue the mystery. Pheagan had warned them that they would face more and more danger as they made progress. The thought of anything happening to Gabrielle made his insides ache. But he knew there would be no keeping her out of it.

He re-dressed the stitched wounds, put on some loose-fitting clothes, and went downstairs to where the activity had centered. He met Ray in the hall.

"Hey, there he is," Ray said. "How are you feeling?"

"Fine. Tired of sleeping, though. How's the search going?"

"We've finished," Ray answered, throwing up his hands in a hallelujah.

"Find anything new?"

Ray shook his head.

"You're up!" Gabrielle said as she entered the center hall from the dining room. She embraced her husband gently and kissed him lightly on the lips. "How are you feeling?" she asked.

"I feel like I need to be doing something," he answered. "Get up on my feet, at least."

"Well, Mom will have dinner ready in a few minutes. We can eat a late supper and then just relax. God knows I was getting tired of going through this house. If I don't open another box or move another piece of furniture again, I won't mind it a bit," Gabrielle said.

"Move another piece of furniture!" exclaimed Danny, reflexively moving a hand to his bandaged forehead. "Jesus, I can't believe I didn't think of it earlier. Get Mike and your mom, then meet me in your dad's room," he said as he took off up the stairs.

He headed to the bedroom that Christian had used. It was an enormous room, furnished with large heavy pieces of beautifully crafted furniture. He went directly to a tall, solid mahogany desk secretary that he had helped Christian move upstairs into the bedroom about a year ago. He pulled down the hinged desktop after pulling out the two supports upon which it rested. Centrally located between the many slotted shelves and drawers was an eight-by-eleven-inch door. He opened it and felt inside, along the base of the compartment. His finger found the hole and pushed down, but there was no give. Then he remembered part of the key to the mechanism. He pushed one of the desktop supports halfway in and tried the hole again. Still no give. He pulled the support back out and pushed the other one in halfway.

The others rushed into the room confused by Danny's sudden actions.

"He showed me this once, but I can't remember it exactly," Danny said, again trying his finger in the hole. This time it worked, and the small wooden trip platform depressed enough to release the entire central compartment. Danny hooked his finger in the hole and gripped the top of the compartment with his other hand, then pulled. It slid out.

"He showed me how this worked once. If I can remember it, we'll be in business." He shook the compartment. "There's something in here, too. I can hear it," he said. He turned the box around to expose the back.

"This box has three secret storage compartments in it. Two in the sides and a shallow one across the bottom for jewelry. But there's a trick to opening them," he said.

After a few moments of fiddling, he had it. The shallow jewelry box slid out first. He removed it completely and poked a finger inside the opening it left. He located the trip pins and a second later both side compartments were free. He slid them out.

Each compartment was about the size of a hardcover book, with a thickness of about an inch and a half. He placed them flat on the desktop and opened one of them. The box was crammed tight with neatly stacked and wrapped hundred-dollar bills.

"There must be thousands here," Ray said in amazement.

Danny flipped his thumb across the edge of one of the piles. "There has to be twenty or thirty thousand in here," he said.

Danny opened the other box. In it was another small packet of bills, and what appeared to be Christian's old military medals that had

96

been awarded him before his trial in 1945. There was also a pack of about twenty old photographs and a piece of paper with the words "Leopard, Fox, Albatross, and Ferret" printed on it. On the back of that paper was a single word in large letters: "CIRCUS."

Danny picked up the old photographs and looked at them.

"I know some of those people," said Denise, looking over Danny's shoulder. "This one is Edna-Marie DeBussey," she said, taking a picture of an attractive dark-haired woman dressed in a long white frilly dress specked with small flowers and dots and standing beside a stone wall. "She led Le Groupe Défi. I told you about her."

She selected another photograph, this one of a short but well-built man with a wide cocky grin. He held a submachine gun in his hands, the sling draped over his left shoulder. A small beret was tipped downward and to the right, adding to the cockiness of his expression.

"This one is Claude St. Jude," she said with a reminiscent smile. "He was your father's best friend. They saved each other's lives more than once. Your father introduced me to him after he had joined the Resistance, on one of the few occasions when we were together. Claude was a wonderful man. I think that if I had not already been married to your father and loved him so much, I would have trapped that man for myself."

"Is he still living?" Michael asked.

"I think so, though I haven't heard from him in years. His address is here in the house."

Denise looked through more of the photographs—pictures of Claude and Christian, some of Edna-Marie and Christian, and others of people she didn't know.

Gabrielle had picked up one picture and was staring at it. The image showed a woman of immense beauty. Christian stood beside her with his arm around her shoulders, her arm tightly around his waist. There was something about the way they touched one another and the look on her father's face that brought tears welling to Gabrielle's eyes. It was a faraway look, and she knew that the woman he was with was the one he had loved so much. It was as though the face were trying to apologize for that truth to the camera, or perhaps to the person looking at the picture. But there was no mistaking the feeling behind those sad eyes, for one who knew them.

"Who is this?" Gabrielle asked.

Denise looked at the picture in silence for several long moments. She, too, could feel the story in Christian's face.

"She . . . was Gabrielle Dupuy," Denise said, looking into her daughter's eyes. "She was so beautiful. I never met her, but I felt as though I knew her. Claude St. Jude told me about her after the war, when I thought your father would die from some hidden grief. I didn't know what to do to bring him back to the living, so I called Claude. He rushed to us immediately, halfway across France. That was when he told me about her, although I had sensed that there was another woman years before. I had thought that it was Edna-Marie, with the war and the desperate state of life in those times, and them being together so much. But I was wrong."

There was another picture of Gabrielle Dupuy standing with a tall, handsome German officer. They seemed to be at a party of some kind.

"Who is that?" Danny asked.

"I don't know." Denise replied. "She . . . knew many Germans. That was her job for the Resistance. To know them, and to learn what she could from them."

There was a picture of a young boy. He was small and looked no more than thirteen or fourteen. He, too, was posed with a submachine gun in his hands and wearing a dark beret.

"I don't know this boy." Denise commented. "But look at his face. Such hatred in the eyes. That war could do that to a child is so sad. So very sad."

"Some of these people must still be alive. Do you think they would help us?" Michael asked.

"I'm certain of it. They loved your father. If they are alive, you can count on their help."

Michael picked up the pictures and the paper bearing the code names. It was here, in his hands. He could feel it. It didn't seem like much of a beginning, he thought. It was like looking at a bare canvas with a single stroke of color. He could not see what the artist's mind had planned. But he knew that one stroke of the brush would be followed by another until the bare expanse closed in and was transformed into a perceivable image obvious to all who beheld it. The canvas was set, the first line in place. The rest would come. He felt it.

After dinner, Michael spent a little time going through some of his old Marine Corps gear. Seeing Pheagan had unlocked the doors of his memory, and now, as he touched and examined certain objects, the memories flooded back strong.

Like many men, he had brought back things that he shouldn't have. As a Dawgs specialist, he had had access to all kinds of weapons and equipment not routinely issued, and certainly less strictly ac counted for. Each team member had been issued a "kit" that contained a unique mix of weapons and devices designed for ease of carrying yet still capable of delivering maximum killing power. Depending on their assignments, any piece of equipment could be made available to them, from the finest infrared night scopes to the most sophisticated explosives.

He had chosen not to bring back most of his kit when he left Nam. He did bring back his KA-BAR fighting knife, and three handguns, however, including a special issue Swiss SIG 9-mm Parabellum automatic, a .357 Colt MK III that he carried as a second gun, and a Smith and Wesson .38 Special Military Airweight, which was standard Dawgs issue as a light backup weapon. Michael had chosen to carry two backup pieces of revolver design because of the foul environmental conditions he was often exposed to. Revolver designs were simpler to clean and held up to the worst of conditions better than automatics, even the extremely well-made Swiss SIG that he had been issued. But by far the most imposing close-range weapon that he had been issued was the extremely compact lightweight Ingram Model 10 submachine gun, which possessed an awesome destructive firepower of 1,100 rounds per minute. It could virtually shred a small group of men with a short, violent burst. He had chosen not to take the Ingram, not because of its illegal status outside the military or law enforcement, but because he had had enough of killing and war and bodies made unrecognizable pulp by the sheer power of the weapons in his hands. The Ingram would have been a constant reminder of that. If he could have, he would have left behind the ability of those bare hands to kill as well, for that had been surely taught, and too often used in the grim business of war. Especially in the dark, secret war conducted by the Dawgs, which made no distinctions among uniform, rank, and sex.

He remembered one particular assignment as he cradled the Swiss SIG in his hands. He had been sent into Saigon to terminate a "tiger lady" who had executed at least ten American officers. Tiger ladies were found in many cities, but this one had caught the interest of the group, because she was believed to be working for a certain South Vietnamese general who was attempting to cover his dirty tracks in the black market and drug business by selectively eliminating American officers he thought dangerous to his swelling income.

It took a month to find her, and Michael remembered the confrontation. She was one of the most beautiful Vietnamese women he had ever seen. She had served a double role for her master, as an expensive prostitute for high-ranking American officers, and as the assassin who struck at her carefully selected paramours days later.

Her unexpected beauty had stunned him for a split second when he broke in on her, finding her naked in the small third-floor room, preparing to earn a day's pay. She was fast, and that one second almost cost him his life, before he blew her away with the Swiss SIG, knocking her through a window to the street below.

The shocked and terrified American officer with her never knew how lucky he was. He stood there in utter disbelief as Michael took a brief second to look out the window at the rock-still body of his target. "No more boom-boom for you, mamma-san," Michael whispered. What a fucking waste of beautiful pussy, he thought. Then he was gone before the American officer could even find his voice . . . or his pants.

Three days later, he paid a visit to the South Vietnamese general. He caught him in the middle of an obviously delightful union with one of his girls. With the speed and silence of a cat, Michael had the self-locking garrote fatally engaged. At first, the girl thought the general was convulsing in thralls of pleasure, but the sudden vision of Michael brought home the reality of what was happening. The KA-BAR silenced her before the second scream left her throat . . . and then found the throat of the general's aide, who had made the fatal mistake of investigating a scream that did not sound like the wild moans of pleasure he was used to hearing through the door.

That had all been part of a day's work for Michael. At first he believed what he was doing was for the best interests of America. But as his time began winding down during the third and last tour of duty, he began to see that what he did would make no difference to what was happening in Vietnam. He began to hate the job. Nothing would save that country. The people running the government and its army were too caught up in a game of greed, grabbing all they could while the grabbing was good. They were selling American equipment before it even came off the ships or out of the transports. Half the drugs going to Vietnam ended up on the black market. No one cared that South Vietnamese and American soldiers would die because those drugs weren't getting to where they were needed. There was too much money to be made to worry about such trivial details.

Those much higher in the government didn't have to bother themselves with fencing what they could steal. They got right into the hard cash that the United States was pushing in. And they weren't shy about digging into that golden pot, either. More of it went into private accounts and back pockets than went into the country. They were too busy living high to realize that they would not live long. Of course, those with enough money managed to make it out before the final curtain fell.

Michael's bitterness grew more intense in his last months in Vietnam. He knew that the American government was aware of what was going on there, and he could not comprehend that they could continue to spill American blood for a cause so totally lost. The South Vietnamese had a good army, but next to no leadership. They wanted to help themselves and could have to a much greater extent if priorities had been straight. It was a hard thing to watch without the power to effect change. It was time for him to get out and he did just that, leaving it *all* behind.

Pheagan had been right about the group not having created the situation there, but Michael didn't know enough about Sub Rosa to separate it from a government that allowed such a thing to persist while handing a complete lie to the American people at home. He grew to truly hate and distrust the system. The group was a part of that, as far as he was concerned. He wanted no more to do with it.

The family gathered in the kitchen before retiring for the evening to plan the next steps, which pointed inevitably toward France.

"We could probably be ready to go within a week, if no matters of the estate delay us," Danny said.

"We'll need to make arrangements for the children," Gabrielle said, staring down into her coffee cup.

"It might be best if—"

"If you didn't even finish what you're thinking," Gabrielle said, cutting off her husband. "Don't you even hint at my staying behind," she warned with an earnest resolve.

"It might get rough, Sis," Michael said.

"Which is all the more reason for me to be there. I'll go, if I have to go alone and follow you two every place you go."

"We can take care of the girls," Ray offered. "I've got nothing pressing in California. We can stay in Princeton while you're away."

Gabrielle smiled her gratitude to Ray and her mother.

"I can make a phone call tomorrow to Claude St. Jude," Denise said. "I'm sure he'll be willing to help in any way possible. He could begin making some of the arrangements for you there."

"You've got the cash we found in the secretary to use for immediate expenses," Ray said. "That was probably the money Christian used to cover his expenses. That's why we couldn't find any financial records of his trips to France."

"If only we knew where in France he went. We'd have a starting place," Michael said.

"Claude St. Jude will be a good starting point," Denise said.

"Your father may even have contacted some of these people when he went over."

"Let's hope so. It could make our job a lot easier," Danny said.

"I think the best thing right now would be for you to tell us as much as you can, Mom," Michael suggested.

"Well, I know a good deal about what happened from the time that your father left for the front with the army until he returned home after being wounded and discharged. He stayed with me only a short time, then left to join the Resistance. From that time on, I'm afraid I can't tell you very much," she said.

"We'll take anything that we can get, Mom. We want to learn it all," Michael said.

"It's easy to remember that terrible feeling of imminent war, especially when we knew from your father's letters that France was illprepared to fight. The government had painted quite a different picture to the people of France. They said that we were ready to meet and defeat the German army. Most of France believed that the Maginot Line was impregnable, and that our brave army would save us from an enemy that they had beaten in the last great war. Within two weeks, the Germans would be licking their wounds and running back into Germany, we had been told. Well, it was quite a different picture, indeed. A picture one could never forget. . . ."

Chapter 14

FRANCE, MAY 1940: War had finally come to France, although it had actually been declared more than eight months earlier. The bombs had begun to fall on French towns and villages, and were tearing French flesh. The French army had been mobilized many months ago, but it had been a farce of monumental proportions. France was no more ready to fight a war now than it had been before the preparations were started.

It took no power of clairvoyance to recognize that an army in which only 75 to 80 percent of its men had weapons—of which only 10 percent were modern and equivalent to the standard issue of the German army—was in a poor position to win a war; or that observation outposts complete with all comforts and amenities, including steam heat and champagne, but with no possible view of the enemy, were a product of almost criminally poor planning.

It was the day following Germany's invasion of Belgium and Holland that the 21st Foreign Volunteers received their first orders. Christian Gladieux had been assigned as a lieutenant to the officers' staff of the 21st Foreign Volunteers because of his fluent command of six languages, including English, German, Polish, Spanish, Czechoslovakian, and Italian. The 21st Foreign Volunteers was comprised of many nationalities, and communication often proved difficult.

The two hundred men of the 21st Foreign Volunteers were a part of the 35th Division of the XII Army Corps. They had been positioned in Mommenheim, in Alsace, awaiting assignment as the inevitable clouds of war gathered. When Belgium and Holland were invaded by Germany, the order was sent down to march with all possible haste toward the Belgian front.

"All possible haste" was a bad joke. Orders had been issued by the High Command to march in an absurd zigzag route, avoiding the more direct and shorter roads to prevent detection by the enemy. A march that should have been ten kilometers was now closer to twenty.

The first token strafings by the jagged-winged Messerschmitts would dispel the High Command's strategy of avoiding detection by the enemy.

At the beginning of their forced march from Mommenheim to St.-Mihiel, most of the roads were relatively clear. But they gradually began to thicken with refugee traffic flowing in the opposite direction. What had begun as an orderly advance to St.-Mihiel became quite the contrary as they approached the beleaguered town. They could hear the deep drone of German planes and the muffled thuds of bombs going off in the distance. Large pillars of black smoke rose and tailed in the wind, and the horizon became a gentle flickering glow as night fell.

They arrived to find St.-Mihiel almost completely deserted. Seeing the orderly pattern of destruction at close hand drove home the sickening reality of this war. Entire blocks were smashed and burning. In some areas, only one side of the street was in ruin, while the other stood untouched, glowing softly in the dancing orange light of the fires. They were seeing the effect of what they had heard and could only imagine from a distance as they approached the town.

After only a short rest, new orders were received to begin an advance to Verdun, thirty kilometers to the north—fifty kilometers by the prescribed zigzag route. Some consolation was offered in the fact that they would be moving under the protection of darkness. They had not yet felt the true bite of the German war machine, but the fear of it had been planted from the destruction they had witnessed in St.-Mihiel and by the sudden appearance of the German planes which had simply harassed them earlier.

They passed through more empty villages, only some of which had sustained significant damage. But the roads had become congested to the point of being almost impassable. Vehicles of all descriptions were abandoned by the roadside because they had either run out of fuel or were no longer able to negotiate through the pathetic clog of humanity. The roads were cluttered with abandoned belongings too heavy to take further, things of little value or importance to anyone but the owners. So many people had packed things they thought to be important, only to find that the important things had been left behind—like ample food and water. Dead animals also littered the roads where they had been crushed by personal vehicles or those belonging to the military. Nothing stopped the tanks—not horses, not cows, not wagons.

But the most appalling sights had been the attacks on the refugee columns by the Germans planes. Sometimes it was a distant road under attack, and one felt relief that the bombs and machine guns were aimed at those other poor souls. But everyone had his turn. The Germans did their utmost to see that the roads remained as jammed and chaotic as possible, to hinder the movements of the French military.

Christian could not help thinking about his wife, Denise, who he knew would be in some refugee column herself, trying to reach the safety of her father's house in the Pyrenees, close to the Spanish border. His mind was tortured with worry over her. He could only wait and pray that she would reach her father's home safely.

It was in Verdun that the first significant signs of army disorder were noticed. The columns of refugees leaving the city were not all civilians. The desertions had begun. Men were going home. Guns, packs, coats, and helmets were found everywhere. Yet the 21st Foreign Volunteers did not crack. Those without arms found them by the side of the road. Equipment was so plentiful that they began leaving some of their own behind. There was no reason to carry the extra weight when the same things could be found further up the road.

It was not until the following afternoon that the order to rest came. The men sat in small tired groups, eating from their supplies of canned sardines and meat. Even these supplies were often inedible. Paint scraped from the cans of meat, which the men called *singe* (monkey meat), showed packing dates of 1914. Christian shook his head in dis-ust and disbelief. Surely, someone must be shot for treason, he thought.

There was a numb silence when the order came to gather up and proceed at once to Grandpré, another march of at least fifty to sixty kilometers. The 21st was to cover the regiment's rear.

It was all part of a cruel joke, Christian thought as the company proceeded to leave Verdun. They were reaching the end of their endurance. At least there was one benefit, he thought. By the time they engaged the enemy, they'd be too tired to be frightened. He could not help wondering if that went into the planning of war.

As usual, the roads were a nightmare. Again, darkness concealed their movements from the German planes, which could be heard overhead. Christian wondered whether the planes he heard had already completed their grim task, or whether they were destined to flatten the next town ahead of them.

Through some minor miracle, the company managed to stay together during the long march through the refugee columns. They set up camp in a graveyard near Grandpré and collapsed from exhaustion.

An enormous Pole by the name of Stephan Zanosko slumped to the ground next to Christian. He rolled onto his side and lit up a cigarette.

"They trying very hard to kill us, hey?" he said in very bad French.

"Someone is, but I'm not sure which side is trying harder," Christian answered in a low voice.

The Pole roared with laughter and hacked a loud cough born of fatigue. "If not the walking, then this," he said, holding up a can of the ancient meat. He tossed it over his shoulder. "I will eat dog before I eat *singe* again."

"You may have trouble finding dogs. I haven't seen more than one or two since leaving Mommenheim. I've always heard that they disappear when a war starts," Christian said.

Zanosko held out another can toward Christian. "I tell you, dog is better," he said, tossing the can in the same direction as the other. "Cat's good too. Taste like rabbit. I will find a dog or a cat," he said, getting to his feet. He tossed two more cans of the *singe* away, and stared hard at the small Russian, Victor Sasmi, who quickly snatched up the four cans.

"Food!" the Russian said in equally bad French. "When the fighting starts, you will wish you had this. You will not have time to hunt dogs and cats," he scolded.

"Ha! That is not food. When the fighting starts, if I cannot find dogs or cats, I will eat Germans," the Pole said, roaring with menacing laughter. "And if there are no Germans, I will eat Russian."

Sasmi gave the Pole a vile stare, and stuffed the cans into his sack. Zanosko started to walk away, when Christian called out to him.

"You cannot fire your rifle. Orders. To prevent detection by the enemy," he said, feeling foolish at the absurdity of the order.

The Pole roared again, louder than any gun could sound. "Zanosko does not need this to kill," he said, laying the gun across his pack.

There were wishes for good hunting as he passed through the company of prostrate men. He laughed loudly to each one.

Zanosko was a good hunter. He returned with four chickens, a helmet filled with eggs, and two white rabbits. There was a feast in the graveyard near Grandpré.

Christian watched the colonel's car stop at a distance. He got up and walked over to it.

"Were those men cooking?" the colonel asked, seeing the smoke of the dying fires.

Christian nodded.

"Orders from Command strictly forbid the starting of fires, to prevent detection by the enemy," the colonel said in his rigid manner.

Christian let the rest of his reprimand slip past him as he made it obvious for the colonel's sake that he was observing horizons on all sides that were marked with smoke.

The colonel caught his meaning too well. He stared with icy eyes at Christian. "Form them up. We march to Ferme St. Denis. Immediately."

"Where is Ferme St. Denis, *mon Colonel?*" Christian inquired.

"I don't know. We don't have a map with proper detail of the area." He unfolded a small Michelin road map and held it out to Christian. With a pencil, he marked a spot on it. "This is where we are now. We must follow the main roads to Dormans. I think it's near there."

Christian stared grimly at a map that showed a distance of what he guessed to be about ninety kilometers between Grandpré and Dormans.

"The men are exhausted. They need rest—"

"They are French soldiers," the colonel interrupted sternly. "Our orders are to proceed at once to Ferme St. Denis. We will do just that."

Christian snapped to attention and saluted. *"Mon Colonel."*

"Put out those fires and form the men. Tell them they are not to fire their weapons unless they are engaged by enemy *infantry*. Keep them together. Short rest periods every fifteen minutes. We will bivouac the men near Verzy."

The colonel tapped his driver and the car sped off.

"The marching will kill us before the Germans get the chance." Christian muttered to himself.

The roads had become pure chaos. They were jammed not only with the pathetic crush of civilians but also with the simultaneous advance and retreat of the French army. Ambulances slithered through impossible openings, their handcord bells ringing in near hopeless attempts to clear the road ahead.

Zanosko occasionally took a few moments to inspect any dead animals that looked recently killed. It was only when he witnessed a fallen horse die agonizingly beneath the treads of an advancing tank that he exercised his skill as a butcher to gather provisions for later.

The night was like a celebration. They could see flames and cannon fire for what seemed to span the entire gap between the Aisne and the Meuse.

The cold night air grew noticeably warmer as they approached a town that was easily the most devastated they had yet seen. Parts of the town were burning fiercely, giving off intense heat. The broken signpost outside the town showed only the letters . . . IVILLE.

Christian checked his watch. It was their break time. He spotted another cemetery and directed his men to it. During their break, a messenger from the motorcycle unit of the division came in search of Christian. The colonel had decided to bivouac the men here instead of at Verzy. The distance was too great for their level of fatigue.

"What village is this?" Christian asked the messenger.

"I don't know," he replied with a disinterested shrug.

"We'll bivouac here in the cemetery. Will the colonel and the other officers be coming up to join us?" Christian inquired.

The messenger replied that he didn't know, shrugged once again, then sped off.

"Find areas away from gravesites and dig in," Christian ordered. "The Germans may not be through with this town yet," he said.

Zanosko went directly to a fresh grave and quickly spaded a body trench in the soft earth.

"You have no respect for the dead," Sasmi's voice accused from behind him.

Zanosko turned his huge body to face the little Russian. "I have even less for you," he growled, holding the spade like a weapon.

Sasmi slinked off into the darkness, cursing in Russian.

Zanosko finished his trench quickly, then cut long strips of his horse meat and headed for the closest burning building.

The rest of the company was still digging in when the German artillery started once again on the town. At first the hits seemed random, but quickly formed a pattern closer to the graveyard, the tremendous noise and concussion inspiring the fiercest expenditure of energy by the men to get quickly below the surface. Then the range was found, and like a stormy sky opening its full torrential fury, the German 77s began pouring in an awesome continuous fire.

All joking of what or who would bring death first was lost in the reality of the deafening explosions ripping the cemetery and the nearby church to shreds.

The men dove into their holes and pressed themselves hard to the shaking earth. Never had they been closer to hell than their baptism by fire was taking them now. The pounding was unending. Shrieks and mortal cries filled the air. The ground shook violently as dirt and stone and debris flew like heavy rain. It went on and on and on.

The men of the 21st were facing their first lesson of war, and they were alone, save for one officer, Christian Gladieux, who had been with them every step of the way. The remaining officers were absent. The bond of faith between men and their leaders was being sorely tested.

As quickly as the incoming fire had started, it was over. In the distance behind them, they could hear the sounds of the French 75s concentrating a withering return fire on the German artillery positions. They had been unable to hear their countrymen helping them. It was, perhaps, the one aspect of this war in which the French maintained the upper hand. Their artillery consistently outdueled the Germans throughout the fighting.

Christian rose from his trench to quickly regroup his men and assess their losses. What had been a perfectly untouched cemetery a short while ago was now a vision of utter destruction.

Gradually heads began popping out of holes, and struggled through earth that had covered others. Broken caskets and parts of long forgotten corpses were scattered everywhere.

Christian counted quickly as he ran from section to section. More and more heads began popping up and bodies emerging, frightened and shaking. The casualties were not as heavy as he had feared.

Sasmi stood over what had been the soft trench of Zanosko. It had taken a direct hit. He searched for a trace of the big Pole, finally jumping into the crater to look more closely. He looked around frantically filled with a surprising concern.

"Have some. It's good," said the booming voice of the Pole from above the crater.

Sasmi looked up to see Zanosko standing there, his uniform torn, blood running down the side of his face, holding out a long strip of cooked horse meat. Sasmi automatically smiled and caught the meat that Zanosko tossed to him.

Christian walked up to Zanosko and clapped him hard on the shoulder. "You lucky idiot. If you hadn't gone to cook your meat, you'd be a dead man. That was a direct hit," he said to the giant in Polish.

He stared down into the crater. "And I thought I had no luck. The house I was in was hit, too. Now I am certain that no German will kill Zanosko. Eat your meat," he said, tossing a strip to his lieutenant.

Christian has just finished collecting the identity bracelets of the dead and had regrouped his men when he saw the colonel's car arrive. With him were the two remaining French officers of the company who had been mysteriously missing since leaving Mommenheim. They had come to survey the casualties. They paid no notice to the looks of contempt aimed at them.

Captain Henry Cassell approached Christian for his report.

"Where were you?" Christian asked. "You belonged with your men."

Cassell was a tall man, quite thin in build, with dark, almost effeminate features. He leveled a cold stare at Christian. "It's not your concern where I was," he snapped at the young lieutenant. "It's not your place to question me. Give me your report."

Christian stared into the face of his superior. "The French army has lost seven dead, twelve wounded and incapable of going on, and twenty-one walking wounded who will advance with the company. But you, *mon Capitaine*, have lost them all. You are their captain. You belonged with them when they needed you."

"That's enough, Gladieux. Your insubordination is going too far."

"I respectfully submit, *mon Capitaine*, that you join your company and take your place as its leader. It will do more good being here to issue orders and to share our hardships than it will to send your orders by messenger while you sit on your soft ass somewhere out of harm's way.

"These men are going to engage the enemy sooner or later, and the support and leadership of their officers will be vital to prevent them from becoming a part of that refugee traffic going in the other direction. These are not maneuvers that we're on. This is a *war*. The bombs going off are real; the dead are real.

109

"Here," Christian said, shoving seven identity bracelets into Cassell's chest. "Write the letters to their wives and mothers and children. Be their captain."

Cassell stood for a long moment in silence holding the bracelets.

"Group your men for the advance toward Dormans. I will march with you. We leave immediately." Cassell said.

Christian saluted his captain and returned to his men.

The company trudged away from the devastated town, too tired to feel, too tired to care. They had just survived hell. Being tired wasn't important anymore. Only being alive was. And feeling tired told them that they were still alive. They did not complain.

Daylight brought another reminder of German superiority. This was the presence of the remarkably invulnerable reconnaissance plane, the little Arado. A heavily armored modified monoplane, it flew at very low altitudes, secure in the knowledge that it could not be damaged by ground fire. Flying at a slow 120 to 140 miles per hour, it became an ever-present spy that reported all French army movements and artillery positions when the duels between the big guns started. The psychological effect was devastating. There was no escaping the German eye. The Arados were everywhere.

Despite the knowledge that the Germans were completely aware of their movements, the idiotic order to march in a time-wasting zigzag pattern was strictly adhered to.

Not far from Dormans, Cassell spotted a small but dense thicket of woods. He hurried his pace and caught up to Christian.

"Those woods," he said, pointing, his breathing telling the tale of his exhaustion, as did the limping of his blistered feet. "That would be a good place to rest the men for a few hours."

Christian looked at the thicket about a hundred yards off the road. He shook his head. "Too confined. We're better off strung out as we are. They can't concentrate artillery on a long line like this. We had better keep on going until we reach Dormans," he recommended.

Cassell's limping was getting worse, fast. He looked back at the weary men and took a measure of his own fatigue and the prospect of going further.

"We'll stop," he said. "Order the men into the cover of the woods."

Christian turned his head to Cassell, then looked to the sky at the pesky Arado in the distance. " 'Coco' is watching. It would be too risky."

"The woods," Cassell repeated, moving off the road and heading for the shady cover.

Christian shook his head and gave the order.

Within fifteen minutes the entire company was concealed there, lying against tree trunks, smoking, eating canned sardines and meat, drinking water or their ration of *gnole,* an alcohol given to each man almost daily.

Contrary to Christian's expectations, things remained peaceful. Then he saw the absurdity that explained why. A second company of foreign volunteers had come up the road behind them and was also approaching the woods. The forest was hardly big enough for two companies.

No sooner had the last man entered the cool shade of the trees, than the German artillery opened up. It took only ten rounds to find the range, and then the carnage began.

The bombardment in the cemetery had been mild in comparison to what the Germans concentrated on the tiny woods. The great massive trees became as deadly as the shrapnel of the exploding shells. There had not been sufficient time to dig in, and the men were caught above ground. They darted frantically, like frightened fish in a bowl, finding hot craters to dive into, or fallen wooden giants to lie behind.

The whole time, the tiny Arado circled at a distance, calling in the results to the German artillery.

It was again the ferocious response of the French artillery which finally ended the assault, zeroing in sufficiently for the Germans to pull up stakes and head for safer ground.

When it was over, Christian unburied himself from a crater that had nearly become his grave, and he looked in disbelief at what had once been a beautiful forest. It seemed that not more than a few dozen trees were left standing, and those were scarred and torn, and were nearly branchless. He had watched trees being snapped off at the tops as if they were mere twigs; he had seen it happen to men.

The floor of the forest became a grim revelation. Bodies lay everywhere. A heavy smokelike vapor hung along the ground. Ghostlike figures crawled about slowly, or writhed with arms and legs flailing out of desperate pain, or lay in the absolute stillness of death. Agonized sounds filled the air.

The harsh throaty engine of the Arado could be heard as it came in for a closer look at the effect of the big guns. The moans and cries were temporarily drowned out as the little "Coco" flew just above what had been treetop level. Christian could see the face of the pilot. For one fleeting moment they looked at one another. The victor and the vanquished. No words could express any better the recognition of their roles in that one instant.

Of the nearly 400 men who had entered the tiny forest, fewer than 250 would walk out. Of those, almost half were wounded to some degree, but would go on with the unit.

Cassell was found sitting against a splintered tree trunk, dazed and unresponsive. He gradually came around and instructed Christian to take temporary command of the two companies' survivors.

Three hours later, the 21st Foreign Volunteers were again marching in search of Ferme St. Denis, without a map or even the slightest hint of where it was.

The next week of the war brought with it a clearer role for the 21st Foreign Volunteers. A section of front along the Canal des Ardennes had been assigned to them between Attigny and Le Chesne. They were to defend the line and keep the Germans north of the canal.

The German army had smashed through Sedan to the northeast, then split their drive. The armored columns pushed north and west, while the infantry went south to split the French forces still further apart. But they got no further than the Canal des Ardennes before finding the defenses of that line surprisingly tenacious.

The 35th Division, of which the 21st was a part, held the important part of that entire line. They blew the bridges on the canal and repeatedly beat back the superior German forces. Completely stopped without the spearhead thrust of their armored units, the Germans called in the Luftwaffe to soften the enemy positions.

The Luftwaffe ruled supreme in the sky. The French air force had been beaten on the ground. There was no challenge to their efforts.

The peaceful silence of the darkly brooding forests of the Noirval was interrupted daily at dawn with heavy bombings by the Luftwaffe, followed by intense artillery saturation before probing infantry advances.

The 21st occupied the most advanced positions closest to the German lines. They could see the arrival of the German armored units sent to help with the breakthrough, and knew that their own 75s had recently fallen silent for some unknown reason. What they didn't know was that everything behind them and to their flanks had now been withdrawn, while they had received no such order themselves. The phone lines were useless. Every bombardment destroyed them, and the repair teams had stopped going out.

During the quiet moments, it was almost possible to forget that a war was going on. The thick portions of the forest at Noirval were like a stop frame in time taken long ago. The forest was filled with rusted reminders of the last great war. Helmets, rifles, swords, even trenches and underground bunkers remained, as though locked in timeless posture, waiting for war to come again.

The severe food problem had also become most acute in the last days. Food used to arrive once daily from field kitchens ten to fifteen kilometers behind the lines. But everything behind them was gone now. No food came whatsoever.

It was the first week of June when the real offensive to break through the stubborn defenses on the Canal des Ardennes was started. The bombings and artillery barrages became particularly savage to soften the French positions to the maximum. It was during the breakthrough drive of the German army, being led by heavy panzer support, that the 21st learned of their abandonment. They fought valiantly, holding their ground to the last possible moment before falling back without the awaited order for withdrawal. Upon pulling back, they learned that the division had already withdrawn without notification.

The retreat was disorganized, and splintered groups made their way south toward Vouziers. All along the way, they passed through villages that had been totally destroyed, which the Germans still pounded relentlessly. The trail of the retreat was easy to follow. It was littered with the signs of a defeated army.

Finally, at Bois de Cernay, the survivors of the 21st met to regroup with the rest of the regiment.

Christian listened to the lies about flank failures and the order to withdraw to straighten the lines of defense with a building rage as Cassell told them to him.

He grabbed Cassell by the tunic and pulled him close to his face. "If you ever leave this company again, I'll shoot you like a dog. Or better, I'll let Zanosko deal with you with his knife, and save my bullet for a brave German soldier. I promise that you will die with this company before I do." He held back the urge to crash his fist into the soft face of his captain, and then released his hold on him.

"What happened at Noirval was not my fault," Cassell protested. "I did not give the order to withdraw."

"Nor did you pass it on." Christian interrupted forcefully. "You don't leave your men to die when the order to withdraw has been given."

The sound of a motorcycle was heard in the distance. Orders had arrived from division. The two men fell silent as the messenger approached them.

Cassell read the dispatch handed him, then looked at Christian.

"We have been ordered to march to Vienne-la-Ville. We leave at once Advise the colonel that we will leave immediately," he said to the messenger.

The messenger saluted and left.

"We were never meant to win this war," Christian said in disgust "I'll regroup the men—and *you* will lead," he said, ramming his index finger hard into the chest of Cassell.

"I will lead," Cassell repeated.

The sounds of war drew near again as they approached Vienne-la-Ville. But the sounds were distant. The Germans had finished with Vienne-la-Ville, at least for the time being.

Like so many other towns they had seen, the patterns of destruction were neatly cut. One side of a street, a small pocket of buildings or small factories, all demolished. The rest stood nearly untouched—and empty. Homes were left with their doors open, either out of haste or out of consideration for some other poor souls who might take refuge there.

When they entered a relatively intact part of the town, the men were rested, and they made for the comfort and shelter of dwellings with roofs and walls, and windows with curtains. Food was found in abundance. Sausages, cheese, wine, and even eggs. Cows heavy with milk were quickly relieved to the benefit of both man and beast, and for a little while, at least, they enjoyed comforts they had forgotten could exist.

Christian found himself in a charming cottage. He fell across the thick, soft bed and felt the last bits of energy leave his body. So much all at once, it was too good to be true.

A small picture on a dresser caught his attention, and he got up from the bed and went to it. It was a picture of a lovely young woman and her husband. It looked like a wedding picture. He opened a drawer and found delicate lace undergarments. He held a pretty bone-white negligee to his face and smelled the gentle fragrance. He thought about Denise. She must be safe by now, he figured. He would allow no other thought to challenge that possibility.

He picked up the picture again and looked at the woman. She was as beautiful as Denise. He wondered whether the man at her side was with her now, or dead in some shattered wood somewhere. He placed the undergarments back carefully in the drawer and closed it.

He looked up into the mirror over the dresser and stared at the strange drawn face looking back at him. It took a moment to recognize that he was looking at himself. He touched his face, as if to verify that

114

was really his. Only his exhaustion stopped him from bolting out of he room and away from the image of what the war had done to him. It was so hard to go on. And it was only he who kept these wonderful men going. He wanted to go downstairs and into the street to tell them ll to go home, but he couldn't do that. They had given so much lready, it wasn't fair to ask them to give more when so few gave nything at all. Yet someone must give. And if not them to stand and ght for France, then who? They would go on and give more, he new—for a cause that was useless.

Orders arrived once again to march an additional ten kilometers) Ste.-Menehould, where the remaining elements of the 35th Division were gathering. They had been ordered to hold the German advance as ong as possible to allow the masses of retreating French army units unneling through the town to escape.

The men were dangerously exhausted. Christian assembled them nd spoke. Cassell stood at a distance and listened.

"We have been ordered to Ste.-Menehould," he began, turning nd pointing to a horizon brightened by explosions and fire. "It's only en kilometers from here, and then we stand and fight. The remaining nits of the 35th are gathering there to prepare a defensive line to allow s many French army units as possible to escape, along with any civil-ns still moving through the city.

"I will not order you to assemble and march until you have eaten nd rested sufficiently for what lies ahead. I will ask that you each dvance to Ste.-Menehould the best way you can, and that you be here by noon tomorrow. There is a large square in the center of the own. We will meet there.

"It has been my honor and privilege to serve with you. We've been nrough a lot together, and I have the utmost faith in each and every ne of you. France could ask for no more than you have offered her, or have reason to be prouder of anyone than you. You have served er well and with love, and for that, I am proud of you. Rest well. I'll e you tomorrow in Ste.-Menehould."

Christian walked away from his men. Cassell hurried to catch up ith him. "I've just learned that the Germans have entered Paris," 'assell said.

Christian grabbed Cassell by the tunic. "Don't you dare tell the en. I warn you. It will destroy anything that they have left."

"They'll hear it. It'll spread like a fire in dry grass," Cassell eturned.

"They've heard every kind of rumor possible in the past weeks.

Three days ago they cheered when they heard that the Russians ha[d]
crossed the border into Germany, and yesterday when they were tol[d]
that the English had retaken Dunkirk. You saw their faces when the[y]
realized that those things were not true. It only intensified the feeling [of]
defeat inside. Let them hear it from the wind, where the rumors fly, b[ut]
not from their officers."

"You really care, don't you?" Cassell asked.

"Yes, I care," Christian answered, nodding slowly. "I care tha[t]
many of those men will die tomorrow, and I care that they believe i[n]
why they must. We can't take all hope from them."

"They know that there is no hope," Cassell said.

"Perhaps, but they fight like there is. And France has not surren[-]
dered yet. We'll fight every day that we can, until . . ." Christian hes[i-]
tated. "We'll fight on for as long as we can, in every way that w[e]
can . . . for as long as it takes."

Cassell stared at Christian as though he were looking at a mac[l]
man. Losing would not be the end of everything, Cassell thought. Att[i-]
tudes like Gladieux's could be dangerous in a France no longer at wa[r]
and realigned with a former enemy. The sooner this farce of a wa[r]
ended, the sooner France could get about the business of fitting into [a]
new Europe. Men like Gladieux hindered that inevitability.

"I'll say nothing about Paris," Cassell said. "See you in Ste.-Men[e-]
hould tomorrow."

The following day, the 21st regrouped intact in the square as o[r-]
dered. They had straggled in at every man's own pace, but all ha[d]
arrived by noon as ordered.

It became immediately evident why Ste.-Menehould had becom[e]
strategically essential to defend. It seemed that all roads of the secto[r]
north and to the east and west led to Ste.-Menehould, and that all th[e]
retreating forces were funneling through, slowed by the constriction [of]
the two passage points—bridges north and south of the city. Everythi[ng]
going through Ste.-Menehould passed over those two bridges, and th[e]
town was packed tight with those fleeing to the south.

The 21st had been given its orders with the rest of the division [to]
concentrate defense on the north bridge. The Army Engineers we[re]
wiring both bridges to slow the advance of the Germans, but the sou[th]
bridge would be left intact until all elements of the 35th had withdraw[n]
across it. The order of retreat put the 21st as the last to withdraw.

There was perhaps an hour of utter stillness from the Germa[n]
guns before the assault started. It was begun when Ste.-Menehould wa[s]
packed to the point of bursting.

True to German form, the dive-bombing Stukas came first. The horrible screams of their dives were an invitation to panic. They knew their targets precisely, hitting the major arteries to further slow the progress of the retreating French army. Following the Stukas, came the most ferocious artillery barrage yet witnessed by the 21st. They could only sit tight and wait. The sensation of being as helpless as prey filled them as the town was methodically shredded by the German 77s.

When the shelling stopped, they quickly crawled out of their concealment and prepared to meet the Germans' advanced units. The situation verged on mad panic when tanks, not infantry, came across the north bridge, which had not been blown. It was to be rifles against tanks. They should have expected it.

A furiously pitched battle ensued, with the 21st holding their positions well. They allowed the tanks to pass them, then concentrated all their firepower on the infantry divisions of the second wave. It was only after the tanks circled back to relieve their pinned infantry that the lines of the 21st were broken and pulled back to the inner defense perimeter.

The fighting was now on a block-by-block, house-to-house basis. The resistance was much more determined than the Germans had expected, and casualties were high on both sides.

Christian had just regrouped about twenty of his men to establish a cross fire when Sasmi charged up to him in near hysteria. He fell at the feet of his lieutenant, fear, anger, and disbelief across his face.

Christian bent down and grabbed him, shaking him to coax the words out.

"They've done it to us now, the stupid bastards," Sasmi finally managed to say. "They've blown the *south* bridge. We have no escape."

The crushing realization was almost too much for Christian. To insure the escape of the other units, they had been sealed in to buy as much time as possible.

"The 35th is being sacrificed," he said. "The cowards."

"Not all of 35th," came Zanosko's deep voice. "I see two-thirds of the division go across. Cassell was with them, and gave order to blow the bridge," he managed in his poor French.

"Then we'll buy them time," Christian said. "Two hours, then we're on our own. We'll fight our way to the river and escape if we can."

He picked out ten men as runners to inform all that they could and to begin as intense a fire as they could bear upon the enemy, then to withdraw to a point below the bridge at the set time.

Other fragmented units had also been caught in the city by the blowing of the bridge. These had been withdrawing units, which now became fighting units out of no other choice.

For two hours, the 21st and other defenders fought stubbornly being gradually pushed back as the German tanks knocked the build ings down around them. When ammunition ran out, the fighting be came hand to hand. Stones, pipes, field knives, and pick shovel: became instruments of death.

Christian, Zanosko, and Sasmi used the last of their ammunitior from a second-floor room as the time for withdrawal came.

"I'm out of ammunition," Christian shouted above the screams o ricocheting bullets aimed at their position.

"Us, too," Sasmi said.

"There's nothing left for us to do, then. Let's go," Christian said just as the floor blew out from beneath them.

The tank that had leveled the shot clanked toward the buildin they were in, its machine guns blasting, infantry cautiously followin behind its protective presence.

The big Pole quickly unburied Sasmi, who was closest to him, the crawled over to Christian and dug him out from a pile of debris.

Christian clutched his ribs painfully, trying to breathe through th crushing pain. Blood dripped from his mouth and down his chin.

Zanosko examined him quickly. He had two small chest wound on the left side, heart high. One exit wound in the back revealed tha one of the objects had passed through him.

Sasmi grasped his right ankle painfully.

The Pole helped Christian to his feet, clutching him to help hir walk.

"Take Sasmi, I can make it," Christian insisted in a painfu whisper.

The Pole released his lieutenant and picked up the Russian like puppy.

"To the river," Christian ordered, coughing up blood as he spok

They made their way through a withering enemy fire toward th rendezvous point. The Germans had already attained a position be tween them and the point of destination, so they made directly for th water.

At the river's edge, they found scores of wounded. Those mo: able to help others responded to Christian's command to do so, an entered the water. Christian slung a badly wounded captain over h shoulder and told the rest who could not be helped to wait until h returned.

Fighting the pain of his own wounds, he carried the captain as the small group of men waded along the shore, passing directly below the German positions. A heavy fire concentrated from across the river helped cover their movements. Once far enough below the German positions, they climbed back onto the shore, where more able-bodied men were clustered.

Christian laid the captain gently on the ground, then turned and headed back into the water, his wounds now large bright spots of smeared red.

"Where are you going?" the captain asked.

"Back for the others. You can make it safely from here."

There was a look of tremendous pride on the face of the man he had just helped. "What is your name?" the man asked.

"Gladieux. Christian Gladieux," he responded.

"You . . . are France, Christian Gladieux. God be with you. My name is Jean Monjaret. I will remember you always."

"Be sure that you live to do so," Christian said, entering the water, Zanosko right behind him.

Christian and the huge Pole made repeated trips back to the upper bank, each more dangerous than the one before, each trip saving French lives. The last two were made after the Germans had complete control of Ste.-Menehould. The extreme sacrifice of the 21st had been well made. The German advance was stopped with the inability of their tanks to go further. It would be at least a day before they could lay pontoon bridges to continue their chase. Many Frenchmen would live because of it.

The pitifully ragged survivors of the 21st staggered into Verrières, the point of regrouping.

For Christian, the last kilometers of the trek were made lying across Zanosko's broad shoulders. His strength had given out to blood loss and the effect of his chest wounds. Zanosko carried him with the last of his own endurance to the church being used as a hospital.

"I owe you my life." Christian said to the Pole.

"You owe me nothing." the giant replied in Polish. "You will be safe here. I must try to find Sasmi, then I will return to you."

"Find the rest of the company." Christian said.

"I will try," Zanosko promised. "Rest, *mon ami*. I will be back."

The Pole had been gone for nearly an hour when Christian first saw Cassell. He was with the colonel and some other high-ranking officers he did not recognize. The group drew closer to him and spoke to the doctor who had attended him. Christian closed his eyes, peeping through a tiny squint. He pretended to be asleep as he listened to their words. He could just barely understand their conversation as the spoke after the doctor had left them.

"What do we do with him?" Cassell asked. "He has been a trou blemaker from the beginning."

"Is there anything damaging in his record?" the colonel asked.

"Outside of his insubordination, no," Cassell replied.

"Does he drink? Drinking could pose a serious danger to the me of his command."

"He doesn't even take the *gnole* when it is rationed. No, it must b something else."

He could not make out their words as they deliberated quietly Cassell again summoned the doctor. They spoke quietly to him, the left.

About twenty minutes later the colonel returned and approached Christian. He came to the cot and sat beside him.

Christian looked up at him as though he had just been awakened

"You are a lucky man, Gladieux. Two severe chest wounds, an you are still alive. The doctor says that you will recover—in time. The war is over for you. You are going home."

"Home? There is a war . . . and I can still fight," Christian insisted

"No, Lieutenant, you cannot fight. Your wounds are too serious, the colonel said. "Besides, Reynaud has resigned. Marshal Pétain ha become premier. He has asked for an armistice. It will be only a matte of days until the fighting has ended and the war will be over for all o us. You are going home a hero. I am personally recommending you fo distinction. There is no more that you can do."

Christian stared up into his colonel's face, with tears of outrage ir his eyes.

"Yes, Lieutenant Gladieux, we will all be grateful when the fight ing is over at last. We will all rejoice."

Christian held back his rage. He would have given anything to stil have had two bullets in his revolver. One for the colonel, and one fo Cassell.

The colonel placed a fatherly hand on Christian's shoulder. "I am proud of you. France is proud of you."

He patted Christian on the arm, then handed him an envelope "This is your safe conduct, granting you permission to return to you home. You are free to go whenever you feel able."

The look in Christian's eyes was anything but joyous, and the colonel took its measure. A flash of embarrassment crossed the colo nel's face. He rose without speaking, turned, and walked away.

For Christian Gladieux, the war had just ended.

Chapter 15

"AND so your father made his way across France after being discharged, to join me at my father's house in the Pyrenees just outside of St.-Jean-Pied-de-Port. I had heard nothing from him since the start of the fighting, and was worried to the edge of madness for him. I can remember, to this day, the feeling inside me when I saw him walking along the narrow road cut into the side of the mountains.

"He had lost almost thirty pounds. His face was drawn and gray, his eyes sunken and surrounded by dark circles. He looked so beaten. His wounds were too serious for him to have undertaken such a journey.

"He came into my arms and cried. It was one of the few times he ever cried to me. I held him and we both cried, your father from sadness and frustration, and I from the joy at having him back alive.

"My mother and I nursed him carefully in the next days. He was in a state of depression over the sacrifices his men had made for a cause that was so futile from the start. The war was over, France had surrendered to the Germans at Compiègne. But he had never accepted it. Then life returned to him suddenly one day when my father rushed into the house almost in tears, telling us that the British had just attacked a helpless French fleet at Mers-el-Kébir. He spoke such words of hatred toward the British. He said he prayed that the Germans would attack and destroy England.

" 'If England falls, we will have lost all hope,' your father said. 'Do you think that they *wanted* to attack the French fleet at Mers-el-Kébir? They had no choice. If they had not, the Germans would have used the fleet against the British,' he said.

" 'They killed Frenchmen!' Papa said.

" 'So did the Germans, or have you forgotten? The British destroyed *weapons*. They're guilty of no crime. *We* are guilty. Guilty of surrendering our fleets intact without a fight or a run for England. We were guilty of letting the German army crush France. I saw the extent of our crimes during the fighting. Put the blame where it belongs. Put your hatred where it belongs. England must survive if France is to be saved.'

"The following week your father packed a small bag and left for Vichy, where the new French government had set up. 'Vichy is where the struggle will begin again,' he said.

"I can't tell you the loss I felt when he left. I thought that I would never see him again. He was stronger, though still not completely healed. He just could not accept the defeat. Many good men believed the way he did. He said that the battle of France had not ended but was, instead, just beginning.

"I watched him walk away on the same road that had brought him home to me. I felt as though my life had just ended," Denise said. She looked down into her empty coffee cup, her energy spent.

It was almost 3:00 A.M. when she finished her story. Silence filled the room as everyone felt the emotions of those dark days. The sense of frustration, of facing such an uncertain struggle, filled them all, for they, too, faced a very similar situation in which they would engaged in a battle of unforeseeable outcome. They were preparing to march back into that same war, looking for answers that lay hidden in its past. Answers which, when found, would help decide the outcome of a very very deadly game with the highest of stakes.

"We've made pretty good progress, considering the time restrictions we've had to work under," the mellow voice of Horatio said to Pheagan. "And you have the boys at Intelligence Central to thank for it," he added. "They've worked through the night on the pendant."

"Thank them for me," Pheagan said. "We'll all be putting in a lot of extra hours before this thing is through. What were they able to come up with?" he asked.

"Close microscopic examination by our experts showed the pendant to be made up of over eight hundred separate glass rods, called canes, which were fused together, then drawn to a much thinner diameter. Each of these canes was individually made, and is unique to this pendant. One of these canes, which had been drawn to near microscopic thinness, proved to be a signature cane. It bore the initials HH.

"A search of computer files turned up three names of master glassmakers with those initials and the required skill to execute the making of such a piece. Only one of the three is a likely possibility, however, as two are in their early fifties, and would have been too young when the canes were made. That leaves us with the name Hans Haupte, of Dresden, who died during the war. According to our experts, he was considered the finest glassmaker in Germany. We're working on his background details now, and should have something shortly."

"But he's dead. What's that going to get us?" Pheagan asked.

"Perhaps a great deal. According to Intelligence Central, the execution of such a piece would have taken at least two people. Either another master craftsman, or perhaps one of the apprentices making up the master's 'chair.' Every master has apprentices at various stages of learning who act as his extra hands. These apprentices were quite probably very young and could certainly still be alive today. We're approaching all angles," Horatio said.

"And what can we learn if we find one of these apprentices?"

"For starters, the number of pendants that were made; exactly when they were made, and possibly even a clue as to who commissioned the job," Horatio answered.

"Well, we already know that four exist," Pheagan said.

"Yes, but we suspect that as many as six could have been made. We need to confirm this. It's probably a long shot, and more than likely we won't come out knowing more than what we know already. But we have to follow it. We have to follow everything at this point."

"What about the rest of my requests?" Pheagan asked.

"Regarding a possible Trinity contact at Bonaventure, we've run through backgrounds on everyone employed there, especially those who were killed in the blast. There was one strong possibility, a member of their subsidiary rights department, but he was one of the casualties in the explosion. It would not be unlike Trinity to eliminate their own contact for the sake of security.

"Regarding the killers, we've come up with two strong possibilities, both known to work for Trinity. These are Renaud Demy, a Frenchman, and Bruno Scalco, a Corsican. We've got files on both of them.

"Demy was last observed in Toronto, before we lost him about two weeks ago. He could have easily driven across the border, and then down to New York. Scalco was spotted leaving Charles De Gaulle Airport in Paris enroute to Kennedy International in New York. He was lost in lower Manhattan on the same day he arrived. We know of at least two other occasions when these two have worked together. They're particularly nasty, especially Demy, whom we've tried for twice in the past, once in Biarritz and again in Geneva. We lost three good men in those attempts. Scalco is an explosives man, so he fits well with what's happened. The timing of their being here is perfect, too. We don't know where either one is now. You'll have complete files on them both in the morning."

"And what about the numbers I gave you?" Pheagan asked.

"You were right. They're both Swiss accounts, with the World Bank of Geneva. We'll have no problem getting the information we need, but the earliest we can expect to have it will be on Monday. By the way, Gladieux's attorney was just in Geneva. He spent two days there. As far as the rest of Gladieux's financial background, the analysis will be delayed because of the bombing at Bonaventure. We can still get what is needed, it'll just take a little longer. We should start getting some kind of a picture by the middle of the week."

"Good. We *are* making progress," Pheagan said, pleased with the early results of his inquiries. "The family will be going to France, probably within the next week. I'd like to arrange for a communication tie to France, and I'd like one of our offices alerted, just in case it becomes necessary for me to go over."

"I would avoid that, if at all possible," Horatio advised. "I don't have to tell you the inadvisability of compromising the cover of someone at your level."

"I know," Pheagan said, "but you and I both know that this is a once-in-a-lifetime opportunity for Sub Rosa. If my being there can make that possibility become a reality, then it's well worth the personal risk to me—and to Sub Rosa—to take the chance of making it happen."

"We'll consider that possibility when the time comes," Horatio said, not willing to accede to the demand this early.

"I'd also like to arrange for surveillance of the Gladieux family when they go over, with a special unit on standby for protective purposes, if it becomes necessary," Pheagan said.

"That can be arranged, but assistance must be given only as a last resort. To help them openly in any way will tip our hand to Trinity, and will most likely end any chance of our success. They will certainly act quickly to terminate the individual we're after if even the slightest suspicion of our involvement arises," Horatio warned.

"I understand. It will be only as a final measure—and only if it's to our advantage to keep them safe. The success of this operation is the only criterion by which that action will be deemed necessary."

"That's acceptable," Horatio said. "I'll speak to you on Monday. Let's say at four o'clock."

"Okay. At four o'clock Monday, then," Pheagan said. The line went dead, and he placed his phone down on the cradle.

He looked down at the notepad he had used to list pertinent facts of their conversation. It was covered with the elaborate symmetrical patterns he habitually doodled while on the phone. One thing curiously stood out as being present in every pattern at the starting point of the intricate designs. This was the set of initials that had been discovered in the pendant: HH.

Chapter 16

NOVEMBER 9, 1938, DRESDEN, GERMANY: Hans Haupte stared at the headline story in the evening edition of the paper. He had read about the death of a man, Ernst vom Rath, the third secretary of the German foreign office in Paris.

Vom Rath had not been an important man to the German government, at least not before November 7, 1938, when he was shot in the Paris embassy by a young Jew named Herschel Grynszpan. Grynszpan, a boy of seventeen, had gone to the embassy to assassinate the German ambassador, Count Johannes von Welczeck, out of revenge for the deportation of his parents to Poland, along with 10,000 other Jews. Grynszpan was young and frustrated, and took the only course of action he believed open to him to protest the persecution of his parents and other Jews within Germany. He could not have known when vom Rath approached him that he was about to shoot a man who was vehemently opposed to the anti-Semitic posture of his own government and who was, in fact, being carefully watched by the Gestapo because of this position. It was a shot heard clear into Germany.

The government's anti-Semitic position to this point had been somewhat restrained since 1933. The Jewish laws had not been as totally restrictive as they would shortly become. The pressure had built slowly to the point of bursting, and vom Rath's death was like a pin to a fat balloon.

The glassmaker shook his head sadly as he read that anti-Semitic

riots had started in Kurhessen and Magdeburg-Anhalt. He had see
the illness start in Germany when the roughneck brownshirts bega
their rowdy tactics in the 1920s. He had watched with disbelief as th
movement grew like a spreading infection until it seized his countr
with its terminal philosophy. It was in the air, such hatred and distrus
so thick that it could be felt.

Haupte heard the bell clang above the door in the studio, followe
by the rapid heavy footsteps of a man making his way toward th
gallery. A second later, the tall figure of his daughter's boyfriend cam
through the doorway and approached him.

"Claus, what are you doing here so late?" the glassmaker askec
"Sonja is at her uncle's—"

"I'm not here to see Sonja," the young man interrupted urgentl
"I'm here to save you."

"Save me? From what?"

"Haven't you heard? Vom Rath has died."

"So, why does that necessitate saving me?" the glassmaker asked

There was frustration all over the young man's face. "Her
Haupte, you must listen to what I say. I know you do not believe in th
changes that Germany is going through. But that will not stop then
from happening. The death of Ernst vom Rath has caused a furor i
Germany. It's going to be like the Reichstag fire all over again, but thi
time instead of a half-witted Dutch communist, it is a Jew. The riot
are starting, and they will get worse—far worse. You must send tha
Jew away from here immediately. Tell him never to come back, and
can protect you," the young man implored.

"The boy is gifted. Being Jewish makes him no less talented—o
German. He is welcome here. He always has been, and always will be
I will not send him away," the glassmaker insisted.

Claus could have grabbed the older man, and wanted to, to shak
the sense back into him. He leaned close to Haupte's face and spoke i
a heavy whisper.

"Tonight, years of anger and hatred will be released. No one wil
stop it. Not the police, not the government. Life for the Jew is about t
change in Germany. You employ a Jew. Everyone knows this. You
even lost one of your best students three months ago because you
wouldn't let the Jew go."

"He has a name," Haupte said icily.

"Will you stop this!" Claus shouted. "I am trying to save you an
your business. Germany has changed, its people have changed. You
must accept that. Send the Jew away—now. Immediately! If not for m

easons, then for another. His father's shop is on the list. Send him
ome to warn his family to leave for their own safety."

"What list? What do you mean?"

"All across Germany, Jewish businesses, synagogues, homes,
lubs—everything, will be disrupted. The Jew will be smashed from
conomic existence in Germany. They will be excluded from every part
f German life—from professions, schools, theaters, public parks—from
verything. There will be rioting and beatings, shops will be smashed
nd arrests will be made. You must be saved from this."

"Why must *I* be saved? I am not a Jew."

"But you employ one, and everyone knows . . . knows your feel-
ngs for him. You treat him like the son you never had. Once this
egins, it will be out of control. I will not be able to stop them if they
ecide to come here to teach you a lesson. I can only warn you. Dis-
harge the Jew—Mendel—tonight. Tell him never to come back. If they
ome here, tell them that you have sent him away after the killing of
om Rath by a filthy Jew. Show them. Make them believe that you feel
his way—even if you don't. Make them believe it, and they will not
arm you or your business," Claus said.

"And you? Will you be out tonight smashing windows and beating
ld men because of their faith?" Haupte asked.

"I am a German. I will do what I must, and what I believe in."

"And what do you believe in?" the glassmaker pressed.

"I believe in Germany. I believe that we are about to attain some
reat destiny, and that Jews will not be a part of it. The sooner they are
ll driven out, the better it will be for Germany. I did not come here
oday to help the Jew, I came to help you."

"Then you can help me best by leaving here now," Haupte said
o the young German. "I have no wish to stand here listening to
he warped logic that will guide the 'New Germany' that you have
lanned. Don't you see that this is wrong? Don't you see—" He stopped
t seeing the expression on the face. Claus saw nothing but a demented
ream. "Leave. Go, please," Haupte said in a soft, sad voice.

"Herr Haupte, I *care* that nothing happens to you. Please, for the
ake of your family, send the Jew away," Claus implored one last time.

"I hope that history will be kind to the old Germany from which
our Germany is arising. I hope that the difference will be recognized,
nd that enough of it will be remembered for the things in it that were
ood. I have no more to say to you. You know the way out."

The young German lowered his eyes from Haupte's. There was a
rief flush of what looked like apology, or embarrassment, before he

127

turned and walked away. The glassmaker heard the bell clang as th studio door opened and closed. He thought about Claus's words for few moments, then went into the studio, where his three students wer beginning to clean up after the late evening work.

He raised a hand to catch young Abraham Mendel's attention The broad-shouldered fifteen-year-old came to him immediately. Th dark features had an expression of concern.

"Come with me, Abraham," Haupte said, turning and walkin into the gallery. Mendel followed him.

"Yes, Herr Haupte?" the polite young craftsman said.

"Sit a moment," the glassmaker said, motioning to a chair by small table in a corner of the room. He went to the table and sat wit the boy.

"Why is it that you did not become a shoemaker like your father? he asked with a weak smile.

"I like to make things of beauty. Have you ever seen a beautifu shoe? I haven't," the boy replied.

"And you do create such beauty—while the world around us grow ever more ugly.

"I have just learned that vom Rath has died. Riots have begun i several cities, and . . ." Haupte hesitated, looking into the innocen face, wondering how to tell him of the sickness that was beginning "And there will be repercussions aimed at the Jewish community. To night, I'm afraid there will be trouble in Dresden. You must leave righ now, to tell your parents to leave their home," he said.

"Leave?" the boy said. "And go where? My father will not leav The shop is all that he has. And where would we go? If there is trouble our home is where we should be. We will not leave."

"You must, or you face grave danger," Haupte said. "You mus leave Germany."

The boy stood up. "Why must Jews always be afraid? My brothe and I have fought before. We'll fight again."

"This is not the same."

"It's always the same," the boy said. "I heard you and Clau speaking while I worked," the boy said. "I will leave so that you won have trouble."

"No," the glassmaker said quickly. "I'm not afraid for myself. Yo are my apprentice before you are a Jew. I'm not asking you to leave fo my sake. I'm asking you to go for your sake, and the sake of you family. You must believe that."

"I do," the boy answered, placing a hand on the old man's shoul der. "But I couldn't stay, knowing that it would bring danger to you

You've taught me a great deal about many things. You've been like a father to me."

Haupte embraced the boy. "And you like a son to me." Tears were in the glassmaker's eyes. "I've held you here too long. I should have sent you out of Germany long ago. I could have arranged apprenticeship for you. I . . . wanted you close for my own selfish reasons. But now you must go. Convince your father. Make him understand that he must take your family out of Germany as quickly as possible." He paused for a long moment, looking into the dark eyes of his apprentice. "I will always think of you, and miss you. Now go."

The boy kissed the old man's cheek and left the gallery. The sound of the bell on the studio door followed shortly.

Hans Haupte sat at the table, buried his face in his hands, and wept. A feeling of such loss and emptiness filled him. It could have hurt him no more if he had just sent away a son.

Nearly an hour passed before the knock on the studio door sounded. The two remaining students had just finished their clean-up duties and were preparing materials for the next day's work. Haupte went to the door and opened it.

Standing in front of Haupte was his former student, Karl Steiner, who had left three months earlier because of the glassmaker's refusal to let young Mendel go. Behind him was a group of at least ten others, carrying an assortment of clubs and sticks.

Steiner put a hand to Haupte's chest and pushed him back into the heat of the studio. "Where's the Jew?" he asked in a menacing tone as the others with him filed into the studio, clubs at the ready.

Haupte stared hard into the face of his former student. "He's not here," he responded.

Steiner saw that the preparations for the following day were not yet completed. He knew that no one went home until the work was done for everyone.

"Liar!" he shouted.

"I told you, he's not here," Haupte repeated calmly.

"Liar!" a second man standing beside Steiner screamed. This man was the obvious leader. He stepped forward and shoved Haupte hard into the railing which separated the walkway from the work area.

"He was released two days ago," said one of the other students, rushing up to his teacher's side. "The filthy Jew was fired," he lied.

Steiner stepped up to the boy and shoved him. "Then why was he seen here today?" he asked.

"He came for the last of his things and his pay," the student said.

"Let the old man answer for himself," the leader shouted.

"I have nothing to say to you," Haupte said. "Now leave here at once."

The leader threw a vicious slap that hit the left side of Haupte's face, knocking his glasses across the floor. In an instant, the student threw himself at the man, landing a heavy punch before the clubs started slamming down on his head, being directed by several of the ruffians.

Haupte rushed to put himself between the attackers and his student, when the leader's club found its mark on the glassmaker's left collarbone. A sickening crack preceded his crash to the floor.

Steiner looked on in shocked disbelief. He had not intended this.

"Find him!" the leader shouted.

The group quickly dispersed through the gallery and private residence above. Steiner rushed to Haupte and knelt at his side.

The old man's eyes rolled up in pain, and he clenched his teeth. "And you've come to this?" he said.

Steiner stared at his fallen teacher and the unmoving student, who three short months ago had been his friend.

The sounds of smashing glass filled their ears. Haupte squinted at the door to the gallery, and could see reflecting fragments of glass flying through the air like horizontal rain. Sounds of smashing and destruction were heard above them, too. Haupte was immediately glad that his wife and daughter were gone.

"I didn't intend . . . for this—" Steiner began.

"Does your hatred go this deep? Or are you simply selling your friends to gain acceptance?" Haupte asked.

"You . . . you don't understand. You never understood."

"He's not here," the leader shouted, hurrying back into the studio "Steiner, take us to his house."

Steiner looked back into his former teacher's face. He wanted to tell him what he felt—to make him understand.

"Get out! Get out," Haupte hissed at him.

Steiner shook his head as though he were confused.

The leader grabbed him by the back of the coat and pulled him up to his feet. "Let's go. Take us to his house."

As the men left the studio, Steiner backed away, his eyes on the face of the injured glassmaker. Steiner's eyes did not show the conviction he wanted to convey. The look was very similar to that which Haupte had seen on Claus's face. It was a look of embarrassment—or shame.

The leader did not relinquish his grip on Steiner's coat, and he was pulled through the door into the street. Only the clanging bell sounded to interrupt the silence of the shock left behind.

The madness that Haupte had sensed growing in Germany had finally surfaced. It was not the destruction of his gallery that started the tears in his eyes. It was the destruction of a country and a way of life, and the rage he felt at being powerless to stop it. The pain of that inner torment seemed as great as that from the broken collarbone. Perhaps some miracle would save Germany, he thought. But the hope was a fleeting one, for the glassmaker from Dresden had stopped believing in miracles long ago.

The news of that night's violence and destruction throughout Germany rocked the world. The unforgettable name of "Crystal Night" was given to the incident because of the tremendous number of smashed windows. The true assessment of the damage was never made public. The numbers that eventually became a part of the record, but which were admittedly low, were: 7,500 shops looted or smashed, 195 synagogues set afire or destroyed, 171 apartment houses set on fire or destroyed, 36 deaths (all Jewish), 36 injured seriously (a number 100 times that was actually closer to truth), and 20,000 Jews arrested (only 20,000 because the existing prisons could accommodate no more).

Hans Haupte stood in the smashed, glass-littered gallery. Countless hours of work had been destroyed in a few moments of sick, senseless rage. The value of the lost pieces was enormous.

He moved slowly through the room, glass crunching beneath his feet as his right hand cupped the left elbow of the tightly bound and slung arm. It would be months before he would be able to resume even the simplest duties of his craft. The student who had come to his assistance was still in the hospital, lying unconscious after seventy-two hours. The second student was told to stay at home until after the insurance company had made an assessment of the damage. It would be a day or two yet before they would come. There was so much damage all across Germany that it would take a great deal of time to assess it all. The Jews would be made to pay for it in the form of fines, so as not to bankrupt the non-Jewish-owned insurance companies throughout Germany.

Haupte walked across the shattered gallery and stooped to pick up a piece of the smashed bird of prey that his talented young apprentice had made. He had never sold the piece, turning down handsome offers for it. He could not bring himself to part with it. And now it lay smashed, along with the greatest part of the gallery pieces. He wished now that he had sold it so that its beauty would have been preserved as it should have been.

He heard the sound of glass beneath feet and turned quickly to face the uninvited guest. Tears of both joy and sadness filled his eyes when he saw the battered face of Abraham Mendel. He rushed to him and embraced the boy with his one good arm.

"I worried so much," Haupte began. He touched the boy's swollen, black and blue face. "What have they done to you?" he asked.

"My father, brother, and I were all dragged into the street and beaten. My father's shop was completely destroyed, though not burned, so at least we still have a roof over our heads," the boy replied.

"The animals. Was Steiner with them?"

"Yes. But it was Steiner who saved our lives. At first my brother and I fought back, but Steiner grabbed me from behind and threw me to the ground, and whispered to me to fake serious injury. Then he managed to do the same to my brother, before turning their interest away from us to smash the shop. He was successful in keeping their interest away from us after that, leading them from shop to shop away from our location."

"And your father?"

"He was not hurt badly. Again, it was Steiner . . ." Mendel said his words stopping as he touched the old man's shoulder gently.

"Broken. But I'll be all right. Hermann was injured coming to my assistance. He has not yet regained consciousness."

"The pigs. It wasn't necessary. Hermann. The gallery. And to do this to you—not even a Jew."

Haupte put his good arm on Mendel's shoulder and directed him to the door of the private residence, away from the broken windows of the gallery. "It's not safe for you to be here," he said.

"I've come to say goodbye," Mendel said sadly.

"Then you will leave Germany?" Haupte asked with a pleased smile.

"Yes. If I can convince my father, the whole family will leave. If not, then I will take my baby sister, Keva, whether they want me to or not. I'll not have harm come to her. I'll kill first," Mendel said with believable emotion.

Nothing meant as much to Abraham Mendel as his little two-year-old sister and his work with Hans Haupte. His work had been taken away; he could do little about that. But he could protect Keva by taking her away from Germany. He would not allow the stubborn insistence of his parents to remain in Germany to endanger her. He would sacrifice his own life if it meant that she would live.

"Where will you go?" the glassmaker asked.

"I have an uncle in Poland, near Kutno."

Such a long journey for two children alone, the glassmaker thought. "You will need money. Come with me," Haupte said.

"No, Herr Haupte, I have saved some money," Mendel answered.

"You will need more. Now come with me," the glassmaker insisted.

Mendel followed the master into his smashed living quarters and to a safe hidden behind a false compartment in a closet. Haupte dialed the combination and opened the thick door. He reached in and pulled out a stack of crisp mark notes. "Take this. You will need it for food, and perhaps to buy influence."

"Herr Haupte, I cannot accept this," the boy said.

"You must. I've underpaid you for years." He smiled. "I want you to have it—for Keva."

The boy accepted the money with inner reluctance.

Haupte reached back into the safe and pulled out a small low-caliber handgun. "And you will also take this. Two children traveling alone must have protection."

"I am not a child," Mendel protested.

"Perhaps not, but you may need it."

Haupte reached into the safe once more and pulled out a small item wrapped in paper and tied with a string. "And I want you to have this," he said, holding it out to the boy.

Mendel took it and untied the string, then opened the paper. He stared down at one of the pendants he had helped to make two years ago.

"They were so beautiful that I kept one," Haupte said. "And because you helped to create it, I feel that you should have this. Please take it, too."

"Herr Haupte, I don't know what to say," Mendel said with emotion.

"Say nothing. Just accept what I offer you. And remember always that as long as I live you will have a friend to come to who will help you in any way possible. Now you will eat something and leave. Waste no time in leaving Germany. This madness could erupt again at any time."

After having a good lunch together, Haupte sent Mendel on his way with his arms full of food for his family. It was again a great moment of sadness for the gentle glassmaker, for he knew that he would never again see the boy who had meant so much to his life.

DECEMBER 1942: A gentle snow fell on Dresden as the general's car pulled to the side of the street in the early-morning stillness. Snowflakes landed and melted on the wrinkled hand protruding through the open rear window. A stream of cigarette smoke trailed upward and out of the staff car window. The general sat patiently waiting, remembering the last time he had come to this street over six years ago. It seemed more like six decades. He had seen a world change right before his eyes. War and destruction had touched it and scarred it, and it would go on for years, he thought, even though the outcome of the war was already clear to those who were not blind or deceived. Sadly, some of the worst tragedies were yet to begin. A country preparing for its own destruction would try to destroy as many of the "enemy" as it could. The death camps had been busy before now, but they would be pushed to the limit to erase undesirable peoples from existence in the time that was left.

The long black police wagon pulled up in front of the glassmaker's shop. German police, under Gestapo supervision, quickly entered the studio. The general didn't have to see through walls to know the drama that was unfolding. He was too far away to hear any of the sounds until the first of them came out into the street. Hans Haupte, his wife, Erna and their daughter, Sonja, were shoved and handled roughly while being loaded into the police wagon. The general could see blood running down the forehead, along the side of the nose, and over the lips of the glassmaker. Frau Haupte and their daughter were the picture of terror and confusion. These lightning-quick arrests often had that result, which was always to the benefit of the arresting party. Less resistance was given, and the use of violence by the arresters maintained the edge of fear needed to hold control over the victim, or victims.

The general crossed their names off the list in the notebook in his lap. Three more lives, for all intents and purposes, had just ended, taking care of another phase of security. He looked at the other names. Karl Steiner, Hermann Vogt, Ludwig Kriessle—all former apprentices of Hans Haupte—were now dead. Steiner was killed on the Russian front, Vogt by sudden heart seizure four days after his severe beating on Crystal Night, and Kriessle was found dead recently in the Elbe River, an apparent victim of drowning after a beating by parties "unknown." Claus Bitterman, the former fiancé of Sonja Haupte, was killed in action in North Africa. Solomon Mendel, father of the Jewish apprentice, dead by gassing at Birkenau, Naomi Mendel, the mother, dead by gassing at Birkenau, and Israel Mendel, the older brother, dead by shooting at Ravensbrück.

Two names remained, only one of which bore true significance. Abraham Mendel, who would be nineteen years old now, and his sister, Keva, who would be six. Of the two, only the boy was of concern.

The last possible trace of the existence of the pendants remained with the young Jew who had helped to make them. Finding him was the final step. But it could be the most difficult one, for the boy had simply disappeared without trace. In all likelihood, the boy was already dead. And if he weren't, perhaps the boy alone wouldn't be so dangerous, the general thought. After all, how much could he hurt them? He was just a boy, how much could he know? The general thought for a moment, then tapped his driver on the shoulder. The car started and pulled away into the snowy morning.

The general ran his pencil through the names of the young apprentice and his little sister. As far as he was concerned, the security matters had just been concluded. An organization the size and scope of the Salamandra would not be affected by the life of a boy. One person never mattered that much.

Chapter 17

I<small>T</small> was nearly noon when the knock sounded on the door of the Gladieux house in Spring Lake. Michael opened the door to find the smiling face of Father Piela.

"Father," Michael began in polite surprise. "Come in. I was just about to make some lunch. Why don't you join me?" he offered.

"Well, I didn't come over to bum a lunch, but I will come in. Besides, I can do without the extra calories," the priest said jovially.

"I was only going to make a bacon, lettuce, and tomato sandwich. That's not a whole lot of calories to worry about."

A flash of temptation crossed the priest's face. "And without the bacon—"

"It's almost like eating air, Father," Michael coaxed.

"You've convinced me."

"Good, let's go into the kitchen."

The priest followed Michael in.

"I'm alone in the house, Father. Sis and Danny have gone to

Princeton to pick up the kids, and Mom and Ray have just left to do some shopping," Michael said.

"I know," said the priest. "Of course, I didn't know where everybody was going, but I saw them all drive by the church on their way out of Spring Lake. I figured you'd be alone, that's why I came over. I wasn't sure if you'd take me up on my request to come see me. You didn't sound too positive."

"So, the mountain comes to Mohammed," Michael said with a smile.

The priest laughed. "In a way there's truth to the mountain part," he said, his hands patting his round stomach.

Michael began removing the ingredients for the sandwiches from the refrigerator. He chose to pass on the bacon as well, opting not to dirty a frying pan, which he would have to clean. He began washing the lettuce and tomato in the sink.

"How are your sister and mother bearing up?" the priest asked.

"Real well. Of course, being so busy around here helps. They haven't had too much time to mope around and let depression set in. I think they're both beyond the worst of it now."

"That's good. And I hear that Danny is out of the hospital."

"Yes, he's fine. He got away with only a few cuts and bruises, but nothing serious," Michael said, turning toward the table with a plate covered with crisp lettuce leaves and sliced tomato. "Did you want that on toast, Father?"

"No, white bread is fine."

"Are you sure? I'm going to toast mine."

"Okay. I didn't want you to go through any trouble."

"It's no trouble at all, Father. What did you want to talk to me about?" Michael asked.

"Are you still planning on going to France?"

"Yes, we are. We haven't made the final arrangements yet, but we should be leaving within the week. Mom has to contact one of Dad's old Resistance pals first. We'll base our plans upon his recommendations," Michael replied.

"And what will you do when you get there?" the priest questioned.

"Take care of business, Father."

"You'll hunt for the killer of your father?"

"Killers," Michael corrected. "At least three. The two who actually killed him, and the one who gave the order."

"And if you find them, will you kill them?" the priest asked almost hesitantly.

136

Michael did not answer immediately. "I only want justice, Father," he said at last, being deliberately vague.

A pained expression crossed the priest's face. "Michael, to kill these men would be wrong. They will be brought to justice—before God."

"So will we all, Father."

The toaster oven bell rang indicating that their toast was ready. Michael carried it to the table.

"You want milk with that, Father, or a beer? They both have about the same calories," Michael said.

"I think the beer," the priest replied.

There was a long silence as both men prepared their sandwiches. It was the priest who finally spoke.

"Do you have any idea who you're looking for?" he asked.

"We think we're after a collaborator who has successfully covered his past for almost forty years. As we get closer to him, the others will surface. He'll try for us, too, if he thinks we threaten him."

"Can you be certain that this is the man responsible?" the priest asked.

"Right now I feel that he is," Michael said. "This guy was responsible for the deaths of hundreds of people from his own Resistance group. It appears that he tried to pin it on my father to cover his own trail."

"The deaths of those people cannot be a part of your judgment against him, my son. There is always killing in war. Perhaps he did the things that he did because of his principles. There are always two sides in a war—two diametrically opposed causes which each side believes in. You must recognize that. If he believed that what he did was right, then his actions are as guiltless as your father's during the war—or as your own were while you were in Vietnam.

"I condone no form of killing, but in calling upon the justice that you claim to be your due, you must weigh those facts as well. War is a sorry madness. Killing is a part of that. The church does not excuse it, yet it does not condemn a soldier because he has killed an enemy," the priest said.

"My father didn't die in a war, Father. He was murdered in his own home, because he obviously knew something that he shouldn't have. I'm not interested in claiming the past as part of the reason for wanting justice. I only claim the death of my father as my right to it."

"It's obvious that your mind and will are set," the priest said. "But there is one thing that I can ask of you. Promise me you will be absolutely certain, beyond all reasonable doubt, that this man is guilty of ordering the death of your father, and that you will stay within the bounds of the law."

Michael stared into the eyes of the priest in silence.

"Surely, it is not too much to ask?"

"No, it's not too much."

"Then promise me."

Michael nodded his head slowly. "I promise that I'll be certain."

If it was a victory at all, it was a small one. The two men finished their lunch together, both looking for lighter topics of conversation, like two friends who had just quarreled and found apology awkward.

They sat in the living room together after their lunch had ended, holding hot mugs of coffee. Michael began telling the priest about the meager evidence that had been found. Before long, he had the most recent findings out, showing them to the priest.

Father Piela examined all of the pictures. Then he looked at the piece of paper with the code names on it. Michael saw the sudden change of expression as the priest's eyes narrowed and a pensive look crossed his face.

"Do you recognize something?" Michael asked.

"Well, yes. At least I think it has some meaning. Do you remember me telling you about your father's troubled period?"

"Yes."

"Well, I told you about a conversation we once had when he said some things about how a man's ideals and beliefs could change so completely. He said something about the cruelty of such a realization and not being able to change certain things that had happened in the past because of those beliefs. Then he said something about loyalty, which I didn't quite hear or understand. Well, this word—'Circus'—I'm sure he used it in part of that statement."

"Try to remember it, please," Michael exhorted.

The priest closed his eyes and pressed his memory hard. " 'Loyalty . . . we lived or died by that simple word,' I think he said. Then came the part that I couldn't make out. But then he said the word 'Circus,' and his face changed as though he had made some sudden realization. 'For what possible reason?' he then said. I'm sure those were his words."

"When did he say this to you?" Michael asked.

The priest thought for a moment. "It was during Lent, a year ago. I remember because the thing which sparked the loyalty statement was our discussion of Easter, and the death of Christ, and Judas's betrayal

138

f Him. We had just been talking of Judas's reasons for betraying Jesus, and about whatever became of him. Yes, I'm sure that was it."

Michael thought about the priest's words. "Judas . . . and what became of him," he mused aloud. "He hanged himself, didn't he?"

"According to Matthew, that is correct. He returned the money the priests had paid him, then hanged himself from a tree. But Mark, Luke, and John do not attest to this," the priest explained. "According to Acts, Judas did not commit suicide, or return the money. He bought property, a field, and there 'fell headlong and burst asunder.' And still again, Papias says that Judas died later of a mysterious disease. It's not really factually clear how he died, or exactly when."

Michael shook his head, unable to see the connection that his father must have made between the word "Circus" and the conversation just related by the priest.

"Circus," he repeated, his mind straining for the slightest clue. He couldn't see it, but he knew it was there. It had to be.

Chapter 18

BILL Pheagan stared out his office window to the city street below. New York was many things. It was the best and the worst of what a city could be. But one thing was certain to Pheagan, it had the most beautiful women in the world. The coming of warm weather and the reduced layers of clothing made that fact eminently visible.

He checked his watch and broke away from his girl watching. It was four o'clock and Horatio was scheduled to call him on the Omega-David line. He tapped the intercom button.

"Yes, Mr. Pheagan," his secretary responded over the speaker.

"Marcie, I'd like for you to hold all calls for about thirty minutes. No interruptions whatsoever, please," he instructed.

"Yes, Mr. Pheagan."

Pheagan sat at the desk and opened the drawer containing the Omega-David phone. He raised it out of the drawer and placed it on the desk in front of him.

Omega Enterprises was equipped with three such special phones with the distinguishing names "Adam," "David," and "George." The Omega-David line was used solely for direct communication to one of two contacts, Horatio being the primary. The Omega-Adam line put Pheagan in contact with the Special Services of Sub Rosa for emergency or unusual requests. The Omega-George line was a free line capable of specific assignment to any office worldwide on a direct basis. The Omega-George line would be the one used for contact to France during the upcoming operation involving the Gladieux family. This was the only one of the three lines that did not filter through the Unitrol complex. Instead, it ran through a larger complex known as Variscan, which was a satellite-integrated system that also fed directly to Intelligence Central, the working heart of Sub Rosa. Omega-George could also be patched to the other Omega lines if needed.

The phone rang on Pheagan's desk. He answered it immediately.

"Please state your identification code and clearance," the voice from Unitrol said.

"Phoenix, seven-seven-zero-four-zero. Clearance triple-Delta-Queen," Pheagan responded.

The customary wait followed for the computer's cross-check.

"Accepted," the voice said. "Please hold."

Pheagan waited for approximately five seconds.

"Hello, Phoenix," came the familiar voice.

"Good afternoon, Horatio."

"We've gotten some preliminary information on the Swiss accounts for you," Horatio began. "The first account is nearly nineteen years old. It was started in June of 1963 with a 250,000-dollar cash deposit. A second deposit of 500,000 dollars was made in December of that same year. The account then remained dormant until April of 1965, when rather heavy levels of transactions were started. The transactions involved varying sums of money, some quite large, but most in the ten- to twenty-thousand-dollar range. All totaled, the money involved was well in excess of the income profile established on Gladieux for the same time period. Intelligence Central has begun a detailed trace of the paper trail of the transactions. It'll take some time, but we'll be able to establish sources and consignees of the monies involved.

"The account activity ceased abruptly in 1978, after a number of odd transactions occurred. Large sums of money, which had been deposited from other numbered Swiss accounts, were immediately returned to those same accounts in the exact amounts originally transferred. The pattern repeated over a two-month period of reduced activity, then was stopped entirely.

"The other account is relatively new. It was opened eleven months ago and had received several sizable deposits over the last six months. Gladieux's attorney arrived last week with a valid power of attorney and closed the older of the two accounts, transferring all funds—amounting to just over two million dollars—into the second account, which was established in trust for Michael Gladieux and Gabrielle Glady-Preston. This account now totals nearly three million dollars. The trust was activated upon the death of Christian, so the money is now available to the two named holders of the account."

"This is very interesting," Pheagan commented. "I can't wait to see the run on the paper trail. What about the code names? Have you got anything on them?" he asked.

"Yes, on some of them. Fox was the code name used by Edna-Marie DeBussey within the Group Defiance circle. The names Ferret and Albatross also belonged to former Resistance fighters of Group Defiance. These are Claude St. Jude and René Pezet, respectively. De-Bussey and St. Jude are still living. Pezet died during the war.

"We've struck out so far on Leopard and Circus. We're still checking every possible angle."

"Then any one of the names could have been his contact—except Pezet, who is dead," Pheagan said.

"Not only possible contact, but also possible suspect," Horatio added. "It is the opinion here that Leopard was the contact, based on the amount of time apparently spent with him by Gladieux."

"Do you have anything else?"

"Yes, two more items. Demy and Scalco, our two leading suspects in the killing, have both been spotted back in Europe. Demy was sighted in Nice yesterday, and Scalco earlier today in Ramsgate, England, boarding a Hovercraft ferry bound for Calais. If we're correct about them, the family should be out of danger in the United States."

"And what is the last item?" Pheagan asked.

"Hans Haupte, the glassmaker, and his entire family were sent to Auschwitz in 1942. Our search indicates that they all died there in 1943. We've begun searches on the apprentices, and have confirmed the deaths of two of them already. We're still working on the remaining two."

"I have a meeting scheduled with the Gladieux family tomorrow. They should be leaving for France on Thursday. How much of this background can I give them?" Pheagan asked.

"Everything is on a need-to-know basis. Obviously, we don't want them knowing any more than they have to regarding our interests in the situation. The less, the better."

"All right, I'll keep it that way. Have my communications been approved on the Omega-George line yet?" Pheagan asked.

"Yes, you'll be patched through Variscan to the Paris office tomorrow. Special Services over there will also be alerted to comply with anything you may request," Horatio said.

"Good. I'd say we're off to a fairly good start, all things considered. Let's hope that a few pieces start to fall into place. I think that with the family in France things will start to happen."

Paul Axel arrived at the Gladieux house in Spring Lake at eight o'clock Monday evening. The business at hand was short and simple. The last will and testament was read to the family. The house in Spring Lake as well as the car and two additional properties were left to Denise, along with all furnishings, except for any personal effects belonging to Michael that were still in the house. The rest of the estate, which totaled $34.6 million by the most current figures compiled by Axel, was divided between Michael and Gabrielle. Stocks, cash, and properties were equally divided, with two one-million-dollar trust accounts set aside for the grandchildren Alexis and Sandra, the trusts to become activated when each girl reached the age of twenty-one.

Axel also delivered documents to Michael and Gabrielle giving them possession of and immediate access to the Swiss account set in trust for them upon the death of their father. This account contained an additional $2.92 million not included in the estate valuation.

When the attorney had finished, Denise and Gabrielle served coffee and pastries. There was a numb silence hanging in the room as the realization of sudden wealth settled in. Paul Axel's words had made it all real. It was still hard to believe.

"I just can't get over the size of the estate," Michael said.

"Yes, it's quite impressive," Axel said. "Your father had a way with his money, almost as though he were guided by a sixth sense. I began taking his advice about five years ago, and I can tell you that he made a believer out of me. If I were you, I'd think seriously about following the projected investment plan you found in your father's safe-deposit box."

Michael nodded. "Yeah, well, I don't have a head for investments. I'll probably do just that to keep the money working, I guess."

"You could always hire professional advisers later. That's an awful lot of money. You could live quite comfortably for the rest of your life with it," the attorney said.

"I was pretty happy without it. I guess it won't make life any harder. But I'd give it all up in a minute just to know what was in my father's mind. Did he ever confide in you as to the contents of the book he was working on?" Michael asked the attorney.

"No, but it seemed to me that he was quite troubled by it in some way. He became concerned about his personal safety, although he never told me as much. He worked very quickly to make sure that all matters of the estate were in good order. I think he was preparing."

"Preparing? To die?" Gabrielle asked in a shocked tone.

"Not necessarily to die. But most of the money that established the trust account in Switzerland was held in a separate account until his death. The trust account was built only within the past eleven months. I helped him set up that account and made the deposits for him. He never said it, but the monies in those accounts could have been set aside for an emergency fund of some kind," the attorney explained.

"Do you think he planned to go into hiding?" Danny asked.

"I repeat, he never said that to me, but he could have hidden well and for a long time with that money."

"Yeah, like maybe long enough for any storm started by his book to blow over," Michael said.

"Did you know that he went to France twice last year?" Danny asked the attorney.

"No, I didn't. When did he go?"

"In July, and again in November," Danny replied.

"Well, the account we just talked about was established in late June. He was apparently aware of the potential danger he would be in before he went over," Axel said. "Your father was a planner. Everything was always very carefully thought out before he did anything."

The meeting with Axel was concluded and he left. Everyone but Michael returned to Princeton for the evening—Danny and Gabrielle to prepare for their upcoming trip to France. Danny was to return with Gabrielle at noon the next day to pick up Michael for their meeting with Pheagan.

Michael took a long run on the beach, then returned to the house and showered. He brought a hot cup of coffee to his room and sat himself on the floor with the old foot locker in front of him. He took out the KA-BAR fighting knife, the three handguns, and small quantities of ammunition for each. He carefully cleaned each weapon and wrapped it in an oiled cloth. Then he sharpened the KA-BAR to a razor's edge and lightly greased the blade. He had begun making his own special preparations for a trip that he was looking forward to.

Michael and Danny, minus the bandages and stitches, and Gabrielle arrived at Omega Enterprises a few minutes early for their appointment but were not kept waiting. Pheagan's pretty secretary greeted them cordially and led them to his office.

Pheagan walked directly to Gabrielle. "And you must be Gabrielle," he said, accepting her hand gently with both of his. "I'm glad that you could make our meeting."

"Thank you, Mr. Pheagan. I did want very much to meet you," she said.

"Please, there are no formalities here. Call me Bill."

"It's a pleasure to meet you, Bill," she complied.

"That's better," he said and turned to the two men. "Mike, Dan, it's good to see you again. Especially you," he said to Danny. "That was a mightly close call you had at Bonaventure."

"Too close," Danny said, taking Pheagan's proferred hand.

"Marcie, would you please bring in another cup for coffee? And have Phil bring in another chair from the conference room, would you?"

The girl nodded and left the office.

A moment later, a heavy-set man brought in another chair and placed it near the others. Marcie entered as he left, poured the coffee, then left the office.

"So, you leave for France on Thursday?" Pheagan asked, already knowing the answer.

"Yes, for Paris," Gabrielle replied.

"Do you speak French?" he asked, knowing that answer as well from the dossiers.

"Yes, Michael and I grew up speaking it. Dan has had a good bit of it in school, too, and after we were married I helped him sharpen it considerably. He's nearly fluent," Gabrielle answered.

"Will you be met by someone in Paris?"

"Yes, by Claude St. Jude," she said.

"St. Jude. He would be Ferret," Pheagan told them.

Surprised looks crossed their faces.

"And going to Paris instead of Marseilles, I'd say that you're going to meet first with Edna-Marie DeBussey."

"That's right," Gabrielle said in amazement.

"Edna-Marie DeBussey would be Fox," Pheagan said.

"And the rest of the code names?" Michael asked.

"We've learned only one other. Albatross. That would be René Pezet. But you won't be meeting him, because he died during the war, in 1944. We haven't been able to crack the other two yet," Pheagan said.

"I'm impressed," Gabrielle commented. "What else have you learned?"

"Quite a bit, actually. I assume that you've been brought fully up to date on all the previous meetings that have taken place?"

Gabrielle nodded. "Yes, completely."

"Good, then we won't have to backtrack. I've got a lot to tell you, so I'll start right at the top," Pheagan said, leaning forward to the legal pad on his desk upon which he had scratched notes of the pieces of material he felt secure in giving them.

"The first item, then, would be Firewatch's reaction to the query regarding responsibility for the trial and death of your father. What we learned here was most interesting. I utilized two contacts, one a spokesman for the organization whom I've had dealings with in the past, and a second very friendly source known only to me, whose information is highly reliable.

"The first source accepted the claim and the responsibility for the events involving your father. He left no doubt that Firewatch was responsible. The second source, however, did not corroborate this. He said that a hasty trial did in fact take place, and he even provided a date. That date was *after* your father had begun receiving his letters, and was just shortly before his death. This does not agree with the content of the threat letters. My source also said that the execution of your father was not the work of Firewatch, and that the claim of responsibility for the deed was in reality a quid pro quo—a payback—for a past favor. Apparently someone, or some group, was in a position to call in a rather sizable marker from Firewatch."

"Then I take it that you're convinced that someone other than Firewatch was responsible?" Michael asked.

"That's right. But at this point, we still don't know who that someone is," Pheagan replied.

Pheagan was fully aware of Trinity's control over these groups, but his level of information was to be withheld from them.

"Are there any leads in that direction yet, other than the clues we've managed to find?" Michael asked.

"A few that are quite slim, but which we are pursuing vigorously. The most important would seem to be one that you've turned up,

145

however. That would be the contact your father seemingly made while in France. Like you, I also believe that the code name Leopard applies to this person. We're pursuing every aspect with regard to the word 'Circus' that we can think of, even to the point of checking every circus that was performing in France during the times of your father's trips abroad, looking for people who may have had affiliations with Resistance networks during the war. We're grasping here, but we have to follow whatever leads exist.

"Another lead we intend to follow was supplied by the glass pendant found on your father's body," Pheagan said, as he began his altered account of the origins of the Salamandra. "This pendant has an interesting history that goes all the way back to Nazi Germany. When it was fully realized that the war was going to be lost, a plan was hatched which was designed to continue the goals of the Third Reich and to orchestrate a comeback. Well, it never happened and this plan was nipped quietly in the bud before it ever got off the ground. A highly placed British agent caught on to the plan, and a key witness attempting to plea-bargain against serious war crimes, helped the Allies pull the string on the entire plot. This witness identified the three people in charge of making it work. The three people were all found shortly afterward, dead from suicide, and found with them were items which identified them. These items were pendants—identical pendants to the one found on your father.

"Of these three men, one was found in the United States, one in England, and one in France. According to the witness, only three pendants ever existed. It's understandable why the surfacing of this new pendant caused such a stir in Washington, especially since the other three pendants are still in place, secretly vaulted by the governments involved. This was a fourth pendant—one not thought to exist," Pheagan said.

"Does this mean that the movement still exists?" Gabrielle asked.

"No, it does not. I think that it confirms quite the contrary," Pheagan said. "You see, the name of the group whose job it was to engineer this comeback was the Salamandra. If it still existed, we would have had signs of its activity. And to expose a pendant now would be utter madness, as it would draw attention to the movement.

"What I think we have here is a unique combination of factors that made life very uncomfortable for the man we're after. Your father had obviously acquired information beyond that which was already known by the governments involved. It threatened to expose a former member of the Salamandra who was a pendant holder unknown to the key witness. Exposure of this past association with the aborted movement would have destroyed this man. I think there's also a good possibility that this man and our collaborator could be the same person.

"Your father had discovered the connection, or was presented with it by his contact, and attempted to use it. But our collaborator cleverly used your father's past, which he knew well, to set up his ploy to draw attention away from himself as both the collaborator and the pendant holder in one move. Leaving the pendant also served as a personal form of signature, a coup de grace between adversaries," Pheagan said.

"And without the pendant in his possession, there's nothing left to link him to the Salamandra," Gabrielle added.

"I'm sure that's what he thought," Pheagan said. "But there's been one more development that could prove him to be wrong. You see, we've learned one very important fact about this pendant that had never been learned about the others, and quite possibly would have never been learned at all if this one hadn't surfaced. It could prove to be a dangerous liability to him in the long run."

"And what have you learned?" Michael asked.

"We know who made the pendant," Pheagan said. "By very close and careful examination, we found a microscopic form of signature on it."

"But how does that help you?" Gabrielle asked.

"I think I see it," Michael said. "A back-door approach."

"Exactly," Pheagan confirmed. "A very slim hope, perhaps, but a hope, nonetheless."

"Wait a minute," Danny said. "How could you have examined his pendant? It's part of the collected evidence."

Pheagan shook his head and opened the center drawer of his desk. He reached in and pulled his closed fist out, then slid the pendant across the desk toward his three clients.

"How did you get this?" Danny asked in amazement.

But Michael wasn't so amazed. Bob Caldwell's name flashed into mind.

"It's a long story, and we had best not go into it right now for the good of a number of people. That pendant is yours to take with you. But guard it, and show it only if you feel you must. It could be dangerous to do otherwise. Exercise your own judgment in how you want to use it.

"And remember one other thing. The code names of these people in your father's Daytimer calendars were there for reasons known only

147

to him. No matter how close they may have been to your father once you must suspect them all. One of them may be the person you're after."

"Jesus," Michael said, "I feel like I'm on a goddamned merry-go round traveling too fast to even see the brass ring we're supposed to grab. I don't know if we're after a collaborator, a pendant holder, or what. I can't see the connection," he said.

"Yes, it's complicated," Pheagan said. "But it will start to sort out pretty fast once we break a few major clues. Then we'll know just who and what we're really after. We're working all the time from the pendant side of it. You'll have to work the collaboration side in France. Right now it seems like an awful tangle, but somewhere inside this mess is a simple knot that will enable us to unravel it all.

"I have more here that can help you," Pheagan said. "This other thing is very important, and unlike the rest of it, we're fairly certain of this information. We've learned the identities of the men we believe killed your father."

Pheagan watched as Michael's expression took a hard set.

"Give me their names," Michael said, moving to the edge of his chair.

"Their names are Renaud Demy and Bruno Scalco."

"Renaud Demy and Bruno Scalco," Michael repeated, burning them permanently into his memory.

"I've compiled dossiers on them for you. These men are extremely dangerous. If you get close to answers, they may come for you. I have only one recommendation to make regarding them. If you see them kill them immediately, before they can act. Because if you don't, they will kill you."

Pheagan's warning hit Gabrielle with enormous impact. Pheagan read the reaction on her face.

"It can only mean that you're getting close to answers if they come into the picture. Their only reason for being there will be to stop you. You won't learn anything from these men, so don't even entertain that thought. Just do it quickly in the best way you can, and worry about any consequences later. The important thing for you is to stay alive.

"You'll need weapons," Pheagan continued. "I can either arrange to have some waiting for you there, or, if you like, you can take your own, and I can provide you with two suitcases which will allow you to conceal them sufficiently to pass any search. You tell me what you want."

Michael and Danny exchanged glances. Gabrielle stared straight down into her lap.

148

"We'll take our own," Michael said.

Danny nodded his agreement.

"Okay, then you can take the bags with you when you leave here today. I also have the dossiers on Demy and Scalco, and your father's Daytimers for you to take back. Is there anything else, or are there any questions?" Pheagan asked.

"Yes, I forgot something," Michael said. "We found some pictures in a secret compartment of my father's desk. You should have them to make copies before we leave. I left them in the glove compartment of the car."

"You can bring them up and drop them off before you leave the city. I'll have copies made and will have the originals waiting for you at the Air France ticket counter before you leave. Is there anything else?"

"I can't think of anything," Michael said.

"Neither can I," Danny added.

Gabrielle looked up and shook her head without comment.

"Then all that's left to be said is good luck and good hunting."

The group collected the things that Pheagan had for them and left Omega Enterprises. They walked in near silence to the parking garage. Five minutes later Michael was on his way back up to Pheagan's office with the photographs. Danny and Gabrielle waited in the car on the street below.

"That was pretty good, forgetting the pictures like that," Pheagan said. "I was wondering how we were going to get the chance to talk."

Pheagan held out a slip of paper. "Here's a number I want you to memorize," he continued. "It's a Paris-based number, but you can reach me directly through it. This line will be automatically scanned for possible wiretap electronically. If the line isn't completely sterile, the connection won't be made. Call at any time, I'll be near enough to answer. I have an apartment set up here in the suite. I'll be using it throughout this entire operation."

"All work and no play. You're going to be a dull boy," Michael said.

"Don't worry about me, I'll make up for it in style when this thing is history," Pheagan returned. "Keep me posted on whatever you learn. Call in regularly, even if the going is slow, because I may have something for you. Do you remember your old identification code and clearance?" he asked.

"Yeah, I remember it."

"You'll need it to get clearance to use the line. If you screw it up, you won't get the connection."

"I remember it," Michael assured him.

"Good. You also know how to use the luggage."

"Right," Michael confirmed.

"If you have any problems or need any special assistance, call me immediately," Pheagan said.

"Ever ready, like in the good old days, huh?" Michael said with a slight trace of sarcasm.

Pheagan just smiled. "Any questions?"

"Which one is the group after—the collaborator or the pendant holder?" Michael asked.

"We want the pendant holder," Pheagan replied.

"Do you really think they could be the same person?"

"It's possible."

"How does the pendant holder interest you?" Michael asked.

"I thought you didn't care?"

"I don't. I'm just curious."

"Then it doesn't matter. If you decide to change your mind about the group, I'll tell you about it when we learn a little more. But right now, at least, it appears that we're after the same man. You for your reasons; me for mine. Just contact me before you do anything permanent if you get lucky, okay?"

Michael nodded. "Like I said, as long as I get what I'm after, I'll play ball."

"I want to wish you luck, Mike," Pheagan said, extending his hand. "I mean that."

Michael took the hand firmly. "I know you do. Thanks."

The two men smiled at one another, then Michael turned and left the office. Pheagan watched him as he made his way through the office and left the reception area. "Good luck," he whispered under his breath. He had the distinct feeling that they would all be needing generous portions of it before this thing was over.

Chapter 19

THE slow banking turn of the aircraft brought Gabrielle out of her restless sleep. Her head still against the reclined seat back, she turned first to the right toward her brother, who stared out the window into the blackness of night over France.

He seemed to be a mile deep in thought, as his eyes looked down to city lights below. She could not know the activity going on inside the quick mind, the fine honing to a razor's edge of preparation that was occurring. Preparation that could mean the difference between living and dying, especially when facing the possibility of coming up against men like Demy and Scalco, whose dossiers he had studied for hours on the plane. Failure to respond instantly, even the slightest hesitation, could be the sudden end to everything. But he had been trained to prepare, trained to react, trained to take a man's life so quickly that even the time necessary for the recognition of danger was often too long a delay for the adversary. Demy and Scalco would not be dealing with an ordinary man. This was Michael's advantage. They would not know how to estimate his capabilities. And the first rule in this game was never to underestimate your opponent.

Gabrielle didn't want to disturb his seemingly innocent concentration, and turned her head to her left toward her husband. Danny had his tray table down and had spread out the pictures that Pheagan had left at the Air France counter for them. She peeked silently over his shoulder as he studied the pictures in turn.

The reduction in airspeed and drop in altitude were noticeable now. They were on the approach path to Charles De Gaulle Interna-

151

tional Airport. The "fasten seat belt" sign went on, followed by the announcement by the stewardess in English and French.

Danny gathered the pictures into a neat stack and raised the tray table to its locked position. He turned toward his wife and, seeing that she was awake, smiled and took her hand in his.

She smiled back and squeezed his warm hand. She felt secure between the two men in her life. And security was a much needed thing.

Ever since hearing Pheagan's words warning them to kill Demy and Scalco on sight, she had been filled with a kind of fear that she had never before experienced. Like her brother, she too wanted very much to unscramble the dark mystery surrounding her father's death. But she had never thought beyond the point of actually learning the facts, to what would follow. The meeting with Pheagan brought home the reality that they were engaging in a virtual hunt in which death was both an objective and a threat. It horrified her.

It had been like part of a strange dream watching her husband and Michael carefully preparing the special bags that Pheagan had given them. She saw a side of these men that she had never seen before. They were preparing to face the danger that had frightened her so with a calm, deliberate ease. It also gave her great comfort to see their strength and lack of fear. But it did not once leave her mind that one or all of them could die in the days or weeks ahead. And that prompted one urgent concern—her children.

Perhaps the hardest moment of her life, besides the death of her father, came when she said goodbye to her daughters. She had done her best to keep up a happy appearance for their sake. Mommy and Daddy were just going on a short trip with uncle Mike to take care of some business for Grandpa. She held them tightly for a long time until she felt the one moment when enough strength would allow her to let them go and she could walk away quickly to the car. The next hardest moment came when the car turned the corner and they were suddenly gone from her sight. She had the horrible fear that she would never see them again.

Her fears had lessened as the plane streaked its way toward France. The knowledge that a friend was waiting to meet them and that others would be ready to help was comforting.

The plane touched down at De Gaulle and the family went through the routine of claiming luggage and passing through customs.

Michael liked airports. There was something invigorating about the activity and the people. It seemed that airports also had the most beautiful women to watch. His eyes stopped on one particularly lovely creature waiting to greet some lucky passenger coming off his plane.

Standing a few feet in front of her was a bull-like figure of a man, his eyes searching the faces of the passengers. At almost the same time, their eyes met, and Michael could see at once that it was Claude St. Jude. Time had not been as kind to him as to Michael's parents. He was considerably heavier than he had been in his youth. But the broad smile that suddenly broke across the tanned and weathered face was unmistakably St. Jude's. The wide gap between the front teeth was clearly evident as in the photos showing his smile.

St. Jude immediately began walking toward them. As he drew closer, Michael could see that the smile, which had at first been a happy one, was now strained, and that tears had formed in the man's eyes.

St. Jude stopped a few feet from them and held out his arms.

Gabrielle could sense his sorrow, and with a renewed pain of her own, hurried into the arms of the man she had never met. They embraced, both crying, sharing their grief.

St. Jude kissed both her cheeks and backed away at arm's length to look at her.

"You have your mother's eyes . . . and her smile," he said in his native French as Gabrielle's smile broke through the tears. "I'm sorry, but I speak very little English."

"We all speak French," she said.

St. Jude turned to Michael and stared up into his face for a moment. He took Michael in a warm embrace, then backed away, holding Michael's right hand in both of his own. "So much like your father," he said in amazement. "It is as though I have gone back in time."

"Monsieur St. Jude, it's a pleasure to meet you," Michael said.

"Please, please, call me Claude as all my friends do. It makes me feel too old to be called Monsieur St. Jude," he said. "Besides, you are like family in my heart."

Next, St. Jude turned to Danny. He took him in an equally warm embrace. "And you are Gabrielle's husband, Danny," he said. "Your mother-in-law has told me about you. You, too, are my family," he said, putting a strong arm around his shoulder.

St. Jude took Gabrielle in the other arm and held her tightly. "I cannot begin to tell you the pain that I feel," he said, the tears again forming in his eyes. "The awful shock, I'm still not over it."

"It was a shock to us all," Michael said.

The Frenchman took his arm from Danny's shoulders and

reached for his handkerchief. He mopped the tears from his eyes and ran it across his nose. "I can assure you that there are many friends of your father who are ready to help you get to the bottom of this filthy mess. Many friends."

"We'll need their help," Michael said.

"Come, I have a car," St. Jude said. "We have a busy night, and you must also get some rest."

The bags were picked up and the group moved a few steps when Michael again saw the beautiful young woman he had noticed before. She was closer to them now, and he could see that she was even more lovely than she had seemed from afar. She was looking right at him with her enormous brown eyes. Her long wavy blond hair hung down over her shoulders and almost to her breasts.

"Nicole," St. Jude said with a flick of his hand. "Please, forgive my bad manners," he said, turning back into the shuffling group behind him, causing them to stop suddenly. "This is my daughter, Nicole." He turned to where he thought she would be, but she had already passed behind him, directly toward Michael.

"Where did she—" He stopped at seeing her hand already extended to Michael.

"I am Nicole St. Jude," she said in accented English.

"Michael Gladieux," came the response as he gently accepted her hand. "It's a pleasure to meet you," he said, meaning it thoroughly.

The eye contact between them continued beyond the handshake, broken only as her father continued the introductions.

The group began to walk again after the introductions were finished.

"Nicole speaks excellent English," St. Jude said. "I was not sure how good your French would be, and I speak so little English that I thought it a good idea to have her along to act as an interpreter."

Michael found it hard keeping his eyes off her as they walked. Their eyes met several times before quickly darting away.

"Have you been to France before?" she asked, turning partially back to Michael, slowing her pace to allow him to come up even with her.

"Yes, I have. But never to Paris," he answered.

"Where in France have you been?" she asked.

"I've been to Nice, and along the coast as far as Marseilles. I've only been as far north as Grenoble, but have spent several weeks touring through Provence."

"We are from Provence," she said.

"Yes, I know. From the Camargue," he returned.

"We live about five kilometers north of Saintes-Maries-de-la-Mer," she explained.

"I've never been to the Camargue," Michael commented.

She turned to him. "I'm sure that you will love every minute there," she said with a pleasant smile.

"I'm sure that I will."

It seemed like a very long ride into Paris for the tired Americans. St. Jude sensed their fatigue, and did not fill the time with much talk.

Danny had taken the front seat beside St. Jude, and was thoroughly involved in seeing what he could. He had never been to Europe, and his behavior was amusing to St. Jude, who quietly pointed out things of interest. He kept his voice low, as he could see in the rearview mirror that Gabrielle had fallen asleep, and he did not want to disturb her.

Nicole had sat between Gabrielle and Michael. The back seat of the rented car was a tight fit for three, and Michael had to sit a little sideways to allow ample room for Nicole. It was necessary to put his arm up over the seat back behind her. To his unending delight, she had nestled herself in close to him, inside the arm. He spent a very long time watching her, looking at her hair and profile, studying the outline of her breasts beneath her clinging top, and in admiring what parts of her legs he could see. Each passing headlight or streetlamp brought a tiny and welcomed reward.

The smell of her perfume was very faint but quite exotic, and he felt the warmth of her body close to his. He began wishing the ride would last forever.

Nicole was quiet throughout the entire trip. Twice she looked up into his eyes, then smiled and looked away. After the second time, she let her weight shift slightly toward him; and Michael gave in to a tiny temptation to let his hand touch her soft, beautiful hair.

At last the car came to a stop in a well-to-do part of the city. Before they could exit the car, a smartly attired man appeared who immediately opened the car doors for them. A second man appeared almost at the same time and began attending to the luggage at the instruction of the first.

Michael looked up at the impressive stone structure standing a short distance behind a stately wrought-iron fence of masterful design. There were at least four balconies that he could see, behind which blazed beautiful large chandeliers, visible through the glass doors and windows.

155

"Is this a hotel?" Michael asked.

St. Jude laughed softly. "No, this is the residence of Edna-Marie DeBussey," he replied.

"She lives here?"

"Yes, and we will be staying here for our short time in Paris," St. Jude said.

The first domestic led them up the steps to the huge double front doors. He took a position just inside them. "Madame DeBussey is waiting for you," he said.

It was like walking into a palace, replete with marble stairway and columns. The walls were laden with ornate tapestries and paintings that Michael wouldn't have dared to estimate the value of. There were Persian rugs everywhere and furnishings that looked to be of museum quality. There were crystal and silver everywhere, and huge mirrors adorning the twenty-foot-high walls.

The three Americans cast quick glances at one another.

"Here, at last," came the pleasant voice of a woman, toward whom they all turned.

A woman of grace and beauty walked through a large doorway. Michael recognized Edna-Marie DeBussey immediately. She had to be about seventy years old, he knew, but she looked as if she had yet to reach fifty.

She stopped a short distance from them, her eyes focused on Michael. She assessed him silently for a long moment, then looked at St. Jude.

The Frenchman smiled and nodded.

Edna-Marie took a few steps forward and kissed Michael on both cheeks. "I would not have believed it if I had been told. You are the image of your father," she said. A brief look of sadness flashed into her eyes. Then she forced a smile. "And you, my dear, are Gabrielle," she said, giving Gabrielle a hug, touching both her cheeks to the young American's.

"Madame DeBussey," Gabrielle said, "what a pleasure it is to meet you."

"No, no, none of this formality," Edna-Marie said, taking Gabrielle by the hand. "I am Edna-Marie."

"May I introduce my husband, Daniel Preston," Gabrielle said.

"And such a handsome man," Edna-Marie remarked, shaking his hand. "I've always thought that Americans were beautiful. Look, isn't he beautiful?" she said gaily.

"It's the apple pie and hot dogs," Danny said straightfaced.

Everybody enjoyed a short laugh, which helped to break the air of formality demanded by the elegance of the surroundings.

"It's almost ten o'clock," Edna-Marie said. "I'm sure that you would all like to be shown to your rooms to freshen up a bit before talking for a little while.

"Alois, would you please show our guests to their rooms, and see to it that their luggage is brought up?" she said to the second domestic.

"Yes, madame," he responded. "Will you come this way please?"

The three Americans and Nicole followed the servant up the wide marble stairway. As they neared the top, Michael looked back down to Edna-Marie and St. Jude, who smiled, hooked arms, and walked through the doorway that Edna-Marie had appeared in. He heard the laughter and greeting of dear old friends too long absent from one another's presence. And life goes on, he thought.

About ten minutes later Michael came down the stairs to be greeted by the first, and obviously ranking, domestic.

"Monsieur Gladieux," the majordomo said politely. "Madame DeBussey and Monsieur St. Jude are awaiting you in the study. This way, please."

"What's your name?" Michael asked as he walked alongside of him.

"My name is Guy, monsieur," he answered.

"Have you been with Madame DeBussey long?"

"Yes, for over twenty years."

"I haven't met Monsieur DeBussey. Is he away?" Michael asked.

"Monsieur DeBussey died in a hunting accident six years ago," Guy answered.

"I'm very sorry," Michael responded.

"Thank you, Monsieur Gladieux. We all still miss him at times."

They reached the doorway that Michael had seen Edna-Marie and St. Jude pass through. Guy saw him in, then left.

Edna-Marie and St. Jude were seated on long sofas opposite one another. Between them was an elegant provincial table, upon which sat a tray with two large pots, cups and saucers, and a plate of pastries.

"Please, Michael, come and sit," Edna-Marie said, patting the cushion beside her. "Would you like some coffee or tea? A little wine, perhaps?" she asked.

"Coffee would be fine, thank you," he replied.

She poured him a cup. "Cream and sugar?"

"No, black, thank you."

She handed him the cup after he had seated himself beside her.

"Your home is beautiful," Michael commented.

"Thank you," she replied. "It is also much too large and empty since the death of my husband."

"Are there no children?" Michael asked.

"We were never able to have any," she said. "And we never adopted, although we talked about it. But we only talked, and too soon the years were upon us. We did enjoy our lives together, though."

"I asked Guy where Monsieur DeBussey was, without knowing that he had died. I hope that you won't take offense."

"Certainly not. Jean-Paul died six years ago at our country home," she said.

"Guy said that it was a hunting accident."

"Not really, although that is the official story of the incident. My husband shot himself. He had a very virulent and painful form of brain cancer. I knew when he left that day that I would never see him again."

"I'm very sorry," Michael said.

"Thank you, but it is not my husband's death that is important now, and I am the one to offer condolences. Your father was a wonderful man and a dear friend."

Just then, Guy reappeared with Danny, Gabrielle, and Nicole. Gabrielle sat beside Michael, with Danny and Nicole taking seats beside St. Jude across from the others.

It took only a few moments to dispense the coffee and tea to the preferences of the others. Then Edna-Marie sat back in her seat and looked at the two children of her late friend.

"Claude has told me the details of your father's death as related to him by your mother. He and I have spoken about what we think could be done to help you. Claude has already arranged a number of meetings for you with people who knew your father, as well as some of those who belonged to the communist group that originally brought the collaboration charge against him. We felt that talking to these people would help you to a better understanding of what happened during those years.

"As I'm sure you know by now, we did have a collaborator in Group Defiance who caused us devastating harm. To be sure, there were many collaborators and informers, and even a double agent sent to us by the British who hurt us badly in the early years. But all of these people were discovered, except for the collaborator you seek."

"And we have never forgotten him," St. Jude inserted. "We, too, want to learn his identity. It was long ago, true, but there are many scores to settle which cannot be erased by time."

"Did either of you know that my father had come to France twice last year? He came in July, and again in November," Michael said.

"Your father? Here, in France?" St. Jude asked in surprise.

"Yes, we had hoped that he had contacted one of you. We feel certain that he had learned the identity of this collaborator."

"If only he had contacted us, he might still be alive today," St. Jude said.

"We found the pocket calendars that he always carried, and in the ones used for those months were listed some code names. Perhaps you can identify them for us," Michael said, deliberately hiding the fact that they were employing outside help from a private source. They had agreed to keep that advantage a secret for as long as possible.

"We can try. What are they?" St. Jude asked.

Gabrielle took the Daytimers from her bag and turned to the pages with the entries. She handed the July Daytimer to Edna-Marie, and the November calendar to St. Jude.

St. Jude was the first to speak. "Yes, three of these are easy. Fox is the code name used by Edna-Marie. Ferret is the code name originally assigned to me when I first joined the Resistance, but it was changed at my insistence to Camargue. I don't think that it was ever reassigned, was it?" he asked Edna-Marie.

"No, it was not. Code names were never reassigned," she answered.

"And this one, Albatross. That was the boy. What was his name?" St. Jude asked, pressing his mind to recollect the name.

"Yes, René Pezet. He was a remarkable agent. He died in 1944."

Gabrielle quickly shuffled through the pictures to the boy with the machine gun slung over his shoulder. "Is this him?" she asked, handing the picture to Edna-Marie.

She looked at the picture and smiled. "Yes, this is René. This was taken in 1941, at the château near Pau."

"This other code name I don't recognize," St. Jude said. "Leopard. Did we have a Leopard?"

"The same name appears in this calendar," Edna-Marie said. "We had a Leopard early in the war, but he died, and the name was never used again."

"Are you sure that he died?" Danny asked.

"Oh, yes. In fact, Christian and I were both with him when he died."

The statement bothered Michael considerably. He had felt certain that Leopard was meant to be the contact that his father had met in France.

"And you're certain that he was dead?" Michael asked again.

"Quite. Your father and I buried him in a shallow grave in a field not far from the winery, where we had taken refuge. There were three other Defiance members with us at the time as well. The Collard brothers were there, and their cousin, Richard Boyer, who also died in the war."

"How did Leopard die?" Danny asked.

"He had received a gunshot wound to the head. We were ambushed by the Germans during a Lysander landing between Riom and Clermont-Ferrand. We lost two others at the landing site, but the rest of us managed to escape. We took refuge in a bombed-out winery not far from Pont du Château. Leopard, whose real name was Paul Romenay, lived for almost two days before he died. It was a terrible wound, and we knew that he wouldn't live. Afterward, we buried him, then went south to Marseilles," she explained.

"And this occurred when?" Danny asked.

"It was not long after the Germans had invaded the unoccupied zone. It would have been before Christmas of 1942."

There was a moment of silence as the Americans felt their disappointment. Then St. Jude broke the spell. "There are no more code names in this calendar," he said.

Edna-Marie looked at her calendar, turned the pages and came to the word "Circus."

"This has significance," she said. "The word 'Circus' was part of the last message transmitted by René Pezet. He sent the message, knowing that he would be caught in the process, and he sacrificed his life to get it to us. Claude, I think that you could explain this better than I, as you were involved with the transmission."

"This particular transmission was made in 1944 by Pezet, whom we all thought to be dead," St. Jude began. "He had somehow escaped from an earlier ambush in his sector and later transmitted a message using an early-generation battery-operated radio believed to have been captured by the Germans long before. The transmission was extremely weak and didn't have the power to carry to England. We were fortunate to have picked it up ourselves. It was a single wavelength radio using a frequency that had not been used in years. We were operating a variable wavelength receiver, which picked up this weak signal. There was no mistaking that it was Pezet sending on the old radio, as every radio operator has his own touch, which is as distinctive as his voice.

"Pezet transmitted that he was in imminent danger of capture, and that he had learned the identity of the collaborator, whom the Ger-nans had code-named Z. This was the same collaborator whom you are after today. The transmission stopped for a moment after we had verified that we were receiving him. Then it began again, quite weak. The word he transmitted as the identity of Z was 'Circus.' His transmissions ceased abruptly after the last letter of the word. We requested a repeat, but no transmission followed. We continued to repeat the request, but he had fallen silent. It was only after the final armistice that we learned he had been killed by the Germans.

"Unfortunately, the knowledge he had of the collaborator's identity died with him. We were never able to understand what he had meant. We tried every code possible, but nothing made sense. We sent it to the British, as well, and they could do no better. The only man understanding its meaning had died, and the identity of Z was lost."

"I think that perhaps the best way for us to help you is to start from the beginning, and to tell you what we can as it actually happened," Edna-Marie suggested. "It's a very long story, and you will need to talk to other people to hear it all. But it may be the only way to piece together the facts with what you may already know.

"I can give you the beginning, from the first time that I met your father. It was a long time ago, after the armistice with Germany had been signed. It was in Vichy. . . ."

Chapter 20

VICHY, AUGUST 1940: The journey to Vichy was a difficult one for Christian. The wound that had been so troublesome and improperly healed continued to bother him. He was weakened and pale, and had very little money when he arrived.

Vichy was bustling with activity. It was a city filled with new opportunities for those fast enough and smart enough to grab for them. The new "French State" was forming. The Third Republic had been abolished. New faces were needed. Influence became a precious commodity, which many men used wisely and others selfishly. What matter that a man forsake patriotism for a chance to establish himself in a position of power? This was a new France in a new Europe. Loyalty to the old France gave way to opportunity in the new one, without shame, without guilt, without hesitation.

Christian had made a wise decision to travel in uniform. It opened many doors, provided many meals and rides on the long roads to Vichy. It also gave him his most important lead once there.

He had tried to find a place to stay for a few days, but there were very few rooms available, and none of those with the privacy he desired. The demand for rooms was high, and so were the prices—too high for the little money he had left. He also needed to eat, and his money could not buy both.

He sat in an open-air café sipping a coffee, trying to decide which was the more important—food or lodging—when he overheard two uniformed men in much the same straits as he discussing the Hotel des Sports, which had been established in Vichy as a rehabilitation center for demobilized soldiers like himself.

He excused himself, saying that he could not help overhearing their conversation, and asked where the Hotel des Sports might be located. Given the address and instructions how to get there, he finished his coffee and left immediately. But it was not thoughts of food or a bed to sleep in that prompted his wanting to go there. The Hotel des Sports would be filled with ex-soldiers like himself. Fighting men who loved France, and who would not accept her defeat. If plans to fight on were going to be made, men like these would make them.

He arrived at the Hotel des Sports only to find it jammed with an odd assortment of souls. Confused, strange people swarmed about everywhere. It was like a house of glass with eyes and ears all around. Too many, he thought, for the laying of plans that required discreetness. He was about to leave when a hand came to rest on his shoulder from behind.

Christian turned to face the man who had touched him, and stared into a face that he recognized, but could not place immediately.

"Lieutenant Gladieux, with the 21st Foreign Volunteers, isn't it?" the short stocky man asked.

"Yes, that's right. I'm sorry, but should I know you?"

"The important thing is that I know and remember you," the man said. "Ste.-Menehould. The river. You carried me to safety, below the German lines. My name is Jean Monjaret. Captain Jean Monjaret."

Christian's face lit up with sudden recognition. "You said that you would remember me."

"Yes, and I lived to do so, as you suggested. I'm very glad to see you. Will you join me for a drink?" Monjaret asked.

162

"Happily," Christian replied.

The two men threaded their way through the strange assemblage of people to a small table occupied by another man. The man rose as they approached.

"Lieutenant Gladieux, I'd like you to meet Jan Burak."

Christian reached out to accept the hand of the smiling, swarthily complected man.

"Lieutenant Gladieux, it is my pleasure to meet you," the man said in accented French.

"Czech, isn't it?" Christian asked, recognizing the accent.

"You have a good ear," Burak commented with a nod. "Do you speak Czech by any chance?"

"Yes, I do. I was assigned to the 21st Foreign Volunteers because of my ability to speak many languages," Christian replied in surprisingly smooth Czech.

"I'm very impressed," Burak said in French. "Please, sit down."

The three men sat, and Monjaret raised his hand, motioning for a round of drinks.

"This is the man that I told you about," Monjaret said. "The brave lieutenant who saved me at Ste.-Menehould."

The Czech nodded and eyed Christian as though looking straight through him and into his soul. "What brings you to Vichy and to the Hotel des Sports?" Burak asked in a low voice.

Christian looked around carefully, unsure whether it was wise to talk where they were.

"Don't let the appearance fool you, Lieutenant. You can speak at this table," Burak said, as if reading his mind.

Christian waited until the glasses of wine were distributed and the girl who had brought them had left. He raised his glass in toast. "To France and the war she is about to fight," he said.

Burak looked at Monjaret, his expressive eyes confirming the opinion that the captain had formed of Christian. "You have come to the right place," he said, extending his glass toward Christian.

The glasses clinked lightly and they drank.

Monjaret left the table and walked to the bar. He returned a few moments later with a key, which he placed on the table in front of Christian. "This is to your room," he said.

"I'm afraid that I have very little money," Christian said.

"*You* don't need money here," Monjaret said. "You look pale and tired. Have your wounds healed?" he asked.

"I'm fine," Christian nodded.

"I'll bet you are," Monjaret said knowingly. "I suggest that you go to your room for some sleep. Food will be brought up to you later, and a doctor will visit you this afternoon. I, too, needed his services when I arrived. There will be a meeting tonight that I think you should attend. I'll stop by your room at ten o'clock to get you. We desperately need men like you, Lieutenant Gladieux. I can't begin to tell you how happy I am that you've come here."

At ten o'clock sharp, a soft knock sounded on the door to Christian's room. He opened it a crack and saw Monjaret standing outside. He motioned to Christian to join him with a sweep of his hand.

The two men moved without speaking to the end of the hallway, then climbed a flight of stairs to the floor above.

They reached a door and Monjaret tapped lightly three times, paused, then tapped once again. It opened and the two men entered.

There were three people in the room. Jan Burak was there, along with another man and a young attractive woman.

"Lieutenant Christian Gladieux, I would like you to meet Madame Edna-Marie DeBussey, and Captain Charles Flandine," Monjaret said in introduction.

The three exchanged greetings and handshakes.

"I've already told them about you, so we can get directly to the business at hand. The purpose of our meeting tonight is to discuss plans for establishing a network of loyal patriots to continue the struggle in France against the Germans. Jan Burak was a member of the Czechoslovakian army intelligence service and was in France when his country was occupied by Germany. He stayed on here to continue his efforts for his country, and has agreed to offer his experience and expertise to help us establish our network. We are all soldiers, with the exception of Edna-Marie, and our knowledge of clandestine activities is naively limited. If we are to hope for a chance of success and survival in the long and difficult struggle ahead, we will need the benefit of his wisdom and suggestions. I will now turn the meeting over to him. Jan, you may have the floor."

The eyes of all those seated in the room went to Burak. He rose, took a few steps to where he could address them all equally, and began.

"There are two kinds of war. The first is the one with which you gentlemen are most familiar and experienced. It is a war between armies. It is the war in which cities are destroyed, bodies are torn, and from which tales of heroism are woven. France has just *lost* that war to Germany in forty-three days. The second kind of war is the one with which I am most familiar. It is the war of information. It is the war of obtaining knowledge of the enemy. And knowledge of the enemy is a factor of vital importance to the final outcome of any great conflict.

"The gathering of intelligence is a long, difficult, and thankless job. Unlike on the battlefield, one does not get to see the immediate results of his efforts. Success is not measured in body counts, or in the numbers of smashed tanks, crashed planes, or sunken ships. Success is measured by only one thing—winning or losing.

"What you must do today, before going a single step further, is to decide on the kind of war you want to fight. France is partially occupied, and if my knowledge of the Germans is correct, it will be fully occupied before the tide of this war will swing. The battle of France, for those of you still here, will become one of resistance. And like war, there are two kinds of resistance. One uses violence and acts of terrorism to hurt and confuse the enemy. The other is, again, the war of intelligence.

"Acts of violence by armies of Resistance fighters have a very important value of their own. But they alone cannot win a war against an occupying force with the strength of Germany. Intelligence *can* win that war. Information of vital importance placed into the hands of those allies capable of meeting the enemy on the battlefields, combined with the efforts of those Resistance networks whose job it is to disrupt the enemy, can kill an occupying force as surely as a deadly cancer.

"A war of information is a difficult one. It is as dangerous to those engaged in it as a war between armies is to a soldier in the field. The enemy will fight back in a war that has no rules. And you will find the enemy to be not only the forces of Germany. France is occupied, and as painful as it may be for you to accept, your enemy will also be France."

There was a noticeable reaction to the statement. Flandine let out a grunt of disagreement. Christian himself could not imagine Frenchman against Frenchman.

"By working in the underground, which will be illegal in the eyes of your government, you will become official enemies of your country. There will be many, a great many, who will not think as you think. They will appease their new masters—and fight you. The French against the French," Burak said. "I know what I'm saying. You decide on the kind of war that you want to fight, then I will help you fight it."

There was a long silence in the room. Christian finally rose to his feet. "We're soldiers," he said. "We know only of the kind of war you say we can't win. We know how to fight. We want to fight."

"Yes, *you* want to fight, but *France* does not," Burak said to more murmurs. "You were there. You saw it, unless you were blind. Did you see the streets when the armistice—the surrender—was signed? There was celebration and joy, as if France had just won the war."

"There were tears and outrage," Christian shot back.

"Yes, there were. But not all Frenchmen shed them or felt it. They weren't all like you, Lieutenant Gladieux. Go out there. Go into the streets now and raise a call to arms. Will the streets of Vichy fill with exuberant patriots ready to face the German Wehrmacht again? Think about the faces of the refugees you saw choking every road in France. Think about the faces of the deserters you saw, and the equipment and weapons in heaps along the sides of the roads.

"How do I know what you saw? you wonder. Everyone saw it, including the Germans. Do you think that a parent glad to see a son spared will encourage him to fight on? The slightest gesture of revolt will be discouraged. They *believe* that they can live under German occupation."

Christian was filled with anger. The words of the Czech were hard to listen to without wanting to charge at him and batter him until he recanted. But Christian had seen what Burak described, seen it in the faces—and felt it in his heart. Burak was right.

Christian slumped and sat back down, his brow furrowed, his eyes looking at the floor without seeing.

"What kind of war will you fight?" Burak asked once again.

"A war of information," Edna-Marie DeBussey said. "A war that will help France to be free again."

"I agree," said Monjaret without hesitation.

"Flandine?" Burak asked.

Flandine looked at Burak for a long moment. "I was in the French Air Force. We were ordered to stand down and not to take our planes up. Perhaps we would not have won, but we could have fought." He nodded to Burak. "We must win this war. I am for a war of intelligence."

"And you, Gladieux. What kind of war will you fight?" Burak asked softly.

Christian looked up at him, then slowly around the room at the others. "I will fight the war which is best for France, for only France matters. If you can teach us how to fight this war, then I will listen and learn. I will fight it to the best of my ability and to the last of my strength. I will fight it until France has won, or until I have died. I will fight your war of information. Now teach us how to do it."

"Yes, now I will teach you," Burak said. "We will begin by divid-

166

ng France into sectors. Everything will be watched. Every troop movement, every train, every ship, and every truck. The Atlantic and Channel coasts were occupied for three purposes: coastal defense, to provide a point from which to launch an invasion of England, and for the establishment of U-boat bases. Supplies will also move in and out of these coasts, but Mediterranean ports will bear the greatest importance in that regard, even though they are not now occupied. They will be occupied when the time is right to German thinking. In the meantime, they will run supply ships under every imaginable flag but German, bound for North Africa and points east. All coastal intelligence will be vitally important to the cause. Every ship, every gun placement, every new airfield.

"All existing airfields must be watched, as well as rail yards. Contacts must be developed within the Vichy French state, within the Deuxième Bureau, and as deeply into police networks as possible.

"Courier routes must be established, crossing points between zones designated, and communications with England set up. Put aside your feelings for England and Mers-el-Kébir and for the sinking of the *Richelieu* in Dakar. England is fighting a war of survival, and she is your closest ally. If England falls, France will be lost.

"You must also recruit link men—railroad operators, commercial travelers, truck drivers, et cetera. People who can move about in normal, everyday activity without suspicion. And you must find radio operators, as many as possible."

"But we have no radios," Monjaret said.

"They will come after you have established yourselves with England."

"There's so much," Edna-Marie said.

"Yes, the work will be long and difficult. And at first you will not recognize your success. But one day you will begin to, and you will find that you get better and better at what you do.

"And now we must start at the top, in what will be the most important part of all—the organization and structure of your Resistance group." Burak paused a moment. "It will need a name," he said.

"Defiance," Edna-Marie volunteered without delay.

"Defiance," Burak repeated pensively. "Group Defiance. It sounds formidable," he said, nodding.

The others joined in repeating it and expressing their approval.

"Then Group Defiance it will be," Burak said, announcing the birth of Le Groupe Défi.

The next hour was spent describing the most effective ways of organizing such a network for intelligence gathering. A very tight network of cells needed to be established, each consisting of a maximum number of three or four individuals.

He proposed a pyramidal structure of organization. Ideally instituted, it would allow only a small area of damage to the network, which could radiate only downward, away from those in the most responsible positions, as the identities of those above would be unknown to all parties below. Only the uppermost levels of leadership would know one another. This was a necessity. Burak also pointed out that recruitment would be an enormously risky business. There were no security clearances available as there were with various governmental departments. Whom to trust and whom not to trust would often be based upon friendship and personal recommendations. Many volunteers would come forward without references. How do you judge them? "There are no guarantees. Experience will teach you whom to believe and whom to trust," Burak told them. "There will be mistakes, and even your most trusted people can change for many reasons. Money, to protect loved ones held hostage, fear, jealousy, many reasons. These mistakes will be costly. But you will learn from them."

The meeting continued well into the early hours of morning. Burak established the order of leadership in Group Defiance before the meeting adjourned. He proposed that Jean Monjaret be the leader of Defiance, with Edna-Marie as second. Below Edna-Marie, he proposed Charles Flandine, followed by Christian, whom he knew least of all.

Burak requested a few additional moments with Flandine and Christian immediately after the meeting. One important issue had to be discussed with them—one that he knew needed to be addressed immediately.

"What did you think of the meeting?" Burak asked.

"Very informative," Flandine responded.

Christian did not reply.

Burak's intuitions had been correct. "All right, out with it," he barked.

"Out with what?" Flandine asked.

"What is it that's bothering you?" Burak asked. "I already know the answer, but I want to hear it from you, along with your reasons."

There was silence. Burak waited.

Finally Christian stood up and walked toward the door, and then turned back to Burak.

"This is not a game," he said. "War—even your war of intelligence—is a serious, demanding business. You put a woman who is barely more than a girl in a position of responsibility that I don't think he can handle," he complained.

"How old are you, Lieutenant Gladieux?" Burak asked.

"I'm twenty-four," Christian responded.

"Also young for a command. Did your men in the 21st Foreign Volunteers respond well to you?"

"Quite well. I had their confidence."

"Edna-Marie is twenty-nine, and she has my confidence," Burak said. "It is my profession to know people, gentlemen. I have had the time to get to know her quite well. She is a very capable young woman, intelligent, hardworking—"

"A woman," Christian interrupted. "Emotional, never having been exposed to true danger, fear, or responsibility. What happens if Monjaret is lost to Defiance? Can she suddenly be responsible for the lives of the people who will depend upon her decisions? There will be casualties. How will she react to them? How decisive will she be under pressure?"

"The only real answers to those questions must come with time," Burak replied. "I said that you will learn whom to trust through experience. Just as you, Lieutenant, learned which men of your company were the most dependable and the least, I have learned which kind of people are cut out for this work and which are not. She needs only a bit more confidence in herself. That will come, certainly from necessity if nothing else. But it can also come from you two men. She must be certain of your belief in her—just as I am certain.

"I know that it is a hard thing for two military officers to take subordinate positions to such a young woman, and that you must have faith in your leaders. I spoke privately with Jean before our meeting today, and probed for his reaction to my intended recommendations. He has known Edna-Marie for a very long time. He knows her strengths and her weaknesses. It was his opinion that she could do the job, even if he were lost to the group for any reason."

"Well, I'm willing to give her a try," said Flandine. "The chain of command can always be re-established if she proves incapable of fulfilling her responsibilities."

"And you?" Burak asked Christian.

"I will make that decision in the next weeks as we begin to establish our sectors. I'll spend time with her and get to know her. I'll see how she handles herself and other people. Remember, I am not the only man who will have reservations about taking orders from a woman. That must be understood and expected."

169

"Only the early sector heads will ever know that it is a woman above them. She will be known only by a code name. But your idea of spending time with her is a good one. If you still have strong reservations after that time, we'll discuss them and make some kind of decision."

"Agreed," Christian said. "When do we start?" he asked.

"Immediately. We go to Marseilles, the first sector of Group Defiance."

Marseilles was a port city of endless possibilities for a young Resistance group. It was also a place of many dangers. But the experience and intuitive knowledge of people that Jan Burak gave to them would make their efforts much easier.

Burak, Edna-Marie, and Christian all traveled separately to Marseilles. Burak went ahead by a full day to meet with expert forgers with whom he had had past dealings. Group Defiance would need them as surely as they needed air. Such skills would be in high demand, and the cost of their services high.

Burak knew that his efforts in France to help establish Resistance networks was vital to the course of the war for his country, too. That was his primary goal in all his activities. He had had sizable funds allocated to him just prior to the fall of his homeland, and had access to considerably more money, which would help in establishing Group Defiance. But the cost of running such a network as this, and others that he hoped to help start, would be enormous. That was another reason why Group Defiance must establish themselves with England. Without money, the group would be ineffective. It would wither and die. His money would help in the beginning, however, until they could learn ways to acquire money, by whatever means necessary, to continue their efforts.

The first trip to Marseilles was made under actual identities for Edna-Marie and Christian. Burak was traveling as a commercial businessman, an importer-exporter working for a former Czechoslovakian company now serving the interests of the Reich. He stayed in a hotel separate from the others, who were traveling with funds he had given them. Their first meeting together in Marseilles delighted Burak, as it showed the rewards of his judgments of these two people.

Edna-Marie and Christian had met together before leaving the Hotel des Sports in Vichy, and had discussed the necessity of acquiring funds. It offered Christian his first surprising lesson as to the capabilities of the beautiful young woman. Together, they devised a number of ways of establishing moneymaking enterprises, which would also serve their purposes of intelligence gathering. The first was to establish an import-export firm in Marseilles, using people knowledgeable in the business. This would allow them to know the comings and goings in the port itself, and generate income to help feed the organization. They also proposed buying several cafés and bars in the vital districts of the port city. Near the docks, the merchantmen and dock workers would be filled with information easily obtained through innocent conversation. Across from the main police headquarters, they would set up a café which would offer the rich prospect of learning what was going on inside the department, as well as establishing valuable contacts within the force, itself. Their ideas went on and on.

Burak listened with quiet satisfaction as they explained their plans to him. He could provide the funds to acquire the bars and cafés. The import-export firm would be more difficult. But this problem resolved itself quickly within the next few days. Burak had been given the name of a man who was well known and trusted by one of the ten men that Monjaret had enlisted. This was a young man from the Camargue named Claude St. Jude.

St. Jude was from a wealthy family in the Camargue that operated one of the largest *manades,* or ranches, in the entire region. It was in the prideful business of raising bulls and horses that the Camargue held its worldwide reputation. The family also had substantial interests in growing rice, grapes, and other produce, which gave Claude, the youngest but most business-adept of the three sons, important contacts in Marseilles.

The young St. Jude was a man who knew the ways of making money, both through legitimate transactions and the suddenly blossoming black market. He had many trusted friends in both.

"The import-export firm will be easy," he had told them. "I know just the man you will need, and who is already in the business. He lost two sons in the fighting, and would like nothing more than the opportunity to stick a knife into the backs of the Germans. This will give you the legitimate business you will need. But I strongly suggest that you establish contacts with my friends in the black market. You will learn a great deal more from them regarding the 'life' in Marseilles, and along the rest of the coast. You will also make considerably more money—and much more quickly."

He also knew people with existing bars in the port district who would be willing to help. The café near police headquarters could also be arranged—for the right price.

Christian was reluctant to embrace the black market proposal, fearing that these men could not be trusted.

"There is loyalty among thieves," St. Jude had said. "And they are no less Frenchmen than you and I."

"Their only concern is in making money," Christian said. "We would be helping them steal things that Frenchmen need."

"They will develop contacts from whom they will learn much. The Germans who deal in the black market will also unwittingly help pay for your efforts against them. The information gained will be a great deal more valuable to France, and Frenchmen, than the goods we steal from them to sell," St. Jude returned.

Christian could not argue the logic. There was so much to learn.

It was evident to them all that St. Jude, with his knowledge of Marseilles and his many contacts, would be enormously valuable to them. He was made the head of the Marseilles sector.

They went next to Toulon, and then to Nice, where similar patterns of birth and growth were established. Friends had more friends who in turn had still more friends who were willing to help. The triangle began to grow downward, level by level, each forming a wider base.

The trio moved north to Grenoble and Lyon, then crossed the demarcation line into the occupied zone. They made their way to Dijon, quickly establishing a sector there, and then pushed on to Paris.

The organization of Paris would be difficult and complex. It would be considered a single sector, but would in reality be four. Paris was the center of activity in occupied France and the seat of power of the occupying forces of Germany. It was also a city that Jan Burak had spent much time in before the war. He had many reliable contacts and used them carefully to establish the sectors that would be the eyes and ears of Le Groupe Défi. He knew precisely the people he wanted for sector heads, and reviewed their qualifications with Edna-Marie and Christian, just as he had with Jean Monjaret before leaving Vichy. Each would be carefully interviewed, and would not know the identities of the other sector heads, except by code name. The cells composing each sector would be known only to the sector heads, Edna-Marie and Christian.

The last of the four people to be interviewed was a woman. It no longer bothered Christian to have a woman highly placed in a position of responsibility. He had become a true believer in Jan Burak's judgment of people, and in Edna-Marie DeBussey. The weeks spent with her had demonstrated most clearly her resourcefulness and keen intelgence. There would be no need for a meeting to further consider the decision to rank her second in command of Group Defiance.

The final interview took place in a small flat rented by Burak. It would be maintained for a few months until the sectors were established and working smoothly. It was late morning when the knock sounded on the door. Christian answered it and came face to face with one of the most stunning women he had ever seen. Her name was Gabrielle Dupuy.

He stood looking at her, wordless from the impact of her beauty. She waited a moment, then, seeing Burak in the room, pushed past Christian, looking at him with an odd expression.

"I'm sorry," Christian said, catching himself. "Please, come in."

"You're a little late. I'm already in," she quipped as she breezed past him.

Gabrielle Dupuy was an independent woman who was as smart and strong as she was beautiful. There was no mistaking any of these qualities from the confident air about her.

It didn't take long for the conversation to reveal that she was well in tune to the changes that were occurring in France.

"The Germans were totally prepared. The earliest divisions coming in spoke French quite well, even to the point of using the proper dialects of the regions they were in. They knew the towns and villages extremely well, right down to the streets and alleys. Even the billets selected for their men had been made in advance," she told them. "They go out of their way to be polite and friendly. It's an awful magic that they practice. The people look at them, and their distrust melts away. There are too many smiling French faces, too many lives returning to normal too quickly. And the Germans do not act like an occupation army. They appear to have come to stay forever."

"That will change," Burak assured her.

"I'm certain that it will. France is to pay an awful price for this dirty business," she continued. "Plans are already being made for the modification of France's industry. Renault will repair German tanks, Michelin will make tires for German vehicles, French workers are to be taken into Germany to work in their factories. Our agricultural produce—meats, cheeses, wines—and anything else of use to them will be poured across the borders into Germany. France is becoming a vassal state. Many Frenchmen will suffer, and many will make fortunes working for their new masters. I know several industrialists who believe that this is the greatest thing to have ever happened to France—and to their rapidly fattening wallets."

Gabrielle Dupuy's many acquaintances permitted her easy access into industrial circles, communications, both printed and radio, theater banking and finance, and even to members of the new French govern ment in Vichy. "I get invited everywhere, to every party that's impor tant," she told them without exaggeration.

"And what about the Germans?" Burak asked.

"They're invited, too, naturally. I've met quite a few already, and it's amazing what a few glasses of champagne and a little attention will get in the way of information. They like French women very much, you know, especially being so far away from home."

Burak was quite pleased, as he knew he would be. Gabrielle could be enormously effective, and completely above suspicion being so close to the Germans. A beautiful, engaging woman like this could kill them figuratively one night with flattery and attention, then kill them in a more literal sense the next with the information she came away with.

Gabrielle was given the code name Ariel, and told that her imme diate contact for the next few months would be Christian, who was introduced to her by his code name—Orca.

When the meeting had ended, the trio felt satisfied with the early results in Paris. Four sector heads had been selected, and the ranks were beginning to fill in below them. Christian was told to concentrate his time between Marseilles and Paris until these important sectors were more firmly established.

Monjaret and Edna-Marie were to begin the difficult job of coor dinating the sectors as they formed. Burak would continue his efforts to establish further sectors with Flandine, and also independently.

They opened a bottle of wine and toasted with satisfaction the birth of Group Defiance, which just four short weeks ago had consisted of five people with a plan. It was now nearly sixty strong and growing. The time had come to alert England of their existence and readiness to help.

The hours had slipped past almost without notice as the group listened to Edna-Marie's story. The three Americans had sat atten tively, drinking in every detail.

"I thought that you were in command of Group Defiance?" Michael asked.

"Yes, I was," Edna-Marie replied. "Jean Monjaret was arrested by the French police a month later, but for reasons unrelated to Group Defiance. He had spoken up against the Military High Command and the French government, charging them with treason for the way the

174

war had been conducted prior to the armistice. He was jailed and later put on trial. I took over upon his arrest."

"What were the results of his trial?" Danny asked.

Edna-Marie smiled. "He was found guilty. But Jean Monjaret was a clever man. He stood in his own defense, calling many witnesses whose testimony proved enormously embarrassing for the military and the government. They never conceded him victory, but a six-month prison sentence instead of a firing squad was victory enough."

"Didn't he take command again?" Gabrielle questioned.

"No, he did not. Like your father, he had been badly wounded in the fighting, and his wounds did not heal well, either. Although he appeared strong at the time of his arrest, he was not. The months in prison affected him badly. He was a skeleton at his trial, though his mind was healthy and strong. The additional term in prison only worsened his condition. He died in his home at Montauban a year later. He never saw the Liberation of France and the significant role that Group Defiance played in achieving that end. He was a wonderful man, and all of us who knew him were greatly saddened. But we had many sad times and mourned the deaths of many wonderful Frenchmen and women who worked tirelessly and bravely in the face of what, at times, seemed to be insurmountable hardships. Every death brought pain and tears, but also a determination to fight on in spite of the difficulties. We owed it to our fallen comrades to continue the fight to the very end so that their sacrifices would not have been made in vain."

"How many people died in the service of Group Defiance?" Michael asked.

Edna-Marie took a moment to search their faces. "Very nearly six hundred," she replied. "Hundreds more suffered terrible hardships at the hands of the Nazis and our own French police. And of those nearly six hundred lives, over two hundred were lost because of the betrayal of a single man. A man known to the Germans as Z, and to René Pezet as Circus."

Chapter 21

It was almost noon when Edna-Marie DeBussey greeted her late
rising guests. She led them to a bright, airy terrace, where Guy had
prepared a tray with coffee and croissants as well as fruits and cheeses.

Edna-Marie told them about the earliest efforts of the fledgling
Group Defiance as they took their breakfast.

"Everything was a mass of confusion. Our first sectors began send
ing in information almost immediately. We had no idea what was im
portant and what wasn't. And, even worse, we had nowhere to send it
We hadn't yet made contact with England. Just assigning code names
and keeping track of our rapidly growing network was difficult enough
with our limited experience.

" 'Don't worry about deciding what information is important,' Jar
Burak told us. 'The English will do that. Just keep collecting it. When
contact is made with England, you will need to present it all, to demon
strate your ability to obtain facts. Then they will ask questions. They
will be simple questions like who, what, when, where, and how.'

"I told him that we would need radios. 'They will come,' he said
'but first you must prove yourselves to them. There will be many Re
sistance groups forming, all sending in information. The same or simi
lar information coming in from many sources will help to confirm its
veracity.'

"So we kept collecting it, and began to devise codes for our sector
to use. The volume of work never lessened, but as we became more
organized, it became a little easier."

"So when did England finally agree to help you?" Gabrielle asked

"It was in October," Edna-Marie said. "Charles Flandine went to

England as our representative. He made his way across the Pyrenees near Andorra with the help of our sector members there. He traveled next to Lisbon, and then to London, where he presented the sizable bundle of reports that had been sent in by our enthusiastic sectors. The English were quite impressed. They happily accepted it and began an immediate analysis of its value.

"Flandine then attempted to meet with De Gaulle. It took a week of persistent effort to get an audience with him, and the meeting was anything but pleasant. De Gaulle refused to acknowledge any group that would not wear the badge of his Free French and pledge loyalty to him.

"Flandine was greatly dejected from the results of the meeting. He had come away without the support of De Gaulle, and felt that the news would crush our young hopes. But very good news awaited him. The British had analyzed our reports, and were extremely impressed. We had provided pieces of information that they had been searching for, pertaining to German activity along the Atlantic coast, and the results of bombing raids on German airfields. The British agreed to help us and to supply us with radios and funds, both of which were desperately needed. Our funds had dwindled quickly, and we were existing on loans and what little income had started coming in from the businesses in Marseilles. The money from Claude's black-market friends was keeping the entire Marseilles, Toulon, and Nice sectors going, but on a dangerously thin budget. Much more money was needed, and quickly, or we faced the real danger of losing some of our sectors.

"Flandine returned with three surprises. The first was news of England's enthusiastic support, along with one million crisp new francs. The second was both pleasant and disappointing. It was a radio. But he presented it to me in a heap of parts and wires. It had been damaged in the drop. And the third was received as pure joy at first, but would later be remembered as one of our sorriest days. He had brought with him an Englishman who was a skilled radioman—but also a German double agent. His code name was Pointer."

"Pointer," St. Jude said with a grunt. "The pig."

"Pointer's French was abominable. I couldn't believe that they had sent him," Edna-Marie continued. "Surely, a man who could speak excellent French was required to help carry any cover identity we would need to create for him. But he made up for his bad French by assuring me that he could repair the radio. Two days later, true to his word, the radio, which was christened with the call letters TOM, sent its first message to England. Our link with England had been

established, and we all beamed proudly, for now we were a true R
sistance group joined in the fight for France."

Edna-Marie explained further how the network of sectors gre
steadily and how the most important sectors received their radios ar
began direct transmission to England.

"When did you become aware of the relationship that develope
between my father and Gabrielle Dupuy?" Michael asked.

"I did not become aware of it for some time," Edna-Marie replie
"Claude was the first to know, I think." She looked to Claude f
confirmation, and also inviting him to pick up the storytelling.

St. Jude nodded slowly. "Yes, it was an unfortunate developmer
I believe that they both tried very hard to avoid the relationship. B
with the war, the desperation, the uncertainty of the future, and th
pressures we all lived with daily, the affinity between them became tc
great. It was at the same time both beautiful and tragic to watch. . . .

PARIS, DECEMBER 1940: The months spent in Paris had been high
productive for Christian. The four sectors, with their numerous patrol
each composed of groups of cells, had solidified into a well-functionir
network. The people were highly reliable, thanks to the contacts tha
Jan Burak had developed and recruited into the network.

Christian regularly spent time with each of his sector heads, car
fully reviewing the information they had obtained and transmitted t
England. Two radios were now assigned to the Paris sector because c
the magnitude of important information being gathered, and th
growth in the number of patrols. There were already over forty agen
operating in this city alone, working diligently to tap the many pote
tial resources of the overall sector. A first-class forgery section had als
been started, which was of tremendous value to sectors all acros
France.

Unlike working in the unoccupied zone, the dangers were muc
greater within the heart of the enemy's command center. Precautior
were complex and painstakingly adhered to. Every sector head had
separate meeting place, the security of which was his responsibilit
The slightest threat to that location resulted in its abandonment an
the establishment of a new one.

The contacts with Gabrielle Dupuy were always the most enjo
able for Christian. Her radiant vitality made being with her sheer plea
sure, and her intelligence and amazing capabilities never ceased t

178

mpress him. She had a shrewd appreciation for what was worthwhile
n the way of information.

Christian had felt the undeniable stirrings within him that had
begun the moment he had first seen her in the flat that Burak had
ented. Every moment spent with her over the succeeding months only
made him more aware of the feelings that were growing inside. Every
ouch of her hand or chance contact with any part of her felt like fire.
He wanted very much to take her close to him and to hold her. But he
knew that if he did he would become lost in the magic of her beauty.

Unknown to him, she, too, had realized the same effects from his
presence. Gabrielle had known many powerful, handsome men in her
ife, but none had intrigued her as completely as this one. She began to
anticipate his visits, looking forward to their time together and to the
hrill of even the slightest physical contact with him. Each recognized
separately the inappropriateness of anything happening between them
but were powerless to stop it.

The meeting place they used was in the apartment of a close and
rusted friend of Gabrielle's, which also added a sufficiently adequate
cover for her visits there. They were provided with a room of their own
o conduct their business in complete privacy for as long as they might
equire.

It had been over two weeks since their last meeting, and a different
kind of nervousness filled Gabrielle on this occasion. An opportunity
of enormous potential had presented itself which was too important to
et pass. The decision to act upon it had tormented her for weeks. But
her strong sense of duty and love for France had precluded any other
choice but to seize the opportunity before her. And now she sat ter-
ified at the thought of telling the man she knew she was falling in love
with that she was about to begin an affair with a German officer for the
ake of her country.

Gabrielle sat on a straight-backed wooden chair, her legs tightly
ogether, shoulders hunched forward, her eyes staring down at the
hands in her lap which clutched nervously at a white lace handker-
hief.

The sound of his footsteps approaching the closed door made her
wish that she could die or become invisible before he opened it.

Then, too quickly, the door was opened and closed again. Chris-
ian stood a few feet from her looking down at the distressed, shaking
woman. He had never seen her this way before.

"What's happened?" he asked, dropping to one knee beside her
hair, his hands gently on her shoulders. There was a look of passion-

ate concern on his face. "What's happened, Gabrielle? Tell me," h
said.

She sniffed once and, placing the frilled handkerchief to her nose
rose from the chair. Christian rose with her.

"Do you remember last month my mention of the name Rudol
Immel?" she asked.

"Immel. Yes. Waffen SS, a captain in the Panzer Group Liet
standarte. On temporary assignment in Paris while recovering from
wounds," he said from excellent recall. "What about him?"

She turned to face Christian. "He has been assigned to the staff c
General Claus von Roeth. Von Roeth's chief responsibility is to com
bat the Resistance efforts mounting throughout France. Immel work
closely with von Roeth, and carries a great deal of responsibility,
Gabrielle said, then paused for a long moment, wondering how to te
him the rest.

"And?" Christian said at length.

"Yes, the *and,*" she said, letting out a long sigh. "And I have a
opportunity to get close to Immel. To get quite close, actually. I know
can learn a great deal from him that will be vitally important to Grou
Defiance.

"I met him over a month ago," she continued. "I've seen hir
several times since, mostly at parties. He likes me. Very much,
think . . . I *know.*"

She looked up into his sharp, searching eyes. "It would be ver
easy to develop the necessary relationship."

The meaning was very clear to Christian. "No! I forbid it," h
said, angry and hurt at the thought of Gabrielle in the bed of a Ge
man. "The danger would be too great, not only from the Germans, bu
from your own countrymen as well. They'd see you as somethin
you're not. They'd hate you, and possibly try to do you harm. And I .
I couldn't think of you with him."

Gabrielle's heart and will melted at the sight of Christian's hu
expression. She could no longer fight the need to be in his arms. "Tak
me! Hold me!" she cried to him, tears beginning to flood her eyes.

He drew her close to him, and in that moment knew how much h
loved her and that he could no longer deny the fact to himself. H
tightened his arms around her and felt her surrender softly to h
strength and protection.

They held one another in silence. No words could have commun
cated better the feelings that had just passed between them.

Christian's hand made a gentle fist in her hair, and he pulled he

180

head back until her face looked up into his. "I forbid it," he said, then kissed her.

Their mouths met with the full passion of the longing that had built up in each of them over the past months.

"Make love to me, Christian," she said in a breathless whisper.

He lifted her gently in his arms and carried her across the room to the divan. For one night there would be no worries of war, no German occupation, no Resistance, and no other existence but their own. For just one night, time and the world would stand still, and nothing would matter but the love between them, this moment and their need for one another.

"Your father came directly to Marseilles after learning about Ismel," St. Jude went on. "I had never seen him so distraught and preoccupied. It was as though he carried within himself some terrible burden.

"I had been to Paris with him once before this. Our success with the businesses in Marseilles had prompted Edna-Marie and Christian to explore similar possibilities in Paris. I went with your father to talk to the sector chiefs to determine the likelihood of setting something up. My firsthand experience would save a great deal of time. I also had a black market connection in Paris that we hoped to recruit.

"During the meeting with Gabrielle, known to me only as Ariel at the time, I saw the way they looked at one another. Their feelings were plainly evident to me, though they had not yet admitted them to one another. Little things were obvious, the lingering eye contact, the way they touched and always seemed to stay close, even the way they spoke. All just innocent little things, but they told the story clearly to me.

"Later, when we were alone, I asked him with as much diplomacy as possible if strong personal feelings had developed between them.

" 'I *am* attracted to her,' your father admitted to me. 'But nothing has happened, and I will not let it,' he said.

"When I saw his face that day in Marseilles, I knew. We had become very close friends and he needed someone to talk to. When he explained Gabrielle's opportunity to gain access directly into the German Command, I immediately realized his painful predicament.

" 'I know that the opportunity is too important to let pass,' he said, 'and if it were any other person I would agree to it instantly. But I cannot with Gabrielle. I just cannot.'

"He realized that the best thing would be to remove himself from

the Paris network entirely, but he had set up those sectors and no one
knew them as intimately as he did.

" 'And what will you do?' I asked him.

"He didn't answer for a long time. Then he finally turned to me
and said, 'I have no choice. She must do it.' His pain was so evident
that it nearly moved me to tears. I embraced him and told him that we
would all be called upon to make difficult sacrifices before the Boche
would be driven from French soil.

" 'But you must take precautions for her safety,' I told him. 'You
must change her code name to one that will not denote a feminine
identity, and for the sake of her sector, you must remove her from it
altogether. Appoint a new chief and transfer anyone she may know by
more than a code name to different sectors completely. If she should be
discovered, the sector must be spared and the danger to herself reduced
by limiting her knowledge.'

"He agreed. Edna-Marie and Jan Burak came to Marseilles that
same week to review our financial situation and to inspect the port
sector. We explained Gabrielle's request, not mentioning your father's
personal involvement with her, and the plan was approved.

"But Burak was too wise to let the true extent of the situation pass
him by. He knew of our strong friendship and when we were alone
posed the question directly to me. I told him the truth, but also said
that I didn't think it wise to remove the responsibility of the Paris
sectors from your father.

"Burak deliberated for some time before finally agreeing with me.
He knew of your father's inner strength and of his immense ca
pabilities. 'Some exceptions must always be made,' he said. 'We could
always make the change if my judgment proves wrong,' he said.

"Burak did not tell Edna-Marie of the situation between Gabrielle
and your father until much later, when he was convinced that the
operation of the Paris sector would not be affected by the relationship.

"Gabrielle's code name was changed from Ariel to Galileo, and
she was given the order to develop the relationship to its fullest extent.
It was a brave and difficult thing for your father to do, but he never
avoided dangerous or difficult responsibilities. He was a rare man. A
wonderful man."

The story of her father's relationship with Gabrielle Dupuy had
touched Gabrielle deeply. She studied the picture of them standing
together. She tried to imagine the pain that he had felt, and she
thought of the pain in her mother's eyes when she had told them of
Gabrielle Dupuy.

She looked for the picture of Gabrielle and the German officer and took it from her handbag.

"We found this picture of Gabrielle Dupuy," she said, holding it out to St. Jude. "Is that Immel with her?" she asked.

St. Jude took the picture and recognized the German immediately. "Yes, that is Rudolf Immel," he said.

"Was the contact fruitful?" Danny asked.

"It proved to be invaluable, as you will learn later. But it also cast Gabrielle in a role that her countrymen took great exception to. She never once revealed to anyone the true double role she played. That wonderful selfless courage cost her her life, and your father a deep sorrow which nearly finished him after the war. It was then that I told your mother the story, in the hope that her strength and understanding would help him through it. It took enormous courage to accept that part of his past and to keep her awareness of it from him. She was wonderful, and without her love and strength to help him, your father might never have recovered from that loss."

"My mother said that his arrest as a covert collaborator also helped to spark life back into him," Michael said.

"Yes, it brought out a healing rage at the absurdity of it," St. Jude said. "It was the communists who did that, the pigs. Your father was no more a collaborator than Edna-Marie or myself or Charles De Gaulle, for that matter," he said with an indignant, angry tone.

"Exactly who brought the charges?" Michael asked.

"It was the communist Resistance group known as the Aile Rouge (the Red Wing), a part of the Franc-Tireurs et Partisans Français, the name of the official communist party's Resistance movement, which operated as a unified front across France. The man who led them, and who was responsible for the charges against your father, was Pierre Falloux, known during the Resistance as Com."

It was on another terrace in France, belonging to his lavish estate just outside of Pont du Château 240 miles to the south of Paris and nine miles east of Clermont-Ferrand, that Pierre Falloux sat in the magnificent sunshine of spring. His right hand held a fork that absently played with the remnants of the midday meal on the crystal plate in front of him. His attention was on the voice coming through the receiver of the phone in his left hand.

He listened quietly to the report that told him of the arrival of the three Americans in Paris. They had spent the night at the residence of

Edna-Marie DeBussey. Claude St. Jude and his daughter had also spent the night.

When the report concluded, Falloux placed the phone back in it cradle without comment. He sat for a moment, the fork still pushing a the debris on the plate. Then he picked up the phone again, dropped the fork, and dialed a number. He waited.

" Yes," the voice answered.

"Our friends have come to France."

"Where are they now?" Demy asked.

"Paris. At the residence of Edna-Marie DeBussey."

"Would you like us to greet them?"

Falloux thought for a brief moment. "No, not yet. They're being watched. I think we should wait to determine just how much they know. Stay available, and keep in touch with your associate. Tell him may have another assignment for the two of you shortly."

"I'll contact him," Demy said.

"I'll let you know if I need you," Falloux said, then replaced the phone.

That the Americans were now in France did not mean much in itself. They might know nothing at all. Yet there was something disturbing in the fact that they had come. He had underestimated their determination. It would be important to learn more about them, so as to avoid misjudging them a second time.

He picked up the phone again and dialed a number. His hand again returned to the fork as he waited for the connection.

"Yes, Ernest Rive, please," he said to the voice answering the line

Ernest Rive was an old friend of Falloux's who was highly ranked in the Direction de la Surveillance du Territoire (DST), the counter espionage force of France, concerned generally with surveillance a points of entry to keep running tabs on undesirables entering or leaving France.

"Hello, Rive speaking."

"Ernest, this is Pierre Falloux. How are you, my friend?"

There was a moment of silence on the line. Rive was a little surprised to be hearing from Falloux. This "old friend" had not contacted him for quite some time, and as he remembered, their last conversation had ended in a storm of disagreement over something that was not important enough to immediately recall.

"I'm fine," Rive said, somewhat cautiously. "What can I do for you?"

"I need some information, Ernest," Falloux began.

What else would it be? Rive thought to himself. Falloux had done him some favors in the past, and he was not shy about calling them in. "How can I help you?" he asked.

"I need information rather quickly on three Americans who have just entered France."

"What are their names? I will check our files."

"No, no. They will not appear in your files. To my knowledge, they are not criminals or fugitives."

"Then I can't help you," Rive said, puzzled. Falloux was aware that the type of information he wanted was not covered by DST operations, unless these people warranted being watched. Falloux also had his contacts within the Deuxième Bureau, who would be more likely to help him. Why hadn't he called them? he wondered.

"I know that you *can* help me, Ernest," Falloux said. "You know the people who can get such information."

"So do you. Why not contact them directly?" Rive countered.

"Because I have very important reasons for wanting the inquiry to be kept completely secret and disconnected from me," Falloux explained.

Ah, the rub, Rive thought. "This must be very important to you, then," he said, recognizing his sudden unexpected advantage. It was rare to get one with Falloux.

"Yes, extremely important," Falloux said. He picked up on Rive's little game immediately. He would play along and give the fool his tiny moment of victory. "Important enough . . . shall we say . . . to remove all obligations?" he threw in for good measure. He could almost feel Rive smiling.

"Then I think that I may be able to help you after all. What are their names?" Rive asked.

Falloux dictated the names, along with sufficient information to eliminate the possibility of a trace on the wrong person with the same name.

"You seem to know something about them already," Rive commented.

"I need to know a great deal more. Their backgrounds, experiences, capabilities. You understand. As complete a dossier as possible."

"Yes, I understand. And this will, of course, remove *all* obligations," Rive said as a statement, not a question.

"Completely," Falloux confirmed. He waited a moment, then added his proviso. "That is, as long as my name cannot be connected to the inquiry. That is of paramount importance."

"I'll take care of it," Rive assured him.

"As soon as possible, then?"

"I'll call you when I have your information," Rive said.

"It was good talking to you, Ernest. I always have admired you fo your efficiency and discretion. I'll await your call."

Falloux placed the receiver down in its cradle. He would have to take into account the risk of using Rive. This was a double game tha he was being forced to play by the presence of these Americans. Hi situation seemed suddenly more tenuous by their involvement.

Pierre Falloux, with all his power and influence, had abruptly become an island in the midst of his dilemma.

Chapter 22

THE itinerary, as laid out by Claude St. Jude, called for leaving Paris the following morning on the first high-speed train to Clermont-Ferrand, where a meeting would be held with the Collard brothers a their farm. Additional former members of Group Defiance would be there as well, to help reconstruct the events of the past.

A second meeting was scheduled to be held with several former ranking members of the Aile Rouge, including Pierre Falloux. The meeting would be held at Falloux's estate in Pont du Château.

From Clermont-Ferrand, they would continue by train to Arles. on the northern edge of the Ile de la Camargue. They would then travel by car to the *manade* of St. Jude, just north of Saintes-Maries de-la-Mer, the capital of the Camargue. They would arrive in time for the holiday of the Pentecost and the feast of Saint Mary Jacobe, the most important and jubilant celebration of the year for the Camarguais.

Edna-Marie would rejoin them in a day or two to again pick up the story of the war years.

The itinerary beyond that point was left open, depending upon what was learned from the meetings, and upon which elements the young Americans wanted to pursue.

Michael, Danny, and Gabrielle did get to spend some time seeing Paris following the afternoon story session. Nicole quickly appointed herself tour guide and did a most splendid job in the short time availble. They got to see most of the important sights and capped the day with fine wine and a good Parisienne dinner on the Place du Tertre in the heart of the artsy Montmartre quarter.

Nicole proved to be as warm and charming as she was beautiful. There was no hiding the attraction she had to Michael, just as there was no hiding the fact that shyness was not a word one would choose in describing the daughter of Claude St. Jude. She had been educated at the finest schools in Europe and had studied for two years in the United States. She was intelligent and spirited and not afraid to go after the things she wanted out of life.

They returned to the lavish De Bussey residence a little spent from the combined effects of their tour, the previous night's story session, and the jet lag rapidly catching up to them. Sleep was the important need now as the following day would be a long one and would start very early.

Edna-Marie smiled with a quiet satisfaction as she watched Michael and Nicole climbing the marble staircase to their rooms, their hands touching lightly. They were fortunate to be young with so much life ahead of them, she thought, and then wondered where all the years had gone. Seeing the grown children of her two friends made her feel suddenly old—and sad that one of them was now gone. It was as though an invisible hand had come from the past to snatch Christian Gladieux away. The three of them had survived so much together. It seemed very unfair for it to end this way for one of them. She shook her head slowly and wiped away the start of a tear. Some things just never ended.

It was almost 8:00 A.M. when Michael and Danny went to breakfast in the dining car of the high-speed train flashing southward from Paris. Both Gabrielle and Nicole chose to pass on the early meal in favor of some additional sleep. Claude St. Jude told the two young Americans to go ahead and that he would join them shortly.

They ordered a large pot of coffee and a tray of hot croissants. They smeared the croissants with fruit preserves, eating as they talked.

"So, what do you think?" Danny asked.

Michael shook his head as he swallowed some of the hot coffee. "It's too early. We don't know enough about the collaborator yet, other than that he was called Z by the Germans and Circus by René Pezet. He hardly fits into any of the background we've been given so far."

Michael absently poked the tip of the croissant with the knife, then put both down on the plate in front of him. "Dan, there's something that I want to tell you. I don't think that it would be a good idea for Gabby to hear any of it, and stop me fast if you see St. Jude coming. This is probably something that I shouldn't be telling you, but I'm having trouble sorting a few things out, and I need your help. know that you'll never let what I tell you leave this table."

"You've got it. Shoot," Danny said, his face serious, waiting.

"During my last two tours in Nam, I worked as a part of a very small but elite unit involved in Special Services. Many of our duties were of a nonmilitary nature and I can't tell you much about the people I worked for, except that they operated independently from Command. I don't know who our orders originated from, but all our assignments came to us through 'coordinators.' My coordinator was a man named Tripper. Those above him, from whom he drew his orders were referred to as the 'group.' It was never clear to us then who composed this group, whether it was a military command or the Pentagon or whatever.

"Of course, I learned later that these people were not military, or even government. Beyond that, it wasn't meant for anyone to know But that's not the point. The point is that these people are interested in what happened to my father, and it has raised a number of questions in my mind."

"First off," Danny interrupted, "how do you know that they're interested? I assume that they've contacted you?" he asked.

"They didn't come to me, exactly, because they knew that I didn't want any more to do with them."

"Wait a minute. You're leaving some things out and creating gaps that I can't quite cross," Danny said.

"It's a very long story that we don't have time to get into now Let's just say that I worked for them body and soul while I was in Nam and then once again about six years ago. I made it plain that I wasn't interested in working for them ever again. For that reason, they knew that a direct approach to me would be rejected. They were very clever in the way they handled it, and I never saw it coming—until we walked into Omega Enterprises. You see, Bill Pheagan was my coordinator in Nam."

"Are you sure he's still involved with this group?" Danny asked.

"Yeah, we talked about it after you left for your date with that bomb at Bonaventure."

"That explains your strange reaction to meeting Pheagan that day."

"Exactly. We've spoken a few times privately since," Michael said "I couldn't understand their interest in my father's death until the

188

background on the pendant was given to us. And I don't think that we've been given the whole story, either. But what I am sure of is that they want the man who originally possessed the pendant. Pheagan told me that much."

Danny's mind worked quickly putting together certain facts. "Yeah, I see it now. Bob Caldwell," he said, nodding. "He maneuvered us right to Pheagan and your group, and that was probably how they managed to get their hands on the pendant, too."

"You're right, but Caldwell doesn't matter here. He did his job well, and being a part of the group isn't a bad thing. What is important is finding out why they want this pendant holder so badly, and how their interest affects us. It's possible that we might not be after a collaborator at all," Michael said.

"Now wait a minute. Based on what Pheagan has told us, the collaborator and the pendant holder could be the same man. Did he tell you otherwise?"

"He said that it was possible that the pendant holder and the collaborator were the same person. But he didn't seem too sure to me. My feeling was that we're dealing with two separate identities here."

"If you're right and Pheagan wants the pendant holder, then that brings us back to the Salamandra. Do you think that it's still in existence?"

"I don't know. The pendant holder could just be a loose end that needs tying up," Michael said.

"Or the organization does still exist, and this guy is in real trouble because of the threat of exposure not only to himself but to the organization as well," Danny surmised.

"That's right. Somehow, my father got the goods on this guy through a contact, or an informer, and threatened to blow his association with the Salamandra through his book about it."

"Then what I think you're saying is that this whole collaborator chase could be wasted time on our part," Danny said.

"No, not wasted. Circus and the other code names are still a part of this, somehow. I think that somewhere in this mess is the key to the identity of my father's contact. That should be our real interest. If we find him, then we get everything that my father knew, and we get to see who was really behind the killing," Michael said.

"And then we change directions and go for him?"

"Yes. But before we run off at a sprint, I press Pheagan for some answers—or he doesn't get our information. In the meantime, the only avenue we have to pursue is the one we're on, trying to find a collaborator, hoping that we'll be able to recognize the lead to my father's contact when it comes."

"And the collaborator? What if we find him?" Danny asked.

"That depends on what we find. If he wasn't involved in my father's death in any way, then I'm not interested in him. My job isn't to extract justice for what he did during the war. There are enough people ready to do that, like St. Jude and his friends. I only want to find him to clear Dad's name of that charge. If he was involved in my father's death, then that's another matter. Then he is my business, and I'll take care of it."

Danny looked up and saw St. Jude approaching the table. "Cut it St. Jude is on his way in."

The conversation ceased abruptly.

"Sit down," Danny said. "The coffee and the croissants are still hot."

St. Jude slid into the seat beside Michael. Danny poured him a cup of coffee, and St. Jude attacked one of the rolls.

"We should be in Clermont-Ferrand within the hour," he said as he chewed.

"You said that we'll be meeting the Collard brothers?" Michael asked.

"Yes, Jacques and Lucien. They own a farm just outside of Clermont-Ferrand. There will be others as well. I'm not sure how many Perhaps five or six."

St. Jude smeared a dab of preserves on the remaining wedge of croissant and stuffed it into his mouth.

"Savon and Leveque will be there, I'm sure. They never miss an opportunity to talk of old times and to drink the Collards' wine. The Collard brothers make magnificent wine and should have gone into the business long ago. I can remember more than one secret meeting in their wine cellar that ended when our wits left us because of it." St. Jude finished chewing, grabbed another roll, and applied preserves to its tip.

"I make it sound as though we had great fun," he said with a serious expression. "And perhaps I shouldn't. Yes, we had fun sometimes. We had to, or go completely mad from the constant fear and pressure. It is difficult for someone like yourselves, who have never lived through an occupation, to understand what life was like in those times.

"It's not a pretty story, like the myth of the Resistance which has become history. Too few of us are willing to recognize the truth and dmit to the shame that was also a part of the real story. Do not get me wrong. The people of France, unlike its government, did not accept Nazi rule. The Resistance was a wonderful effort of courage and suffering for which every Frenchman has the right to be proud. But there were other truths that must also be admitted. Vichy's collaboration was fact; the actions of our own police in their ruthless attempts to smash the Resistance were fact; and our treatment and surrender of Jews, especially non-French Jews, was fact. It goes on.

"France was a pool of normal people, with normal fears and normal amounts of courage, and to pass judgment on how France and its people behaved can only really be done by ourselves. It is our pride, and our shame, that we must live with.

"It is impossible to try to understand both sides of the situation without being unfair to either one," the Frenchman continued. "You must serve one side or the other. History honors only the winning side, because it is written by the winner. In winning, the myth of the Resistance made all Frenchmen feel good and proud. The conspiracy of silence was forgotten, the double lie, then and now, ignored. Had the war gone the other way, the collaborators would have been the heroes, and we the criminals.

"When you talk with the others and hear their stories, you must keep in mind that these are stories that have been told a hundred times. Little events grow with each telling, until they are major reasons for our winning the war. But I think that you both have the wisdom and the understanding to come away with the true picture. Edna-Marie and I will always tell you truth, just as it happened. The Collards, too, are notoriously honest men, as you will see."

"Did you ever suspect anyone of being Z?" Michael asked.

"I've thought about that often." St. Jude replied with a pensive look in his eyes. "I once suspected Jan Burak. Once Pointer was revealed and had been disposed of, we underwent massive changes. We had to. Our networks were decimated by his treachery, almost to the point of completely destroying Group Defiance. It had to be someone near the top who had information on the overall network. The results of Z's betrayals were too devastating, often taking complete sectors right from the top on down to the small fish. Only breaks at the top could do that. A break anywhere else could spread only downward, and with limited results. The betrayals were too complete."

"You said 'once' suspected. Did your opinion change?" Danny asked.

"Well, yes, it had to. Jan Burak was killed by the Germans, and the betrayals continued until the war neared its end. Then they stopped completely and suddenly.

"We racked our brains, set traps that should have revealed an identity, but they never worked. Z was much too smart. And he nearly got us all on more than one occasion. I was betrayed and caught twice I escaped both times, once nearly being killed. Your father helped save me both times. Edna-Marie was betrayed and captured, as was your father. But through much luck, and the aid of friends we never suspected of providing help, your father and Edna-Marie also escaped. At one point, the three of us ran like a pack of rabbits with the Germans behind us constantly. We managed to elude them by the narrowest of margins. I am sure that if his treachery had lasted much longer, we too would have fallen victim to him."

"And you don't know why he suddenly stopped?" Danny asked.

St. Jude shook his head. "Perhaps he knew that the war was lost for Germany, and sought to protect himself."

"Or he wasn't as high up as you thought, and his source of information dried up," Danny said.

St. Jude raised his eyebrows and nodded. "A possibility. But whatever our chances of learning his identity back then, they are surely reduced now by the cover of time."

"René Pezet learned the identity," Michael said.

"Yes, little Pezet did. And he tried to give it to us. If only we knew what he meant."

The farm of Jacques and Lucien Collard had been in their family for almost a hundred years. The old stone house that had been their home as children was now lived in by Jacques, the eldest brother, and his wife. A second stone house stood sixty feet away, and was the residence of Lucien, his wife, and his mother-in-law.

The farm had been all they ever really loved and wanted in life. It supported them adequately and allowed them the marvelous sense of independence held so dear by so many Frenchmen. They lovingly and knowingly tended their fields, growing their crops and raising enough cows, pigs, and chickens to supply their own needs. Their income from the sale of their crops was modest but sufficient.

Guests were always welcome. The kitchen table of Jacques Collard was spread with a dozen bottles of wine, loaves of bread, plates of cheese, and enough glasses to accommodate additional neighbors, who often dropped in when interesting people came to visit the brothers The presence of Claude St. Jude—the noted Resistance hero Ca-

192

nargue—and others from Group Defiance would have been enough to
»ring out the curious; but the coming of the three Americans—the
children of Christian Gladieux—was like a visit by royalty. The kitchen
vas packed with people standing around the table at which the Re-
istance heroes and the Americans sat.

The greeting upon their arrival had been a warm one. Embraces
nd kisses and even tears welcomed them.

Word of Christian's death had spread quickly, and everyone was
villing to help his children in any way that they could. When the
»xcitement of their arrival had subsided, they all settled around the
able to glasses of wine, toasted their fallen comrade, and got down to
he business of discussing ways in which they could help. The conversa-
ion began with general comments about the communists during the
Resistance.

Jacques Collard was a stocky, rugged-looking man with a com-
»letely bald head. He was inherently intelligent, possessing a sur-
»risingly keen insight into the characters of people. His alert blue eyes
nad a quality which hinted unmistakably at the wisdom behind them.
_ike Claude St. Jude and Edna-Marie DeBussey, he had formed an
mmediate, favorable impression of his American guests.

"There was always a great rivalry among Resistance groups,"
acques Collard said. "Especially between the communists and non-
ommunists. We never trusted one another. They, of course, had a
'ertain advantage, in that they had experience in operating as an un-
1erground before the war. But we all gained that experience as time
vent on, often at the expense of severe lessons. Our advantage over
hem was that we had a much more efficient network of communica-
ion. They had few radios, and often had difficulty in delivering their
nformation to the appropriate parties. They also served the interests of
Russia primarily, which for a long time was engaged in an intense life-
nd-death struggle. We, on the other hand, had many more radios,
hough they never seemed to be enough. But we contacted England
1irectly with our information. We worked for the British, actually, not
De Gaulle. The British had prior claim to what we learned.

"At first the communists took a rather calm posture," Collard con-
inued, his speech accentuated by frequent hand gestures. "But they
:hanged their style quite suddenly when Russia was invaded. You must
inderstand that before Russia was invaded they wanted to do nothing
o endanger the fragile agreement between Russia and Germany by
vhich they mutually agreed not to attack one another. That was vitally
mportant to Russia, who was playing for time. Acts of violence against

193

the Germans by communist groups would have put a great deal o stress on that situation.

"When Germany finally invaded Russia in June of 1941, the com munists became a guerrilla force almost overnight. Their theory wa that every additional German soldier and tank that had to remain ir France to help keep order was one less that invaded Russia. They alsc did not trust the British as we did, so until it became evident that the allies were to play a vital role in the survival of their Mother Russia they were unwilling to share what they learned. They were alway involved in a double game. They wanted to win the war and for Franc to be liberated, but they were equally interested in getting as mucl control as possible in the France that would emerge from the war. The called for drastic purges after the Liberation to create a vacuum which they hoped to fill. They were interested in removing as many of the politically elite as possible—of which they considered your father to be one."

"Are you saying that my father had political ambitions?" Michae asked.

"You must understand," Collard went on, "that France had los almost its entire prewar government. Those with experience whc served in Vichy would be lost to the future of France. The new politica wave would come from its heroes. Your father had great potential though I do not know if it was his ambition. But knowing him, and hi love for France, I doubt that the call to fill the country's need woulc have gone unheeded.

"They singled him out, realizing his potential, and used our unfor tunate circumstance of the traitor Z to discredit him, casting a cloud o doubt over him that destroyed his chances before they could be born."

"Wasn't the political motivation of the charges recognized then?" Michael asked.

"Certainly," St. Jude replied. "The charges were preposterous Their evidence was so weak that it was an embarrassment to them. Bu they did not have to win to achieve their objective. They succeeded ir naming him, and in casting doubt on him. We who knew him wer never suspicious, but to the rest of France, which had gone crazy anc hatefully looked to punish, it was enough to cause doubt, despite the success of his defense. It was a clear victory to them."

"And they never went after Edna-Marie or you?" Gabrielle asked

"Well, in those days, a woman in politics was not threatening despite her tremendous leadership of Group Defiance. And I was fron the Camargue. If you know anything about Frenchmen at all, you wil understand that the Camarguais are not political people. We despise bureaucracy in any form. We are fiercely independent and have a long history of opposing government in general. But your father was a man who could have achieved any goal in politics that he desired. *He* was their threat as far as Group Defiance was concerned."

"You make it sound as though they never believed the charges they brought against him," Michael said.

"I don't think they did," Jacques Collard said with conviction.

"Then why did they kill him?" Gabrielle asked bitterly.

"That is a question I cannot answer," Jacques replied.

"I think it would help our friends," St. Jude said, "if we could fill them in on the details of our efforts against the Germans. Edna-Marie and I have begun, and have described the birth of Group Defiance, and the establishment of the early sectors up to the arrival of Pointer.

"I think that what we need to do, without giving every little detail, is describe the chain of significant events that affected Group Defiance, and which involve the charges against Christian. By following a reasonably accurate chronological order of events leading up to the betrayals by Z, perhaps we can uncover a clue to his identity."

"After all these years?" Lucien Collard said. "That will be impossible."

"Perhaps not," Michael said calmly. "I'm sure that, with the exception of Edna-Marie and Claude, you people are unaware of the fact that my father knew who the collaborator was."

The sound of astonished voices told Michael that he was correct.

"We think he was killed because of that knowledge and that he learned it here in France. If he was able to learn that identity after all these years, then we're certain that we can, too."

"When was he here? Who did he see?" Lucien Collard asked.

"He came twice, in July and again in November of last year. We don't know who he talked to, but we feel certain that he obtained his information from someone," Michael replied.

"Why would he not come to us for help?" Jacques Collard asked, deeply puzzled.

"We can't answer that," Michael said.

The room was alive with excitement from the news that Michael had just given them.

"Please, please," St. Jude said, banging his glass on the table to restore order. "We can be of little help behaving like this."

The voices in the room calmed, and St. Jude called on Jacques Collard, who had been the head of the Clermont-Ferrand sector, to begin the story of the occupation.

St. Jude judiciously kept their stories to the point of time in question, so as not to overload the Americans with information. "The story must progress as it actually occurred in time, to help our friends," he frequently reminded the others, who often jumped great expanses of time in their excited recollections.

It was early afternoon when the meeting broke up. St. Jude, sensing Michael's impatience at the slow development of facts, tried to ease his disappointment. "You must understand, Michael, that to get a complete picture of what happened in those days, you must learn the entire story. Yet, to heap it upon you all at one time and out of sequence would serve only to confuse you and make your job impossible," he said.

"I understand, Claude. Honestly, I do. But I just can't help being impatient. We haven't even touched upon Z yet."

"I know. But what is more important is that you have begun to understand the man who was your father. You can sense the effort and devotion he put into our struggle. It demonstrates the absurdity that he was the collaborator. Take heart. The story will open up soon. Tonight you meet with members of the Red Wing and Pierre Falloux at his estate in Pont du Château. It is less than fifteen kilometers from here. The information you need will begin with them."

The words of Claude St. Jude did little to comfort Michael. When everyone had left, he excused himself to walk for awhile in order to sort through the flood of seemingly disconnected facts filling his head. He had gone no more than a few hundred yards when Danny called out to catch his attention. Michael turned to see his brother-in-law trailing behind him along the low stone wall separating the fields of the Collard farm.

"Hope you don't mind company," Danny said, catching up to him.

"Not at all. I just needed to get out to take a little walk."

The two men walked for a few moments before Danny turned to Michael. "You know, it suddenly dawned on me when we were in the house that your feelings are probably right. For some reason, the story you told me about your last meeting with Father Piela popped into my head. Your father seemed to have realized who the collaborator was back then. And that was when? Around Lent?" Danny asked.

"Yes, that's what Father Piela said," Michael replied.

"That was months before he came over for the first time. I wonder why he didn't contact any of his old Resistance buddies with the news of his discovery?"

"Maybe he wasn't really sure of his facts," Michael replied.

196

"And maybe he didn't come over here for the collaborator at all," Danny said. "Maybe he came solely for the information pertaining to the Salamandra."

"You're forgetting the Daytimers. Circus is mentioned specifically, along with the other code names. They're all Resistance-related," Michael said.

"Yes, that's true. And I believe that he *did* confirm his suspicions while he was here. But I've thought about what you said on the train this morning. We might *not* be after a collaborator. And what bothers me is that I can't see how we're going to recognize the link between your father's contact and this whole story that we're being presented with."

"The same thing has been bothering me. He meant something by these code names, or he wouldn't have used them. But we do have one thing going for us. We're here, and whoever it is who was so concerned about what my father knew doesn't have the slightest idea of how much we really know. Enough bluff and bravado on our part might just force him into the open to make a move on us. I think that we'll find out fast enough when we've come close to something."

The estate of Pierre Falloux at Pont du Château was imposing in its size and elegance. The three Americans had not been prepared for this at all. Knowing that Falloux was a communist had precluded such imaginings of wealth.

Michael noted as they drove through the large wrought-iron gateway that the estate had the appearance of a defensible compound. An attendant at the gate was armed with an automatic weapon. The walls surrounding the property were topped with an electronic intruder-detection system neatly worked along the uppermost surface. He noticed personnel at various points along the wall patrolling the perimeter, accompanied by trained attack dogs. There were trees spaced in pairs at regular intervals all along the perimeter, except at the corners, where they were clustered in groups of about six or seven. The house itself was huge and sat well back into the property, close to one of the far corners. It was situated at an angle, which Michael noticed corresponded closely to the irregular angle of the rear property line and wall. To the right of the house sat several connected structures that appeared to be garages and security personnel quarters. The kennels were, no doubt, situated behind these.

The car pulled up the long arcing driveway and stopped in front of the house. Michael could hear the sounds of dogs emanating from behind the garages. He had been right about the placement of the kennels. From the sounds, there had to be at least six to eight dogs in addition to those out on patrol.

Michael turned back to the rented car and Claude St. Jude, who remained behind the wheel. "Aren't you coming in?" Michael asked.

"St. Jude set foot in the house of Pierre Falloux?" Jacques Collard said from beside Michael. "I don't think so. If ever a hatred existed between two men, it is between these two."

Michael bent down to the passenger's window and looked into the car at St. Jude. "Is this true? You won't come in?" he asked.

"You don't need me to learn what you must learn," St. Jude said.

"But this meeting might take some time," Michael said.

"If I know Falloux, it will not last a moment longer than it has to. If this were not your first meeting with him, I would go in with you, just to annoy him. But you must understand that we truly dislike one another. My presence now would perhaps limit his willingness to talk to you. I will have my satisfaction from his knowing that I am insulting his hospitality. Jacques and Lucien know all his stories and tricks. You are in good hands. When you come out, I will help you sort the truth from the lies. But remember, it was this man who inspired the charges of collaboration against your father after the war."

Michael turned back to the house, looking at it as though it held an enemy that he had long wanted to fight. He turned to Danny, who gave a slight nod.

The three Americans and the Collard brothers ascended the stairs to the door of the huge house. Nicole had stayed behind at the Collard home because there wasn't room in the car. St. Jude would never have let her enter Falloux's home, anyway, to be raped by his eyes.

They were met at the door and led through the house to a large terrace behind the house. A large swimming pool lay just beyond the terrace. Three men sat at a table awaiting them. One man, his head neatly bald down the middle, sat with an air of icy confidence about him. He was a short, squat man, impeccably dressed in very expensive clothing. He glanced at his watch as the five guests approached.

"Ten minutes late," he said, rising to his feet to greet them. "That scoundrel St. Jude must have driven from Clermont-Ferrand. He knows that I detest the lack of punctuality and made you late on purpose. It's not your fault," Pierre Falloux said, extending his hand to his guests.

Falloux introduced the two men with him. They were former ranking members in the Aile Rouge.

Jacques Collard made the introductions of the Americans.

198

Falloux took a moment to exchange glances with Michael. Then he quickly settled his guests and ordered wine for everyone.

Michael could see instantly that Falloux was a man accustomed to running things. He didn't talk to his help, he talked *at* them.

"Tell me," Falloux began, directing himself to Jacques Collard. "St. Jude refused to come into my house, didn't he? He thinks that it will bother me," he said before Collard could reply.

He summoned one of his servants. "Bring a glass of wine out to the car. If he refuses it, pour it out on the ground and return here," he ordered. Pierre Falloux was not to be outdone.

"My friends here say that you wished to talk to members of the Aile Rouge. What is it you wish to talk about?"

Michael was amused by Falloux's brusqueness. He had been here hardly a minute and the man was already annoying.

"We've come to talk to you about my father," Michael said in slow, perfect French. "I understand that it was the Aile Rouge that made the accusation that he was a covert collaborator during the war. We'd like to learn what it was that made you believe that about him."

"What it was? What it was?" Falloux said in a loud, mocking tone. "Why, my young man, it was simply that your father was guilty of collaboration with the Boche."

Michael felt a hot rush of anger and fought back an urge to strike back immediately. Something inside told him that he was being tested.

"Monsieur Falloux, we are only interested in facts, not opinions. The fact is that he was declared innocent in a court of justice, with both sides being presented."

"Well then, if the fact is that he was innocent, I can see no reason for this meeting," Falloux shot back.

"Monsieur Falloux, I'm not leaving until I drink your wine and hear your side of the story," Michael said calmly. "We've come here to talk, not to argue. My father was murdered because of the belief that he collaborated with the Germans. Your statement that he *was* guilty is not enough of an answer to our question. You say that he was guilty; we would like to hear the evidence."

"It would change nothing," Falloux said. "If I could prove to you that he was guilty, would that make you feel better? If you learned positively that he was not guilty, would that put your mind at rest? There is no winning in this. It is better that you go on believing that he was innocent, and I that he was guilty."

"That's not enough," Gabrielle spoke up, unable to sit back and listen to Falloux's evasion. "If you believe that he was guilty, then you must be willing to defend your position. We're not here to attack you or to attempt to change your mind. We simply want the facts that made you believe him to be a collaborator. You're right. It won't change a thing. It won't bring our father back, and it won't change your mind, or ours. But it might give us pieces to a puzzle that will help us find the real collaborator."

"My dear woman, the real collaborator is dead," Falloux said, unyielding.

"Have you no respect for the love that these children have for their dead father?" Lucien Collard asked. "What would it cost you? An hour of your time? A piece of your memory? These children have lived through the death of their father, killed for a crime that the courts of France said he did not commit. Don't mock their love and their sorrow by this cold behavior. Help them. Answer their questions with honesty and the conviction of what you believe to be truth," he said in a scolding tone.

Michael was surprised by the sudden words of Lucien Collard. Since meeting him, he had hardly heard the man say more than a few sentences.

Falloux remained silent for a long moment, then he looked at Gabrielle. "Madame Glady-Preston, forgive me." He looked from Danny to Michael. "Yes, I will tell you what I know."

"Thank you, Monsieur Falloux," Michael said. "Now, if you could, would you tell us what led you to believe that my father was the collaborator known to the Germans as Z?"

Falloux began to describe those compromising events. The first was an incident involving a time when desperate members of his Resistance group approached Group Defiance for assistance. They had gathered conclusive evidence that Germany was about to invade Russia. Rumors to that effect had been picked up by many Resistance groups across France. But the communist groups had managed to gather hard data to back up the rumor. They had even obtained the invasion code name, Barbarossa, and the target date set for June 22, 1941. They urgently needed to transmit the information to Russia, but were without radios. The only course left open was to try to get the information to Russia through Britain.

The rumors previous to this had never been taken seriously. It was the general feeling that an invasion of England would be the next major step taken by Hitler. It was foolishness to invite a two-front war. But the Aile Rouge possessed the evidence to prove that it would happen. The decision was made to help the communists, using the newly established radio in Vichy, going by the call letters CAT.

The arrangements were made with the Aile Rouge, who sent three of their members to the secret radio location. They gave the details to the Defiance radio operators, who coded it and began transmitting. There were seven people involved that day, four from Group Defiance. One of them was Christian Gladieux, who had made the final decision to use the CAT radio.

In the middle of the transmission, the power was suddenly cut. The Vichy police, with the help of Gestapo advisers, were onto the operation. The significance of the power cut was plain to the Defiance people. The police were trying to locate the radio's position. By cutting power to sections of the city at a time, they could confirm the section in which the radio was operating by the sudden cessation of transmission, which they monitored. They then selectively restored power to smaller sections until the transmissions commenced, then began a thorough search, utilizing the directional homing devices given to them by the Nazis.

The people in that room knew precisely what they were up against, and worked feverishly to complete the transmission. Expecting the imminent location of their position, Christian gathered all the coded messages, logs, code books, and other raw data yet to be sent, and made an attempt to escape the tightening search pattern. Not long after he left, the door splintered open as the final code was sent off. The entire group, with the exception of Christian, was taken. All were later shot in prison. This event, in itself, only raised slight suspicion. But Falloux went on.

Another event was a rather spectacular escape from the low-security prison at Evaux-les-Bains in the Massif Central. It was really nothing more than a fortified hotel used to temporarily house prisoners. On that occasion, six members of Group Defiance had been captured, including Edna-Marie DeBussey and Christian. The communists considered it quite suspicious that only Christian was taken to Evaux-les-Bains, while the others were held under tight security. He somehow managed to escape, completely undetected, simply vanishing from custody. The others also managed to escape a day later, but only because of the timely help of patriotic members of the police force where they were being held.

A third escape was described, in which Christian and three other Group Defiance members were suddenly boxed in at a rail station. This was after the occupation of the free zone. The Germans had been tipped off and were waiting for them. Again, only Christian escaped.

By this time, the communists were highly suspicious of his good luck. They began to pay close attention to his whereabouts. When the betrayals of Z began, they noticed close correlations to his being near major catastrophes. Christian was in the north when the Paris sectors of Group Defiance were smashed. When Marseilles went down for the second time, he was there, just managing to escape again with Edna-Marie and St. Jude. The three of them began a frantic pattern of close escapes, barely getting away with their lives. The communists claimed that the Germans always knew where they were, because Christian had kept them informed. They also said that sectors of Group Defiance were falling regularly during this time. They claimed that Christian was leaving his information behind during the escapes. The Nazis would get their information, crush the mentioned patrols, then chase them again, until the next message was dropped.

Falloux described one incident in which the forgery section in Paris was betrayed. The Nazis obtained vital codes and identities, which had devastating effects on Group Defiance. This, too, was just after Christian had been there.

And lastly, the communists brought up the actions of Christian after the Liberation of Paris, in which he went on endless missions, deep behind German lines. They claimed that he was seeking to escape France, but was refused help by the Nazis.

The three Americans listened intently to the story related by Pierre Falloux. Occasionally facts were added or corrected by his two friends in attendance, who seemed to be there just for show.

Michael scratched frequent notes as Falloux talked, marking certain areas that he would question St. Jude about later.

They had stayed outside on the terrace as the darkness set in. Michael could not help noticing how, in the darkness, the distinct features of Falloux faded, until it was difficult to see what he really looked like. The darkness, Michael thought, can change so much when the mind must begin to fill in parts that the eye can no longer see. Handsome features can become ugly; ugliness beauty. The mind has a mysterious eye.

The meeting was concluded, and everyone began to file into the well-lit house. Michael and Danny lagged behind with Falloux.

"Are you still a member of Firewatch?" Michael asked, well out of earshot of the others.

Falloux stopped and looked into the icy cool eyes of Michael. He did not answer for a moment. The young American was clever, he thought. And he was no fool. "No, I have not been a part of Firewatch for many years. I no longer have the energy for such enthusiasm. How did you know that I had been a member of Firewatch?" he asked.

Michael smiled without answering. "Did you have anything to do with my father's death?" he asked.

Falloux hesitated again. "I gave up witch hunting soon after the war, though I still cheer the hunters when they have success. No, I had nothing to do with the death of your father, and I don't like the fact that you have even asked the question."

Again Michael did not comment, and he walked into the light coming through the open French doors. Falloux and Danny followed him closely. Then Michael stopped again and turned to Falloux.

"Have you ever seen this before?" Michael asked, pulling the pendant from beneath his shirt and extending it toward Falloux as far as the chain around his neck would permit.

Pierre Falloux reached calmly for the pendant. "What is that? Let me have a look at it," he said coolly, taking it in his hand and examining it. "No. I've never seen it before," he said nonchalantly, letting it fall back to Michael's chest.

"I thought that perhaps you had. It's a very rare item, you know, with a very interesting history."

Falloux stared at Michael blankly, as though totally missing the point. But beneath the cool exterior was a live wire tapping every nerve in his body.

"Thank you, Monsieur Falloux. You've been very helpful. I hope that you will consent to see us again sometime if we should need your help," Michael said.

"Perhaps, if it can be arranged," Falloux returned.

Falloux watched as the three Americans and the Collard brothers were led from the house. When they had gone from view, he closed his eyes and put his left hand to his forehead, his thumb and fingers gently rubbing his temples. He blew out a long breath.

He had hoped it wouldn't get this far, that the pendant would simply melt away in some evidence drawer somewhere. But now, with it out in the open, his battle for survival would continue. Indeed, he was an island now, surrounded by those who would hunt him, and by those who would judge his ability to survive this unexpected test. He could turn nowhere for help, and if the battle became pitched enough, or if the outcome fell under the slightest doubt, the "others" would demand that his oath of death be honored.

He had misjudged the family of Christian Gladieux. But before he could "deal" with them, he had to determine just how much was bluff on their part, and how much they really knew.

"Have you heard from Gladieux yet?" the voice of Horatio asked over the Omega-David line.

"Yes, he called in shortly before boarding a train for Clermont-

Ferrand," Pheagan replied. "By now he'll have met with former members of Group Defiance, and also with former representatives of a communist group that called itself the Aile Rouge—the Red Wing. This is the group that originally brought the charges of collaboration against Gladieux in 1945. The leader of the group back then was a man named Pierre Falloux. We probably ought to run a quick book on him to see if it gets us anything. Mike has also met with St. Jude and Madame DeBussey and established that Leopard was the code name of an agent who was killed in 1942. His real name was Paul Romenay. According to Madame DeBussey, there was no doubt that he died, so there must be some other meaning to it. Leopard must not have been Christian's contact. They also learned that the word 'Circus' was a part of a radio transmission made by the agent René Pezet, code name Albatross, who had discovered the identity of the real collaborator, known to the Nazis as Z. Pezet was killed making the transmission, and it was never clear whether that was his entire message or not. In any event, the transmission was extremely weak and didn't carry to England, so there's no confirmation of its content. Unfortunately, whatever he meant by it was never understood."

"Perhaps we had better run it by the British ourselves to see whether or not it was received," Horatio suggested.

"Okay. It won't hurt to double-check. Has Intelligence Central had any luck with the code names Leopard and Circus?" Pheagan asked.

"No, but I think we should pursue this Paul Romenay. Perhaps there was something about this man, known only to Gladieux, that holds the true significance of his using the code name. It's worth a try. If we get enough information, we may hit upon something later by cross-reference."

"What have you found on the Swiss account and the pendant?" Pheagan asked.

"The paper trail on the account is staggering. We've begun establishing an association matrix to see if any of the many sources and consignees link up again elsewhere. We've begun individual traces on all of them. Needless to say, it could be months of work. But it would be work well worth doing. It's still early to posit a theory on the account, but I'm sure it's going to be an interesting one.

"Regarding the pendant, we've traced one of the remaining two apprentices. Ludwig Kriessel died in November of 1942, less than a month before the arrest of Hans Haupte. Kriessel's death was an unsolved homicide. The last apprentice, Abraham Mendel, left the service of Haupte in November of 1938, shortly after the riots of Crystal Night swept across Germany. He seems to have disappeared completely. A trace of the family shows that his father, mother, and brother were all concentration camp victims in 1942, a very coincidental year for many of these people. According to the records of the Jewish registrations, there was also a sister to Mendel, by the name of Keva, who was two years old in 1938. She also disappeared at the same time as Mendel. The records also show there was an uncle living in Kutno, Poland, whom we've begun tracing. It's possible that young Mendel went to Poland to escape the persecution in Germany," Horatio said.

"And jumped right into the fire," Pheagan commented.

"Probably quite true. Less than a year later, the Nazis conquered Poland, and the Jews were rounded up. He may not have escaped, even if he succeeded in leaving Germany."

"It looks like our chances are getting pretty slim on the pendant approach," Pheagan said, disappointment evident in his voice.

"I wouldn't give up on it so soon. Until we've determined what happened to Abraham Mendel, there's still hope."

Pheagan wondered as he listened to Horatio's words. Could they really hope to find a boy who disappeared forty years ago in a world that was being torn apart by war? It would take more than hope, he knew. It would also take luck—and no small measure of it.

Chapter 23

DRESDEN, NOVEMBER 12, 1938: Abraham Mendel made his way carefully through the streets and alleyways of Dresden after leaving the glassmaker. In his arms he carried the two sacks of food that he had been given for his family.

The times were dangerous for a Jew, especially traveling alone through non-Jewish neighborhoods. There were still groups of young toughs wandering about, not quite rid of the frenzy of hatred that had erupted on Crystal Night.

Mendel hadn't really seen them after turning down the alleyway, but the sound of rapidly scuffling feet on the street behind him sent him into almost instinctive flight. A quick peek over his shoulder just before making a sharp cut between two buildings told him that his reaction had been a correct one. Three boys in their mid-teens were chasing him with sticks in their hands.

Mendel was swift, but his uncertainty of the passageways between and behind buildings hindered his progress. He was easily capable of outrunning them, even with the packages he carried, but each delay at choosing his path of escape allowed them to gain on him.

They were too close now for hesitation, and he turned between two buildings on the full run. It was a long narrow corridor down which he sprinted, pulling away from his pursuers. It opened into a small court—and his escape was abruptly ended. The court was closed off by a high wall, too high to negotiate fast enough to escape the toughs behind him. He turned to face them, his chest heaving, his head pounding. He clutched the packages tightly.

The toughs slowed to a walk once in the court. They approached him, fanning out to cut off any lateral attempt to get around them. Their faces were glistening with sweat from their chase through the cold November air. They breathed hard, their eyes bulging from exhaustion and the thrill of bagging their prey.

Mendel backed away until he sensed the wall behind him, then remembered the gun. A quick debate flashed through his mind. To draw the weapon might scare them off—or provoke attack, and an even worse result for his possessing it. He remembered the words of Karl Steiner, words that had possibly saved his life on Crystal Night, telling him to absorb punishment, then fake serious injury. But what if they didn't stop? What if they searched him and found the gun? They weren't in the street now, they were in an isolated court with no witnesses. These ruffians could well beat him to death in their savage desire to spill Jewish blood, and no one would see them do it. He would be just another Jew found dead.

He knew that if he drew the weapon he must be prepared to use it. He forced the look of fear from his perspiring, bruised face and flashed a sudden smile of icy satisfaction.

The toughs all reacted the same to the change in expression, stopping their advance. There was an unnerving quality in the smile and the look in his eyes, as if he knew something they did not. For a moment, at least, it was a standoff. But after a few moments, the tough directly in front of him began to advance again.

This one was obviously the leader, Mendel decided. He was bigger than the other two and seemed to command by his very presence. This was the one to frighten to send them scurrying.

206

"Nice of you to find a place so out of the way, Jew boy," the leader said, ignoring Mendel's expression.

"It was nice of you to follow me to where I wanted you," Mendel returned with a chilling confidence. He hesitated a moment in reaching for the gun, for the expression on the face of this boy left little doubt that he would be forced to use it.

He let the package in his right arm drop to the ground, the eyes of his adversary going quickly down with it. In a flash, the gun was up and pointing squarely at the chest of the bully.

"Not all Jews are afraid, Nazi bastard," Mendel hissed.

Mendel had made three fundamental errors. The first was not releasing the safety on the gun; the second was letting the bully get too close to him before pulling the weapon; and the third was that he had spoken, instead of immediately firing the gun.

The response of the tough was one of attack. The stick crashed down across Mendel's forearm, causing a sudden numbing of his hand, though he managed to hold on to the gun. In an instant, the boy was on him, grabbing for the gun. Mendel pulled the trigger, only then realizing that he had forgotten the safety.

The second package crashed to the ground as the other two assailants joined in the struggle, their well-aimed sticks scoring blows to the side of his head and back.

With all of his strength, he pulled the gun in toward his stomach and yanked it violently away from the first tough. He fell to his knees, the three boys jumping on him, sticks and fists flying full force against him. He hunched over, pulled the gun to his lower chest and looked for the safety, found it, and released it.

He spun forcefully, throwing one of the boys off him, and jammed the gun into the chest of the leader.

The sound of the discharge was muffled by the boy's coat. A look of sudden shock filled his face as he fell backward clutching at his chest. He flopped to the ground, rolling painfully.

Mendel leveled the gun at the face of another attacker and held it steady, as the boy backed away.

The movements of the boy on the ground slowed, then stopped.

In an instant, the remaining two attackers were scurrying for the mouth of the alleyway, running for their lives.

Mendel did not fire at them. The sound of the first shot had not been loud. A second or third shot would definitely bring attention.

He quickly stuck the gun into his coat pocket and picked up his packages. He sprinted back down the alleyway and turned in the direction that would take him toward his own neighborhood. He knew it would be only moments before the other two boys returned with the police.

He entered another alleyway and soon emerged on another street. He slowed his pace so as not to bring more attention than the yellow armband with the star of David would by itself, then took a moment to get his bearings. He found a recognizable landmark and turned down a side street. Within moments he had melted into surroundings he knew, and had picked up his pace again. His excitement was laced not only with fear but also with a wonderful satisfaction for having fought back so decisively. He had shown them that a Jew would fight—and win.

Naomi Mendel stood in the wrecked living quarters behind the badly smashed shop staring at the packages of food her son had just put on the table in front of her.

"Where did you get this?" she asked suspiciously.

"I went to see Herr Haupte. He insisted that I bring it to you."

His little sister, Keva, was clutching at his leg, babbling excitedly in her happy baby language at the joy of his being home.

"They smashed his gallery and home, too," he told them.

"Why?" asked his father, lifting himself painfully from the bed in the corner of the room, his face still swollen and bruised from the beating on Crystal Night. "Herr Haupte is not Jewish."

"Because . . . I worked there," Abraham answered sadly. "Everyone knew that I worked there, and how much he liked me."

"So deep, their hatred," his father said, shaking his head. "It will never change. Throughout our history we have lived with hatred Pogrom after pogrom. Russia, Poland, Germany, all across Europe and Asia. It will never change."

"Why must you always bury your head in the past? You make it sound as though enduring these violations is a sacred obligation. When will Jews all over the world rise up and fight back?" he asked angrily, tired of hearing the helpless lament of Jewish history.

"Silence," his father commanded. "Have I raised you to question the will of God? To doubt His wisdom?"

"Do you call this *wisdom?*" Abraham asked loudly.

"Abraham!" his mother spoke up. "Do not talk to your father this way."

"You stick your face in your books," Abraham continued, ignoring his mother, "you search for desperate interpretations in the Talmud and the Torah and the books of Moses to justify being a race of cowards. We are God's chosen people, but chosen for what? Chosen like lambs for sacrifice and slaughter? Chosen to be beaten and humiliated before others?"

"I will not have this in my house," his father screamed, his voice strained to cracking, his face livid with anger. "Do you call your ancestors who made their stands at Masada and Beitar and Machaerus and Herodium *cowards?*" he asked.

"Where is that courage now? Why can't we be lions instead of lambs so that one day our descendants will have an equal pride in us?" Abraham asked, almost in tears.

His older brother, Israel, approached him, breaking his silence. "Stop this now," he said, taking his brother by the shoulder. "Come with me. You need to cool off, before your mouth runs off even further without your brain."

He turned his younger brother toward the shop and separated Keva from Abraham's leg. "Stay with Momma," he said softly.

Immediately, the small child began to cry as the two of them walked away. She ran to her mother, disappointed at seeing Abraham leave the shop. She had a very strong attachment to her brother, as he had to her. He was the center of her little world.

Israel whisked his brother into the street and away from the boarded-up shop.

"I can't—"

"Quiet," Israel interrupted. "Let's walk a little first."

Israel had always been a strong influencing factor in his younger brother's life. Abraham pocketed his anger and did as his brother said.

They walked for a few minutes along the street of smashed, boarded-up places of business. The streets had been cleaned by the Jewish residents of the neighborhood, and few dared to stay out on them now.

"Are you feeling any better?" Israel asked.

"No," Abraham said, stopping and facing his brother. "How can you listen to him speak that way?" he asked. "God's wisdom. God's will. Pray for His help. What good did prayers do when they smashed everything that we own and dragged us out into the street and beat us? What good are prayers at stopping the sickness that has gripped Germany? They'll stop nothing. Something very terrible is going to happen. Nothing will stop it. Nothing except what it grows upon—force. This will stop it," he said, thrusting the gun out for his brother to see.

"Put that away!" Israel ordered in a harsh whisper, slamming his brother in the chest. "Don't let anyone see you with that."

The gun quickly disappeared into his open coat and under his belt.

"Where on earth did you get that?" Israel asked.

"Herr Haupte made me take it," Abraham replied.

"Well, get rid of it immediately. If you're caught with that thing you'll end up in jail—or worse."

"I won't get rid of it."

"Yes, you will," Israel insisted.

"I would be dead now if it weren't for this. Because of it, I'm not dead, and one of them is."

"*What?* You've shot someone?" Israel asked in shocked disbelief.

"I defended myself. Look at my head. See where they hit me? Did Momma say 'What happened to your head?' when I came home? No. She asked me where I had gotten the food, thinking that I had stolen it. You saw her face."

"Did anyone see you do this?" Israel asked urgently.

"Yes, there were three of them. I could have shot them all, but I didn't. Shooting the one did the trick."

"Are you sure that he was dead?" Israel questioned.

Abraham thought for a second. "No, I didn't take the time to check him. But he stopped moving. I got out as quickly as I could, before the other two returned with the police."

Israel shook his head in disbelief. "Abraham, what have you done?" he asked sadly.

"I fought back to stay alive," Abraham replied defiantly. "Don't you understand? I would be dead now if I hadn't. I fought back! Just as all Jews should do. If we fought back every time they came, they'd stop coming fast enough. We should hit them, and hit them hard. That's the only way to get space to live."

"Listen to you. You sound like one of them. Drunk on the power of that piece of metal under your belt," Israel said.

"Yes, it's power. Power stronger than prayer. Prayers don't work Israel, they really don't. Why can't you see that? What will it take for Momma and Poppa to realize that? Must you or I or Keva be killed in the streets before they'll wake up? I almost *was* killed today. Would that have made them see the sickness in Germany?"

"Poppa sees what he knows has been a part of our history for as long as it has been recorded. Pogroms are not new to us," Israel said.

"Poppa is so typical," Abraham said. "He buries his head in the sands of the past, refusing to force change. 'We must fulfill the obligations of our faith. Protect the laws of Moses.' What bullshit. It's not our obligation to let ourselves be slaughtered like sheep. We do not uphold our beliefs, our faith, and the laws of Moses by becoming fertilizer Moses wandered the deserts for forty years, not because he couldn'

210

find the Promised Land. He did it to build an army strong enough to take it, and to hold it. Yes, Jews were heroic at Masada, and Beitar, and Machaerus, and Herodium. But heroics of the past can't save us today by hiding behind them. We must fight again. Now. Before it goes too far."

Israel placed his hand on his brother's shoulder. "I don't disagree with you, little brother. But your words will never change Poppa. He will never think like you, and he will never leave Germany. But you must. And soon. Your two attackers who got away can identify you. If they do, you'll never live to go to prison. You must get out of Germany now."

"My mind was already made up to leave Germany before this happened. I'm leaving tonight—and I'm taking Keva with me," Abraham said.

"Keva! You can't take Keva," Israel said. "Think of what it would do to Momma and Poppa."

"Poppa may very well wish to fulfill his obligations as a good Jew by waiting for what will come. Momma can make that choice, too. But I'll not let them make that choice for me, or for Keva," Abraham said.

"So *you* will make her choices? *You* will expose her to the danger that you must face? How is that better for her?" Israel asked.

"The danger is here, inside Germany, Israel," Abraham said, grabbing his brother by the shoulders, "you know that I'm right. Can't you feel it? Can't you feel that something terrible is going to happen? The danger is here. I would die before I let anyone hurt her. They will have to dodge my bullets, my fists, and my teeth before they will ever come near her."

Israel maintained a long silence, weighing his brother's words against the possibility of retaliation that he knew could result if Abraham was identified by the two who got away. They would come for him, but they would all draw the punishment. Abraham was right. Keva must go.

"I don't like it," Israel said at last. "You're little more than a child yourself. It will be hard enough for just you traveling alone. With little Keva, it may be impossible. But you're right. She must go, too. For her safety."

"And you?" asked Abraham. "Will you come with us?"

"No, I can't. Someone must stay with Momma and Poppa. They'll need me, whichever way it turns out. And now we must plan quickly. There's very little time."

They considered the possibilities available to them. There was really only one place that Abraham could go where Keva would be properly cared for. That was to Poland, to their Uncle Yakov in Kutno

"Kutno must be almost five hundred kilometers from here," Israel said. "It's at least a hundred and eighty kilometers to the Polish border Much too dangerous. If they'll be looking for you, and we must assume that they will, then you'll have to cross the closest border. Czechoslo vakia. It's about eighty-five kilometers to the new Sudeten border."

Israel thought frantically, mentally mapping out a safe route into Poland. "It won't work," he said, shaking his head. "It's too damned far. Keva will never make it."

"I have money. Once inside Czechoslovakia we can travel by train Look. Look how much I have," Abraham said, holding out the wad of money that the glassmaker had given him.

Israel stared at the money in his brother's hand. "Where did you get all of that?" he asked in amazement.

"Herr Haupte gave it to me. He insisted that I take it to help the family leave Germany," Abraham replied.

"That makes twice that he may have saved your life. And you said that prayers are not answered. This is good. With that much money you will be able to travel all the way to Kutno by train. But first you must get to Prague. I'm not sure how far it is. Perhaps a hundred and twenty kilometers. From Prague you must go to Ostrava, and then north into Poland to Katowice. From there you can get to Kutno, I'm sure.

"Your trip to Prague will be the most difficult. You must cover almost a hundred and twenty kilometers by foot. Alone, you could make that in three days. But with Keva, I don't know how long it will take. You must pack enough food for at least three days from the food that you brought home today. You will have to get more along the way somehow. And you must do one more thing. You must remove the yellow armbands from your clothes and Keva's. You must draw as little attention as possible."

"I wish you were coming with us," Abraham said to his brother.

"Perhaps when you arrive at Uncle Yakov's, Momma and Poppa will think differently. If so, then we'll join you as quickly as possible But I cannot leave them here alone," Israel said.

"I understand."

They looked at one another and embraced.

"Israel, I . . . I love you. I've never told you that before. But I always have, even when we fought like cats."

"I know. I know. And I love you, too, you idiot," Israel said with emotion filling him. "Be very careful, and write to me when you get to Uncle Yakov's. And give Aunt Zoshia a big kiss and a hug for me— you can get your arms around her," he said with a sad smile.

212

"I will," Abraham promised.

"Now let's go back home. Make peace with Momma and Poppa and agree with anything they say. Take this night to be with them and to tell them that you love them. Let it be one last night of happiness to remember."

It was nearly 2:00 A.M. when Abraham and Israel rose quietly from the bed they shared. Their parents slept soundly behind the drawn curtain separating their bed from the rest of the large single room that was their home.

The two boys silently gathered a small bundle of clothing and packed it into a sturdy sack designed to be carried on the back. On top of the clothing they stuffed enough food for three days. Then Israel used one of his father's sharp leather knives to remove the armbands from the coats that Abraham and Keva would wear. Then he put the knife in the bag as well.

Abraham gently dressed his little sister as she slept. He took her small blanket and wrapped it around her, then lifted her into his arms. Her immediate squirms quieted quickly as he put her to his chest, her head tucked snugly against his neck.

He walked to the center of the room that had been his home for his entire life. He turned slowly, looking at it in the quiet darkness, planting every detail in his memory. Then he put a short note on the table for his parents and turned toward his brother, who was tiptoeing into the shop. Abraham followed him, carrying little Keva.

The two brothers embraced again tightly, their eyes wet with silent tears. Israel pushed back the dark hair of his little sister's face and looked at her for a long moment, then kissed her cheek softly.

Abraham and Israel's eyes met one last time. They shared a moment in which words would have been an intrusion. Then Israel turned away and returned to the back room and lay down again on his bed. He listened with all his concentration to the faint sounds of the door as it opened and closed. Then he buried his face in his pillow to hide the sounds of his grief. Unlike his brother, Israel Mendel believed that prayers were answered. At least some of them were. Perhaps this one would be, asking that his brother and sister be allowed to escape the dark, ominous cloud above Germany.

The journey to the Czechoslovakian border was an extremely difficult one for Abraham Mendel. In the back of his mind he kept recalling the words of his brother, who had said that the distance to the Sudeten Czech border and to Prague could be covered in three days if he were alone.

213

It didn't take the young glassmaker's apprentice long to realize just how heavy a sleeping two-and-a-half-year-old could be. But Mendel was determined to put Germany and its black shadow behind him as quickly as possible. He correctly realized that a sleeping Keva would be infinitely easier to handle than when awake. He decided to put as much distance behind him as possible under the protective veil of darkness. He could rest when the sun came up and it was time to feed his little cargo.

By dawn, he had gone over fifteen kilometers and felt as though he had lost half of his life's energy. Keva wiggled to life with the first bright rays of sunshine in the cold November air. To Mendel's surprise her momentary confusion gave way to a child's delight at the strange adventure she was undertaking with her brother. He put her down and straightened his stiff, tired back, feeling the uncountered weight of the backpack nearly pull him over. Keva's cooperation was marvelous. She walked alongside her brother, holding on to his hand, laughing and squealing with glee at the wonders of the country. This allowed them nearly an hour of additional travel before they broke from the road to eat.

After eating and taking a short rest they started out again. He let Keva walk as much as possible, slowing the pace to her speed so as not to tire her too quickly. When she did tire, he picked her up and carried her, walking as fast and as hard as he could. There would be plenty of time to rest after crossing the border.

Lunch had been eaten on the move, and dinner was delayed for as long as possible. The early dusk and the onset of the cold from the loss of the sun made rest and warmth a necessity, which Abraham gave in to. He found a nice spot well off the road near a small brook that meandered through a large pasture to the edge of a small stand of trees. They settled near the trees, where he quickly gathered kindling and started a small hot fire. He told Keva wonderful animal stories and fairy tales as he prepared hot food for them in the one pot he had taken. The chance to rest was most welcomed and needed.

He estimated the distance that they had covered to be about thirty-two kilometers. If he could manage one more full night of travel like the last, they could be halfway to the new German-Czechoslovakian border by morning.

They ate a good, hot dinner of sausages and potatoes, then settled near the warm fire for some rest. He would wait until she was sound asleep, then start out for the next big push.

Within an hour she lay tightly cuddled at his side, sleeping soundly after her first hard day away from home. He let her sleep awhile, then quietly left her side to repack their things and smother the fire.

He picked her up, again feeling the soreness, seemingly exaggerated by the pain and exhaustion he knew lay ahead for him. But one more night would put them halfway out of Germany. He wrapped her in the blanket and put her in the most comfortable position and started out once again. No pain, no fatigue, no cold of the dark night would stop him now. He intended to be in Czechoslovakia by the morning after next, whatever the cost to his body. He would concentrate on movement, counting the steps if he had to, each one bringing him closer to escape.

When the sun came up, he walked, half asleep, automatically putting one foot in front of the other like a machine, ignoring the tremendous aching in his back, sides, and legs. He had stopped feeling the cramps in his arms long ago, thinking only of taking the next step, passing the next tree or the fence he could see in the distance ahead. He saw no one to ask where he was, and his tired brain refused to do the arithmetic to establish the distance he had covered.

He came to a crossroad and stared up at a sign, his tired eyes struggling to read it clearly. It said Usti, two kilometers, and pointed to the west. It nearly brought tears to his eyes. He had passed the old border of Czechoslovakia. He had gone even farther than he had hoped he could. It made all the pain worthwhile to know that one more day like the last would put him out of Germany. He wished that Israel could only see how far he had gone. He would have been so proud.

Keva awoke shortly, and they rested in the cold morning air beside a fire. He fed his sister, but did not eat, himself. He would allow himself one meal per day to help conserve food, hoping to make it all the way to Prague with what he had brought.

He lay back and let every muscle relax. He had never felt so tired or sore in his life. He thought for a moment about his parents, and a terrible feeling of guilt coursed through him for causing the tremendous pain and worry that they must be going through. But his guilt was followed by anger at their stubborn insistence to remain in Germany amidst the horror that was taking form. Suddenly, he didn't feel tired anymore. Obsessed with walking farther and farther away from Dresden, he quickly gathered their things. Every second they were stopped was one less step they would take. Within minutes, the fire was out and they were again walking. He began retelling some of the animal stories he had told little Keva the night before. She loved his stories and listened intently, her little feet walking two steps to his one. He would tell the stories and make up new ones as long as she would listen and walk. Every second, every step adding to the mental arithmetic h constantly performed.

The second day was very much like the first. She walked as far a she could, then he carried her. She cried for Momma, and they stoppe to rest and to eat and to tell stories. He began counting the hours unt nighttime. Although he knew the pain it would bring, he also knew tha their progress would be much faster while Keva slept.

The following morning yawned brightly to life, with Abraham Mendel hardly aware of it. He had pushed himself to the limits o physical endurance through the night. He walked mechanically, on step and then another, on the verge of collapse. He looked and acte drunk.

A recurring sound kept snapping him out of his trancelike stride Finally it drew quite close and loud. It was a voice.

"Young man, are you all right?" the wrinkled old face of a mar asked.

Mendel stared into the face, unresponding.

"I said, are you all right?" the old man asked louder.

Mendel began to snap to consciousness as Keva started squirming in his arms.

The old man took the child from him, and Mendel reached out to take her back, but stumbled in his exhaustion and fell to the ground All he could see was an unclear image of a man holding Keva. In a slow, groping motion he began reaching for the gun to stop the man he couldn't understand, and who was taking his sister.

"Put her down," Mendel shouted, still unable to find the gun.

"Oh, German," the old man said in recognition. "Wait a minute wait a minute, young fellow. I'm not going to hurt her," the man said in excellent but accented German. "I'm only trying to help you."

Mendel looked into the man's face, who was now kneeling by his side. His mind began to clear.

"You were in the middle of the road. I was in my truck and saw you. You looked like you needed help," the old man said.

"Where are we? What country?" Mendel asked.

"Czechoslovakia," the old man answered, puzzled.

Mendel lay back, his hands going to his eyes. He began to cry with such joy that it frightened the old man.

"I'll take you to a doctor," the old man said.

"No, no. I'm all right. Just tired and happy. Unbelievably happy You see, I've just left Germany. Dresden. And I'm trying to get to Prague. I'm just so happy to be out of Germany."

It was then that the old man noticed the marks from the stitching

216

on the sleeves of their coats, and it became immediately clear to him.

"You've come all the way from Dresden? On foot with this child?" he asked in disbelief.

"Yes, we left two days ago."

"Two days!" the old man said in utter amazement. "My boy, you are no more than twenty kilometers away from Prague now. I don't know how you managed to come so far with a small child in so short a time, but I can tell you one thing. You will not *walk* into Prague. I will drive you."

KUTNO, POLAND, 1938: Yakov Mendel was a printer. He was the owner of a small shop, but enjoyed a comfortable life. He lived in a good neighborhood, in a nice large apartment. His children had always dressed well and had good schooling.

It was not that the Jews had not had a difficult time in Poland, for they had suffered through the endless persecutions that had always been a part of their history. For 700 years they had endured ghettos and special taxes, exclusion from normal society, and incidents of beatings and murder. But that was a history common to most Jews.

Poland, as a country, had struggled through a bloodstained history of repeated invasions and wars. Jews had fought alongside Poles for *their* country. And despite the prejudices of the past, and those that still existed, the three and a half million Jews living in the Republic of Poland had become a vital part of the nation as a whole.

Yakov and Solomon Mendel were brothers, but had never been particularly close. They saw each other maybe once in every five years, and seldom wrote to one another.

Yakov, like Solomon, had two sons and a daughter. The boys—Samuel, twenty-two, and Ben, twenty—worked with their father in the print shop. Ruth, his eighteen-year-old daughter, worked in a bakery.

Yakov Mendel stood over a stack of freshly run sheets inspecting the quality of the work, his large bowl pipe hanging from his mouth. The bell of the shop door sounded as it opened and then closed. He finished reading, then looked up, seeing a dirty, disheveled young boy standing before him with a small child in his arms.

The pipe nearly fell from his mouth when he recognized the tired, drawn face of his nephew, whom he had last seen four years ago.

"Uncle Yakov, I need your help," the boy said, his eyes filled with tears. "I've left Germany, and I'm never going back."

Yakov stopped everything. Samuel and Ben were left to tend the shop while he rushed Abraham and Keva home to his wife.

"Does your father know that you've come here?" Yakov asked as they hurried along the street.

"I left a note telling them that I was leaving Germany. But I did not say where I was going. Israel knows. I told him that I would write to him as soon as I made it to Kutno," Abraham said.

"Your parents must be insane with worry. And to take your little sister was madness," Yakov said. "Children. What crazy notions fil their heads these days," he said disapprovingly.

"This was no crazy notion, Uncle Yakov. There is a madness in Germany that has spread too far to ignore." Abraham stopped walking and grabbed his uncle's arm. "Didn't you hear what they did? Crysta Night? They smashed our shop and hundreds more. My father, Israel and I were dragged into the streets and beaten. A man in our neighborhood was killed, ten people hospitalized, and almost a hundred arrested. They did this all across Germany, and no one stopped them The police watched with smiles on their faces."

Yakov looked down, saddened by what he heard. "Come, it's best if we talk further in my home and not on the street. It's just around the corner."

They arrived at Yakov's apartment and went through the entire shock and explanation again with Aunt Zoshia.

She was a big, typically Polish-looking woman with long dark hair, marvelously warm, caring eyes, and a backside as big as a barn. She held Keva with the tenderness of a mother. Yakov and Zoshia had never seen Keva before, as she had been born after the last visit of Abraham's family.

Zoshia's first reaction was anger at Abraham for running away, and especially for exposing Keva to such danger. Her second reaction was to feed them, then throw them both into a hot bath. After hearing Abraham's story, she looked at her husband with an understanding sympathy, and also with the question of what to do about the situation.

"I will wire Solomon and Naomi in the morning," Yakov said, "to tell them that they are both safe. Then I will write him a letter explaining to him what Abraham has told us about the situation in Germany."

"I've already pleaded with them to leave Germany. But they refused to leave. They will *never* leave Germany," Abraham said.

"And you will not go back," Yakov told him. "I will ask your parents to come to Poland. The choice must still be theirs."

"And Keva?" Abraham asked. "They will want her back."

Yakov thought for a long moment beneath eruptions of smoke from his pipe. "They will have her back—if they decide to come to Poland. The danger is too great in Germany. Herr Hitler has set a course of madness that inspires such hatred as you've described. I'll not send that innocent, beautiful child back into that. You will both stay with us. We can make room, and I can use another good pair of hands at the print shop."

Yakov looked at Zoshia and the way she held little Keva. "And I think Momma will enjoy the company, too," he said with a knowing smile.

The wire was sent and Yakov's letter followed shortly. Letters and more wires were exchanged at a rapid clip, Solomon and Naomi demanding that the child be sent back, but refusing to leave Germany to come to Poland. Yakov finally sent one last letter telling them that he would guarantee the return of Keva when the situation in Germany improved to his satisfaction. In the meantime, she would remain in Poland and be well cared for.

After a few days of desperately needed rest, Abraham started work with his uncle in the print shop. A month passed and Abraham demonstrated a remarkable quickness to learn the trade. He also astounded his uncle with the engravings he did in his spare time on discarded plates. His talent was awesome. He could duplicate almost anything with startling exactness.

Yakov made prints of some of these engravings, and to his surprise they sold immediately. Abraham began making larger engravings on new plates, and they too sold impressively well. Abraham began doing special orders for letterheads and stationery, as well as coats of arms and special seals. Within three months, he had added another dimension to his uncle's business and made an impressive reputation locally.

But all the while that life had improved so much for Abraham Mendel since leaving Germany, the dark clouds that had threatened his homeland began to drift over the rest of Europe and toward Poland.

In January of 1939, Hitler formally asked Poland to abandon rights to the old German port of Danzig, which had been essentially stripped away from Germany with the establishment of the Polish corridor in June of 1918 by the Treaty of Versailles, separating Germany from East Prussia. But the Polish refused to be intimidated. They were not afraid, and truly believed that they could defeat Germany in a war.

Tension built quickly, despite the ten-year Polish-German nonaggression treaty that had been concluded between them in 1934. The treaty was not worth the paper it was written on, and the Polish War Department began preparations.

On March 15, 1939, German troops invaded Czechoslovakia and occupied Prague. Bohemia and Moravia were taken over, and on March 17, the province of Slovakia, which only three days earlier had declared its independence from Czechoslovakia, became a "protectorate" of Germany. In Hitler's own words, "Czechoslovakia has ceased to exist."

It was the culmination of a brilliant power play in which Hitler had made utter fools out of England's Chamberlain and France's Daladier, who just five and a half months earlier had met with Hitler and Mussolini in Munich and had virtually partitioned Czechoslovakia through the signing of the Munich agreement. Hitler had succeeded in wresting away from Czechoslovakia the disputed Sudetenland, without so much as inviting the Czech government to attend the meeting that carved up their country and was a prelude to its eventual extinction.

On March 22, German troops occupied the old German city of Memel in Lithuania, forcing its return to Germany by signed treaty. The Polish government recognized the pattern of Germany's ploy, and saw a similar move on Danzig as a real possibility. They took immediate measures. On March 28, they announced that any attempt on the part of Germany to alter Danzig's status without Polish consent would lead directly to war. Three days later Britain extended a unilateral guarantee to Poland against German aggression. Poland was prepared not to back down.

On April 28, Hitler rescinded the Polish-German nonaggression treaty of 1934. Crisp warnings were issued back and forth between Germany and Poland. Unrest mounted quickly in Danzig, and rumors of an impending Nazi coup in the city swept through Poland.

An incredibly complex game of negotiation followed in which the major powers scrambled to align themselves. England's aim was to head off war by presenting an imposingly strong alliance prepared to act against Germany. Germany's aim was to open the way for an invasion of Poland, and Russia's design was to buy time and obtain the best guarantee possible to exercise her "influence" over the greatest area of eastern Europe.

Throughout the summer, as diplomats bluffed, bargained, threatened, and prayed, it became clear that Poland was the center square on the board. Britain and France had guaranteed assistance in the event of attack, and had begun to mobilize their forces after the March takeover of Czechoslovakia. Poland, too, had begun preparations, but had been advised by its two major allies not to call a general mobilization. The Polish War Office set about enacting a quiet alert among its reserves. Armies were deployed in key areas of defense, and the tense business of waiting began. Waiting and hoping. Hoping that the proper combination of alliances would avert the threat of war, which grew more imminent by the week.

Yakov Mendel sat by his radio, which was now always set at either Radio Deutschland or the BBC, listening to a German broadcast of a particularly inflammatory nature, decrying the barbaric treatment of ethnic Germans throughout the Polish Corridor, citing incidents of murder, beatings, even rape of defenseless young Aryan girls. It was a live broadcast, frequently interrupted by cries of outrage or patriotic cheers from a loud audience, which added greatly to the effect of the words. "Seig Heil! Seig Heil!" The words echoed in thunderous unison.

Yakov looked up at young Abraham, now sixteen years old. He could see the pained realization in the face of his talented nephew that his escape had not been complete.

"This is not Germany," Yakov said. "We can fight them here. And they will not be fighting just Jews. They will fight an entire Polish nation. Our army is strong and determined," he said.

His consoling words were interrupted by Samuel, his eldest son, who entered the apartment in an urgent rush. "The reserves have been called up," he said. He looked to his younger brother Ben, now twenty-one. "We've been called up to assemble at Lódź."

Yakov Mendel hid his shock well. He stood up, facing his two boys. "Then the time has come," he said. He turned off the radio, cutting off the loud shrieks of German unity and devotion.

Tears welled up in Zoshia's eyes. She looked on silently, then turned to unpack their uniforms.

"Britain and France will help us," Samuel said confidently. "If the Germans are foolish enough to attack Poland, we'll chase them clear back into Berlin. They'll learn their lesson quickly."

"When must you leave?" Yakov asked.

"We group up to leave at two," Samuel replied.

"Then you will eat one last good meal. And we will offer prayers to God that our strength will prevail," Yakov said.

There was a great mixture of emotions in the Mendel household as the two sons of Yakov and Zoshia left, joining other confident uniformed reservists to go to the train station in Kutno. There was sorrow

and hope, fear and pride, and the true belief that the forces of Polan
would prevail if conflict erupted.

But in the heart and mind of Abraham Mendel was the sickenin
realization that he had not really escaped anything at all. He held hi
little Keva tightly. She was now three years old, and totally unaware c
the dangers growing once again around her.

The next weeks were spent in high anxiety. Yakov and Abrahar
worked hard and long hours in the print shop to get out the work of th
growing business.

The situation in Poland continued to slide dangerously nearer th
brink of conflict. Then on August 23, 1939, the shocking news of th
signing of a nonaggression pact between Germany and Russia mad
the strong possibility of war with Germany seem a certainty.

The door was now open for Germany. Russia would not oppos
them and was happy with the concessions Germany had secretly mad
to them.

At 4:45 A.M. on September 1, 1939, German forces crossed th
border into Poland without a declaration of war. They unleashed a nev
and daring form of offensive warfare called blitzkrieg. The first wav
brought a terrorizing level of destruction from the air, followed on
hour later by armored columns and panzer divisions.

The flat terrain of Poland and the absence of the usual rains of th
season were perfectly suited to the German "lightning war." There wa
little in the way of natural barriers on its frontiers to stop the German
army from racing across its hard dry surface. Even the presence of th
seasonal rains would have greatly aided the Polish cause, for most o
the roads were dirt, and while horses and rifles couldn't stop tanks an
armored columns, mud could. No rains—no mud.

The blitzkrieg was an unprecedented success in modern warfare.

Abraham Mendel held his little sister close to him to conserve a
much body warmth as possible. She was wrapped in the same blanke
that had provided warmth when they left Germany almost a year ago

His mind struggled with the sobering realization that he was agair
in the midst of the madness that they had seemingly escaped. They had
gained nothing but perhaps a little time—and a little happiness.

It was almost night and the darkening woods were cold. Mende
had not started a fire for fear of being detected. The fighting in tha
area had stopped too recently and there were German patrols every
where. He had learned that in the daylight the soldiers never botherec

222

im. Even during the fighting, German motorized columns just drove
y in the opposite direction. But that was during the daylight. There
vas no telling what they would do in the darkness when all they could
ee was a campfire. They might take them for combatants and open
re.

His decision to leave the refugee columns with their constant dan-
er of attack from the air had been a wise one. He had also correctly
ealized that Warsaw was not the place to flee to. Besides his wonderful
ift of talent, he seemed also to be blessed with an instinct for survival.

The decision to leave Kutno had been an easy one for the Mendel
amily. The bombs that started tearing the neighborhood to pieces be-
ore the sun came up on September 1 told them that there was no
uture in staying where they were. Yakov and Zoshia could not believe
he vision that greeted them as the family left the house. By some
niracle, their building and the one next to it were the only two left
ntouched by the German bombs. There was little doubt that the
lames consuming the neighborhood would eventually reach the build-
ngs.

The streets of Kutno were a scene of madness. People were
creaming, crying, praying, and running in all directions. Rumors of
he advancing German army instilled panic.

"We must go to Warsaw," Yakov had said. He held Zoshia ten-
erly as they walked, both of them sick with worry over their two sons.

They left with meager possessions gathered in urgent haste, and
vith what food they could carry. The refugee columns had thickened
uickly, and massive confusion was apparent everywhere. The Ger-
nans did their best to keep things that way with their attacks on the
olumns.

The sight and sound of the screaming Stukas had an immense
sychological effect on the civilian population. The vision of the sud-
len destruction and horror was shattering. It was during such an attack
hat two of the fearsome Stukas made long strafing runs right down the
enter of the tangled mass, inflicting heavy civilian casualties. In that
ttack, Zoshia and her daughter Ruth were killed, and Yakov Mendel
vas mortally wounded. Abraham was made sick at the vision of what
veapons could do to human bodies.

He sat with his Uncle Yakov across his lap, holding him tightly
nd rocking him back and forth as though trying to put an infant to
leep. Tears streamed down young Mendel's face, his anger and sorrow
hoking in his throat. He could see the lifeless torn bodies of his aunt
nd cousin a few feet away, and knew that Yakov was dying.

He stayed with his uncle until all signs of life had left him. Keva clung to Abraham's back like a young chimpanzee to its mother as he sat holding his uncle. He looked at the lifeless form of the kind, gentle man who had taken him and his sister in without hesitation and had shown them such generosity and love. He kissed the bloody head o Yakov, then laid him to rest beside the bodies of Zoshia and Ruth.

Mendel made up his mind to head southeast toward Rumania There was no hope in Warsaw, only containment and entrapment There was no safety in the thick refugee columns, only attack, which was drawn to them. Alone he and Keva would draw little attention Poland was lost. They must again go for freedom, which lay about 430 kilometers distant. There would be no trains to take, little food avail able, and danger all around them in the form of German soldiers and desperate refugees. He still had the gun that Hans Haupte had given him, and he knew that to be caught with a weapon would place him in a great deal of trouble. But he would not give up his only means o defense.

So he and Keva left the refugee column, starting their long trek toward Rumania. The memory of the pain and exhaustion of their flight from Germany had seemed hardly forgotten, and now it was starting all over again. Keva was bigger and stronger now, and could walk for much longer periods of time. But when she tired, carrying her was more difficult. Nonetheless, Abraham plodded on with the same determination that had driven him on his exodus from Germany.

Progress through a war-torn country crawling with soldiers and refugees was a great deal slower than the straight-ahead flight out o Germany. They managed to stay out of the way of the fighting, though the sounds and sights of it were everywhere. When it came too close they walked away from it, regardless of direction. The route became a long, crazy zigzag, which made progress impossible to estimate. Staying alive became more important than counting days or kilometers trav eled, and staying alive meant keeping away from other people.

They continued to travel the safest routes possible, living on what bits of food they could scavenge and from grains stolen from farms at night. Abraham even dared raids, stealing eggs and occasionally an overly protective hen, whose neck he would quickly snap.

This pattern continued for weeks as they made their way unknow ingly right through the central zone of entrapment being formed by the successful pincer movement of the German armies.

Once past Lublin, Abraham tried to maintain as straight a line toward Rumania as possible, correcting for their zigzag maneuvers once out of danger. It was as they neared Tómaszow that they came in contact with moving German columns which just ignored them. Seeing that they took no notice of a boy and a small child traveling alone, Abraham began staying nearer the main roads. This greatly accelerated their progress.

Abraham had told Keva to speak only German when the soldiers were near. It paid off immensely when one challenge was issued by a German officer.

"We're German," Abraham spouted boldly, and handed him a quickly invented story of how he and his little sister had been separated from their parents near Lublin. He told the officer that they had been wandering about for days looking for the German lines for their safety. Keva's German cries for Momma added greatly to the credibility of his story.

They were given food and told that everything from this point to the south and west was now "German," and that the war was nearly over. Most of the remaining Polish armies had surrendered. They were advised not to go southward or to the east, because retreating Polish units had advanced in that direction to get to Rumania, and the Russians had invaded from the east. There would undoubtedly still be fighting in those areas until all the Polish forces had capitulated.

They headed west as advised until well out of vision of the German officer who had spoken to them and helped them, then turned back to the southeast. They moved as fast and as hard as they could for two days, before finding a large stand of trees in which to take shelter and rest. They were too exhausted to go farther without a long period of rest. Abraham estimated that they were perhaps 115 kilometers from the Hungarian border, and twice that from Rumania. He rethought his plan as he cuddled his sleeping sister. Hungary was much closer, and for the moment just as free as Rumania. He could reach the Hungarian border in three days after their long rest. Once in Hungary, travel would again be easier, as he had a little money, which would allow them to put as much distance between them and the German army as possible by rail. They could then make their way into Rumania.

He closed his eyes to sleep, holding Keva as close to him as possible to keep her tiny body warm. It was in that twilight between sleep and wakefulness that the first sounds of the music came to him. At first it was like a dream, the sweet sounds of the violin distant but clear. The music was lovely, almost sad. He did not open his eyes or force concentration upon it, fearing that the dream would end and the music stop. But it continued for a long time, and he listened to it, thinking about the glassmaker. Then the music stopped. A few moments later it started again, and he opened his eyes. The music was not a dream, it was real—and coming from deeper within the same forest. Somebody else was in the forest with them.

Mendel removed the gun from his pocket, released the safety, and held the gun in his fist. He was too tired to move, otherwise he would have investigated the sound. He would do that in the morning to determine whether the forest was safe enough to spend the next day in. He closed his eyes and allowed himself to rest, listening to the beautiful music, letting it take him.

When he awoke in the morning, he could not remember the music stopping a second time. He must have fallen asleep listening to it. There was no trace of it now, but he had gotten a distinct impression as to the direction from which it had come. The wind was blowing from that direction now, and carried the smell of smoke and the aroma of cooking.

Mendel picked Keva up in his arms and checked the gun, then began to move through the forest in the direction of the other mysterious occupants. He whispered to Keva to remain silent.

The smells grew stronger as he progressed, and sounds began to filter through to him. Smoke became faintly visible and he could hear voices, the neighing of horses, and sudden laughter as though a joke had just been told.

He crept quietly through the underbrush until he saw images. They were Gypsies. He could see five small wagons. There were two fires burning with not very much smoke. He counted at least twelve adults, and there were a number of children, covering a wide range of ages. Everyone seemed to be gathered into large circles; they were eating from big common bowls set upon large round wooden discs. They reached and picked at the food with wooden spoons and pointed knives.

The smell of their food was wonderful. He could see the hunger in Keva's bright little face, and felt it in his own stomach. He knew very little about Gypsies, but most of what he had heard said that they shouldn't be trusted.

"Don't move, and don't turn, or I will kill you," a deep voice said in Polish from behind them.

Mendel froze, his hand tightening around the gun.

"And drop the gun," the voice ordered.

Mendel let the gun fall from his hand.

"Now turn around slowly so that I can get a look at you," the voice behind them said.

226

Mendel turned to see a tall thin man standing ten feet behind him. He hadn't even heard him. In his hands was a double-barreled shotgun. The man looked to be about forty years old, had dark skin, and eyes so black that they didn't appear to have pupils. Long black hair hung in tight curls down around his neck, nearly touching his shoulders. He wore a hat and loosely fitting colorful clothing.

"Two children," the man huffed, lowering the gun. "What brings you here to spy on us?" he asked.

"I heard music last night. A violin," Mendel replied. "I was investigating the source. We stopped in the forest to rest. We're trying to get to Rumania."

"You have an accent. German," the man said.

"Yes, we are German. But we are running from the Germans. We left Germany almost a year ago to come to Poland to live with my uncle."

"Why?" the man asked.

"Because we're Jewish."

"When did you last eat?" the man asked after a long assessment.

"We used the last of our food a day and a half ago."

The Gypsy looked at the face of the little child, then to Mendel. "Pick up your gun and put it away. You are welcome to eat with us."

Silence greeted them as they entered the camp with their captor host. He spoke to the others in a language that Mendel couldn't understand. Then the men around one bowl of food adjusted their positions to make room. The tall Gypsy pointed to the space. "Eat," he said to Mendel.

At the same time an older woman came to Mendel to take Keva from his arms. There was distrust in Mendel's eyes.

"What a beautiful child. What is your name, little one?" the woman asked in a kindly voice.

"Keva," the child replied.

"Come, darling Keva. I will see that you eat and are warmed by the fire."

Mendel sensed a kindness in her and allowed his sister to be taken from his arms. He then went to the space provided for him. A knife was held out to him. He accepted it and sat on the ground and followed the lead of the others as they used their knives to spear pieces of meat and potatoes.

The man who had found them introduced himself as Barbu. He was the chief of this family. The woman who had taken little Keva was named Sera.

Barbu briefly explained to the others what Mendel had told him,

227

and immediately the questions started. They wanted to know more about what was going on in other parts of Poland.

Mendel answered as best he could, saying that the war was all over. He told them about the remnants of Polish forces trying to fight through to Rumania, and about the entry of Russia into the war.

They listened with great concern.

"We, too, are going to Rumania," Barbu said.

"I was told that there is heavy fighting between here and Rumania and that there are Germans and Russians everywhere," Mendel said.

"We can get past them," Barbu said with confidence. "We will go through the mountains into Hungary. They will never find us in the mountains."

"They don't seem to be concerned with small groups of civilians," Mendel said. "They passed us by without any interest two days ago."

"When the fighting has stopped, they will be concerned," Barbu said knowingly. "Being a Jew, you will not be safe."

"We passed them once because I told them that we were German. They didn't detain us."

"The next time they will. You can stay with us until you have rested and gained some strength. Then you must go south toward Hungary."

The conversations continued throughout the rest of the morning. Then one of the men sat on a pile of wood that they had cut for their fires and began playing his violin. Mendel watched intently as the man became lost in his music and vision. He was a superb musician.

Mendel found these people generous and interesting. He pitched in to help them with their duties, the most important of which was the repair of two wagons. They had been in this forest for almost a week, trying to avoid the conflict that was ripping Poland.

Keva was well taken care of by Sera. The child was immediately comfortable in her maternal presence. It wasn't long before she was laughing and playing with two other small children.

"She's a wonderful child. Pretty and intelligent," Sera said to young Mendel.

"Thank you," he returned. "She's everything to me."

"She is lucky to have a brother like you. But I feel that she will need more to survive," Sera said.

Mendel looked into the Gypsy woman's eyes. She took his hand and opened it, palm upward. She stared into his hand for a long time. "You have a brother in Germany, and parents who are very worried for you," she began.

Mendel was not impressed. It was obvious that his parents would be worried. Keva could have told her about his brother.

"You have seen the death of family. I see three people. A man and two women. One is a child to the man. There are two others—boys, or young men—also dead now. They were sons to the man."

Mendel was shocked by her accuracy and began to pull his hand away, but she held it firmly.

"You must not leave Poland. To do so will mean your death now."

Mendel jerked his hand away, staring hard at the woman.

Then she pulled his hand back to her and opened it again. She seemed to be looking right through it. "You must go north," she said finally.

"We can't go *north*," Mendel insisted.

"You must. In the north you will be caught—but you will live."

Mendel looked at her for a long time, frightened by her prediction. "I don't believe you," he said at last.

She looked back into his hand. "You are an artist. You create much beauty. You were taught by a man, a good friend who helped you to leave Germany. You both share a secret that will bring danger—great danger. This danger will follow you."

Mendel began to sweat now. "And my sister?" he asked.

"Her future is not in your hand. But I have looked at hers. She will live a long and happy life. But she must go south," Sera said.

"South!" Mendel repeated.

"You will both live. But you must not stay together. Her escape is south. Yours is north."

Mendel took his hand away. He shivered from the impact of her words. He could not accept what she had told him. Keva would stay with him, she had to. And they would go south.

That night after dinner, he sat with Keva near one of the wagons. He held her close to him, thinking about Sera's words. The thought of any harm coming to her brought tears to his eyes. He thought of the danger that the Gypsy woman said he shared with the glassmaker, and he remembered the look of distrust in the eyes of the young officer who had come that day with the old general to pick up the commission. How could Sera have known?

He rummaged through his pack until he felt the small packet of string-bound paper that Hans Haupte had given him. He pulled it out and opened the packet. He stared at the pendant for a long time, then he removed it and used the heavy string to make a necklace. He secured the pendant to it and then placed it over his little sister's head and slipped it below the collar of her shirt. Some feeling he had made him think that it would protect her. Then he held her again for a long time.

Later that night, the group of Gypsies sat around a fire playing their instruments and singing. They all seemed to be smoking pipes including the women. The men drank liberally, their childlike joy growing more and more ebullient with the effects of the liquor.

Mendel could see Barbu and Sera off to one side in serious discussion, their heads turning occasionally toward Keva, asleep under one of the wagons, then to him.

A little while later Barbu came over to him carrying two bottles and sat beside him. He handed one to Mendel. "You must pay no mind to the words of an old woman," Barbu said, his eyes pointing to Sera. "You are a brave young man and have your own ideas of how to help your sister and yourself."

Barbu raised the bottle to his mouth and gulped down a large quantity of the alcohol. "Come, drink with me to the safety of your journey," he said, holding out his bottle.

Mendel extended his bottle, clanking it against Barbu's, then took a long pull as he had seen Barbu do. The contents went down his throat like liquid fire. His eyes popped open as he gasped for breath.

Barbu laughed loudly and slapped him hard on the back. "You drink like a Gypsy. I like that," Barbu roared. "The next swallow will be more gentle. Come, drink to Keva, and to life."

The next swallow was smoother, and the ones that followed became even easier. He began filling with a warm optimism. After all, had not Barbu said that the words of the woman were not to be taken seriously? Every drink helped him put her words further away until he couldn't even remember them.

He became extremely mellow, and the songs and the dancing and the laughter made him feel happy again in a way that he hadn't been able to feel in a long time. The music played, Barbu laughed and raised his bottle again and again, and all fears melted into numbness.

The sounds of the birds singing intruded gently into the clouded brain of young Abraham Mendel. Slowly, his head began to clear and his breathing came as shallow, rapid efforts trying to stay ahead of the mounting nausea. He had never felt so thoroughly sick in his entire life. His head felt as if a balloon was inside, expanding to the point of popping. His stomach felt awful, and every part of his body felt as if it was encased in lead.

He propped himself up on one elbow, holding a hand to his

pounding head, moving his thick tongue in and out of a foul-tasting mouth. He forced one eye open, blinking from the bright sunlight of day, then opened the other. He began to breathe deeply to quell the nausea rising in his stomach.

He looked around through eyes that had difficulty focusing and became suddenly aware of a horrible fact. The wagons were gone. He jumped up, wobbling and unsteady, and looked around frantically. They had left sometime in the night—and had taken Keva with them. He ran through the growth bordering the small clearing, shouting her name through his mounting sickness. He circled the clearing completely before coming back into it and falling to his knees and letting out a pathetic cry. He writhed and sobbed with a terrible sorrow. He had failed so miserably to protect his sister. He remembered his words to Israel, saying that he would die before letting harm come to her. He wailed and threw dirt and grass over himself, pounding the ground with the fury of a man gone mad. He raised himself on his knees, throwing his arms out toward the sky, screaming at God to make him die, to punish him for failing in his sacred trust.

He collapsed to the ground, his face in the dirt, sobbing in unbearable agony. Why? Why had God let this happen?

He looked for the gun, but it was gone, too. If it had been there, he would have used it on himself. He wept until all his strength was gone, calling the name of his little sister over and over. "Keva, Keva. Please, Keva, forgive me."

Chapter 24

CLAUDE St. Jude used the time on the train ride to Arles to counter the points of "evidence" raised by Falloux as proof of Christian's guilt, and to answer questions.

"The escape of your father in Vichy was no mystery," he said. "He was following precisely the correct course of action in saving the code books, transmission logs, and intelligence data of that sector. That was the first priority. All those brave men who were captured that day knew well the risks of their actions. The message that was being transmitted

231

was of vital importance to the British, and that was why they stayed to the end to complete the transmission.

"No one expected the invasion of Russia—except the communists. We and the British were certain that an invasion of Britain would take place first. This news was, therefore, vital to the British. Hitler could not invade in the east and the west simultaneously. It meant that England would be saved from invasion, allowing them to prepare for an offensive against Germany. It removed a great burden from British strategists.

"Your father's escapes cannot be held in evidence in any way, for then we would have all been equally suspect. All of us, Edna-Marie, myself, many of our people, made escapes time after time from situations that seemed hopeless. They seemed spectacular then, but were often just the product of our good luck and less than perfect planning on the part of the enemy. We found help in many unexpected quarters. The enemy couldn't account for that. They never knew where the 'help' would come from until it was too late, and then they quite often never could figure it out."

"Falloux made a point about my father being taken to a low-security prison in the Massif Central—Evaux-les-Bains, I think it was. He said it was highly suspicious that he alone was separated from the others and taken there," Michael said.

"Your father was separated from the others because he was to be taken to Paris. Being wanted in Paris was a bad sign for him. His cover had been blown by a chance encounter with SS Captain Rudolf Immel, which is part of another story that I will tell you later. It was not suspicious to us in the least. As far as Edna-Marie was concerned, they were not aware that it was she that they had arrested—or she, too, would have been taken to Evaux-les-Bains.

"It was strictly their incompetence that allowed your father to escape so easily from them. Had he not escaped when he did, he would have ended up in Paris in the hands of the Gestapo. He undoubtedly would not have survived the war.

"As for his presence in areas where we suffered losses to the enemy, that, too, is easily explained. On at least half of those occasions he was there specifically to save what he could. We were warned in advance of many of those collapses by Gabrielle Dupuy, who was very successful in learning of these things before they occurred. We could not save everyone, because the Germans had set clever traps. To go anywhere near them would have resulted in capture. We were helpless. We could only sit by as our comrades were taken, hoping that none of them would be broken during interrogation, which would have resulted in further losses."

"What about the forgery section in Paris? Falloux felt certain that my father had betrayed them," Michael said.

"It was Z who did that. He also translated the codes that were captured at that time as well. It was Z who betrayed the Paris sector the second time, resulting in the smashing of nearly every patrol. Only your father's tireless work, at great danger to himself, helped to quickly rebuild the sector, otherwise it would have been lost for good."

"And your escapes with Edna-Marie and my father with the Germans so close behind you? He claimed that the Germans knew where you were because my father told them, and that he dropped messages for them to find, resulting in the losses of other sectors," Michael said.

"The communists could have said that about Edna-Marie and myself as well. All three of us were together—running, dodging, hiding. If they had wanted to discredit any one of us instead of your father they could have presented almost the identical case. It was the devilishly clever Z who made these betrayals, neatly putting the blame away from himself."

"And my father's work behind German-held lines after the Liberation of Paris?" Gabrielle said. "That was after Gabrielle Dupuy had been killed, wasn't it?"

"Yes, it was. The Aile Rouge would have had no knowledge of your father's state of mind at that time. He was driven like a madman. I was sure that he wanted to die, and that he took such risks to punish himself. Falloux said it was attempted escape. In a way it was. But not from France because of collaboration. It was escape from himself and the undue guilt he felt over Gabrielle's death.

"I think you can see for yourselves that the evidence against your father was ridiculously circumstantial, and that by merely changing the name at the top of the charge, and a few of the locations, it could have been brought against any one of a hundred Resistance fighters.

"I worked very closely with your father, as did Edna-Marie. He was a man of enormous courage. I know, as surely as I am here with you now, that your father was no collaborator. I would bet my own life on that. It can be said with no more certainty and feeling than that."

There was now no doubt in Michael's mind that the entire theme of collaboration was pure cover, not remotely believed by the killer. It was without question a matter of the pendant and what his father had known about it and its holder. They were not after a collaborator at all.

It was early morning when the train pulled into the ancient city of Arles, situated beside the Grand Rhône River on the northern edge of the Camargue. The group traveled across the Ile de la Camargue toward Saintes-Maries-de-la-Mer in St. Jude's car, which had been left in Arles. St. Jude's *manade,* or ranch, was five kilometers north of the capital city.

It was an enjoyable drive. The weather was perfect and the air streaming in through the open windows felt and smelled wonderful. St Jude spoke proudly of the Camargue as they drove, artfully mixing history and legend. The Ile de la Camargue had been famous since Roman times for its marvelous fighting bulls and its wild white horses which became symbols of the Roman legions. Roman officers rode upon the magnificent white stallions of the Camargue. Caesar's Sixth Legion fought under the emblem of the bull, inspired by the courageous, fearsome Camarguain bulls. Some Roman soldiers were even given land in the Camargue as a reward for heroism during the conquest of Marseilles in 49 B.C.

It was a proud past, and to this day Camarguais raised and preserved the bulls and horses in much the same way as their pre-Christian ancestors. The pastures remained communal, stud services were still provided free to neighboring *manadiers,* and there was no stealing of another man's stock. There continued a strong code of honor and trust, which the true Camarguais never violated.

Claude St. Jude owned one of the largest single *manades* in the entire Camargue. His bulls were famous for their exceptional courage and pugnacity in the ring, and were always in demand.

St. Jude told his guests about the 1,000 bullfights held each year in the Camargue and the neighboring region of Languedoc. Unlike the bullfights of Spain and Mexico, these bullfights were bloodless. Each *manadier* received a fee each time one of his bulls appeared—the fee usually dependent upon the bull's reputation in the ring.

The objective of these bullfights was to remove a rosette, called a *cocarde,* which was hung between the horns and rested on the head of the bull. The brave of heart who attempted to snatch it were called *razeteurs,* a word that signified in local dialect coming as close as a razor to the skin. They fought largely for the honor, and the small purse of a few francs meant little to the winners. They, like the bull, developed a reputation of courage and daring that meant a great deal more than the prize.

For many *manadiers,* other means of deriving income were also necessary to support themselves. In the case of Claude St. Jude, the income from his bulls, through fees and sales, was quite substantial. Yet he had other interests in many ventures, ranging from part ownership in a large salt-extracting company to the growing of rice. He was a true mix between old-world Camarguais and shrewd entrepreneur, who could get the best out of both lives. He raised the finest fighting bulls and sold the finest meat—from those bulls not meeting his high standards of pugnacity. He owned large acreage in the Petite Camargue, the area just west of the Petit Rhône River, where enough rice was grown annually to meet the needs of all of France.

He had also preserved the winemaking business his father had started out of love for the art, but which had, for the years he lived, never been completely successful. It became a thriving business shortly after the war when Claude took over the responsibilities of the entire *manade*. Claude's two brothers were killed by the Germans late in the war and he was the sole heir. When his father became incapacitated by a sudden and severe stroke in 1947, Claude assumed the responsibilities of running the family affairs. His business sense, well honed by the experience he gained during the war as the financial brain of Group Defiance, helped him steadily expand the family's base. He had worked long and hard during those years, and now he enjoyed being a gentleman of leisure.

Michael could see, in both St. Jude and his daughter, the wonderful sense of belonging they felt in the Camargue. This was their home—their life energies emanated from here. All that they were and wanted was right in this beautiful soggy delta, where the past and the present peacefully coexisted.

St. Jude frequently checked his watch as they sped toward Saintes-Maries-de-la-Mer.

"I would like very much for you to see the *abrivado*," St. Jude said to his American guests. "The feast of the Pentecost is starting. It is something that everyone should see once in his lifetime."

"What is the *abrivado?*" Gabrielle asked.

"The running of the bulls through the streets to the arena," St. Jude replied. "I am running two bulls this year. One of them is Satan, the finest young bull I have ever had. Sixteen fights so far. Not once has the *cocarde* been taken from his horns. He is fierce and intelligent, a true pleasure to watch. He performs for the crowd. They love him."

St. Jude looked at his watch one more time. "We will make it in time. This is the best time of the year to be in the Camargue. I hope you will like it."

And like it they did. There was a carnival atmosphere in the air. The streets of Saintes-Maries-de-la-Mer were filled with tourists, colorful Gypsies who annually made the pilgrimage here for their beloved patron Saint Sarah, and Camarguais, who turned out in great numbers for the festivities. Many of them were dressed in the traditional Arlesian fashion so pridefully continued over the generations.

The group sat around two tables put together on the terrace at

Boissete's café. The street was jammed with people awaiting the *ab rivado.*

Nicole sat quite close to Michael with her arm over the back of hi chair, her fingers tracing gently over the well-defined muscles of hi shoulder and neck.

St. Jude talked constantly, describing the proceedings and th events that would follow over the next few days, all the while watchin his daughter. He had noticed throughout the past days his daughter' growing attraction for Michael. She had never been one to hide he emotions, often to the point of St. Jude's displeasure. It took a lot o getting used to as she grew up, especially when she left home for he advanced education. The fierce independence and free-spirited natur of the Camarguais was truly manifested in her. She had her lat mother's beauty, and her father's determination to go after the thing she wanted in life, especially men. He would have fits when she woul come home wearing clothes that left little of her to the imagination But his rantings would do nothing to change her spirited ways. Sh dressed as she liked, sunbathed in the buff when she felt like it, an traveled at will where and with whomever she pleased. St. Jude learne to put up with her ways. He loved her too much to risk driving he away with his protestations.

The shouts in the street announced the arrival of the bulls. Like moving wave, the crowds became suddenly mobile, racing to escap the bulls. The young and brave charged after the bulls trying to pul their tails. Firecrackers exploded all around, bags of flour flew throug the air, and light sticks poked and snapped at the bulls, taunting them

The café crowd rose to its feet as the bulls neared, and the sound of festive mayhem increased in intensity. There were eight black bull charging, flanked by cowboys, or *gardians,* astride small but remark ably quick horses. The flour bags were directed at the *gardians* to dis tract them, as the bravest youths tried to detain the bulls.

The crowd at Boissete's café suddenly parted as an angry bul veered and charged. People scattered into the café and onto parke cars or into trees. Another bull appeared close behind the first, turnin toward the café terrace. Tables and chairs flew as it angrily slashe through the air with its horns, people scurrying out of its path. One bo grabbed the animal's tail, another took it by the horns. His effort ended in an impromptu flight across the café terrace, while the othe youth was dragged some twenty feet before finding the sense to releas the bull's tail. Then as if from out of nowhere, a *gardian* appeare covered with white powder from several direct hits of the flour bags and he deftly prodded the rampaging bulls with his long pole triden

236

back onto their path toward the arena. The excited smile on his powder-white face told of his enjoyment in the rough but good-natured fun.

As suddenly as they had appeared, the bulls were gone, with much of the crowd trailing after them.

"That one was Satan," Nicole said breathlessly, her lovely chest heaving from the evasive maneuvers.

"How could you tell them apart?" Michael asked, laughingly. "They all looked alike."

"We know them," she guaranteed. "Is he not beautiful?"

They followed the crowd to the arena, where Satan kept his string of ring victories alive, taking on at least twenty white-clad hopefuls at one time. He was unlike any other bull—strutting and snorting like a king, chasing his opponents all around the ring, tossing two of them clear over the protective barrier. He kept all of his adversaries running for their lives for the entire fifteen-minute time limit. At the end of the program, he was named the best bull.

St. Jude beamed with pride. He was mobbed with congratulatory handshakes and claps on the back.

"I told you. I told you that he was magnificent. Come, children. Let us go back to Boissete's before it becomes impossible to get a table," St. Jude said, clamping strong arms around Gabrielle and Nicole's shoulders. "We must have the finest bottle of wine in celebration."

"He sure takes his bulls seriously, doesn't he?" Michael said to Danny as they fell in behind the others.

"About as seriously as Nicole seems to be taking you," Danny said, seeing the look in her eyes as she glanced back at Michael.

"You think so, huh?"

"You bet. And Papa sees it too. I don't know how he feels about it, so I'd go slow. We're going to be here awhile, and we wouldn't want to do anything to upset St. Jude," Danny said.

Michael nodded that he'd behave.

About ten minutes later they were seated at Boissete's and St. Jude was proposing a toast to Satan's success. Life at the café had picked up again, and there was once more music and merriment everywhere.

St. Jude noticed Michael's amused curiosity over the Gypsies, whose singing and dancing and music helped greatly in maintaining the festive spirit. "Have you never seen Gypsies?" he asked.

"Yes, I have. But never quite like this," Michael replied.

"We welcome them here as friends. They are much like Camarguais in many ways. They are free and spirited, and dislike the trappings of bureaucratic nonsense. We had two Gypsies working with us in Group Defiance during the war from among these very people. Immensely brave men, both of them."

"What became of them?" Gabrielle asked.

"They were betrayed by Z. They were masters at evading the Germans, and we used their skills when the British began flying in with the Lysanders. They were cousins, Fernand and Dego Simone. They were in charge of arranging the sites for the Lysander landings and bringing the supplies, or people dropped off, safely out of the area. They used many ingenious methods, including canoes, like Indians. They drove the Boche crazy, until they were betrayed. They both died. Dego was shot and killed during the arrest, and Fernand died in prison. He was brutally tortured but refused to speak even a single word through his entire ordeal. He was finally shot by the Gestapo at Fresnes Prison in 1944. I don't remember the month."

"Do these same Gypsies come to Saintes-Maries-de-la-Mer every year for this holiday?" Gabrielle asked.

"Yes. You see, this is the feast of the two Marys, for which the city is named. It celebrates the miracle which saved them. Legend has it that in 40 A.D., Mary Salome and Mary Jacobe, who were both close followers of Christ and the first to arrive at the scene of his Resurrection, were banished from the Holy Land. They were set adrift in a boat without oars or sails, and totally without provisions. By a miracle of God, they somehow managed to land safely in the Camargue. According to Gypsy tradition they were accompanied by a black servant named Sarah. She is their patron saint.

"Tonight they will gather in the church to maintain an all-night vigil. They will burn candles and cover her statue with garments and gifts. In the morning, twenty mounted *gardians* will escort them and their saint to the beach to be sprinkled with water from the Mediterranean to celebrate her safe arrival on these waters.

"The following day, the twenty-fifth of May, is the feast of Saint Mary Jacobe. The archbishop of Aix-en-Provence will be here, and the statues of the two Marys will be taken to the waters in their sculptured boat. They will then be splashed with the waters, and the archbishop will bless the sea."

St. Jude told many interesting stories to his guests. Then he stopped in the middle of one when an old Gypsy woman entered the café.

"That is the wife of Fernand Simone," he said, pointing her out. "She is an Andalusian Gypsy," he told them as they watched her read the palms of some tourists. When she finished, she moved to another table, managing to perform another reading above the protests of the client.

"I will introduce you to her when she finishes," St. Jude said.

"Maybe she'll read your palm, big brother," Gabrielle teased.

"That's a lot of hocus-pocus," he said, dismissing it.

"For the most part, you are right," St. Jude said. "But I have seen her and heard her at times when it made me wonder."

"Oh, come on, Mike. It's just fun. Why don't you let her try?" Gabrielle insisted.

Michael just shook his head.

When she had finished, St. Jude caught her attention. She smiled and walked over.

"Monsieur St. Jude, how wonderful it is to see you," she said in a tired, scratchy voice. She wore an outrageous floral dress with an old red coat over it, for which the weather was much too warm. Her long scraggly hair hung down below her shoulders, with a green scarf covering the top of her head and tied in the back. Her face was old and weathered and cracked from the sun and wind of decades of travel and hard living.

"Madame Simone," St. Jude said, standing to greet her. "Come, sit. I would like you to meet someone." He quickly commandeered a chair for her from another table and she sat.

"Wait," Gabrielle said excitedly. "Before you tell her who we are, let her read Michael's palm."

"No, no," Michael protested.

"Come on, we insist," Gabrielle said.

"Yes, you must," Nicole added.

"Go ahead, be a sport," Danny urged.

Michael let out a sigh and reluctantly agreed. He held out his hand.

Madame Simone took it and stared into it. After a long silence she began. "You are not from here. You come from across the ocean. America. I see a very long life, but one with many dangers. There is happiness ahead for you, despite your doubts." She looked up, finished.

Run-of-the-mill hogwash, Michael thought. He thanked her and put five francs in her hand.

"Monsieur. This will not even feed one of my ten children," she protested.

Michael gave her another five.

"That is better," she said, then turned to St. Jude. "So, what are you up to, you old horse thief?" she asked with a crooked smile.

"It is I who should call *you* a thief," he kidded back. "I told them how wonderfully you read, and you give them a foggy-eyed performance. These are important friends of mine. They will think that you are a fraud and that I am a liar," he said with a mock frown.

She turned to Michael. "You are from America, no?"

"Yes," Michael answered.

"Their accents were easy," she said, waving a finger at Gabrielle and Danny. "You, however, speak like a Frenchman. The rest was routine. Tell me, are you really interested in knowing what is in your future?" she asked through a squint.

"Yes," Gabrielle answered for him.

The old woman smiled at her, then looked back at Michael. "Are *you* interested?" she asked, suddenly sounding quite serious.

"I don't believe in it. And if I did, I doubt that there's wisdom in knowing what lies ahead."

"I will make a deal with you. For ten more francs I will read your cards. I will tell you first the past. If you believe, then I will continue to your present. Then you decide about the future."

Michael looked into the dark eyes. He held her stare and knew that she could stare him right into the ground if she wanted to. "Why not," he said at last, handing her the ten francs.

The old woman produced a worn pack of cards, handed them to Michael to shuffle, and turned the first one over on the table.

"I see that there was great confusion in your life," she began. "Very deep confusion. You were much troubled by it." She turned over another card. "And I see war. War with much killing. Three. The number three. Three wars? No. It is the same war three times."

Michael was hearing this but not believing it. She was saying things that she couldn't have learned from mere observation, no matter how good she was.

"You were searching, trying to find your way out of your confusion," she said, then turned another card. "There is also great learning. Great learning, but after the war. I see a man. You don't want to see this man. But you do."

She stared hard at a new card for several long moments. "I see the place of war again, but there is no fighting. There is still death, still suffering. You see it. You hate it. You hate the man who sent you there, and the men who guide him."

She looked up into his eyes. "Your hatred is wrong. These are not evil men," she said, then looked back to the next card.

"I see happiness from your learning. The confusion is over. I see

240

rees, a jungle. Much like the place of war. But you are happy here. There is no war, no killing." Then her face grew intense as the next ard was turned. "It is interrupted by great sorrow, sudden pain and nger. Hatred."

She looked up into his eyes. "This is the present," she said, and vaited for his decision on whether to continue.

"Go on." Michael said.

"There is death. The death of . . . of a father?" she said, looking up t him.

Michael was shaken by her accuracy.

"You search again. For a man." She looked up. "You seek ven-eance." She looked back to the next card. "I see the same man from before, the one you dislike. He is a friend. Trust him. He wants to help ou."

"The man I'm looking for, can you see him?" Michael asked.

"He sees you. He knows you are looking for him. Be very careful, I ee danger." She turned another card and her eyes lightened. "Unex-ected happiness. It is close to you, very close to you. Do not shut it ut. You will need this." She turned the next card and stared very hard t it. Then she looked up to Michael. "This is the future. Do you wish o hear it?"

Michael thought for a long time, then shook his head. "No, I don't vant to hear it."

"You are wise," she said in a near whisper. She turned, looking ard at Danny and Gabrielle, then back to Michael. She scooped up he cards, rose suddenly, and walked away, leaving the café.

"Why did she do that?" Gabrielle asked.

Michael suddenly felt frightened. He got up and took off after her. le followed her as she weaved through the pedestrian traffic. He aught up to her and grabbed her by the arm, turning her around. 'Wait," he said.

She looked into his face, her expression flat and hard.

"What is it? What did you see?" Michael asked.

"Do not lose your wisdom now. Only a fool wants to know what is n his future," she said with a look coming to her face that was like the xpression of a mother whose child was on the brink of sudden heart-break.

"You frightened me back there," Michael admitted.

"Don't be afraid. They were only words. Never fear words. I saw nuch courage in your cards. You will need to be strong. Your future is long one, I guarantee you that much."

Suddenly, her eyes locked on the pendant showing through th opening in his shirt. She reached out and touched it. "Where did yo get this?" she asked.

"Why do you ask?"

"Because . . . I have seen another exactly like it."

"Where?" Michael asked urgently. "Please, tell me. It's very im portant that I know."

"Yes," she said. "It is the key."

"Where? Please, where?" Michael implored.

"Two years ago in Italy. Near Schio. A Gypsy woman was wearin it."

"How did she get it? Did she tell you?" Michael asked.

"She said that she had always had it, for as long as she coul remember," the old woman said.

"Who is she? How can I find her?" Michael asked in rapid order

"Hungary, Rumania. Perhaps Yugoslavia. She belongs to the fam ily of Barbu Denska," she replied.

"How can this family be found?"

"All Gypsies in that area know Barbu Denska. Finding him wi not be difficult."

"What is her name? And how old is she?"

"She is perhaps in her mid-forties. Her name is Keva Wolenska.

"Keva Wolenska," he repeated to imprint it in his brain.

Michael turned and looked back toward the café, but could nc see Danny or Gabrielle. When he turned back, the old woman wa gone. He spotted her passing between a group of people, then hu riedly rounding a corner. He took off after her, wanting to know mor He rounded the corner in time to see the passenger side door on battered old pickup truck slam shut. The old woman's face appeared i the back window as the truck began to speed off.

Michael started to run after the truck, but it quickly disappeare around a corner, and he gave up his futile chase. His heart pounded i his chest from excitement. He grabbed the pendant, clutching it tightl in his fist.

"It is the key," she had said. *The key.*

Chapter 25

MICHAEL held back the Gypsy woman's information until he could speak to his sister and Danny alone. That was not until they had arrived at St. Jude's home early that evening.

It was a large old home with an impressive, easy elegance about it. It was not grand and imposing like the residences of Edna-Marie and Pierre Falloux, but it was unmistakably upper-crust Camarguais. There was a warm, lived-in air that made the Americans feel immediately comfortable.

Nichole showed them to their rooms, and they quickly settled in. They took a few moments to freshen themselves, then Michael went to Danny and Gabrielle's room to tell them what he had learned.

"That Gypsy woman was scary," Gabrielle said as soon as Michael entered. "She knew so much. About Vietnam, and the rain forest. About Daddy's death, and us looking for someone."

"Listen," Michael interrupted, "I learned something very important when I went after her. She saw the pendant around my neck and said that she had seen another one just like it two years ago in Italy. She said that it belonged to a Gypsy woman named Keva Wolenska."

"Another pendant?" Danny said. "That means there are *five.*"

"That's right. She told me that the Gypsy woman belonged to the family of Barbu Denska, a well-known Gypsy who apparently moves about through Hungary, Rumania, and Yugoslavia."

"Great! That's only three countries we have to scour looking for her," Danny said.

"We don't have to do anything. Pheagan can take care of that part of it. The old woman said that Barbu would not be hard to find."

"When are you going to give him the news?" Danny asked.

"Right now, if St. Jude has a phone that I can use in privacy. can't wait to tell him and hear his reaction."

St. Jude showed Michael to his study, where a phone could b used in complete privacy. He dialed the special number Pheagan ha« given him, gave the necessary codes and clearances, got the go-ahea« after the computer line check, and waited for the phone to ring.

"Tripper," came the voice.

"Three rings. Not bad," Michael said.

"I'm a man of my word. Have any luck?"

"Some. We've met with more Group Defiance people and hav had our meeting with Pierre Falloux. The charges filed against m father in 1945 were outlined to us, and frankly, they're a lot of cra The real reason behind the charges was to eliminate my father as political opponent. The communists were engaged in a power play t get as much control in France as they possibly could during the imme diate confusion following the war. They acted fast to eliminate th competition, as well as some old enemies."

"What about Falloux? Did you get any feelings about him?"

"He's a real sweetheart," Michael said sarcastically. "He sur didn't have any love for my father. He was the one behind the accusa tion, but he denied any connection with his death. I even tried flashin the pendant on him, but if it did anything to his blood pressure, didn't show enough for me to pick up on it."

"What do you *feel* about this man?" Pheagan asked.

"I want to learn more about him. A lot more."

"He was connected to Firewatch until about 1975," Pheagan saic

"I know. We tried that one on him and he admitted it to us. H also said he was no longer involved, or interested in witch hunts."

"We've begun a workup on him. Just keep on the way you'r going regarding him. We'll let you know how his blood pressure runs, Pheagan said.

"Getting close to him won't be easy. The guy lives in a veritabl fortress, complete with high walls, electronic intruder control, arme security, and attack dogs. I got a good look at the layout of everythin except the inside of the house. I made a sketch of the grounds."

"Still have the old instincts, huh?" Pheagan commented. "Sound like there's a little Glad-jo coming to life, after all."

Michael ignored the remark. "I think it's time you started tellin me more about what you're really after. What the group is after," h said.

"You know I can't do that right now," Pheagan told him.

"I think you have to. Every feeling we're getting tells us we're not after a collaborator at all. It all points to the pendant holder. We realize that my father's contact is crucial to the whole thing, and that he must be found. We also know that it would help us a great deal to know more. Specifically about what you're not telling us," Michael said.

"That part of it doesn't make a bit of difference. It won't help you find the man you want any faster. And as I see it, the collaborator *is* important to you. You don't *know* that he isn't involved. And even if he turns out not to be, you'll need to break his identity to clear your father's name."

"That's secondary now. What comes first is getting the son-of-a-bitch who gave the order to kill my father, then the two guys who did it. You say it doesn't make a difference what I know? Would it make a difference to you if I blew the guy you're after away without talking to you first?" Michael asked.

"You said that you wouldn't do that," Pheagan said.

"Well, now I'm saying the only way I'll guarantee that I won't is if you start sharing some information with me."

There was a long silence at the other end. It was a little early to worry about a threat like this, Pheagan knew. But it could be a problem later. "I'll have to talk to my people," he said.

"Good, you do that. How are you doing in your search for the apprentices?" Michael questioned.

"It's down to one possibility. We've confirmed his last-known whereabouts in Poland. The name is Abraham Mendel. He was the youngest apprentice of the glassmaker's chair. He was also extremely talented. He left Germany in 1938 when he was fifteen, and went to live with an uncle in Poland. He left Dresden to escape the persecution of the Jews, taking his little sister with him."

Little sister. The words struck a chord in Michael's brain. "How old would this sister be if she were alive today?" Michael asked.

"She should be forty-six," Pheagan answered.

Michael felt a surge of excitement with the answer to his question. He began to sense the connection. "I have something that I was saving for the end, but this sounds like the right time for it."

"Good news, I hope," Pheagan said dryly.

"I think you'll find it interesting. There's another pendant floating around somewhere in Hungary, Rumania, or Yugoslavia."

"What? Are you sure?"

"Yeah, and it belongs to a Gypsy woman in her mid-forties. Get ting the picture?"

"Go ahead. Did you get a name?"

"It's Keva Wolenska."

Keva! Pheagan's heart nearly exploded. *"That's her!* That's th girl! Mendel's little sister's name was Keva. It has to be her," he sai excitedly.

"She's part of the family of a Gypsy named Barbu Denska. M source says that he's very popular among the Gypsies of the area, an that he should be easily found."

"How on earth did you manage to learn that?" Pheagan asked i complete amazement. He was impressed.

"Let's say that it was almost in the palm of my hand," Micha replied.

"Mendel and his sister just vanished when Poland was invade He could be with the Gypsy, too, though it's probably too much t hope for. I'll get on it immediately," Pheagan said, hardly able to con tain his excitement.

"What if he's not there and she doesn't remember him? She we only three at the time." Michael said.

"We'll have to wait and see. Right now we're going through Ger man arrest records for that time and combing labor and concentratio camp lists. There are so many that it seems almost endless," Pheaga said.

"Well, good luck. Get back to me on my 'request' for informa tion," Michael said. "I think we'll work together a lot better if we pu on the same end of the rope."

"I've been saying that all along. Call me the day after tomorrow. should have something for you by then on both your request and th girl."

"Okay, I'll call. Good luck with the Gypsy woman."

"We're about due for some. Stay careful on your end."

Michael rejoined his sister and Danny before going into the livin room to join St. Jude and Nicole.

"Well, how'd it go?" Danny asked anxiously.

"We may have hit the jackpot," Michael announced. "The searc for the apprentice has narrowed to one candidate, a young Jewish bc named Abraham Mendel who fled Germany in 1938, taking his litt sister with him. They ended up with an uncle in Poland, then bot vanished when the Germans invaded in 1939. The girl's name wa Keva."

246

"It has to be her," Gabrielle said. "What did Pheagan say?"

"He agrees with you. He hopes that the apprentice will be with the same family, though it's not likely. I guess he'll try to get a lead as to where Mendel can be located—if he's still alive."

St. Jude had wine waiting downstairs for his guests. When everyone was situated comfortably in the large homey living room, he began another part of the story.

"It was early 1942. Things were going fairly well for us. Our main sectors in Paris, Marseilles, Bordeaux, Vichy, Brest, and Normandy were well established and were obtaining outstanding information.

"Gabrielle Dupuy had gradually—and successfully—developed her relationship with Immel. By this time, Edna-Marie was fully aware of your father's troubled situation, and wisely had him take some time to get away to be with your mother. It seemed to help him considerably.

"The new year was only several months old when we began to get the first taste of Pointer's treachery, although we had no idea that it was he who was responsible. Our Paris sectors were the first to go. At once, your father made for Paris to assess the situation and see what could be done to rebuild the sectors as quickly as possible. Gabrielle Dupuy, who operated independently of the four sectors there, was untouched by the catastrophe. It was to her that he went. . . ."

EARLY 1942, PARIS: For Christian, each meeting with Gabrielle was at the same time like heaven and hell. Heaven because of the precious moments they spent together, and hell because of the knowledge that she would be going back to *him* when she left.

The disaster that had befallen the Paris sectors only served to heighten the urgency of being together. They held one another tightly, drawing from the strength that each gave to the other. At last, when they were able to discuss what had happened, Gabrielle told him what she had been able to learn.

"Paris has been betrayed. All the sectors are lost," she said. "They've caught nearly everyone. The few who managed to escape are known to the Germans, and are in hiding. They will need help in getting to the free zone."

"Who did this?" Christian asked with a smoldering anger.

"I don't know. But it was definitely from within. The sectors were completely blown. From what I was able to learn, the Germans got their first information months ago, and carefully observed key people.

247

They had been given the names of the uppermost people in the sector. They patiently watched and were able to work their way downward. I was the French police who did most of the work under Gestapo super vision. It was the French police who made the arrests," she said.

"And our people, who has them?" Christian asked.

"They are still in French custody. Vichy is cooperating fully with the Germans," Gabrielle answered. "The French police are conducting the interrogations, and the Germans will have full access to any infor mation obtained."

"Damn them for doing this to their own," Christian said angrily He maintained a short silence. "Have any of the radios survived?"

"No. They were all taken in the raids."

"No radios and every cell blown. We have to start over again from the very beginning. I'll have to bring people in from the outside. Ha the forgery section fallen with the others?"

"No, thank God. Our traitor is apparently unaware of it."

"Or the Germans are too smart to take it now," Christian coun tered.

"Is there anything that we can do for those that were taken?"

"Perhaps. We have strong contacts in Vichy and in the Deuxième Bureau who may be able to help. We must do all that we can to see that they remain in French custody," Christian replied. "In the mean time, you must work to try to discover the identity of this traitor."

"I will," she said, again going into his arms. "Please hold me Christian. Promise me that you'll be careful. I couldn't live if anything happened to you."

Christian held her and kissed her passionately. At least for these few moments they would be safe and together. He kissed her again and again, then lifted her in his arms and carried her to the bed.

Each time they made love, they were filled with such fire and intense need for one another that nothing existed outside their room They brought one another to higher and higher peaks of ecstasy, for getting the fear and the torment of the world outside. In those mo ments, Immel didn't matter, France didn't matter, and tomorrow didn' matter. There was only the sense of the moments they shared together

They fell asleep in one another's arms when the lovemaking had ended. It was Christian who awoke first. He watched her as she slep peacefully. She was so brave . . . and so serenely beautiful. He loved her beyond everything.

It was usually about this time that the thoughts of Immel began He wondered if Immel watched her the same way that he did now, and

248

whether the German loved her. He wondered if she and Immel brought one another to the heights that they seemed to achieve so naturally, or whether she just pretended to enjoy his lovemaking. He wondered whether Immel was gentle with her. And, yes, he always wondered whether she loved Immel, even in some way that she wouldn't admit to herself.

He gently eased himself away from her and walked across the room. It was impossible to have these thoughts of Immel without having to move to dissipate the jealousy and anxiety that filled him. He paced and thought and built a hatred for the man he had never met, but with whom he shared so much.

"You're thinking of *him* again, aren't you?" she said softly.

He turned his head and looked over his shoulder at her.

"You mustn't," she told him.

"I know, but I'm only human. I can't help it."

She could hear the hurt and repressed anger in his tone. These were the worst moments together, always following the best. "Christian," she said softly, "there have been other men in my life. You don't hate them, I'm sure. Never have I given myself to a man as totally as I have to you, and loved so deeply. I've given that only to you."

"I know. But how do you expect me to feel?" he asked. "To know that you're leaving here to go back to him. It kills me inside to think of it."

"We can't think of these things. When I leave here, I think only of doing my job for France, and about the next time that you and I can be together. I don't torment myself with thoughts about you being married, and that when you're with your wife you make love to her."

"I have been with my wife exactly ten days since joining the Resistance in August of 1940. Ten days," he repeated.

"And you have never thought of her? Wanted her in your arms? Wanted to make love to her?"

"And do you think of me when you reach climax with Immel? Or do the colors of France burst before your eyes as you moan in pleasure?" he said caustically.

"Stop this! Stop this!" Gabrielle said, breaking into tears.

He stood looking at her, melted by her crying. How could he have said those things to her? He rushed to her, taking her in his arms.

She squeezed herself hard against him.

"I'm sorry, so sorry," he said. "I . . . I didn't mean those things. I love you. I love you so much that it kills me inside."

"I know," she said, sniffling, trying to bring herself under control.

"Christian, you need only know one thing and carry it with you always. I love you more than my life. If I could be granted but one wish in my life, it would be to spend it with you, only you. I have never known a greater love or have had such happiness before, and never will I again."

He held her tightly. He loved her so much. "We have these moments, and each other," he said. "That's enough for a king—and a lifetime."

The following day Christian was joined in Paris by Jan Burak, who had narrowly escaped capture in Argenteuil just days before. They carefully reviewed the situation and formulated a plan of action that could re-establish the Parisian sectors within a week to ten days, if there were no sudden setbacks. Two radios could be made available from Marseilles, as four new ones had just arrived from England. They were much smaller and lighter in weight, and could be transported more easily than the large first-generation radios. They had been destined for other sectors, but would be reassigned. Paris was too important to be without at least two radios.

With their plans made, the two men separated. Christian was to spend the night in Paris, then head back to Marseilles to join Edna-Marie and St. Jude, who was now administering financial affairs for the entire Group Defiance network. Christian would give his report, then outline the plan to rebuild the Paris sector. The hardest news to give would be that they had a traitor in their midst. It would be imperative to find him quickly and take appropriate action.

The following morning, Christian went out for breakfast. When he returned to the flat, his landlady greeted him with a message. "Monsieur Burdette," she called, catching him as he was climbing the stairs to his room.

"Yes, Madame Bronte," he said, turning on the stairs to look down at her.

"You had a phone call while you were out this morning," she told him.

A phone call! "Yes, Madame Bronte. Who was it?" he inquired, trying to hide his alarm.

"A woman. She said it was important that she talk to you immediately. Her name was Madame Galley."

Madame Galley. That would be Gabrielle, no doubt, the Galley being taken from the code name Galileo. "I do not know a Madame Galley," Christian said. "Did she leave a number for me to call?" he asked.

The old woman looked at him suspiciously. "I do not want to know your business, monsieur, but this woman seemed quite upset. She said that you could meet her at this address at noon," the woman said, holding a slip of paper out to him.

He came down the half-flight of stairs, took the paper, and read the address. It was a café on Rue du Faubourg that they had once gone to.

"Well, I don't know this woman," Christian said, crumpling up the piece of paper. "She said nothing else?" he asked.

"No, but she did ask for you by name. She knows you."

"Well, I'm leaving Paris this morning for Rouen," he lied. "If she calls back before I leave I'll talk to her. But I am certainly not going to this place to meet a woman that I don't know. Thank you anyway, Madame Bronte."

The old woman shook her head. "Men," she muttered, turning to her door, sure that he was having an affair with some married woman.

Christian was up the stairs in a flash, glad to be away from her. He couldn't use this place again. He would have to find another.

At half past ten he left the building carrying a small bag with his belongings. He went to the train station and deposited the bag with the left-luggage clerk, to be picked up later that day. Then he went to the café to find Gabrielle.

He stood in the doorway of the café looking for her, but she wasn't there. Suddenly, he felt a pinch on the backside.

"Mathieu, it's so good to see you again after so long," her voice said from behind him.

He turned to face her. She looked beautiful and was smiling radiantly. But in her eyes he could see that there was trouble.

"Come, let's find a table," she said, walking around him before he could speak.

They found a table against a side wall and made small talk until they had ordered some lunch. When the waiter had left, Gabrielle reached across the table and held his hand in both of hers. "I have just learned that Marseilles has been betrayed. The police are going to strike today with the help of the Gestapo," she said.

"Gestapo? So, Vichy is selling out."

"The Gestapo are acting only as advisers, without authority or jurisdiction. They cannot take possession of evidence, or custody of prisoners in the unoccupied zone, unless officially turned over to them by Vichy decree."

"Marseilles betrayed. Who was it?" he asked.

"The same person who betrayed Paris. I haven't been able to find out who it is yet. But I do know that it was the same person."

"There's no way that I could get there in time."

"It may already be too late," she said.

"How complete will it be?" he asked.

"Not as complete as Paris. But there were important names given Edna-Marie DeBussey, Claude St. Jude, Jan Burak, Charles Flandine and . . . Christian Gladieux," she told him.

"My God," he said, stunned to silence. "And Edna-Marie and Claude are in Marseilles now. If they are caught—" He cut his sentence at seeing the sudden alarm in her expression. Her eyes were fixed on the entrance to the café.

"What is it?" Christian asked.

"It's Rudolf. He's with some other German officers. He's going to see us, I'm sure."

Christian couldn't resist the urge to get a look at the man who had been the poison in his gut for so long. He turned slowly to see him.

There was no doubt which one was Immel. At the same instant Christian turned to look at him, Immel saw Gabrielle. A hot flash of jealous hatred shot through Christian as he eyed the German. He had imagined all kinds of faces and shapes. He had not expected him to be so good-looking or to have such commanding presence.

Immel said something to his fellow officers, who started for a table at the other side of the café. He headed directly for Gabrielle and Christian.

"He's coming over here," Gabrielle said. "For God's sake, behave yourself," she said, seeing the look in his eyes.

"Rudy, what a wonderful surprise. I'd like you to meet Mathieu Burdette. Mathieu, this is Captain Rudolf Immel."

Christian stood with the introduction, as Immel snapped his heels together, giving a swift tip of the head.

"Monsieur Burdette, it is a pleasure to meet you," the German said with a courteous smile.

"And a pleasure to meet you, as well. Imagine, the entire time we've been sitting here, Gabrielle has been carrying on about this mysterious captain of hers. And now I actually get to meet you. I think that you've fairly stolen her heart," Christian said with his magnificent lying eyes playing every bit the part.

Immel gave a slight smile. He was handsomely Aryan, with light brown, almost blond hair, and sharp blue eyes. He had strong, chiseled features with a narrow squared chin having a slight cleft. A two-inch dueling scar ran down his left cheek. The scar was a symbol of courage, coming from a fraternal initiation during his university days. It added a rugged quality to his handsomeness.

"Rudy, please get a chair and sit," Gabrielle insisted.

"Join us for lunch, perhaps?" Christian invited.

"I will sit, but only for a moment. I must rejoin my friends," he said in very good French.

"Are you certain that you can't join us? I'm sure that your friends will understand," Christian said.

"Thank you, but no. I really must get back to them shortly." Immel grabbed an unused chair from another table and brought it over. He sat, eying Christian carefully.

"We were supposed to be talking about old times," Christian said. "But all that she's talked about is you."

"Really. What has she said?" Immel asked.

"Well, she started—"

"Mathieu, please. You'll embarrass me," Gabrielle said, blushing.

"I didn't think that *anything* could embarrass you," Immel said, taking her hand in his. "That *is* what you said."

"Did she say that?" Christian asked. "Lies. All terrible lies. I've seen her embarrassed many times. Do you remember when you and my brother were swimming in the river near our uncle's place and I happened by and found your clothes?" he asked Gabrielle.

"Mathieu! Please, stop that," she said with believable urgency.

"This sounds interesting," Immel said with a smile.

"I could tell you some funny stories," Christian said with a smile. Inside, he wanted to cut off the hand that was touching Gabrielle.

"It almost makes me wish that I didn't have to return to my friends. Perhaps we can talk again some time," Immel said, rising to his feet. "I really must go. It was very nice talking to you."

"It's been a pleasure," Christian returned, fighting back the urge to grab Immel by the throat.

"Enjoy your lunch, and I do hope that we meet again sometime. Gabrielle, I'll see you later."

There was a certain look in Immel's eyes when he looked at Gabrielle that hurt Christian to see. He was sure that Immel loved her.

They both watched as the German walked away.

"If I ever see him alone, I'll kill him," Christian whispered.

Gabrielle wanted to reach across the table to take his hand, but didn't dare with Immel in the same room. "You must leave Paris, immediately," she told him.

Christian nodded. "Yes. And I must try to get to Marseilles."

They finished their lunches quickly, both forcing themselves to e: food that they did not want. They stood and walked to the entrance c the café. Christian smiled and gave a wave to Immel, who returne acknowledgment with a dip of his head. Then Christian gave Gabriell a brotherly hug and a kiss on the cheek, and they departed in differer directions.

When they had left, Immel took out a pad, wrote the nam Mathieu Burdette, and added a short physical description. Then h closed the pad, returned it to his pocket, and resumed his attentiv interest to the conversation of his friends.

"Your father was helpless to stop what happened in Marseilles, Claude St. Jude said to his American guests. "At the very time he wa hearing about it, we were running for our lives. Marseilles was badl hit. Our businesses, however, were untouched."

"How did you manage to escape?" Gabrielle asked.

"One of the earliest arrests was seen by one of our people, who, i: fact, was on her way to that very same address. She saw the polic vehicles and wisely kept walking past, and went directly to a phone The word spread quickly, but for many it was too late.

"Edna-Marie and I were at a newly rented apartment in the Ol: Port, which was not on their list. We made our way out of Marseille on the fishing boat of a friend.

"Within days, more sectors fell, more radios were lost, as wer very valuable people. But perhaps the worst shock of all came from information obtained by Gabrielle Dupuy in Paris. All of the Defianc prisoners taken in the smashing of our sectors had been delivered int: the hands of the Gestapo. Vichy had cut a vile deal with the Germans Our people were imprisoned and interrogated by Gestapo experts Some were eventually shipped to German concentration camps, bu most were not lucky enough to have at least a chance at survival. The were made to endure brutal treatment and torture before dying at th: hands of both their German and French captors.

"It is most difficult to describe the feelings that we all had a learning this. The betrayal, the crime of Vichy's sellout, the deaths of s: many of our friends. It was crushing and demoralizing. And the wors shame of it all was that it was the French police who had done this t: their own people in serving their new masters. For the first time in m: life, I wept and wished that I were not a Frenchman."

Chapter 26

A BRIGHT, beautiful morning had dawned over the Camargue. After a hearty breakfast, Nicole asked Michael if he would like to join her horseback riding in the Camargue. It sounded wonderful, and he said that he would be happy to.

Claude St. Jude was going to be driving into Arles to pick up Edna-Marie, who would be joining them for the next few days. Gabrielle saw the opportunity to spend some time in Arles, and jumped at it. Danny took advantage of the chance to spend time with St. Jude, whom he wanted to know a little better. He had begun to detect the slightest trace of anxiety in him, which Danny was sure arose from Nicole's obvious interest in Michael. It would be important to determine if this was, in fact, the case, and head off any difficulties before they became more profound. They needed a happy, cooperative Claude St. Jude to help them.

St. Jude hadn't seemed to show objection to Michael's decision to stay behind with Nicole. He even made a point of being sure that Michael was provided with a gentle horse, as he had had little riding experience. And he admonished Nicole to remember that her guest was not as adept at riding as she, and not to go galloping off at her accustomed breakneck speed.

"That one, she is as wild as the horses of the Camargue," he had said, shaking his head. "Go at your own pace," he advised Michael. "And trust the instincts of the horse in the marshes. It knows better than a man the areas of safety and of danger."

"Don't worry, please. I'll be doing all I can just to hold on. I'll gladly let the horse go anywhere it wants to," Michael replied, smiling.

255

St. Jude seemed to like Michael a great deal, Danny thought. But he was also very paternal and protective regarding his daughter. He hoped Michael would use good judgment.

Michael's skill astride a horse was a bit better than he had confessed. Though he had not ridden much, he was possessed of a keen sense of balance and a great deal of coordination.

It pleased Nicole to see his quick adjustment. After a little learning by trial, Michael demonstrated fairly good control, even while at a medium gallop. Taking that as evidence enough that he could ride Nicole took off at a high-speed gallop. Michael's horse followed without cue, and he was quickly relegated to a role of "hanger on," just as he had told St. Jude.

As they dashed and splashed across the marshes and flooded plains, Michael started to get the rhythm of the horse and began to exercise more control. It became great fun as he chased after her, never able to catch her. Nicole's skill on a horse was outstanding.

After a long splashing frolic, they slowed their mounts to a walk as they came to an area of firmer ground covered with tall swaying reeds They let the wind blow into their faces, carrying the sound of the rustling tall grass and the smell of the marsh. It was all wonderful Time had not changed this place since it was carved into being.

"See there," Nicole said, extending her arm.

Michael looked into the tall reeds to where she pointed. He could see the tops of the heads of at least ten of the beautiful white horses for which the Camargue was famous. They were feeding on the tall grass shoots that many *manadiers* still used to thatch their roofs. Entire houses had once been built with the stiff grasses.

"Is it not beautiful here?" she asked in her accented English.

"It's magnificent. I can see why Camarguais never leave."

"Oh, some do. The young, mostly, going to the cities. I almost left," she said, with the sounds of the horses' heavy breathing and the soggy clopping of their hooves as backdrop.

"I've seen many places," she said. "Each one was different and interesting. I wanted to live in them all. But the Camargue in my blood always burned hottest, and I returned. I always return."

"That keeps your father happy," Michael said.

"Yes. It is his dream that I take over the *manade* one day. He would like nothing better than for me to marry the son of some other *manadier* and live out my life here. But no one is good enough for me he thinks."

"Is that why you haven't married?" Michael asked.

Nicole shook with laughter. "God, no! Life is too much fun to end t with marriage and children. Perhaps I've sampled too much of it to :ver settle down," she said. "I enjoy going where I like, when I like, ιnd with whom I like. I enjoy men. Certainly too much to settle for *ne*. Besides, I haven't found one yet that is everything that I want in a ιan. I want too much. Perfection."

They came to a spot with low grass and a large stand of trees. In he distance several of the white mares grazed idly on samphire and narsh plants, their dark foals close by their sides.

"How long do they stay dark like that?" Michael asked.

"About three years," Nicole replied. "That is also the age at which hey are first saddled and broken."

They stopped their horses and dismounted, letting the animals graze on the low green grass. They looked at one another and laughed ιt the sight of themselves. They were both speckled and covered with he dark mud of the marshes.

Michael walked over to a tree and sat on the ground, leaning back ιgainst the trunk. Nicole followed him and did the same. They sat in :ilence for a while, letting the marsh wind cool them. Then Nicole spun ιway from the tree and lay on the ground with her head across Michael's legs.

"My father likes you very much," she said. "He admires your determination to find your father's killers. But I think at the same time ιe is a little afraid, not knowing what you'll do when you find them."

"And you?" Michael asked, letting his fingers run through her soft ong hair.

"I'm afraid, both for you—and of you a little bit," she replied.

"Afraid *of* me?" Michael asked in surprise. "Why?"

"Because in your eyes I sometimes see a hardness belonging to a man who could do anything, even kill. The old Gypsy woman, Madame Simone, was right about war, wasn't she?" Nicole asked.

"Yes, she was. I was in Vietnam for thirty-nine months. That was :hree tours of duty," Michael replied.

"You are either very courageous or very stupid," she said.

"A little bit of the first and a lot of the second."

"I think not," Nicole said, sitting up and moving closer to him. 'You are not a stupid man, Michael. And I also said that I was afraid 'or you. I think that you are beautiful," she said, placing her hand on :he side of his face. "Beautiful for loving your father so much, and beautiful for defending his honor so gallantly. And you are beautiful because . . . because you are simply beautiful. I see a wonderful sen- :itivity in you, from the way you see such beauty here in the Camargue.

257

You are chasing after such ugliness, and I am afraid for your safety."

They were now face to face, looking into each other's eyes.

Michael wanted to tell her not to be afraid for him. He felt dishonest in letting her think that the Glad-jo in him did not exist. If she could see that part of him, she would mount her horse and ride away as swiftly as possible, he thought.

But he chose silence, and he put his hand into her hair and gently pulled her face forward and kissed her.

Nicole gave herself willingly to the kiss, pulling herself tightly against him. In that moment something special seemed to exist between them, perhaps not unlike what had existed between Christian and Gabrielle. They were being swept by a force stronger than themselves.

Their lips parted, and Nicole quickly kissed him again, but very softly, her tongue repeating a shortened version of its sensual performance, then lightly tracing his lips. She smiled at him and touched her cheek gently against his. With her lips near his ear, she whispered, "I think it's time we went home."

Their lovemaking was as magical and surprising as their first kiss had been. As if by instinct, they knew the ways to please one another. There was an amazing gentleness to the strong American that Nicole had not imagined in her fantasies of him. And in her, he had found more than he, too, had imagined.

They lay in each other's arms, wonderfully spent and gratified. They kissed tenderly, and caressed one another for hours, neither wanting to look at the clock and the approaching time when they knew the others would be returning.

"They'll be back before too long," Michael said, gently stroking her hair.

"Why are Americans always so preoccupied with a clock and punctuality?" she pouted.

"My only concern with time right now is that it isn't moving slow enough," Michael said. "But I think it would be to everyone's best interests if we were dressed and waiting downstairs when they return."

"Okay," she said, sitting up in the bed. "But I protest most ardently."

He looked at her beautiful breasts and body, then began kissing her again. "We could keep this up forever," he said, stopping himself. "We can resume this discussion later."

"And soon," she added. "I get lonely at night."

"You'll get a lot more than that if we're not downstairs when your

258

father gets back." Michael said. "Come on. Pretty Lady. let's get your little buns dressed and downstairs. I know." he said, cutting off her next words. "You protest most ardently."

Their timing couldn't have been better. No more than fifteen minutes had passed when the car pulled up in front of the house.

Danny was the first into the house, carrying Edna-Marie's bag. One look at Michael and Nicole together left him with the unmistakable impression that his warning to go slow had been wasted. Eye contact with Michael all but confirmed it.

"Shit." Danny muttered under his breath.

Greetings were warmly exchanged when Edna-Marie entered. St. Jude took her bag upstairs and showed her to her room. Then he returned downstairs while Edna-Marie freshened up.

"How was your ride?" St. Jude asked Michael.

"It was great. I couldn't get over the beauty of the marshes. I can see why you're so contented living here. It's truly a remarkable place. I hope to see a good deal more of it," Michael said.

"I'm sure that you will."

"How was Arles?" Michael asked his sister.

"Beautiful—like something out of a Roman history book. You have to see the arena," she began, and continued giving him her impressions of Arles until Edna-Marie came downstairs.

Over dinner they reviewed the discussions that had taken place in Clermont-Ferrand and Pont du Château for Edna-Marie's benefit. They also brought her up to date on the part of the story that St. Jude had told them the night before.

Edna-Marie picked up the story again as they sat at the table over coffee and after-dinner drinks. She told them that weeks of intense activity followed the losses due to Pointer's treachery, as they went about the rebuilding of the smashed sectors. The three of them were now fugitives, their names on a wanted list. They traveled under false identities, always apart from one another, and in carefully prepared disguises created specifically for their new identities.

They worked long, hard days and nights, but were amply rewarded when every sector again became functional. The British replaced the lost radios and sent badly needed money. Group Defiance was bouncing back.

It was at about this same time that more bad news was received. There had been fourteen executions at Fresnes Prison, ten of those being Defiance people. Accompanying that news was information that another five had been released. They had seen this trick before. The people released were doubtless let go to be followed, hoping that they would lead to other cells in the Group Defiance network. The word went out immediately to avoid any contact, whatsoever, with these people. Some of them could also be traitors now, having dealt with the enemy to save their own skins at the price of their friends'.

It was mid-1942 when the British began the Lysander operations for Defiance. Lysanders were widely used to help Resistance groups all over France. The Lysander was a small, relatively slow-flying plane used by British Intelligence to bring agents, supplies, presents, and dispatches in and out of France. The wonderfully brave pilots of these planes virtually hedgehopped their way to carefully selected landing sites all over France. The beauty of the Lysander was that it could land and take off in surprisingly little space, and on rough, unprepared fields. Its lightness and maneuverability, as well as the skill and courage of the pilots, made it an invaluable tool to both the British and the French. Unarmed and fitted with a large auxiliary fuel tank, it relied only upon the ability of the pilot to outwit German Luftwaffe on night patrol.

"It was always very inspirational to us when one of these planes came in safely. It was a piece of Britain right here in France. It was so much more than the invisible air waves which we could not touch," Edna-Marie said.

"At first the landings in the unoccupied zone were simple and uncomplicated. Once all of France became occupied, however, the Germans quickly made things difficult. They put wooden stakes and trenches across fields ideal for use, and had some success. They also managed to discover landing sites through informers, and would lie in wait to catch both the plane and the Resistance fighters meeting it. It was just such a trap that proved fatal for poor Leopard and almost got us all."

Their conversation was interrupted by the ringing of the phone. St. Jude jumped up to get it, taking it in the study so as not to disturb Edna-Marie's storytelling.

A few moments later St. Jude came rushing back into the room in a state of great excitement. "I have just spoken to Jacques Collard. He said that Immel has been discovered in France."

"Immel? In France?" Michael repeated.

"Yes, near the town of Cuisery in Burgundy. He has apparently been living there in isolation for years. He was discovered by the communists. From what Jacques told me, threats have already been made against him by both the Red Brigades and Firewatch. They are demanding that he leave France, or else."

"They don't waste any time, do they?" Danny said.

A wry smile crossed St. Jude's face. "Against Immel? He is lucky that they did not shoot him on sight."

"How soon could we get to see him?" Michael asked.

"Tomorrow is the feast of the Marys, and I am irrevocably committed to the ceremonies. But it should be possible for you to leave by car first thing in the morning. Cuisery is about a four-hour drive. I know the director of the Poste de Police there. I will contact him in the morning to tell him that you are coming. Edna-Marie and I can join you there later by train."

"Do you think that Immel would know the identity of Z?" Michael asked.

"It is possible," Edna-Marie replied. "Though I don't think it is likely. Immel left France in January of 1943, having been reassigned to the Russian front. Z had only just begun to work his treachery, and Gabrielle Dupuy had been unable to learn anything regarding Z from him. There is always the possibility that he *did* know something, however. We will have to wait and see."

Chapter 27

GEORGES Blanc was the director of the Poste de Police in Cuisery. He was sixty-two years old, comfortably overweight, and quite content to sit out the few remaining years of his public service behind the desk of his quiet post. Life was good in Cuisery. There was little major crime, and virtually nothing by which a man of ambition and planning could distinguish himself to the notice of his superiors in the Police Judiciaire. But this did not disturb Georges Blanc, for he had neither ambition, nor plans for advancement beyond his current station. He had achieved his rank by the mere distinction of being there so long, having joined the Poste de Police in Cuisery in 1946, just after the war. And though his record was not distinguished in any significant way, it was also unblemished.

It was just three days ago that the easy stillness of his post was disrupted by the discovery of the presence of former SS Colonel Rudolf Immel, convicted war criminal, living in quiet solitude only a few kilometers south of Cuisery.

A quick investigation revealed that Immel had been in formal residence, unnoticed as it was, for the past eight years. He had applied for a French resident permit under his own name, which was automatically granted under the then-established protocol of the Common Market Treaty. Immel had made no attempt to hide his identity, though he had neglected to enter into record that he was a convicted war criminal, having been tried and found guilty before a U.S. military court at Dachau in 1945 of the mass murder of seventy-one American prisoners in the Ardennes Forest near Malmédy during the Battle of the Bulge.

Immel's presence had been discovered by a storekeeper—a communist and a holder of the Brown Book, a publication listing all alleged Nazi war criminals, published by the East German communist party. Immel had left his name with an order requiring a special requisition. The store owner, suspicious of the obvious German accent, thumbed through the book, and to his delight found the name in clear prominence.

The situation came to Director Blanc's immediate attention. Despite his efforts to keep the issue from being blown out of proportion, it became common knowledge all across France within a few days when *L'Humanité*, the newspaper of the French communist party, splashed the news in large headlines for all to see. Blanc's office suddenly became a hotbed of activity and ringing phones. Extremist groups like the Red Brigades and Firewatch threatened violence unless Immel was expelled from France immediately. For some, it seemed that the war had never ended.

But Georges Blanc was not of the same belief. The war was over as far as he was concerned. In all the years that Immel had quietly lived outside Cuisery, he had never once caused complaint, keeping to himself while he earned a meager but sufficient income translating books into German. This supplemented the pension he received from the German government for his service in the military.

The mayor of Cuisery and other officials of the town agreed with Blanc, stating that they saw no reason to demand that Immel leave France. With that statement came a flood of protests from the communist groups, accompanied by quite serious threats of action.

St. Jude's call to Blanc the next morning had made the situation plain to the interested parties in the Camargue. Though the danger did not seem immediate, it was very real. The three Americans were on the oad within the hour, with St. Jude and Edna-Marie planning to join hem the following day, after the feast of the Marys was concluded.

It was midafternoon when the Americans arrived at the office of George Blanc.

The short, plump police official received them immediately, his round face and bald head wet with perspiration from the unusual heat of the spring day. The purpose for their visit and reason for being in France had been explained, and he greeted them warmly.

Blanc closed the door to his hot little office after the introductions had been made. He sat behind his neatly kept desk, wiping away the steady flow of perspiration with a damp, wrinkled handkerchief. A small fan strained in the background to cool the stuffy room.

"We appreciate your seeing us so promptly," Michael said.

"It is no problem at all," Blanc replied. "I have had my secretary arrange for rooms for you, as Claude said that you would be staying for one or two nights."

"Thank you very much," Michael said.

Blanc acknowledged with a flick of his plump hand. "It was no trouble."

"Have you spoken with Immel?" Michael asked.

"Yes, I have. I felt it my duty to inform him of the threats being made against him. But he is unafraid and will not leave. He lives in a small but comfortable house which he built himself. It has been his home for eight years, and he has no intention of leaving it."

"What is your assessment of the situation?" Danny asked.

Blanc hesitated a moment, lighting a cigarette. He blew out smoke, extinguishing the match. "I think that we will have serious trouble in Cuisery if he does not leave," he said.

"Then you think that they'll follow through on their threats and try to kill him?" Michael asked.

"I think that at first they will try to scare him. But they won't. He is truly unafraid. He was a German officer, highly decorated, who saw much action during the war. He is still very sharp and strong. When they realize that he will not run from them, then they will try to kill him."

"Can you protect him?" Gabrielle asked.

Blanc shook his head. "I have a very small department. I can't spare men to guard his home. I have offered to bring him into Cuisery, where I can give him protection, but he fears, and probably quite correctly, that they will burn his house and belongings if he leaves."

"Then he's left alone to make a stand," Michael said.

Blanc nodded, puffing his cigarette. "That's about it. Of course, I've issued stern warnings to all those making threats that any act of violence will be in violation of French law and subject to action by the police. But that won't stop the really serious-minded. When their patience runs out they will act."

"Can we see him, to talk to him?" Michael asked.

"I can take you there, but I cannot promise that he will talk to you. Many people have tried to see him in the past three days, mostly reporters and news people. He has spoken to a few, but refuses to see any of them now," Blanc said.

"We'd still like to try."

The Frenchman leaned forward and crushed out his cigarette. "I have a car ready to leave whenever you would like," he said.

Within minutes they were on their way, and Blanc used the time driving out to give them a rundown on the former German officer's record.

Rudolf Immel had been an officer in the Waffen SS, with a classic background. He was born the son of a Prussian army officer, raised with discipline, loyalty, and a sense of duty instilled in him by the example of his father. At eighteen he was a member of the Hitler Youth. He attended the Junkerschule, emerging as a commissioned lieutenant with a military career planned. He became a member of the Schutz Staffel—the SS—which developed into two distinct branches; the black-uniformed concentration camp guards, and the Waffen (military) SS, of which he was part.

He was assigned to the Liebstandarte panzer division, and saw extensive action in Poland, where his heroism won him many decorations and a captain's rank. He later saw action in France, spearheading the rapid advance of the panzer divisions through Sedan and then westward toward Paris. He received multiple wounds in the heavy fighting which smashed the last-gasp resistance of the beaten French armies, again being decorated for acts of extreme courage and daring.

It was during his recuperative period that he was temporarily assigned to the staff of General von Roeth in Paris to combat the efforts of Resistance groups springing up across France. Immel proved to be quite adept at his new job, and remained on assignment until January of 1943, when he briefly fell from grace with his superiors over his failure to protect and deliver a very important scientist being transported back into Germany.

Immel was then reassigned to his old Liebstandarte command just at the time when Waffen SS panzer divisions were first used as a uni-

ed block in February and March of 1943, in the Manstein coun-
eroffensive in Russia, which recovered Kharkov.

These battle-toughened panzer divisions then began an incredible
ecord of performance, being rushed back and forth between Eastern
nd Western fronts, serving in France, Italy, and Russia, carrying out
n emergency role, being thrust into one major offensive after another,
onstantly being whisked between fronts and thrown immediately into
onflict. Liebstandarte became the most renowned division of them all.
They were used mercilessly, fighting themselves to virtual destruction.

The last great battle of Liebstandarte began in December 1944, at
he Battle of the Bulge, in which Immel's group spearheaded the offen-
ive in the Ardennes. He was a full colonel now, commanding the 1st
Panzer Regiment of the 6th Panzer Division, equipped with the superb
King Tiger" heavy tanks. It was here that the infamous massacre of
American POW's occurred at Malmédy, for which he stood trial and
was found guilty.

Surviving the Battle of the Bulge, the remaining units of Liebstandarte fought gallantly, counterattacking the Russians in Hungary in
arly 1945, fighting themselves to final oblivion. A mere twelve tanks of
he once dreaded Liebstandarte Division limped away to remain at
war's end. Immel was arrested in Austria and put on trial at Dachau
before a nine-man United States military court, along with seventy-
hree other officers and men. He was found guilty of the deaths of
eventy-one American prisoners at Malmédy (as the identities of only
hat many could be positively confirmed), and was sentenced to death
by hanging. But one legal maneuver followed another for five years,
eeping him from execution, until his sentence was commuted to life
mprisonment. Immel had won the greatest battle of all—for his life.

Five years later, a board was convened consisting of three West
Germans, an American, a Frenchman, and an Englishman, and clem-
ncy was recommended. He was free after nearly twelve years of im-
risonment.

Unlike many of his fellow war criminals, he did not change his
name. His pride and personal honor would not permit it. This resulted
n more charges being brought against him for actions in France and
taly involving more mass killings. The trials were lengthy, but he won
reedom in each of them, because it was decided that, just as his de-
ense had stated repeatedly, the deaths were the result of acts of war
during the heat of battle, and were not atrocities.

He was next brought under fire by the Soviet Union and Hungary
or similar charges, but could not be extradited to face trial, and he
remained a free man.

Years followed in which he took jobs, quickly working his way up the ladder of responsibility, demonstrating strong capabilities, only to have it all pulled out from under him each time because of his past. Finally, he gave up and looked for a place where he could live his life quietly, without the haunting presence of those terrible episodes. He found it in Cuisery, where he managed a comfortable, happy existence with the first peace he could remember in what seemed his entire life. He had eight years of that peace, before leaving his name on an order sheet in the wrong store. It proved to be an invitation back into the hell he thought he had left behind.

It was a long walk from where the car had to be parked. Immel's house was almost a kilometer off the road. They passed through a large pasture and a narrow stand of trees before the house came into view across another large pasture.

Immel could be seen in the distance swinging an ax with strong rapid chops. He was taking down a five-foot-high row of what had been thick, well-maintained border pine running across the front of his property about forty feet from the house. It was no mystery to Michael what he was doing. He was removing possible cover for the enemy and increasing his field of observation from the house. The man was getting ready to make a stand.

With what Michael knew about warfare, he could have made that inviting pine row a death trap for anyone coming near it.

A large German shepherd started barking as the group crossed the pasture. It was a particularly mean-sounding dog. Immel stopped his work and looked across the field at the approaching party. He dropped his ax and disappeared into the house, emerging a few seconds later with a double-barreled shotgun. The German walked back to his property line, and waited for his uninvited guests to draw nearer.

"Herr Immel, it is I, Georges Blanc," the round little police captain announced in rather good German as they drew closer.

Immel had known that much, recognizing Blanc from the moment he first spotted them. It was the other people with Blanc that concerned him.

They heard Immel voice some kind of command to the dog, who went immediately to his side, still barking fiercely. Immel leveled the gun at them as they approached.

"Herr Immel, there is no need for the gun," Blanc said to him.

Immel stood tall and straight. His hair was as white as snow, the shoulders broad and still strong. The sharp eyes still had the intensity of their youth. He looked remarkably like the photograph they had of

266

him, as though time had done little to change him except to whiten the hair and add a few lines around the eyes and mouth. The cleft in the chin and the scar on the left cheek still dominated the handsome, rugged features.

He held the gun steady. The group had stopped at about twenty yards.

"Good afternoon, Captain Blanc," Immel said. "What brings you here today?" he asked in good but accented French.

"These are friends of mine. They mean you no harm. They wish only to talk to you," Blanc explained over the loud barking and mean snarls of the angry dog.

"No interviews," Immel said gruffly.

"No, no, you don't understand," Blanc said, looking nervously at the dog, who seemed ready to charge at them. Blanc had never liked dogs.

Immel did nothing to quiet the dog. The louder and more fearsome it seemed, the greater the distraction to these people. He meant to have every advantage possible.

"They have not come here because of the events of the past days. They have come to you because they need your help," the Frenchman said.

"My help?" Immel said, then laughed.

"Let me talk to him," Michael said to Blanc.

Blanc nodded and gestured to go ahead by pointing a hand forward at Immel, at which the dog nearly broke at him, but held close to its master's side. Blanc backed away a few steps behind the American.

"My name is Michael Gladieux, and this is my sister, Gabrielle, and her husband, Daniel Preston," Michael said in perfect German. "My father's name was Christian Gladieux. The name may not mean anything to you, but you met him during the war. He was a member of Group Defiance in the French Resistance. He was recently murdered. A charge of collaboration was made against him as the reason for his murder. We've come to France to find those responsible for killing him, and to clear his name."

Immel remained silent, seemingly unimpressed by what he had heard. He looked at these people closely, then stared hard at Michael's face. "Hold, Schatzi. Down," he commanded the dog.

The dog stopped barking immediately and lay down, distrust still in its eyes, grunts and whines coming from its throat.

Immel checked the gun and swung it away. "I don't know how I can help you," he said. "But you are welcome here."

"Thank you," Michael said, smiling.

Immel bent down and patted the dog. "Stay, Schatzi. Good dog," he said in German.

The dog lowered its head to its front paws, its tail wagging ever so slightly from the praise of its master.

"You may come in, if you like," Immel offered, dropping into French.

The group approached, Blanc still keeping a cautious eye on the dog. They followed Immel toward his house.

It was an attractive house, about forty feet long, one level, and made of stone. The quality of the masonry was outstanding. The design was imaginative, and the entire area inside the property line was meticulously landscaped and cared for. There were even flower boxes along the windows filled with brightly colored flowers. Attractive curtains hung in the windows.

They entered the house and found it surprisingly well decorated inside. Immel was a man of good taste and obvious talent, as much of the furniture was homemade and quite well done.

He led them to a large sunlit living room, where they sat. Along one wall was a massive stone fireplace, the walls to either side covered with old photographs and mementos from the war years. By one of the tall windows sat a long desk upon which were neatly piled books and papers and a typewriter. This was where he worked in the mornings and evenings translating other people's work into German.

"Now, how do you feel that I can help you?" he asked in his gutturally accented French.

"We were hoping that you could tell us something about the collaborator code-named Z by your people during the war," Michael said, hoping that Immel would show signs of recognition. But he didn't, and waited for Michael to continue.

Michael briefly described the death of his father and the threats that had been made against him prior to his murder. He made no reference to the pendant, but did tell him about the missing outline and manuscript materials, explaining that he felt certain his father knew the identity of the true collaborator, staying carefully with that theme.

The German listened noncommittally, then rose to his feet when Michael had finished. He walked to the window by the desk and looked outside for a long moment, as though he were expecting someone. Then he turned. "I'm sorry," he said at last, "but I can't help you. I remember Group Defiance, and that there was a collaborator known as Z who was quite helpful to us. But I left France in January of 1943 to rejoin my command on the Eastern front. I never knew the identity of Z. I could not tell you if it was your father or not."

"Do you at least remember our father?" Gabrielle asked, the disappointment obvious in her face.

"It was a long time ago. I was assigned to Paris for a short time during the war. Ask me if I remember Paris, or Russia, or the Ardennes, or any of the dozens of major battles I fought in, and I could tell you about them. But one man, a Frenchman, whom I *might* have met once? No, I'm afraid I can't help you," he said.

Michael listened to the words, but something in the man's eyes said they were not the truth. Perhaps he was just seeing what he wanted so much to see. He rose and paced slowly toward the fireplace. He stopped in front of the pictures on the wall and saw something that told him that Immel remembered those days in Paris a great deal more than he was willing to admit. It was a picture of a radiantly beautiful Gabrielle Dupuy. He turned and walked back to his sister. "Give me the pictures," he said.

She found them in her bag and handed them to her brother.

Michael looked through them, finding the one of his father standing alone. He handed it to Immel. "Do you recognize this man?" he asked.

Immel took the picture and studied it. "No," he answered.

Michael was sure that he saw recognition in Immel's eyes. He flipped through the pictures again, found the one of his father standing with Gabrielle Dupuy, and showed it to him. "And now?"

It was unmistakable this time.

"You shared more than a war with my father, Colonel Immel. I think that you remember him quite well," Michael said.

Immel stared at Michael for a long moment, then looked back to the picture of Christian and Gabrielle. He turned his head toward the wall to where the picture was hanging. "She was the most beautiful woman I have ever known. I loved her very much," he said, his eyes far away in the past.

"So did my father," Michael said.

"Yes, I know. I knew it from the first moment I saw them together."

"Can you help us, Colonel Immel?" Michael asked.

"Perhaps. I'll tell you what I can. I never knew the identity of Z, as he became operational shortly before I was transferred out of Paris, and he reported through another department of von Roeth's office. But I can tell you one thing of which I am absolutely certain—your father was not the collaborator Z.

"Please, sit down," Immel said to Michael, gesturing toward the chair. "This will take some time. I will get some glasses and wine."

Pierre Falloux slammed the phone down and pounded the desk with an angry fist. Damn it! he thought. Because of some idiotic over-zealous store clerk, the discovery of Immel living in France had become hot news. The timing couldn't have been worse. He had just received a report telling him that the three Americans were with Immel now.

Falloux got up from his desk and began pacing the room, thinking about the possible significance of this development. He had made the mistake of underestimating Gladieux's children once already. They seemed to be able to pick up on the smallest clues and oversights, turning them into potential threats to his existence.

He decided not to take any more chances than he had to. Everything was at stake. The smallest error on his part now would be the end of him. The Committee would demand it. They would even "arrange" it if he did not immediately execute his sworn oath to the Salamandra.

He had already stretched their patience as far as it would go, assuring them that all traces of Gladieux's outline and manuscript had been successfully removed. If they knew that Gladieux's children were trying to retrace his steps on the scent of the same mystery, they would not hesitate to withdraw the one opportunity they had given him to save himself. They would not wait for him to fail the test; they would demand action at the first sign of danger. And finding Immel could be that first sign. He had to act quickly before these new developments came to the attention of the Committee.

He walked back to his desk and dialed a number.

After several rings, the other end came to life. "Yes," the voice answered.

"Have you contacted your associate?" Falloux asked nervously.

"Yes, he's in Dijon, waiting," Demy answered.

"Have him meet you near Cuisery tonight. I have an urgent job for you. It must be taken care of immediately."

Chapter 28

R UDOLF Immel proved to have an excellent memory. It became immediately evident as he recounted the story of the time when he first met Christian sitting with Gabrielle in Paris.

"Your father put on a very good act," he said. "It was almost believable. But I knew Gabrielle too well, the little things about her, things that reveal little truths. She was very nervous. I could see that.

"I tested him immediately by holding her hand. His eyes did not lie as well as his tongue did. I watched them closely after leaving them, making careful notes on your father's description so that I could remember him later."

"Did you suspect my father so quickly?" Michael asked.

"No, not of being in the Resistance. The juices working inside me were not of a professional nature. What I felt was jealousy. It was only later, when I recognized your father from a photograph taken from the military file of one of the identities given to us by a well-planted double agent, that I confirmed his connection to the Resistance," Immel explained.

"That was Pointer?" Michael asked.

"I see that you know a good deal already," Immel commented.

"We've made progress. But we need to learn a lot more."

"Excuse me for interrupting," Danny said. "But once you became aware of Christian's involvement, didn't you suspect Gabrielle?" he asked.

"Yes, I did," Immel replied. "But I kept these suspicions to myself. I later confirmed that fact by setting a little trap, which worked perfectly."

"Then you knew that Gabrielle was a part of the Resistance?" Michael asked.

"Yes, *I* knew, but Command didn't."

"Why didn't you arrest her?" Michael asked.

Immel stared down at the photograph of Gabrielle and Christian for a long moment before answering. "Because I loved her," he said.

From the background that had been supplied by Georges Blanc, and the impression he had formed of Immel, Michael was surprised by the unexpected weakness in this man.

"You were fighting a war," he said. "She was the enemy."

"It was 1942, and we were *losing* a war," Immel corrected. "There were many of us who were not blind, especially in the military. I knew what I should have done, but also knew how much I loved her. And it would not have changed the outcome of the war to have arrested her."

"You never confronted her with this?" Danny asked.

"Yes, but it was not a confrontation actually. I made a statement to her that made my awareness of it plain. It was one of the last things I ever said to her, when I was leaving for the Russian front. I could never have lived with the knowledge that I had sent her to her death. It wasn't until many years after the war that I learned she had died," the German said, then fell sadly quiet.

"You mentioned setting a trap," Michael said.

"Yes. I used Pointer to confirm my suspicions about Gabrielle. It always intrigued me how such a fool could have been as successful as he was," the German began. "I decided to use him when he made the incredible blunder of turning up in Paris, radio and all, when he was supposed to be operating in Normandy. And he was continuing to transmit as though he was still in place. It was only a matter of time before his cover would have been blown.

"I prepared a blind memo to von Roeth, advising him that Pointer, who was known to us as Vulcan, had come to Paris, seriously risking compromise of his double role. I recommended that he be sent at once to Algeria, by way of Marseilles, with the story that he had been reassigned by urgent order from British Intelligence; otherwise, we risked losing him completely by his blunder.

"Gabrielle and I were staying together at the time, and I left the folded memo inconspicuously among my papers. I reasoned that if she was an agent for Group Defiance, she probably went through my papers regularly. If she did, and discovered the memo, then Pointer would be revealed as a double agent and intercepted before arriving in Algeria. His immediate departure would allow him ample time to get out of France before Defiance could have discovered his betrayal by their own efforts. If he made it to Algeria, then I would consider my

272

suspicions about Gabrielle to be wrong, and he would be safely in place elsewhere.

"Well, he left Paris a few days later by order from von Roeth. He never made it to Algeria. He simply vanished. Group Defiance had intercepted him in Marseilles, interrogated him, and disposed of him," Immel said.

"How were you able to confirm that?" Michael asked.

"It was confirmed several months later by Z," Immel replied.

"Was Z planted by German counterintelligence?" Danny asked.

"No, he was developed from within the ranks of Group Defiance," the German answered.

"How?" Danny asked.

"I don't know, he wasn't my agent. He reported through another section of von Roeth's office, headed by a Hauptmann Dieter Liepart. Somehow, he had managed to entice Z to inform, either through an offer of money, or some form of extortion. We did that often," Immel replied.

Michael's brain had zeroed in on the name that Immel had just mentioned. Dieter Liepart. *Liepart. Leopard.* Could the similarity be simple coincidence?

"Go back to this Captain Liepart," Michael said. "What became of him?"

"I don't have the slightest idea," Immel responded.

"When was Z developed?" Michael asked.

"Near the end of 1942. A few months later, I was on my way to Russia."

Michael looked at Danny, who by this time had made the connection. Both were thinking the same thing. This could be an interesting lead for Pheagan to follow.

"And Liepart was still in Paris when you were transferred?"

"Yes, he was."

"Was he also in the SS?"

"No, he was Gestapo. He had not been in Paris very long when I left."

"Does the word or possible code name Leopard mean anything to you?" Michael asked.

Immel thought for a few seconds before shaking his head. "No, but Group Defiance often used the names of animals as code names. Many Resistance groups did."

"What about the word Circus?" Michael asked.

Immel shook his head again after some thought. "Another code name, I imagine. There were so many."

"Did you ever see my father again?" Gabrielle asked.

"Yes, just once, shortly before I left for the Russian front. In fact it was your father who was responsible for my . . . 'reassignment,' " Immel replied.

"I had been given the responsibility of seeing to the safe transfer of a scientist who was being brought back into Germany from Spain. His name was Dr. Max Schrict. He was a physicist, I learned later, who was to help in our atomic research and experimentation. Our intelligence had learned that the British were aware of our original plan to fly him into Germany across the Alps. The plan was secretly changed and he was transported by land to Clermont-Ferrand, where he was to be safely put on a specially armored, heavily guarded train taking him to Mulhouse, where another command would take charge.

"We were unaware that the British had broken our code and were onto the change. They very cleverly followed through on the attack on the decoy plane, which flew according to the original plan, shooting it down over the Alps. We had every reason to believe that we would succeed in our deception.

"Clermont-Ferrand was a critical point in the operation, as Schrict would be there for two hours before boarding the train and being taken from my responsibility. About an hour before the arrival of the train we received a communication that our plan had been discovered, and that an attempt was to be made on the scientist's life in Clermont-Ferrand. He was already under heavy guard, but we increased our security to the maximum, completely securing the perimeter of the train station. Special units were dispatched to inspect every rail section and bridge between Clermont-Ferrand and Mulhouse, and the station was crawling with our troops."

"How did you become aware of the attempt?" Danny asked.

"Liepart's office was informed by Z. He didn't divulge the nature of the attempt. Presumably, he didn't know this. But he did know that it would take place in Clermont-Ferrand," Immel answered.

"And I take it that the attempt was successful?" Danny asked.

"Quite," Immel replied. "It was remarkable, one of the best demonstrations of marksmanship that I have ever witnessed. We were seconds away from success when Schrict was killed by a shot fired from nearly four hundred meters away. He was hit right in the head. The bullet passed so close to me that I felt the disturbance of air. We never even heard the shot over the noise at the station. I learned the following day that it was your father who fired the shot."

Michael listened with awed surprise. He had not known that his father was so proficient with a rifle.

"How did you learn that it was my father?" he asked.

274

"I received a telephone call from someone identifying himself as .. He told me that it was your father who had fired the shot and that he had been badly injured in a fall while making his escape. He also told me where he was hiding. I left immediately after talking to him."

"Why did Z call you instead of Liepart?" Michael asked.

"I don't know. He just gave me the information, then hung up."

"And then you arrested my father?"

"No. I confronted him alone. I intended to kill him. It had become personal matter to me. Although I didn't know at the time who Max chrict was, it had been made plain how important he was. It had been ny responsibility to get him on that train, and I had failed. My career as over, I reasoned, because of that failure, and I fully expected to be rought back to Berlin to be shot. I wasn't about to accept defeat vithout taking my measure of retaliation against the man responsible or it.

"I went to the place where your father was supposed to be hiding, ut he wasn't there. There was evidence that he had been there, so I aited. He returned several hours later, and I surprised him. We strug-led briefly. In his weakened condition I was easily able to defeat him. ut as I stood over him, ready to kill him, I hesitated to savor the final atisfaction. I found myself taking more pleasure in the thought of illing him because of what he had meant to Gabrielle than because of hat had happened in Clermont-Ferrand. And that saved his life. It as only because of her that I didn't kill him when I had the chance. ecause she loved him, because I loved her, because the war was lost, nd because I was lost. I thought of what it would have done to her if I illed him. I couldn't do that to her.

"We were gladiators, your father and I, and although I stood over im with the power of life and death in my hand, I realized that it was e who had won. I left him there and returned to Paris as quickly as I ould."

Immel continued his story, telling them that orders were awaiting im in Paris to report immediately to the Eastern front to rejoin his ormer command in the Waffen SS group Liebstandarte. Fighting in Russia looked good compared to the possible alternative of being shot 1 Berlin.

The orders for immediate departure did not leave time for even ne last night with Gabrielle. He returned to the apartment they hared, but she was not there. He quickly packed his things and tried to ompose a letter to leave for her. His attempts were useless. He just ouldn't find the words to say what he felt. He crumpled the last poor effort and threw it into the wastepaper basket. He went to his bags and was about to pick them up when the door opened.

Gabrielle walked in and saw his bags on the floor beside him. She looked into his eyes, confusion and surprise written plainly on her face.

There was a long moment of awkward silence before he told her that he had been ordered to report to the Eastern front.

"Why? I don't understand," she said, flushing from the shock of his news.

Immel did not answer. He looked at her, forgetting that she had been the enemy, knowing only how much he loved her. He held his arms out to her, and she rushed into them. They held one another tightly.

For Gabrielle, it was a moment that she always knew would come. It had been unspoken between them, a fact deliberately ignored. Rudolf Immel was a fighting soldier, a commander of one of the fiercest, most frightening combat units in the war. Fighting was in his blood. A desk in Paris, complete with its paper wars and invisible enemy, wasn't his style or preference. Although he displayed a talent for conducting such silent warfare, he preferred the hellfire of the front line, where one could immediately assess the results of his efforts.

"Rudy, did you request this?" she asked.

"Request to leave you?" he said. "I would rather pray for a hundred years of war than to leave you," he replied.

"Then why?" she asked.

"It's a long story, and I'd rather spend the time holding you."

"Must you leave now? So soon?"

"Immediately," he answered.

She put her head against his chest and closed her eyes. It was a moment of truth for her. Painful truth. For in the double life she lived she had come to know two men so very different yet so much alike. She had been drawn to one irresistibly, and she loved that man. She had gone to the other not out of love for him but out of a sense of duty and love for her country. This man was the enemy. But within that enemy was also a man that she had come to know and regard separately.

At first it was the enemy who held her and kissed her and made love to her. It was the enemy for whom she had pretended wild, passionate satisfaction. But the man was always there. And the man had been a gentle, considerate lover.

A separate war had started between her heart and her mind. The heart saw the man, the mind recognized only the enemy. She hated herself when her pretense gradually yielded to true explosive passion, when guilt-riddled, sleepless nights became comfortable and warm when the feeling of being used turned to one of giving and sharing; when she looked forward to seeing him and became aroused from watching him; and when hating him became undeniably wanting him.

In this war her mind never surrendered—until now. It was telling her what her heart had known all along, that she loved this man, too.

She looked up into his face, her eyes flooded with tears. "Rudy . . . I love you," she said, for the first time being able to truly mean it.

He smiled at her. "I know that you do, and I love you, too. But you've always known that."

He felt a terrible sadness inside. He sensed that he would never see her again. And in that moment of seeing her, and loving her, he felt glad that he hadn't killed Christian.

"I just want you to know that being with you has meant so very much to me. I tried to put it on paper, but I'm an oaf at such things. I may have the heart of a poet when it comes to you, but I don't have the brain of one, or the gift of his words," he said.

There was no mistaking the look in her eyes. If Rudolf Immel had ever been certain of anything, it was that she loved him.

He smiled and kissed her once, a long and tender kiss, then released her and picked up his bags. He walked to the door, the soft sounds of her sorrow being choked back behind him. He put one bag down and opened the door, then picked up the bag again. He looked back at her for a long moment, then spoke.

"Christian is at the bombed-out Bouchard winery outside of Pont du Château. He's badly injured. Go to him, he needs you."

She looked back at him with a look of absolute shock on her face. "You knew?" she said.

He smiled and nodded. "I knew that you loved him from the time that I first saw you together. I knew the rest shortly after. No one else is aware of it."

"But if you knew, why . . ." Her question trailed off.

"Because I love you that much," he answered. "Goodbye, Gabrielle. Thank you for the love that you've given me. I'll remember you always." He gave a last look, then the door closed and he was gone.

The love that Immel had felt for Gabrielle Dupuy was evident in his voice and on his face as he told them his story.

"I'm afraid that there is no more that I can tell you," Immel said.

Michael nodded. "I thank you for telling us what you have. And I thank you for your honesty."

There was a moment of reflective silence before everyone rose from their seats. Immel accompanied them to the door.

"What was the nature of your father's manuscript?" Immel aske Michael as they walked.

"We don't know. But it was threatening to someone. Enough t get my father killed," Michael replied.

"It's a pity that such a survivor of history should come to tha end," the German said. "I hope that you find what you've come fo Your father was a man of courage. It should not end this way."

"Thank you, again, Colonel Immel," Michael said with a smile c gratitude.

Goodbyes were said all around and the group filed out of th house, Michael being the last along with Immel.

"Have you ever heard of the Salamandra?" Michael asked him i German.

Immel stared at Michael for a moment. "No," he replied.

Michael reached into his shirt and pulled out the pendant. "Hav you ever seen this before?" he asked, continuing in German.

Immel looked at it for a moment. "Is that a part of your mystery? he asked.

"It's the key," Michael returned.

Immel did not break eye contact, nor did he speak.

"Will you come with us? I know your situation here," Micha· said.

Immel gave a crooked smile and shook his head. "I'll be ready fc them. They don't scare me."

"May I come to see you again?" Michael asked.

Immel squinted pensively.

"There's a little more to this that I'd like to talk to you about. Michael said, not sure of the reaction he was trying to elicit.

"Perhaps tomorrow," Immel said, continuing to stare into M chael's eyes.

Michael nodded and smiled. "Tomorrow, then. Good evenin, Colonel Immel."

Michael remained strangely silent on the short trip back into Cui ery. There was something about that last brief exchange with Imm· that stayed with him. It wasn't anything that he had said, unless pe haps it was his agreeing to talk with him another time when the who story had seemingly been told. He kept replaying the entire exchang trying to put his finger on what it was that bothered him.

After checking into their rooms, the three Americans went to th small outdoor café of the hotel for a few drinks before having a la dinner.

Gabrielle remained unusually quiet. Her mood was rather low. She had been thinking about her father, and missing him. The spells of grief still came to her, though they were manageable.

"Why so quiet, Sis?" Michael asked.

She shrugged and sipped her drink. "There was so much about his life that we didn't know. The story of Gabrielle Dupuy is so sad. To think of what he must have gone through. It makes me just . . . just . . . sad," she said, her eyes misting over.

"Yeah, I know, Sis. I miss him too."

After a few moments of pensive silence, Michael turned to Danny. "What did you think about the name, Dieter Liepart?"

"I think that it sounds close enough to be worth pursuing. Pheagan could probably get a fast rundown on the guy," Danny said. "When are you going to call him?"

"I was going to call him tonight, but I might wait a day. I've got another date to see Immel tomorrow," he announced.

"Is that what you two were talking about back at the house as we were leaving?" Gabrielle asked.

"Yes. He asked me about Dad's manuscript. He wanted to know what it was about. Then I asked him about the Salamandra and showed him the pendant. He didn't look at it for more than a split second, but he sure looked at me hard enough to see what was in the back of my head. After that I told him there was more to the story that I wanted to talk to him about. That's when he suggested tomorrow. He could have just said there was no more to talk about, and have been done with it. But I don't think he wanted to be done with it," Michael said. "Maybe I'm just reaching for straws or—"

Michael's words were suddenly cut off by the sound of gunfire in the distance. It was far away, and to the untrained ear would have sounded like firecrackers exploding many blocks distant. But both Michael and Danny knew the sound of gunfire, and there was no mistaking it in their minds.

"Shit!" Danny said, jumping to his feet. "They're trying for him tonight."

In a second, Michael was up and both of them were sprinting for St. Jude's car.

The distant sounds had escalated. There was the rapid tattoo of many weapons, including automatic weapon fire, and the occasional loud boom of a shotgun could be heard. They scrambled into the car and screeched away before Gabrielle could catch up with them. She hesitated a moment, listening to the dreadful sounds of the drama

279

unfolding a few kilometers away. She turned and ran into the hotel and went to the desk.

"Captain Georges Blanc. I need to speak to him immediately," she said nervously. "It's a matter of life or death. Hurry. Please, hurry."

Chapter 29

THE orange glow in the distance told them that the fire had started. It was not a small fire, to be sure. The sounds of gunfire had grown sporadic. There would be a short eruption of shots, abbreviated bursts, a boom, pops from handguns. Then there was the explosion, and large yellow and orange glow. The gunfire stopped after that.

Michael and Danny continued at a reckless pace. The last part of the trip would have been impossible for them in the darkness, as they weren't sure of the way. But the bright glow from the fire provided an easy beacon to home in on.

The car skidded to a halt on the stone and dirt road. They got out of the car quickly, ready to encounter Immel's attackers. Michael snapped back the slide of the Swiss SIG, putting a round into the chamber, and Danny's Smith and Wesson .357 Combat Magnum was out and ready, its stout four-inch barrel menacingly attentive.

They moved quickly across the first pasture in a low crouched run, reaching the protective cover of the trees from where they could command a good view of the area around Immel's house. If they were lucky, they'd be able to catch the attackers in the open. There hadn't been any gunshots since the explosion, and judging from the vision of Immel's blazing house, they were too late to help the former SS colonel, unless he had taken the fight into the open.

The explosion had been extremely powerful. Most of the standing walls had been knocked down from its force, and a fiercely intense fire was raging.

"Let's separate and approach from opposite sides, just in case someone stuck around to confirm their work. Let's try to get one alive if we can," Michael said.

They separated to the extreme edges of the woods, then moved cautiously toward the house. In the distance they could hear the sound of European sirens from Blanc's police cars.

The light from the fire provided good visibility. It became obvious that none of the attackers had stayed around. After confirmation of that fact, the two Americans came together at the front property line, near the partially removed border pine. The heat from the intense blaze could be felt from their vantage point.

Michael shook his head as he released the hammer of the Swiss SIG and returned the weapon to its shoulder holster. "Somebody has had a much better sense of timing than we've had right from the start," he said.

"Somebody knows every move we're making," Danny added, replacing his piece in its holster as well. "Do you think he made it out?"

Michael shook his head. "From the sounds of the gunfire, there were enough men to surround the house. They'd have gotten him if he tried."

Danny looked down to the ground about ten feet in front of them. "He had some advance warning, I'm sure," he said, pointing to the dead dog.

"I doubt that the fight took place in the open," Michael said. "It wouldn't have lasted as long."

The sound of the sirens stopped. A few minutes later Blanc appeared, sweating and puffing from his run across the pastures and through the woods. His men fanned out and surrounded the burning house.

"Did you see anything?" he asked, gasping for breath.

"It was over when we got here," Michael said.

"I didn't think they would strike so soon," the fat policeman said. "Certainly they would have tried to scare him first."

Michael and Danny just looked into the blazing remains of the house without speaking.

"I guess there is little that can be done here until morning," Blanc said. "You may as well go back into Cuisery. I will leave some men here and return at first light to begin an investigation."

"Would you mind if we came back in the morning?" Danny asked.

"Not at all."

"Thank you," Danny said, then looked at Michael. He could see the frustration and disappointment in his brother-in-law's face. How much longer could they hope to go on with every promising lead being taken from them before it could be developed?

"Come on, Mike. There's nothing we can do here now. Let's ge back to Cuisery and contact Pheagan," Danny said.

"Yeah, all right," Michael replied, the disappointment obvious in his voice. "At least we got to talk to him once."

He reflected a moment further and thought about something tha Immel had said in reference to his father. For someone who had sur vived so much history and a war like that, this was no way for it to end The same could be said for Immel. But at least he had had a chance to die like the true soldier he was.

Michael shook his head and turned away, wondering if this wa: the first sign that they had come close to something. If they had, he stil couldn't recognize it.

The match flared, touched the tip of the cigarette, then was blowr out in a stream of smoke. Renaud Demy dragged hard on the cigarette inhaling deeply, and picked up the phone. He dialed the number and waited.

"Hello," answered Pierre Falloux. There was an unmistakable touch of apprehension, which Demy measured immediately.

"This is your friend. The commission has been completed," he announced.

"Are you positive?" Falloux asked.

There was a short silence.

"I said that it was completed," Demy returned, perturbed.

The silence came from Falloux's side this time. He could feel the exception to his question as surely as if he were seeing Demy face to face and reading it in his eyes.

"How many associates were supplied?" Falloux asked, wanting to know the extent of the cooperation that Firewatch had been willing to give after his application of pressure.

"Six."

"Six? There were to be ten," Falloux said, upset by the news.

"It was very short notice. Next time, give me a few days, and I car get men of my own. Professionals, who know their work." It was ob vious that Demy was not pleased with the execution of the operation or the level of proficiency of the men supplied by Firewatch.

"Did you take care of establishing credit?" Falloux asked.

"Yes, at least one. The commission may have provided another At least two others were . . . left impressed by his skill."

"Good, that is exactly what I wanted."

"What about the family?" Demy asked.

There was a momentary pause. "Not yet, I think. I must make one final determination. Stay ready. You may as well begin alerting some of your people. This one can be handled your way when the time comes, but it will be soon," Falloux said.

"Good. Call me when you need us," Demy said.

"Oh, I will. I certainly will."

Demy hung up the phone and crushed out the half-smoked cigarette. What a stupid little game this was becoming, he thought. The family should have been taken care of as soon as they arrived in France. It would have been the moment of greatest advantage. There was no doubt in his mind that they had come to France knowing danger awaited them. Each day that passed would allow them extra preparation, even if it was only mental. But Falloux had said it would be soon. For Demy, it couldn't be soon enough.

At almost the same time that Renaud Demy had spoken to Falloux, another phone conversation had begun. This one was being relayed across the ocean by satellite through the Variscan system of Sub Rosa.

"You're being followed," Pheagan announced before Michael could speak.

"We figured that out for ourselves," Michael replied. "We haven't made the tail yet, but we will, now that we know he's there."

"We've already made three of them. We're running them through the computers now," Pheagan said.

"Three of them?"

"Yes, we spotted the first one in Paris. He left off at the train station in the morning. You were picked up again in Clermont-Ferrand, then again in Arles," Pheagan explained.

"We must be getting important," Michael said. "I take it you already know we've been to Cuisery?"

"I know that you went there, but I don't know why yet," Pheagan said.

"Colonel Rudolf Immel, Waffen SS. He commanded a panzer division in Hitler's elite Liebstandarte, the 1st Regiment of the 6th Panzer Division. He should be an easy book. Immel was convicted of war crimes in 1945 at Dachau by a U.S. military court for the massacre of American prisoners at Malmédy during the Battle of the Bulge," Michael said. "He turned up living quietly in France. He's the German officer in the pictures we gave you. Immel met my father during the war and provided us with some additional background."

Michael summarized the story that Immel had told them. He gave Pheagan the name Dieter Liepart, captain in the Gestapo, and explained their thoughts about the similarity in the names Liepart and Leopard.

"We'll get to work on both Immel and Liepart immediately,' Pheagan said.

"I can give you the last page in Immel's file," Michael said. "Mark it 'Killed in an attack by parties unknown.' Give it today's date."

"Are you sure he's dead?"

"Based upon what I've seen, I'd say it's a sure bet. We'll know in the morning when the authorities go through what's left of the house. I doubt that he'll be recognizable. It'll take a while to confirm it,' Michael said.

"Did you get anything else out of your meeting with him?"

"Just the feeling that he wanted to talk a little more. We were supposed to see him again tomorrow."

"I see," Pheagan mused. "Good timing, to say the least. That could be significant. If I were a betting man, I'd say that your visit to him could have helped trigger the incident."

"Why don't you just grab one of the people who have been following us and 'talk' to him?" Michael suggested. "You might be able to verify that."

"It's not that simple."

"Which leads me to wonder why," Michael commented.

"Yes, I knew that you would," Pheagan retorted dryly.

"I think it's time we had our little talk," Michael said.

On a need-to-know basis, Pheagan had been told. "Will you work with us on this?" he asked.

"I've been working *with* you since I started paying you a thousand bucks a day."

"Cut out the horseshit. You know what I'm asking," Pheagan shot back.

"I thought I made that point quite clear," Michael said. "I don't ever want to work *for* the group again."

"Listen to me," Pheagan said sharply. "You're out there busting your ass, collecting your facts and getting nowhere fast. What you've been able to turn up of importance, so far, would be useless to you without us. We're making progress, real fucking progress. As slow as it may seem to you, it's still taking us to where we both want to be. It doesn't make a goddamn bit of difference why we both have to get there, as long as we get there. You've been running off at the mouth like you think you can get there alone. Well, you can't get there alone. You need us."

"Why don't we just see about that?" Michael threatened. "You've

284

known me for a long time, Pheagan, or Tripper, or whoever the hell you are. You know I don't bluff when I say I'm going to burn ass. This is Glad-jo talking to you now, pal. Glad-jo. And I ain't stupid. I know I'm running point for you right now. I know you didn't grab the first tail you made on us because you *can't* grab him. We're the whole fucking show. That's what you want them to think. And do you want to know what else I think? I'll tell you.

"I think that the Salamandra still exists, and that you and your bosses are scared shitless of them. I think you can't risk letting them know you're onto them, or you lose it all. I'm not the one who can't do it alone, *you* are. Now, do we talk, or do I fire your ass and go the rest of the way alone?"

"You won't get there without us, Mike. We both hold parts to the puzzle," Pheagan said.

"I'll bet I have as good a chance as you. I'll grab one of the tails and bite his goddamn fingers off one at a time, until he tells me who he works for. Then I'll do the same to his boss, and his boss's boss, until I get there. I don't have to play by rules. I'll kill everyone I think has the slightest chance of being the guy I'm after. And when I get close, let them send in Demy and Scalco. They can kill an old man in his library, and other poor unsuspecting sons of bitches, but they'll find Glad-jo tougher than they could ever imagine."

The need to know, Pheagan thought. But whose need? Michael was right. Glad-jo *was* running point for them. If the Salamandra, or Trinity, as he had always known it, became aware of Sub Rosa's involvement, the pendant holder would be terminated immediately. Their chance would be lost forever. There was need, all right, but it wasn't as much the need of Michael Gladieux as it was the need of Sub Rosa.

"All right, you win," Pheagan said. The time to tell Michael Gladieux about Sub Rosa had come. He must be made to understand the seriousness of the situation being faced.

"And don't give me any double talk," Michael warned. "Because the second I think you're handing me a line of shit, the conversation is over. And I mean over."

"You'll get the truth. But I must ask that you keep it to yourself, and not share what I tell you with Danny or Gabrielle."

"I'll agree to that, unless it becomes necessary to share that information to ensure success. I trust Danny completely."

"I'll have to risk living with that, I guess. But I assure you, Mike, it would be a lot simpler for everyone if you were able to withhold the information. It's important that you understand."

"I hear you, but winning this little war is also important. You have my word that I'll hold it as long as I can."

"Fair enough. I trust you," Pheagan said, then took a long breath. "It started a long time ago, Mike, with a small group of men dedicated to preserving the very heart and strength of this country—its private sector. They were men of tremendous wealth and power, who recognized the many dangers in the world. They united themselves, forming sizable secret trusts to help finance their efforts, and embarked upon a course of self-preservation and watchfulness. To symbolize the secrecy of their intentions, they called themselves Sub Rosa. . . ."

Chapter 30

FRAIL white columns of smoke rose slowly from the smoldering ruins of what had once been the home of Rudolf Immel. A large coterie of people had gathered to poke through the wreckage. The brief sensation had drawn a lot of attention throughout all of France and much of Europe. It had swiftly developed into a delicate situation. Many eyes were on France, waiting to see how the matter would be handled. What had happened was the worst of all possible events. The French government would suffer international embarrassment because of its inability to protect a German national living within its borders. It didn't matter that Immel had been a convicted war criminal. He had paid for his crimes to the satisfaction of international law.

Georges Blanc was the picture of worry as Michael and Danny went to him.

"Quite a crowd," Michael said.

"Yes, quite," Blanc said with a troubled frown. He nervously lit up a cigarette. "They've sent in people from the Services Régionaux headquarters, from the Gendarmerie Nationale, and the Central Commissariat. Even the Constituency Commissariat has sent someone," he said, blowing out a huge cloud of smoke.

"All that's missing is the Police Judiciaire," Michael said.

"They will be here later this morning," Blanc complained. He would be held responsible for allowing this to happen, he was sure. There had not been a single blemish on his record. And now this. He puffed nervously on the glowing cigarette.

"Maybe it would be better if we left," Michael suggested.

"No, no. You must stay," Blanc replied quickly. "You were the closest to what happened here. Whatever you have seen or heard will be important."

"It was over when we got here," Michael said. "We told you that last night."

"Yes, I know you did. But for the official record . . . you understand." He broke a weak smile.

"Certainly we do," Danny said before Michael could protest.

"Excuse me, please," Blanc said. "I will be back shortly."

The Americans watched as Blanc walked away to talk to his men, who had been conducting their search for clues since dawn.

"We told him what we saw last night," Michael said, irritated.

"Calm down," Danny said. "The poor guy's just trying to save his ass. Right now, there's a lot of important people here, and he doesn't look too good to any of them. Immel was his responsibility, and he knows it. This should have never been allowed to happen. There's going to be egg landing in a lot of faces over this. All of these departments are here trying to protect themselves. That poor son of a bitch is thinking about his pension."

Just then, shouts emerged from a thin stand of trees at the back of Immel's property. One of Blanc's men had found something. A crowd quickly gathered around the discovery. It was a body.

Blanc was bent over the corpse when Michael and Danny got there. He stood up after a few moments and turned to the Americans. "Have either of you ever seen this man before?" he asked, as if they were his two star witnesses.

They drew nearer to look at the body, which was locked in an ugly death pose. He had died from a bullet wound to the side of the head.

Both said that they had never seen him.

Blanc handed the dead man's wallet and some other papers that had been found to one of his men. "Find out who he was," he ordered as another one of his men approached.

"Pardon, mon Capitaine, but we have found blood in two different locations. It seems that others may have been wounded in the fighting."

Most of the entourage marched off behind Blanc. A police photographer remained to take pictures of the corpse. Two other men, reporters, also tried to take pictures, but were dissuaded by a rather large, angry-looking policeman. They took his meaning and raced off, spitting curses as they ran.

Danny bent down to get a closer look at the head wound. "That was done with a handgun at close range. I'd say from less than a foot away."

"Immel had a handgun. I saw it on a table as we were leaving. It looked like a Luger Parabellum. This could mean that Immel made it out of the house," Michael said optimistically.

"Well, this man died right here. His position suggests response to impact. If he had been moved, he'd have straightened out. Immel could have made it out of the house . . . or somebody else killed this guy," Danny said.

Michael squinted at his brother-in-law after the suggestion.

Another shout arose from the smoldering debris of the house. A second body had been found. Michael and Danny headed over immediately.

The body had been found beneath a large pile of charred debris. It was gruesomely burned beyond recognition and had shrunk to a length of about thirty-six inches. Lying under it was what remained of a shotgun—Immel's shotgun.

"So much for his getting out of the house," Danny said. He kicked around in the rubble near the body and uncovered a handgun. It was a Luger Parabellum. It drew immediate attention.

Danny gestured to Michael to follow him. The two men walked out of the rubble and toward the back of the house. Danny was searching along the ground. "I seriously doubt that they'll be able to get any ballistics from that weapon," he said. "After what it's been through, it probably isn't capable of operation anymore."

"What are we looking for?" Michael asked.

"Casings. To try to determine how much firepower was concentrated at the house from behind it," Danny answered.

They came to a three-foot-high stump of wide diameter. The ground around it was covered with used bullet casings.

"There's no way that Immel came out the back," Danny said. "I figured as much, anyway. It's not likely that he'd have left the house, only to return to it while it was surrounded and burning. That would have been suicide. That tells us something, doesn't it?" he asked.

Michael nodded. "Someone else blew away the dude in the trees."

"That's for damn sure. Now all we have to do is figure out why."

Michael looked at his watch. "We'd better give our statements to

Blanc," he said. "St. Jude and Edna-Marie will be arriving in Tournus later this morning. We have to pick them up."

"Then let's do it," Danny said. "We've gotten all that we need out of here for now. I'm sure that Blanc will tell us what he learns later."

They headed back into Cuisery after giving their statements, picked up Gabrielle at the hotel, and left for Tournus. Blanc had provided them with directions, telling them also how to find the train station once there.

They told Gabrielle of the findings at Immel's place and that he had been killed. It truly depressed her to think that he was dead. It was another small part of her father's life that had been so suddenly erased.

Michael had shared bits of his conversation with Pheagan with them, though he had not said anything about the sensitive information pertaining to Sub Rosa, the pendant holder, or Trinity. He had kept his word to Pheagan, and would, as long as it wasn't in the family's best interests to do otherwise. But he had made no promise to Pheagan about sharing theories arrived at from the awareness of that information.

They talked about Pheagan's belief that their visit could have inspired the attack on Immel. Danny's exercise in logic had already brought him to the same general conclusion. They also discussed the theory that the same people who had killed Christian and the people at Bonaventure could have been connected to Immel's death and the killing of the man in the woods.

Michael gave his thoughts on it as he drove. "It fits the pattern," he said. "We must have been close to something that we can't recognize. I've thought about everything that Immel told us, and the only thing that stands out is our learning the name Dieter Liepart."

"What about your feeling that Immel wanted to talk to us some more?" Danny asked.

Michael shook his head. "I just don't know. It was only a feeling."

"Your feelings have been pretty respectable up to now. I wouldn't quit on them yet," Danny said. "You could have been right. Maybe he did have something more to tell us."

"I just don't know," Michael said.

"Well here's something to think about," Danny said. "We're definitely going the wrong way."

"What?"

"I said, we're going the wrong way. Look at that sign. It says that we're approaching Romenay. According to this road map here, that puts us south of Cuisery."

Michael checked the sign. It said Romenay, all right. "Blanc said to take N75, didn't he? Check the piece of paper he gave us."

Danny unfolded it and read it. "Yep. He said N75, all right. But he also said to take it west out of Cuisery. We're going south. According to this map, the road bends south just east of Cuisery. We got on the wrong way."

"We'll change that fast enough."

A few seconds later they were speeding back in the right direction.

"It's possible that Immel could have told us something more," Michael continued. "But seeing as he can't now, we're left with what we have. This Gestapo guy Liepart could be a good bet. If Z reported through him, then he must know who Z is. That'll solve part of our problem. Then we have to worry about the pendant holder and my father's contact. I really don't know if learning the identity of Z will help us with those aspects of the mystery."

"Unless they *are* connected in some way," Danny said.

"I still have trouble with that theory. If he was connected somehow, why would the pendant holder push him into the open?" Michael asked.

"I can think of two reasons," Danny said. "First, he could have really believed that we wouldn't follow up on it, and that it would all die with your father. Second, he could be in a position to kill the collaborator if we get too close to him."

"It's the same triangle, no matter how you look at it," Gabrielle said. "The pendant holder, the collaborator, and the contact."

"And we still can't recognize the clues," Michael said. "I'm beginning to wonder whether we'd recognize them if they were neatly laid out on a map for us."

What he didn't realize was that they had just, in fact, had one of the elusive clues right in their hands and failed to recognize it. It was like all things obvious—invisible.

The short ride back to Cuisery from Tournus was used to fill Edna-Marie and St. Jude in on the events that had taken place without discussing any of the possible theories.

The three men sat in the lounge of the hotel waiting for the women to join them for lunch. They ordered a round of drinks.

"It must have been quite a surprise learning Immel was living in France," Michael said to St. Jude.

"To say the least," the Frenchman answered. "I had always thought that he was killed in Russia. He never did figure into the

290

picture of Group Defiance again after leaving France. It was too bad that he was unable to give you information pertaining to the identity of Z."

Michael took a sip of his drink, capturing one of the ice cubes in his mouth. He rolled it around with his tongue as he slowly turned the glass round and round on the napkin.

"What can you tell us about a Captain Dieter Liepart?" he asked.

St. Jude held Michael's stare for a moment, as though thinking about the question. "Liepart? Let me see. It seems that I should know the name. Liepart," he repeated.

"Immel had given us his name," Danny said. "He was in the Gestapo, and had been assigned to the staff of von Roeth a short time before Immel was ordered to the Eastern front."

"Yes, of course, now I remember him. I might be wrong about him, but I think that he actually took over Immel's responsibilities. We never had direct exposure to him, however, as we did to Immel. Because of Gabrielle Dupuy, Immel's name came up quite often. Liepart helped to direct the German efforts against us. But we were just one of many groups that they were forced to try to deal with," St. Jude said.

"I take it, then, that you wouldn't know what became of him?" Michael asked the Frenchman.

St. Jude shook his head. "No, I wouldn't."

"That's too bad," Danny said. "Immel felt sure that Liepart would have known the identity of Z."

St. Jude shrugged. "I wouldn't know. But if he did, then he would certainly be the man to find, it would seem."

A moment later Edna-Marie and Gabrielle arrived in the lounge and joined them at the table.

"When will you be meeting with Georges Blanc again?" Edna-Marie asked.

"Either tonight or tomorrow morning," Michael answered. "He said he wanted us to stick around for at least today, in the event that any more questions should arise that we might be able to answer."

"Would you excuse me for a moment?" St. Jude said. "I have to call Nicole. I told her that I thought we'd be home tonight. I had better tell her that we'll be staying the night so she won't become worried." He left the table and headed for the hotel lobby.

"Have you ever heard of a Captain Dieter Liepart?" Michael asked Edna-Marie.

"Of course," she replied. "He worked with von Roeth in Paris. A particularly nasty man, that one. He was responsible for ordering the executions of many of our people after they had been caught and questioned. The struggle against Defiance became almost a personal matter to him. He was a great deal more effective against us than Immel had been, because he could use the treachery of Z to his advantage.

"It was Liepart, in fact, who had come to Marseilles when the sector was first decimated by Pointer's betrayal."

"Would you know what became of him?" Danny asked.

"He was captured trying to escape from Paris just before the Liberation. He was shot," Edna-Marie answered.

"Dead. I should have known it. So, what else is new?" Michael said, shaking his head.

"Was he shot after being put on trial?" Danny asked.

"No, he was captured, interrogated, and summarily executed against a wall, along with a few dozen other Germans and known collaborators. Of course, for the record, the deaths of the Germans were not 'executions.' That was something that Pierre Falloux could have told you about. It was the Aile Rouge that captured him. Falloux personally interrogated him, before . . . Liepart's 'escape attempt.' "

"Falloux?" Michael asked, then looked at Danny.

"Oh, yes, the communist groups were particularly busy shortly before and after the Liberation of Paris, dealing with collaborators and such. They worked hard all across France."

"Immel told us that he felt that Liepart knew the identity of Z," Danny said.

"That is possible. But if he did, Falloux would have learned it without a doubt. It was never mentioned at your father's trial. In fact, your father would have never been arrested if Falloux had that information. The real collaborator would have been on trial," she said.

"I think we need to talk to Falloux again," Danny said to Michael.

"And soon. Like right after we're free to leave Cuisery," Michael said, then turned back to Edna-Marie. "Immel told us about the time he confronted my father after the scientist Max Schrict was killed. He mentioned a bombed-out winery near Pont du Château. Was that ever rebuilt?"

"No, it never was. We could go there if you'd like to see it," she offered. "As long as you want to see Pierre Falloux again, we'll be quite near it. It was the same place that I told you about earlier, where your father and I went into hiding with Leopard after the ambush in which poor Paul was shot. He died there.

"It would also be a good idea to talk to the Collard brothers once

gain, too. They could tell you about the scientist, perhaps better than
nyone."

St. Jude returned to the lounge looking somewhat annoyed. "That
irl," he said, shaking his head as he sat at the table. "She has no sense
f responsibility. She was supposed to remain at the *manade*. I have
nportant calls coming in. And where is she? Off somewhere with her
ousin, who is to be married next month. A wedding dress is more
nportant than the affairs of the family business," he said.

"I'm sorry. I should not interrupt," he apologized.

"If it's important for you to get back—" Michael began.

"No, no. A little business is not as important as helping you," St.
ude insisted.

"Immel told us about Pointer's disappearance in Marseilles. Did
ither of you know that it was all part of a trap he had set to test
jabrielle Dupuy's association with my father?" Michael asked.

"Why . . . no," Edna-Marie responded in total surprise.

"Did he say that?" St. Jude asked in like amazement.

"Yes. It's true."

"Incredible. Why didn't he have her arrested?" St. Jude asked.

"He loved her that much. A few months later he was on his way to
Russia. It didn't matter after that," Michael said.

"Now, I might be wrong, but if I have the story right, so far, Z's
•etrayals began after Pointer's discovery. Is that correct?" Danny
.sked.

"Yes, almost immediately," St. Jude replied. "It was about mid
)ctober when we intercepted Pointer in Marseilles after being alerted
•y Gabrielle. He took his capture with remarkable calm. I must say
hat he had more courage than I had given him credit for.

"We drove him straight to Clermont-Ferrand, figuring that they
vould never think to search for him there. We took him to the Collard
arm where we interrogated him in the wine cellar. At first he denied
.ll of our charges, claiming that he had been en route to Algiers under
•rders from British Intelligence. But his pretenses ended when your
ather arrived with communications from England denying his claims.
Vfter that he calmly answered all of our questions."

"He just told you everything?" Danny asked.

"Everything. He told us how he had acquired the most damaging
nformation while repairing the broken radio after arriving from En-
;land. He had gone through Edna-Marie's papers and learned enough
o wreck the Paris and Marseilles sectors, as well as others. He had
•earned the actual identities of most of our top people. He detailed all

of his betrayals and even told us about the Nazis' plan to invade the free zone on November eleventh.

"He was not ashamed of what he had done. I remember that he smiled with a smug satisfaction and told us that it was only a matter of time until we would all be taken by the Germans. I have felt anger many times in my life, but never as I did on that day . . ."

CLERMONT-FERRAND, 1942: "You filthy swine," Claude St. Jude said, no longer able to tolerate the smugness of the Englishman. He rushed across the small wine cellar at Pointer, grabbing him and yanking him out of his chair. He threw a vicious blow to the Englishman's face, sending him crashing into a wall. Immediately, he was on the prisoner, raining blow after blow upon him, spitting curses like a mad man.

Christian was quick to step in, pulling St. Jude away. Both Collard brothers helped in restraining the ranting, bull-like St. Jude.

Christian helped stand Pointer against the wall, allowing him to recover.

Pointer cracked a half smile and squinted hard at St. Jude. "If you think that I've hurt you, wait. Von Roeth would not be sending me to Africa unless he had developed another more important contact."

"What do you mean?" St. Jude screamed, struggling to free himself to get at Pointer once again.

"I simply mean that there is a traitor who will hurt you far more than I have," the Englishman said.

"Who? Who is it?" St. Jude shouted, breaking free and slamming the prisoner across the face. "Tell us who it is," he demanded, crowding the prisoner and throwing another punch.

"I don't know who it is," Pointer said, holding his hand to his split lips, again finding himself on the ground.

"Don't lie to us. Tell us," St. Jude demanded, shaking Pointer furiously, before being separated from him once again.

"Do you really think that they would tell *me?*" Pointer laughed, blood dripping down his chin. "You're a fool. A bloody fool."

"We have all day, all week, if necessary, to question you," Christian said. "You may as well tell us what you know."

"I've told you everything," Pointer grunted painfully, his arms wrapped tightly around himself. "Von Roeth isn't stupid. He wouldn't tell me if he had developed an informer. I know that he has, that's all. I earned it from someone else in his office who knew no more about it than I do now. It could be anyone at all. Even you," he said to Christian.

Christian looked down at the Englishman. Perhaps Gabrielle could be successful in obtaining this information for them, he thought. In any event, they would learn no more from Pointer, he was sure.

"Stay with him," Christian said, handing his gun to Lucien Collard. "If he moves or attempts to stand up shoot him."

Lucien Collard smiled. "With great pleasure," he said.

The rest of them filed out of the wine cellar to discuss the matter. All but St. Jude felt that they had learned what they could from Pointer. The only things of importance that the Englishman knew were the details of his own betrayals. They had all of this now. Christian expressed his belief that Pointer would not know the identity of the newly developed traitor, stating that it would have been foolish to reveal that information outside of von Roeth's office, especially to an agent of diminished value to them.

"We have nothing to lose by trying," St. Jude insisted. "If he knows nothing, then we learn nothing, and all it will have cost is time. But if he does, then we will learn a great deal. I say that we work on him to try to force more information from him. Let me talk to him. I will quickly learn whether he knows more or not."

"Are you sure that you don't just want to punish him for what he has already done?" Jacques Collard asked.

"Yes, that's part of it. Can you say that you don't want to batter him and kick him and kill him for what he has done to our friends?" St. Jude said to Collard.

"Yes, I despise what he has done to our friends, and we will kill him because we must. But to torture him when there truly is no reason is not right. His death will be his punishment, and that should be enough, otherwise we make ourselves no better than the Germans," Collard replied.

"No reason?" St. Jude asked. "Another traitor is reason enough."

"Claude, I know how you feel," Christian began. "But you must recognize the absolute foolishness required on the part of von Roeth to reveal that name to Pointer. The Germans are not fools."

St. Jude thought angrily for a few moments but in the end agreed.

Now all that had to be determined was how to dispose of Pointer. Talk of killing him was easy, but it was now time to pick the hand that would do it.

"Give me the gun, I'll do it," St. Jude said, his anger still burning.

"Are you sure, Claude?" Christian asked, knowing that it was his anger speaking.

"I will do it," Claude insisted, but his eyes were uncertain.

Christian nodded. "I'll inform Pointer that he has five minutes to make whatever peace he feels necessary in his heart and mind."

Christian re-entered the wine cellar, relieving Lucien Collard. The two men were alone now.

"You have two minutes to make your peace with God, if you believe in God," Christian said.

Pointer smiled weakly. "Just because I am your enemy doesn't mean that I don't believe in God. Nor does it mean that what I did for my country was any less heroic than what you now do for yours. To you, what I did was reprehensible treachery. To me, it was my duty. I am as much a soldier as you, fighting for what I believe in. The difference between us is that I have been caught and you have not.

"I won't need two minutes," Pointer said after a brief moment of silence between them. "I'm quite ready. But I would ask one favor, as a last request between two soldiers."

"What is it?" Christian asked.

"That you permit me a final moment of personal honor. That you leave the gun and one bullet with me," Pointer requested.

Christian stared back at him without answering.

"I assure you that nothing can possibly happen," Pointer said. "There is no other way out of here but that stairway behind you. With only one bullet, I couldn't possibly hope to attack an entire band of armed men."

Christian continued looking at him in silence.

"Certainly, it is not too much to ask between soldiers," Pointer said.

"Perhaps not," Christian replied.

"Then you understand," Pointer said with a smile.

"I do understand," Christian said, leveling the gun at Pointer and pulling back the hammer. "I understand that we are alike in our fight for our countries, be it on different sides. Putting myself in your place, I know exactly what I'd do with a gun in my hand. I'd take you with me as a last victory. We are alike. Too much, in fact, to deceive one another that easily."

"You misread me. I am not that brave," Pointer said.

"And I am not that foolish."

The report was heard outside the wine cellar as a muffled bang. There was no doubt as to its meaning. The book on Pointer had just been closed.

Chapter 31

Edna-marie used a good part of the afternoon to describe the hectic weeks that followed Pointer's capture, telling of their efforts to protect as many people as possible from the betrayal of which they had been warned. This new task was an enormous one, creating severe organizational problems because of the already difficult rebuilding job under way. They worked twenty hours a day trying to beat the November 11 deadline of the coming German invasion of the free zone, all the while maintaining the flow of intelligence data into England. The Allied invasion of North Africa was approaching, and information regarding ship and cargo movements along the Mediterranean was vital to the Allies.

Things progressed well, despite the demanding work schedules they imposed upon themselves. But as November 11 approached, they nearly suffered complete tragedy.

"On November seventh, your father, Charles Flandine, myself, and several others were captured at Montélimar. It was during this period of custody that your father was separated from us to be taken to Evaux-les-Bains, from where he later successfully escaped," Edna-Marie said. "We were all extremely lucky on this occasion, as assistance came from a least expected source.

"The commandant at the headquarters that we were taken to remained most adamant with the Gestapo agent, insisting that all evidence and prisoners remain in French custody until official notification, in writing, was received by his office. This infuriated the German. The two men argued heatedly until the Nazi left in a rage, swearing that he would return the next day with the papers he needed. 'In the meantime,' the commandant told him calmly, 'we will begin the interrogations.'

"The interrogations were a demonstration of cooperation that nearly made me cry. They actually helped us sort out the material into piles of importance. The most sensitive materials were burned in the stove heating the room. Others that were known to exist by the Gestapo agent, and which would surely be missed, like our radio plan diagram, could not be burned. But time was permitted us to recopy this with false information. Other papers of a less vital nature were left to be handed over when the official request came.

"The German did not return the next day as promised, but did on the following day instead. That was on November ninth. That morning, before his arrival, the commandant gathered us together in the interrogation room and informed us that your father was to be taken to Evaux-les-Bains. The rest of us were to be taken to Castres Prison, from which escape would be impossible. He told us that your father's identity had been discovered, but that Flandine and myself were still safe. He said that an escape would be arranged for us before we reached Castres Prison."

"What about these men who helped you?" Gabrielle asked. "Surely they could not have avoided getting into trouble," she said.

"We told them what we had learned about the November eleventh invasion of the free zone," Edna-Marie explained. "We asked them to go into hiding and to join us. But they had already made plans to join the Maquis.

"As a final bit of news before returning us to our cells, we were told that the Allied invasion of North Africa had successfully begun on November eighth. The interrogation room was a scene of joyous, though quiet, celebration and tearful embraces. For the first time, we felt the wonderful realization that our efforts had been successful and that the tide of the war was turning.

"Then, just before we separated, there was a moment of concern for your father. We were worried about him being separated from us. It was a bad sign.

" 'Don't worry,' your father said. 'I have been given a detailed plan of Evaux-les-Bains. I would have to be an idiot not to be able to escape. Don't worry about me. Take care of yourselves; your escape will be a great deal more dangerous,' he said.

"Your father left that afternoon with his escort, and escaped the next day as easily as he had said he would. The rest of us escaped the ollowing day with the good help of our new friends," Edna-Marie explained.

"And your capture in Montélimar, was that a betrayal by Z?" Danny asked.

"It is possible, but I don't think so," Edna-Marie replied. "If it had been Z, the identities of Flandine and myself would have been discovered, I'm certain."

"And what about Charles Flandine?" Danny asked. "He doesn't seem to be central to much of the story as you've given it so far. I thought that he was next in command behind you?"

"Yes, he was, originally. But he spent a great deal of time traveling between Spain, Portugal, and England, acting as our liaison with the British. He was much more valuable there, and your father certainly became the true second in command. Had anything happened to me, Christian would have taken over. That was acceptable to Flandine," she explained.

"Did Flandine survive the war?" Gabrielle asked.

"No, he did not," Edna-Marie said sadly. "Both he and Jan Burak were betrayed the following year by Z. Both were shot in prison."

"Claude was already acting as the next in command behind your father, so when Flandine was arrested, it became just the three of us running Group Defiance in reality."

"What about below you?" Michael asked. "The three of you were in danger so often that you could have all been taken, or killed. What would have happened if you had been?"

"We had taken precautions. A chain of command had been established below us, though it changed often because of the losses we suffered. Group Defiance would have carried on," Edna-Marie replied.

"Z could have been in that layer of the organization," Michael said.

"At one time or another, we suspected everyone," St. Jude offered. "But whoever he was, he was extremely clever. He somehow managed to continually obtain information, avoiding detection."

"But there weren't that many people it could have been," Danny said.

"That is exactly what we thought," St. Jude answered. "But it still didn't help us to find the traitor."

Michael remained silent, looking at St. Jude and Edna-Marie. "Trust no one," Pheagan had warned them. "No matter how close they may have been to your father once, you must suspect them all. One of them may be the person you're after."

He looked at the two friends of his father's. Then one more thing they had been told filtered back into awareness. Immel had talked to Z And Immel had said that it was a man's voice he had heard. Michael looked at St. Jude and wondered.

Michael and Danny met with Georges Blanc that evening. He had learned that the man found dead behind Immel's house was a known member of Firewatch. He also told them that the bullet killing him was a .38 caliber.

That neatly answered the important question of whether Immel could have killed him. Immel's Luger was a 9-mm. This information fit perfectly with what they had expected.

Blanc said that he could see no reason why they couldn't leave Cuisery whenever they liked, as long as they remained available by phone for the next few days.

Michael and Danny returned to the hotel with the news that they were free to leave Cuisery. They learned from Edna-Marie that Pierre Falloux had agreed to meet with them a second time. The meeting was scheduled to take place at Falloux's estate during the early afternoon of the next day. That would permit leaving for Pont du Château the following morning. They could travel at a leisurely pace and arrive in plenty of time to see the old ruined winery before going to Falloux's.

After dinner, the group walked together in the pleasant night air.

"What do you hope to learn from a second meeting with Falloux?" St. Jude asked.

Michael thought for a moment before answering. "I think that he knows a great deal more about the identity of the collaborator than he lets on," he replied.

"What makes you think that?" St. Jude asked, puzzled.

"Captain Dieter Liepart. Falloux's men caught him just about the time Paris was being liberated. They interrogated him before killing him, and I believe that Liepart knew who Z was. If Falloux was the kind of man I think he was, he got that information," Michael answered.

"He couldn't have," St. Jude insisted. "It wasn't brought up at the trial of your father."

"Of course it wasn't," Michael agreed, "because it had nothing to do with my father. Falloux accomplished his goal by creating enough doubt over him to eliminate any political threat. He's been sitting on that information ever since."

"Why would he do that? Falloux would have had the collaborator killed if he knew who it was, I'm certain of it," St. Jude said.

"Maybe, and maybe not. There might have been something to ₁in from him by holding it over his head all these years," Michael ₁ggested.

"He has everything that he could possibly want now," St. Jude ₀jected. "Falloux has money and power. He wants for nothing."

"Some people never have enough power," Danny said. "And ₀wer over people is more bankable than cash to men like that. He ₀uld virtually own this man, if Mike is right in his theory."

The group walked for a few minutes in silence.

"Did you ever get your call through to Nicole?" Gabrielle asked.

St. Jude snapped out of some deep thought. "Pardon? Were you lking to me?" he asked.

"Yes. Did you ever speak to Nicole to tell her when we would be turning?" Gabrielle repeated.

St. Jude slapped his forehead at the reminder. "I left a message for ₂r. But there's no telling with that girl. I'd better call again. Thank you ₀r reminding me. I will call her immediately. Please, excuse me. I will ₂e you all at breakfast. Sleep well," he said, then headed straight back ₀ the hotel.

The group continued walking without conversation. After a few ₁inutes the women excused themselves and headed back to the hotel, ₀aving Michael and Danny to themselves.

The two men walked for awhile before Danny spoke. "That's a ₂etty interesting theory that you're working on," he said.

"Do you remember what Pheagan told us after he contacted his ₁urces in Firewatch? He said that Firewatch's claim of responsibility ₁as in reality a quid pro quo, that someone was in a position to call in ₁ sizable marker. Well, he was in a position to call in a second marker ₀m the same people over this Immel deal. He's got to be pretty big ₁d powerful to do that, especially when he's not afraid to have one of ₁rewatch's own men be knocked off to be sure that the rap was hung ₁ them. A guy with the smarts and the instincts to control a group like ₁rewatch has probably dedicated his life to gaining the upper hand ₁er people and maintaining it."

"And you suspect Falloux?" Danny asked.

"You saw the way he talks to people. He's a man used to being in ₀mplete control. He fits the profile."

"I can agree with that, but you have no proof," Danny said.

"Not yet. But then if he's smart enough, we may never be able to ₂t anything solid on him. All we can do is test him. Try to rattle him a ₀tle, see what he does about it."

"He doesn't seem to be the type to get rattled."

"Yeah, well if he is our man, he'll get good and rattled if he think we're onto him. This might just be the time to run a bluff by him to se how good he is at his poker. If he panics, we'll learn about it fas enough," Michael said.

"Then I think it's time that Gabby went home," Danny said.

Michael looked at his brother-in-law. They had been thinking th exact same thing. "So do I, pal. So do I."

Chapter 32

Two large stone pillars marked the location of the long-abandone lane leading to the bombed-out ruins of the Bouchard winery. It wa only the presence of the vine-covered pillars that hinted that a lane ha once existed at all. It had been a gravel lane, which had long sinc grown over and was only vaguely distinguishable through the fores surrounding the old site.

They left the car by the road and walked along the old lane, high stepping through the combined tangle of the previous year's dea growth and the emerging spring greenery.

It was a wonderfully pleasant day, bright with sunshine, with nearly cloudless sky above. A gentle breeze weaved through the shad forest as the group walked the long lane to the ruins, almost a half-mil from the road.

"This was certainly way out in nowhere," Michael commented.

"Yes, but in those days it wasn't so inconspicuous," Edna-Mari explained. "The lane was much wider and perfectly cleared. A larg sign hung above the pillars and a wrought-iron gate stood betwee them. This forest wasn't nearly so thick, and you could see the winer from the road in the winter when the trees were bare. But it did serv us well and offered us the protection we needed."

They continued walking through the low growth until the fores around them seemed to open up into a large glade. In the center of th opening were the forgotten remains of the Bouchard winery. What ha been its high stone walls were barely above ground level. Here an there a higher portion of wall still stood, but no overhead structur survived at all. It looked as though it had been abandoned during th early stages of construction.

To the side of the old remains of the winery was an equally ruined structure that had once been a large house. About seventy-five yards behind the house was an old barn, barely visible through the trees. It looked to be in fairly sound condition, having all its walls and a reasonably intact roof.

"This doesn't look like it could have provided any shelter at all," Michael said. "Did you use the barn?"

"No," said Edna-Marie. "Much more of the structure had been standing at the time, including some areas with a roof. But when the Bouchard family decided not to rebuild on this site after the war, they had much of the remaining structure taken down and the stone transported to the new site, about six or seven kilometers from here. The house had been nearly as totally destroyed as you see it now, but we had sufficient cover in the winery."

Edna-Marie led them to a portion of the ruins in which they had taken shelter. "There was enough room for all of us here. There was a table and a few chairs to use, and we made beds out of hay taken from the barn. We slept on it and covered ourselves with it to protect us from the cold," she explained.

Gabrielle stood in silence, her hands in her coat pockets, looking around at the remnants of the old walls, remembering the stories they had been told about those times. There was a warm gratification in sharing what had been a tiny but important part of her father's life. How wonderful it would have been to have come here with him, to hear him tell the stories they were now learning about his life.

"Is this where Leopard died?" she asked.

"Yes. Right here, in fact," Edna-Marie said, pointing to the exact spot beside what had once been a wall. "He lived for two days, never regaining consciousness. We knew that he was dying. All we could do was wait for it to happen. We kept him as comfortable as possible, but I don't think he felt anything."

They stayed a few moments more before St. Jude looked at his watch.

"Is it time to leave already?" Gabrielle asked, not wanting to.

"I'm afraid so. As it is, we'll probably be a few minutes late for our appointment," St. Jude replied, a tiny trace of a smile evident. It would be just enough to irritate Falloux again. Even little victories had their glory.

Pierre Falloux sat at his large desk scribbling notes rapidly as Rive spoke to him over the phone. He had succeeded in piecing together fairly informative briefs on the three Americans.

Falloux continued to listen without interruption as Rive slowly fed

him the details, which laid out a clear picture of two men considerab
more capable than Falloux had at first expected.

Gabrielle Glady-Preston was also not to be underestimated. Sh
was a highly intelligent young woman, successful in a writing caree
and no doubt as determined as her brother to arrive at the answers fc
which they searched. Words were the weapons her father had used. I
that regard, Falloux could consider her no less a threat.

These people presented a greater danger than he had imagine
They were truly capable of developing information from even sma
clues. But the same questions remained in Falloux's mind that ha
been there before hearing from Rive. Were they here only to try
solve the mystery of their father's death, or were they here to try
discover what he had known? Were they after a killer, a collaborato
or a pendant holder? And if the latter, did they know the significanc
of what they were after? And finally, but perhaps most important of a
were they acting alone, or with the help of others? These were a
questions that he had to try to answer before turning Demy and Scalc
loose on them.

The car pulled through the guarded entrance almost ten minut
late. St. Jude guided it slowly down the long drive to the oval an
stopped in front of the house. St. Jude again remained in the ca
refusing Falloux's hospitality.

The group was received and again led through the house to th
expansive terrace, where Pierre Falloux was waiting for them. He ro
to his feet as they approached, taking first the hand of Edna-Marie.

"Madame DeBussey, it is a pleasure to meet you once again," h
said quite politely. Then he took Gabrielle's hand. "Madame Glad
Preston, it is good to see you again so soon."

Gabrielle tipped her head with a smile, but without comment.

"Monsieur Gladieux," Falloux said, taking the firm handshake c
the American. There was a brief moment of assessment between then
a polite crossing of swords. The Frenchman repeated a similar e
change with Danny.

Falloux made a gesture to his servant to bring wine for his guest

"So, what is it that you wish to talk to me about so soon after yo
last visit?" he asked, looking at Michael.

"We'd like to talk to you about a German officer—"

"Immel?" Falloux interrupted. "I'm sure you are aware that he
now dead," he said. "I can't say that I'm sorry for him. The man was
butcher. It wasn't only American soldiers that he was guilty of killin
you know. He had also committed atrocities in Italy and Poland, and,
would wager, in Russia as well."

304

"Yes, we know all about Immel," Michael said. "We spoke to him the day he was killed. But we didn't come here to talk to you about Immel. We came to talk about a Captain Dieter Liepart."

"Liepart?" Falloux said pensively, sipping his wine. "Yes, I remember him. What would you like to know?"

"He was captured by the Aile Rouge, wasn't he?" Michael asked.

"Yes, it was the day before the Liberation of Paris. He had stayed at his post to the bitter end, destroying documents of arrests and execution orders that he had signed. We were quite fortunate in grabbing him."

"We understand that you also had him shot," Danny said.

Falloux smiled crookedly. "He was killed trying to escape," he said. "But yes, you are right. We shot him. It is a pity that a man can die only once. We would have liked killing that one over and over again."

"Why didn't you turn him over to the Allied Forces coming into Paris?" Danny asked.

"What good would that have done?" Falloux asked gruffly. "They would have arrested him, put him on trial after the war, convicted him, and given him a sentence which would have later been reduced. Then they would have pardoned him and set him free, just as they did with Immel. No, we knew what to do with him. There was no question of his guilt."

"You interrogated him, did you not?" Edna-Marie asked.

Falloux looked at her for a moment before answering. "Yes, we did."

"And during your questioning, did you talk about Z?" she asked.

Falloux looked at her again, but longer this time. "Now I see what you're getting at," he said. "You think that he knew the identity of Z, and that we obtained the information from him." He laughed, slapped his knee, then leaned forward in his chair. "Christian Gladieux *was* guilty."

"But you never heard that from Liepart," Michael said. "Otherwise you would have used it in your evidence at the trial."

"That is correct. Liepart didn't tell us anything about Z. He didn't know the actual identity of the traitor. And I can assure you that we used highly persuasive methods. We had hoped to learn that from him, I confess, although we had enough evidence of our own to be convinced of Christian Gladieux's guilt.

"I'm very sorry to inform you that if you are staying in France solely to search for the collaborator Z, you are wasting your time," Falloux said. "You may as well go back home to America and forget this thing."

"You will never give up the act, will you?" Edna-Marie asked "You know as well as anyone that Christian Gladieux was not guilty o collaboration. We countered your evidence point by point to the satis faction of the courts of France."

Falloux looked squarely at Michael. "What do you hope to ac complish in France?" he asked. "Is it vindication you seek? Or is i revenge?"

Michael looked at him hard for a moment, wanting to confron him openly with what he felt to be truth. But it had to wait, and h knew it.

"We want the truth. We want to know who the real collaborato was so that we can clear my father's name. And we want to know wh was responsible for his death," Michael replied.

"You already know that. Firewatch has claimed responsibility And I will believe to my dying day that it was your father who betraye Group Defiance time and time again. So, to talk with me in the hope o learning otherwise is a waste of your time and mine."

It was pointless to carry on this conversation. Everyone realized it But conversation had been only part of Michael's reason for wanting t see Falloux again. The biggest part of that reason still lay ahead o them. And he knew that he would have only one opportunity, for i was doubtful that Falloux would agree to see them again.

Michael finished his wine and rose from his chair. The other followed. "Thank you for your time, Monsieur Falloux," Michael said He leaned close to Edna-Marie as they moved away from their chairs "Take Gabrielle outside," he whispered.

Without saying a word, Edna-Marie took Gabrielle's arm and hur ried her ahead of the others, while Michael and Danny deliberatel held back their pace. Falloux was directly behind them. They botl turned back toward the Frenchman when Edna-Marie and Gabriell were out of earshot.

"I don't know why you insist on sheltering the real collaborator," Michael said. "We'll find him, despite your lack of cooperation. W know that Liepart was aware of the identity of Z. Immel confirmed tha bit of knowledge—among other things."

Other things! Falloux's eyes squinted slightly. "I've told you al that I know," he insisted.

Michael smiled. "But we haven't told you all that *we* know," h said, pausing to let the meaning settle into Falloux's brain. "The col laborator is only of secondary importance. We know why my fathe was really killed. It has nothing to do with a collaborator, or Firewatch Does it, Falloux?"

306

Falloux's heart began pounding wildly. Perspiration beaded instantly on his upper lip and forehead.

Michael reached into his shirt and pulled out the pendant. "This is the key," he said. "It unlocks many mysteries, many dark secrets, and one man's past. It holds a story that few people know. But my father knew that story, that's why he was killed. And we know the desperate gamble that this pendant represents for one man's survival. We know, Falloux. We *know*."

Falloux's face was unmistakably flushed. "Why do you go on with this meaningless gibberish?" he asked. "I don't have the slightest idea what you're talking about. Pendants, keys, secrets—you don't make any sense." His distress was not well hidden.

"Not all my father's notes were lost. Enough was left behind to tell a very interesting story. A few parts were left out, but the pieces are falling into place quite nicely now," Michael exaggerated to add strength to his bluff.

"What notes? What story?" Falloux asked, sounding angry now. "At least make some sense."

"Come on, Dan. I think that we've made all the sense we have to for now," Michael said, then turned and rapidly walked away to join Edna-Marie and Gabrielle.

Falloux did not follow them. He remained on the sunny terrace watching them walk away. His legs were trembling and his throat was dry. He had learned enough to realize that they knew a great deal more than he would have ever thought possible. Too much to let it go further. It was time that they were stopped.

Nicholas Tarnes was a naturalized American citizen. He had lived in Boston, Massachusetts, for over fifteen years, teaching economics at Boston College and leading a quiet life. He was well respected in his environment of academe, was a favorite instructor among the students, and had a beautiful, loving wife. His life was a happy one.

It was no secret that he had been born Nicolae Tarnescu in Rumania forty-seven years ago, and that he had left his country with little more than the clothes on his back. He worked his way across Europe, saving as much money as he could, then came to America. The only possession of value that he carried with him was a diploma from the Academy of the Rumanian People's Republic showing that he was a doctor of economics. It was his ticket to the American dream. And that dream came in search of him shortly after his arrival in the United States.

Nicolae Tarnescu was approached with a very simple proposition.

If he agreed to act as a special analyst on Rumanian affairs for a small group of interested people, he could be given a teaching position at a prestigious American college. It was a simple enough arrangement, and he needed work. And so it was that his association with Sub Rosa came about.

Nicholas Tarnes had been on vacation in Greece when he received the telegram. He contacted the number provided and was asked if he'd be interested in undertaking a small assignment in Rumania, in exchange for which his vacation expenses in Greece would be totally reimbursed. He listened to the details and accepted, after being told that his presence in Rumania had already been cleared through special channels and that there would be no danger to him.

That was how Nicholas Tarnes came to see Rumania again, and how he came to sit at the table of the Gypsy Barbu Denska.

It was on the eastern decline of the Carpathian Mountains, not far from Fǎlticeni, that the family of Barbu Denska was located.

Barbu Denska was now eighty-two years old, though Tarnes would not have guessed it to look at him. The tan weathered face looked strong and middle-aged, the curly black hair had only the beginning traces of silver, and the wiry, thin frame stood straight and tall.

"So, you come a very long way to talk to Barbu Denska. What could it be that interests you?" the Gypsy asked, pouring out drinks for his visitor and himself.

Tarnes remained silent as he accepted the drink. "Thank you," he said, raising it to his host. The two men drank to one another.

"I've come looking for a woman known to be a part of your family," Tarnes began. "Her name is Keva Wolenska."

Barbu regarded his visitor cautiously as he relit the ever-present pipe. "She is my daughter," he said, refilling both glasses. "Why do you wish to see her? She is not a thief, you know."

Tarnes smiled. "I know that. She's not in any trouble."

"Then why do you wish to see her?" the Gypsy repeated.

"You say that she is your daughter. I hope that you won't take offense, but is she your natural daughter?" Tarnes asked.

The Gypsy looked at him for a long time. "Why do you ask this?"

"I take it, then, that she is not your daughter."

"Answer my question," Barbu said.

"She wears a pendant that we believe once belonged to a young boy by the name of Abraham Mendel. He had a sister named Keva who disappeared in 1939 when she was three years old. The age would be about right from the description I have of your daughter. We're trying to locate this boy. We hoped that he would be here, too."

Barbu puffed vigorously on his pipe, looking Tarnes over.

"The last known whereabouts of Mendel and his sister was in Poland at the time of the German invasion," Tarnes added. He could sense that the Gypsy was still unwilling to cooperate. "We only want to locate the boy, who would be about sixty now."

Barbu paused for a long moment, rubbed his head in thought, then spoke. "Keva would not remember him. She was only three when they were separated. We raised her like our own."

"Then Abraham Mendel is not with you?" Tarnes asked.

Barbu shook his head. "No, he is not here."

"Do you know where he is?" Tarnes asked.

"The last time I saw him was in Poland in 1939, in a small wood outside of Tomaszów. We had met the two of them the morning before, and shared food and conversation with him. We got to drinking that night, and I suspect that it was the first time that he had ever had the spirits. He drank well, like a Gypsy. I liked that. But it was too much for him, and he passed out. We made him comfortable and packed our wagons. We left before the sun had risen, keeping the girl with us," Barbu explained. "I never saw him after that."

"But he was alive?" Tarnes asked.

"Oh, yes. But in the morning he may not have wished it so."

"Why did you take the girl?" Tarnes asked.

"I doubt that you would understand," the Gypsy said, puffing out a great cloud of smoke. "But it was not simply to steal a beautiful child. That is not our way. We have certain beliefs that most people do not understand. Beliefs in predestiny, in vision. One old woman in our family named Sera had such powers. She saw quite plainly that if the child and the boy stayed together they would both die. The only hope for the boy was to go back to the north, from which direction he had come. That was against his every instinct. But the girl had to go south to live.

"Sera was immediately taken with the child, and could not bear the thought of any harm coming to her. She explained to me what she had seen, and we decided to save at least the girl."

"And you don't know what became of him?" Tarnes asked.

"No. We left him there."

"What was Sera's vision regarding the boy?"

"That he would go north, be captured, but not die. If he went north, then he probably lived," Barbu replied.

"North," Tarnes said to himself. "So far the records that we've examined don't show an arrest of the boy. Sounds like a dead end," he said.

The Gypsy thought for a moment, then spoke. "Perhaps not. You see, the boy had a remarkable talent. I remember, when he was quite drunk, he took great pride in showing me identity papers which he himself had forged while working for his uncle, who was a printer. remember examining them very closely and being amazed at the qual ity of his work. If he used these papers and was arrested it could ex plain why you could find no record of his arrest."

"False papers? Why would he have a need for false papers?" Tarnes asked.

"To hide the fact that he was a Jew. That was what he said," Barbu replied.

"Do you remember the name? This is very important. Please try to remember it," Tarnes said.

"That is quite easy, actually. You see, he chose the name of a city in northeastern Poland called Wilno. The name was Paul Wilno," the Gypsy said. "Of course, Wilno is now called Vilnius, and is part of Lithuania. But I remember Wilno so well because my father died there three years before the war."

Tarnes scribbled the name down. "This information could be tre mendously useful," he said. "I'd like to talk to . . . your daughter, if may."

A troubled look crossed the Gypsy's face. "She will remember nothing," he said. "Even if you could spark a tiny flame of recollection would it help you? Would it help enough to justify destroying the lov that she has known all of her life by telling her that she had been stolen from her brother?" he asked.

Tarnes looked back at the Gypsy with true understanding and compassion. "No, I can't imagine that it would," he admitted. "Would I be able to at least meet her, to see her? Perhaps have a picture of her I promise that I'll say nothing about the real reason for my coming to see you."

The Gypsy smiled and poured out another drink for each of them "Not only shall you meet her, but you will also meet her husband, her two lovely children, and a beautiful grandchild. Then you will under stand why it was better to break the heart of a boy to save the life of this little sister."

Tarnes smiled and raised his glass. "To life."

"To life," Barbu repeated.

Both men downed the contents of their glasses.

Barbu Denska smiled with approval. He liked a man who could drink like a Gypsy.

Chapter 33

Jacques and Lucien Collard walked with Michael and Danny after having been told the story of what happened in Cuisery. The four men entered the Collards' well-stocked wine cellar, where Lucien filled two jugs from a huge barrel for the houseful of guests who had turned out to greet the heroine of Group Defiance, Edna-Marie DeBussey.

Edna-Marie, Gabrielle, and St. Jude were back at the house with the many interested observers and former Defiance members who turned out to meet their former leader. It was a joyous reunion.

"Sit, have some wine before we return," Jacques Collard said, gesturing to the small table and chairs in the center of the room.

Lucien filled glasses for each of them as they sat at the table.

"To your father," Jacques toasted.

After drinking the toast, Michael placed his glass on the table and looked at the two Frenchmen. "Immel had told us about an event that happened in Clermont-Ferrand in January of 1943," be began. "It involved a scientist that the Germans were trying to get back into Germany. He gave us the story from his side. Could you tell us the Defiance side of that story?" he asked.

"Most certainly," Jacques Collard replied. "I know it very well. In fact, there were circumstances that forced last-minute planning right here at this table. We were in near panic. The whole event almost never occurred at all. . . ."

TAUVES, JANUARY 1943: The plane appeared overhead in the clear night sky, too obvious for the liking of the three men waiting on the ground. The chutist allowed as much free fall as possible to reduce the chance of detection. He pulled the cord, then for several frightening seconds watched as the chute trailed, flapping and crackling, but failed to open. Finally, it blossomed wide with the sharp jolt from its sudden grab of air, stopping the descent of its wearer. He looked down to see the ground much too close for his speed, and a sloping terrain not well suited for even a more controlled landing. He hit the sharp incline with a jolting thud and a sudden burst of pain to both his ankles.

He writhed on the ground, then was pulled and dragged quite unexpectedly further down the slope by the chute, which was now opened from ground-level wind blowing across the incline. He pulled frantically on the lines, bringing them in toward himself to close the chute. Each sudden jolt compounded the pain from his injured ankles as he tumbled further down the slope. The chute finally unfurled and fell flat, ending his unexpectedly rough introduction to French soil.

He released the buckles securing the harness and pulled himself out of it. He grabbed his ankles, biting his lips hard enough to make them bleed, trying to remain as quiet as possible. He knew the verdict regarding the ankles.

The Englishman heard the sounds of people coming from the other side of the ridge he had just missed. He fought back his gasps of pain, fearing that the men approaching could be German. All of France was now occupied. He knew that the night had been clear enough to allow the plane to be easily spotted, and he wasn't sure by how much he had missed his mark. He pulled out the Webley .38 and aimed it at the ridge above him, ready to shoot the head off the first German to appear.

The voices became more distinct. They were French.

"English. English, where are you?" Jacques Collard tried calling in a loud whisper, straining to see in the darkness.

The third Frenchman came over the ridge and looked down. Christian had found the Englishman. He was hunched on the ground, his gun raised and ready.

"Don't shoot, you are quite safe," Christian said quickly in English, his hands raised to show he meant no harm.

The Englishman lowered the gun, and nearly passed out from the pain.

By the time Christian got to him, the Collard brothers had attained the ridge and were coming swiftly down the slope toward them.

"Are you injured?" Christian asked.

"It's my ankles. I've broken the bloody both of them," the Englishman moaned in mixed anger and pain.

"What's wrong?" Jacques Collard asked as he approached, hearing the Englishman's moans.

"He thinks he's broken both his ankles," Christian replied. "Get him on my back, I'll have to carry him."

The Collard brothers lifted the Englishman, who clenched his teeth near to breaking. He put his arms around Christian's neck, and his legs around his waist. Christian held the Englishman's legs as gently as he could, then started up the incline.

Jacques Collard gathered the parachute, and Lucien picked up the equipment the Englishman had carried.

It was just over forty kilometers to Clermont-Ferrand from where the drop had occurred, near Tauves, and it was almost 3:00 A.M. when they arrived at the Collard farm. They carried the Englishman into the wine cellar, where Madame Collard quickly set up a cot. The boots had to be cut off, and the damage was assessed. There was no doubt that both ankles had indeed been broken. They were beginning to discolor and swell now that the boots were off.

"I'm afraid it's botched." The Englishman winced. "There isn't time enough to get another man in here. Tomorrow morning was the only decent chance we had. You'll have to radio London to call for an air strike on the train. I'm afraid that Gerry will have a tight escort arranged. It won't be easy."

Christian picked up the tool of the Englishman's trade, turning the well-balanced precision rifle in his hands. He examined the unattached scope. "We may still have a chance," he said. "Explain the details of your plan."

The Englishman looked at Christian. "You won't be able to get within three hundred yards of the train station. I'm afraid you wouldn't have a chance," he said, reading the Frenchman's mind.

Christian looked at the large 24X scope, and at the rifle again, then nodded. "I can do it. What is it firing?"

"Mercury-tipped explosive. Seven millimeter, special load, and quite hot. For the man who can place it, a thousand yards could get a kill," the Englishman replied.

"Jacques, you know the train station. Assuming that it will be well guarded, where would the shot have to be taken from?"

Collard thought. He picked up a splinter of wood and drew a rough sketch of the station and surrounding area on the dirt floor of the wine cellar. "They will be using this siding to leave northbound. I would say . . ." He hesitated, mentally filling in the details of the station. "Perhaps, from right here," he said, scraping an X on a rectangular shape. "This building is at least three stories high. From the roof it could be done."

"How far is it?"

Jacques shook his head. "I don't know. Three hundred meters at the very least. I think more. Four hundred, maybe."

Christian looked at the Englishman.

"The scope is sighted to four hundred," the Englishman said. "But there are a dozen factors. Without an intimate knowledge of the weapon and its performance with the special load, it would be impossible. The density of the air, the wind—there are just too many things. It isn't quite as easy as putting the cross hairs on the target and squeezing the trigger. At these distances, the margins for error are extremely small."

"Assume four hundred meters. I want you to describe the performance of this weapon with the load you have prepared under every set of conditions that you can think of," Christian said.

The Englishman looked at Christian, doubt in his eyes.

"What other alternative is there?" Christian asked. "We will radio for the air strike, anyway, in the event that I fail. We have nothing to lose."

The Englishman nodded. "I guess we'll have a bloody go at it then."

Christian smiled. "Don't worry, English, I have used a rifle before."

"Right. We'll begin with trajectory . . ."

Christian used the cover of the early-morning darkness to gain entry to the building suggested by Jacques Collard. He quietly climbed the stairs and gained access to the roof. He waited until the first rays of sunshine began to brighten the sky, then crawled to the edge of the roof and peered over at the train station.

It was already crawling with German troops. He could see that a large perimeter was being established. Collard had picked the perfect spot. Though the angle was quite oblique, the view to the siding that they would use was clear and unobstructed, except for a few electrical lines. He ran a quick mental calculation. Based on what the Englishman had told him, he could expect a drop of about forty-four inches from the muzzle at this range. Mentally picturing the path of the bullet's flight, he determined that the lines should be no problem.

314

He laid the rifle down and surveyed the roof for possible routes of escape. If their perimeter extended out far enough from the station, the stairs might be too slow. He crouched and walked along the roof edge furthest from the train station and looked over the side. There was another roof just one story below to which he could easily jump by hanging down over the edge where he was now standing. That would leave only two stories to the ground. Even a simple drain would allow him to negotiate only two stories. He would take this route.

Christian moved back to the center of the roof, cradled the weapon, and sat back against a chimney. When the sun was fully up he'd go back to the front edge of the roof and survey the scene, then make his final preparations. He curled himself into a tight ball against the harsh cold and prayed that the wind, as slight as it was, would die down. It was one factor he didn't want to have to compensate for.

He tried recalling everything the Englishman had said. He had already known about the mirage effects that would be caused by the cold. This resulted from the bending or refracting of light as it passed through air layers of different temperatures and densities. Cool air bent light rays downward, warm air upward, causing the target to appear in a different place than it actually was. At this distance, there could easily be multiple effects from the different temperatures existing between the building he was on and the station. The wind could also move the target image, as well as physically deflect the bullet, and there was no real way of knowing what wind currents would sweep across the range of fire. But he had listened well to the Englishman, and would analyze the situation carefully when the time to act came. The Englishman had been right; the job would be a difficult one.

Time had never moved more slowly for Christian. His fingers and toes were beginning to hurt from the cold, the hands stiffening. He shoved his hands under his armpits to help keep them warm, occasionally removing one to wipe across his sore, running nose. What he wanted now more than anything was to be in Paris, snuggled in a warm bed with Gabrielle. Just the thought of her warmed him.

When the sun had finally made a full appearance, he went to the front edge of the building and stared out at the train station. To the very best of his judgment, he put the distance right at 400 yards. A few yards plus or minus would make only a minor difference in trajectory. The margin was more than adequate if enough of the target was visible. A head or torso shot should score a kill without question with the load being used.

There was now a complete absence of wind. He raised the scope

and surveyed the area closer to the target and in between, looking fo
any signs of wind. Anything, a moving piece of paper, a bare twig o
branch pushed slightly, anything. It all looked quite calm. At least one
thing was going right.

There were now a great many uniformed soldiers in sight, as wel
as men in plain clothes whom he immediately marked as Germans. He
could see civilians being directed away from the station, despite inef
fectual protests.

Christian checked his watch. There was almost an hour unti
the train would arrive. He moved the scope across the windows of the
station house, hoping to catch a glimpse of the man whose picture the
Englishman had shown him. And for the first time, Christian though
about the *man* he was going to kill.

Max Schrict had been a professor at the University of Goettinger
in the spring of 1933, when he saw his world begin to collapse. A
lifetime of happiness in his home and work ended when the Nationa
Socialists dismantled what had been the very cradle of nuclear science
in blind pursuit of their hatred and prejudice. They forced the resigna
tions of Jewish professors and scholars and drove them out of the
scientific community completely, rejecting their theories as "Jewisł
physics." This attitude dominated Nazi thinking, and most certainl
played an important part in keeping them from developing the mos
potent weapon ever devised by the minds of men to that point ir
history. These same *Untermenschen* that the Reich had discarded
would help the enemies of Germany reach the successful development
of that same weapon in America.

But Max Schrict was not a Jew, he had only married one, which
wasn't quite as bad. He was not dismissed from his post, but was en-
thusiastically invited to continue his work. He did so for nearly three
years, his family enjoying a measure of protection by the semi-closed
environment of university life. But the atmosphere had become suffocating, sterile, and uninspiring. He had witnessed a great injustice
and finally felt that he could not stay in the spreading shadow of it. He
resigned his post and, fearing for the safety of his family, left Germany
in 1936, first going to Switzerland, where his foresight had led him to
deposit the bulk of a large inheritance. From Switzerland he went next
to France, where he found a position instructing physics at the Sor-
bonne. Life was improving, the shadow of Nazi Germany was safely
far away, and he was again finding the satisfaction he enjoyed in the
world of academe.

But the dark threat of Germany and the awareness of imminen

316

war forced yet another change in his life. When Poland was invaded, he made up his mind to take his family yet further from Germany. Through some old friendships, he was able to find a position in Spain, which had just emerged from its bloody Civil War, and was now trying to rebuild. Spain had just ended its war, there was no more heart or will to fight in another one. He knew that when war broke out, Franco would make a formal declaration of neutrality. He felt safe at last.

He had three years of happiness before the black hand of the Fatherland reached out for him. And it did so quickly and cruelly, by taking his wife and children away from him. They were spirited quickly back into Germany before Schrict was contacted with the "offer."

Germany was on the wrong path to the atomic bomb. In 1938, Dr. Otto Hahn found that uranium atoms bombarded with neutrons would give off atomic energy. Professor von Ardenne, working in the Reichspost laboratory, envisioned the possibility of a bomb, but the ideas were dismissed. Other men, like Professor Werner Heisenberg, head of the Kaiser Wilhelm Institute atomic research laboratory, knew that a bomb could be made, but exaggerated the problems in order to discourage the ministry from trying to make one. Some men chose this path of deception out of conscience, others out of secret anti-Nazi sentiment, and yet others because they were afraid of the consequences of failure to produce what they said could be done.

There were many problems standing in the way of nuclear progress in Germany. But one man in the Ministry of Science was prepared to take the bold risk of pursuing "non-Aryan" theories in the attempt to find the correct path to the bomb. It would be done very quietly and funded secretly until enough proof of success was available to force aside the pitifully stupid prejudice that was ultimately leading them to failure. This man knew it could be done, just as Heisenberg, von Ardenne, and others had known. He needed the right man to head the secret research, which would begin where others had left off. The man he chose was Max Schrict, and he approached him in a way that would *insure* his cooperation.

More than Schrict's cooperation would be required if he was to see his family alive again. Success was the only acceptable level of performance. There had been no choice left him. Max Schrict was on his way back to Germany to work along the right path to the bomb, while others wasted time and money on the heavy water experiments, which were ultimately doomed to failure.

There was a sudden rush of activity outside the station. Christian raised the scope and watched a small convoy of staff cars, armored cars, and a troop carrier pull up to the station house, then move behind it and out of his view.

They must be bringing Schrict in, he thought. People were rushing everywhere in response to orders coming from inside the station house. Then, to his complete surprise, Immel appeared in the doorway, taking several steps forward toward the tracks.

A flutter of jealous hatred flashed through Christian at the sight of him. At least *he* hadn't been with Gabrielle while Christian thought of her.

Immel began issuing orders and waving an arm, pointing here and there.

Christian wondered why the sudden rush of activity had started. He doubted that they would be onto him. Even if they were, they wouldn't look for him this far out, he thought. He playfully placed the cross hairs on Immel's forehead. What a magnificent scope it was. He smiled. Who knows, maybe he would take the extra time to get off a second shot at Immel. It would be worth the added risk.

Immel turned and disappeared through the doorway again. Christian continued to watch the activity around the station. The perimeter was being expanded. Several troop carriers had now pulled up and more men were fanning out. They began searching buildings and—*damn it!* They were taking higher positions on rooftops. They *must* be onto something. But how could they have known?

He stayed low and crawled back behind the big chimney he had sat against earlier. It would give him cover from detection from the other rooftops. He looked at his watch. Fifty-five minutes left, if the train stayed on schedule.

He attached the scope to the rifle by its precision mounts. He would make his windage adjustments visually. He then loaded four of the mercury-tipped 7-mm "hot" cartridges into the magazine and snapped one into the chamber with the bolt. He engaged the safety then waited. This was the worst part, he knew—the waiting. He hated it.

It was five minutes before the arrival of the special armored train that was to carry the scientist across France. Immel walked impatiently to the door and looked out. He looked at his watch and shook his head.

"Corporal, where is the troop train I requested?" he asked a nervous little man near the radio.

"They've been delayed, Hauptmann Immel. There had been some sabotage to the tracks. The repairs are completed and they are on their way," the corporal responded.

318

"Sabotage," Immel grumbled. "These French are like mosquitoes. f it moves, they bite it."

He looked around the perimeter and at the rooftops covered with is men. With all these men, he thought, we have been unable to find a one assassin. He wondered who the odds really favored at a time like his—one man acting alone or a whole army. If only that troop train vould hurry.

It was time. Christian crawled back out to the edge of the roof. till no train in sight, and still no scientist.

He waited another minute, then saw it in the distance. He listened, hen turned his head and listened again. There was the sound of an- ther train, but coming from the opposite direction. His line of sight revented him from seeing the other train, but it had to be as close as he first. That could mean disaster. If either train arrived at the plat- orm before Immel and the scientist emerged from the station house, e'd have no shot. His vision would be completely blocked.

He drew himself up into a comfortable position, ready to bring the ifle over the high edge of the roof cap. Once up and taking aim, he'd e vulnerable to being spotted, and perhaps sniped at himself. There vere men on rooftops less than 200 yards from his position.

The sound of the second train was much louder now, though it still ouldn't be seen. He released the safety on the rifle. Then he saw the econd train. Both were moving at about the same speed, and seemed o be about the same distance from the platform. He guessed that he ad less than a minute before they would reach the platform and he vould lose all hope for a shot.

At the same instant of this realization, Immel came through the loorway followed closely by four officers and a man in civilian clothes.

Christian raised the rifle immediately, put his eye to the scope, and wiftly moved it to the form in civilian clothing. He raised the cross airs to the face and then down to the chest—and then sharply back to he face. It wasn't Schrict! He wore glasses like the scientist, but it vasn't the man in the picture.

Christian went immediately to the faces of the officers. The first ne, no. The second, no. The third was directly behind Immel and he ouldn't see him. The fourth, no. Back to the third. It had to be him. mmel was a clever bastard, he had to give him that much.

He took his eye from the scope to spot the trains. Less than thirty econds left. He trained the scope on the back of Immel's head.

"Come on, move. Move, you bastard. Move!" Christian muttered, s though begging would make him do it.

Fifteen seconds.

"Move! Move!" he said under his breath. But the head stayed directly in front of the officer's face.

Ten seconds. It had to be now, Immel or no Immel. Perhaps the bullet would score them both.

The trains rapidly approached one another, their brakes squealing loudly. Mere seconds before they would crisscross.

The finger began the squeeze, Immel's head turned to look at the approaching train, and the cross hairs fell on the face of Max Schrict.

Boom!

The trains crossed, but not before Christian saw Schrict's face begin to explode. The crossing trains blocked Christian's view of Immel's shocked reaction at seeing the shredded face of the scientist and feeling the sudden wetness of his blood and flesh splattering about. The bullet had scored the right cheekbone an inch and a half below the cross hairs. The shot hadn't even been heard by Immel above the sound of the trains.

Christian threw down the rifle and sprinted across the roof as a bullet exploded against the chimney, followed closely by the sound of the shot. He could hear more ricocheting bullets and shots as he swung over the side of the roof cap and lowered himself to arm's length, then let go. He landed and rolled onto his back, then got up and raced for the edge of the second roof. He reached the corner and looked over.

Damn! The drain was broken.

He had only minutes to get out. There wasn't time enough to enter a window and make for the stairs. He looked at the ground. There were boxes and wooden crates piled high near some steel drums on the ground two stories below. He didn't hesitate, and jumped for the boxes and crates, hoping they would break his fall.

He crashed into the crates, splintering through them, and slammed into the edge of a steel drum. He bounced off and to the ground, stunned and unable to breathe. He lay without moving for a few moments, then began to slowly assemble his wits.

Still unable to breathe, he removed his bleeding legs from the crates and rolled onto his stomach. He coughed, tasted blood, coughed again, and saw it splatter from his mouth.

He forced himself to his feet and made himself breathe through the crushing pain. He had to get out fast and find a place to hide.

One step, then another, on painful bleeding legs. More steps, then a run. His chest hurt terribly as he forced air into his lungs. There was no choice. He put the pain aside and ran to escape. He ran for his life.

320

Chapter 34

I T was near midnight when the car pulled into the *manade* of Claude St. Jude. Edna-Marie and Gabrielle had fallen asleep on the trip back. Michael sat in the front with St. Jude, who drove, while Danny sat in the back with Gabrielle nestled comfortably under his arm.

There had been conversation early in the trip when the women were awake, mostly about seeing old friends again and about the Group Defiance members who had turned out at the Collard farm. But for the most part the trip was undertaken with a minimum of talk.

Michael and Danny had each thought separately about the many things they had learned in the past few days. They had talked in private earlier about their feelings regarding Pierre Falloux, and the story they had heard from the Collard brothers. Both men had agreed that Falloux's reaction had not been nearly so cool as the first time when he had been confronted with the pendant. This time he had demonstrated unmistakable tension. Michael felt certain that he had found his man. If he was right, they could expect him to move on them shortly. They'd be ready for it. Pheagan could also start a concentrated effort on Falloux as soon as Michael could speak with him the next day.

They also discussed a further aspect of the story that had been given to them by the Collard brothers. The Collards had told them that London had been notified of the mishap to their agent, and that an attempt would still be made on Schrict. They called for the RAF strike in the event of failure.

The thing that interested Michael about this part of the story was that they had decided not to risk transmission of the important message from Clermont-Ferrand, just in case it was intercepted and decoded by the Germans. Instead, they called Claude St. Jude in Marseilles by phone and gave him the information in code, which he got off to London via Spain.

This struck the first strong chord of suspicion in Michael, who began recalling to Danny parts of Immel's story as it had been told to them. Someone had notified the Germans of the attempt shortly *before* it was due to take place. Beside the Collards, who else even knew of the attempt and new plan?

That could also offer some possible insight into the bitter relationship that existed between Falloux and St. Jude. If Falloux knew the identity of Z, and used that knowledge to exercise leverage of some kind over him, then that could explain their enmity.

Michael's logic had scored heavily in Danny's mind, though it had not left him fully convinced. It had been conjecture, not proof. And proof was needed.

The car coasted to a stop in front of St. Jude's house. Danny awakened Gabrielle to tell her they had arrived. Edna-Marie also awoke with the stopping of the car and Gabrielle's movement.

"Oh, that sleep felt good," Gabrielle said as she got out of the car and stretched her muscles.

St. Jude opened the trunk and handed out the bags. "Nicole must still be awake. The lights are on," he said.

No sooner had he finished his sentence than the front door opened. "I expected you hours ago," Nicole said. "I was beginning to worry."

"Not to worry, my little dove. We stayed at the Jacques Collard farm longer than we expected to," St. Jude replied.

Nicole walked out to the car to help with the baggage. "Can I take anything?" she asked.

"We have it," St. Jude said, hugging her with a free arm and giving her a kiss on both cheeks.

The others started for the house as Michael closed the trunk. Nicole inched up to him and put an arm around his neck and gave him a short kiss on the lips. "I missed you," she said.

Michael smiled at her and winked, then noticed that St. Jude had seen it all. He also noticed the stern expression on his host's face before he turned away to enter the house.

Danny had seen it as well. "Terrific," he mumbled under his breath. It was exactly what they didn't need to happen.

Nicole encircled one of Michael's arms and walked him into the house. "Would anyone like some coffee or something to eat?" she asked.

"I don't know about the rest of you, but I'm going to bed," Edna-Marie said with a tired yawn.

"So am I. Good night," St. Jude said brusquely, and headed for the stairs without looking back at the others.

"I think we should all go to bed and get a good night's sleep," Danny said, putting an arm around his wife's shoulders.

Gabrielle nodded and took her husband by the waist as they headed for the stairs.

"Bed sounds wonderful," Nicole whispered to Michael.

"I don't think so, Pretty Lady. Your daddy didn't seem too keen on the way you said hi to me."

"Nonsense, I'm a big girl."

"Boy, is that ever the truth. But I think we had better use a little discretion," Michael said.

"By discretion, do you mean as in the better part of valor?" Nicole asked, smiling.

"Put it any way you like. This is your father's house."

"It's my house, too," Nicole rejoined.

"Come on, upstairs. We're going to bed. Me to mine, and you to yours."

"But I missed you," Nicole purred.

"I missed you, too. But momma didn't raise this child stupid."

"Okay, have it your way," Nicole pouted. "I'm going to turn out the lights. I'll see you in the morning," she said, walking out of the room.

Sleep did not come quickly to Michael. He lay awake for hours thinking about what they had discovered. He also thought about Nicole, and how wonderful it would have been to just carry her to bed. Sleep finally came, overtaking a mild fantasy of her.

His sleep was restless at first as a collage of the bits and pieces played through his brain in a distorted dream. He saw Falloux and St. Jude killing his father and taking his papers. They divided them up like money and laughed over their success. Then the dream somehow turned to Nicole. Beautiful Nicole. Michael was with her in a bright white room on a round bed with white covers and satin sheets. They were kissing and touching one another tenderly. There was a large two-way mirror on one wall, and Michael was looking into it, at himself and Nicole making love. Suddenly, he saw right through the mirror. Falloux and St. Jude were standing there—Falloux smiling with a savage delight and laying sheets of his father's papers down on a table in wager, St. Jude's face angry and stern as he watched. He threw down matching amounts of paper to meet the wager. Falloux roared with laughter as St. Jude met his bet, and threw down more and more, each time St. Jude matching the amount, growing more frantic with rage.

Then the mirror was gone, and the room was no longer white but dark and warm. There was just Nicole and her kisses and her mounting passion. He felt her hand caressing him, her lips kissing his chest, and then his stomach. It felt so real as she gently stroked him, her soft lips and tongue working downward, closer . . . until it was almost too real to be a dream.

Michael came suddenly awake to her presence, and she raised herself to kiss him deeply, her hot naked body against his. He wanted to protest—but took her in his arms and kissed her. She responded with the hot passion that was such a wonderful part of her, and for that night it didn't matter where they were—they had each other. And right now he wanted that more than anything.

Michael opened his sleepy eyes to the bright sunshine pouring through the window. The brightness made him squint and blink. He picked his head up off the pillow with a start, realizing that Nicole was still with him. She was half on top of him and stirred slightly as he moved.

"I hate to break up such a beautiful scene, Pretty Lady, but it *is* morning, and you have to go," he said.

"Nonsense," she said sleepily, running her hand down his chest and over his stomach, to begin her artful caresses. He responded with a substantial erection.

"You see," she whispered, kissing his ear. "He wants me to stay, too."

Oh, God, Michael thought. If ever a woman had driven him crazy, it was this one. He prayed that the sun would fall from the sky to give them even a few minutes more of night.

She began kissing his chest and working her way downward again when his hand caught her chin.

"This is definitely going to hurt me more than it is you, but you have to go. If your father catches you here, he'll shoot me," Michael said.

"Are you sure I can't convince you?" she asked, her hand expertly adding to her persuasiveness.

324

"I'm more than sure that you could. But like I said, it's time for you to get back to your room. Now get your things on."

"What things?" she asked.

"What do you mean, 'What things?' Your clothes, or your night-gown. Whatever it was that you wore," he said.

"I don't wear anything when I sleep," she said, tracing his tight, firm stomach with her tongue.

"You what? Oh, shit!" Try explaining this one, he thought. "We've got to do something fast."

She jumped up to her knees in front of him. Seeing her beautiful breasts and body nearly melted him but before he could say anything she was up and putting on one of his shirts, which barely covered the essential parts.

"I'll see you at breakfast," she said and went to the door without buttoning the shirt. She opened the door and stepped out into the hallway.

Before the door closed, he heard her say good morning to some-one, and was sure that he was going to be dead before the next minute was over.

Gabrielle and Danny stood in the hallway watching as Nicole nonchalantly said good morning and walked past them after coming out of Michael's room.

Danny's jaw nearly dropped to the floor when he saw what was just beginning to be covered by Nicole's buttoning efforts as she walked past. It drew a swift elbow from Gabrielle.

"Down, boy," she said. "You had all you could handle last night."

"So did your brother, it seems, the lucky bastard."

No sooner had Danny said that and absorbed a second well-aimed elbow, than he saw St. Jude standing a little further down the hallway. His face was red and angry.

"Good morning, Papa. It's going to be a lovely day," Nicole said, walking past him without the slightest trace of shame.

"Good morning," her father said, following her with angry eyes.

When she had gone into her room, he turned to look at Danny and Gabrielle, then lowered his eyes to the floor and walked past them to the stairs.

They watched as he went down and moved out of sight. They looked at one another.

"Now what?" Gabrielle asked.

"I don't know what to think," Danny said. "You go downstairs to breakfast. I want to talk to Mike."

"What do I say?" Gabrielle asked, hopelessly puzzled.

"You didn't see a thing. Forget that it ever happened. What else can you do?"

She shrugged her shoulders.

"I'll be down in a few minutes," Danny said. "Play it cool."

"Play it cool," she repeated, shaking her head. "What line did she stand in when they gave out the parts?" she mumbled, starting down the stairway.

Danny walked to Michael's door and knocked, then opened it. "It's a fine mess you've gotten us into," he said, walking in. "Her old man was right out there watching the whole show."

Michael shrugged apologetically. "She came into my room last night when I was asleep. Next thing I knew, she was all over me like napalm, only hotter. And let's face it, I'm only human."

Danny just shook his head. "We've got a few things to talk about."

Michael nodded. "Start at the top."

"The *top* is getting Gabrielle out of France and back home," Danny said.

"Have you spoken to her about it yet?"

"No, I haven't. I figure we have to come up with a pretty imaginative way to bring it up, or it's not going to work."

"I think we have a problem even considering it now," Michael said. "Let's just for a second assume that it is Falloux we're after, and that we've shaken him enough to provoke him into trying for us. He's demonstrated, so far, the presence of mind to cover all bases. Don't you suppose he'd consider Gabrielle to be as much of a threat to him as the two of us? The second she left, she'd be in danger, compounded by the fact that we wouldn't be able to protect her," Michael explained. "If she stays, she'll face the same danger that we do, except that we're here to take care of her. Remember, we're expecting it to happen, all we have to do is spot it before it starts. That's a greater advantage than any of the others had."

Danny thought for a second. "Okay, then she stays. But we remain armed every second and stay close together."

"The weapons might be a little hard to explain to Edna-Marie and St. Jude," Michael said.

Danny smirked. "Not for you it won't be. In fact, don't be surprised if old Claude isn't waiting for you with a shotgun and a priest."

"Yeah, well his little girl has been around, and I'm sure he knows it. He might not like it, but that isn't going to change Nicole, and he knows that, too."

"Well, it won't help matters any," Danny said.

"And it might not hurt, either," Michael commented. "If he is Z, and he is in league with Falloux, then a little provoked anger might just work on him as well."

"You really think you have them, don't you?" Danny asked, recalling Michael's case against St. Jude.

Michael nodded. "For the first time since my father died, I think I know where we stand. We still need the proof, especially regarding St. Jude, but the feeling is definitely there. There's still one more person to find. That's the contact. I want to know exactly what my father knew, and see to it that whatever he tried to accomplish gets done."

"You mean the story of the pendant?" Danny asked.

Michael nodded again without speaking. Of course, he now knew that story, thanks to Pheagan. The contact would make all the parts complete. Sub Rosa would have what they needed, and he'd have the people he was after. As far as Demy and Scalco were concerned, he was sure he wouldn't have to find them; they would find him.

The scene at breakfast was not what Danny had expected. Aside from one brief angry stare when Nicole joined the group at the table, and kissed Michael after her good mornings to everyone else, St. Jude seemed remarkably civil, though at times pensive and distant. The table talk was trivial in nature until breakfast was completed.

St. Jude spoke just as everyone was preparing to leave the table. "Seeing as we have nothing planned for today, I think that it would be wise to use the time to give you as much of the remaining story as possible. If there is anything at all to learn about the identity of Z, it must come from this. I am sure that you will want to resolve this matter as quickly as possible, so that you can return home to America," he said. "Shall we say, then, in one half-hour on the terrace?"

Just as Nicole and Michael were leaving the dining room, St. Jude spoke again to his daughter. "Nicole, I would like to speak to you," he said, his eyes on Michael.

"Perhaps I should stay," Michael said to Nicole.

"Nonsense. Go with the others. I'll see you later," she replied.

"I don't think so. This is something for both of us."

"Don't be silly. Go freshen up."

"I wish to speak only to my daughter," St. Jude said to Michael.

Michael exchanged one quick glance with a rock-faced St. Jude and left the dining room, still hesitant to leave Nicole to face him alone.

"Yes, Papa?" Nicole said with an innocent smile.

"Not here. In the study," he said, extending an arm in the proper direction. He followed her into the room and closed the doors behind him.

"Yes, Papa?" Nicole repeated, but this time without the innocent smile. Instead, a tough, serious expression replaced it.

"Your behavior is disgraceful," St. Jude hissed.

Nicole's expression did not change, nor did she speak. She just waited patiently.

"How could you do a thing like that in your own home?"

"A thing like what?" she said.

"Stop this right now. You know what I'm talking about. Have you no shame? You disgrace the name of St. Jude by acting like a . . . like a common tramp," he said. "And in this house. You go to a man's room in the night, a man whom you hardly know. And then this morning, you parade almost completely naked in front of guests. How could you do that? How could you shame me so?"

"Did it shame you to make love to my mother before you married her?" Nicole asked. "Did that shame the name of St. Jude?"

"That has nothing to do with this," he said angrily, his face reddened. "That is not the same."

"I'm sure that you made love many times before you were married. Did that make Mama a common tramp?"

"You have no right—"

"It is you who have no right to tell me how to act when it comes to how I feel for a man," she interrupted sternly.

"Your mother and I loved one another."

"And did you not consider that perhaps I am beginning to love this man?" she asked.

"You haven't known him long enough," St. Jude objected.

"How long must one know someone to recognize the goodness inside?" she asked. "I'm a big girl, Papa. I've always acted the way I've wanted to with men from the time I felt old enough to make those judgments for myself. I'm not a tramp, and don't you call me one again. I'm old enough to go anywhere I care to, to be with any man I wish, and to do so without worrying about obtaining your consent.

"I'm not your little girl anymore, Papa. We can never go back to that. I live here because I love you and I love the Camargue. But that does not mean that I'll stay forever. When I find the right man, I'll go with him, wherever it is that we must go together."

The hurt and the anger balled up inside of St. Jude. There were tears in his eyes from the pain of what he had just heard. He couldn't control her anymore; she wasn't a child. She was a woman. He could no longer be protective or demanding. How does one stop a child from growing? he wondered as tears rolled down his cheeks.

"And is this the man?" he asked through clenched teeth.

"I don't know yet. He's like no one I've met before. There is something very special about him, like there must have been about his father, from the stories I've heard," she replied. "I know that I want to love him very much, and that I'm starting to without being able to help myself. I . . . hope that you can understand that."

"When he leaves, will you . . . go with him?" St. Jude asked.

"He hasn't asked me to."

"If he does, will you go?"

Nicole thought for a moment. "I . . . don't really know. I only know that I want to be with him very much."

St. Jude closed his eyes in a moment of extreme pain, his head rolled to the side as he turned away from her. "I . . . I have nothing more to say right now. I . . . need to think, to be alone for awhile," he said.

She walked up behind him and put her arms around his shoulders and kissed his cheek. "Did you not love his father?" she asked.

He turned his head, his eyes filled with tears, and nodded.

"Then love Michael, too. I love you, Papa. You were the first man in my life, and will be the only man to be a part of it entirely." She kissed his cheek again and left him, closing the doors behind her.

St. Jude looked at the doors, their image blurred by the tears in his eyes. Did you not love his father? he heard her voice ask again in his mind.

"Yes, I loved him—like a brother," he answered aloud, and wept for the truths he could no longer change.

Chapter 35

Michael was the first to reach the terrace. He waited nervously for Nicole to arrive. He felt that he should have been firmer and insisted upon facing St. Jude with her. He turned to the sound of the glass doors opening. It was Danny and Gabrielle.

Danny shook his head. "I can't figure it. I expected all hell to break loose. You were lucky, my boy. Damn lucky."

"Yeah, I know. But you can bet he wants to be done with us as quickly as possible, for more than one reason," Michael said.

Gabrielle gave her brother a puzzled look. "You're doing it again, both of you. You're not telling me things. What was that last remark about?"

"We'll tell you about it, but not right now. They'll all be out here any minute," Michael told her.

"When do you contact Pheagan next?" Danny asked.

Michael looked at his watch. "It's only about four A.M. there now. I'll call him about midafternoon, that'll make it morning there. He'll have a full day to get started on the things I have to tell him."

"It sounds to me like you two have a lot of explaining to do," Gabrielle said. "And don't think for a minute that I'm going to let you get away without doing it."

The glass doors to the terrace opened again and Nicole walked out. Michael went to her immediately, concern on his face.

"He was just being silly," Nicole told him. "There's nothing to worry about. He knows that he has to treat me like an adult; he just doesn't want to admit it to himself yet."

"I can't tell you how bad I feel," Michael said.

"Bad? About what has happened between you and me?" Nicole asked.

"Not about that, not for a single minute. I mean about hurting your father. I would never want that."

"Well, there's an understanding now. He knows . . . how I feel about you," she said, her marvelous large brown eyes looking into his. She took his hand, and they walked to the circle of chairs that had been set up for them.

"I would like to apologize for this morning," Nicole said to Gabrielle and Danny. "Not for having been with Michael," she said, smiling up at him, "but for showing a lack of respect for your feelings. I am truly sorry. I should have been more considerate and discreet."

"We understand," Gabrielle said softly. "It was a bit of a surprise, but we weren't offended."

The glass doors opened once again, and St. Jude escorted Edna-Marie out toward the chairs. He appeared quite composed, though not his usual smiling self.

"Now then, where should we begin?" Edna-Marie asked.

"We've heard the story of the scientist from the Collard brothers, but only up to where my father escaped," Michael said. "Perhaps you could pick it up from there," he suggested.

"Claude, I think that you could tell it best, as you were involved," Edna-Marie said.

As he was involved? Michael thought to himself. He hadn't heard it that way. "The Collard brothers hadn't mentioned that you were involved in that operation," he said.

"I wasn't, really. At least not in the actual execution of the plan. But I did notify London immediately after being informed of the necessary changes. I wasn't given the details of your father's involvement, of course, but knew that there was little chance of success. So, I finished sending the message and left immediately for Clermont-Ferrand," he said.

"But wasn't that extremely dangerous?" Gabrielle asked. "You were wanted, and they were looking for you."

"Yes, that is true. I don't really know what it was that I hoped to accomplish, and it was foolish on my part to run such a risk. But it was a good thing for your father that I did. . . ."

CLERMONT-FERRAND, JANUARY 1943: A badly injured Christian Gladieux made his way painfully from the building from which he had just shot the scientist. He was out of the area by the time the Germans arrived on the scene, though signs of his being injured were evident, and the gun was found on the roof.

Christian made his way the two blocks to where he had instructed Lucien Collard to leave his trusty old motorcycle. He found it and, though in great pain, was able to get out of the city before it could be sealed shut. His first thoughts were to get help. He realized from the sudden activity at the station that the plan had somehow been revealed, and he ruled out going to the Collard farm, on the chance that it had been betrayed as well. So he sped aimlessly along country roads, not knowing exactly where to go, until he saw the road sign to Riom. That instantly reminded him of the nearly disastrous Lysander operation less than two months earlier in which Leopard had been killed. His first thought went to the ruined Bouchard winery, where they had successfully hidden after that near tragedy. He sped off for it.

The pain grew significantly worse, and he began to cough up more blood. Dizziness followed, making control of the old battered motorcycle extremely difficult and dangerous. He abandoned the bike not far from Pont du Château, concealing it in the woods. Then he began the trek on foot, staying off the roads and traveling through the bare forests and fields.

He continued moving, though it became a great deal more painful and difficult as time passed. The bleeding stopped for a while, then started again, and he was beginning to grow weak. The injured legs were rebelling and the broken ribs made breathing extremely painful, but he kept moving. The cold had become worse, and it was starting to snow quite heavily. He had to find shelter before losing consciousness, for it could easily mean his death in this kind of weather.

Thirty minutes later, feeling at the end of his strength, he saw the ghostlike image of the winery through the trees and the whipping snow. He headed for it and, once safely there, collapsed and fell unconscious on the floor.

It was dark when Christian came to. He found himself on a thick bed of straw, with a blanket over him. He looked around with a start and saw the face of Claude St. Jude looking at him, a weak smile breaking.

St. Jude came to his side immediately. "Thank God, I thought you were dying," his friend said, sounding greatly relieved.

Christian squinted and looked at him with puzzlement. "How did you find me?" he asked.

"When you did not show up at the Collard farm, I thought abou the places you might choose to hide. I guessed correctly, though the others don't know yet. We had no idea that you had been injured. You were lucky to get this far."

Christian nodded, feeling grateful to have a friend near.

"You need a doctor. I know one in Pont du Château who can be trusted. I will go to him and then contact the others to let them know that you are safe. I won't be gone long," St. Jude promised.

"No, don't go yet," Christian said. "Stay a while longer. Until morning."

"But you need help, and you need it now."

"Right now, I need you here more, my friend."

St. Jude nodded. "I'll stay until morning. I have no food or water, I'm afraid," he said.

Christian shook his head to say that he didn't need either.

St. Jude nodded once again, and sat beside his friend to wait for the morning.

The two men were asleep side by side when the dawn broke. St. Jude came quickly alert and checked Christian. He seemed to be all right, and St. Jude thought it best not to awaken him. Sleep was the best thing for Christian now.

He arranged the blanket to be sure that Christian would be warm in the bitter cold, then left the shelter of the winery to go for the doctor.

It was nearly an hour later when he returned alone. The doctor was unable to come because of an emergency, but agreed to see Christian later in the day. Though he had agreed, his willingness was not as enthusiastic as St. Jude had hoped it would be. The doctor said that he would see Christian, but not at the winery. He must be brought to town, which was a dangerous proposition. St. Jude would not risk such a thing until evening. That meant another full day without medical help for his friend. He stopped on the way back to buy some things to help in the meantime.

Christian was still sleeping when St. Jude returned. He checked his friend and found him feverish. He opened the bag containing bandages and salve for the leg injuries, and removed some small packages of food.

He prepared a kind of sterno by mixing a small amount of kerosene with a thick petroleum jelly, making it into a paste, then put it into an old empty can. He lit it, then laid three flat pieces of wire across the mouth of the can to form a small triangle above the flame. He then placed a metal cup filled with water on the can and poured some tea leaves into the cup. It wasn't exactly a stove, but it would make hot tea and give off warmth.

It was about that time that Christian woke up. He realized that St. Jude must have already left and come back when he saw all the things on the table.

"How are you feeling?" St. Jude asked him.

"I hurt, but I'll make it," Christian replied.

"You'll feel better after you've eaten and had some hot tea. I've been to the doctor. He will see you this evening, but we have to go into town. And he won't see you at his office, so I've arranged for a place."

Christian nodded, and coughed. No blood came up; that was a good sign. But the coughing had been terribly painful, and it still hurt a good deal to breathe.

St. Jude gave him the hot tea and food, and made sure that he was comfortable and warm. He had parked the car in the old barn so that it wouldn't be seen, and he went out regularly to check that no one was coming down the lane to the winery.

Together they waited until darkness. Christian told St. Jude the story of what had happened to the Englishman, and how he had taken his place. He described how he had gotten only the slightest glimpse of the scientist after firing the shot when the trains crossed, completely blocking his view. He was sure he had killed him. Only a fraction of a second's delay would have meant failure.

"Well, if our luck holds out, they won't look for you here. You said that Immel was there?" St. Jude asked.

"Yes. It was Immel, all right. I didn't expect to see him there," Christian said. "I didn't even know that he was in Clermont-Ferrand."

"That doesn't matter. You did what you had to do, now we must get you taken care of," St. Jude said. He looked at his watch and at the darkness outside. "It's safe to leave now."

CLERMONT-FERRAND: The German orderly entered the room and approached Immel. He stood politely by as Immel spoke to the other men in the room.

"I want every house in the entire area searched again," he shouted. "The gunman was injured and couldn't have gotten far. He must still be in the area."

"Herr Hauptmann, there is a call for you," the orderly said softly at the first opportunity.

"All right. All right," Immel said in a temper. "It's probably Berlin again, wanting to hear it for the tenth time." He stormed out of the room behind the orderly and picked up the phone.

"Hauptmann Immel?" the voice inquired in a raspy whisper.

"Yes, yes, this is Immel," the German said impatiently.

"I have some information regarding the assassination in Clermont-Ferrand," the voice said.

"Who is this?" Immel asked.

"The man who did it is Christian Gladieux. He can be found at the destroyed Bouchard winery near Pont du Château. He was badly injured in a fall during his escape," the voice informed him.

"Who is this?" Immel asked again.

"A friend. You can trust my information."

"Who are you?" Immel repeated loudly.

"I am Z. Goodbye, Captain Immel. Happy hunting," the voice said, then the phone went dead.

Immel slammed down the phone, then started back into the room to rejoin his men, but he stopped short of the door. He thought for a long moment, then entered the room.

The men looked at him, waiting for him to speak.

He looked back at them. "Well, you have your orders. Get out of here, you idiots. Find him!" he shouted.

When they had all left, he walked back to the door. "Josef," he called, summoning his orderly.

"Yes, Herr Hauptmann."

"I want my car brought around immediately. I won't be needing a driver. If there are any calls for me, I'll be on my way back to Paris," he said.

"Yes, Herr Hauptmann," the orderly snapped, spinning quickly to carry out his orders.

Immel walked back into the room, closing the door behind him. He went to his briefcase and pulled out a pile of maps, sorted through them, and found the one he wanted. It was an enlarged detailed map of the Clermont-Ferrand area, extending to a full twenty-kilometer radius. He consulted it for a few moments, finding what he was looking for, then put his things back into the briefcase. He put on his scarf, coat, and hat and left the office.

The orderly returned just as Immel closed the door behind him. "Your car is ready, Herr Hauptmann."

"Thank you, Josef. Now get Hauptmann Radl, quickly."

Five minutes later, after having left orders to continue the search

through the next day, he was on his way to Paris. There would be one
stop, however, in Pont du Château, to even a score once and for all.

P ONT DU CHÂTEAU: "You are a lucky man," the doctor said, completing the last binding around Christian's chest. "It will probably take a
few months for you to recover properly. You must find a place where
you can get complete rest."

Christian nodded. "Thank you, doctor. Thank you very much."

"Yes, yes. We all do our part," the doctor said. "I suggest that you
stay here for a few days at least. Monsieur Plante says that you can stay
in the loft of his garage. That should be sufficient, as long as you keep
warm and eat. There is little more that we can do. Time must now do
its mending. Keep the chest tightly bound for at least four weeks, or
you risk more serious damage."

"I understand. Thank you."

When the doctor had left, Jean Plante and his wife sat with Christian. Madame Plante fed him some hot, rich soup.

"You will be in great danger keeping me here," Christian said.

"We must all do our part for France," Jean Plante said, his tired
old face not hiding his worry well.

"Be still now. You must eat and then sleep," the kindly wife said.
She turned to her husband with a reproachful frown. "And he will not
stay in the garage. It will be much too cold for him there."

"I can keep the stove burning," the old mechanic said.

"That would be stupid! The police would spot that as being unusual immediately. And besides, you don't have enough fuel. No, it is
settled, he will stay here, in your mother's old room in the attic."

These were kind, wonderful people trying to do their best, Christian thought. But they would be in grave danger keeping him here,
especially now, after what he had done. They would be shot immediately for their efforts to help him.

When they had turned in for the night, he quietly left the house
and headed back to the winery.

It was a long walk, and he was still quite sore. He wished that St.
Jude had remained to drive him back, but he had left to inform the
Collards of the situation, in the belief that Christian would remain with
the Plantes for at least the next few days.

It took Christian well over an hour to reach the winery. He was
cold, and hoped that St. Jude had not returned to remove the things

that they had left there. The blanket would be a blessing if it remained.

He walked down the lane, shivering from the cold, and went into the small intact portion of the winery that had served as his shelter. He opened the door and stepped into the dark room.

He was suddenly grabbed by two strong hands and shoved hard into the wall. He recoiled from the impact, and turned to face his attacker. Two heavy, vicious blows hit his shoulder and ribs. He crumpled from the searing pain, but managed to roll away, avoiding a kick.

He couldn't identify his attacker in the darkness, but he could make out quite clearly the boots of a German officer.

Christian rose and tried throwing a punch, but received another blow to the ribs. The pain was too great and he fell once again, the grasping hands of his attacker tearing his shirt and ripping away his neck chain as he fell. This time the kick scored full force to the stomach, and Christian rolled in beaten agony, the taste of blood fresh in his mouth again. He rolled to his back and stared up at his attacker. It was Rudolf Immel.

Immel stood over him, holding a piece of torn shirt and the broken chain in one hand, his drawn gun in the other. He glared down at the Frenchman, exchanging the unspoken hatred of their double rivalry.

Christian knew that he was looking at death, and waited for it, a look of defiance across his face, a look of having won the contest over Max Schrict, and of knowing the true victory regarding Gabrielle.

Without explanation, Immel put the gun away, and threw the chain to the ground. He stared at Christian a moment longer, and Christian could swear that he read defeat in the German's eyes. Then Immel turned and was gone.

Christian lay on the ground breathing painfully, blood dripping from his mouth. Then he heard Immel's car start up from behind the winery and drive off. For whatever reason, and it bordered on miracle, Christian Gladieux had been spared.

"Your father was found the next day by Gabrielle Dupuy, who was frantic with worry over his condition. Following his instructions, she got him to the Collard farm, where he was well taken care of.

"Christian was then taken to St.-Etienne, where Edna-Marie joined him a day later," St. Jude said, looking to Edna-Marie, to turn the story over to her.

"He was a frightful sight," she said. "He looked on the edge of death. We knew that a long period of rest was needed and that staying in France would not be safe for him, so we arranged for a Lysander operation to take him out. It took place just north of Firminy, and I cried as I saw the plane lift off safely," Edna-Marie told them. "I knew that he would be safe in England and be able to recover to good health. But when he left, I saw much of my strength and self-confidence go with him.

"Claude took over your father's responsibilities while he was gone. We suffered disappointingly heavy losses almost immediately. It was perhaps an omen of how difficult a year 1943 would ultimately be."

Edna-Marie continued the story, telling them about the sudden onset of costly betrayals. They became almost daily occurrences, with sector after sector falling, even the newly and carefully organized ones. Old hiding places and addresses were even being hit. It was as though the Germans were being provided with a complete plan of the network a small piece at a time.

Then Defiance managed to intercept a series of German memos, largely obtained by Gabrielle Dupuy, who had quickly established new contacts after Immel's departure. The memos confirmed the presence of a well-placed informer who was designated as Z. It was Z who was responsible for the sudden level of success being enjoyed by the Germans.

Then Edna-Marie told them of an event that had nearly destroyed her remaining confidence. Claude St. Jude was captured in a shootout in which three of seven Defiance members were killed. Another memo was intercepted, boasting of the capture of the "prize" Defiance agent known as Camargue. The memo clearly indicated that the capture was made possible by Z.

"It was a desperate time for me," Edna-Marie said. "My two towers of strength were gone. Group Defiance was suffering terrible losses at a pace that would soon consume it if they continued unabated.

"Nearly two months had passed since your father left France. We were still successful in obtaining information, but our falling sectors were not being rebuilt, and our effectiveness was starting to drop off. It appeared that the Germans were beginning to win their war against us.

"Flandine was in England at the time of Claude's arrest. Fortunately, Jan Burak appeared in Marseilles when he heard the news of our losses. He gave me a great deal of strength to carry on through those dark hours. Then, as if by miracle, your father returned from England. He looked so beautiful, so strong and fit. I felt revitalized and alive. I was suddenly filled with fight and energy.

338

"We began a rapid rebuilding of our cells and sectors, at which your father was capable of working miracles. Throughout the entire war he continuously picked up the threads of what remained from broken sectors and weaved a healthy, efficient network from them.

"Then Charles Flandine returned from England with news that Group Defiance had been formally militarized by De Gaulle as part of the Free French army. It was a moment of tremendous jubilation.

"Flandine told me privately how terribly impressed De Gaulle had been with your father. He felt certain that he had had a most positive effect on De Gaulle's decision.

"Then we learned another bit of news that ignited us. Claude, who was being held at Castres Prison, was going to be taken to Paris by order of von Roeth, himself. The memo, which had been intercepted, said that Claude had been stubbornly uncooperative, despite intensive interrogation. Von Roeth wanted the Gestapo experts in Paris to go to work on him. He was growing impatient in his war against Le Groupe Défi. The details of the transfer were included in the memo, and your father quickly organized a daring rescue, which caught the Germans completely off guard.

"Claude was in terrible condition. He had been beaten and tortured during the interrogations," Edna-Marie said.

St. Jude's eyes were down, his mind far away at this point, his fists tightly clenched as though he were recalling those terrible moments.

Edna-Marie fell silent, waiting for St. Jude to pick it up. It took a moment for him to realize her intent. When he did, he began haltingly.

"You . . . cannot imagine the things that they did to people," he said, shaking his head. "Women with nipples torn from their breasts—men too." He nodded. "Vile objects shoved into anuses and women's genitals, fingers hideously bent and broken, burns inflicted on every part of the body. And the things they did to the eyes . . ." He lowered his head, still shaking it. "And many of these interrogators were Frenchmen. They made you wish for death, and laughed at your suffering."

There was a long moment of silence, in which St. Jude settled himself. Then Edna-Marie began once again.

"We learned from Claude that thirty more of our people had been shot at the fortress at Bondues by French firing squads. It was terrible news, which angered us and filled us with a determination to carry on for all those who had died.

"We went on the run after that. It was at this time that our string of narrow escapes began. We were so harried that at times it seemed we were almost always out of breath. We would find a safe place, take refuge, and work endless hours trying to plan countermoves and trying to reorganize sectors. And all the while, our brave and wonderful people continued sending in their vital information to Britain.

"But our losses continued. It was an extremely serious dilemma The Germans were hurting us badly, thanks to Z, and we were power less to stop it.

"And then, after nearly three months of constant running, we re ceived the terrible news that the Marseilles sector had been completely crushed—all of the businesses, everything. And to add to the tragedy Jan Burak and Charles Flandine were betrayed and caught near Mont pellier.

"In all of the war, there had never been a point so low. We were totally despondent, weary from running and the narrowness of ou escapes, often only by minutes ahead of the Germans.

"It was time to separate. We could do no more good staying to gether. Were we to be caught, with the state of the network as it was Group Defiance would have perished completely. So we separated each knowing the things we must do. I went to Pau to establish a new headquarters. Your father went to Paris to begin a third rebuilding o the sectors there, and Claude went to Marseilles, with the difficult job of rebuilding the totally destroyed and critical Mediterranean por sector.

"Without realizing it, we had done the best possible thing. Ou rebuilding began again, with the three of us working separately. Group Defiance began coming back slowly, and with surprising strength.

"And then disaster struck again in the form of Z. Claude and nine other members of the rebuilding Marseilles sector were betrayed and trapped. A terrible gunfight took place. Four were killed, Claude and two others were badly wounded, and two got away to tell the story.

"Claude had been taken again, and from what we had heard, wa nearly dead. And this time there was nothing that we could do to help him."

Chapter 36

A COLD silence hung over the table following lunch. The women had excused themselves to freshen up before the resumption of the tory session. The three men sat for several minutes without speaking before Michael looked at Danny, then rose to his feet.

"Monsieur St. Jude, I would like to apologize for what happened earlier today," he began. "There is little that I can offer in defense of my actions, except . . . except that your daughter is a remarkably wonderful and beautiful woman, and that I am quite taken by her. I never meant you any disrespect, or wished to hurt you in any way," Michael said sincerely.

St. Jude looked at him for a long moment, then rose to his feet. "I have many things, Michael—money, property," he said, sweeping an arm slowly as though to encompass all his possessions. "But of all the things I have, only one is important to me. Only one is my happiness. That is my daughter. She is my life. She is a wonderful girl, so very much like her mother. But she is wild and impulsive. She has always been that way. She has always done and lived for herself.

"I . . . I cannot hate you for what happened. I know my daughter, and the effect she has always had on men. And perhaps I . . . should realize that she is a grown woman. I am not too old to remember how I felt about her mother when we were young and falling in love. And I am no hypocrite who would deny that we showed our love for one another before we married. But I am also a father, and you can't understand, until you have a daughter of your own whom you will love as I love Nicole, how a father feels when he senses that he is beginning to lose her.

"I cannot hate you, and I will not. You are very much like your

father, and I loved him like my own brother. But I will not apologiz
for the pain that I feel. What you and Nicole choose to do is betwee
you. I know that I am powerless to stop it. I also know that I shouldn'
try. You are young and have your whole lives ahead of you. If yo
bring each other happiness, even if it is for a short time, that is to you
benefit. I will not take that away. I've seen too much pain and sorrov
to know how few and precious such moments truly are. I ask only tha
you respect her, and that you never hurt her. She is all that I have. Sh
is my life."

The two men remained standing, looking at one another.

"I will promise you that, Monsieur St. Jude," Michael said.

St. Jude nodded without smiling, then turned and walked away.

Michael watched until he walked around the side of the house
then he sat back down. "That says it, I guess," he said.

Danny nodded. "I have to admit to feeling a bit confused. W
may have jumped the gun a little bit about him before hearing th
whole story."

"You mean about St. Jude being betrayed by Z twice himself?"

Danny nodded. "He went through pure hell: torture, nearly ge
ting shot to death. I'd say that puts a slightly different slant on thing
wouldn't you?" he asked.

Michael remained silent, deep in thought.

"Well, do you agree, or don't you?" Danny asked.

"On the surface it would seem that you're right. But I'm still no
convinced," Michael replied. "Z was a remarkably clever fellov
Clever enough to have set himself up to cement his cover."

"I'd say that setting himself up to go through what St. Jude di
would be pretty extreme, wouldn't you? I don't know, Mike. Tha
clever I think I could be—but that brave? I doubt it quite seriously.
Danny said, shaking his head slightly.

"You'd be surprised at what you'd do to stay alive."

"Perhaps, but don't lose sight of the fact that there is still anothe
suspect who was not caught as a result of betrayal by Z, and who kne
everything that St. Jude knew, and more," Danny said. "Her cod
name was in the Daytimer, too."

Michael was silent again, thinking. Yes, Edna-Marie was a suspe
herself. Either one of the two could have "dropped" information f
the Germans while they were running. Once they had separated, eith
one could have also continued feeding information to the Germar
quite easily. But on the one side, the second betrayal of the Marseill
sector, in which St. Jude was working, would have truly been a clev

342

move on his part. The shootout may not have been a part of his plan, and just developed. Getting shot was just bad luck, which turned out to be one of the best things that could have happened to him. It certainly made it impossible for anybody to point a finger at him.

The extent of his wounds could have been a well-kept secret. He certainly hadn't volunteered any information about it. But what continued to focus Michael's suspicion on Claude St. Jude was the story of what had happened after the killing of the scientist. He had the distinct advantage of being able to combine the stories told him by St. Jude, the Collard brothers, *and* Rudolf Immel, putting the pieces from each into a more complete picture.

Michael began shaking his head. "I don't buy it being Edna-Marie," he said. "It's St. Jude, all right. It has to be. He knew about the altered plan to get the scientist in time enough to warn Liepart in Paris. He didn't know the details, or he probably would have given them. Once he came in from Marseilles and spoke to the Collard brothers, he was then aware of what had happened, and that my father was the trigger man. Then after finding my father, he learned from him that Immel was in Clermont-Ferrand. The call to Immel was placed only *after* St. Jude had become aware of those facts."

"We're not exactly sure when that call was placed," Danny said.

"We sure as hell are," Michael countered. "Immel gave us that answer. It's probably the biggest clue we, or anyone else, has ever had as to the identity of Z. Do you remember what he told us about that call?"

"Yes, I do," Danny replied. "He told us that he got a call informing him that it was your father who had shot the scientist, and that he had been badly hurt during the escape. He was also told where to find him."

"Immel was told that my father had been injured in a *fall* during his escape. Who else knew that?" Michael asked.

Danny thought for a moment. "No one else could have," he replied.

"Exactly. And as for *when* the call was made, Immel said that he left immediately after receiving the call. Pont du Château is a short ride from Clermont-Ferrand. He got to the winery late at night, when my father wasn't there, and waited for him. That would put the time at about when my father was in Pont du Château being patched up and resting at the home of the Plantes," Michael said.

"But there's one flaw here, Mike," Danny countered. "St. Jude was on his way back and, granted, could have made the call to Immel.

But he had arranged for your father to stay at the Plantes' home for a least a few days. If he thought your father wouldn't be at the winery why would he have sent Immel there?"

"I can think of two possible answers to that," Michael said. "First he may not have expected my father to stay at the Plante home, afte all. We only have St. Jude's word that that was the plan."

"He wouldn't have left your father to walk back in his condition," Danny offered.

"That's true. And that's why I think my second reason is closer to the truth," Michael said.

"And what is that?" Danny asked anxiously.

"He didn't want my father to be caught," Michael said.

Danny stared at him for a few moments. "Yes, I'm beginning to follow your meaning," he said at last. "He accomplishes two things by doing that. First, he performs his duty to the Germans as he was expected to do, only above the call of duty because of the value of his information. Second, he makes sure that in doing so he doesn't really hurt your father, having made certain that he was safely away from the winery."

"You've got it exactly. They were truly good friends. Perhaps too good to have a one-on-one betrayal weigh on his conscience. That's probably also why Edna-Marie, Gabrielle Dupuy, and my father were never really betrayed in a fashion that resulted in their actual capture He cared too much for all of them. My father leaving the Plante house almost blew his good intentions," Michael explained.

"It makes a lot of sense," Danny admitted. "And, of course, without Immel's side of the story we could never have known. It's a part of the story that no one has ever heard before."

Michael smiled at his brother-in-law. "I think we've got both of our birds marked. All we need is a little more evidence."

"And a contact," Danny added.

Michael nodded. "And a contact," he repeated, "who, somehow ties into the word Leopard."

It was Edna-Marie who continued the story when the group had once again assembled on the terrace.

"Your father was in Paris at the time of Claude's capture in Marseilles. He didn't learn of it until later, when we met again in Pau.

"He had been working tirelessly trying to rebuild the sectors in Paris and to locate Gabrielle Dupuy. She had simply disappeared after your father was sent off to England. Her information kept coming in

344

through a contact that was established to work solely with her, and who was not taken when Paris fell. She never met with this contact, who couldn't have identified her if they stood beside one another. The contact was simply given a coded message over the phone when Gabrielle had information, then he picked it up at one of the dead drops that had been arranged between them. Though she continued to be highly effective, we had quite completely lost track of her."

Gabrielle Dupuy had suddenly found herself left with so little. The two men that she loved were gone from her life at almost the same moment. She could have survived the loss of one of them, but to lose them both was too much for her to bear. To fight off her deep depression, she chose tireless, unending work. She knew that there were many German officers who drooled with envy each time they had seen her and Immel together, knowing full well the relationship that had existed between them. Even von Roeth had patted her lovely ass on more than one occasion, the suggestive gleam in his tired old eyes as evident as the weak bulge in his pants. They all possessed information that France needed to win the war, and she knew the delicate art of obtaining it. Now she would be theirs, too, whoever wanted her—as long as they had the information that she needed. For her, there was nothing left but the war, and winning it.

Gabrielle Dupuy had no way of knowing that Christian had returned to France. She had thought his injuries too severe to make that possible while the war lasted. And when he did return, his life was so hectic with mad dashes and escapes, and endless hours of work when running was not necessitated, that he could not get to Paris to find her. It was only after the disaster in Marseilles and the joint decision for Edna-Marie, St. Jude, and himself to separate that going to Paris became possible.

The amount of work there left little time for him to search for her, though he did try. He left coded messages with her friend, at whose apartment they had regularly met, and also with her special contact. She had not been back to the apartment or even contacted her friend since Christian left France. Her assigned contact hadn't heard from her in weeks. It was as though she had disappeared.

Then another terrible disaster struck. The entire forgery section in Paris fell. Every person involved was taken, and even worse, which they weren't to learn until later, meticulously kept records had fallen into German hands. No one knew of these records except the man who had kept them, and even he didn't know how damaging they would become to Le Groupe Défi—once the traitor Z began interpreting them for the Germans. It nearly sounded the death knell for Group De fiance, which had relied too heavily upon the one forgery section be cause of its speed and quality of work.

Christian went to Pau immediately, where he was told of St. Jude's capture just the week before. He was deeply upset by the news. They had no idea what had become of their friend. There wasn't the slightest hint of where the Germans might be holding him. This was the second time that they had caught this prize, and they were not about to lose it again.

Then, suddenly, Gabrielle resurfaced with another memo she had intercepted which indicated that St. Jude was alive and about to be secretly transported to Paris. He had been under heavy guard in a prison hospital for nearly eight weeks. After interrogation in Paris, he was to be taken into Germany. There were no details on the date or method of transport to be used in getting him to Paris. But at least they had learned that he was alive.

"Your father again returned to Paris," Edna-Marie continued "The sectors were again functioning, and we hoped that some information regarding Claude's transfer to Paris could be learned in time to help him.

"Claude, perhaps you had better take over from here," she suggested.

"I had been kept in complete isolation in Castres Prison since my capture in Marseilles, and actually could have been moved before the time selected. But I pretended to be in worse condition than I was really in, and had the help of a loyal French doctor to convince the Germans of that fact.

"It was only by the sheerest luck that I managed to escape a second time, thanks to the foolish bravery of five young patriots bent on doing their part against the Germans. They nearly killed me in the process, thinking that I was a German, for the Boche had dressed me in one of their uniforms. But in the end, it was both their bravery and their fear which saved me," St. Jude recounted, then told them the story.

The Germans had taken great precautions to keep the movement of Camargue a secret. To lose him a second time would be unforgivable, and those having the responsibility were keenly aware of the fact.

It was just after the last daily visit by the prison doctor that they came for him. They ordered him to dress in a German officer's uniform, and even took the precaution to bring in another prisoner to occupy the bed of St. Jude. The prisoner was heavily sedated to guar-

ntee his sleeping through to the morning, when St. Jude's removal
rom the prison would first be detected. By that time, he would be in
'aris.

He was placed in a car with three other Germans—two officers and
. driver. The car left Castres Prison in the early evening without escort,
o as not to attract attention, and sped off for Paris. It stopped one time
tear Moulins for fuel, then continued its high-speed trip northward
oward the darkened City of Light.

Once in Paris, they kept to obscure, dark streets as they made their
vay toward the heart of the city. It was as they approached Pont Neuf
on the Quai de Conti that fate awaited them.

The Quai de Conti is one of many short streets that parallels the
River Seine along its southern bank nearing the Cité, the largest of
he islands on the river, upon which the Cathedral of Notre Dame and
he huge complex of buildings known as the Palais de Justice stand in
iistoric majesty. The Quai de Conti is a quiet, narrow cobbled street
oordered on one side by trees and high stone walls, and on the other
side by the Seine. A low stone curb was all that separated the roadway
rom the waters of the river. Along the wharf, small barges and boats
loated and were intermittently docked.

Concealed at a point where the street took its sharpest bend were
four young patriots, armed with a shotgun, a rifle, a handgun, and an
automatic weapon, all secretly "borrowed" from their fathers. They
were waiting to ambush the first German car to come their way. A fifth,
the youngest, waited further up the road ahead of the bend, sitting atop
the wall behind the remaining cover of an autumn-colored tree.

They had waited for three consecutive nights to strike out in their
private rage at the occupiers of their country, wanting very much to do
their part for France.

They waited nervously, silently, each dealing in his own mind with
what he had come to do. It was nearly 4:00 A.M. when the shrill whistle
of their lookout on the wall sounded. Suddenly there was an explosion
of nerves. A car carrying Boche was actually driving straight into their
ambush. They moved into position quickly, raising their weapons for
the attack on the car that would appear at any second.

The driver of the car was tired. The officer beside him was half
asleep. Only St. Jude and the officer next to him were fully alert in the
back seat.

The car rounded the bend, and before the driver's mind could
focus on the sight greeting him, the hail of bullets and buckshot started.
The windows of the car blew inward, and St. Jude saw the face of the
driver shredded by the shotgun blast. As the car passed the attackers,

347

the eruption of gunfire was deafening. St. Jude felt a sudden burst of pain in his right shoulder, then the car veered sharply to the left, going over the low curb, hitting the back of a barge, then plunging into the water.

The gunfire continued to pour into the car as it tilted downward into the dark water and began to sink rapidly. St. Jude watched as the officer beside him tried to exit the car and was hit by a sudden rush of bullets.

He knew in that instant that to try to get out of the car would mean his death. He waited, holding his breath as the car went down fighting his panic to escape. When the car slipped below the surface, he made his move. He opened the door and began kicking to try to get deeper below the surface of the water. Another short burst from the automatic weapon sounded and he felt a sharp burning pain in the back of his left thigh. St. Jude kicked as hard as he could, stroking frantically and awkwardly with his manacled hands. He sighted a barge in the reflecting surface of the water above him, and made for the outward side of it.

He surfaced to hear the scuffling of feet moving quickly on the barge and looked up to see the double barrels of a shotgun trained on his face.

"I'm French! I'm French!" St. Jude screamed frantically.

The youth looked down at the face in the dark waters. Two more of his comrades joined him on the barge. "He's wearing a German uniform," one of them shouted.

"No, no. Don't shoot. I'm a member of Group Defiance. I was a prisoner of the Germans being secretly transported into Paris," he blurted out. "See, look," St. Jude said, raising his cuffed hands as high as the injured shoulder would permit.

"Cover him," the youth with the automatic weapon said to his friend with the shotgun. "If he tries anything, kill him."

Two of the youths pulled the wounded St. Jude from the water and looked him over suspiciously. The manacled hands lent a great deal of credibility to his claim.

"Quickly, we must get out of here," St. Jude said urgently.

It was after they were safely away and hiding in the apartment of the sister of one of the youths that St. Jude succeeded in fully convincing them who he was, and of the tremendously valuable service they had just unwittingly performed for their country.

The youths did their best to temporarily treat his wounds, apologizing repeatedly for having shot him. That fact, perhaps, terrorized them more than what they had just done to the three Germans. They feared, unrightly so, that Group Defiance would take retaliation against them.

"You did a wonderful job," St. Jude told them, to ease their minds. "Believe me, I would gladly suffer these wounds three times over to be out of their hands. I have been in their prisons before; I know what they can do to a man to make him talk. In giving me this little pain, you have saved me from a great deal more, and probably saved my life as well."

The one youth explained that they would all have to leave the apartment, as his sister was unaware that they were using it. She was spending the night with a boyfriend, but would be returning that morning.

St. Jude looked around the room at the bloodstained rug and furniture. "Well, you won't be able to keep it from her for long," he said, his meaning immediately clear. "I hope she's a patriot," he added.

"She is. But she'll be as angry as a hornet. She doesn't even know that I have a key to her apartment."

"It will be daylight in a few minutes," St. Jude said. "It won't be safe for me to move about on the streets until dark. I'm afraid I'll have to stay here until nightfall."

A look of worry flashed across the youth's face. "I'll make her understand, I'll wait for her on the street and explain—"

"Not on the street," St. Jude interrupted. "The wrong ears might overhear you. Let her come in, then I will help you explain," he said. "For the sake of safety, you had all better stay here until after sunrise."

When the youth's sister returned to the apartment, she proved to be quite understanding, but not before delivering a fierce scolding to her young brother and his friends for having taken such foolish and dangerous actions. She then saw to it that St. Jude's wounds were properly cleaned and bandaged.

"I understand your anger over your brother's risky actions," St. Jude began when they were alone.

" 'Foolish' is the word I used," she said, her anger still evident in her pretty face.

"I won't argue, but it was that foolishness that saved my life. You don't really know who I am, and probably don't care, but those boys did a tremendous service to their country."

She shook her head slowly. "He's too young to die. He's only a boy."

"He's a man now, you can be sure of that."

She looked up at St. Jude as she placed the last bandage on his shoulder. She smiled at the bull-muscled Frenchman with the handsome face. "You will need to see a doctor, and then to contact you friends. You can stay here until you are fit enough to travel," she tol him. "Now tell me, just how do I get word to your friends that you are safe?"

St. Jude paused in his story a moment. There was a distant look ir his eyes. Then he looked at Nicole and smiled.

Nicole smiled back.

Michael didn't quite understand the significance of their subtl communication, but was glad to see them sharing a meaningful mo ment.

"That marvelous, beautiful young woman was to become you mother," St. Jude said to Nicole, though he knew she was already aware of the fact.

After a few more moments of quiet reflection, St. Jude continued "My stay became longer than expected when I developed a high feve and infection. I was not strong, due to the previous wounds that I hac suffered, and my resistance was low. Colette brought a doctor to me who re-dressed my wounds and succeeded in getting the manacles of my wrists. Then Colette took care of me.

"She managed to get a message through to Gabrielle's contact, as per my instructions. I felt certain that your father would get word through him. I didn't expect that your father and Gabrielle would both get the message on the same day, or that they would both come to my assistance without knowing that the other would be there. That was the last time that your father ever saw her . . ."

Paris, october 1943: A gentle knock sounded on the door. Colette answered it to find a stunningly attractive raven-haired woman standing there. Gabrielle Dupuy entered the room quickly and rushed tc Claude's side. He was sleeping.

"He's on fire," she said, touching his sweating face and forehead, "How long has he been here?"

"Two days. A doctor has already seen him and treated his wounds. We can only wait and hope that the fever breaks soon," Colette replied.

Gabrielle could see the basin of water and the towels and washcloths that had been used as compresses and to wipe away his perspiration. It gave evidence of the constant attention that Colette had been giving him.

"Has he been eating?" Gabrielle asked.

"No, but he is taking fluids. He seems very weak."

"He's already been through a great deal without the added complications of these wounds. How did he get them?"

Colette explained what had happened on the Quai de Conti.

"You've done a marvelous job of helping him. I don't know how to thank you," Gabrielle said.

Colette did not respond, but instead took her place beside him and began applying the compresses again, with a great deal of concern in her eyes. Thanks were not necessary.

Then another knock sounded on the door. The two women looked at one another with a start. "Are you expecting anyone?" Gabrielle asked.

Colette shook her head.

Gabrielle removed a low-caliber automatic from her bag and put it into her coat pocket, her hand cradling it, ready to use it. "Answer it," she whispered.

Colette moved swiftly to the door as a second series of knocks sounded. She opened it a crack and peeked out. "Who is it?" she asked.

"I am a friend," Christian whispered.

"How do I know that?" Colette asked.

"I received your message regarding our mutual friend. I am with Group Defiance. I am called Orca," he replied.

Colette felt the hand of Gabrielle on her shoulder, and backed away from the door. Christian opened it and stepped in, and was stopped by the sudden vision of Gabrielle.

She pushed the door closed and took him in a desperate, tight embrace.

Christian's heart pounded with the combined worry over St. Jude and the sudden joy of seeing Gabrielle.

Colette watched as the two embraced, the love between them clearly evident. "I will leave the two of you alone with your friend. I'll be back in a little while," she said. She picked up her coat and in a moment was gone.

Only then did Christian kiss Gabrielle, over and over again, with a flood of combined love and relief.

"Why? Why have you been so impossible to find?" he asked.

She placed her forefinger to his lips to silence him. "That is not important now. We must help Claude."

Christian looked away to St. Jude, who was now awake, but very weak and wet with perspiration. He went to him immedi-

351

ately, Gabrielle close behind, explaining what she had been told by Colette.

A weak smile crossed Claude's face as they drew close enough for him to recognize them. "Am I in heaven, or are the two of you really here?" he asked.

"We're here, my friend. We'll take care of you. You'll be all right," Christian said.

Gabrielle began applying cool compresses.

"Where is Colette?" St. Jude asked. "Where is she?"

"She'll be back. She went to get some things," Gabrielle replied.

"You're here. I feel safe now," St. Jude said, patting Christian's hand. "Now I can rest." He closed his eyes and fell into an immediate sleep.

"He needs sleep and time," Christian said. He could not help bringing to mind the time ten months ago when it was Claude who gently nursed him in the intense cold at the winery, and how, after his encounter with Immel, Gabrielle had suddenly appeared to take care of him. Ten months. It had been that long since he had last seen her.

"You look well," Gabrielle said. "I didn't think that I would see you in France again until after the war." There was a strange distant quality in her voice.

Christian took her hand and led her away from the bed, then took her in his arms again and kissed her. But the kiss was different. It started out the same, with the enormous passion and giving that always filled them both, but it grew suddenly cold and mechanical, as though her passion were being dampened.

Christian looked down at her for a moment. "You're not staying in Paris any longer. You're coming away with me," he said.

There was pain in her eyes, as though some great struggle was occurring within her. "I can't," she said.

"You will," Christian countered. "I thought I had lost you forever. I won't let that happen again, now that I've found you."

"I have work to do," she said.

"Damn the work," Christian said. "You're leaving Paris. I *order* it."

The conflict within Gabrielle Dupuy was an enormous one. The biggest part of her wanted to hold Christian and never let him go, to go anywhere with him that he wanted, so long as it was to a place safe from war and the threat of losing each other again. But another part of her had already been scarred by the pain of losing Christian—and Rudolf Immel. It could not bear to endure another loss. It was that part

352

of her that had pushed her into the beds of one German after another, that forced false sighs of pleasure as they used her body, making her want to die from the shame and disgust that filled her. It was that part of her that shut off the natural flow of passion with Christian, because it wanted protection from the pain of another loss and punishment for the things she had done to shame herself and make her unworthy of his love.

"Those are the words of Christian Gladieux my lover," Gabrielle said, "not the words of Christian Gladieux the Resistance fighter of Group Defiance. If I leave now, we'll lose all hope of obtaining the information within my reach. You know I'm right."

"I know that I love you, and that France is going to win this war without the information you give to us. I can't let you do this to yourself any longer. I have to know that you're safe. Come with me to the South of France. I can get you safely across the Pyrenees into Spain, where you'll be safe until the war is over. You must do this for yourself . . . and for me," Christian implored.

"And will you come with me to Spain?" Gabrielle asked, already knowing the answer to her question.

Christian stared at her. "I . . . I can't. There's too much to be—"

"Exactly, my darling. I love you, Christian," she said, going again into his arms. "But you must understand that I can no more stop fighting this war than you can. We both face dangers daily. And we live with them because we're left no choice."

"But your dangers are so much greater. Can't you realize that? The risks I take are visible, recognizable. Yours aren't. France sees you as something that you're not. Something to be hated, to be ashamed of . . . to be dealt with. I love you too much to let anything happen to you."

The door opened, interrupting them, and Colette entered with a small package.

Gabrielle used the interruption to her advantage. "Goodbye, my darling," she said. "Take good care of Claude." She backed away, forcing a smile through her tear-filled eyes. "I love you," she mouthed without sound, then turned and left the apartment.

Christian felt as though his heart would break. He started for the door when St. Jude let out a loud moan, followed by another. He was in obvious pain. Christian turned back to the sight of his helpless friend and went to him.

Colette and Christian comforted him, and he again fell off to sleep.

Colette looked across the bed to Christian's face. "You love her no?"

Christian looked back at the door that she had gone through "More than my life," he answered. And he knew that he had just seer a part of his life leave him, for he now felt sure that he would never see her again.

Chapter 37

"T RIPPER," Pheagan said, answering the long distance call.

"Still sitting by the phone? I must not be giving you enough to do," Michael said.

"Some of us just get our work done faster than others. I expected a call from you yesterday. What happened?"

"We got tied up between talks with Pierre Falloux and the Collard brothers. Then we drove straight through to St. Jude's place. It was late when we got back and I was beat to hell. It was a productive time for us, though. How about you? How'd you make out on the Gypsy girl?"

"We located Barbu Denska and talked to him. He remembered the boy."

"Then she was the apprentice's sister?"

"Yes, but she didn't remember a thing."

"What about the pendant?" Michael asked.

"She had it. Photos brought back confirmed it as a match for the four already known to exist."

"That makes five."

"More importantly, it tells us that her brother did work on them with the glassmaker, Haupte. It gives some life to our back-door theory."

"Get back to Barbu Denska. Did he tell you anything that might help you find the apprentice?" Michael asked.

"He put us as close as we've been, so far. Denska gave us a false identity that Abraham Mendel was preparing to use. The name was Paul Wilno. We then quickly found the name in the German arrest

354

records. It seems that a Paul Wilno was arrested in Lódź, Poland, in 1942 while working for the underground."

"There could have been a hundred Paul Wilnos in Poland."

"There could have been. But this Paul Wilno shared a characteristic which is too striking to disregard as mere coincidence. You see, Abraham Mendel forged all the documents for his new identity himself. Denska commented that the work on those documents was exceptional. The Paul Wilno who was arrested in Lódź was an expert forger. One of the best working for the underground."

Michael felt a rush of excitement. "Well, what happened to this Paul Wilno?" he asked impatiently.

"He was sent to Theresienstadt in Czechoslovakia."

"That was a concentration camp, wasn't it?" Michael asked.

"Yes, but it wasn't a death camp. The Germans established Theresienstadt as a 'model' camp, which they displayed regularly to the media. The longer he stayed there, the better his chances were of surviving."

"I take it from what you're telling me that you haven't gotten any further on him," Michael said.

"We're just getting into the Theresienstadt records. He was probably sent to that particular camp because of his talents. The Nazis ran a rather impressive counterfeiting operation making American, British, French, and South American currencies. Most of the highest-quality plates were secretly prepared in Theresienstadt by gifted prisoners. They tried to cover the activity as the war neared its end. I doubt many of these talented prisoners survived. Being a Jew would have then become a double liability to him. He could very well be dead."

"But at least we know he survived part of the war. If he was strong enough he could have survived, unless he was specifically marked for death," Michael surmised.

"That's right. From everything we've gotten on Mendel so far, it appears he was a pretty resourceful fellow. If he was stronger than the average long-term prisoner, and was sent to a large enough camp, he just could have made it. We'll know more shortly, now that we have a line on him. We still hope to find that back door," Pheagan said.

"And after the events of the past few days, we think that we may have just gotten our foot in the front door, as well," Michael said. "Dan and I believe that the man you're after is Pierre Falloux."

"Explain," Pheagan said.

"We managed to shake him up a little during our last visit," Michael said. "We approached him at first with the information that

Immel had given us about Liepart. We learned that the Aile Rouge had captured Liepart, interrogated him, and then summarily executed him. We implied that we thought Falloux must have known who Z was. Later, when Dan and I were alone with him, we all but made that accusation, and followed with a bit of heavy bluff regarding the real reason my father was killed, saying that his notes weren't totally destroyed. He reacted like a kid in a candy store caught with his pockets stuffed with things he didn't pay for. There was also a much more visible reaction to our comments regarding the pendant and its hidden past. That shook him this time."

"That's quite interesting," Pheagan said, holding back further comment. Pierre Falloux had become more than a leading suspect to Sub Rosa, as well. The wiretap they had established on him when his name had first come into prominence was paying off quite handsomely. They knew about his contact with Ernest Rive in the DST and his wanting to develop information on the Gladieux family. But what had been of the greatest value were his contacts with "his friend"—whom they knew to be Renaud Demy. Sub Rosa knew that Falloux had ordered the killing of Immel—the "commission." It had become academic that he was also behind the killing of Christian Gladieux and that the family now faced grave danger.

Pheagan was remaining cautious here. Were this information to be given to Michael, Sub Rosa would run the risk of Glad-jo taking matters into his own hands, despite having given his word not to. To lose Falloux now would be catastrophic to the new hopes being kindled by their early success. The longer they could monitor Falloux, the greater their chances would be that someone from the Committee of Trinity would contact him. Assuming they could recognize that contact when it occurred, it could open a new door to perhaps a second identity of a Trinity Committee member. Falloux would be their access deeper into the heart of that organization.

Sub Rosa also kept alive the hope that Michael and his family would be able to uncover the identity of the contact that Christian had developed to get his information. There was no telling how much information could be obtained from that source.

"You had better start taking precautions," Pheagan warned. "If you are as close as you think, he may begin taking steps to protect himself."

"We're aware of that," Michael returned. "We think he's already started by taking out Immel."

"What makes you think that?" Pheagan asked, impressed by their insight into the facts.

"Because we believe that Firewatch was deliberately set up in the mmel affair. They, no doubt, took part in it. But a body was left ?ehind that was not the work of Immel. Someone killed this man and eft him there to implicate Firewatch—for a second time. We haven't igured out why Falloux wanted Immel dead yet. Perhaps it was to try o prevent any connection being made between himself and Z. We're ,ure that he knows who Z is, but for some reason never exposed him. There may be some kind of connection between them which Falloux ias been exploiting all these years."

"Your chances of learning that will be greater once you've figured)ut who Z is," Pheagan said.

"We've got a theory there, too. We feel that it's Claude St. Jude. We've been afforded an entirely new slant to the story by virtue of vhat we learned from Immel. It's mostly just little things, but when we it them together, a definite picture starts to form. We have yet to ?stablish his motive for working with the Germans, to cement our heory, however."

"His brothers could have been motive enough," Pheagan told him. 'We've discovered that St. Jude's brothers were both arrested at the :ime the Marseilles sectors were first smashed in 1942. Captain Dieter Liepart was the Gestapo adviser in charge of the arrests. You'll remem- ?er that St. Jude's name had been given to the Germans by Pointer. Liepart could have used his brothers' lives as the bait to get him to :ooperate."

"And St. Jude acted as though he couldn't recall the name when we first asked him about Liepart," Michael said.

"I don't see how he couldn't have known it," Pheagan added.

"It would fit perfectly. The betrayals by Z began shortly after that."

"According to the records, his brothers both died in Ludwigsburg Prison in November of 1943. I don't know if that will help you at all, but you should know it," Pheagan added.

"Why don't you have your people try to find a possible connection between Falloux and St. Jude," Michael suggested.

"We'll start on it. There's one more thing here that could be signif- icant, I think. It has to do with the transmission that was sent by Al- batross containing the word 'circus.' We questioned some contacts in Britain about the transmission, and it seems that part of it *was* received in London. As you had the story, it was not. Is that correct?"

"Yes, go on."

"It was a very weak signal, and was not picked up in its entirety. The letters that they received were C, indistinguishable, R, C, indistinguishable, and S. They worked with Defiance on trying to decipher its meaning but were unable to help them."

"Did they disagree on any of the letters?" Michael asked.

"No. As I said, the signal was extremely weak and was almost lost entirely. The information given to them by Defiance fit perfectly with the letters that they did receive."

"That was Morse code, wasn't it?"

"Yes. The final conclusion was that it was indeed the word 'circus' that was transmitted."

"What about the code name Leopard? Have you had any luck with it?"

"No more than you have, I'm afraid. It wasn't Dieter Liepart, or the Defiance agent Paul Romenay. Both are long dead. There has to be another meaning."

Michael thought for a moment. Two words, two hidden meanings, and both so important to final answers. "Is there anything else?" he asked.

"That's about all that we have as of now. When will you be calling in next?"

"Probably in a couple of days. We don't have any meetings scheduled. If anything important comes up, I'll call."

"All right, talk to you then. And remember what I said. Your lives could be in danger."

"We'll be ready. Talk to you later."

Pheagan listened to the dead receiver for a moment, then placed it back in its cradle. If his feelings were right, matters would begin to resolve themselves quickly from this point on. It was time, Pheagan knew, to call in the special team he had put on alert and to get them to France. It would be only a matter of time until their services might be required.

In the meantime, another angle would be pursued with a great deal of vigor. The "back door," which had once seemed unreachable, was now becoming a clearer possibility. The odds were still slight, but definitely existent. It all depended upon the survival instincts of a boy—Abraham Mendel.

POLAND, 1944: Abraham Mendel pressed his face to the small hole in the side of the boxcar to suck in as much air as his lungs could hold. He had fought a constant battle to defend his position at the hole for the ntire two and a half days of confinement since leaving Theresienstadt. He had kicked and scratched and punched to hold his ground. The air inside the boxcar was almost unbearable. The two tiny vents in the roof did little in the way of ventilation, and the incredible stench of feces and urine and sweat and vomit defiled what little breathable air there was. It was spring, and the sun on the roof heated the stuffy interior of the crammed boxcar to near oven-intensity.

The only relief came when the train made one of its many stops on its meandering journey, and the doors opened for a few moments letting in fresh air, but only for as long as it took to shove still more people into the stuffed confines. Children and small adults were piled on top of those standing. Occasionally a little room would be made when an individual passed out or was just too weak to stand any longer and would somehow manage to slide to the floor, or a parent unable or too tired to hold a child any longer would lose his grip. The floor meant death for those on it, and a little more room for those standing on the dead.

Mendel was a good deal stronger than the average prisoner because of certain advantages he had been able to maintain at Theresienstadt, which were mainly extra food and nonexertive duties. His talent as a forger was in high demand, both by the Reich and by other individuals with secret plans to avoid the aftermath of the twelfth hour approaching Germany. Besides his work on counterfeit currency plates, he had obtained additional "advantages" by preparing false identity papers, which had been his specialty while in the Polish underground. There were a few Germans who had begun to worry about their necks as much as their Swiss accounts. And Abraham Mendel was no fool. He did nothing for nothing, and enjoyed more than a fair measure of special treatment. That is, until one man, smarter and more powerful than the rest, sought to eliminate every little part of his past, which, unfortunately for Mendel, included those who had helped establish his future. The counterfeiting operation was about to be closed down anyway, so the departure of one Jew from the project would be inconsequential. Paul Wilno, forger extraordinaire, Jew, was sent to Auschwitz-Birkenau for "resettlement." It brought an abrupt end to what had been an otherwise tolerable hell.

By camp standards, Abraham Mendel had been a wealthy man. Things of tradeable value were easy to come by for him. Things like extra food, clothing, a pair of shoes, cigarettes, a bowl (which was a man's life in the camps), soap, newspapers, books, scraps of paper, and a hundred other things that in normal life were taken for granted. These goods assured him of other necessities that made life easier. He had lived a level above that other hell. But that had all ended. He was down in it with the rest of them now. Compared to what he was about to experience, life in the prestige camp of Theresienstadt would seem like a happy memory.

The swaying of the boxcars and the endless clackety-clack of the wheels on the track began to slow. The train was nearing its destination. Mendel felt for the paper in the waistband of his pants. It was a letter of introduction that was supposed to guarantee him special treatment at his new destination. It briefly described his skills and was signed by a rather influential officer to whom he had tendered his services. It could also guarantee his death, and he was aware of that. He would wait to make the determination of just what to do with it later. He was still phsyically strong. That in itself should be worth something—time, if nothing else.

The train slowed to a crawl and he pressed his eye to the hole as the screeching, grinding sounds of the brakes began. He saw what seemed to be endless rows of identical wood and brick barracks laid out in a sea of mud. They were precisely alike, with numbers on them to differentiate one from another. He saw the tall watchtowers spaced at regular intervals with their floodlights and machine guns, and the double rows of high electrified fence. The size of this camp was staggering. How many more like this were in existence, he wondered. And how many people did they hold? It was difficult for the mind to grasp the scope of it all.

The train stopped and the compartment began to fill with low anxious murmurs. Then came the hard metallic sound of the door clasps being unfastened, followed by the press toward the doors for the expected rush of air and a chance to breathe, to move an arm or a leg, perhaps even to have some water or bread. Even some of the dead, who had been too tightly jammed to fall, seemed to shuffle forward the inch or two possible.

Suddenly the doors slid open, and those closest to them were literally hurled out by the force of the press behind them. Loud shrieks and guttural commands began, and with them the brief tattoo of automatic weapons directed at those unfortunate enough to fall from the boxcars to the ground. Some of those falling out had already been dead before the doors were opened, and the bullets couldn't hurt them anymore.

The gunfire stopped and order was quickly restored. The harsh commands were now directed at the people in the boxcars to exit quickly and to form up in close lines. The awful stench emanating from the boxcars made the guards closest to them nearly retch. Even the dogs seemed to hesitate going nearer, until commanded into action to help maintain a semblance of order. Ever-present German order.

The dogs snarled and barked and snapped at the prisoners as they hurriedly obeyed the commands being shouted at them. Occasionally, a dog would be commanded to attack a random figure to impress upon the other prisoners the necessity to respond instantly to orders. The dogs were never stopped until the lesson was gruesomely complete.

The boxcar was nearly empty when Mendel moved away from his small air hole. Only then could he see the full extent of the hardships of the trip. There must have been at least thirty dead in his boxcar—mostly the elderly and children and those who had been in extremely weakened condition at the start of the journey. But the most devastating was the vision of beautiful, innocent children who had had no chance at life, lying dead. He hesitated a moment, watching one grief-stricken mother trying to pick up her dead baby. She seemed incoherent, oblivious to the frantic shouts being directed at her. Mendel thought about his little Keva and wondered if she had been trampled to death on the floor of a crowded boxcar somewhere, or whether Barbu the Gypsy had managed all these years to avoid capture. He was almost grateful that she had been kidnapped.

The sudden sound of the shot that ripped a hole in the woman's head restored Mendel's attention and prompted his rapid leap from the boxcar.

The lines were hurried along toward two tables where the process of selection was being carried out. An SS doctor sat at each table, quickly assessing the physical condition of the prisoners. The old, the very young, the lame and weak, and women with young children were directed to one side, while the strong were sent to another. Occasionally, a particularly attractive girl would be sent to a third line. These women would carry out duties in the camp brothel until they became diseased or pregnant or too weak to perform satisfactorily. Several young boys were also selected for similar duty.

Mendel knew well the fate of those people directed to the one side. He managed to stuff the letter into the back of his pants before approaching the table.

The doctor looked at him once, then asked him to open his shirt. He looked at the number tattooed on his arm and squinted at him. "Where did you come from?" he asked, suspicious of his surprisingly strong stature.

"Theresienstadt," Mendel answered.

"How long were you there?" the doctor asked.

"Two years and one month."

The doctor continued to squint suspiciously. He took Mendel's hands and turned them palms up. He examined them for a moment. "What were your duties there?"

"I . . . was a printer," Mendel answered cautiously.

"A printer?" the doctor repeated, his eyes almost smiling. "Give your name and number to that guard. Then go to that line," he said, pointing to the second line. It was the line of life.

After giving the name Paul Wilno and the identification number tattooed on his forearm, he went to the line as instructed. He looked back at the mass of people that had just been unloaded. There were thousands of them. He could see bodies being dragged out of the box-cars and piled in heaps on long flat wagons pulled by tractors. There had to be at least a thousand dead. Perhaps one in every five or six had died in transit, he estimated.

It was a poignant sight watching families being torn apart. Husbands being separated from wives, children being torn from their mothers, except in the case of very young children. Some of the guards tried assuring these people that they would be reunited after registration and delousing procedures were completed.

By now the awful stink of the boxcars was replaced with a new stench. It was the smell of burning flesh. He had come to know the smell well in Poland. He now understood why the dogs were so nervous. The smell of death was everywhere.

Those scheduled for delousing were marched to the baths, passing by the camp orchestra, which was composed of prisoners dressed neatly in white and blue uniforms, playing gay, spritely tunes. The ragged procession was marched to Birkenau, about two miles away, to its attractively landscaped grounds. It was a death march toward the gas chambers awaiting them.

For the lucky ones like Mendel, chosen because of their strength to work in factories of the I. G. Farben Chemical Works and the Krupp fuse factory, or on general labor details, the slogan above the camp entrance contained a grain of truth: *Arbeit Macht Frei* (Work Makes Free). As long as one was strong enough to work, he lived. It was carefully worked out, almost to the month, just how much labor could be obtained with the bare minimum of food. Six months was a reasonable expectation, assuming a minimum of twelve to fifteen hours of work per day. It was cheaper to replace workers than to feed them.

Abraham Mendel wasted no time in disposing of the letter he had carried with him from Theresienstadt. His first trip to the latrine pits found the letter performing a rare and useful service as toilet paper. If they wanted to dig through shit to find it, then let them. He would not hand them his death warrant.

The first night at Auschwitz made unmistakably clear the obvious differences between life as he had come to know it at Theresienstadt, and life as it would be now. Triple-layered wooden platforms served as beds. Men crowded in with room enough to lie only on their sides. It was almost impossible to move, once positioned, and any attempts to do so were met with curses and well-aimed elbows. The only advantage to the arrangement was the shared body warmth in the cold of the evenings.

The night was alive with sounds. Sounds of men coughing their lives away, trying to muffle their deep hacking to prevent the *Kappos* from recognizing that they were sick. Being sick was as good as being dead when it was discovered. Sick men didn't work. Men who didn't work didn't eat. Men who didn't eat went to the showers and ended up being spread across the fields to fertilize next year's potatoes. There were other sounds, too. Sounds of men crying, of men praying, sounds of struggle over the possessions of a man who had just died. There were ugly sounds. Obscene animallike grunts of men engaging in homosexual activity, be it voluntary or forced. There were sounds of men relieving themselves in their food bowls, then dumping the contents to the floor at the head of the bed. The weak just let go where they lay, unable to manipulate the bowls and their bodies to do otherwise. There were sounds of shots in the night taken at those who had given up hope and had chosen the swift death of a tower bullet or the electricity of the fences. There were many sounds, except for laughter. Had any of these men ever laughed? Most couldn't remember what it was like to have a happy thought.

The shrill whistles brought an end to the five hours of sleep. *Kappos* slammed the sides of the bunks with their clubs to hurry the men out to daily roll call.

They stood in the grayness of early morning, stooped, skeletal bodies, their ears sticking out from their shaven, bony heads like handles. They shivered in the cold morning rain, most with only their baggy single-layered pajamalike uniforms to protect them from the elements. At least it was spring, and the promise of warm weather lay ahead.

After roll call came the mad rush to breakfast, which consisted of hot discolored water that passed as coffee and a piece of bread. Next came the rush to the latrine pits, where the morning struggle was as desperate as the cramming for position on the sleeping platforms.

Mendel was first assigned to work in the old burial pits, which were being reworked in an attempt to hide them. They spent endless hours digging, removing skeletal remains, and regrading, but the pits always looked the same. The lye that had been poured over the bodies prevented anything from growing, the ground was depressed, and even after regrading would sink again.

He spent the first weeks assessing the inner society within the camp. It was similar to Theresienstadt, but a great deal more complicated here, necessitated by the larger number of people. An order of dominance existed everywhere—on a barracks level, on a section level, and even all the way up to the camp level. There were leaders and achievers in each group—individuals capable of intimidating those weaker than themselves. There were also "soldiers" who enforced the will of the leaders by virtue of their strength. They extracted tribute, in the form of food, hidden valuables, sexual favors, or anything amounting to gain at another's expense. It was a way of life no different than in any other form of nature; the strong dominated the weak.

Anything could be made available, and everything cost something. For the right price, a man could buy the privilege of using a real latrine instead of a pit. He could have the luxury of squatting over a fifteen-inch hole at the same time as five other people to relieve himself in style. He could buy a cup of water to drink or, for a special price, buy enough water to wash with before it was sold to the next five men in line to drink. A full ration of bread was strong currency. Another man could buy a shirt for a hidden piece of jewelry; an act of oral sex could gain the shoes of a dead man, or his pants. For those with enough to offer, even women were available from the female barracks. Anything could be bought, except freedom, though some were fool enough to try. All they ended up with was a "shower" and a chance to recycle through nature a little faster than the next fellow.

Mendel's advantage was his strength. If nothing else, his time in Theresienstadt had benefited him that much. That, together with his intimidating eyes, was enough to keep the "soldiers" interested elsewhere. Mendel followed his own rules for survival, which were simple: Don't make friends; don't get involved in anybody else's problems; don't speak unless it is necessary; and flatten the first guy who tries to intimidate you. It was a successful formula. Months passed with his only worry being to stay alive by caring for himself.

Mendel's next assigned duty was a prime one. He got to shovel hit out of the latrine pits. The job came just at the right time, too, as all weather started to settle in and the temperature began to drop. The mell of the pits was hard to take, but the biodegradation was exother-nic, that is, heat-giving, and it was warm work on cold days. Being a *Scheisskommando* was top notch.

It was in late November of 1944 that Abraham Mendel, known only as Paul Wilno, was summoned to the infirmary at the order of Dr. Roland Meyer. He reported as ordered. The penetrating warmth of the doctor's outer office was a great deal better than the knee-deep shit pile. Mendel sat with his hands crossed in his lap, waiting.

"The doctor will see you now," said a grim-faced corporal, eying Mendel suspiciously as he approached the door to the doctor's private office.

Mendel entered the room and walked up to Meyer's desk. He tood there silently, cap in hand, his red bowl hanging from his waist, waiting for the good doctor to finish reading the file in front of him. It was the same doctor who had examined him during the selection pro-ess at the rail siding.

Meyer looked up at Mendel, who now displayed the typical stoop and floppy ears. He was a great deal thinner than when Meyer had first een him. A few teeth had fallen out and he had the customary body ores common to the poor diet. But the eyes were the same, sharp and challenging, though set deeper into dark-ringed sockets.

"So, Wilno. You've been with us for—what is it—almost seven months now. Not quite the life you enjoyed in Theresienstadt, is it?" he asked, a smile crossing his round face.

Mendel stared back without answering.

"Your life here was not as bad as it could have been. I made sure of that. Hold out your hands," Meyer ordered.

Mendel held out his hands, palms facing upward.

"Palms down. Hold them out," Meyer told him.

The hands were still surprisingly steady. Only a trace of a tremor howed. That was good. The fingers were straight and unbroken. Also excellent.

"Why did you not present the letter given to you by Major Fuchs when you were tranferred out of Theresienstadt?" the German asked.

"It was a long trip without food. I ate it," Mendel lied flatly, lowering his hands.

The doctor smiled, then his round stomach bounced in silent aughter. Meyer sat back in his chair and lit up a cigarette. He assessed Mendel without speaking for several long moments.

"I'll be frank with you, Wilno," Meyer said. "I have several friends who are interested in your services."

"I'm a *Scheisskommando*," Mendel replied.

"Do you wish to play games, or hear my proposition?" Meyer said, puffing on his cigarette.

"I'm listening," Mendel replied evenly. He was about to be in command of this conversation, and he knew it.

"Good. Of course, no one can force your cooperation, but should you decide to . . . make your talents available to the needs of my friends, there could be some special privileges arranged for you," the German said.

"I'm still listening," Mendel commented.

"Your duty will be transferred to the infirmary on a permanent basis. You will have good food, a warm place to work, and all of the rest that you need. The materials you require will be supplied, and you will work in complete privacy. All of this is, of course, strictly between you and me. Out there, your life will be the same as it is now, for reasons of . . . shall we say . . . your protection and mine?"

Mendel was reading him clearly now. There had been no real news of the war, outside of the typical camp rumors. This could only mean that Germany was losing quite seriously. Escape was being planned by Meyer and his friends.

"How many identities will you require?" Mendel asked.

Meyer smiled broadly. "Four," he replied.

"They'll cost you all that you said earlier, plus one thousand deutsche marks apiece," Mendel said boldly.

"You are not in a position to make demands," Meyer snapped harshly, the smile suddenly gone from his face.

"And my guess is that you are not in a position to refuse them," Mendel came back at him. "Germany was losing the war when I was at Theresienstadt. I doubt that the situation has improved. The war is going to end, and probably soon. Now do you want my services, or don't you?"

"You are not the only man in this camp who could help my friends," Meyer informed him.

"Perhaps, but I am the best, as you've no doubt learned from Fuchs."

Meyer's face was red with anger. He allowed himself a few moments to regain his calm.

"I'm not blind, Colonel," Mendel said before the doctor could speak. "The activity at Birkenau has stepped up feverishly. The trains come in every day now." Fewer and fewer people are selected for labor. More and more workers are assigned to camouflage the pits, crush bones, and then disappear themselves. The end is near, Colonel," Mendel said, then waited.

Meyer knew that the assessment was an accurate one. He had, in fact, just heard that orders had come down from Berlin to begin dismantling the ovens and gas chambers, to blow the structures and grade over them to erase all trace of their existence.

"Agreed. One thousand deutsche marks apiece," Meyer said at last, giving in to the terms.

"Not in currency," Mendel qualified. "Paper currency will be useless after Germany falls. I want the equivalent value in gems. Diamonds, to be precise."

Meyer gritted his teeth, then nodded to the new conditions. "How long will you need?"

"It's been a while. A few weeks to regain my strength and to exercise the fingers with pens—" Mendel stopped, seeing the concerned expression on Meyer's face. The end was that close! "When must you have them?"

Meyer eyed the clever Jew. "Shall we say by the first of the year?"

"That should be possible, provided you can obtain the necessary seals and stamps. Otherwise, it will take longer," Mendel replied. "I will have to make what you can't supply."

"How much longer?" the doctor asked.

"Perhaps as much as two weeks," Mendel replied.

The doctor thought for a few moments. "That should still be satisfactory. Prepare a list of what you'll need. I'll get all the materials you'll require, and will try to get the necessary seals and stamps."

"Then we have a bargain?" Mendel asked.

"We do," the fat doctor replied, a trace of relief evident on his face. "You will begin today by eating a good meal and taking as much sleep as you wish. From this moment on, you are working for me. Present this letter of authorization to the guards each morning," he said, handing the letter to Mendel. "I have arranged for a small room for you. Hot food will be brought to you there, as much as you care to have. Are there any questions?" Meyer asked.

Mendel shook his head.

"You're excused," Meyer said.

Mendel turned and walked to the door.

"Wilno," the doctor called out to him.

Mendel turned to face him.

"It was a good thing for you that you chose to dispose of Fuchs' letter. You would be dead now if you had presented it."

And you would be out of luck, Herr Doktor, Mendel thought to himself. Destroying the letter had not saved him, he knew, for these same people could very well want him removed after he had finished his work for them. But he could buy time now. He only hoped he could buy enough of it.

So the standard of life had again improved for the gifted Jew who had the eye and the hand to duplicate almost anything with startling exactness. Outwardly his life went on unchanged. But anyone who had made it a point to watch him closely would have seen the improvement in his color and the slow return of his strength.

Meyer stopped in regularly over the next weeks to deliver the materials he had obtained for Mendel and to check on his condition. He was amazed as he watched the exercises and drills that Mendel repeated over and over with the fingers and pens to restore the ultimate level of skill. Then Mendel began practicing simple duplications, which made Meyer smile with joyful approval.

Mendel began his work by making the necessary seals and stamps that Meyer had been unable to obtain. Pleased that work on the commission had started, Meyer asked when the papers would be completed.

"The papers will be ready by the middle of January as promised," he guaranteed, knowing full well that he could buy additional time simply by doing the good doctor's papers last.

"Good. Good," Meyer said nervously. "If there's anything you need, let me know immediately."

Mendel smiled when the doctor left the room. He guessed that there were fewer than four weeks left before Auschwitz would be liberated. They had already begun to dismantle some of the ovens. Vigorous efforts were being made everywhere to cover their dirty work. Soon the enemy reconnaissance planes would be spotted overhead and the panic would begin in the ranks. But the good doctor, who had sat behind his little table exercising the power of life or death so ruthlessly and without guilt, would stay to wait for his papers that would never be finished. It was a race for time for all concerned. When the moment was right, Mendel would disappear into the camp. The roll calls were already haphazard and disorderly. He would never be found.

And he worked his plan to the letter. He provided the first completed set of papers in rather fast time after finishing the seals and stamps.

Meyer was delirious with joy. It looked as if all the papers would be finished before the deadline. Then the second set was completed, and the days rolled by.

Mendel teased the doctor with parts of the completed work on his set of papers. That same day, the first Russian aircraft were spotted overhead.

The third set was completed and handed over to Meyer.

"When will the last set be ready?" the German asked excitedly.

"In three days," Mendel promised. "When do I receive payment for the first three sets?"

"When the fourth is completed," Meyer replied. "You will be paid for all four sets at the same time."

"I think not," Mendel replied. "I would like it now."

A stern look crossed Meyer's face. "Don't play games with me, Wilno."

"I'm not playing games," Mendel protested innocently. "I saw the Russian planes overhead again today. I'm worried that things may happen too fast. You will have the means to carry out your plans in sufficient time, I guarantee you. And your papers are coming along perfectly. By far the best of the bunch. I just want to be sure that I am paid. It will be all that I'll have to start—"

"You will have payment when the last set of papers is completed and handed over to me," Meyer said with finality.

"Then shall we say . . . two days?" Mendel said in the ultimate tease.

He could see the nervous joy in Meyer's face.

"Two days," Meyer agreed, then left the room.

Mendel had never expected to be paid. The time he had bought was payment enough. He would work one more day to satisfy Meyer. Then he would disappear on the next.

He estimated that he would need only a few days before the Russians would show up. Many of the higher brass had already left the camp, leaving behind other hastily promoted poor bastards to take the brunt of the Russian arrival. There would be a mad dash to escape at the last moment, he was sure, for no one wanted to be here when that moment came.

Mendel worked diligently the one day as planned, and announced that the papers would be ready as promised. He ate a last large meal and returned to the compound, but he walked clear across it to a barracks where he wasn't known and disappeared into the anonymity of that human misery. He would have given anything to see Meyer's face

369

in the morning when he didn't show up, and then again later when it was announced that he could not be found. What a moment to miss.

The sounds of fighting could be heard in the distance. Abraham Mendel had successfully hidden for three days. The roll calls had been stopped, the work details had ended days ago, and the guards had even stopped patrolling through the compound. In fact, fewer and fewer were even seen along the perimeter. He doubted that Meyer was still in the camp; he was probably running as fast and as scared as he could by now.

All semblance of order had gone from the camp. *Kappos* and leaders, along with their "soldiers," met swift justice at the hands of those they had bullied so relentlessly. The few remaining guards simply watched from outside the compound, letting things take their course. No smart German would enter the compound now. Not after the greetings that had been prepared for the last few who tried.

On the morning of January 22, 1945, there were no whistles to wake them. Instead, there were the throaty sounds of Russian fighter planes flying in low formation over the camp. Then came the sounds of the Russian tanks and the vision of strange uniforms swarming to the rescue, searching with a savage intent for any Germans too foolish not to have run in the night.

It was the moment that Abraham Mendel had lived for. He had *survived.* His time in hell was over. But he could not smile or cheer, for now he saw the enormous reality of the horrors that he had managed to push out of his mind for so long. He saw it all in a flash of stored memory. The indescribable cruelty; the loss of all human dignity; the piles of corpses; the faces of those who had chosen death on the electrified fences, or by the bullets of the tower guns, rather than live an existence which was not life at all; the grim, methodical way in which the Germans relentlessly practiced an exercise in inhumanity that would scar the history of mankind forever. No, Abraham Mendel could not smile or cheer. He could only weep with the sorrow that he had put aside so well and for so long.

The Russians brought food and doctors. For many it was too late. No amount of food would have saved bodies that could no longer tolerate it. Typhus and pneumonia and the cold continued to claim the weak. They died by the hundreds each day, and the doctors were helpless to stop it.

The prisoners continued to live within the compound, for the Russians were not prepared to do anything with them. A war was being fought, and although its outcome was no longer in doubt, every effort was being made to end it as quickly and decisively as possible. Even when the war was formally over, it changed nothing. The prisoners of Auschwitz, mostly Jews by now, remained just that—prisoners, even though the gas chambers and the crematoriums were gone and the gates were left open. The fences no longer carried the killing voltage, and had even been torn down in places. There were no more machine guns or floodlights or snarling dogs to keep them in terror. But a different terror existed, a terror of venturing out. They had forgotten that another kind of world could exist for them. This was all they knew. Where would they go? To cities that had been smashed? To countries that had forsaken them? Who was left to go back to? Relatives who had died in Birkenau, or Bergen-Belsen, or Dachau, or a hundred other places that had been a part of the "master plan" of the master race? They had been spread out and dispersed to a degree beyond precedent.

With the coming of warm weather, some began to venture out. Most returned. Within the camp, a semblance of normality had begun to take shape. They organized schools within the compound for the precious few surviving children. Religious services were conducted regularly. Programs in music, dancing, art, and theater were started. The culture that had been so long suppressed began to surface. Abraham Mendel saw a wonderful transformation occurring, and for the first time in his life felt the pride of being a Jew. He saw in these people a part of them that had never died—their heritage, their sameness. There was a deeply rooted strength that sprang from their common faith. Faith. It was the same thing he had called weakness in his father.

He remembered the arguments he had had with his parents and recalled the words of his father that had sent him off in a rage of misunderstanding. That same faith he had blamed for bringing them death was now bringing life. Only there was so much more power in his than he had ever thought possible. If only he could see his father and his mother and Israel again to tell them . . . to tell them . . . The thoughts of family brought thoughts of Keva. His beautiful little Keva. He felt such a terrible guilt that he wished the fences were still alive with voltage so that he could throw himself upon them. Even if his family had been lucky enough to survive, he knew that he could never face them again after losing her. Abraham Mendel knew that he could never go home.

Men started coming to the camp to talk to the people about Palestine. These men were from the Mossad Aliyah Bet, and were here to take their people "home." The enthusiasm of the people was tremen-

dous, but the obstacles to them were greater. "Eretz Israel" did no
exist. Palestine was their home—but only in their hearts and minds. A
world of politics stood between them, Arab oil and hatred stood be
tween them, and a world that did not understand stood between them
But these people had just emerged from a lesson in faith that provided
a determination and strength that would eventually overcome al
obstacles. A new fight was beginning for them, but with an old familiar
theme—survival.

When it was learned by these men from the Mossad Aliyah Be
that Paul Wilno was an accomplished forger, they drafted his services
into use. The old Abraham Mendel would never have been interested
the one born in Auschwitz in 1945 was.

Special passage was arranged for him to La Ciotat, France, situ
ated on the Mediterranean coast between Marseilles and Toulon
where one of the largest Jewish refugee camps in Europe was con
structed. La Ciotat was one of the critical elements in a plan being
formed that would challenge the stubborn British position opposing
establishment of a homeland for the Jews of the world. A never-ending
attempt to get their people into Palestine illegally was starting and
would become an enormous struggle between the wills of both sides
Identity papers would be needed, a great many of them. The Polish
Jew Paul Wilno would be an important part of that operation.

The camp at La Ciotat had been selected by the Mossad Aliyah
Bet for a number of reasons. The most notable were that the French
government had adopted a sympathetic posture on the Jewish home
land issue, and that being in France, La Ciotat was not under British
jurisdiction, as most of the other camps situated in occupied Europe
were. La Ciotat was also on the Mediterranean coast, which provided
many points of possible debarkation for the refitted refugee ships tha
would attempt to run the British blockade of Palestine. It was also
chosen because of the large number of refugees available from which
desirable, able people could be selected who could best carry on the
struggle in Palestine. As it stood, the British allowed a token trickle o
Jews into Palestine. But these were always people that they selected
They were usually the elderly or the weak. People who would pose les
possibility of threat once there.

Mendel liked these men from the Mossad Aliyah Bet. They had
the strong faith he so admired, and they had the hearts of lions, which
fitted his beliefs well. They were not timid or frightened, and knew tha
strength and the willingness to fight were essential to their dream and
their survival, just as a frightened, angry young boy had known once in

n alley in Dresden in 1938. These men would never dig their own graves and wait meekly to be shot, or march without protest into gas chambers. They might die, but they would die fighting as the Jews of Warsaw had.

The months passed and Mendel worked feverishly with other men of similar talents. The refugee ships would set sail, then would be detected and given close escort by the British navy until they reached the territorial waters of Palestine, where the battle of wits would begin. Desperate, heroic efforts would be made, most often ending futilely, sometimes successfully. It was always expected that the ratio of success would be a low one. That only served to make each attempt more important. Those caught were usually sent to displaced persons camps on Cyprus or in Europe, or were sent back to the points of origin. It was a war of wits and attrition in which the Jews had nothing to lose and everything to gain. No matter what the outcome of each small battle, the British lost something in the eyes of the world. The courageous efforts of these determined people began to draw more and more sympathy from all parts of the world.

The dream that now filled Abrham Mendel was to take that risk himself one day. He wanted to get to Palestine so badly that he could think of nothing else.

He requested to go on each ship making the run. His requests were always denied because of the value of his work in La Ciotat. So he worked, day after day, week after week, month after month, the dream becoming a desperate physical need. Palestine was his air, and he was suffocating.

So Mendel worked on, waiting and hoping, and preparing one special set of papers that would be his own. It was a set he had made with utmost patience and skill, creating with every line and letter a piece of an imaginary life that he would remember forever, for it would be his life. It would be his escape from the terrible guilt of losing his baby sister; escape from the guilt of ignoring his Jewish heritage for so long; escape from Paul Wilno, survivor, who had even worked for the Germans for favors that he had guarded so selfishly; and escape from a danger that an old Gypsy woman had once said would follow him always. He was not sorry that he had survived, but he was not proud of the way he had done it.

It was a day like any other day for Abraham Mendel when word arrived that his latest stack of completed identities would be needed within the week. Another try would be made from Toulon. Mendel prepared the required number of identity kits and sat staring at the worktable at which they had been made. He would wait no longer. I that moment Abraham Mendel made up his mind to be on that ship There were enough talented forgers at La Ciotat and other settlemen camps to carry on the work without him. He was through being prisoner. A new life awaited him in Palestine. A life without shame o reason to hide. A life that would let him fight for the things he wante and believed in. Palestine was a home he had never been to, but it wa a home that he knew he would never leave. No one would stop hir now, not the Mossad Aliyah Bet, nor the British.

The *Misty Witch* was an old tramp freighter that had seen its be days before the start of the First World War, managing somehow t stay afloat and in use by the British until being bought at nominal co by a small exporting firm in Rotterdam. She was supposed to be pu into limited service along the North Sea, Channel, and Atlantic coast The British kept careful tabs on her whereabouts. Their suspicior about her ultimate purpose were confirmed when she arrived in A cachon, France, for refitting. It took little time to realize that she wa being refitted into a refugee runner, so when she finally set sail fc Toulon, they readied themselves for her run to Palestine.

After leaving Toulon with her human cargo and skirting the Med terranean coast in the darkness of night, the newly named *Maiden c Hope* rounded the Iles d'Hyères and set a course toward the norther tip of Corsica. It was as she passed between Bastia and Livorno that th first British vessel was spotted. It was a light destroyer, and it kept clos accompaniment through the Tyrrhenian Sea. As the *Maiden of Hop* passed through the Strait of Sicily she was joined by two other Britis vessels, both heavy cruisers. The *Maiden of Hope* sailed on with dete mination through international waters, now flying the white and blu Star of David, not attempting to hide her already plain intent. She wa safe so long as she remained in international waters, and her captai knew it.

There were 550 refugees crammed into her stuffy confines, whic made the crowded barracks conditions of the camps seem mild t comparison. But there were no complaints among the refugees, wh would have put up with worse for the chance to reach Palestine. Th captain, Stephen Michalopolis, never expected to fool the British. A far as he was concerned, the real drama would begin just outside of th territorial three-mile limit of Palestine. He knew that if he made it t that point he could give them a surprising run for the coast. Dee within the bowels of the *Maiden of Hope* were two auxiliary engines that had been secretly put in at Arcachon and were capable of increasing her steady eight knots to almost nineteen for a short all-out run toward shore. The *Maiden of Hope* drafted a great deal less than the British vessels and, if she got enough of a lead, could not be followed in through the reefs when Michalopolis beached her.

Abraham Mendel sat in the crowded, stinking hold of the *Maiden of Hope* unable to fight off the memories of the boxcars. Only the knowledge that there was hope at the end of his journey helped preserve his sanity. But the one struggle that even hope could not conquer was his obsessive need for *air*. There was no hole to breathe through to lessen the stench of sweat and vomit.

Many of the refugees were weak and sick, not taking well to sea travel. The numbers of them passing out below decks grew alarmingly, and the deck was reserved for those most in need of it. As soon as someone topside was revived sufficiently, he would again be moved below to make room for someone else in need. The children were given the most time above, as they suffered a great deal more than the adults. For that reason, the children had been put together in one area of the ship to make rotating them above an easier process.

Mendel began developing a severe phobia of the enclosed confines below decks in which air was not available to him. His fear of suffocation became so extreme at one point that he actually considered killing someone in order to take the person topside in a faked attempt to "save" him. It was only passing out himself that saved him from the insane idea that his brain had concocted.

The salt air filled his lungs and the warmth of the sun on his face and arms brought him gently back to consciousness. He kept his eyes closed, his body still, and breathed slowly and deeply, not knowing how long he had been on deck. He began wondering how long he could fake unconsciousness just to stay above decks in the air. Then he felt hands shaking him. "Wilno. Wilno, wake up!" a familiar voice said.

He opened his eyes, but had to close them against the bright sunshine. He squinted through tiny slits at the faces looking down at him. There were two of them, both men he had come to know well at La Ciotat. Their names were Yosi Cymerman and Eugen Yary.

"Look," Eugen said, pointing over the rail. "There are British ships out there."

Mendel sat up quickly and looked.

"We'll never make it," Eugen said. "We've come so far . . ."

"We'll make it, if we have to swim," Mendel said with determination.

"They can't bother us until we enter the three-mile limit," Yosi said.

"What if they stop us before reaching the three-mile limit?" Eugen asked with worried concern.

"They can't. It's against international law," Yosi replied.

Mendel laughed. "Yosi, you're a fool," he said.

"What do you mean?"

"I mean that the British will stop us any time they feel like stopping us, international law or not. What the Germans did was against international law, too. But that didn't stop them. There is no law, only the will of men."

Yosi looked back at Mendel. "They'll have to sink us to stop us. And if they try to board, we'll fight them to the last man. I'm through with the camps, Paul. I would rather die than spend another day in one."

Spoken like a fool, Mendel thought. But perhaps he, too, was becoming such a fool, for the thought of being returned to another camp was indeed a bitter one compared to the freedom lying ahead for them.

"We'll make it to Palestine," Mendel said. "We haven't come this far to be denied."

The time below decks was easier for Mendel after seeing the British warships. From that moment on, air was a secondary concern. Getting to Palestine was the only thing that mattered. Yosi and Eugen stayed with Mendel after finding him on deck. Even though Mendel at twenty-three was a few years younger than they, they looked up to him. There were certain leadership qualities about him that were evident to anyone who came to know him.

Speculation and rumors ran all through the ship for the next two days. They ranged from certainty that the British were going to sink the *Maiden of Hope* in order to make a lasting impression on future refugee runners, to word that the British had finally partitioned Palestine, which was, in reality, not to happen for another two years. Fears and hopes rose and fell like the swells of the sea. The only certainty was that they were on course for Palestine and that three ships of the British Royal Navy had been in close escort since the Strait of Sicily.

Mendel and his friends managed another short visit topside after the three of them had become quite peaked from the increased pitching and rolling of the vessel. People were sick everywhere, and a system of quick rotation was started to try to alleviate the situation.

What Mendel and the others saw topside was an incredibly angry sky and the unmistakable signs that they were in for a terrific storm. That would mean everybody below decks and even worse mayhem ahead when the water really got rough.

But what Captain Michalopolis saw was the chance he had been waiting for. They were approaching the three-mile limit and would soon be in heavy seas. The British, he knew, would give a much wider berth in the rough seas for the safety of all ships. If the distance was great enough, and he could sneak an extra bit of a lead, then he could kick both auxiliary engines in and fly before they were aware of what he was up to. It would be hell below decks, and the debarkation after beaching would be much more difficult in the storm. But it could just be the chance of success that they needed.

Michalopolis sent men below to request the previously appointed section heads to meet in his quarters. He laid out his plan as simply as possible. Their choices were to risk using the cover of the storm to make their dash and to run the *Maiden of Hope* aground as close to shore as possible, or to ride out the storm and increase the risk of being caught and towed into Haifa by the British. He made it plain that the surf would be rough and that there could be casualties. The children would all be fitted with life jackets to help them in the water, and would each be assigned to an adult to help get them safely ashore.

After a short discussion, the decision was made to make the run for shore. They had come almost 2,000 miles to get to Palestine. Perhaps it was God's will intervening for them now, to give them a chance against such unfavorable odds.

Michalopolis ordered them to tell everyone and to ready the children. He returned to the bridge and signaled the engine room to start the two auxiliary engines. He ordered a slight increase in speed to start pulling away almost unnoticed from the British ships, which had already widened their berths considerably. One cruiser remained positioned well off to starboard, the other well off to port. The sleek little destroyer was well aft of the *Maiden of Hope*. The destroyer, Michalopolis knew, would be capable of chasing them in much closer to shore than the cruisers. But he would also have the biggest lead on it if he timed it properly.

And time it properly he did. The commander of the destroyer was just beginning to notice the widening of the distance between them in the now full-blown storm. Visibility was poor, and he was about to order slightly more speed when Michalopolis opened the old runner to full steam.

The heaving British vessels were no match for the sudden swiftness of the old tramp as she bore away from them in the storm, quickly reaching her top speed. It was madness to make a run in seas like this The warships opened up their boilers but the *Maiden of Hope* slid steadily away, being tossed and battered by the heavy seas. Her speed was too great and her jump too well timed. The destroyer cut after her building to maximum speed well ahead of the heavier cruisers, which were hampered in their efforts by the storm.

Michalopolis headed the creaking, groaning old tramp toward the most dangerous waters, which he had come to know from over thirty years of seamanship. The distance between the two ships narrowed significantly as the *Maiden of Hope* plunged into the reef- and shoal-infested region. The commander of the destroyer radioed the position of the landing attempt to waiting shore patrols of British troops, who immediately began racing to the area. The destroyer pressed hard after the tramp steamer beyond the point of her own safety. But the speed of the old vessel was too great to permit it to be caught before the level of danger became too high, and the destroyer was forced to break off its chase. It suffered a minor scrape against a reef as it zigged its way back toward the safety of deeper water. The British had been beaten on the water by the wily Michalopolis. All that remained now were the shore patrols—and the storm.

The waters grew increasingly angry as the old ship bore in toward shore. Michalopolis had little idea of where the dangerous reefs and shoals were now, and followed instincts honed by time and experience He ordered every possible ounce of steam that could be generated to increase their chances of riding over anything they might strike.

Luck held out for the *Maiden of Hope* until 600 yards from shore when she struck a reef. The old mistress of the sea groaned and cried her port side splitting open as she glanced off the main point of the reef with a violent lurch. Her momentum carried her beyond it, but she had been mortally wounded.

She began taking water as the scramble to her decks started. The impact had knocked nearly everyone off his feet and prompted a panicked rush topside.

Michalopolis kept the old vessel heading straight for the closest point of land. The *Maiden of Hope* limped onward, starting to list to port. It grew worse by the moment as her bow began to ride lower and lower, making her even more susceptible to the hidden dangers. Her momentum carried her over a second reef, but she lost her props and all rudder control. She was helpless now in the angry, slashing waves struggling forward as though following the mental commands of her captain.

378

A final reef ended her courageous run, but not before she had gotten to within one hundred yards of shore.

The scramble over the sides began. Lights from the British lorries could be seen racing toward them.

It was mayhem in the pounding surf. The refugees struggled against the powerful forces of the sea, being pushed helpfully forward at times and washed back at others, all the while struggling and flailing for life. Those who could not swim were lost quickly. Others were smashed against rocks as they got closer to shore.

The British troops reached the shore directly in front of the old *Maiden of Hope*, which was now being battered to pieces by the sea. They could just barely see her in the driving squall and dusklike darkness. They spread out quickly to intercept survivors coming ashore all up and down the stony beach, who had been scattered over a two-hundred-yard area by the tricky surf and its undercurrents. Some troops began firing shots into the air over the refugees, while others went into the water making courageous efforts to help those struggling in the surf, too spent to go further.

It was a sight of awful desperation, accompanied by the gruesome vision of failure. It wasn't until days later that an official estimate had been made. Of the 565 refugees and crew, 324 had made it safely to shore and were apprehended, 167 had been confirmed drowned, either washed up on shore or recovered in the water, and 74 were missing and presumed to be dead.

Abraham Mendel, the boy who had left Dresden to escape Nazism and who had survived nearly three years in the dreaded concentration camps, was among the missing . . . presumed dead.

Chapter 38

EDNA-MARIE DeBussey glanced through the glass terrace door and saw Michael sitting alone in the long shadows of the setting sun. She opened the doors and stepped out to join him.

Michael rose when he saw her approach.

"Please, stay seated," she said, gesturing with a hand for him to sit back down. "I hope you don't mind a little company?"

"Not at all. It was getting downright lonely out here," he fibbed. The fact was, he wanted very much to be alone with his thoughts. He was deeply troubled about his growing feelings for Nicole and the probability that her father was one of the people he was after. He was also beginning to believe they would never find the contact who had been so useful to his father.

Edna-Marie sat beside him and placed her hand on his. "We have a few minutes yet before dinner, and I wanted to talk to you," she said.

"You have my undivided attention," he returned, smiling.

She looked into his eyes for a long moment, then her smile faded. "We haven't been very helpful, have we?" she said, more as a statement than a question.

"That's not true, you've been a tremendous help," Michael answered.

She frowned and shook her head slowly. "We're no closer now to solving the mystery of Z than we were during the war. So much remains covered by time. The clues are even less obvious to us now than they were then. Only our memories are left to serve us, and you. It's not enough. I feel as though we've failed you," she said sadly.

Michael squeezed her hand. "You've done all that you possibly could to help us."

"I'm afraid that there is little more we can do. The remainder of your father's story will be told tonight, but very little of it will pertain to Z. We left off in October of 1943 with Claude's escape in Paris. I went to England the following month and returned to France after the invasion of Normandy. For some reason, Z was never a factor again in the war."

They were interrupted by the sound of the terrace doors opening. It was Nicole. "There you are. Dinner is ready," she announced, holding out an arm to invite them in.

Michael and Edna-Marie rose together. He extended a forearm to her, which she took, and they walked into the house.

Conversation during dinner was light and St. Jude seemed more at ease, which made Michael feel a good deal more comfortable, although he could not dispel the constant suspicion he felt toward the man. Michael looked at Nicole and smiled to cover the dark feelings inside.

Following dinner, Edna-Marie picked up the final part of the story.

"It was nearly a month before I saw your father again," she began. "And what a terrible month it was. The Germans had begun waging a frantic war against the Resistance in France, extracting harsh reprisals against innocent Frenchmen for the successes enjoyed by any Resistance group.

"They were becoming quite successful and sophisticated in their efforts to locate our radios during transmission, and they had begun making major infiltrations into the most important Resistance groups. They leveled some of their most intense efforts against us, and hurt us badly. Sectors fell with depressing regularity, radios were lost, and I was harried by the Germans so badly that I seemed constantly on the run.

"The loss of each radio further worsened our situation. Intelligence reports built up faster than we could code and transmit them. It was not uncommon for sectors still having radios to be holding forty or fifty pounds of backlogged intelligence reports. I, myself, at one point, carried over sixty pounds of reports with me simply because the information could not be transmitted."

"Why couldn't you send it out by Lysander?" Danny asked.

"Lysander operations had been suspended in the summer of 1943 because of high casualties. The British could not replace pilots as fast as they were being lost, and the Germans had become much mor successful at stopping such landings," she replied.

"How did you manage?" Gabrielle asked.

"Not very easily, I can assure you. And the British were requestin; mountains of information. We knew that an Allied invasion of Franc was being planned, and we did all we could to comply with thei requests.

"The remaining radios began transmitting more frequently an with much longer code groupings than previously dared, which greatl increased the risk to them. Priority was given to the information re quested by British Intelligence, with the rest being constantly re-evalu ated so that the most important went out first.

"I had two very narrow escapes that month before reaching safet in Avignon. It was there that I met Christian. I must have been ; frightful sight to him. I had lost a good deal of weight and my face wa drawn and lined with fatigue, worry, and depression. I can't tell yo the wonderful feeling it gave me to be with your father again. He wa so much a part of my strength. I remember that we sat on a high clif overlooking the Rhône and the curious bridge to nowhere, whicl looked as if it had been started in the middle and was left with no be ginning and no end. It seemed symbolic of Group Defiance, in a way So many of the brave and wonderful men and women of our begin nings were gone. We stood fractured, barely clinging to life, yet wen on and on. Ahead of us lay such uncertainty that I wondered if any o us would survive to see the end of the war. We had all used up mor than our share of luck.

"Your father saw how badly in need of a long rest I was, an suggested I go to England for a while to 'cool off' the trail of the Fo; that the Germans were so hot after. I protested, though I knew he wa; right. In my state I was nearly useless to Defiance; I could not rur much longer without being caught. That would have been a terribl blow to the morale of our people. So, reluctantly, I gave in to hi; argument.

"Christian managed to persuade the British to make a Lysande run for my benefit, and they jumped at the chance to get the Fox t England. Within a week, I was in London.

"I hadn't imagined how important my stay in London would b and how much good I could do for our people from there. Had known, I would have gone sooner.

"My desk became a madhouse clearing center for thousands o transmissions from Group Defiance. I had never had a clearer pictur of the overall functioning of our network. I was able to pull together the loose threads from England, tightening the fabric of Group Defiance, directing its efforts with greater precision than I'd ever dreamed possible. I met with many of our agents, and was able to send them back into battle laden with important questionnaires, personal heartening messages, much-needed money and supplies, and gifts for all my children.' Group Defiance, though badly mauled, reached unprecedented levels of efficiency.

"The pace continued for months. And with each agent that I sent back into France, I felt a wrenching guilt, for I was sending them back into the danger that I no longer shared. News of each loss only compounded my guilt, and, as important as my work in London was, I felt the need to get back into the struggle, to share the dangers I was asking my people to face. I finally asked to return to France after receiving news of the Atlantic sector tragedies and the first reported loss of the magnificent little Albatross, but the request was refused.

"It was in the spring of 1944 that memos telling of the long silence of Z were intercepted by Gabrielle Dupuy. But the losses continued without his treachery, as the benefits of his betrayals were long-lasting to the Germans."

"Are you saying that Z just suddenly dropped out of sight?" Danny asked.

"Yes, though it was never clear exactly how long he had been silent. But the last major betrayal attributed to him was in January of 1944, when the Atlantic sectors were smashed."

"Do you think there's a possibility that Z could have been killed?" Michael asked.

She thought for a second. "We suffered many casualties during that time, and it could be possible. More likely, he recognized the opportune time to save himself and seized it. The ultimate outcome of the war was clear. Even escape into Germany would not have been a guarantee of safety, as many collaborators discovered. No, I think he felt secure enough in his cover to remain in France, assuming his legitimate role in the Resistance," she replied.

"That would put his disappearance somewhere between January and spring," Michael mused aloud. "Please, excuse me. Continue with your story."

"It wasn't until after the Allied invasion of Normandy that the British allowed me to return to France. Lysander operations had been resumed several months prior to the invasion, and within a week I was flown in on a dark, overcast night and landed on a tiny field near

Poitiers. I was again on my beloved French soil, breathing the clean, wonderful air of the beautiful Poitou countryside. Within hours, I was reunited with Christian and Claude, who had been informed of my return by a coded message broadcast by the BBC.

"The following day, we laid out a new battle plan for Group Defiance. It called for three main objectives. Group Defiance was to advance ahead of the Allied invasion forces, sending back information of enemy movements, concentrations, and defensive positions, wherever possible identifying specific divisions and units of the Wehrmacht, especially panzer groups; Group Defiance was to maximize their intelligence gathering in the South of France, in preparation for another Allied landing, and were then to precede the Allied advance as in the north; and lastly, they were to advance members of the group as far into German-held territory as possible to rally those in Defiance being cut off by the German withdrawal, and to try and save as many as possible who had already been taken and were still being held in French prisons.

"Claude left immediately for the south to prepare the Mediterranean sectors for the massive effort they were being asked to put forth in preparation for the Allied landing there. New patrols would have to be quickly assembled to act as intelligence teams advancing ahead of the Allied forces. All sectors north along the Rhône Valley and above Dijon would be put on alert to make careful observations of German movements. The way would be well paved with loyal French patriots. Depending upon the advances of the two armies, a rendezvous site would be set for myself, Christian, and Claude and transmitted by radio.

"Christian and I raced north into Brittany to where the U.S. Third Army under General George Patton was engaging the enemy. We established contact with Patton's intelligence headquarters and began our advance ahead of the U.S. army. Our information was radioed back or hand-carried by teams of couriers directly to Patton's G-2.

"In order to pass freely into and throughout enemy-held territory we carried identification supplied by British Intelligence showing us to be loyal collaborators. We even carried weapons and radios openly and were congratulated for our loyalty to the Reich as we passed German checkpoints, all the while carefully noting the movements and strengths of the various divisions that we encountered. This information was relayed to Patton's waiting G-2, which enabled the Third Army to select routes of advance.

"By July thirty-first, Avranches had been captured and the Third

384

Army began its wide sweep across the Brittany peninsula. The advance proceeded methodically to the southeast to Orléans on the Loire and then toward the Seine south of Paris. By August twenty-third, Paris was boxed in by large Allied forces to the northwest and southeast. On August twenty-fifth, Allied forces entered the city, finding it largely under the control of unified Resistance units. Most importantly, they found the city and its bridges intact. The order by Hitler to completely destroy Paris and its bridges was deliberately ignored by the commandant of Paris, General Dietrich von Choltitz, who could not reconcile within his own conscience such wasteful destruction in a lost cause. Paris had been liberated.

"In the south, the Franco-American Seventh Army under General Alexander Patch had landed on the Riviera on August fifteenth and advanced rapidly up the Rhône Valley. Claude and his Defiance patrols pushed relentlessly ahead of them, sending back vital information. Patton's Third Army had pushed east and captured Verdun, besieged Metz, and reached the Moselle River, where Patch's Seventh Army met up with them.

"Word of the Liberation of Paris was met with wild joy by Frenchmen everywhere. Perhaps in all of France there was only one loyal Frenchman for whom the news brought a dreadful concern. That man was your father. His concern was for the welfare of Gabrielle Dupuy, for he knew that reprisals would be swift and cruel against known collaborators. The hatred was intense, inflamed by the awareness of victory over the occupying forces of Germany. I recognized his concern and allowed him to go immediately to Paris in an attempt to find Gabrielle and to provide protection until the story of her heroic efforts could be made known.

"Claude arrived in Verdun, where I had established Defiance headquarters to organize the next phase of the advance. He missed Christian's departure by a day.

"Claude, perhaps you had better tell it from here," Edna-Marie said.

"Could you first tell us about the 'Circus' transmission?" Michael cut in.

St. Jude nodded and began immediately. "On the advance northward ahead of Patch's Seventh Army, I had set up the radio and just finished transmitting my reports to his G-2 section. I was preparing to contact our group in the north, and was trying to pick up news about the situation in Paris. It was then that I happened upon the broadcast from Albatross.

385

"There was no telling how long he had been transmitting, trying to make contact on the single wavelength of the old radio that he was using. The signal was very faint, only the long dashes of the Morse code were clearly distinguishable. I fine-tuned to the frequency and shot back a coded recognition. I had recognized the call letters of the radio, and hoped that my return transmission would be received.

"The reply began with a return code, indicating to me that it was Albatross sending. I had communicated with him frequently enough to know his 'hand,' especially after our internal communications network had started. He began transmitting out of code, which was never done. I understood the reason, however, when he transmitted that he was in immediate danger of capture. I verified reception of his signal out of code to save him time. There was a long delay, which made me fear that I had been too late, but he started again. He transmitted that he had learned the identity of Z. Then he sent the word 'circus' and his transmission suddenly stopped. I verified reception and asked for a repeat of the message, as it didn't make any sense to me. He never came back, despite my repeated requests," St. Jude explained.

"You said that the signal was very weak. Were you certain of the letters transmitted in the word 'circus'?" Michael asked, recalling Pheagan's information from British Intelligence regarding the transmission.

"Although parts of the preceding message were unclear, I was able to understand all the letters in the word 'circus,' though I didn't understand why that one word would be transmitted in English, when the rest had been in French," he replied.

Michael thought for a moment before asking his next question. "When you acknowledged receipt of his signal, did you identify yourself?" he asked.

St. Jude shook his head. "No, I did not. Just the call letters of the radio and the Defiance code."

"And you said that London did *not* pick up the transmission?" Michael questioned further.

"No, they did not. Later, after the fighting had stopped in France we contacted London regarding the transmission, hoping that they could shed some light on the mystery. But they were unable to help us."

"The radio that you were using, Claude, was this the one that you routinely operated?" Michael asked.

"Yes, it was. It was one of the first variable wavelength sets that we received. It was essential to have a radio of this type during the ad vance ahead of the Allied forces to permit contact with as many of our radios of fixed or limited wavelengths as possible," St. Jude answered.

Michael nodded at the response, mentally filing what he had just learned. "What happened after you rejoined Edna-Marie in Verdun?"

"She told me that your father had started back toward Paris in an attempt to save Gabrielle Dupuy. I left immediately to try to help him. Finding a single person in that city would have been a difficult job for ten people, much less for one. It was a good thing for him that I did follow after him, too, for when I finally caught up with him, he was being held prisoner by another Resistance group. He had been questioned by them, and his collaborator identity card was found on him. They were convinced that they had caught a genuine collaborator. They were itching to tie him to a tree and shoot him, and were losing patience with him when I arrived. I verified his story, and even radioed Edna-Marie in Verdun and Intelligence in London to confirm that Orca was indeed one of the leaders of Group Defiance. After they let him go, we raced the rest of the way to Paris."

St. Jude paused for a second and a sad expression came to his face. "It would have been better for your father if he hadn't gone. . . ."

P ARIS, SHORTLY AFTER THE LIBERATION: It was on a steam-driven lorry burning charcoal as fuel that Christian and St. Jude made their entrance into Paris. From a distance the capital looked like a dead city. There were few signs of normal life; no smoke coming from factory chimneys; little visible vehicular traffic; and an air of somnambulism in a populace still numbed by the reality of the Liberation. People walked down the middle of streets alone or in groups looking from side to side, as though inspecting some strange planet they had suddenly found themselves on.

There were makeshift barricades on nearly every major street. Barricades made of wood and tangled wire, of disabled cars and overturned buses, of carts on their sides and furniture piled high. It was the work of Parisians sensing their freedom, answering the call to battle.

But the most unusual sight of all was the vision of French and American uniforms. The only German uniforms to be seen were on those still being rounded up and paraded through the streets in full view of angry, taunting citizens. It was a dramatic change from the last time that either man had seen Paris.

Their immediate problem was to locate Gabrielle. There were already mobs roaming about rounding up known collaborators and people being pointed out by others as suspects. No form of proof was needed, just the accusation and the pointed finger. Some of the worst known collaborators were dealt with swiftly by the sudden crack of a revolver, or a quickly assembled firing squad brandishing a ragtag arsenal of weapons. Resistance people and others with newly found courage roamed the streets with guns in plain view, ready for German or collaborator alike.

Occasionally there would be scenes of an angry mob hustling about a column of marching prisoners. Rocks and insults were hurled at those who had lived high during the occupation by serving their Nazi masters so well. Men and women were shoved and punched, spat upon and cursed as they were led to awaiting confinement and public humiliation. Women collaborators had their heads shaved and chests painted with swastikas, or were stripped and made to parade naked in front of their jeering countrymen. The most hated women never made the columns; they suffered a more tragic fate. It was precisely this danger to Gabrielle that Christian was trying to head off.

Christian and St. Jude rushed madly about, carefully checking faces in the columns they came across. But Gabrielle was not among them. They went first to the apartment she had shared with Immel and had remained in after his departure. But they learned that she had not lived there in almost a year. They were given a second address, and found that her stay there had been only a short one. A third address was obtained, and yes, she had lived there up to the present, but spent most of her nights with the filthy Boche that she whored for. An angry mob had already been there ahead of them looking for her, but she was not there. The Nazi whore was probably running as fast as her legs would carry her for Germany, they were told.

She had seemingly dropped from sight. Then Christian realized that perhaps she had gone to the old apartment where they used to meet. Her friend knew that she was no collaborator. She may have found safety there. They headed directly for the address.

Christian's worst fears were met when they turned onto the block of their former meeting place. He saw the angry mob outside of the building, throwing rocks and other objects at the windows, while others vented their pent-up anger on the prisoners in their column. The two of them broke into a sprint for the building. There was no doubt as they drew nearer that the apartment they had used was the object of the scene. A large white spot from a well-aimed bag of flour marked the outside wall just above the third-story windows, serving as the beacon for the mob. The stairway and stoop were lined with people waiting to be among the first to administer some form of punishment to the "collaborators" inside.

Christian bolted up the outside stairs three at a time, St. Jude closely behind. He pushed and shoved people aside as he struggled to get by them, receiving jabs and pokes back from those not willing to give up their prime locations. He fought his way through the doorway and made for the first flight of stairs, just as a wild cheer went up. A body sailed over the railing, landing with a hard thud on the stairs in front of him. It was Gabrielle's friend Joan Orsay. The lifeless, staring eyes and open mouth greeted him. She had suffered a brutal beating before being dropped over the railing.

Christian let out an enraged cry and fought his way up the stairs, climbing over people, throwing punches at them in his blind rage.

"Stop! You don't know what you're doing! Stop!" he screamed in a dreadfully agonized voice.

He continued up past the half-flight landing and up to the first floor, then began struggling to gain the second floor. The people on the stairway were now fighting back, landing blows with fists, clubs, and hastily thrown kicks. He fought his way through the gauntlet, his face cut and bleeding, his bottom lip torn from a well-aimed fist. He managed to reach the second floor, St. Jude still struggling a flight behind him, absorbing even more punishment than Christian had received.

A wall of men stopped Christian as he tried to go up the stairs to the third floor. He was met with a barrage of fists and thrown back into the angry waiting arms of men behind him. It was only the sudden cheers rising on the stairway above them that momentarily distracted his attackers.

Gabrielle's partially nude, battered body was being passed down the stairs above the heads of those handling her limp form. The screams and cheers were wild and frenzied, animallike.

Christian used the distraction to draw his two handguns and fire a rapid series of shots into the air. The blasts were nearly deafening in the narrow stairway and the angry cries were suddenly stilled from the shock of his actions. There was a brief moment of total silence as the lifeless body of Gabrielle fell to the floor in front of Christian. He stared in horror and immeasurable grief at the battered body of the woman he loved—a hero of the Resistance. He let out a pathetic cry as he took her in his arms.

"You fools!" St. Jude's voice boomed, breaking the utter stillness surrounding Christian's grief. "You've just killed an agent of Group Defiance. You've killed a hero of France," he screamed.

The name of Group Defiance was known to all Frenchmen.

"She was a German whore," came a voice from the stairs above them.

Christian looked up at the man who had made the statement. The man was making his way down the stairs toward the landing, his followers parting to let him pass.

"She slept with half the German officers in Paris," the man continued, the scratches on his face plainly indicating that he had been one of those to administer the beatings to the two women.

A growl emanated from Christian's throat. In an instant he was springing at the man.

The man swung viciously with a stick he had carried, hitting Christian squarely across the head. The stick snapped from the force, but did not stop Christian, who was possessed with a strength born of madness.

The man was big and strong, but could do nothing against the incredible strength inspired by Christian's rage. He was shaken like a rag dummy as Christian's hands tightened around his throat. His eyes bulged and the facial veins popped like balloons as Christian started choking the life out of him.

"She was our agent. She saved hundreds of French lives," Christian hissed into the man's face as he squeezed.

St. Jude was on Christian, trying to stop him from killing the man. Onlookers stood by in shock as Christian lifted the man by the throat and flung him over the railing. He crashed onto people crowding the stairway below, which saved his life.

Christian threw wild fists of rage, scoring those closest to him as he pushed his way past St. Jude to again take the lifeless body of Gabrielle in his arms.

There was a sudden rush of murmurs that swept wavelike down the stairway and to the street outside. A stunned silence followed, broken only by the sobs of Christian Gladieux, immersed in his grief.

"We didn't know," a weak voice said from the stairway above them.

"Didn't know? *Didn't know?*" Christian repeated. He looked hatefully into the faces staring at him. His eyes moved slowly from face to face.

"What did any of you ever know?" he asked angrily. "What did *you* do for France when you were needed? Where were *you* when the Germans were *here?* When they were winning and strong and prepared to stay forever?"

The faces stared back or looked away in embarrassment.

"Is *this* your courage? The Germans are gone. You attack a defenseless woman, crying for a justice that you now righteously claim." He paused, staring hard at them. "You don't deserve justice—you deserve pity. Pity for being cowards, for doing nothing while your country sank into a darkness that will forever be its shame. Pity because your country's sins were *your* sins for not opposing them. *You* are the guilty ones. Guilty for your silence and lack of courage."

An utter silence followed as people stood motionless, feeling their shame. The silence was everywhere, even on the street below. Slowly people began to turn and leave the building without speaking. The hallway filled with the sounds of feet shuffling in reverent silence, the faint sounds of soft crying coming from somewhere below. On the street, the column of collaborators was led off with a remarkable absence of anger and violence.

Within a few minutes, Christian and St. Jude were alone with the body of Gabrielle. Joan Orsay still lay dead on the stairs below.

Christian cried, his rage spent, kissing and stroking the face of his Gabrielle. Tears poured down the face of Claude St. Jude as well. He was powerless to help his friend. He could only share the grief. Grief over his friend's tragic loss, grief for all the others who had been lost, and a grief far worse that only he could know.

Christian looked up in the face of his friend. "See what they've done," he said, choking in his sorrow. "Tomorrow they will be the heroes. Twenty years from now they will have won the war. I hate them all," he said, placing his cheek against Gabrielle's in a final expression of love. "Oh, God, I hate them all."

There was a long silence in the room after St. Jude finished his story. Then Edna-Marie spoke softly. "The rest is unimportant," she said. "We pushed on only to discover the terrible truth of what had happened to our comrades being held by the Germans. As the Allies were winning in Normandy, Defiance prisoners had begun paying the price for that victory. Hundreds were executed in the prisons in France. Hundreds were shipped into Germany, where the same fate awaited them. The rest of the war is history. The Battle of the Bulge, the advance across the Rhine, the final defeat and surrender of Germany—all mere history now.

"As for your father, he was grief-stricken. The war didn't matter, France didn't matter, nothing mattered. He did come back into the fight, pouring every ounce of his strength into the effort, advancing far beyond the Allied forces. He became obsessed with saving others, only to learn time after time of the tragic fate of our fellows. We saved a few, but for most it was too late."

She paused for a moment, looking around the room at the silent faces. "That is the whole story of Christian Gladieux," she said. "France could have asked no more of him, and few would have given so much. He was no traitor to France."

The whole story of Christian Gladieux, Michael thought. No, they didn't know the *whole* story. There was still more to be learned, and it had yet to be given an ending.

Chapter 39

Michael stared at the two sheets of paper that he had just covered with every scrap of pertinent fact known to him. What a tangle it was. Code names, places, dates, people known and unknown. Of course, to him most of it made sense now, but it still did not provide the conclusive answers they needed. They still hadn't found the most important piece to the puzzle—his father's contact. Nor had they any truly concrete evidence to support their suspicions about Falloux and St. Jude, though in his mind Michael was certain about both of them. Everything they had to this point was circumstantial.

A knock sounded on his door. "It's open," he said.

Danny opened the door and stepped in. "Not bothering you, am I?"

"Not at all. Come on in. How are Mom and the kids?" Michael asked, knowing that Dan and Gabrielle had just called home.

"Your mom is fine, so are the girls. Alexis gave Sandra a black eye two days ago, otherwise nothing exciting has happened. What are you up to?" Danny asked, seeing the sheets in Michael's hands.

"This is everything we have. We ought to be able to get our answers from this information. I've been over it and over it, and I just can't get anywhere with the contact and the name Leopard."

"Well, Gabby is just finishing downstairs. When she comes up, I hink it would be a good idea if we three went over it together," Danny uggested. "She's getting pretty serious about wanting to hear it all. I lon't think we can put her off any longer."

"It's probably as good a time as any to tell her, I guess," Michael tgreed, holding out the sheets to Danny. "See if I've left anything out."

Danny had spent a few moments carefully checking the sheets vhen he heard the door to his room open. He stuck his head out of Michael's room and caught Gabrielle's attention with a soft whistle. "In here, Babe."

"Secrets again?" she asked as she entered the room.

"Not this time, Sis. You're going to hear it all," Michael told her.

"I could have told you that," she replied. Danny was right, she neant to know.

"Before we start, I want you to look those sheets over when Dan las finished with them. They represent everything we've learned so far. There are certain facts that only Danny and I are aware of and under-:tand right now. What I need from you is to be sure that nothing has ›een left out from the parts that you do know and understand," he told ier.

She turned to look at her husband, just as he looked up from the heets.

"Did you get this stuff from Pheagan?" Danny asked, regarding he information contained on them that he had never seen.

Michael had included everything from his last conversation with ²heagan, as well as some of the confidential background he had been ;iven. He added only enough of it to give them a clearer picture of the ›ignificance of the pendant, its holder, and the Salamandra. Sub Rosa vas not developed beyond what Michael had already divulged to Danny.

Michael nodded his answer to Danny's question. "Did I leave inything out?" he asked.

"Not that I can see. It seems clear from what you've got here that ⁄ou've settled on your two suspects."

"Yes, I have, but I'm willing to listen to arguments," Michael said.

Danny handed the sheets to Gabrielle without comment. Both nen sat quietly as she read them slowly, digesting every word with :are.

When she had finished, she looked up into her brother's face. "I :an't believe it! Falloux and *Claude?* Are you certain?" she asked.

"I'm not sure that we'll ever be certain, Sis. But based on what ve've gotten from Immel, the Collards, and St. Jude himself, that's the vay it looks," he replied.

Shock and disappointment showed clearly on her face. "I hope you're wrong about Claude, for your sake and Nicole's."

The point didn't have to be expanded.

"St. Jude may not matter if it turns out there's no connection between him and Dad's death. If he's not a part of it, then he's not our business," Michael said.

"And if he is a part of it?" Gabrielle pressed.

"Then he's my business and I'll take care of it. As I see it, the two important things we're after are the pendant holder and the contact," he said.

Danny accepted the sheets from Gabrielle and looked at them. "We've got the whole story now. There still isn't a clue as to who the contact is," he said. "With this Salamandra angle, he may not even be a part of the Resistance at all."

"And I'm out of answers on how to approach it," Michael added.

There was a knock on the door, which Michael answered. Nicole stuck her head in, gave him a quick kiss, and smiled at Danny and Gabrielle. "You have a phone call," she said.

"A phone call? Here? Who is it?" he asked.

"Jacques Collard. He says that he has something important to talk to you about," Nicole said.

Michael shot a quick glance at Danny. "I think you had better come along," he said, then looked at Gabrielle. "Both of you."

Nicole led them to the study, then left them in privacy.

Michael picked up the phone. "Hello, Jacques? Michael Gladieux here."

"Hello, Michael. I apologize for calling you so late in the evening, but we have some information regarding Immel that we're sure will interest you," Collard said.

"Has Blanc confirmed the identity yet?" Michael asked.

"No, the medical and dental records have not arrived from Germany. But I think it will not matter when they do," he said.

"What do you mean?"

"I mean that Immel is not dead," Collard answered.

"*What!*" Michael said, shocked.

"I have a friend in Cuisery who works for Blanc. He made the photographs taken of the body available to us. What we saw made us very suspicious," Collard said.

"We viewed the body, too, but saw nothing suspicious in it," Michael said.

"It had to do with the way the body was lying and the position of the shotgun," Collard went on. "Immel was left-handed, yet the gun lay across from right to left."

"That's very little to make such an assumption from," Michael said.

"There's more, my friend," Collard said calmly. "We decided to do a little investigating ourselves. We went to the site of the house and began a search. We found enough proof to make us certain that he did not die."

"What kind of proof?" Michael asked skeptically.

"A tunnel. The entrance to it from the house had been situated in the floor of a closet which had been buried by debris when the roof fell in. We found it, however, and entered it. It was just large enough for a man to crawl through on his hands and knees, but very well made and supported. It led to a root cellar that was not visible from the outside. It had been expertly camouflaged like many of the machine gun pits that the Germans used around important defensible positions. There were signs of blood in the tunnel, and indications that he had cleaned and dressed a wound in the root cellar. It appeared to us that he had left this hiding place not more than a half a day before we discovered it," Collard explained.

"Then he *is* alive," Michael said in amazement.

Danny and Gabrielle had expressions of equal surprise on their faces.

"Yes, it would seem so," Collard replied.

"It's imperative that we find him, Jacques. Do you think your people could help us?" Michael asked.

"We've already begun. He will probably not be far. From the amount of blood that we found, we know his wound was not a small one. He will need to get some help somewhere," Collard said.

"Jacques, I can't thank you enough for what you've done for us," Michael said.

"It is the least that we could do for you—and for your father. He was our friend."

"Get in touch with us if you should learn anything. If you could discover that he's still alive, then the people who tried to kill him can, too. Especially when the medical and dental records coming from Germany arrive and make the truth evident. He must be kept alive. We have to talk with him," Michael said.

"We'll keep him safe if we find him," Collard assured Michael. "We'll contact you if we learn anything at all."

"Thank you, Jacques. Good luck."

Michael placed the phone back on its cradle. "Immel's alive. He escaped through a tunnel he had made, probably when he built the house. We may get the chance to talk to him yet. Let's hope he knows something that can help us."

"And that we find him first," Danny added.

"And that we find him first," Michael repeated.

A great deal would depend on being the first to find Rudolf Immel.

"I must go," Nicole whispered into Michael's ear, kissing it softly. "It is nearly four A.M., and Papa will be up very soon. Satan will be fighting tomorrow in Aigues-Mortes, and my father must first attend to some business in St.-Gilles. He will be leaving before dawn, and I don't want to make matters more uncomfortable for you," she said, smiling. "I will see you at breakfast."

Michael pulled her close to him and held her for a long moment. "I wish we could just stay this way forever," he said.

"Perhaps we will," she said with a catlike grin. "I think that will be up to you."

She looked down into his face, her hair hanging down around him. "I love you," she said, giving him a quick kiss, then was up and putting on her robe as she moved for the door. A second later she was gone.

Michael felt pleasantly exhausted. He put his troubles out of his head for awhile, letting only one thought remain. Nicole. He drifted off to sleep with a mental picture of them riding and splashing together through the Camargue.

He heard the sounds of St. Jude in the hallway, and then the truck starting which would pull the trailer transporting Satan to Aigues-Mortes. He heard the sounds, recognized them perhaps, but sank deeper into sleep and dreams.

His mind drifted, taking him to the rain forest. With those visions came a sense of relief, of being able to breathe. The rain forest was good, he was happy there, untouched by the events of a sick world. The worst things he experienced there were the nightmares, or the sudden flash memories triggered by a smell or a sound. Smells like the beautiful mixed fragrances of rain forest flowers blending with the smell of vegetative rot. It was exactly like that in the highlands of Vietnam. Or some sound of the rain forest—the birds, the insects, the big hunting cats calling out their victory after a kill, the screaming monkeys . . . the helicopters. He could almost hear the *whop-whop-whop-whop* of the rotor blades as they darted like overgrown dragonflies, carrying troops, delivering death and destruction to points below, ferrying piles of grotesque bodies and bone-tired men too scared and exhausted to care. If he remembered one thing when he thought about Vietnam, it was the helicopters—*whop-whop-whop-whop.*

It was as though he had been drowning when he suddenly gasped for air. He emerged from the dream, though still more asleep than awake. But the sound remained in his head—*whop-whop-whop-whop.*

Go away, he willed. But the sound remained distant and constant. "Go away!" he said out loud to dispel it.

Whop-whop-whop-whop.

His eyes opened and he looked to the window. The dawn was just beginning to break. He was totally out of the dream now, and yet he still heard the sound.

Whop-whop-whop-whop-whop-whop-whop.

In an instant he was out of bed, pulling his pants on. He went to the window and looked out but couldn't see anything. The sound was still there, and it was real. The other side of the house, he knew. He grabbed the Swiss SIG and ran out of the room and up the hall. He pounded twice on the door to Danny and Gabrielle's room, then opened it.

Danny jumped up startled, staring in confusion at his shirtless brother-in-law.

"Company! Let's go," Michael said, then was gone.

Danny came instantly awake, fumbled quickly with his pants, then went for the Smith and Wesson. "Gabby. Gabby, get up!" he shouted.

His wife sat up in the bed.

"Get Edna-Marie and Nicole out of bed, quickly," he ordered.

"What's—"

"Do it fast!" he said, then was off after Michael.

Michael entered Nicole's room, which had a window facing the side of the house that the sound was coming from.

She jumped up, surprised, and watched as he ran to the window. "What is it? What's wrong?" she asked.

Michael looked out and saw the helicopter lifting off and peeling away to wait at a point more distant.

"Get out, fast! Get everyone into the bathroom," he shouted, spinning and rushing out of the room.

It was only then that she heard the helicopter's faint sound and saw the gun in Michael's hand.

Michael met Danny in the hallway. "They're already down. I don't know how many or how they're armed," he said. "We've got to get downstairs, fast."

The two men spun and raced for the stairs, going down them three and four at a time.

"Kitchen," Michael said, pointing for Danny to go in that direction, while he went toward the terrace doors. He heard the glass smash just as he rounded the corner near the archway to the room. Two men were outlined against the opening of the terrace doors when he got there.

Boom! Boom! The Swiss SIG roared. One man was blown back through the glass doors.

Crack! The other man fired back, missing narrowly.

Boom! The Swiss SIG answered, driving the man over a potted plant near the wall.

Michael crouched and raced to the shattered terrace doors. There were no other intruders visible. Then he heard the sound of the front door being smashed open. He raced out of the room and toward the main entry just in time to see three men sprinting up the stairs toward the bedrooms.

Boom! He ripped off a shot at the last of them, but missed. He tore off after them.

The first man up the stairs was Bruno Scalco. He rapidly and systematically began kicking in the bedroom doors as he came to them, throwing in hand grenades.

The explosions began going off, followed by the second man raking each darkened room with automatic weapon fire. The third man had turned to intercept Michael. But the Swiss SIG spoke first, dropping him at the top of the stairs.

Scalco continued going room to room with the grenades as Michael started up the stairs. The man following Scalco turned and raked a burst across the top of the stairway at Michael, who had ducked beneath stair level as the man turned. The burst ended with the clip being emptied. In a flash, the man had the spent clip out and reversed. The second clip, taped upside down to the first, was rammed home.

Boom! Boom! The Swiss SIG barked before the man could snap the first round into the chamber. The shots hit him squarely in the chest, splattering his blood on the wall as the hollow points blew gaping holes out of his back at the close range.

Scalco kicked in the last bedroom door and threw in the grenade, turning instantly to see Michael, and managing to successfully dodge the hasty shot fired at him. Scalco could see by the locked back slide that the clip was empty. He drew his handgun and started back down the hallway toward Michael. A wide grin crossed the Corsican's face, the advantage fully his.

398

He raised the gun to fire when he was suddenly hit from the side by Nicole, who had charged out of the bathroom like an Ohio State linebacker. Before he knew what had hit him, she had her nails dug into his face, and the added impact of Edna-Marie's charge drove him against the wall.

The Corsican threw a vicious elbow sweep at Nicole, hitting her in the ribs, and tried aiming the gun at Michael, who was already halfway down the hallway toward him.

Edna-Marie reached for the gun and pulled it off target as it discharged. It fired again and again into her, as she clutched Scalco's wrist.

By this time Gabrielle was on him as well, and the combined strength of the two women pulled Scalco almost to the floor. The gun went off again as Michael got there, Nicole falling off with a whimper.

Michael delivered a swift series of strikes, which scored the Corsican in the windpipe and eyes, then a savage smash to the side of his neck, just below the right ear. Scalco was jarred back, badly damaged by Michael's blows, and fell into a sitting position.

Michael's well-aimed kick caught Scalco square in the face, slamming his head into the wall. In an instant, Michael was on him and had wrenched the gun away. He jammed it straight into the face of the Corsican and pulled the trigger, blowing the back of his head all over the wall.

Edna-Marie lay rock still on the hallway floor, her eyes open and fixed. Nicole was holding the inside of her left thigh, her hands covered with blood.

Gabrielle stared in shock at the mess that had been made of Scalco by her brother's swift, brutal attack. She was uninjured.

"Take care of them," Michael shouted, then raced for the stairs.

He heard a series of rapid shots from downstairs. Danny had intercepted someone in the kitchen. It sounded as if a small battle was raging. Then the sound suddenly stopped.

Michael heard the helicopter again, much nearer the house this time. He ran into the kitchen in time to see Danny administer a punishing blow to an intruder he had engaged hand to hand. There was another body on the floor. Michael fired twice at the man Danny had been fighting, knocking him against a cabinet. The man flopped dead to the floor.

Michael and Danny ran out of the house just in time to see the helicopter rise and peel off. Michael futilely fired the last remaining shot in Scalco's gun at the moving craft. They stood there, both breathing heavily as they watched it move off, untouched.

"I wounded one of them. There was at least one more who didn't even make it into the house," Danny said. "I'm sure from the dossiers that it was Demy."

"We've got casualties," Michael said, turning and racing back into the house, Danny close behind. They ran up the stairway back to where the fight with Scalco had taken place.

Nicole was sitting against a wall, crying and looking at Gabrielle, who was trying to administer assistance to Edna-Marie.

Gabrielle's eyes were flooded with tears of anger and desperation as she futilely tried CPR techniques to keep Edna-Marie breathing.

Michael threw the gun aside and knelt beside the former Resistance leader to take over Gabrielle's efforts.

Danny felt for a pulse in the throat, and checked her eyes. The pupils were fixed and dilated. She had no pulse. He touched a finger to the open eye. There was no reflex response.

"Come on, Baby, breathe," Michael was saying, tears beginning to form in his eyes.

"She's gone, Mike," Danny said softly.

"Come on, Baby. You can do it," Michael said.

Danny put his hand on Michael's shoulder and shook him. "Mike," he said firmly. "It's too late. She's gone."

Michael looked up into Danny's face, an expression of pain and anguish in his eyes. He turned and looked at Nicole, who nodded that she would be all right.

Michael lifted Edna-Marie's head and upper body into his lap and pulled her close to him. He recalled her words about feeling that she hadn't helped them enough and had failed to lead them to the answers they had needed. "You beautiful, noble woman, you'll never know how much you've done," he said to the gallant Edna-Marie DeBussey, who had just saved his life at the cost of her own.

Chapter 40

It was perhaps the third ring of the telephone that roused Pheagan out of his slumber. He swatted the alarm clock once or twice before realizing that it was the Omega-George phone making the intrusion. He squinted at the illuminated dials on the clock face. It was almost 2:00 A.M.

"Shit!" He was suddenly alert and racing across the darkness toward the phone as it continued ringing.

"Tripper," he said into it.

"We were hit this morning at St. Jude's place," Michael said.

"What? What happened?"

"They hit us at dawn. Nine of them were brought in by helicopter."

"How bad was it?" Pheagan asked, almost afraid to hear.

"Edna-Marie DeBussey was killed. Nicole St. Jude was wounded in the thigh. That's all we suffered. They lost seven killed and one wounded, but he escaped with the last attacker."

"Give me the details," Pheagan said.

Michael went on to describe the attack and their successful defense against it. He told him how the women had saved his life in the hallway against Scalco.

"And you say that Demy was there as well?"

"Yes, Danny positively identified him as the one who got away clean. I didn't see him myself, but both Danny and I have spent a lot of time with the dossiers you gave us. I don't doubt the identification."

"What about St. Jude?

"He was on his way to deliver one of his bulls to Aigues-Mortes.

401

He's been notified of the attack and is on his way back now. He should be here any minute," Michael replied.

"How bad is his daughter's wound?" Pheagan inquired.

"Flesh wound to the inside of the left thigh. She'll be all right. Listen, I want my sister, Nicole, and Danny taken out of here. Can you arrange it?"

"I sure can. In fact, I think it's time I come to France, and that Sub Rosa becomes a more active partner in this deal. We could have prevented what happened if we had stepped in sooner," Pheagan said.

"You couldn't have known." Pheagan felt a twinge of guilt. He *had* known that some kind of attack was imminent, though he would not have guessed it to take place so soon.

"Besides," Michael continued, "we'd have had to get down to this sooner or later, anyway. I'm just glad we were able to handle them and take out Scalco. That's one less to worry about."

Able to handle them, Pheagan thought. What an understatement that was. They chewed them up. It was a sure bet that Renaud Demy had learned respect for these two guys. He'd be smarter and tougher the next time.

"What's your situation there now?" Pheagan asked.

"Well, the house is a fucking wreck upstairs, but we can still stay here. There are police all over the place, and St. Jude's *gardians,* or cowboys, I guess you'd call them, have set up an armed perimeter around the place. Falloux couldn't hit us here again unless he had a B-52," Michael replied.

"Good. That will help in keeping Sub Rosa less visible for a little while longer. Once we've been connected to the situation, it'll be over for Falloux. Our chances of being able to use him to get deeper into the Trinity Committee level are growing slimmer by the minute," Pheagan said.

"You mean because of what happened this morning?"

"Yes. His troubles are just starting, and soon you won't be his biggest worry. His own people will be. Up to now, he's been pretty successful at keeping his tracks covered on all sides. It was important to him that the other Committee members be unaware of the true extent of the danger that he was in. Well, he can't hide it anymore, not after blowing his chance to end the entire threat in one sweep. His days are definitely numbered, although he may feel that he still has a chance.

"Our biggest hope now is that either he'll contact them, or that they'll contact him before it happens. The worst thing that could happen would be for him to suddenly find enough personal courage and honor to uphold his oath of death," Pheagan said.

"He could always run," Michael suggested.

"He'd never get the chance. Besides, it's our objective to demonstrate to Trinity the ability to penetrate their Committee. If he's going to die, then we have to do it, and make it known to them that it was Sub Rosa who was responsible for it. But we have to wait until the last possible moment, in the hope that a contact to the Committee will be made. If we move too soon, we may blow the only chance we'll ever get. If we're too late, then we lose our chance to show them that we can strike at their heart. We'll have just been observers of a situation we couldn't take advantage of," Pheagan said.

"What about the apprentice?" Michael asked. "You felt that there could be a back door of some kind."

"That's still a possibility. In fact, that was one of the things I wanted to talk to you about."

"Go ahead, I'm listening."

"We contacted the Israeli Mossad and got extremely lucky. It seems that one of their people, named Eugen Yary, knew a Paul Wilno from a displaced persons camp in La Ciotat, France, right after the war. He was a forger like the Paul Wilno we're looking for. It seems that Yary and Wilno were together in an attempt to run the British blockade of Palestine in 1946. The attempt was a disaster as they tried to beach in a storm. Yary was separated from Wilno and another man named Yosi Cymerman. He thought that the other two had drowned, but he met Cymerman two years later. According to Cymerman, he and Wilno made it to shore together in the storm and managed to elude the British. They likewise thought Yary had drowned. Cymerman and Wilno separated soon after that.

"To make the story short, we have the name of a man who could be the apprentice we're looking for. It would take a quick trip to Israel to find out. I was hoping that you'd want to be the one to make that trip," Pheagan said. "Your family and Nicole would be well-protected during the time you'd be gone. We'll get them out of Saintes-Maries-de-la-Mer in a way that will keep security matters well guarded. No one would know that you'll be in Israel."

"There's been another development here," Michael said. "Immel is alive."

"What? Are you sure?"

"Positive. Some former Defiance people found an escape tunnel in the ruins of his house. There were signs that he had been wounded. But he definitely made it out. The medical records on Immel should be in France any time now, and then it'll become common knowledge that he survived the attack. I think we have to find him before Falloux gets

403

a second chance at him. I still have the feeling that he could tell us something."

"I can start a lot of people looking for him," Pheagan said. "And we can protect him if he's found."

"And you'll do all this if I go to Israel?" Michael asked.

"I'll do it even if you don't go."

"Protect the family *and* start the search for Immel?"

"That's right. I realize that Falloux is your prime reason for being in France, but I also think that you want to complete what your father started. You can do that by helping us now," Pheagan said convincingly. "Your father and Sub Rosa wanted the same thing, Mike."

"And Falloux? Will you guarantee that he'll be mine when the time comes to take care of him?"

"Only two things could prevent me from keeping a promise like that. And that's if he killed himself, or if Trinity gets to him before we can. Discounting those two possibilities, he's yours. You have my word."

Michael thought for a few moments. "Okay, you have a deal. Make the arrangements. I'll need a complete dossier on this apprentice."

"You'll have every scrap we've got."

"Okay, when will you get here?" Michael asked.

Pheagan checked his watch. "I can be there at about ten o'clock this evening, your time. I'll have security people with me. Your family will be safe from that point on."

"See you tonight, then. Go back to bed," Michael said, then the line went dead.

Pheagan held the phone and looked at it. He felt as though he had just won the lottery. "Welcome back, Glad-jo," he said, then placed the phone down in its cradle.

Claude St. Jude stepped into the study, then closed the doors behind him just as Michael finished hanging up the phone.

Michael looked into his face. A kaleidoscopic range of emotions was plainly evident. His eyes were red from crying; there was fear and anger and puzzlement.

"Nicole is okay," Michael said.

"I know, I've just come from her. Danny and Gabrielle told me what happened. I . . . cannot properly express my gratitude for your actions in the face of what happened," St. Jude said, tears welling up in his eyes, his speech halting from the emotion.

"It wasn't enough," Michael replied, the reference to Edna-Marie's death plain.

"After so much, so very, very much . . ." St. Jude said in a near whisper, his silent crying forcing him to stop. After a few moments he regained his composure, a hard quality suddenly coming to his eyes and face. "I want to know why a thing like this happened in my home," he said angrily. "It wouldn't have happened if you weren't here."

Michael stared at him for a moment before answering. "You're right, it wouldn't have happened if we weren't here. But we wouldn't be here if my father hadn't been murdered, and if you hadn't agreed to help us. If we had known that something like this was going to happen, we would never have stayed here to endanger you, Nicole, Edna-Marie, or your property."

"The property is meaningless. Buildings can be repaired or rebuilt. But Edna-Marie DeBussey was killed, here, in my home. My daughter was almost killed as well. I demand to know what is going on. There's more than a search for an unknown collaborator. And I want to know who did this," St. Jude demanded.

"You deserve some explanation," Michael replied. "It has to do with the real reason my father was killed. It goes deeper than a charge of collaboration. That was only the ruse used by the killer to cover the real motive. Of course, we weren't entirely sure of that when we first arrived, so we set off on the only course available. That was to find the real collaborator."

"What is this real reason?" St. Jude asked.

"My father had discovered another identity while in France. The identity of a man guilty of far worse crimes than the collaborator he tried to hide behind and use as his diversion. My father tried to expose that identity in a book, but was stopped before its completion. I'm not at liberty to tell you more right now," Michael explained with deliberate vagueness.

"Then do you mean that you were never really after the collaborator?"

"Yes, we were after him in order to clear my father's name of the charge. But he was not the man responsible for the death of my father. The man who was is also responsible for what happened here today. He's desperate, trying to protect his secret."

"And do you know who this man is?"

"Yes."

"Who is it?" the Frenchman asked with a vindictive interest.

"I'm sorry, but I can't tell you that right now," Michael answered.

"You must tell me," St. Jude said.

Michael stared at the angry bull-like man in front of him. If St. Jude were involved in the setup of his father, then he already knew the answer to his own question. If he wasn't, however, but had merely been used by Falloux, then his reaction could very well tell the story.

"I can tell you that this man not only used the collaborator as a ruse to cover the killing of my father, but he also knows Z's identity. It was his ultimate plan to lay the full blame on him not only for the crimes of collaboration during the war and the murder of my father but also to set up Z to take the full rap for what my father had learned about him. Z would have been a dead man unable to refute the evidence that this man had cleverly prepared against him."

St. Jude's jaw unconsciously fell half open. He stared at Michael without speaking a word.

That was all Michael had to see. "You'll excuse me now, I'm sure," he said, and walked past St. Jude and out of the study.

Let him chew on that for a while, he thought. And we'll see what he does next.

"You must be a crazy fool to call me here like this," Pierre Falloux said angrily into the phone.

"You filthy slime," St. Jude hissed. "You murdering pig."

"You sound very self-righteous for a man who ruthlessly betrayed hundreds of his own people during the war. You have no right to call anyone filthy slime or a murdering pig. You are the worst example of both," Falloux said back.

"I should have killed you in 1944."

"*You* kill *me?*" Falloux laughed. "You forget that it was I who could have had you killed in an instant. It turned out well for both of us that I didn't, though. We both made a great deal of money, thanks to your connections. You should have stayed involved; you'd be twice as rich as you are today."

"And just as dead if your men had succeeded this morning," St. Jude said.

"Who has been telling you that nonsense?"

"I know that it was you," St. Jude insisted.

"A very unfortunate incident, but you are wrong. If I had wanted you dead, you would have been that way years ago."

"I know your double game, Falloux. It was you who had Christian Gladieux killed to prevent him from exposing your involvement in drugs," St. Jude accused, thinking he had made the real connection.

"Be quiet, you fool," Falloux said. The idiot, he thought. Someone

406

had planted just enough of a seed in his pea-sized brain and he had fallen for it.

"You fool, you're being used," Falloux said. "Someone else must know the little secret that we've shared for all these years. You're just killing yourself."

"It was you who had Gladieux killed, wasn't it?"

"No," Falloux lied.

"It was you. That's why you contacted me after the news of the killing became known. You wanted my help to save your skin while you pinned the blame on me," St. Jude accused.

"You've been talking to someone with a very active imagination, Claude. The truth is exactly as I told you it was. When Gladieux was killed, I expected that the mystery of the identity of Z would be probed. It was for both our sakes that I contacted you. We both stand to lose by it being discovered that you were the real Z. You for obvious reasons, and me because of the mutual advantages we shared by virtue of my knowledge of that fact, as well as my not having turned you over to France for the just punishment that you deserved," Falloux said.

"You made me believe that Christian's family was in France solely to hunt me down, while the truth was that they were after you. Then you tried to kill them, and me—and my daughter—when they got close to you," St. Jude said.

"Do you honestly believe that I would try to kill you and your lovely daughter?"

"I know that you tried!" St. Jude fumed. "But you failed. And I'm warning you now, Falloux. I've prepared a letter making a full confession of my crimes, and I name you and every dirty transaction that you've been a part of. I tie you to the drugs you grow richer from by the day. If anything happens to me, or to my daughter, that letter will go straight to the highest authorities. And I'm telling you this as well. If anything happens to the children of Christian Gladieux, I will also release that letter."

"Gladieux's children are no concern of yours," Falloux shot back crisply. "And I have this to say about your letter. Your sword has two edges. Your daughter will never be harmed so long as you hold the letter. If, however, that letter ever reaches the authorities while she is living, I *will* have her killed. Even if it is after your death. So, my dear Claude, what I am telling you is that you can very well guarantee the safety of your daughter with that letter. But you can also kill her with it if it ever surfaces."

Falloux's counterthreat against his daughter hit St. Jude like a dagger. Nicole was his life.

Falloux listened to the long silence. He knew he had won that little skirmish. "Goodbye, Claude. Don't ever call me here again," he said, slamming down the phone.

Yes, he had won that battle, but he was losing his war. He could do nothing more about it until Demy called in. He looked at his watch. That would be in less than one hour. One hour could seem like a lifetime. He wondered how long "lifetime" meant for him. It wouldn't be long if he didn't win, and win quickly, and without a trace of doubt remaining. He was no longer confident that he could win to that degree. But he was sure of one thing, he knew that he would stop at nothing to try.

Chapter 41

THE large strong hands patted a lightly scented cologne to the freshly shaven face. The brain ignored the stinging sensation as the cold, dark eyes surveyed the cleanness of the job. He used a finger to lightly groom the thick mustache that covered the remarkably faint scar of the harelip he had been born with. He was one of the few lucky ones whose features seemed to be completely natural. Only a close examination revealed it on the handsome face. There was no trace of it in his speech.

Renaud Demy was an attractive man if judged by his appearance only. He was six foot three, 230 pounds, and powerfully built. He had been an outstanding athlete as a youth, was bright and always at the top of his class, and he enjoyed a large measure of success with the ladies. No one would have imagined him becoming a terrorist and a killer for hire.

He toweled off his hands and packed his shaving kit, then put on a shirt. He picked up the key to his room and walked out, locking the door behind him, then went to the main desk in the hotel lobby and asked the operator to put through a call for him. He went to the booth she indicated and waited for the phone to ring. It took about three minutes.

He picked up the phone on the first ring. A second later, Falloux answered. "This is your friend, again," Demy said.

"You're an hour late," Falloux said, perturbed.

"I was busy," Demy returned, unfazed.

"You fool! I thought you said your men were professionals? I've already heard that you failed. You made a bigger mess of this than you did of the previous commission," Falloux said scornfully.

"We underestimated the family," Demy replied in a cool, even tone.

"That's the second time you've underestimated the opposition. It was fortunate for us that the first one was an old man, otherwise he might have driven you off as easily as the family did. As it turned out, the reports have it that you managed to retire only one old woman."

"We failed to take them by surprise. They were ready for us, and the advantage was theirs. They cut my men to pieces before they even penetrated the house. Only one team managed to reach their point of assignment," Demy said.

"Two men against nine. It's inexcusable," Falloux derided.

"Had they been asleep as expected, they would all have been sanctioned."

"Well, they weren't asleep. The report I have is that they retired seven of your men, including your close associate. You botched it good, and may not get such a chance again."

"Eight were retired," Demy corrected. "Another was badly impressed. He . . . was persuaded to leave us over the Etang de Vaccarès. I won't misjudge them again. I'll take care of it myself, this time."

"You had better, and soon. Very, very soon," Falloux warned.

"It'll get done, I guarantee it."

"It had better!"

"I said that it will," Demy returned sharply. "And, my friend . . . don't ever call me a fool again, or I'll cut your throat as you sleep."

Falloux felt a sudden twinge of fear course through his body. "Don't you dare threaten me."

"Be assured it is no threat. It is a promise."

Even Pierre Falloux knew enough not to beat a dog when its teeth were bared. "I pay you quite handsomely. I expect results. I'll double your usual bonus to take care of the matter quickly. Don't fail me this time," he said in a calmer voice.

Demy smiled. He knew a frightened man when he heard one. "You get the money ready. I made a promise, and I'll keep it."

It was nearly ten in the evening when the large helicopter put down at the home of Claude St. Jude. Michael and Danny walked out of the house into the darkness to greet Pheagan. He stepped out of the

409

craft as the blades swished overhead. He was accompanied by four
other men.

"Mike, Dan, glad to see that you guys are okay," he said, shaking
their hands."

The three men walked into the house through the smashed terrace
doors and went to the living room, where everyone was gathered.

Pheagan greeted Gabrielle warmly with a hug. "Are you all
right?" he asked her.

She nodded that she was, but the strain was apparent in her eyes.

"You're all going to be fine from here on out. I've made arrangements for you," Pheagan said.

"Bill, let me introduce you," Michael interrupted, then made the
introductions to St. Jude and Nicole.

"Glad to meet both of you," Pheagan said. "I've heard a lot about
you. Mike has briefed me on everything that's happened. I've made
arrangements to take all of you to a place where you'll be safe until we
determine the full extent of the threat to you."

St. Jude stood up and looked first at Michael then at his daughter,
a confused expression on his face.

"Papa, Monsieur Pheagan has come to take us to a place of safety
until the danger can be investigated," she translated.

"He speaks very little English," Michael explained to Pheagan.

"I will not leave my home," St. Jude insisted.

"It would only be temporary, until we have a better picture of our
situation," Michael explained.

"I will not leave. There is plenty of protection here now."

"Yes, I agree, but we wouldn't want a second attempt made here.
Your men would be put in great danger. The men who came here were
professionals. We can't be sure that they won't try again as long as
we're here."

"Then you leave. I'm staying," St. Jude said with finality, then
walked out of the room.

Michael turned to Pheagan. "He won't buy it. He's staying."

"That's his choice. As for the rest of you, I suggest you seriously
consider my offer," Pheagan said.

"Nicole?" Michael asked.

"I . . . I cannot leave Papa," she replied in English.

"Oh, yes you can, sweetheart," Pheagan returned. "You can't do
him any good staying here, especially injured as you are. You'd only be
a liability to him. Besides, I doubt that a second attempt would be
made. It's just a precaution that we're taking to help us control the
variables a little better. I'll leave two of my men here with him if he

410

nsists on staying. He'll be safe enough. But as for the rest of you, I hink we'd better do it my way," he said.

Danny looked at Michael. "Do you go along with that?" he asked with some skepticism.

Michael nodded. "Right now I do. Especially for the sake of the girls. We can reassess our situation and go from there."

"Okay, then we'll do it," Danny said, not quite believing that he had heard Michael agree so readily.

"I suggest that you get your things ready, then," Pheagan said.

"Sis, why don't you go into Nicole's room and pack a few things or her?" Michael asked.

"I will help," Nicole said. "I can make it up the stairs with assistance."

"Dan and I will get you up the stairs," Gabrielle said. "I'll help you gather some things while Dan puts ours together."

"What's left of them," Danny chipped in.

"You guys go ahead. I'm already packed," Michael told the others.

Pheagan waited until he and Michael were alone in the room. "Is there someplace where we can talk more privately?" he asked.

Michael nodded. "Yes, in the study."

Pheagan followed Michael to the room. It was empty, and they entered, closing the doors behind them.

"What do you have?" Michael asked.

Pheagan smiled. "Plenty. You're going to be very pleased," he said.

"I can't wait," Michael said dryly. "Start at the top."

"The top is that you were right about St. Jude. He was the collaborator."

"You've got proof?" Michael asked.

"The horse's mouth. He contacted Falloux today. We got the whole scoop on the connection between them, too, although Intelligence Central had already begun to make progress along those lines."

"Then he *was* involved in my father's death," Michael said, a hard set coming to his eyes.

"No, he wasn't involved. That's been established without a doubt. St. Jude contacted Falloux after the attack here. Apparently you had talked to him and spooked him about Falloux, although he didn't say as much. Whatever you said to him worked. It became quite plain that St. Jude hadn't even known that Falloux was the one who had your father killed, and went as far as to accuse him of it. He knows nothing about the Salamandra, either. He thinks the reason Falloux killed your

411

father was because Christian had found evidence tying Falloux to dru;
movements through Marseilles. St. Jude's only guilt in this affair ha
been in trying to cover up his past. He was under the impression tha
Falloux's only interest was in hiding the connection between them
which might have been revealed if St. Jude's identity as Z was dis
covered."

"Then you're positive that he wasn't involved in my father';
death?"

"Absolutely, just as there's no doubt about him being Z. So,
don't think that this will be of interest to you," Pheagan said, holding
out a folded piece of paper upon which was typed the transcript from
the "circus" transmission.

Michael opened it and looked at it. "It interests me, all right. Ever
though it may no longer be needed to prove his guilt to me, it ha;
always remained a critical piece of evidence to the people of Le
Groupe Défi. You might also say that it has become a point of pride
for me to solve it, especially after all the trouble it's given us."

He read it in its entirety. The first thing that stood out was the fac
that St. Jude had indeed identified himself, as well as his radio, by its
call letters. That explained the delay on Albatross's part, as he recognized that he was contacting the traitor himself. The coded word was a
clue developed on the spot by the clever little Pezet, which he hoped
would be solved by others while not being immediately recognized by
Z.

"We've played with the possibilities," Pheagan began, "and have
come up with something interesting. It is probable that the word 'circus' was not the word transmitted at all. We took the information
British Intelligence gave us and have come up with a second word
based upon the incomplete parts of letters as the British received them
That word is 'cercis,' " Pheagan said.

"Cercis," Michael repeated.

To a biologist who had devoted much of his study to plant and
tree types, it suggested something immediately. Cercis was a genus of
tree that enjoyed a degree of notoriety because of the role it was believed to have played in history. The connection was suddenly clear
He recalled his conversation with Father Vincent Piela about the time
that his father had seemingly made the important discovery regarding
the word "circus." They had been talking about Judas and what had
become of him. Popular theory was that he had hanged himself from a
tree. The tree upon which he chose to take his life forever thereafter
was referred to as the "Judas tree." Its proper name was Cercis. Cercis—Judas—St. Jude. St. Jude had recognized the connection, however,

412

and had simply changed two letters to form a well-known English word.

"What will you do about him?" Pheagan asked.

Michael didn't answer right away. The situation was complicated by his feelings for Nicole. "Well, one thing's for certain. Beyond the discovery of his collaboration, he's not my concern."

"You're going to let him get away with it, then? Because of the girl?"

"No . . . I don't think I could do that. Not after hearing the story and knowing what he did to so many people. But, in this case, the justice isn't mine to extract. I'll talk with him, and then see that the proof gets put into the right hands," he said.

"Le Groupe Défi?" Pheagan asked.

Michael nodded.

"It'll turn out the same," Pheagan said.

"I know," Michael said, then paused. "But perhaps it will be easier for Nicole if I give him the alternative of honor—a chance to confess his guilt and face up to it, or resolve it himself."

"You're getting soft, Glad-jo," Pheagan kidded.

"Don't you believe it. What else have you got?"

"Demy has contacted Falloux. Our pendant holder is desperate. He apparently feels that he still has a chance if Demy can get rid of you guys fast enough. No doubt he'll have plans for St. Jude as well."

"What are your plans for Danny and the girls?" Michael asked.

"We'll take them out in the chopper tonight to a place where we can protect them without being too visible. We have a few days, if we're lucky, before Sub Rosa's involvement becomes known."

"And Demy?"

"He won't be a factor as far as your family is concerned. He won't be able to find them, much less get close to them," Pheagan replied.

"I can draw him in once I'm back from Israel. He'll come for me fast enough," Michael said. "What about Immel?"

"He's dropped out of sight. I have a team positioned not far from Cuisery to get to him when he's located. The records from Germany arrived in Cuisery today. They'll probably realize that he's still alive by late morning. Falloux will find out immediately, then the hunt will start. I guess it'll depend on just how bad he wants to find Immel. You already know who Z is, so he can no longer prevent that from happening."

"What about this apprentice? If I'm being watched, they might put two and two together."

"I'm certain they don't have the slightest idea he might still be alive. As for you, one of the men I brought with me will stand in fo you, just in case our departure is observed. All they'll know is that you and your family were lifted out. You'll be taken out later under cove and will depart directly for the airport, where one of our planes i ready to take you to Israel. I expect you'll need two days there," Phea gan explained.

Michael nodded. "Keep your fingers crossed that this guy is the one you want, and that he can tell us something."

"Here's the file on Mendel," Pheagan said, handing Michael a manila envelope. "You'll be met in Lod. From there you'll be taken to the man we think is Mendel. Handle it the best way you can."

Michael thought for a moment, then looked directly into Pheagan's eyes. "I'll be needing a 'kit' when I get back," he said.

An almost inperceptible smile came to Pheagan's lips. He nodded slowly. "It'll be ready." This was getting to be like the good old days Glad-jo was getting ready to go hunting.

They left the study and returned to the living room, where the others had gathered. It was only then that Michael noticed that one of the men who had come with Pheagan was about equal in size and build to himself, and sported a remarkably similar beard. He was the stand-in.

"The helicopter is ready. Let's go," Pheagan said to the group.

They began picking up their things with help from two of Pheagan's men. Danny looked suspiciously at the man who resembled Michael in general appearance.

"How long are we going to need these baby sitters?" Danny asked Michael as they began walking through the house.

"No more than a few days, I hope," Michael said.

"I don't get it. Why are you so willing to step out of it all of a sudden?"

"We're not stepping out of it," Michael responded. "Things have just gotten a little too hot too fast. I want to get Gabby and Nicole out safely, and then you and I can jump back in after we've evaluated the situation.'

That didn't sound like the Michael he knew. Danny was beginning to realize that Michael Gladieux never stepped back from anything. He had the uneasy feeling that something wasn't right.

The group walked out of the house and into the darkness. The rotors of the helicopter were now swishing forcefully in preparation for the takeoff. Michael had lagged behind, and now he stopped just outside the house as his stand-in moved to the center of the group and

414

ook a position beside Nicole, who was managing well with crutches. He watched them go the remaining distance.

Their bags were put in and Nicole was helped aboard, then Gabrielle. Both of Pheagan's men were now in, and only he and Danny emained on the ground by the open door.

"What's going on?" Danny asked above the loud chopping noise of the helicopter, unable to hold back his suspicions.

"Get in," Pheagan told him.

Danny looked back at Michael, who was watching from the terrace. "What the hell are you up to?" Danny asked, turning back to Pheagan.

"Get in, Dan. We know what we're doing," Pheagan responded.

By this time Nicole and Gabrielle had noticed that Michael hadn't approached the helicopter with them. Gabrielle looked into the face of the stand-in, and then turned with an expression of alarm back toward the door. "Mike! Mike!" she called out.

Pheagan grabbed Danny by the arm and shoved him toward the door. "You're going to blow it for him. Now get in," he ordered.

Danny looked across the dark expanse to the cool expressionless face of his brother-in-law. He understood it now. Michael had always intended to go the last part alone, and was guaranteeing it now.

Before he could say another word, he felt himself being grabbed under the arms and lifted backward into the helicopter. Pheagan pushed in with him, in time to stop Gabrielle's rush for the door.

"No! What are you doing?" she screamed, trying to fight past him.

The door was slammed shut and the helicopter lifted instantly from the ground, then hung suspended for a moment.

Michael stood at his distance, feeling guilty for the deception he had just been a part of. He raised a hand to shield his eyes from the wind and debris generated by the powerful sweeping rotors. He saw the faces of the three people he loved most in the whole world press to the windows to stare down at him. He raised his other hand and waved as the helicopter cleared tree level, then peeled off and away.

He watched it for as long as he could in the darkness, until its lights became tiny specks and faded. No amount of guilt could have lessened the relief he felt as they sped away to safety. Pheagan would take care of them now. The rest was up to Glad-jo.

Michael turned and walked back into the house just in time to see St. Jude enter his study. There was no point in putting off what had to be done. He went to the study, opened the door, and stepped in.

St. Jude was sitting behind his desk. The Frenchman was a sorry picture of anxiety. Michael couldn't tell if it was sadness or fear dominating him.

Michael walked up to the desk, staring without expression into St. Jude's tense, sweating face. It was St. Jude who broke the silence. "So, she has gone, then?" he asked, his voice cracking slightly.

Michael nodded. "She'll be safe with my friends."

St. Jude broke eye contact and looked down at the surface of his desk. After another long silence, the folded piece of paper with the transcript of the "circus" transmission slid across the desk into his field of view. He looked up at Michael with a question in his eyes.

"You had better have a look at that," Michael told him.

St. Jude picked it up, opened it and read it. The theory about the word "Cercis" was plainly spelled out, and Michael had penned in his interpretation of its meaning.

The Frenchman's hands were trembling now, and a slight twitch had started in his left cheek. He was perspiring profusely. St. Jude looked up into Michael's eyes, fear and defeat visible in his own.

"Why?" Michael asked.

"Why what?" St. Jude replied, swallowing dryly. "This means nothing."

"Perhaps not. But I have proof."

St. Jude stared at the American in silence, his eyes challenging him to produce his evidence.

"Your phone conversation with Falloux today was taped. We've had a tap on his line since he first figured into the picture," Michael said.

St. Jude's hand went into his lap and a gun came up with it, pointed at Michael's chest.

Michael didn't register the slightest surprise.

"How long have you suspected?" St. Jude questioned.

"For some time. But we didn't have proof before now."

"What made you believe it was me?" the Frenchman asked.

"A number of small bits and pieces that began adding up. It had to be one of the three of you. I knew it wasn't my father. Edna-Marie had no motive, but you did. We had learned about your brothers, whom you never mentioned. We also knew that it was Liepart who had arrested them. Your pretending not to know him was a mistake. Immel gave us important parts of the puzzle, too, which when added to the stories told by yourself and the Collard brothers regarding the Max Schrict affair, pointed to you as being the only one who could have contacted Immel in Clermont-Ferrand."

Michael's words were registering on St. Jude's face like well-aimed darts.

"You were very clever in your double game, too. Especially when you betrayed yourself to the Germans twice. That really kept us confused. It was the perfect cover. All the while you were in their custody, you worked safely, giving them the latest codes and betraying newly formed sectors. You even endured some torture to add strength to your cover. It was brilliant. And then when you were shot in the last capture, you all but cemented your cover. That was a remarkable display of courage. And your timing was perfect."

St. Jude was visibly trembling now. "It was more a product of fortunate miscalculation and the failure to duck on my part," he conceded.

"But it was brilliant, nonetheless, especially the way the Germans handled the situation in their memos and telegraphs. Who would have suspected you? And the whole time that you were recovering, you were feeding them information. You were right there when they discovered the information after smashing the forgery sector in Paris. They merely brought it to you and you turned it into a pot of gold for them.

"But the high point of your cleverness came when you allowed Z to disappear after your escape in Paris the second time. I suspect that you made that decision on the spur of the moment," Michael submitted.

St. Jude squinted up at the young American, impressed with his accuracy. "You are quite right. The opportunity presented itself to make it appear as though I had been inadvertently killed. The outcome of the war was obvious, and I had to save myself, after all. I no longer trusted Liepart, and suspected that my brothers were already dead, anyway, and that I would be killed in the end. It was the only chance I had to save myself."

"But one thing puzzles me," Michael said. "Edna-Marie said that the Atlantic sectors were betrayed after your escape. That doesn't fit."

St. Jude shook his head. "The *arrests* were made after my escape. The information that led to them came from the fall of the Paris forgery section. René Pezet had organized his sectors so well that it took months for the Germans to establish the information they needed to make all of their strikes."

"And my father's betrayal to Immel. Why did you do it after going to such pains to help him?" Michael asked.

"Your father was supposed to have stayed in Pont du Château. Had he not returned to the winery, he would have never been found. I never intended for him to be caught," the Frenchman said. "I never betrayed Edna-Marie or Gabrielle Dupuy, either. They . . . were my friends."

It was precisely as Michael had theorized. "They were *all* your friends, Claude," he said.

An expression of immense shame came to the Frenchman's face. "Yes, they were all my friends." He paused a moment, then began again. "Did you come here to kill me?"

"No, I didn't come to kill you. My interest lies in those responsible for killing my father."

"And you know who that is?"

"Yes. It was Falloux and two of his men. One was killed during the attack on us here," Michael answered.

"And why have you come to tell me all of this if you did not intend to kill me?"

"Because of Nicole," Michael replied.

St. Jude's lower lip began to tremble, and his eyes filled with tears. "Does she know?" he asked, his voice choked with emotion.

"No, and I don't intend to tell her."

"Despite my betrayals, I also did my part for France," the Frenchman said. "That cannot be ignored. Surely, it must mean something."

"That's not my judgment to make. You were a traitor, Claude. You sent hundreds of your own people to their deaths. You can never reconcile that," Michael told him.

St. Jude lowered the gun and laid it on the desk. "And I suppose that killing you will solve nothing," he said with resignation. He sat for a moment, then buried his face in his hands and wept. It was the grief of almost forty years coming out. "How can I ever face her again?"

Michael picked up the gun, removed the clip, and engaged the safety. "Did you never think that this day would come?" he asked.

St. Jude looked up, his eyes wet and red. He could not answer the question. "Nothing is left," he whimpered.

Michael placed the gun on the desktop with the single round still in the chamber, and laid the clip beside the gun.

"*Honor* is left, Claude," Michael said.

After staring at the gun for a long moment, St. Jude looked hard into Michael's eyes. "And Nicole? I must know," he said.

Michael nodded. "I love her."

St. Jude pulled the gun closer to him and again stared at it. "Thank you," he said, without looking up.

Michael looked at the pitiful figure of the broken man. There were

418

no words left to say. Without speaking, he turned and left the room.

Pheagan's man was waiting for him just outside the doors.

"Are you ready to go?" the man asked.

Michael turned and took a slow look around the house of Claude St. Jude and let out a long silent breath. "You bet. Let's get out of here."

Chapter 42

THE flight into Lod airport was uneventful. Michael used the time on the private jet to study the file on Mendel and to start planning his method of approach. It was nearly 2:00 P.M. when the plane landed.

Michael took his small bag from a storage compartment and walked to the door of the plane. As he came down the steps he was approached by a young Israeli in military uniform. The man was a *segen,* or lieutenant, in the Israeli army.

"Mr. Gladieux?" the strong-featured young man asked, stepping up to him.

"Yes," Michael replied.

"My name is Conrad Volrick. I'll be your escort while you're here," the man said, his English good enough to sound like an American's.

"Call me Mike, okay?" Michael said, extending his hand,

Conrad nodded and took the handshake. "Come with me, I'll get you through customs," he said.

Michael followed as instructed. The young officer showed a card to the men in customs, and they were waved through.

Within minutes they were heading southeast toward Jerusalem in a dust-covered Land Rover.

"It's a pity that you won't be here long enough to enjoy Israel," Conrad said. "There's an awful lot to see and experience."

"Perhaps someday I'll be able to come back to see it," Michael said. "Unfortunately, my business is rather specific, and there's little time to spare right now."

"So I understand. The man I'm taking you to is named Benjamin Zell. He is one of the administrators at the kibbutz of En Gedi. From the facts we've been given, and from what we've been able to learn ourselves, the chances of you finding the man you're looking for are not good," the young leiutenant said.

"What about this Benjamin Zell?" Michael asked.

"We were lucky to come up with him. We've shown photographs of him to Eugen Yary and Yosi Cymerman, whom I'm sure you are familiar with by now. They both feel that he could be the man, but were tentative. Thirty-six years is a long time to remember a face."

"What can you tell me about him?"

"Well, he's got quite a fine record in Israel. He distinguished himself with honor in the wars of 1948 and 1956, and then again as a major during the Six Day War of 1967 in the fighting for the Golan Heights. He was a member of the Knesset when the Yom Kippur War broke out. He served only one term, preferring to return to En Gedi. He's a man of the land, not the conference table. He has devoted his life to En Gedi, making it green and prosperous. Benjamin Zell is a fighter. And he doesn't hide the fact that he came to Israel on the *Maiden of Hope,* being one of a handful to make it ashore and past the British in the storm," Conrad explained.

They made good time to Jerusalem, then traveled east past Bethany and to the south of Jericho. They turned south above the northern tip of the Dead Sea, and continued along its western bank. Much of the scenery possessed a desolate beauty, as though it belonged to a faraway planet. The heat was intense, rippling the light and making the golden glowing hills of Moab, visible in Jordan across the dying sea, seem to dance. They continued along the desiccated, crumbling cliffs on the Israeli side until a spot of green became visible on a high plateau. It grew larger and more distinct as they drew closer. It was En Gedi.

Somehow, Michael had not been ready for what he saw. He had expected the En Gedi kibbutz to resemble a small farm. But it was a great deal more, with well-made buildings, gardens, schools, and many of the things one would find in a city, but on a smaller scale.

"When do we get to see Zell?" Michael asked.

"Tonight, at his home. You're supposed to be a writer gathering research material. That's all he's been told. You'll have to take it from there. I'm sure that you'll be able to spend a good part of the day with him tomorrow, too, if it's necessary," Conrad explained.

Night had begun to fall over En Gedi when Michael and the young lieutenant arrived outside the apartment building in which Benjamin Zell and his wife lived. There was a magnificent stillness in the air, which Michael took a moment to appreciate. He looked out to a vast horizon upon which a pale yellow sun was preparing to slip away, turning a cloudless silver-gray sky into a deep blue darkness.

He followed Conrad along the neatly trimmed sidewalk to the Zells' apartment. Conrad knocked softly.

After a moment's wait the door opened, revealing the tanned, smiling face of a woman in her late fifties. "Welcome to En Gedi," she said with a broad smile. "Won't you come in?" Her English was excellent.

Michael followed the young lieutenant in.

"You would obviously be Lieutenant Volrick," she said, extending a hand to Conrad. "And you are Mr. Gladieux."

Michael smiled and tipped his head as he accepted her hand.

"My name is Sarah. Benjamin will be right with us. Please, come into the living room and make yourselves comfortable."

The apartment was as thoroughly modern as anything one might expect to find in Tel Aviv or the most recently developed parts of Jerusalem. It was amazing to Michael how these people had scratched out a piece of barren earth and converted it into a productive oasis, complete with modern conveniences.

They followed her into the living room. "Please, be seated," she said.

Michael noticed the many pen and ink sketches adorning the facing wall behind the sofa. He bent close to examine a few. They were originals, signed "Ben Zell." He turned to Sarah Zell. "Your husband did these?" he asked.

"Yes," she said with a proud smile. "He's always sketching or painting in his spare time. I've got boxes full of them."

"They're truly outstanding," Michael commented, turning back to examine them. It was when he turned away again from the wall that he made the discovery that started his heart pounding. On the wall opposite him were three long shelves covered with glass miniatures. There were larger pieces, too, so fine in detail that they looked as though they had been sculpted. He was about to ask if her husband had made them, also, when Benjamin Zell entered the room.

He was a tall man with a head of thick hair well into graying. The face was tanned and weathered from years in the harsh sun and wind, with wrinkles and cracks like those of an aging mariner. There was strength in the face and the dark, sharp eyes.

"Good evening. My name is Benjamin Zell," he said in heavily accented English. The accent was unmistakably German.

His wife made the introductions.

"It's a pleasure to meet you," Michael said, taking the hand extended toward him. The hand was toughened from the years of hard work, yet it possessed a certain gentleness in its touch.

"Please, sit. Make yourselves comfortable," Zell said.

"I was just admiring your drawings. They're excellent," Michael told him.

Zell smiled. "Thank you very much. It is a relaxing hobby."

"Have you had formal training?" Michael asked.

"My father was an artist, a sculptor. I watched him often as he worked and sketched. I learned from observation."

Mendel's father was a shoemaker, Michael recalled.

"I take it from your accent that your childhood was spent in Germany?"

"Yes, in Hamburg."

Mendel was from Dresden.

"I admire a talent like yours," Michael said.

"Thank you. But I understand that you have a talent of your own. You are a writer?" Zell asked, changing the subject from himself.

"Yes, I am."

"Now, that is a talent I wish I had. Tell me, you come to Israel to do a book? Is it about Israel?"

"I'm here to gather research material for my book, but it's not about Israel, exactly. It's rather complicated to describe the overall story quickly, but one of my major characters will be an Israeli agent working for the Mossad," Michael invented. "His background will be developed rather extensively, going into his family and experiences during the war. I plan to take him through those experiences to Palestine and the forming of the state of Israel. I'm not entirely sure how I want to handle it, yet. That part of his background is quite flexible. I was hoping to pick up ideas while conducting my research here."

"And how long do you plan to remain in Israel?" Zell asked.

"I hope that a few weeks should be enough," Michael responded.

Zell nodded. "And why have you chosen En Gedi?" he asked.

"It was recommended to me, actually. I have very little knowledge of Israel. I'm not even sure if En Gedi is the best place to begin," Michael replied.

"Anywhere that a Jew is willing to talk is a good place to begin," Zell said, smiling. "How may we help you?"

"Well, I guess tonight it would be best just to talk about Israel a little bit. If you have time tomorrow, perhaps you could describe some of your experiences to me."

"Do you mean experiences in the concentration camps?" Zell asked.

"No, there's already a wealth of information available on that. What I had in mind was more on what happened immediately after the war and the actual coming to Palestine. I need to know what it was like during the early days of struggle in the fight to establish Israel."

Zell nodded again. "Yes, I can tell you about my experiences. There are many stories that you can hear from many people. I am sure that you will find what you need during your stay."

Michael opened his duffel bag and removed a small tape recorder. "Would you mind if I record our sessions?" he asked.

"Not at all. Where would you like to begin?"

"I guess with your thoughts about Israel and En Gedi, and why you chose to come here," Michael said.

Zell thought carefully about where to begin, bringing his hands together at the fingertips in front of him.

Michael turned on the tape recorder and waited.

"I think there are a few points I should make before beginning. Points about Israel, its Jews and its Israelis," Zell said.

"You say that as if they're two separate entities," Michael commented.

"In a way, they are. There is a difference in the mind between a Jew and an Israeli. We share the same heritage and pride, but there is a difference in commitment. The Jew recognizes the religion as the state. He clings to the past as the essence of Jewish life. The Israeli, on the other hand, is a realist who turns from the past to face the dangers of the present. He recognizes that the gun is as important as the Torah to our survival. The Torah *offers* strength of character and will; the gun *is* our strength. We are a people of great determination and abounding pride. We do what we do because there is no other choice. Few men could have looked upon barren, wasted rock and envisioned what exists in En Gedi today. Fewer still would have attempted to make it possible.

"We had a long and difficult struggle to become a country, but now we are one. And we will remain one through our strength and uncompromising determination.

"As for En Gedi, we chose to come here because to us the soul of Israel is found in this life. It is a simple theory that we apply. We believe that just as our heritage is a shared thing, so must our ownership and labor be. We make a collective, cooperative effort to work this hard land. Together we share in its joys and sorrows, its gains and

423

losses, its harmony and its dangers. We are one here, in equality. You need only look at En Gedi and the very many places like it to see the success of the theory.

"For those with the will and understanding, Israel is the Promised Land. But it was never meant to be handed to us. We must make it green and make it prosper. Many come here expecting to find the milk and honey ready for the taking, only to find hard work and more hard work. Those without the heart of an Israeli find a wasteland that has been oversold to their expectations. Those that are of heart see what it can be, and what they can make it become."

"And what did you expect when you came here?" Michael asked.

Zell sat for a moment in silence before answering. "I came as a very angry young man, looking for a home. I came prepared to take it, if necessary, and to fight to keep it. That was a long time ago, but I remember the feelings quite well. It was in 1946 that I came to Palestine. It was an act of ill-fated desperation for over five hundred of us. We came on a ship, bound and determined to run the British blockade. That ship was named the *Maiden of Hope . . .*"

It was difficult for Michael to sleep that night. He had begun to feel certain that Zell was Abraham Mendel when he had first seen the collection of glass pieces. But his story was so convincing and filled with details of the life of Benjamin Zell that he seriously began to wonder. Details about friends and relatives lost in the war, even about efforts to locate them years later, only to learn that he alone remained.

Michael would be spending time with Zell tomorrow. He knew that if he was to learn the truth, he would have to force the conversation in the direction he wanted it to go. He felt uncomfortable about the dishonesty he had used on Zell to this point, though he recognized the necessity of it. But a great deal more was at stake here than personal feelings, his own or Zell's. Tomorrow would tell the tale, and he would be going back to France either with or without what he had come for.

It was late morning when Michael met with Benjamin Zell for the second time. They met again at his apartment.

"I hope that you do not mind that we meet so late in the day," Zell said. "I had some duties to attend to at the vegetable packing plant."

"It's no problem, Mr. Zell. Any time that's convenient for you is acceptable to me," Michael said.

424

"What would you like to talk about? Perhaps you have questions?" Zell asked.

"Well, I've been thinking a lot about my character. I guess I'd like to try a few things out on you. Perhaps you could just give me some suggestions on certain points, or tell me if something about him seems unrealistic. He's a very complicated fellow, and I don't want to make his past seem too incredible." Michael said.

Zell nodded. "Yes, I will try," he said with sincere interest.

"First, I want him to have some kind of double life. In other words, he is living under a different identity now than he had before coming to Israel."

"He will be a criminal?" Zell asked.

"No, not exactly a criminal, although I haven't fully worked out what it is that he's trying to hide from. When I do, I'll tie it into the story somehow. Of course, he'll have survived the camps, perhaps a work camp or two and one death camp that he will have been sent to near the end of the war. I was thinking of using either Dachau or Auschwitz. You were in . . . ?"

"Auschwitz," Zell answered.

"I need to find something special about him that will have been a big factor in his survival all of these years," Michael said.

"I do not think I understand," Zell interrupted. "What do you mean by 'something special'?"

"Well, something quite unique like . . . like . . . maybe a skill of some kind that was important to the Germans in the camps he was in."

"Many people survived without any special skills at all," Zell commented. "Survival became a skill in itself."

Michael nodded pensively. "Yes, but it lacks drama. I need something that I can build into the story."

"Make him a doctor," Zell suggested. "Doctors were very important to the Germans. Many prisoner doctors even helped them with their terrible experiments on humans, and the sterilizations of young men and women."

"Yes, but I think that it's too obvious. It has also been well used in American fiction. I need something else. What other kinds of professions were useful to the Germans?" Michael asked.

"Most skilled trades—electricians, carpenters, masons, plumbers, nurses. There were many. But these would offer very little in the way of dramatic effect. Perhaps a scientist, like a chemist, or a physicist?"

Michael nodded. "Yes, that's more like what I need. I can really do something with that. A few others also came to mind while you were speaking. I had come up with a person having strong black-market ties, or an art expert. Perhaps even a forger. They would all have good possibilities, don't you think?"

Zell nodded agreeably, without comment.

Michael raised his eyes upward, pretending to be deep in thought. "Of course, the art expert would be interesting. He could have knowledge of stolen treasures never found after the war, or even of expert duplications of certain masterpieces. Hidden treasures are always interesting. On the other hand, the forger has promise, too. He could have knowledge of the existence of counterfeit currency plates. Perfect plates. Or even a huge sum of printed money that had been hidden away. Or, better yet, the identities of high-ranking Germans who used his services to arrange for their escapes. Would they have used prisoners for counterfeiting and making false identity papers?" Michael asked.

"Counterfeiting, yes," Zell answered. "Several camps had counterfeiting sections. I believe that Auschwitz even had one. I had also heard that one was in operation at Theresienstadt. However, I doubt that the Germans would have trusted a prisoner to prepare identities that they would be hiding behind after the war. That would have been too great a risk. And if they had, such a man would have not been permitted to live. The art expert, in all likelihood, would have been killed as well," the Israeli commented.

"Unless the forger's services were in demand right up to the end. He could have survived," Michael said.

"Not highly possible," Zell remarked pensively.

"And he could have easily prepared another identity for himself to hide under after the war, couldn't he? Yes, I like that. Hiding to keep himself alive, afraid that if his real identity came out, he'd be killed by those he had helped escape in order to save themselves. That could be tied in a dozen ways. In fact, when attempts were made to run the British blockade of Palestine, weren't false identity papers provided?" Michael asked.

"Yes, they were. However, they were surrendered to the Mossad Aliyah Bet upon safe arrival in Palestine for their reuse. Of course, those identity papers on people caught by the British were seized to prevent their further use."

"My character could have prepared a secret set to use upon his arrival after turning the one set in, couldn't he?" Michael tried.

Zell nodded. "A possibility," he said, his eyes narrowing slightly.

They were interrupted by the ringing of the telephone.

"Excuse me one moment," Zell said, then left the room.

Michael used the break to examine the glass miniatures and the larger pieces. They were absolutely breathtaking in their detail and execution. Only a master could have done such fine work.

"I'm very sorry," Zell said, returning to the room, "A minor problem at the plant. Continue, please."

"By the way, I meant to ask you earlier if you made these beautiful glass pieces?"

Zell stared at Michael for a moment. A sudden flash of suspicion crossed his face, then quickly vanished. But it wasn't before Michael had taken its measure.

"No, I did not. I have acquired them gradually over the years. There is a man in Tel Aviv who makes them," he answered.

"They're magnificent. You'll have to give me his name. I'd like to bring a few like these back home," Michael said.

"Certainly. But I warn you, he has become very expensive. I haven't been able to afford one in years."

"Well, maybe I'll get just one, then," Michael said. "The man who made these has a most unique talent, wouldn't you say?"

Zell leveled a hard stare at Michael. "Who are you?" he asked. "And why are you here?"

Michael looked back into the serious eyes. There was no fear in them. He was glad to see that.

"My name *is* Michael Gladieux."

"But you are not here to research a book."

Michael shook his head slowly. "No, I'm not," he replied.

"Why have you come to En Gedi to see me?"

"I'm looking for a man. A man that I must find for a very important reason."

"And you think that *I* am this man?"

"Yes, I do."

"You think that I am the forger?" Zell asked with a short grin.

"I believe that you were once known as Paul Wilno."

Zell's reaction to hearing the name was obvious in his eyes. "And why is it important that you find this Paul Wilno?" he asked.

"It's not Paul Wilno that I'm after."

Zell looked at Michael with a confused expression. "You say that you know I was the forger you described earlier, and that my name was once Paul Wilno. You say that you must find this man for a very important reason, and then you say that you are not looking for him. What are you saying?" Zell asked.

"I need to find this man for two reasons, actually. One is to tell him something that I'm sure he will want to know. The other is to see if he can tell me something that is of great importance to my country, to Israel, and to the whole world."

"You are not writing a book, my friend, you are living one," Zell said. "I am sorry, but I still do not understand you."

"I mean you no harm. I also have no intention of trying to make anyone else aware of the fact that you are not Benjamin Zell. You must believe that."

Zell stared at the young American without comment.

"You were once Paul Wilno, were you not?" Michael asked.

There was a great struggle behind the eyes of Benjamin Zell as he stared at Michael. "Yes, I was once Paul Wilno," he admitted. It seemed to cause him physical pain to say the words. "But I am no longer. I have been Benjamin Zell for the last thirty-six years."

"Thank you. Thank you very much for your honesty," Michael said with deep sincerity.

"I am not proud of the things I did," Zell went on. "But I am alive. A man will do many things to stay alive."

"Mr. Zell, you don't have to explain to me. I know about men faced with survival, and what they're capable of."

Zell squinted hard at the young American. "Then what is it that you *do not* want with Paul Wilno?"

"I am looking for a young boy."

"A boy?" Zell repeated as though totally perplexed.

"A boy from Dresden."

Zell's face went white and his jaw dropped open. There was a look of utter disbelief on his face.

"A boy who was wonderfully talented and had the finest glass-maker in all of Germany for his teacher."

"No! I know nothing of a boy from Dresden," Zell said, an edge of anger in his voice.

"A boy who left Germany, taking his little sister, Keva, with him to escape the pitiful treatment of Jews."

"No! You're wrong . . . about me. I have never been in Dresden."

"A boy who went to Poland to live with his Uncle Yakov, until Germany invaded that country, ending the short happiness he had found."

"Stop this!" Zell said, his voice rising.

"A boy who tried to escape with his sister again, getting as far as a forest outside of Tomaszów. He met a band of Gypsies there."

428

"No! No!" Zell shouted, his chest heaving, his eyes growing wild.

"A boy who awoke the next morning to find that his little sister had been taken from him."

"No! No . . . no . . . no," Zell said, his voice becoming a near whimper.

Michael reached into his shirt and pulled out the pendant. He held it out to Zell's face. "A boy who gave this to his sister. She's alive, Mendel. Your sister is alive."

"Keva! Keva!" Zell cried, clutching the pendant and pulling it to his chest, snapping the chain from around Michael's neck. Zell went to his knees, weeping.

Michael knelt beside him, placing a hand on the man's shoulder. 'Barbu Denska kept her safe all those years, raising her as his own daughter. If he had not taken her, she would have died in the war."

Zell looked up, his eyes red and suddenly bloodshot, tears streaming down his face.

"She's had a good life. She has a fine husband and beautiful children of her own now." Michael reached into his shirt pocket and pulled out the picture that had been taken by Nicholas Tarnes.

Zell took it, his hands trembling, his eyes straining to see through the tears. "She's beautiful," he said, sniffling like a child with a cold.

"She has no memory of that day," Michael told him. "She's alive and happy in a way that few people can ever hope to be. You need not feel guilt or pain any longer."

Zell stared up into Michael's eyes and smiled. "How? How did you find me?" he asked.

"With much difficulty, I can assure you."

Zell was breathing deeply now, regaining his composure. "You said *two* reasons. This was the first, and I will be eternally grateful to you for it. Now what is the other reason, and how can I help you?"

"I only hope that you can. It has to do with this pendant. This is not the pendant you gave to Keva. It is one of five identical ones known to exist, including your sister's. Did you help make it?" Michael asked.

"Yes. Yes, the master and I made them all ourselves. That was in 1936. But the pendant I gave to Keva was an extra one, secretly made by Herr Haupte."

"Then they don't know that it exists."

"That is correct," Zell said, nodding. "They wished for the utmost secrecy. I can still remember the night that they came for them. It was snowing very heavily. It was in December," Zell answered.

"Who came for them?"

"Two German officers. One very old, and one young. A general and a lieutenant."

"Do you remember any names?"

"I never heard their names."

"Do you know who they represented?"

Zell shook his head that he did not.

"Can you tell me anything more about them?" Michael pressed.

Zell thought for a long moment. "The young one had hate in his eyes. He was very suspicious of me. I could tell from the way he looked at me with those cold, hard eyes. He had an ugly arrogance about him, obvious from the moment I first saw him. Upper-class Prussian Junker, complete with dueling scar and riding crop."

"Dueling scar? Where?" Michael asked excitedly.

"Right here," Zell said, running his finger along the line on his left cheek.

Immel! Michael fell back from his knees into a sitting position. That was it! The connection! Immel was a part of it. He was the contact! He could even know the names of the remaining two identities in the triumvirate.

Michael hurriedly looked through his things and found the picture of Rudolf Immel standing beside Gabrielle Dupuy.

"Is this the man?" Michael asked, praying that the memory of Abraham Mendel would be clear enough to remember the face from so long ago.

Zell took the picture and studied it, then handed it back to Michael. "That is the man," he said.

"You've helped me more than I could ever tell you," said Michael, reiief and exhilaration apparent in his voice.

"You said that this will help your country and mine?" Zell asked.

"Yes, it will. I can't tell you more right now, but I promise that if I ever can, I will come to Israel personally to tell you about it."

"It has to do with the people holding the pendants?"

"Four pendant holders have already been found, and you have just helped put us nearer to finding the final two," Michael replied.

Zell shook his head. "No, not two," he said. "You said that four have been found, and that two remain."

"That's right," Michael said.

"No, that is not right. You see, it was not six pendants that were made for them. It was *twelve.*"

Chapter 43

P HEAGAN," came the voice over the long-distance line from France.

"Damn, but your people are good!" Michael said on the phone from En Gedi.

"You seem to be in a good mood, which can mean either that you've found what we're after, or you found yourself a hot little sabra to help while away your time under an olive tree. Which is it?" Pheagan asked.

"We found Mendel," Michael answered triumphantly.

"Mendel! It was really him!"

"You bet. And I don't know how you guys found him," Michael said. "It was just unbelievable."

"Was Zell able to tell you anything of value?"

"Yes, he was. And it's all crystal clear now. Immel is the contact. He's the man we've been looking for. I finally figured out why we kept missing on the code name. Leopard was never meant to be a person. It was a place. Leopard's name was Paul Romenay. Immel lived outside of Cuisery—which is only a hop, skip, and a jump away from the town of Romenay. There's no doubt about it. Mendel even identified him in a picture as being one of two men who picked up the finished pendants in 1936. He was a part of the Salamandra. Do you know what that means?"

"Yes, it means that we may get all the identities. The whole triumvirate in one swoop."

"You're right, but not entirely," Michael said.

"What do you mean?"

"I mean it may be possible to learn the identities of the entire Committee of Trinity, if, in fact, Immel knows them, and if we find him first."

"And the not entirely part?"

"The Trinity Committee, in all likelihood, is not a triumvirate. There were twelve pendants made besides the one held by Keva Wolenska."

"*Twelve!*" Pheagan gasped.

"That's right, twelve. That leaves seven unaccounted for, assuming that Immel is a holder. The Committee is a great deal larger than you thought."

"Jesus Christ!" Pheagan muttered. "We could never have learned it all through Falloux. At best, we might have established one, maybe two more identities. That would have left us thinking we'd nailed the coffin shut, and we wouldn't even have been close."

"That's right. You'd have hurt them plenty, which is what you originally set out to do. But now you have a real chance to strike a death blow," Michael told him.

"If we find Immel," Pheagan said, his voice pensive.

"What's the situation with him?"

"Still no trace of him. We got a little lucky, though. The news that the body found in the house wasn't his didn't come out until today. It gave us an extra day, although we haven't been able to take best advantage of it. They'll probably lose another day going over ground we've already covered. That may still let us find him first."

"Listen, why don't you contact the Collard brothers. They may be able to help. There are still Defiance people willing to do what they can. I think, if you explain the situation to them regarding Immel, and that you need him alive, they could be valuable. You wouldn't have to tell them any of your reasons. They would do it just to help."

"We'll try it. We'll have an opportunity to see them tomorrow. I don't expect that you could know, but St. Jude committed suicide right after you left his *manade.*"

"I . . . had a talk with him. I told him we knew the truth about him being Z. I expected it would happen. Has his death been connected to the collaboration?"

"No. He left no letter. Nothing. My men set it up to look as though it was accidental. They set out some cleaning materials, and with the clip out of the gun, it looked like he was preparing to clean it when it went off accidentally. The police believed it, too."

"How is Nicole taking it?" Michael asked.

432

"Very hard, Mike. Claude is being buried tomorrow on the *manade*. We're taking her in to attend."

"I understand. You have no choice," Michael said.

"Danny and Gabrielle want to be there as well," Pheagan told him.

"I can understand their wanting to, but I think it would be too dangerous to bring them back into sight right now," Michael objected.

"I know. I'm afraid they're both pretty insistent on it, though. We can have plenty of protection available, plus there will be hundreds of people there. It's a definite risk, but I think it's one we can handle," Pheagan said, with more confidence than he inwardly felt. He knew that the risk would be a grave one, and that Demy would be a lot smarter this time around.

Michael thought for a moment. "Well, I don't like it. I hate to take such an unnecessary risk. But they're both stubborn as hell. When they want to do something, they're going to do it. I guess it'll have to be all right."

"Perhaps for Nicole's sake, too, it might be best. Especially since you can't be here."

"What time is it set for?" Michael asked.

"There's a church service set for nine A.M. I'll get Nicole and your family in and out as quickly as possible. They shouldn't be exposed for more than a few hours at the most. And besides, I would think that Demy will be busy enough trying to run down Immel."

"Okay. Just be careful. And, Bill, try to protect Nicole from the truth about her father, will you? There's no need for her to be saddled with that for the rest of her life."

"Sure thing, Mike. See you tomorrow. Have a good trip, and don't worry about things on this end. We'll keep it tight."

"I hope so. See you tomorrow."

SAINTES-MARIES-DE-LA-MER: The security aspects of covering the funeral of Claude St. Jude were a nightmare for the entire time that Pheagan's charges were in Saintes-Maries-de-la-Mer. The church was mobbed with people, the streets outside were packed, and even the procession route through the city had been lined with the many people who had known St. Jude and wished to pay their final respects.

Pheagan hoped desperately that if Demy or any of his men were observing the proceedings, it was from a distance. An up-close observation of Michael's stand-in would certainly not hold up to someone who knew the face well. At a distance, however, the resemblance was a great deal stronger, especially since the stand-in was wearing Michael's clothes and was almost always at Nicole's side.

Pheagan breathed easier only when the party reached the *manade* where a secure perimeter had been established using local police, St Jude's hired men, and Pheagan's people. He was sure that events from this point on were controllable.

It was, perhaps, the knowledge that St. Jude had been the traitor Z that afforded Gabrielle the strength to be at Nicole's side almost constantly. Both she and Michael's stand-in maintained an almost continuous physical contact with Nicole, who still needed crutches. Gabrielle could see in Nicole the same picture of grief that she herself had been at the death of her own father. The tears streaking Gabrielle's face were more for the beautiful daughter of St. Jude than for the man.

Danny hovered close by most of the time, keeping a watchful eye over the women, but also scanning the faces of the hundreds of people looking for Demy. He didn't put it past Demy to make an attempt at such a moment of weakness.

The Collard brothers reported that they believed Immel to be out of the Cuisery area, though they could offer no suggestion as to where he might be, unless he had made his way to Switzerland. They did not expect that he would stay in France longer than he had to. It was their bet that he would make for the protection of Germany and old friends as quickly as possible.

Jacques Collard stood beside Pheagan during the graveside ceremonies. They were a good distance behind the throng of people Danny was with the women, as was Lucien Collard.

"It was him, was it not?" Jacques Collard asked Pheagan in heavily accented English.

Pheagan nodded in response.

"It was a suicide, then?"

"Yes, but the official version will remain unchanged. And I think it best that the fact of his guilt remain buried with him," Pheagan said "It would serve no one to have it otherwise. Your mystery is solved and a form of sentence has been carried out. There has been enough pain and shame."

"And Michael, he is agreeing with this?"

Pheagan nodded again. "He wants it this way."

"And the honor of Christian, will that be satisfied?" Collard asked.

"Yes, it will. We have the identities of the people responsible. It will all be taken care of very soon to the complete satisfaction of Michael and the memory of his father," Pheagan responded.

"To think that so long after the war it would still cost this, the lives of Christian and Edna-Marie. It is too sad. But it is finally over," Jacques said.

"Over for you, perhaps. We still have to find Immel."

"I think that you may never find him," Collard said.

"We'll find him, all right. We have to, and we won't stop looking until we do."

"Then we will continue to help you. If he is still in France, it may be to the north that he has gone, to the part that he would know best. France is an easy country for a man to hide in when he does not wish to be found."

When he does not wish to be found. The accented phrase of Jacques Collard played back in Pheagan's mind. Perhaps that was not the case at all. Maybe he wanted to be found by the right people. If so, then he could be quite near, waiting for the right moment to make his whereabouts known.

Renaud Demy raised the powerful binoculars and studied the scene around the burial site from his concealed position on a high knoll almost five hundred yards away. He watched the figures closest to Nicole St. Jude. They had all come into the open again, just as he had expected they would. The fools! It would be their last mistake, he thought.

He switched his field of view from the gravesite to the helicopter that had flown them in. It sat, watchfully attended, its big rotor blades drooping from their weight. Well planned on their part, he thought, to use the helicopter. He had watched them leave the ranch of Claude St. Jude on the night of the suicide. It had been a surprising move to him then. But his observations that night had made his plan today possible. He was expecting the helicopter. In fact, he was hoping for it. He would soon close out a part of Pierre Falloux's problem, he thought. Then that would leave only Immel to deal with once and for all.

Grief-stricken, Nicole was led away from the gravesite by Gabrielle and Michael's stand-in, who was playing the part perfectly. Despite the shock of the deception on the part of Michael and Pheagan, Danny and Gabrielle played their parts admirably.

The party retired to the house for about thirty minutes before appearing again. Pheagan wanted to spend as little time as necessary

435

away from the safe compound he had arranged for the protection o
the family. They were just a one-hour helicopter ride away from com
plete security. The sooner they left, the better Pheagan would like it.

"When is Mike due back?" Danny asked as they walked towar
the waiting craft, its rotors now limbering up for the flight.

"He should be airborne by now," Pheagan said in response. "He'l
be touching down in France in about four hours. I'll have you al
together about an hour after that."

"How did he make out?"

Pheagan wondered just how much Danny actually knew or ha
figured out for himself. He had proven to be a smart and capabl
operator. Pheagan allowed himself to toy with the thought of ap
proaching Danny on behalf of Sub Rosa. They could always use me
of his caliber.

"He hit the jackpot," Pheagan replied.

Danny smiled widely, shaking his head. "I wouldn't have playe
the odds of that happening with *your* money."

"Sometimes we get lucky. It had to happen sooner or later the wa
we were going."

"Where does that leave us?"

Pheagan thought for a second. "That depends on whether we fin
Immel or not. If we don't, then we play a waiting game. But for al
practical purposes, your part in it is over. You and Gabrielle can g
home shortly knowing that you've done what you set out to do. Yo
did a fine job with so little to work with."

"And Mike?"

"That's up to him. I'd like to see him out of it, too. But I don'
think he'll buy that. He's going to want to deliver the coup de grac
personally. I can't blame him for wanting to," Pheagan said as the
neared the helicopter.

The sounds of the helicopter's engine and rotors picked up sharpl
as the party began boarding.

"I'd like to be able to help, to kind of look out for him," Dann
said above the noise.

Pheagan clapped him on the back. "Don't worry about him. I
there's anyone who doesn't need looking after it's him. Besides, I'v
already arranged for a more than ample baby-sitting service. He'll b
fine. Before you know it, you'll all be stateside trying to figure out wha
to do with all the money you have. This job is just about over. The res
is a mop-up," he exaggerated.

Danny climbed into the craft, taking an outboard seat. Gabriell
was across from him, her arm consolingly around Nicole.

436

Nicole sat quietly, her head down, her eyes swollen and red. She couldn't understand *why* her life had been so affected by the arrival of these people from America. Everything had happened so fast. She had met a man and felt the beauty of falling in love, survived the violent attack on their home, and seen the death of the noble and gallant Edna-Marie DeBussey; and now she attended the funeral of her own father.

Gabrielle squeezed her gently, offering soft words of consolation.

Nicole leaned her head against Gabrielle's shoulder, her sobbing starting softly again.

"I know, I know, It'll pass, Nicole. Just let it all come out," Gabrielle coaxed gently.

Danny had been watching his wife. It was wonderful to see her strength returned to her enough to help Nicole through her grief. He smiled inwardly, and knew just how much he loved Gabrielle. He was glad that this nightmare was ending for them. It would be good to get home, to be with the girls again, in America again, and alive again.

The helicopter lurched slightly as it rose from the ground. It hung a moment, turned ninety degrees, then started on a low course that would take them over the northwestern corner of Les Impériaux Réserve.

Renaud Demy lowered the binoculars, convinced that the entire party had boarded the helicopter. He placed the binoculars on the ground to his left, then turned back to his right to the Soviet SA-7 GRAIL man-portable missile. He lifted the one-piece, two-component missile and launcher, armed it, and raised it into firing position. He began tracking the helicopter moving slowly at low altitude across his field of view.

Demy placed the sights on the target, tracked it patiently for a few additional moments, then fired. The *shhwompff* of the rocket and the thirteen-meter backblast went unnoticed within the perimeter of the St. Jude *manade*.

The helicopter made a sudden violent diving maneuver as Pheagan heard the frantic alert of the pilot.

"Smoke signature, ground level, nine o'clock!"

In that one instant, Danny knew with horrible certainty what was happening. He had barely enough time to look at Gabrielle and her frightened reaction to the sudden diving maneuver of the craft. Barely enough time to think how much he loved her and about his beautiful children.

The explosion and concussion were tremendous as the side and back of the helicopter disintegrated in the violent red-orange ball of fire.

To those on the ground, it was an awesome sight as almost half the craft simply vanished in the blast. The rest of it spun and tumbled in hideous motion as it plummeted the short distance to earth, slamming to the ground amid the tall reedy grasses of the Camargue.

There had been no time to react on board the craft. For those not killed instantly, there had been only the realization of the rending explosion, followed immediately by the helpless tumbling descent and the crash.

There had been no secondary explosion on impact, though a violent spray of flame seemed to cover nearly everything. Pheagan found himself on the ground, still strapped to his seat about sixty feet from the burning wreckage. There was intense pain in his left arm and shoulder as he struggled to free himself. Just as he rolled out of the detached seat, he saw a dazed figure crawling out of the burning heap. It was Nicole.

He raced toward her as fast as he was able, chancing the possibility of a secondary explosion. He got to her and grabbed her with his good arm and began dragging her away. He looked back over his shoulder for other signs of life, but could see none.

He managed to get her a safe distance away, then started back. He wasn't halfway when he heard a loud hissing sound, and then the wreckage blew up, the force of the explosion knocking him off his feet.

He rolled to his stomach, balled up and covered his head as the spray of debris hit. He then crawled as rapidly as he could to escape any spreading of flames. When safely away, he turned to view the blazing wreckage. It was then that he noticed that another body had been thrown clear as he had been. He hurried toward it. It was Gabrielle, and she was covered with flames.

He threw sand and dirt on the body and began rolling her along the ground slapping at the burning clothing. He managed to extinguish the flames and quickly felt for a pulse in the neck. She was still alive.

There were two more muffled explosions, then just the sounds of the fire. Pheagan fell back into a sitting position, his right hand holding his injured left shoulder, blood streaming down the side of his face. He stared into the hypnotic inferno that was once their helicopter, knowing that the rest were beyond hope. Six people hadn't shared the miracle that had spared Nicole, Gabrielle, and himself. He had seen Michael's stand-in literally blown apart when the missile hit, along with one of his other men who simply vanished with the back of the helicopter.

438

Tears of rage came to his eyes as he saw the figure that had been Danny Preston, still strapped in his seat, engulfed in flame and ravaged by the explosions to a point that he no longer looked human. He looked down at the pitiful limp figure of Gabrielle and knew that she wouldn't live. He looked back to Nicole, who was mercifully unconscious now. She seemed remarkably intact, and he knew that she would survive.

He wiped the stinging tears from his face and breathed deeply, the shock beginning to set in. He slumped back as he heard the first sounds of help coming. The sky began swirling and closing in, and he could feel himself slipping. But one thought stayed in his mind. Michael Gladieux would be landing in France in four hours. What could he say to him? How could he explain his failure to keep Michael's family alive? He almost wished he had not survived to face that moment.

Chapter 44

"**Y**ES, what is it?" Pierre Falloux said gruffly into the phone, his anxiety venting itself in irritability.

"This is your friend," came the easy reply.

Falloux swallowed nervously. His very existence could depend on this news. "Well? Well?" he demanded, his hands and face sweating.

"It's finished," Demy announced calmly.

"All of them?" Falloux asked before Demy had stopped talking.

"Yes, all of them. And the girl."

Falloux let out a breath of relief. His cold sweaty hands were shaking as he unconsciously reached for the pen in front of him and began tapping it on the desk pad. "You are sure? There is no doubt?" he questioned.

"Positive. They were airborne when the SA-7 made contact."

"Did you make a sight inspection?"

Demy frowned at the foolishness of the question. "Of course not. The scene was crawling with police and interested parties. There wasn't time or the need for such foolishness. I told you, it was an airborne hit."

Falloux was silent, his mind trying to determine the significance of the presence of the helicopter.

"What do you make of the helicopter?"

"Some kind of security arrangement contracted after the unsuccessful event at the house," Demy replied.

Hired protection. Falloux deliberated on the possibility. The Americans could certainly have afforded to hire a private security service. Their sudden appearance right after the attack fit well, too. Even taking them out to a place of safety made sense.

"It may even have been the saint who hired the security service to look after the girl, as well as the family," Demy suggested.

Yes, that would be like Claude to do that, especially in light of the conversation they had had, Falloux thought. That was it, it had to be. He was merely trying to protect his daughter. And his death could have been accidental, as the newspapers were claiming.

If St. Jude had left the confession he had threatened to leave, it would have been a big item in the news, and the police would, no doubt, have already paid a visit to Pont du Château. Falloux began to breathe easily once again.

"Whatever the reason," Demy said, "it is beyond importance now. Your problems with the family are over. All that remains is to find the German, then the matter will be completely settled."

Falloux pushed the pen aimlessly as he digested Demy's last words. One more obstacle, then he would have beaten his long odds. One more man to find and remove, and he would have demonstrated his ability to emerge from the entire mess completely secure.

"How long will it take to find him?" Falloux asked.

"Not long. If I've figured him right, it could be very soon. There will be no doubt left this time."

"Good," Falloux said with a relieved smile. "Find him, my friend—and take proper care of him."

The Sub Rosa Lear set down sleekly on the runway in Fréjorgues, just southeast of Montpellier. It taxied toward the commercial terminal, then veered to the south toward a waiting Mercedes limousine bearing diplomatic plates and embassy flags, stopping about fifty feet from the car. Two men got out of the vehicle and approached the aircraft as its door opened, folding down into a ready stepway.

Michael stepped out and hesitated, seeing the two strange faces. He looked to the car in search of Pheagan and saw no one but the driver. He didn't like it.

"Mr. Gladieux, we've been sent by Tripper," the man closest to Michael said.

Michael remained motionless on the steps, surveying the faces in front of him. "Tripper was supposed to meet me. Where is he?"

"He's been detained in Arles," the man replied.

"Arles? There's no reason for him to be in Arles."

The two men looked at one another, then back to Michael. "I'm afraid that there's been a problem, Mr. Gladieux. It's vital that you reach Arles immediately."

Michael squinted down at the two men, still not trusting them, "What do you mean by a problem?"

"There's been another attack."

"Attack!" Michael repeated with a fearful anxiety. "When? What happened?"

"It happened today in Saintes-Maries-de-la-Mer, right after the funeral of Claude St. Jude. They were on their way out when the helicopter was hit by a man-portable missile. I'm sorry," the man said.

Michael stared at him with an expression of pained disbelief.

"There's no time to waste. Your sister is still alive, but her condition is gravely critical. There isn't much time."

"And Danny?" Michael asked, almost in a state of shock as he began moving toward the car.

"I'm sorry," the man said, shaking his head. "He never knew what hit him. Tripper and the girl also made it by some miracle, though both were injured. Six other people weren't so lucky, including the one standing in for you. The official release stated that all on board were killed."

Michael was crushed by the news. Everything around him blurred as he reached the car and slumped into the back seat. Danny dead! Gabrielle dying! It wasn't possible. He didn't fight back the tears that began flooding his eyes. Only one thing was important now. That was to get to his sister while she was still alive.

The diplomatic status of the limousine allowed it to speed with immunity toward Arles.

A cruel memory played in Michael's head as the sights outside the car blurred by unnoticed. He recalled those days in Vietnam when he seemed to enjoy a kind of immortality, while those around him died with alarming regularity. Had he brought that same luck to France with him? he wondered. And had it just claimed those most dear to him?

He felt as if he was in a bad dream, his mind screaming out to be awakened. Please, it can't be true! Not Gabrielle! Not Danny! God no . . . not them.

He thought about their children as he wiped the tears from his face. Those beautiful children. They were so young—too young to be left alone. They'd never remember their parents when they grew up. It was so unfair. He should have insisted on going to France alone. Damn it! *Damn it!*

The limousine pulled to the curb in front of the hospital in Arles. Michael opened the door and sprinted in, his escort close behind. Jacques and Lucien Collard were waiting for him inside the doorway.

"Come, quickly," Jacques said without greeting. The three men turned and hurried through the lobby and up a flight of stairs. Collard pointed the way as they entered the hallway and Michael went on at a run. He moved swiftly down the hallway, seeing Pheagan standing at the end of it, in front of the doors to the intensive care unit.

Pheagan looked a mess. His head was bandaged, his left ear was under a huge pile of gauze and tape. His left arm was tightly bound to his side. His face had bruises and minor cuts, and reddened areas where he had been burned. His right hand was also heavily bandaged from the burns he had suffered while putting out the fire on Gabrielle.

The eye contact between them was an entire conversation. Pheagan's eyes were filled with sorrow and defeat, apology and guilt. It hadn't been his fault, but he had failed to protect Michael's family as he had promised to do.

Michael stopped in front of Pheagan. His red, bloodshot eyes weren't accusing, exactly, though Pheagan's guilt made him think they were.

"How is she?"

"She's holding on."

"How . . . bad?" Michael asked, his eyes searching for the miracle.

Pheagan shook his head. "She's not expected to live, Mike."

Michael steeled himself to the truth of the situation, and nodded. He walked past Pheagan through the doors into the intensive care room.

It was a fair-sized room with six-foot-high partitions separating beds. There were about eight beds in the room, only three of them occupied. He spotted Gabrielle's bed and walked over to it. A doctor and one of the nurses turned away from the bed as Michael approached, the second nurse making adjustments in the intravenous drip rate.

The doctor finished giving some instructions to the nurse, then looked up at Michael, who towered over him. "You are her brother?" he asked.

Michael nodded.

The doctor put a hand on Michael's arm and coaxed him a few steps away from the bed.

"How long does she have?" Michael asked, his voice strained.

The doctor shrugged. "It could be any time. She's still breathing well on her own. That's a good sign. We can put her on a respirator if it gets difficult. We're just trying to keep her comfortable, but I doubt that she feels anything."

"There's no hope?" Michael asked.

"Where there is life, there is always hope. I say that as a man who has seen many strange things happen. As a doctor speaking to you in a purely clinical sense, I say that there is very little. She has burns over forty percent of her body, severe internal injuries and bleeding, possible skull fracture, and many severe lacerations. She may also lose the right leg if she survives," he replied.

Michael closed his eyes and blew out a long slow breath. Then he looked past the doctor to the bed. "Can she hear anything?" he asked, his voice almost breaking.

"She doesn't respond in any way. But I would suggest that you try talking to her. It is possible that she will hear you, even though she is unable to let you know that she can."

"Is there anything else that you can do for her?"

The doctor shook his head. "Not really. As long as her heart beats, we can keep her alive. But right now she's doing it all on her own. I think that we should leave it that way for as long as we can. In the end, I doubt that heroic measures will change matters."

Michael nodded, a fresh flood of tears welling up in his eyes.

"Talk to her. Let her know that you are here and that you will stay with her," the doctor said. "If she hears you, it could lift her will to live."

Michael thanked the doctor and approached the bed. He bent down close to examine her face. Her left eye was completely closed, the right one opened just a slit. The eye was moving from side to side across the opening. It would stop occasionally, then start again after only a moment. Her face was swollen, and there was a tube in her nose, through which darkened blood and fluids were passing into a large bottle beneath the bed. Her breathing was loud and mechanical, the lower jaw dropping with each inward gasp. He had seen enough death to know that he was looking at it again.

He bent closer and kissed her cheek.

"I'm here Gabby. It's Michael. I'm here to take care of you You're going to be fine, Baby, just fine," he said, the last words choking off as he said them.

He looked into the right eye as it moved aimlessly. The pupil was about halfway dilated. He stared into it, and it stopped, as though to look at him. He watched the pupil for signs of contraction, but there were none. The eye held him for a moment without focusing, then began its movement again.

He wanted to talk to her, but couldn't without crying. So he waited until his composure returned.

Looking at her, he thought of his father, of how he hadn't had the chance to see him alive one last time to tell him that he loved him, and of all the other things he wished he had said. He thanked God that Gabrielle had lived long enough for him to get to her. He would not let this opportunity go to waste.

He breathed deeply, until he felt his control return, then began stroking her hair and holding her left hand.

"Gabby, honey, I want you to know that I'm here with you, and that I love you. I think that you can hear me, Gabby. I love you, Sis," he said, then was forced to stop once more by the wave of emotion sweeping him.

He let out a little silent laugh, and kissed her cheek again. "You know, Sis, I was just remembering way back when we were little, to that Christmas when Dad dressed up like Santa Claus for you. I remember you being so surprised to learn that Santa spoke English with a French accent. I even remember what you got for Christmas that year. It's all you talked about for months and you must have written a dozen letters to Santa, to be sure he wouldn't forget. It was wonderful."

It seemed like hours that he sat and talked to her, holding her hand and stroking her hair. He reviewed the memories of their life together that were the most treasured and important to him, and told her how he had marveled at watching her grow, becoming more beautiful each year. It was time well spent, he left nothing unsaid.

He sat silently beside her now, thinking about her. He had never had more sharing moments with her. Never felt more love.

The nurse interrupted him to take her blood pressure and temperature. The blood pressure had fallen significantly, and she was burning at 105°F inside. Funny, he thought, how she was like fire inside as her body fought for life, while she felt so cool, almost cold on the outside.

The nurse checked her left foot and toes. Michael watched as she did so, and noticed that the toenails were blue. It wasn't much longer before he noticed that her fingers and fingernails were turning blue, as well. It was death coming, claiming her slowly, from the extremities first.

"It's okay, Sis. I'm with you," he said. "It will be gentle, Baby. I promise you, it'll be gentle."

He looked at her through his blurred eyes. He could almost see her healthy smiling face through the obscured vision. He blinked, and the happy smiling face was gone. She looked so peaceful.

He listened to the mechanical sound of her loud breathing, the jaw still dropping and rising. The eye had stopped moving now and had dilated further.

He held her cold hand, while wiping away the cold sweat from her head with a towel.

"Relax, baby sister. Just relax and don't trouble yourself. I'm here, I'm here," he said. "It's going to be a piece of cake, Baby, I promise you. There's nothing to be afraid of. There's a whole new experience waiting for you to be born into. No fear, no pain. Just relax."

There was a sudden break in the rhythmic cadence of her breathing, sending an electrifying jolt through his nerves. She stopped breathing completely for about ten seconds, then began with a loud gasp and heaving of her chest, followed by a second and a third, before the steady rhythm returned.

The nurse came over immediately.

"It's close," Michael said softly.

The nurse checked her toes again and her fingers, then took a blood pressure. She looked up and nodded her agreement. "Soon," she whispered.

Michael continued caressing her forehead and hair for several minutes. The cadence of her breathing was much slower now. He kissed her forehead and cheek and put his lips close to her ear and whispered softly that he loved her.

She breathed in deeply, then out. There was a long pause. Then she breathed in deeply again, and suddenly smiled, then breathed out, the smile just as suddenly gone. Another longer pause followed, nearly ten seconds. Then she breathed again and smiled faintly once more. Then her expression went blank and a last breath eased gently from her lips. The jaw remained open, the eye fixed and fully dilated.

Michael waited for nearly a minute before bending over her to kiss her again, his eyes streaming with silent tears. "I love you," he said. "Goodbye, Gabby. My beautiful, beautiful baby sister. I'll love you forever."

Pheagan was still outside the intensive care unit when Michael walked through the doors. Michael said nothing for a few moments, his eyes telling all the story there was. He walked to a window in the small waiting room and stared out without really seeing anything. Pheagan came to his side.

"How are *you* doing?" Michael asked, breaking his silence. "You look like hell."

"I feel like it, too," Pheagan replied, then paused for a long moment. "Mike . . . I'm . . . I'm sorry that any of this happened. I said that I'd take care of them for you, and I couldn't keep that promise."

"You didn't fire the missile. But I know who did. How is Nicole?"

"She came out remarkably well. She's in a room upstairs. She'll be all right," Pheagan answered.

Michael nodded and looked back out through the window. "You know, I never felt more love for my sister than I did in there. I know that she knew I was there and could hear me talking to her. It was really something, but I could feel the moment her life left her body. I was sure that she was happy, and smiling, and telling me that she loved me, too. Sounds crazy, I guess, but I felt it as sure as I'm standing here," he said, tears running down his cheeks.

"It doesn't sound crazy. It sounds beautiful, Mike."

"It doesn't end with death, Bill. I know it now," Michael said, then turned to face Pheagan. "I want that 'kit'; can you get it?" he asked.

"It's ready, Mike. And I don't see any reason why you need to wait on Falloux any longer," Pheagan said.

Michael nodded. "Good, because I wouldn't have waited, anyway. It's time for Glad-jo to do a little night walking, and when I get back, this thing is going to be over," Michael said.

"For Falloux, I'm sure, but what about finding Immel?" Pheagan asked.

"Don't worry about Immel. He wanted to talk to me again, I know it. He's hiding someplace where he knows I'll find him," Michael said.

"Do you think you know where he is?"

"I think I do. And I know who else will be there before too long, too. And I'll be waiting.

Chapter 45

IT was nearly 11:00 P.M. in Pont du Château as Glad-jo studied the grounds of Pierre Falloux's estate in the dim light of the moon's first quarter. He paid close attention to the patterns of the security patrols moving around the perimeter of the property. Each patrol consisted of a single guard and one Doberman pinscher. There were four patrols constantly circling along the high wall surrounding the property. He timed four passes, which averaged eighteen-minute intervals. He knew from his first visit that there were probably twice that many dogs. His concern was that the dogs patrolled alone or were in the house. It wasn't that he was afraid of the dogs; no true professional is. He knew how to handle them. But with so many, if the dog made any sound whatsoever, it would alert the others, and that would be trouble.

He waited patiently, perched high in his tree behind the house, just where the wall passed closest to the terrace where they had had their meetings. Michael checked his watch, then studied the house and the various windows with lights still burning in them. Falloux could be in any one of those rooms.

He unfolded the sheet of paper, provided by Pheagan, showing the layout of the house. He was primarily interested in three rooms. The first was Falloux's bedroom on the second floor. Then came the large study on the main floor, and a smaller study on the second floor. He was biding his time, knowing that Falloux's whereabouts would be limited to one of these rooms as the hour grew later.

Michael was comfortable in his high point of observation. He was nearly invisible in the darkness, dressed completely in black, his face and hands darkened with lampblack. A small backpack held his "kit." It contained the things he needed for night operations. Everything wa specifically designed to be light and compact in size. Around his wais was a black field belt holding the Swiss SIG, the smaller Airweigh backup gun, two smoke grenades, two fragmentation grenades, clips t the Swiss SIG and the Ingram in the bag, and two coils of rope of thin diameter but great strength. To his right thigh was strapped the razor sharp KA-BAR. On his feet he wore high-topped black canvas boot with ultrathin rubber soles. They were light, flexible, silent, and af forded excellent traction on any surface.

He removed the backpack, pulled out a compact pair of infrare binoculars, and began a more detailed surveillance of the grounds. I wasn't long before he spotted the first solitary dog on patrol. It was jus as he had expected. He watched it move swiftly and nervously in seemingly erratic pattern, never coming in contact with the other pa trols. He had seen dogs like this in action before. Many of them were trained not to bark, patrolling in near perfect silence. They were the type that didn't prevent you from entering. They'd sit and even watch you do that. It was after you were in that they went to work. Getting out was your problem.

His patience paid off nicely, as he spotted two more dogs during the next thirty minutes. That made it four patrols, three independent dogs outside, and only a guess at what was inside. Michael would have wagered that at least two more dogs patrolled inside the house.

He studied the house again as more of the lights went out, and waited until the last window in the servants' wing went dark. The ligh in the window of the upstairs study continued to burn brightly. There was a small balcony outside one end of the room, with glass door leading into it. Michael studied the back of the house and the roof fo possible points of approach. He decided that the safest route would be to reach the roof at the far side of the house nearest the garages and kennels, where the darkest shadows were, then to cross to the other side of the house along the roof using the shadows of the chimneys. He would then lower himself onto the balcony and gain entry.

He repacked the infrared binoculars and removed a small, com pactly folded crossbow. He hooked it to the field belt and put the backpack on again, then silently climbed down the tree to a point about five feet above the wall.

The top of the wall had two separate types of intruder detection systems. The first was a wide strip of pressure-sensitive wire mesh run ning along the cap of the wall. About a half-inch below the mesh was a metal bar. The mesh was strong enough to support the weight of a bird or small mammals like squirrels, cats, and most raccoons, which might commonly use such a wall in their hunting and movement patterns. The weight of a person, however, would bend the mesh down to the bar, making contact and setting off a pinpointing alarm.

The second system consisted of a series of infrared senders and receivers set at intervals along the top of the wall. A small invisible beam of light ran between elements at a point high enough to let small animals pass below it, but low enough to catch a man tryng to scale the wall. Between the two systems, climbing the wall at any point was nearly impossible.

Michael unclipped the compact crossbow from his field belt and grasped the string, then pulled back on it evenly and forcefully until it locked back. He removed the smaller length of coiled rope and secured one end of it to the sturdy ten-inch projectile bolt, and the other end to the tree he was in. He loaded the bolt, and looped the remainder of the coiled rope over a short projecting rod that he folded down from the bottom of the stock. He raised it, took aim at the thick body of the nearest tree on the estate side of the wall, and fired.

There was a dull thud as the bolt was driven deeply into the body of the tree. Michael quickly took up the slack, tightening it with all his strength, then sat patiently to see if the sound had drawn attention.

He used the time to quickly repack the crossbow and to remove the infrared binoculars again, then he climbed to a point higher in the tree to begin another surveillance.

He saw one of the solitary patrol dogs approaching rapidly past the pool area to investigate the sound. It sniffed and slinked around silently for about two minutes before moving off. Next he watched the routine pass of a patrol. It went under the taut line above them without noticing it in the darkness. He watched them move off, then moved swiftly down the tree.

Michael put on a pair of dark leather gloves, grabbed the extended line with both hands, crossed his legs over it, then pulled himself hand over hand along the line, passing over the infrared beam on the wall. He made the tree on the other side and swung himself to a strong bough, then surveyed the area carefully.

Convinced that he was unnoticed, he dropped to the ground, looked around once quickly, and sprinted in a low crouch across sixty feet of open ground to the cover of neatly trimmed shrubs bordering the pool house. He looked around cautiously once again, then moved to the edge of the shrubs closest to the large terrace. He moved silently

449

across the terrace to the house, then along the length of the house to the side nearest the garages. The building that housed the security personnel still had lights burning. He had no idea how many people could be inside. Probably at least enough to form relief patrols, he figured.

Michael looked up the side of the house to the lowest point of the roof. He removed the second coil of rope with the closed grappling hook attached to one end. He unfolded the arms of the hook and prepared to release a sufficient number of coils of rope to enable him to swing the hook, when his eyes caught a flash of movement at the corner of the house just ten feet away.

It was one of the dogs. It rounded the corner, having probably spotted him from its position near the wall. The dog looked almost startled to see him so close. It did not bark, but instead snarled and bared its teeth menacingly. It took a few steps toward Michael, who did not hesitate to act. He threw his left arm out with the coiled line in his hand. The dog lunged for the moving arm. Michael released the line with the dog's leap and jammed the gloved hand straight into the dog's mouth, while throwing the right arm forcefully around the back of the dog, pulling it toward him. He shoved the hand as far down the dog's throat as he could with all of the combined force of the pushing left and pulling right arms. The locked pair tumbled to the ground, the dog kicking frantically and gagging violently from the hand going down its throat. Michael's right arm slid up behind the dog's neck. He raised the left arm forcefully while jerking the right arm toward him with all of his might. The action was fluid and swift, there was a snap and a muffled whimper, then the dog fell absolutely still, dead from a broken neck.

Michael picked himself up and wiped a hand across his left cheek where one of the dog's claws had scratched him during the brief fight. There wasn't a great deal of blood, though the pain was considerable.

He grabbed the dog and dragged it as close to the house as he could, leaving it in the dark shadows. He found the rope again, checked the area once more, then turned back to the house. The first toss of the hook caught securely on the roof, and within seconds his strong, conditioned body scaled up the rope, his legs and feet using the side of the stone house in his silent ascent. He quickly pulled the rope up to the roof, coiled it, and attached it to his belt again; then he began moving slowly along the roof.

He stopped in the shadows of each of the many chimneys he encountered, using each occasion to survey the visible ground area to make certain he was still undetected. He went the last distance to the point directly above the balcony outside the upstairs study, having marked in his mind which of the chimneys was situated closest to it.

Michael secured the line to the chimney, then went over the edge of the roof and lowered himself to a point just beside the balcony, which kept him out of the light shining through the doors, and left him still invisible to the ground patrols. He climbed silently onto the balcony, still remaining out of the direct light, and peered in through the corner of the glass doors. He saw Falloux sitting pensively at a desk, the phone in his hand.

He removed his backpack and laid it on the balcony. He crouched low and dared his first exposure to the lighted background of the doors as he cautiously reached for the latch to see if it was unlocked. It moved downward freely, answering his question. He darted back quickly out of the light.

He tried listening to the conversation through the glass doors, but could not hear it clearly. He removed a small tape recorder from the backpack and a little plastic pouch containing an earpiece with a suction microphone. He connected the jacks and attached the suction microphone to the glass doors, then turned on the tape recorder and inserted the earpiece in place. He could now hear Falloux clearly as he watched him through the doors.

"Yes, it was on the news this evening," he said. "You did well. There is just one more job to finish, and then you can take a long vacation."

Falloux listened, Michael wishing that he could hear the other side of the conversation, though he knew it was being recorded by Pheagan's wiretap team.

"You make it sound as though you know where he is already. Have you found him so soon?" Falloux asked, then listened. He wanted very much to know where Immel had managed to hide, but knew better than to ask the question over a telephone.

"You've done well, my friend. Handle this in your own way, just be sure it gets done properly. He was clever enough to escape you once already. Don't let it happen again."

A brief moment of silence followed while Falloux listened to the other end.

"You also had confidence in the men that you hired to handle the job at the saint's place."

Pausing to listen.

"If they are that good, then you should have used them earlier. It could have saved you a lot of trouble and me a lot of unnecessary worry. How many will you have?" Falloux asked.

"Yes, I would think that should do it. Be certain that the job is clean and complete. I'm counting on you." Falloux nodded to Demy's final comments.

"Yes, yes, the cost is inconsequential. They will be paid whatever you promised them. I will expect to hear from you in the morning, then. Your money will be ready and payment made in the usual way. It has been a pleasure doing business with you, as it always is. A bit expensive, perhaps, but then all things are relative, no? I will expect to hear from you in the morning. Good luck," Falloux said, hanging up the phone.

Michael removed the earpiece and turned off the tape recorder. He reached for the Swiss SIG, removed the silencer from the pouch on his belt, and screwed it into the barrel.

He looked the grounds over one last time, then began reaching for the handle to let himself in, when the phone rang suddenly. Michael instinctively pulled back from the handle, returning to his position out of the light.

Falloux answered the phone and Michael turned on the tape recorder once again, sticking the earpiece back into his ear.

"Yes," the Frenchman answered, expecting that Demy was calling him back with some forgotten detail.

Michael watched as Falloux sat up sharply in his chair. Something had surprised him. He hung up the phone and stared at it nervously.

From the darkness, Michael watched as Falloux opened a drawer and pulled out what looked like a remote phone speaker attachment, which he hurriedly connected to the small jacks mounted on the side of the phone. Falloux then sat back, waiting.

It appeared to be a scrambler of some sort. Of course, Michael realized, that was how the Committee must contact him. It made Pheagan's wiretap useless without the proper decoder.

Michael waited, knowing that with the use of the scrambler speaker, he'd be able to hear both sides of the conversation in its entirety. Perhaps his tape recording of the conversation would be of value to Pheagan.

The phone rang again, and Falloux picked it up, pushed a button on the scrambler box, then hung the phone up again. The connection was now live through the box.

"Good evening, Number Three," came the voice. It sounded unnatural, as though the scrambler also served to disguise its tonal quality.

452

"Number One, I was not expecting your call," Falloux said, sounding a bit perplexed, though confident.

"You haven't called in for some time. I thought that perhaps it would be best to call you for an update. As you know, the Committee is very interested in your situation," Number One said in a mild accent made difficult to distinguish because of the artificial quality of the voice. It was guttural, almost German, though not quite, to Michael's ear. Swiss, perhaps.

Falloux sat well back in his chair. "For all practical purposes, the matter has been resolved. The final detail will be taken care of tonight. By morning, the matter will be history," he said.

"I see," the voice said evenly. "Perhaps you could explain in some detail the steps taken, so that I may inform the others?"

"Certainly," Falloux replied. "You already know that all of Gladieux's papers, including the outline and manuscript, have been destroyed, and that all those with access to them have also been removed. Gladieux's son and daughter came to France, along with the daughter's husband, in search of the identity of the collaborator Z, whom their father was accused of being. They came to me on two occasions regarding this collaborator. They also had the pendant in their possession, and asked if I had ever seen it before, and if it suggested any possible connection to the identity of Z."

"*They* had the pendant?" the voice asked.

"Yes, they did. So, you see, it did not draw the attention that the Committee had feared it might," he replied.

"Go on," the voice instructed.

"They spoke to former members of Group Defiance, and poked hopelessly around. They were, of course, following a harmless trail, as far as the Committee was concerned," Falloux said.

"The Committee does not consider speaking to Rudolf Immel as being 'harmless,'" the voice said back.

A sudden spike of anxiety shot through Falloux. The Committee knew that the Gladieux family had talked to Immel. But how? he wondered. He wondered how much more they knew.

"You must understand that Immel played a part in the story of the father's past. The untimely discovery of his presence in France made me expect that they would visit him," Falloux said quickly, almost nervously.

"Is that why you tried to have him killed?" the voice asked. "Because you did not consider that meeting dangerous?"

"Yes, I ordered the action, but only to remove the possibility of his becoming a threat. They came here immediately after seeing Immel.

All they had learned from him were a few details of the past pertainin
to their father and Group Defiance," Falloux said.

"Yet, when it was discovered that Immel had in fact escaped you
attempt, they enlisted the help of former Defiance people to find him
Why would they do that if they had learned nothing to interest them
Can you explain?" the voice pressed.

Falloux had no ready answer to the question.

"Did you know that they had also hired a private agency to assis
them in their investigation?" Number One asked.

"I . . . well, after the attempt . . . on their lives, it became obviou
that they—"

"Before the attempt, Number Three," the voice cut in, interrupt
ing Falloux's stammering reply.

"Before?" Falloux repeated.

"And if they were not a threat, why did you attempt to remov
them in Saintes-Maries-de-la-Mer?" the voice asked. "Are you awar
that your phone is being tapped? Our electronic scans have just con
firmed this. We have no way of knowing how long this surveillance ha
been taking place, or what they may have learned. Do you still believ
they were merely looking for a collaborator?"

Falloux was shaking now, his face red and sweating.

"They were after *you*, Number Three. *You*, not the collaborator,
the voice said.

"That's not poss— They couldn't . . . they're dead. I had them
killed," Falloux said.

"They knew about your connection to the death of their fathe
They knew a great deal more than you thought."

"But they're all dead now. And Immel will be taken care of to
night by Demy and over a dozen of his men. Whatever they knew i
gone with them, and the threat from Immel will be ended. With hi
death, all possible danger to the Committee will have been remove
completely. Certainly you must realize this?"

"We realize a great many things, Number Three. We realize tha
you are not out of danger until Immel *is* dead. We realize that a privat
agency of some kind was, and possibly still is, involved in the investiga
tion. Do you know what that can mean?" the voice asked.

"I . . . I swear to you that no threat will exist to the Committe
after Immel has been dealt with. There can be no possible dange
beyond him."

"And the private agency?"

"Their clients are dead. They have no reason to continue," Fal

454

loux insisted. "Please, believe me, I would never let the Committee come into danger. I . . . I would carry out my oath of honor first, to end it all with me. I know that I am safe now. You are safe—the Committee is safe. You must see that," Falloux blurted with an unconvincing confidence.

"We are endeavoring to learn more about this agency now. If you are right about the investigation ceasing, and if Immel is successfully removed, you may very well have saved yourself. But if you are wrong about the agency, or if Immel is not killed immediately, then your life is forfeit. You will carry out your oath swiftly, or we will do it for you. There are those already calling for that. I have extended myself dangerously on your behalf solely because of your past importance to us. But there cannot be the slightest margin for doubt in this test of your survival. And you must understand that," the voice said.

"Yes . . . yes, I do. I do," Falloux said, shaken. "I promise that the matter will be resolved tonight. You will see. The Committee will not be endangered further."

"You are right. The Committee will *not* be endangered. We will not permit that. Is that clear?"

"Yes, I understand fully," Falloux said, his voice struggling for control.

"Then we will wait, Number Three, and we will be watching carefully."

"I will not fail," Falloux insisted. "You will see. The Committee will see."

"You have one day to resolve the Immel matter," the voice said coldly. "Then we shall see about the rest. Goodbye, Number Three. Good luck."

"Good—goodbye," Falloux said, but the connection was broken before he had finished.

Falloux sat back in his chair, still trembling. Michael turned off the tape recorder and watched him for a long time before the Frenchman finally moved.

Falloux disconnected the scrambler and put it back into its drawer. Then he walked to the wall at the far side of the room, and moved a picture attached to that wall by hinges, revealing a wall safe. He turned the dial of the combination lock and opened the door. His hand went in and pulled out a small-caliber automatic. He turned it in his hands, regarded it pensively, then placed it on the table below the safe. Then he pulled out some papers and folders and began hurriedly to look through them.

Michael knew that two things were vital. First, Immel *had* to be found before Demy could get to him. Second, Falloux could not die by his own hand or in any way that would seem accidental. The Committee must not misconstrue his death to be a sign of his failure. They must think that Falloux had succeeded, at least long enough for Sub Rosa to take the play as far as it would go. If the Committee suspected their danger, they could all carry out their oaths of death after appointing successors. Sub Rosa would have won nothing.

Michael readied the Swiss SIG and reached for the door handle.

Pierre Falloux was systematically separating the papers he wanted when he heard the sound behind him. He spun to face it. The shock of seeing Michael nearly staggered him.

"You!" he gasped. "You . . . you're dead!"

Thud! the silenced Swiss SIG coughed.

Falloux's head snapped back, and he was driven against the table behind him. He flopped off to the floor.

Michael walked up to the body and inspected it. There was a hole in Falloux's head, just above the right eye. He was as dead as a stone.

Michael went quickly to the safe, reached in, and emptied the contents. He found a sizable amount of cash, negotiable bonds and certificates, and other items of immediate value. It appeared that Falloux was planning to run rather than take his own life. He would have bolted like a frightened deer at the first indication of failure on Demy's part.

Michael scattered items that would have been of little value to a thief on the floor, then rifled through every drawer in the room creating the appearance of a robbery. When he had finished, he went to the desk and picked up the phone. He dialed a random number to eliminate the dial tone, then raised the phone.

"This is Glad-jo. Tell Tripper to have the tap removed immediately. Falloux has been taken care of. Tell him that I'm going for Immel tonight. Demy is making his move, and with plenty of help."

He paused and thought for a second, hoping that he was not wrong about where he had guessed Immel to be hiding. There was only one place he could think of that Immel would expect him to recognize as having been important to both his father and the German at the same time in both their lives. He could be wrong, but he was certain that Immel had wanted to talk to him again, and felt little doubt that the former German officer would choose a place that Michael would find.

"Tell Tripper that Immel is hiding at the old Bouchard winery just outside of Pont du Château. There's an old barn behind the ruins. That's where I'll be and where Demy will come. Get word to him immediately," he said, placing down the phone. The boys minding the wiretap would be on the phone to Pheagan in a hurry.

Michael moved swiftly to the glass doors, after turning out the study light to help further conceal his movements on the balcony. He gathered his gear and prepared to make his descent to the ground. He looked back into the darkness at the lifeless body of Pierre Falloux lying on the floor. Only then did he realize that when he had shot Falloux, he had not had his revenge in mind. He had thought only to ensure the success of Sub Rosa's attempt to destroy Trinity. He had missed the moment of satisfaction. Perhaps Pheagan had been right. There was still more Glad-jo left in him than he would even admit to himself. The same Glad-jo who cared so long ago, cared today as well.

Demy would be the one, he vowed, to take the brunt of his vengeance. Vengeance for the murder of a father, for the murder of a beautiful sister, and for the murder of Danny.

A single battle remained that would settle all scores. A battle between two men who had been bred to kill. Demy's advantage lay in a team of men, while Michael's was in the fact that Demy didn't know he was still alive. It was a fight that he was looking forward to.

Michael pushed off the balcony and glided swiftly and silently to the ground. He moved with catlike ease through the shadows, making his way back to the trees near the wall. In moments he had made his escape as easily as he had come, disappearing into the darkness that Glad-jo knew best.

Chapter 46

"TONIGHT? Are you sure?" Pheagan asked excitedly.

"Positive. The wiretap picked it up from Demy himself. Then Glad-jo plainly indicated the same thing, advising that the attempt would be made at the Bouchard winery outside of Pont du Château," the man said.

"God damn it! The team is in Cuisery. Get me that map," Pheagan said with urgency.

The man grabbed it and hurriedly spread it across the bed over Pheagan's legs.

"Where the fuck is Cuisery?" Pheagan said, beginning a frantic search.

The man's finger shot out and hit the spot on the map. Pheagan quickly noted the distance between Cuisery and Pont du Château, his eyes jumping up to the scale of miles.

"Shit!" he said. "It has to be a hundred miles. How many men did you say Demy will have with him?" he asked.

"Fifteen, including himself. And they're seasoned," his man replied.

"Mike won't stand a chance without the team's help. Is there still a helicopter in Cuisery?"

"No, but I can get one there fast," the man said.

"Then do it, and get them on it immediately. There isn't a minute to waste. Everything depends on stopping Demy and keeping Immel alive. We won't get a second chance," Pheagan said.

"The team is battle-ready. They'll be on their way as soon as I get the bird in," the man said, turning and leaving Pheagan's room at a run.

A hundred fucking miles, Pheagan thought to himself. "Mike, I hope you've got enough Glad-jo left in you to hold out until the team gets there," he whispered, staring at Pont du Château on the map. "Just hold out, pal. Just hold out—for all our sakes."

The gentle light from the quarter moon was to his advantage right now, but he knew that it wouldn't be once the action started. At least the foliage on the trees helped to reduce the light in the forest, Michael thought as he completed the trip wire to the second grenade trap he had set. He wished that he had about ten more grenades to help reduce the odds against him.

He knew that surprise would be his biggest advantage, and if he timed his strike properly he could panic the enemy for a short time. Every second of confusion would help him.

He looked at his watch, then removed the infrared binoculars from the backpack and thoroughly scanned the area. There was still no sign of them, but it wouldn't be long before they arrived.

Michael lowered the binoculars and looked at the barn. There were no signs of life, but he knew that Immel had to be in there. There was nowhere else he would have gone where Michael could have figured to find him. He prayed that his gamble had been correct.

He picked up the compact Model 10 Ingram submachine gun and his pack and moved silently toward the barn. Though small in size—only 10.5 inches in length with its retractable rear stock in the stowed position—the diminutive Ingram possessed the most fearsome firing power of any submachine gun made, having a rate of fire of 1,100 .45-caliber rounds per minute. Its thirty-round clip took just under 1.7 seconds to empty, becoming a shredding rush of bullets. If anything could put fear into a group of men, it would be the sudden eruption of that first salvo coming unexpectedly out of the darkness.

The barn was fairly large in size, and getting into it could be a problem. Michael suspected that Immel could be armed, and he might not wait to ask questions before opening up on anyone trying to enter.

He approached the barn silently and moved around it looking for a point of entry other than its doors and windows. He had gone three-fourths of the way around when he spotted what he thought was just what he needed.

There was a rotted barrel standing nearly against the weathered side of the barn. Behind it was a hole that looked large enough for a man to crawl through. He approached it and laid the pack down, then lowered himself to his stomach.

He squeezed between the barrel and the barn and listened patiently at the hole for a few moments for any sounds. He was about to try entering when he heard a muffled cough. He froze as a hot flash of nerves shot through his body in startled response to the sound. He waited a few moments until he could calm himself, then poked his head through the hole slowly and with the greatest caution. It led into a stall of some kind. Its sides would provide added cover for him.

Silently, he began inching his way in, pausing with each forward movement to listen. He moved again and listened, moved a little further in and listened yet again. He repeated the slow process until he was inside, then moved to the mouth of the stall.

There was another cough of longer duration. When it stopped, he poked his head around the end of the stall and saw Immel sitting on the ground, propped against a thick beam that rose to help support a loft. Immel's head was back against the beam, his eyes closed. He appeared to be in a great deal of pain.

The German suddenly bent forward and began another racking cough, which he tried to muffle with the back of his left arm. It grew worse and he flopped to his side as the spell continued. When it finally ended, he attempted to sit up again against the beam. He turned to look back to locate the beam, when he saw a man beside him on one knee.

Immel let out a startled cry at the sudden appearance. He hadn't heard the faintest sound.

"I'm not here to harm you," Michael said quickly, grabbing Immel by the upper arms to prevent an attack response. He saw instantly that his touch caused a great deal of pain to the former German officer. The entire right shoulder and upper chest area of his shirt were stained with blood, old and new.

"Easy, easy," Michael said. "I'm here to help you."

Immel squinted through the tired, blurry eyes and recognized Michael "You! I knew! I knew you would come," he said, expressing great relief nearly to the point of tears.

"Shhh," Michael said, raising a hand to quiet him. "It's okay, I'm here. But we won't be alone for very long. They know you're here, and will be coming soon. We don't have much time to get ready for them."

The look of fear returned to the German's face.

"Don't worry, they can be handled," Michael assured him.

Immel leaned to his side, wincing from the pain, and reached into his back pocket. He pulled out a small battered notebook and held it out to Michael. "Take this and leave," he said. "Leave quickly. This is what you have come for."

Michael accepted the notebook from Immel without opening it. "I've also come for you," he said.

"No, you will have no hope of escape with me. You must leave to save yourself," the German insisted.

Michael pulled the KA-BAR from its sheath. "You'd better let me do something for that wound," he said, cutting away the shirt over it.

"It's no use. Go, before it is too late."

Michael ignored Immel and peeled away the shirt, removing an old blood-soaked dressing to reveal an ugly wound in the upper chest, just below the collarbone. It was discolored and pus-filled. It had become infected and smelled rather bad.

"You have to get to a hospital," Michael said.

"Listen to me," Immel said. "If you leave quickly with the information that I have given you, you can complete what your father died for. If you stay, you will die, and it will have all gone to waste."

"There's another reason for my staying," Michael returned. "The man who killed my father—and my sister and her husband—will be here soon."

Immel's face saddened. "I . . . am very sorry to learn about the

460

deaths of your sister and her husband. I am sorry about your father as well. But he and I both knew the dangers we faced in trying to do this thing. You do not understand its importance. That is why you must leave, especially now with the added deaths of your sister and brother-in-law. It will all have been for nothing if you do not," he persisted.

"I do understand. I know the whole story about the pendants and the Salamandra. And I know what this information is," Michael said, holding it up.

"You could not," Immel replied.

"But I do. These are the identities of the Committee of Trinity. Am I correct? And it's your aim to kill Trinity."

Immel looked at him in amazement. "Yes . . . yes, that is right. But it is also much more. You see, it is not enough to know only the identities of the Committee. Trinity cannot be stopped with just that information. There are successors to the Committee who would carry on. It's all there, including the names of the successors. You will also find the sources of Trinity's funding outlined, their banks, their plan of action and the timetable established for that plan. That is why you must leave. You do not know what will happen if you fail. The world will change, governments will fall. Chaos and confusion will spread all across the globe.

"The plans of Trinity have been greatly altered because of the successes of its enemies and many of the nation-states against it. Victories like those of the Israelis at Entebbe and Beirut, or of the Italians against the Red Brigades when Dozier was kidnapped have put Trinity on the defensive, making them all the more dangerous.

"Trinity has set a new course. One which is far more threatening and aggressive than anything in the past. A wave of terrorism unparalleled in human experience is about to be unleashed. Whole countries will face the danger of being destroyed. The weapons are ready. Nuclear weapons, biological and biochemical weapons of the worst kind. They will stop at nothing. They seek to win the final victory once and for all. Nothing will stop it. Only the destruction of Trinity can do that."

"When is all of this going to take place?" Michael asked.

"It will start early next year with a wave of political assassinations all across the globe. Then it will escalate quickly. The timetable is set for two years. Two years! That is all the time left. It cannot be stopped once it has started. It must be ended now, before the plan can begin. Do you see now why you must leave? If you don't, and Trinity is not stopped, the world as we know it today may not exist in two years."

Michael looked at the notebook in his hand and stuffed it into his breast pocket. What he had just heard had changed things drastically. His revenge was no longer the most important thing. He did not doubt for a moment that what Immel had told him was true. Pheagan had painted the picture quite clearly for him.

Michael knew that the ultimate goal of Trinity was the destruction of existing institutions of power by the ruthless application of massive terror, and then the continued use or threat of it as the means of social control. Social control—but not on the scale attempted by Robespierre during the French Revolution, or even by Hitler or Stalin in modern times. This was an attempt to achieve social control on a *global* scale. The plan was ambitious, enormous—and made frighteningly possible by the high technology of the weaponry available to them. Whole cities could be destroyed and major governments toppled by inflicting such enormous and overwhelming acts of violence that they would be rendered powerless in the face of populations mad with fear. What was to stop them from destroying Washington, Moscow, London, Paris, and every other major seat of power with a "basement bomb," or canisters of biological or biochemical weapons as easily transported into the heart of a city as a truckload of melons? The possibilities were terrifyingly real—and now so was the plan.

Trinity had patiently built the mechanism for this plot over the last forty years. Every little terrorist group with a cause, and the balls to plant a bomb, was useful. Trinity had begun conditioning people to fear at a planned rate. Every act of terrorism added to the effect until people could no longer walk past a row of lockers without wondering if a bomb had been planted in one, or whether some glassy-eyed fanatic had left an explosive device in a parcel in the department store where they were doing their Christmas shopping. Everyone was affected by it to a degree and thought about it at one time or another.

Men like Demy were their ants. Skilled ants, to be sure, but ants just the same—spent like small change by Trinity in the march toward the greater objective. These groups controlled by Trinity were filled with people willing to die for their own beliefs and believing that it was really for *your* sake that they blew you up. Trinity had used them all so well, with such simple perfection.

Michael realized that all sides had done their small part to help them. The U.S., the Russians, the British, the Israelis, and the Palestinians—anyone who supported them with words, who secretly or openly funded them, or hired them, or even just used their methods. We had all used them against one another. And they laughed all the while. It didn't matter whom they worked for on any given day; the effect was the same. And they were always quite prepared to bite the hands that fed them. There was no loyalty to any quarter. Everyone would be a target when the time suited them. No one was safe. And now it was ready to explode in everyone's face with a big, big bang.

Even in the war against them our successes served only to drive them to a point of desperation, making the alarming possibility of a terrorist Armageddon a tangible threat. What if we couldn't stop them this time? What would happen? What would be left? Once the weapons were employed, it wouldn't matter who was left. There would be such massive disorder that their way would be the only way it could work. It would take decades to re-establish a global system of order. It was too frightening to envision.

"There are a lot of questions that I want to ask you," Michael said.

"There is no time. You must leave before it is too late. Only you can stop them now."

Michael rose and stared down at the German. Immel was right, he knew. The chance to get Demy would have to wait, and perhaps be lost forever. But a world was more important than one man's revenge.

Michael picked up his backpack and turned to leave, then turned back to Immel once again. He removed the Swiss SIG from its holster and the three clips that he had carried and placed them in his lap. "It may not be enough against them, but at least it will give you a chance," he said.

Michael turned and walked to a window, raising the infrared binoculars. He looked out through the broken panes of glass. It was too late. He saw at a distance that Demy and his men were approaching cautiously. By the time he could get out of the barn they would be close enough to spot him if he wasn't careful.

He dropped the binoculars into the pack and let it fall to the floor. "They're here," he said, turning to Immel.

"You *must* try to escape," Immel said urgently. "There is no time to waste. Go immediately."

Michael turned and moved swiftly toward the hole he had entered through. If he could get into the woods, he could get away when Demy's men turned their attention to the barn. They wouldn't be looking for him.

Michael dropped to his stomach and quietly crawled through the hole. He moved swiftly into the darkness of the forest and crouched low to wait for the attack to begin to cover his escape. He watched as Demy's veterans began to fan out quietly to surround the barn.

They split up into five groups of three. Demy and his team would enter the barn. The others would position themselves in the forest at the corners of the structure, where all sides could be watched from a safe enough distance to initiate a cross fire in all directions without endangering one another.

The first two corner teams got into position as the last two moved through the trees and undergrowth. To the untrained ear they moved in near silence, but to Michael's keenly developed senses their positions were as clear as if they had been marked with signal flares.

One team was moving directly for him. If he bolted, they would spot him. If he remained where he was, they'd walk right over him. He had waited too long. There was no choice now but to take them by surprise. He was back in the fight, whether he wanted to be or not.

The trio moved cautiously through the woods, their attention concentrated on the barn. Suddenly, a figure in black popped up in front of them, no more than twenty feet away. Before they could overcome the initial surprise of the unexpected presence in the trees, the silence was shattered by the furious discharge of the Ingram as the clip emptied into them, shredding them with near explosive force.

Michael dashed away swiftly to escape the exposed position given away by the flashes of the Ingram. He discarded the spent clip and inserted another as he ran. A sudden rush of gunfire erupted from one of the corner positions and from Demy's team at the spot that Michael had just left.

There were shouts of confusion and shots starting to go off in all directions. His attack had been so unexpected that a flash of panic had filled Demy's men. Michael knew that they would recover from it in short order, however, as he raced to his next position.

The other corner team, which had not yet reached position, had panicked to a surprising degree. They bolted in three different directions, one of them running right into the fire of another corner team, who had seen him only as a shadow and heard his thrashing movements. They sent him straight to hell. A second member of the panicked team ran through one of the trip wires that Michael had set. The explosion occurred at almost the same instant that Michael fired the next furious burst, catching the third man. The impression was that there were a number of attackers.

Demy shouted orders for the corner teams to spread out to establish a more effective field of fire. Then he crouched low and rapidly tried to assess his situation. Another explosion sounded as the second trip wire was hit. The gunfire intensified, though no one had a real target.

Michael moved in closer, crouched as low as he could while still permitting himself swift movement. The two positions from which he had fired were being thoroughly raked. It wouldn't take them long to realize that they were being attacked by one man.

Demy had already reached that conclusion. He saw no return fire being directed against his men and knew that the explosives had probably been traps. He also knew that it was not Immel conducting the fight against them. Immel could not possibly have moved with the speed necessary to get between the points of fire he observed. Immel would still be in the barn.

He quickly assembled his entry team and they began a sprint for the barn.

Michael spotted them and fired the half-empty Ingram. The man behind Demy was dropped by the short burst, but Demy and the other man continued unhurt.

Return fire concentrated immediately on the flashes from the Ingram. Michael bolted, knowing that Demy and his man had gone for Immel. He could no longer remain outside and hope to keep the German alive. He took three rapid strides before the impact of a bullet knocked him sprawling to the ground. The initial shock of pain in his right arm was replaced by a deadening numbness. He grabbed the empty Ingram in his left hand and crawled frantically for the cover of the barn, which would shield him from the gunfire.

Demy and his man went directly for the barn door. His man kicked at the old, rotted wood. It took several kicks to splinter enough of the door to allow entry. Demy dove through quickly, rolling out of the feeble light into the blackness of shadow.

Immel opened up with a rapid series of shots from the Swiss SIG, too late to get the darting figure of Demy, but catching the second man and knocking him back through the opening.

Demy fired his handgun back at the flashes and heard a short painful cry. He rose to advance, firing again at the spot, when the Swiss SIG fired from a new position. The shots ripped at Demy, the first missing completely, the second grazing his right forearm. He dove away, losing his gun, and moved into the darkest shadows.

Immel held the Swiss SIG, its slide locked back with the last shot emptying the clip. He had lost the other clips in his escape after being hit in almost the same spot as his initial wound. He staggered and dropped to his knees from the intense pain, then crawled into a stall to hide.

Michael reached the side of the barn, his arm hanging limp and bleeding badly. He moved along the barn, turning the corner that would take him to the opening by the barrel. He had to cover twenty feet to reach the hole. He gritted his teeth and began a sprint for it.

Fire from two positions concentrated on him immediately. He slammed into the side of the barn amidst the splatter of bullets and pitched forward, his momentum carrying him nearly to the barrel. He winced and almost cried out from the pain of the two hits he had suffered, one in the right thigh, and the other in his lower right side. He lay stunned for a moment, unable to move.

Then there was a sudden eruption of intense gunfire, which helped to restore his wits. A furious firefight had just begun with gunfire coming from deeper in the woods. There was no mistaking the familiar sounds and fire patterns from the M-16 assault rifles that silenced the gunfire from one of the two positions that had caught Michael. Pheagan's team had arrived, and Michael knew that the situation outside was no longer his worry.

He rolled to his stomach and located the Ingram. He struggled to insert another clip, and began crawling toward the hole in the side of the barn, biting through the pain from his wounds and compelling his body to move. Feeling was beginning to return to the wounded right arm, and it was all pain. He tried forcing movement of it as he crawled. He found the hole, fought back the gasps from his pain, and crawled through the opening.

Inside the barn a deadly game of cat and mouse had started. Neither Immel nor Demy could see one another. The German huddled in the stall he had crawled to, hunched over from the agonizing pain of his wounds. The noise from the intense fighting outside covered the sounds of his loud breathing, as well as the sounds Demy was making as he moved slowly, searching the darkness. His eyes had not yet adjusted to the diminished light inside the barn. The wound to the Frenchman's forearm had caught only flesh, and, though it was painful, he still had use of the arm and hand.

Michael saw the tall figure of Demy pass the mouth of the stall as he made his way through the entry hole, but by the time he was inside, the figure was gone. He dragged himself forward as quietly as possible to where he had seen the figure, and pulled the Ingram up with his left hand. He forced the right hand to clench a feeble fist, then opened it, and stiffly raised it to the wounded side. He took a deep breath and came out of the stall to follow the path he had seen Demy take.

Like Demy, Michael's eyes needed to adjust. Even the gentle light of the moon had accustomed them to more light. He began moving forward, limping heavily, prepared to fire at the first upright target to present itself.

The fighting outside was beginning to slacken. From the sounds of the weapons, it appeared that Pheagan's men were rapidly gaining control. Michael would have settled for having just one of them inside to help him with Demy. As badly wounded as he was, he knew he would have little chance in a hand-to-hand struggle. His success now would depend on sighting him and using the Ingram.

He heard a loud sudden movement and a brief struggling, followed by the choking, gasping sounds of strangulation. He pinpointed the sound and rushed at it. Demy's figure became visible, but was too shielded by Immel to risk firing the Ingram.

Michael lunged at the two figures, crashing heavily into them. Demy lost his grip on the garrote from the sudden impact and was jarred away. Michael tumbled over Immel, losing the Ingram in the darkness, and came to his feet quickly to respond to Demy's attack, which was instant.

The Frenchman hit him like a bull, knocking him forcefully into the side of the stall. Michael bounced off the backstop and got his left arm up in time to deflect a vicious blow. Demy followed quickly with a sweeping kick to Michael's wounded side and a fast series of thrusting blows that crumpled him to the ground. Michael's speed of response and attacking capabilities were greatly impaired by his wounds, or he could have stood his ground and dealt back severe punishment. Unable to breathe from the kick, he rolled along the ground to avoid Demy's next kick. After the miss, Demy moved with Michael and threw another kick as the American rose. But Michael had anticipated the kick and absorbed it against his left rib cage, catching the leg with his arm. He forced the wounded right arm into service and threw a vicious finger slash straight into Demy's eyes, then drove a forceful thrust to the solar plexus, taking the Frenchman's wind. Demy toppled as he was caught by the unexpected swiftness and power of Michael's next backhand blow.

Michael was on him in an instant, knowing that he couldn't match the Frenchman in his condition. On the ground Demy would have little leverage, and the advantage of his greater strength would be neutralized.

Michael slammed Demy across the bridge of the nose, then threw another savage strike to the eyes, badly damaging the left eye. The Frenchman let out a demonic howl and threw Michael completely off him and across the stall in a tremendous surge of strength.

Michael struggled to his feet just as Demy charged in a growling, snorting rage, throwing a furious barrage of thudding blows. Demy threw an eye slash of his own, which gashed Michael's left eyelid and nose, and then relentlessly battered the wounded side and arm. Michael knew that he couldn't sustain such punishment, but he also knew that he couldn't fall. To fall against Demy at this point was to die.

He tried blocking the Frenchman's brutal blows, then caught the slightest opening and threw a short but powerful jab to the throat. Demy retched and backed away involuntarily, leaving himself open to the best kick that Michael could manage with a wounded leg to act as a pivot. It wasn't forceful, but it caught Demy just right and he was sent crashing into the side of the barn. Michael closed in rapidly only to see the Frenchman spin toward him with a weapon that his hands had found by chance in the darkness. The pitchfork came up at Michael as he charged.

It was only the slit of light coming through the window that permitted Michael the fleeting glimpse of the tines flashing up at him. By instinct, the left hand shot out to meet the weapon.

Demy drove the rusted tines through the blocking hand with a forceful lunge. Michael cried out sharply as he pushed the hand out to the side, deflecting Demy's thrust at his chest.

Demy yanked the weapon to clear it, but Michael's desperate grip held tightly, his arm strength keeping the tines harmlessly to the side and away from their fatal duty.

Unable to drive the weapon into his foe, Demy yanked the handle sideways, away from Michael, the pierced hand going with it and pulling Michael off balance. Demy lowered his shoulder and bulled into Michael, ramming him into the side of the stall with crushing force, and pinning him to further restrict his defensive efforts.

For a moment their snarling, bleeding faces were just inches apart, their eyes locked onto one another's. Demy's left eye was formless from the strike Michael had scored to it. The right one burned with rage as it stared at him. The advantage that Demy held was plain as he struggled to free the pitchfork. He twisted the handle and yanked downward, tearing it free as Michael's injured right hand fumbled weakly to grasp and control the handle of the KA-BAR strapped to his thigh.

The moment the tines ripped free of the hand, Demy backed away slightly from his press against Michael. The powerful shoulders began an upward lunge when the face of the Frenchman suddenly changed, an expression of shock and horror replacing the sensed victory as Michael's KA-BAR struck deeply into his lower abdomen.

468

Michael let out a blood curdling yell as he yanked the razor-sharp fighting knife upward with all the strength remaining in the wounded arm, then yanked again. The KA-BAR sliced through the belt on the second yank and ripped upward, stopping against the breastbone of the Frenchman.

Demy's mouth fell open and an awful gasp escaped as he dropped the pitchfork and stumbled backward, his hands clutching to keep his insides in place. He staggered a few steps, blood pouring out over his arms, splattering down his legs and to the ground. He wobbled and toppled to the ground, writhing and gasping as his life ran out in a dark spreading pool.

At almost the same moment, the doors at both ends of the barn burst open and four figures in black darted in at the ready. Bright beams of light went on and flashed frantically around the interior of the barn, one coming to rest on Michael's battered face. Another found Demy's agonizing body, while a third found Immel sprawled on the ground but still alive.

"Secure," said the man shining the light on Michael.

Michael stared back into the blinding light, his chest heaving, blood dripping down his face. "Secure," he responded hoarsely, knowing without seeing the man behind the light that he was addressing a former Dawg, like himself. They were all former Dawgs. The "help" that Pheagan had arranged was the old team that had been assembled in Vietnam. The other four had remained active with Sub Rosa over the years. They had come, to the man, to help one of their own.

The barn was suddenly flooded with light as two Porta-lights went on. Within moments, two more were on, and the scene was entirely visible.

One of the four men went immediately to Michael to tend his wounds, while a second went to Immel. The man who had addressed Michael went to Demy's twitching body. The Frenchman was in the last stages of clinical life. The man then walked over to Michael and the Dawg assisting him.

Michael slumped into a sitting position against the side of a stall. "Secure," he whispered, putting his head back and closing his eyes. Secure, he thought. It was over. He had gotten the men who killed his father, and Sub Rosa had gotten what it was after. He shook his head, tears coming to his eyes as he realized the price he had paid. His wounds were nothing, they would heal. But he had lost the people he loved most in the world, and nothing could bring them back. Tears streamed down his face as thoughts of his father, Gabrielle, and Danny filled his head, the pain of their deaths suddenly fresh in his memory.

He wondered now if it had all been worth it. To Sub Rosa it had been; to the world it would be; but to him—he wondered if it could ever be. There was sometimes a fine line between winning and losing, just as there was between being a hero and being a coward. The difference was often unrecognizable, though it ultimately didn't matter unless you survived to worry about it. Being alive was, after all, a victory by any standard. In that sense, he had won. But it was a victory he would never celebrate.

"What's the body count?" the team leader asked as he applied the finishing touches to the temporary dressings of Michael's wounds.

"Fifteen, counting him," the other Dawg answered, pointing to Demy.

"That's the bunch of them. Call in, get both helicopters in here fast. We've got ten minutes, if we're lucky, before this place is crawling with authorities."

The man nodded and left the barn.

The team leader made a final inspection of his work on Michael and patted him on the left shoulder. "You'll live," he announced.

"How's he?" Michael asked, nodding toward Immel.

"That depends on how much information you need to get from him yet," the man answered.

Michael raised the heavily wrapped left hand and tapped his breast pocket. "It's in here. Everything," he said.

The man undid the button on the pocket and removed the notebook, then put it into his own pocket. "I'll see that Tripper gets it immediately. You won't be taken to Arles, and probably won't be seeing him for awhile. Any messages to go along with it?" he asked.

Michael just shook his head, then turned to look at Immel.

"That shoulder of his is a fucking mess," the Dawg said. "I wouldn't be surprised if gangrene has set in."

Michael had suspected as much from the smell when he had attended to the wound earlier.

"I'll leave you two alone for awhile. We've got some details to take care of outside. There aren't any more trip wires to worry about, are there?" he asked.

Michael shook his head. "I set two. Demy's men hit them both."

"You'll be taken out as soon as the second helicopter arrives. It should be here in a shake," the man said, rising to his feet.

"Thanks," Michael said.

The man smiled. "No sweat. I gotta call in," he said, then turned and walked out of the barn.

470

Michael would have been dead without them, and he knew it. He still couldn't believe that they had shown up. The whole team. Pheagan never ceased to amaze him.

Michael pulled himself over to where Immel was propped up. The German opened his eyes and looked at him, his face tight and drawn from pain. Blood ringed his neck from the unsuccessful garrote attack that Michael had interrupted.

"Why did you risk coming back?" Immel asked through his pain.

"I ran into Demy and his men outside. I had no choice," Michael replied in German.

Immel squinted at him. "I think you had a choice," he said. "You could have gotten away after your friends arrived."

Michael thought back to his reaction to seeing Demy and his men breaking for the barn. His only thought had been to get back inside to save Immel. The German was right. There had been a choice.

"I guess I had to know the answers to a few questions," he finally said. "I wouldn't learn them with you dead."

"I'll answer them if I can," the German said weakly.

"You did send for my father, didn't you?" Michael asked to clarify a point before starting.

Immel nodded.

"Why did you choose him to help you?"

"May I first ask you one question?" Immel inquired.

"As long as you answer my questions. Go ahead."

"You said that you knew the story of the pendants and the Salamandra, and about the Committee of Trinity. How did you learn that?"

"That would require a very, very long answer," Michael said.

"Can you try briefly?"

"Let's say that I had a lot of good help. The pendant that I have around my neck, and which I showed you at the end of our visit, was found pinned to my father's body. The appearance of the pendant sparked considerable interest from certain quarters, especially when the only three thought to exist were found to be still in place," Michael explained. "These were the three pendants that surfaced following the secret testimony given at the Nuremberg trials, and which provided the first knowledge of the existence of the Salamandra."

"Falloux did not expect that any connection would be made," Immel added, his breathing loud and labored.

"That's right. He gambled on odds he figured to be a sure win."

"And now he will be most dangerous," Immel said.

Michael shook his head. "Falloux is dead."

471

"By his own hand?" Immel asked with a worried urgency, fearing that Falloux's suicide would tip off the Committee and possibly inspire enactment of emergency contingencies that would foil the success he thought he had just guaranteed.

"No. I killed him. I made it look like a robbery-homicide. It will not be interpreted as the carrying out of his oath of death."

Immel regarded Michael through his squint, impressed by the things he seemed to know. "And after learning of the Nuremberg-Salamandra connection?" he asked.

"Let's just say that that was where my 'friends' became interested. That's another story in itself, how we came together on it. Let it be enough that we did, okay?"

Immel nodded and grimaced suddenly from pain. A few moments passed, then he gestured for Michael to continue.

"My friends theorized a possible connection to Trinity, and quite correctly believed that the identity of a Committee member was in jeopardy of being exposed because of what my father had learned. At that time, Trinity was believed to be run by a triumvirate, but we learned otherwise later."

Immel shook his head. What he was hearing was incredible. Michael's "friends" knowing about Trinity and the existence of a Committee suggested only one possible answer to him. "Sub Rosa?" he asked cautiously.

"Sub Rosa," Michael repeated.

"You are a part of Sub Rosa?" Immel asked in amazement.

"Let's say that I worked for them once, a long time ago, and that we came to a mutual agreement to help one another out," Michael explained.

It was perfect, Immel thought. Sub Rosa was the only group capable of striking at Trinity in exactly the right way with the information he had given them."

"Go on," the German said.

"The pendant was traced to the glassmaker, Hans Haupte, by virtue of a miscroscopic signature cane incorporated into it. A thorough investigation was begun which led to the trail of his apprentice, who was found."

"The apprentice—the boy! You found him? Alive?" Immel asked in utter disbelief.

Michael nodded. "Yes, and it was from him that we learned that twelve pendants had been made. He also identified you as one of the German officers who picked up the finished commission. You had ac-

472

companied an older general. That was how we finally figured out that you were my father's contact. We also knew that you had escaped the attempt on your life. Your escape tunnel was found, and we knew that you had been badly wounded. The rest was the result of putting the facts together."

"And the winery?" Immel asked.

"That took a while to figure out. Oddly enough, it was our most troublesome clue that helped give me the answer. That was the word Leopard. I finally figured out that it was intended to be a place and not a person. That place was Romenay, which was very near to where you lived. Later, when the facts began falling quickly into place, and after my sister and her husband had been killed, the same word popped into my head. This was where the agent Leopard had died during the war. But the important aspect of that thought was that this was also the place where you had encountered my father. It was the only place I could think of that you would go with the hope of my finding you."

"You are very much like your father," Immel said. "He would be very proud of you."

"And that brings us back to my question. It's your turn to do the talking," Michael said.

Immel nodded. "Yes, about why your father was chosen," he said, pausing a moment to gather some strength. "I *am* a pendant holder. The 'old general' was one of the original Salamandra Committee members. I had been selected to become his successor.

"There were twelve pendants, as you know. The Salamandra was governed by the Committee of Six. With the outbreak of a world war imminent, a great opportunity to take advantage of its effects was presented. The Committee decided to select and place its heirs very carefully, to guarantee the greatest measure of influence possible in the world that would emerge. Twelve heirs were selected, each bearing one of the pendants made in 1936. The Committee wisely distributed the potential heirs on both sides, so that no matter what the outcome of the war the ascendancy would be guaranteed. It was believed that Germany would be the ultimate loser in the war, so the heirs were distributed with nine going to the expected winning side, and three going to the other. When the war ended and the existence of the Salamandra was unexpectedly discovered, action was taken quickly to avert disaster. The decision was made to sacrifice three of the chosen heirs to save the others. The false suspicion that the Salamandra had been a Nazi-inspired plot helped greatly to hide the true purpose of our existence. We did nothing to discourage the belief."

Immel paused again to rest. It was obvious that he was growing weaker. "To sacrifice three of the pendant holders was not a grave risk to us, as not all of the pendant holders were meant to rise to Committee level anyway," he began again. "It was always intended that only six would. I did not because of my conviction as a war criminal, though I continued to hold the pendant and remained useful to the cause," Immel said, stopping suddenly. He coughed heavily for a few moments, spitting up blood as the spell ended. Several seconds passed, and he seemed to grow more comfortable.

Michael nodded. "Go ahead."

"It was after the war had started and Germany had such startling success that the attitudes of the Committee began to change. The old general watched those attitudes develop to his great sadness. He confided in me in a way that perhaps he shouldn't have, in the hope that the true purpose and philosophy of the Salamandra, as originally set down, would be upheld by the heirs, who would take over upon the deaths of their sponsors. He revealed to me the name of another Committee member who was the youngest among them and who thought as the general did. I kept that name all through the years, and, unknown to me, he had kept mine. He lived until last year, dying in a plane crash in Austria. Just before his death, he summoned me to come to him secretly. It was then that he told me of the sad course that had been set upon, which he could no longer reconcile with his conscience. He gave me a detailed record of the decisions and activities that the Salamandra adopted after Nuremberg—and released me from my oath of death to uphold the secrecy of the Salamandra. He begged me to help him stop them, and then gave me the means by which to do it. He gave me everything that I gave you, including the name of his successor, who also died in the same plane crash. And so I set myself to the destruction of the Salamandra—of Trinity—and enlisted the aid of your father," Immel said.

"And now my original question. Why my father?" Michael asked.

Immel paused for a few moments before answering. "I had never forgotten your father," he began slowly. "He was a most difficult and capable adversary. I respected him very much and felt also that I could trust him."

"But what made you think that he'd agree to help you?" Michael questioned.

"I knew that he would. You see, we shared more than a time in history, a war, and the love of a woman," Immel said, his eyes narrowing as though his mind were going back in time. "We shared a great deal more. We shared a purpose that made us both enemies and brothers at the same time."

Michael stared into the German's face without understanding.

"Do you have the information I gave you?" Immel asked.

"I've already turned it over to the team leader. It'll get into the proper hands much faster through him," Michael replied.

Immel continued looking directly into Michael's eyes. "Your father's name is in that book. He was a pendant holder."

The shock was electric. His father a pendant holder! It couldn't be true.

"He, like myself, did not rise to Committee level because of the collaboration trial and the suspicion that would hang over him afterward.

"That was why I did not kill your father the day I found him here. In our brief struggle, I tore away his neck chain and saw in my hand the symbol of our brotherhood. I knew that the pendant holders of the Salamandra must live at all costs. I could not kill him, though I wanted to."

Michael's mouth was open and he stared numbly at the German. "Did . . . did you reveal to him your common bond?" he asked.

"No, for it was never meant for us to know the identities of one another until reaching Committee level. I could have killed him and no one would have known. But my sworn loyalty prevented it. I knew that my fate had probably been sealed by my failure to protect the scientist in Clermont-Ferrand. I expected to be shot. To lose a second pendant holder when it could be prevented would have been a tragic error on my part. As it turned out, however, the course of events that followed also prevented your father from reaching the Committee level, as well as the position in France's government that was being prepared for him. Like myself, he continued to hold the pendant afterward, still serving a very useful purpose to the brotherhood, though his role in its future leadership had been lost." Immel's voice was growing steadily weaker. He closed his eyes and paused for a long moment to summon what strength he had left.

Michael looked away. "My father—a part of this," he muttered to himself in pained disbelief.

"There is something that you must try to understand," the German began after measuring Michael's reaction. "When your father joined the Salamandra shortly before the war, it was not dedicated to the destructive philosophy that it is now as the Trinity that you know. Its intent was good, constructive. Europe was headed for unavoidable war. The Salamandra hoped to heal the wounds that would be left by the conflict, to unify whatever emerged into a politically and economically strong coalition dedicated to world peace and security."

"But the Salamandra changed," Michael said.

"Yes, it changed. And the pendant holders like your father and myself were the 'offspring' of those who had set the original direction. The new path was chosen by the Committee of Six—and without all of its members in total agreement."

Michael thought for a moment, then looked up. "And Falloux's accusation against my father at the war's end?" he asked.

"Falloux's sponsor had violated a principle by telling him that your father was a pendant holder, and his adversary for a Committee position. Falloux acted quickly to remove your father as a threat. You see, each Committee member sponsored two potential heirs. Only the better of the two would rise to Committee level upon the death of the sponsor. Your father was easily the better of the two, but he was also a man of principle who would oppose the new goals of the Committee. So the sponsor intervened, successfully sidetracking your father."

"And you said that my father continued to serve a useful purpose. How did he do that?" Michael asked, hoping the German's strength would hold out.

"He was a brilliant writer. His gift of words and persuasion enabled him to reach people by the scores of millions over the years, and in many countries. Examine his earliest books carefully, study the changing times during which they were written. You will see and understand the role he played in shaping the thinking and attitude of a population.

"It became the long-range plan of the Committee to begin molding the world population slowly, gently at first, using world conditions, both naturally evolving and those engineered, to bring people to the proper level of vulnerability and need; to make them distrustful of their governments and insecure in the outlook for their future; to create the necessary weaknesses in them to make them dependent, desperate, and ready to *follow*. They will always follow when their fears are great enough.

"And in this aim they were tremendously successful, exploiting every opportunity with subtle skill. Your own country was, and is, the classic example of their success. They changed your whole society," Immel said.

"I can't believe that," Michael replied. "Those changes weren't engineered."

"Weren't they?" Immel asked, a knowing expression showing

hrough the pain on his face. "Look at the last thirty years, at your own generation. You went through the nineteen fifties with the suspicion of communist plots everywhere, and the almost paranoid fear of atomic warfare and its effects on the world. The strain of the racial unrest began to be felt like at no other time in your previous history. In the nineteen sixties it began to bloom, and as young adults you found ourselves shocked by the assassination of a President, by the murder of a great civil rights leader, and by the growing reality of a war in Vietnam. The moral fiber of your country was being tested and torn. It couldn't hold up to the pressures being placed upon it. Your belief and trust in your government was shattered by Vietnam. It grew worse in the seventies, when your faith in the system was irreparably damaged by Watergate and other corruptions. You were made bitter by the manipulations of big business, so well typified by the conspiracy of an oil crisis, and by shortages and crises in everything from coffee to sugar. And real fear began entering your lives from the violence of terrorist groups, both major and minor, who made you wonder if you were ever truly safe from their violence. You were being manipulated just like everyone else in the world. And today your children grow up seeking escape from the pressures around them and find it in drugs, alcohol, sex, and rebellion—rebellion against you, against the system, against everything. What kind of a world do they have to look forward to? They see today's world as a bad place, being crushed by inflation and troubled economies, torn by violence and unrest, sitting on the brink of some sudden, convulsive change. It has to change for them to have any chance at all. They know it. You know it. Trinity knows it."

"Are you saying that Trinity was responsible for creating these conditions by controlling events in the world?" Michael asked.

"Yes, either directly causing them or by carefully exploiting those that were not their doing," Immel replied, his face beginning to look like the mask of death as his strength ebbed slowly away.

"And you're also saying that my father was a part of this exploitation?" Michael asked.

"Not knowingly. He was never privileged to know the plans of the Committee. He merely built his stories around the topics chosen by the Committee. They used his nature of high principles to their advantage, knowing he would dig into the issues and unwittingly deliver precisely the message they intended. They had found the way to use his ideals in a way he would have never agreed to. But I believe he began to sense this on his own, and very gradually fell away. During the past ten years, his association was limited to the transfer of funds through a special account set up in Switzerland in his name. His involvement in

477

the laundering of these funds was not active, though the account activity would make it seem so. This he did solely for his own protection for the oath of death was still over him. He could not completely disassociate himself. He realized that the Salamandra was no longer representative of the ideals to which he had been drawn before the war. And, after all, the United States was now his country, not France. He eventually took the very bold step of refusing further transaction through the account."

The Swiss accounts, Michael thought. It was a sure bet that Sub Rosa had meticulously gone through the records of their transactions, which meant that Pheagan probably already knew about his father's involvement.

"And you sent for my father, knowing that he would help you after learning about the plan of Trinity to begin their massive effort against the world," Michael stated.

"Yes. And our plan began well, but the tentacles of Trinity were spread too far, and your father's attempt was stopped. My cover remained safe for a while, but became suspected by Falloux after your arrival in France. The rest you know," the German said, gasping to catch his breath.

"You now have the means by which to complete the job started by your father and myself," he continued. "I am sorry only that I will not live to see it."

Immel smiled and began a deep racking cough, spitting up a great deal of blood. He fell back and rolled his eyes toward Demy's body. "He has succeeded, despite your efforts," he said.

"I'm sorry," Michael said, staring at him.

They were interrupted by another voice.

"It's time to get you out of here," the team leader said, rushing back into the barn with two other members of the team.

Michael was scooped up in a sitting position by two of his fellow Dawgs and was whisked out of the barn at a run toward the helicopters. There had been barely enough time to see the team leader standing over the German with Michael's KA-BAR in one hand and Demy's handgun in the other, and the KA-BAR being dropped at Immel's side.

The German watched as Michael was carried from the barn, then looked up weakly at the Dawg standing over him. Immel nodded without expression. "I understand," he said, then closed his eyes.

Michael barely heard the shot over the sounds of the chopping whirling rotors and the roaring engines of the helicopters. One look at the first chopper told him the story of what was being left behind, however. The bodies of ten of Demy's men were piled into one craft. They were leaving behind the scene of a successful mission by Demy. It would appear as if the German had staged a terrific defense, killing four of Demy's men before Demy and Immel had killed one another in the barn, the rest of Demy's men having gotten away. The story might not hold up in the end, following a thorough investigation, if one was made. But even if the story didn't hold up, it would still buy the time necessary for Sub Rosa to strike against an unprepared Trinity Committee and its heirs.

Michael was lifted into the second helicopter as the first with the bodies of Demy's men lifted off. The team leader and the last remaining Dawg sprinted from the barn and into the clearing as the first signs of smoke and flames became evident in the dried-out old structure. They boarded the chopper, which lifted off immediately.

The scene below was lost quickly in the darkness as the craft rose swiftly upward, then tipped sharply and accelerated. For a brief moment before leveling off, Michael got a glimpse of the dark road below, dotted by the string of lights speeding along it toward the old Bouchard winery. The authorities, no doubt, racing to the scene.

He closed his eyes and let his head fall back, feeling the wind in his face and the vibration from the helicopter. He wished that some sudden, loud noise would startle him and that the vibrating motion of the helicopter would miraculously become the shuddering sway of his research platform caught in a sudden tropical storm. He prayed for the sound of the heavy rain hitting against the plastic top of the platform and for the wetting spray to splash through the insect netting and hit his face to wake him from this terrible dream. He wanted very much to open his eyes and find himself in a different part of the world, and to know that his father, Gabrielle, and Danny were still alive—to know that this whole thing had never happened.

But it would never vanish like some interrupted dream, or like the two helicopters swiftly melting into the darkness, carrying the story of what had happened away with them into secrecy. What had happened had been real, terribly real. And Michael Gladieux would forever carry the memory of it with him.

To a world more fortunate than he, it would be a thing that never happened. They would never know the details of the drama that had unfolded during the past twenty-five days, culminating on that night, or of the importance of the information contained in a small battered notebook tucked securely in a breast pocket. They would never know the price that had been paid to obtain it, or from what suffering, fear and sorrow they had been spared by those sacrifices. They would never know as they slept and dreamed their dreams how close they had come to sharing the same ugly nightmare—and living it. How dangerously close they had come to what might have been.

Epilogue

THREE MONTHS LATER, SPRING LAKE: Michael Gladieux sat back pensively, his legs crossed, his feet up and resting on the railing of the upper level of the beach pavilion. He listened to the rhythmic roll of the surf and watched the hypnotic, timeless grace of the ocean's rise and fall as the endless parade of waves moved shoreward. There were still a few stragglers left on the beach enjoying the last moments of the day. This was the time, besides dawn, that Michael liked best on the beach. It was beautifully peaceful and private.

He had come to the beach every day since his return home, following the two-month stay at the private clinic in Interlaken, Switzerland. He had done a great deal of soul searching regarding his priorities in life as his wounds healed, and later during his long visits to the beach. It wasn't that his priorities had been poorly set or were without meaning, for neither was the case. His work in the rain forest in the interests of science and conservation had been tremendously important and gratifying. But he had suddenly found himself without the motivation to return to it. Like the innocence and youth that had been stolen from him by the war in Vietnam, his father's death and the events that followed had tapped his vitality and drive, and had forced him to face truths and priorities that he had selectively eliminated from his mind. He found himself once again confused and uncertain of his purpose in life.

He loved the rain forests, but hated the memories they evoked; hated the memories but loved the excitement inspired by them; loved the excitement but hated the need he felt for it. He was at war within himself. It was as if two men existed in him and could not coexist as one. One saw the purpose of the war that Sub Rosa fought against powers of evil, and belonged to it; the other wanted only to be left alone, to feel free from having to carry the weight of the world on his shoulders. Both had paid a terrible price, which only one could begin to understand.

Footsteps sounded on the stairs behind him, but Michael didn't turn to see who was climbing them. He didn't look as he heard the sound of a chair being dragged over to be set beside him, and didn't look as Bill Pheagan sat.

Both men sat for several long moments without speaking.

"I trust that all went well with the Committee?" Michael began, breaking the silence.

"It was a piece of cake," Pheagan replied. "Every Committee member and every heir. We've got Trinity's financial sources and every route of transfer under surveillance. Nothing moves that we don't know about or can't trace completely. It'll get us much deeper into the organization—what's left of it."

"So, your worries are over. Now what will you do for excitement?" Michael asked.

"Oh, there's still plenty to do. There are still hundreds of individual groups out there that are as dangerous as ever who are still fighting. We haven't ended the war by a long shot," Pheagan said.

"Then what did you win?" Michael asked, looking at Pheagan for the first time.

"A great deal, actually, While we haven't ended the war, we have removed the biggest threat of losing it."

"And if they reorganize?"

"They may try, but there are too many little chiefs now. They could organize to some degree, perhaps even splinter and become several groups, but they'll never pose the collective threat that Trinity did. At least not in our lifetime. They'll carry on day to day and we'll fight them day to day. We can handle it on that basis. We'll win, we'll lose, but mostly we'll win."

"And the weapons that Trinity had planned to use?" Michael asked.

"Safely in hand," Pheagan answered. "They could always obtain more, and even wipe out a major city if they wanted to, but without the massive, concerted effort that had been planned, it will never be as truly world-threatening as the situation we faced. Like I said, it's day to day, and we can live with that kind of war. The core is gone, their causes are divergent. The world will always have its mosquitoes."

There was another long silence.

"Did you know about my father's involvement before learning of it from Immel's information?" Michael asked.

"We figured out that he had been peripherally involved in the financial transactions from the audit of the Swiss accounts. But we also knew that he had ceased involvement completely," Pheagan replied.

"Why didn't you tell me that he was a part of it?" Michael asked.

"What good could that have served? If you hadn't learned it from Immel, you would never have found out. We didn't want you hurt by it if you didn't have to be. We had hoped that you wouldn't be hurt by it in any way, but it . . . just . . . didn't work out that way."

"No, it didn't work out that way," Michael repeated, staring out over the water.

There was another long moment of silence between them.

"What about you, Mike? You look like you've recovered well from your wounds. Will you be heading back to the rain forest?" Pheagan asked.

"Yeah, as soon as the arm and leg are stronger," he replied. But it didn't sound very convincing.

"I guess it'll be good to get back, huh?" Pheagan asked. "Away from the system, from people."

Michael remained pensive, then cocked his head to look at him again. "I don't know if anything can be good again," he said.

I know, Pheagan's eyes seemed to say. "It'll get better," he said after a pause.

Michael just nodded and looked back to the water.

"Well, I guess I'll be going," Pheagan said, leaning forward in his chair. "I just wanted to stop by to see how you were getting along and to tell you how we made out. I . . . also wanted to tell you that it *was* worth it all, Mike. We stopped their plan cold. It wouldn't have been possible without you—without Dan and Gabrielle. It wouldn't have been possible without your father. It doesn't even matter that he was ever involved. *He* made it possible to stop them. His dying made it possible. And even if he had been a man who had made no other contribution to the world in his life, it would have still been the greatest gift to his fellow man that he could have given. It made up for a lot— for everything," Pheagan said.

"Thank you," Michael said, nodding slowly. "It means a lot to hear it said."

Pheagan rose to his feet and stretched. "I'll be heading out. Take care of yourself. And . . . uh . . . you know where I am if you need me for anything," he said, expecting the acid stare and the bitter "Don't call me, I'll call you," reply. But it didn't come.

482

"Thank the team for me, will you?" Michael said, instead.

Pheagan smiled. "You bet," he answered.

"And thanks for stopping by."

Pheagan threw a short wave and started to walk away. He stopped near the top of the stairs and turned back to Michael. "Oh, there was one more reason for my visit. I brought along an old friend of yours who wanted to see you," he said, looking at Nicole St. Jude as she came silently to the top of the stairs.

Michael turned to look at Pheagan, and saw Nicole. He rose instantly to his feet.

She rushed to him and came into his arms. They held one another tightly, without speaking, tears in the eyes of both.

"Take care, Glad-jo. The pleasure has been all mine. In fact, it's been an honor knowing you and working with you," Pheagan said, tossing a lazy salute. He turned and started down the first steps.

"Hey, Pheagan," Michael called after him. "You never sent me a bill," he said with what was almost a smile.

"Didn't I? That's funny, it must have slipped my mind. I'll put it in the mail one of these days when I get around to it. Take care of yourselves, you two. And, Mike, remember, if you need me for anything, give me a call."

"I never thanked you for all that *you* did, and I want to," Michael said. "Thanks. And I mean it."

Pheagan smiled weakly and nodded. He looked at the two of them for a moment, feeling that Michael would never quite make it back to the rain forest and the memories it must hold. He was a man who wanted to forget. Having Nicole with him was the best thing for him—for both of them.

"See ya," Pheagan said.

"You probably will," Michael answered.

Pheagan started down the stairs, a smile breaking across his lips. You know, he thought, I bet I will at that.